Praise for the Virgin River series
by Robyn Carr

"The Virgin River books are so compelling—
I connected instantly with the characters and just
wanted more and more and more."
—#1 *New York Times* bestselling author
Debbie Macomber

"Carr's leisurely paced, low-key story charms by
virtue of its characters…who are only a phone call
away."
—*Booklist*, starred review, on *Virgin River*

"Carr has hit her stride with this captivating series."
—*Library Journal* on the Virgin River series

Praise for the Whiskey Creek series
by Brenda Novak

"It's steamy, it's poignant, it's perfectly paced—it's
When Lightning Strikes and you don't want to miss it."
—USATODAY.com's *Happy Ever After* blog

"*This Heart of Mine* is a potently emotional, powerfully
life-affirming contemporary romance that can be
read and enjoyed on its own, but it also serves as an
excellent addition to Novak's popular Whiskey Creek
series."
—*Booklist*, starred review

"One needn't wonder why Novak is a *New York Times*
and *USA TODAY* bestselling author. Just read
Come Home to Me."
—*Examiner.com*

For more titles by Robyn Carr, such as:

The Virgin River series

The Grace Valley series

The Thunder Point series

and

The Sullivan's Crossing series

visit www.robyncarr.com,

and look for her next Sullivan's Crossing novel,
available soon from MIRA Books.

For more titles in Brenda Novak's

Whiskey Creek series

and many other books,

visit brendanovak.com,

and look for her next novel, introducing
The Silver Springs series,
available soon from MIRA Books.

ROBYN CARR
BRENDA NOVAK

HOME *to* YOU

MIRA®

MIRA

ISBN-13: 978-0-7783-3049-3

Home to You

Copyright © 2017 by Harlequin Books S.A.

The publisher acknowledges the copyright holders of the individual works as follows:

Virgin River
Copyright © 2007 by Robyn Carr

When Lightning Strikes
Copyright © 2012 by Brenda Novak

www.MIRABooks.com

Printed in U.S.A.

CONTENTS

VIRGIN RIVER

Robyn Carr

This novel is dedicated to Pam Glenn,
Goddess of Midwifery,
my friend and sister of my heart.

One

Mel squinted into the rain and darkness, creeping along the narrow, twisting, muddy, tree-enshrouded road, and for the hundredth time thought, *Am I out of my mind?* And then she heard and felt a thump as the right rear wheel of her BMW slipped off the road onto the shoulder and sank into the mud. The car rocked to a stop. She accelerated and heard the wheel spin but she was going nowhere fast.

I am so screwed, was her next thought.

She turned on the dome light and looked at her cell phone. She'd lost the signal an hour ago when she left the freeway and headed up into the mountains. In fact, she'd been having a pretty lively discussion with her sister Joey when the steep hills and unbelievably tall trees blocked the signal and cut them off.

"I cannot believe you're really doing this," Joey was saying. "I thought you'd come to your senses. This isn't *you,* Mel! You're not a small-town girl!"

"Yeah? Well, it looks like I'm gonna be—I took the job and sold everything, so I wouldn't be tempted to go back."

"You couldn't just take a leave of absence? Maybe go to a small, private hospital? Try to think this through?"

"I need everything to be different," Mel said. "No more hospital war zone. I'm just guessing, but I imagine I won't be called on to deliver a lot of crack babies out here in the woods. The woman said this place, this Virgin River, is calm and quiet and safe."

"And stuck back in the forest, a million miles from a Starbucks, where you'll get paid in eggs and pig's feet and—"

"And none of my patients will be brought in handcuffed, guarded by a corrections officer." Then Mel took a breath and, unexpectedly, laughed and said, "Pig's feet? Oh-oh, Joey—I'm going up into the trees again, I might lose you…"

"You wait. You'll be sorry. You'll regret this. This is crazy and impetuous and—"

That's when the signal, blessedly, was lost. And Joey was right—with every additional mile, Mel was doubting herself and her decision to escape into the country.

At every curve the roads had become narrower and the rain a little harder. It was only 6:00 p.m., but it was already dark as pitch; the trees were so dense and tall that even that last bit of afternoon sun had been blocked. Of course there were no lights of any kind along this winding stretch. According to the directions, she should be getting close to the house where she was to meet her new employer, but she didn't dare get out of her swamped car and walk. She could get lost in these woods and never be seen again.

Instead, she fished the pictures from her briefcase in an attempt to remind herself of a few of the reasons why she had taken this job. She had pictures of a quaint little hamlet of clapboard houses with front porches and

dormer windows, an old-fashioned schoolhouse, a steepled church, hollyhocks, rhododendrons and blossom-
ing apple trees in full glory, not to mention the green
pastures upon which livestock grazed. There was the
pie and coffee shop, the corner store, a tiny one-room,
freestanding library, and the adorable little cabin in
the woods that would be hers, rent free, for the year of
her contract.

The town backed up to the amazing sequoia redwoods and national forests that spanned hundreds of
miles of wilderness over the Trinity and Shasta mountain ranges. The Virgin River, after which the town
was named, was deep, wide, long, and home to huge
salmon, sturgeon, steel fish and trout. She'd looked on
the internet at pictures of that part of the world and
was easily convinced no more beautiful land existed.
Of course, she could see nothing now except rain, mud
and darkness.

Ready to get out of Los Angeles, she had put her résumé with the Nurses' Registry and one of the recruiters
brought Virgin River to her attention. The town doctor,
she said, was getting old and needed help. A woman
from the town, Hope McCrea, was donating the cabin
and the first year's salary. The county was picking up
the tab for liability insurance for at least a year to get
a practitioner and midwife in this remote, rural part of
the world. "I faxed Mrs. McCrea your résumé and letters of recommendation," the recruiter had said, "and
she wants you. Maybe you should go up there and look
the place over."

Mel took Mrs. McCrea's phone number and called
her that evening. Virgin River was far smaller than what
she'd had in mind, but after no more than an hour-long
conversation with Mrs. McCrea, Mel began effecting

her move out of L.A. the very next morning. That was barely two weeks ago.

What they didn't know at the Registry, nor in Virgin River for that matter, was that Mel had become desperate to get away. Far away. She'd been dreaming of a fresh start, and peace and quiet, for months. She couldn't remember the last time she'd had a restful night's sleep. The dangers of the big city, where crime seemed to be overrunning the neighborhoods, had begun to consume her. Just going to the bank and the store filled her with anxiety; danger seemed to be lurking everywhere. Her work in the three-thousand-bed county hospital and trauma center brought to her care the victims of too many crimes, not to mention the perpetrators of crimes hurt in pursuit or arrest—strapped to hospital beds in wards and in Emergency, guarded by cops. What was left of her spirit was hurting and wounded. And that was nothing to the loneliness of her empty bed.

Her friends begged her to stave off this impulse to run for some unknown small town, but she'd been in grief group, individual counseling and had seen more of the inside of a church in the last nine months than she had in the last ten years, and none of that was helping. The only thing that gave her any peace of mind was fantasizing about running away to some tiny place in the country where people didn't have to lock their doors, and the only thing you had to fear were the deer getting in the vegetable garden. It seemed like sheer heaven.

But now, sitting in her car looking at the pictures by the dome light, she realized how ridiculous she'd been. Mrs. McCrea told her to pack only durable clothes—jeans and boots—for country medicine. So what had she packed? Her boots were Stuart Weitzmans, Cole

Haans and Fryes—and she hadn't minded paying over a tidy four-fifty for each pair. The jeans she had packed for traipsing out to the ranches and farms were Rock & Republics, Joe's, Luckys, 7 For All Mankind—they rang up between one-fifty and two-fifty a copy. She'd been paying three hundred bucks a pop to have her hair trimmed and highlighted. After scrimping for years through college and postgrad nursing, once she was a nurse practitioner with a very good salary she discovered she loved nice things. She might have spent most of her workday in scrubs, but when she was out of them, she liked looking good.

She was sure the fish and deer would be very impressed.

In the past half hour she'd only seen one old truck on the road. Mrs. McCrea hadn't prepared her for how perilous and steep these roads were, filled with hairpin turns and sharp drop-offs, so narrow in some places that it would be a challenge for two cars to pass each other. She was almost relieved when the dark consumed her, for she could at least see approaching headlights around each tight turn. Her car had sunk into the shoulder on the side of the road that was up against the hill and not the ledge where there were no guardrails. Here she sat, lost in the woods and doomed. With a sigh, she turned around and pulled her heavy coat from the top of one of the boxes on the backseat. She hoped Mrs. McCrea would be traversing this road either en route to or from the house where they were to meet. Otherwise, she would probably be spending the night in the car. She still had a couple of apples, some crackers and two cheese rounds in wax. But the damn Diet Coke was gone—she'd have the shakes and a headache by morning from caffeine withdrawal.

No Starbucks. She should have done a better job of stocking up.

She turned off the engine, but left the lights on in case a car came along the narrow road. If she wasn't rescued, the battery would be dead by morning. She settled back and closed her eyes. A very familiar face drifted into her mind: Mark. Sometimes the longing to see him one more time, to talk to him for just a little while was overwhelming. Forget the grief—she just missed him—missed having a partner to depend on, to wait up for, to wake up beside. An argument over his long hours even seemed appealing. He told her once, "This—you and me—this is forever."

Forever lasted four years. She was only thirty-two and from now on she would be alone. He was dead. And she was dead inside.

A sharp tapping on the car window got her attention and she had no idea if she'd actually been asleep or just musing. It was the butt of a flashlight that had made the noise and holding it was an old man. The scowl on his face was so jarring that she thought the end she feared might be upon her.

"Missy," he was saying. "Missy, you're stuck in the mud."

She lowered her window and the mist wet her face. "I… I know. I hit a soft shoulder."

"That piece of crap won't do you much good around here," he said.

Piece of crap indeed! It was a new BMW convertible, one of her many attempts to ease the ache of loneliness. "Well, no one told me that! But thank you very much for the insight."

His thin white hair was plastered to his head and his bushy white eyebrows shot upwards in spikes; the rain glistened on his jacket and dripped off his big nose. "Sit tight, I'll hook the chain around your bumper and pull you out. You going to the McCrea house?"

Well, that's what she'd been after—a place where everyone knows everyone else. She wanted to warn him not to scratch the bumper but all she could do was stammer, "Y-yes."

"It ain't far. You can follow me after I pull you out."

"Thanks," she said.

So, she would have a bed after all. And if Mrs. Mc-Crea had a heart, there would be something to eat and drink. She began to envision the glowing fire in the cottage with the sound of spattering rain on the roof as she hunkered down into a deep, soft bed with lovely linens and quilts wrapped around her. Safe. Secure. At last.

Her car groaned and strained and finally lurched out of the ditch and onto the road. The old man pulled her several feet until she was on solid ground, then he stopped to remove the chain. He tossed it into the back of the truck and motioned for her to follow him. No argument there—if she got stuck again, he'd be right there to pull her out. Along she went, right behind him, using lots of window cleaner with her wipers to keep the mud he splattered from completely obscuring her vision.

In less than five minutes, the blinker on the truck was flashing and she followed him as he made a right turn at a mailbox. The drive was short and bumpy, the road full of potholes, but it quickly opened up into a clearing. The truck made a wide circle in the clearing so he could leave again, which left Mel to pull right up to…a *hovel!*

This was no adorable little cottage. It was an A-frame with a porch all right, but it looked as though the porch was only attached on one side while the other end had broken away and listed downward. The shingles were black with rain and age and there was a board nailed over one of the windows. It was not lit within or without; there was no friendly curl of smoke coming from the chimney.

The pictures were lying on the seat beside her. She blasted on her horn and jumped immediately out of the car, clutching the pictures and pulling the hood of her wool jacket over her head. She ran to the truck. He rolled down his window and looked at her as if she had a screw loose. "Are you sure this is the McCrea cottage?"

"Yup."

She showed him the picture of the cute little A-frame cottage with Adirondack chairs on the porch and hanging pots filled with colorful flowers decorating the front of the house. It was bathed in sunlight in the picture.

"Hmm," he said. "Been a while since she looked like that."

"I wasn't told that. She said I could have the house rent free for a year, plus salary. I'm supposed to help out the doctor in this town. But this—?"

"Didn't know the doc needed help. He didn't hire you, did he?" he asked.

"No. I was told he was getting too old to keep up with the demands of the town and they needed another doctor, but that I'd do for a year or so."

"Do what?"

She raised her voice to be heard above the rain. "I'm a nurse practitioner. And certified nurse midwife."

That seemed to amuse him. "That a fact?"

"You know the doctor?" she asked.

"Everybody knows everybody. Seems like you shoulda come up here and look the place over and meet the doc before making up your mind."

"Yeah, seems like," she said in some self-recrimination. "Let me get my purse—give you some money for pulling me out of the—" But he was already waving her off.

"Don't want your money. People up here don't have money to be throwing around for neighborly help. So," he said with humor, lifting one of those wild white eyebrows, "looks like she got one over on you. That place's been empty for years now." He chuckled. "Rent free! Hah!"

Headlights bounced into the clearing as an old Suburban came up the drive. Once it arrived the old man said, "There she is. Good luck." And then he laughed. Actually, he *cackled* as he drove out of the clearing.

Mel stuffed the picture under her jacket and stood in the rain near her car as the Suburban parked. She could've gone to the porch to get out of the elements, but it didn't look quite safe.

The Suburban's frame was jacked up and the tires were huge—no way that thing was getting stuck in the mud. It was pretty well splashed up, but it was still obvious it was an older model. The driver trained the lights on the cottage and left them on as the door opened. Out of the SUV climbed this itty-bitty elderly woman with thick, springy white hair and black framed glasses too big for her face. She was wearing rubber boots and was swallowed up by a rain slicker, but she couldn't have been five feet tall. She pitched a cigarette into the mud and, wearing a huge toothy smile, she approached Mel. "Welcome!" she said gleefully in the same deep, throaty voice Mel recognized from their phone conversation.

"Welcome?" Mel mimicked. "Welcome?" She pulled the picture from the inside of her jacket and flashed it at the woman. "This is not that!"

Completely unruffled, Mrs. McCrea said, "Yeah, the place could use a little sprucing up. I meant to get over here yesterday, but the day got away from me."

"Sprucing up? Mrs. McCrea, it's falling down! You said it was *adorable! Precious* is what you said!"

"My word," Mrs. McCrea said. "They didn't tell me at the Registry that you were so melodramatic."

"And they didn't tell me you were delusional!"

"Now, now, that kind of talk isn't going to get us anywhere. Do you want to stand in the rain or go inside and see what we have?"

"I'd frankly like to turn around and drive right out of this place, but I don't think I'd get very far without four-wheel drive. Another little thing you might've mentioned."

Without comment, the little white-haired sprite stomped up the three steps and onto the porch of the cabin. She didn't use a key to unlock the door but had to apply a firm shoulder to get it to open. "Swollen from the rain," she said in her gravelly voice, then disappeared inside.

Mel followed, but didn't stomp on the porch as Mrs. McCrea had. Rather, she tested it gingerly. It had a dangerous slant, but appeared to be solid in front of the door. A light went on inside just as Mel reached the door. Immediately following the dim light came a cloud of choking dust as Mrs. McCrea shook out the tablecloth. It sent Mel back out onto the porch, coughing. Once she recovered, she took a deep breath of the cold, moist air and ventured back inside.

Mrs. McCrea seemed to be busy trying to put things right, despite the filth in the place. She was pushing chairs up to the table, blowing dust off lampshades, propping books on the shelf with bookends. Mel had a look around, but only to satisfy her curiosity as to how horrid it was, because there was no way she was staying. There was a faded floral couch, a matching chair and ottoman, an old chest that served as a coffee table and a brick and board bookcase, the boards unfinished. Only a few steps away, divided from the living room by a counter, was the small kitchen. It hadn't seen a cleaning since the last person made dinner—presumably years ago. The refrigerator and oven doors stood open, as did most of the cupboard doors. The sink was full of pots and dishes; there were stacks of dusty dishes and plenty of cups and glasses in the cupboards, all too dirty to use.

"I'm sorry, this is just unacceptable," Mel said loudly.

"It's a little dirt is all."

"There's a bird's nest in the oven!" Mel exclaimed, completely beside herself.

Mrs. McCrea clomped into the kitchen in her muddy rubber boots, reached into the open oven door and plucked out the bird's nest. She went to the front door and pitched it out into the yard. She shoved her glasses up on her nose as she regarded Mel. "No more bird's nest," she said in a voice that suggested Mel was trying her patience.

"Look, I'm not sure I'd make it. That old man in the pickup had to pull me out of the mud just down the road. I can't stay here, Mrs. McCrea—it's out of the question. Plus, I'm starving and I don't have any food with me." She laughed hollowly. "You said there would be adequate housing ready for me, and I took you to mean clean and stocked with enough food to get me through a couple of days till I could shop for myself. But this—"

"You have a contract," Mrs. McCrea pointed out.

"So do *you*," Mel said. "I don't think you could get anyone to agree this is adequate or ready."

Hope looked up. "It's not leaking, that's a good sign."

"Not quite good enough, I'm afraid."

"That damned Cheryl Creighton was supposed to be down here to give it a good cleaning, but she had excuses three days in a row. Been drinking again is my guess. I got some bedding in the truck and I'll take you to get dinner. It'll look better in the morning."

"Isn't there some place else I can stay tonight? A bed-and-breakfast? A motel on the highway?"

"Bed-and-breakfast?" she asked with a laugh. "This look like a tourist spot to you? The highway's an hour off and this is no ordinary rain. I have a big house with no room in it—filled to the top with junk. They're gonna light a match to it when I die. It would take all night to clear off the couch."

"There must be something…"

"Nearest thing is Jo Ellen's place—she's got a nice spare room over the garage she lets out sometimes. But you wouldn't want to stay there. That husband of hers can be a handful. He's been slapped down by more than one woman in Virgin River—and it'd be a bad thing, you in your nightie, Jo Ellen sound asleep and him getting ideas. He's a groper, that one."

Oh, God, Mel thought. Every second this place sounded worse and worse.

"Tell you what we'll do, girl. I'll light the hot water heater, turn on the refrigerator and heater, then we'll go get a hot meal."

"At the pie and coffee shop?"

"That place closed down three years back," she said.

"But you sent me a picture of it—like it was where I'd be getting lunch or dinner for the next year!"

"Details. Lord, you do get yourself worked up."

"Worked up!?"

"Go jump in the truck and I'll be right along," she commanded. Then ignoring Mel completely, she went to the refrigerator and stooped to plug it in. The light went on immediately and Mrs. McCrea reached inside to adjust the temperature and close the door. The refrigerator's motor made an unhealthy grinding sound as it fired up.

Mel went to the Suburban as she'd been told, but it was so high off the ground she found herself grabbing the inside of the open door and nearly crawling inside. She felt a lot safer here than in the house where her hostess would be lighting a gas water heater. She had a passing thought that if it blew up and destroyed the cabin, they could cut their losses here and now.

Once in the passenger seat, she looked over her shoulder to see the back of the Suburban was full of pillows, blankets and boxes. Supplies for the falling-down house, she assumed. Well, if she couldn't get out of here tonight, she could sleep in her car if she had to. She wouldn't freeze to death with all those blankets. But then, at first light…

A few minutes passed and then Mrs. McCrea came out of the cottage and pulled the door closed. No locking up. Mel was impressed by the agility with which the old woman got herself into the Suburban. She put a foot on the step, grabbed the handle above the door with one hand, the armrest with the other and bounced herself right into the seat. She had a rather large pillow to sit on and her seat was pushed way up so she could reach the pedals. Without a word, she put the vehicle in gear and expertly backed down the narrow drive out onto the road.

"When we talked a couple weeks ago, you said you were pretty tough," Mrs. McCrea reminded her.

"I am. I've been in charge of a women's wing at a three-thousand-bed county hospital for the past two years. We got all the most challenging cases and hopeless patients, and did a damn fine job if I do say so myself. Before that, I spent years in the emergency room in downtown L.A., a very tough place by anyone's standards. By tough, I thought you meant medically. I didn't know you meant I should be an experienced frontier woman."

"Lord, you do go on. You'll feel better after some food."

"I hope so," Mel replied. But, inside she was saying, *I can't stay here. This was crazy, I'm admitting it and getting the hell out of here.* The only thing she really dreaded was owning up to Joey.

They didn't talk during the drive. In Mel's mind there wasn't much to say. Plus, she was fascinated by the ease, speed and finesse with which Mrs. McCrea handled the big Suburban, bouncing down the tree-lined road and around the tight curves in the pouring rain.

She had thought this might be a respite from pain and loneliness and fear. A relief from the stress of patients who were either the perpetrators or victims of crimes, or devastatingly poor and without resources or hope. When she saw the pictures of the cute little town, it was easy to imagine a homey place where people needed her. She saw herself blooming under the grateful thanks of rosy-cheeked country patients. Meaningful work was the one thing that had always cut through any troubling personal issues. Not to mention the lift of escaping the smog and traffic and getting back to nature in the pristine beauty of the forest. She just never thought she'd be getting this far back to nature.

The prospect of delivering babies for mostly uninsured women in rural Virgin River had closed the deal. Working as a nurse practitioner was satisfying, but midwifery was her true calling.

Joey was her only family now; she wanted Mel to come to Colorado Springs and stay with her, her husband, Bill, and their three children. But Mel hadn't wanted to trade one city for another, even though Colorado Springs was considerably smaller. Now, in the absence of any better ideas, she would be forced to look for work there.

As they passed through what seemed to be a town, she grimaced again. "Is this the town? Because this wasn't in the pictures you sent me, either."

"Virgin River," she said. "Such as it is. Looks a lot better in daylight, that's for sure. Damn, this is a big rain. March always brings us this nasty weather. That's the doc's house there, where he sees patients when they come to him. He makes a lot of house calls, too. The library," she pointed, "Open Tuesdays."

They passed a pleasant-looking steepled church, which appeared to be boarded up, but at least she recognized it. There was the store, much older and more worn, the proprietor just locking the front door for the night. A dozen houses lined the street—small and old. "Where's the schoolhouse?" Mel asked.

"What schoolhouse?" Mrs. McCrea countered.

"The one in the picture you sent to the recruiter."

"Hmm. Can't imagine where I got that. We don't have a school. Yet."

"God," Mel groaned.

The street was wide, but dark and vacant—there

were no streetlights. The old woman must have gone through one of her ancient photo albums to come up with the pictures. Or maybe she snapped a few of another town.

Across the street from the doctor's house Mrs. McCrea pulled up to the front of what looked like a large cabin with a wide porch and big yard, but the neon sign in the window that said Open clued her in to the fact that it was a tavern or café. "Come on," Mrs. McCrea said. "Let's warm up your belly and your mood."

"Thank you," Mel said, trying to be polite. She was starving and didn't want an attitude to cost her her dinner, though she wasn't optimistic that anything but her stomach would be warm. She looked at her watch. Seven o'clock.

Mrs. McCrea shook out her slicker on the porch before going in, but Mel wasn't wearing a raincoat. Nor did she have an umbrella. Her jacket was now drenched and she smelled like wet sheep.

Once inside, she was rather pleasantly surprised. It was dark and woody with a fire ablaze in a big stone hearth. The polished wood floors were shiny clean and something smelled good, edible. Over a long bar, above rows of shelved liquor bottles, was a huge mounted fish; on another wall, a bearskin so big it covered half the wall. Over the door, a stag's head. Whew. A hunting lodge? There were about a dozen tables sans tablecloths and only one customer at the bar; the old man who had pulled her out of the mud sat slumped over a drink.

Behind the bar stood a tall man in a plaid shirt with sleeves rolled up, polishing a glass with a towel. He looked to be in his late thirties and wore his brown hair cropped close. He lifted expressive brows and his chin in greeting as they entered. Then his lips curved in a smile.

"Sit here," Hope McCrea said, indicating a table near the fire. "I'll get you something."

Mel took off her coat and hung it over the chair back near the fire to dry. She warmed herself, vigorously rubbing her icy hands together in front of the flames. This was more what she had expected —a cozy, clean cabin, a blazing fire, a meal ready on the stove. She could do without the dead animals, but this was what you got in hunting country.

"Here," the old woman said, pressing a small glass of amber liquid into her hand. "This'll warm you up. Jack's got some stew on the stove and bread in the warmer. We'll fix you up."

"What is it?" she asked.

"Brandy. You gonna be able to get that down?"

"Damn right," she said, taking a grateful sip and feeling it burn its way down to her empty belly. She let her eyes drift closed for a moment, appreciating the unexpected fine quality. She looked back at the bar, but the bartender had disappeared. "That guy," she finally said, indicating the only customer. "He pulled me out of the ditch."

"Doc Mullins," she explained. "You might as well meet him right now, if you're okay to leave the fire."

"Why bother?" Mel said. "I told you—I'm not staying."

"Fine," the old woman said tiredly. "Then you can say hello and goodbye all at once. Come on." She turned and walked toward the old doctor and with a weary sigh, Mel followed. "Doc, this is Melinda Monroe, in case you didn't catch the name before. Miss Monroe, meet Doc Mullins."

He looked up from his drink with rheumy eyes and regarded her, but his arthritic hands never left his glass. He gave a single nod.

"Thanks again," Mel said. "For pulling me out."

The old doctor gave another nod, looking back to his drink.

So much for the friendly small-town atmosphere, she thought. Mrs. McCrea was walking back to the fireplace. She plunked herself down at the table.

"Excuse me," Mel said to the doctor. He turned his gaze toward her, but his bushy white brows were drawn together in a definite scowl, peering over the top of his glasses. His white hair was so thin over his freckled scalp that it almost appeared he had more hair on his brows than his head. "Pleasure to meet you. So, you wanted help up here?" He just seemed to glare at her. "You didn't want help? Which is it?"

"I don't much need any help," he told her gruffly. "But that old woman's been trying to get a doc to replace me for years. She's driven."

"And why is that?" Mel bravely asked.

"Couldn't imagine." He looked back into his glass. "Maybe she just doesn't like me. Since I don't like her that much, makes no difference."

The bartender, and presumably proprietor, was carrying a steaming bowl out of the back, but he paused at the end of the bar and watched as Mel conversed with the old doctor.

"Well, no worries, mate," Mel responded, "I'm not staying. It was grossly misrepresented. I'll be leaving in the morning, as soon as the rain lets up."

"Wasted your time, did you?" he asked, not looking at her.

"Apparently. It's bad enough the place isn't what I

was told it would be, but how about the complication that you have no use for a practitioner or midwife?"

"There you go," he said.

Mel sighed. She hoped she could find a decent job in Colorado.

A young man, a teenager, brought a rack of glasses from the kitchen into the bar. He sported much the same look as the bartender with his short cropped, thick brown hair, flannel shirt and jeans. Handsome kid, she thought, taking in his strong jaw, straight nose, heavy brows. As he was about to put the rack under the bar, he stopped short, staring at Mel in surprise. His eyes grew wide; his mouth dropped open for a second. She tilted her head slightly and treated him to a smile. He closed his mouth slowly, but stood frozen, holding the glasses.

Mel turned away from the boy and the doctor. She headed for Mrs. McCrea's table. The bartender set down a bowl along with a napkin and utensils, then stood there awaiting her. He held the chair for her. Close up, she saw how big a guy he was—over six feet and broad-shouldered. "Miserable weather for your first night in Virgin River," he said pleasantly.

"Miss Melinda Monroe, this is Jack Sheridan. Jack, Miss Monroe."

Mel felt the urge to correct them—tell them it was Mrs. But she didn't because she didn't want to explain that there was no longer a Mr. Monroe, a Dr. Monroe in fact. So she said, "Pleased to meet you. Thank you," she added, accepting the stew.

"This is a beautiful place, when the weather cooperates," he said.

"I'm sure it is," she muttered, not looking at him.

"You should give it a day or two," he suggested.

She dipped her spoon into the stew and gave it a

taste. He hovered near the table for a moment. Then she looked up at him and said in some surprise, "This is delicious."

"Squirrel," he said.

She choked.

"Just kidding," he said, grinning at her. "Beef. Corn fed."

"Forgive me if my sense of humor is a bit off," she replied irritably. "It's been a long and rather arduous day."

"Has it now?" he said. "Good thing I got the cork out of the Remy, then." He went back behind the bar and she looked over her shoulder at him. He seemed to confer briefly and quietly with the young man, who continued to stare at her. His son, Mel decided.

"I don't know that you have to be quite so pissy," Mrs. McCrea said. "I didn't sense any of this attitude when we talked on the phone." She dug into her purse and pulled out a pack of cigarettes. She shook one out and lit it—this explained the gravelly voice.

"Do you have to smoke?" Mel asked her.

"Unfortunately, I do," Mrs. McCrea said, taking a long drag.

Mel just shook her head in frustration. She held her tongue. It was settled, she was leaving in the morning and would have to sleep in the car, so why exacerbate things by continuing to complain? Hope McCrea had certainly gotten the message by now. Mel ate the delicious stew, sipped the brandy, and felt a bit more secure once her belly was full and her head a tad light. *There,* she thought. *That is better. I can make it through the night in this dump. God knows, I've been through worse.*

It had been nine months since her husband, Mark, had stopped off at a convenience store after working a long night shift in the emergency room. He had wanted milk for his cereal. But what he got was three bullets, point-blank to the chest, killing him instantly. There had been a robbery in progress, right in a store he and Mel dropped into at least three times a week. It had ended the life she loved.

Spending the night in her car, in the rain, would be nothing by comparison.

Jack delivered a second Remy Martin to Miss Monroe, but she had declined a second serving of stew. He stayed behind the bar while she ate, drank and seemed to glower at Hope as she smoked. It caused him to chuckle to himself. The girl had a little spirit. What she also had was looks. Petite, blonde, flashing blue eyes, a small heart-shaped mouth, and a backside in a pair of jeans that was just awesome. When the women left, he said to Doc Mullins, "Thanks a lot. You could have cut the girl some slack. We haven't had anything pretty to look at around here since Bradley's old golden retriever died last fall."

"Humph," the doctor said.

Ricky came behind the bar and stood next to Jack. "Yeah," he heartily agreed. "Holy God, Doc. What's the matter with you? Can't you think of the rest of us sometimes?"

"Down, boy." Jack laughed, draping an arm over his shoulders. "She's outta your league."

"Yeah? She's outta yours, too," Rick said, grinning.

"You can shove off anytime. There isn't going to be anyone out tonight," Jack told Rick. "Take a little of that stew home to your grandma."

"Yeah, thanks," he said. "See you tomorrow."

When Rick had gone, Jack hovered over Doc and

said, "If you had a little help, you could do more fishing."

"Don't need help, thanks," he said.

"Oh, there's that again," Jack said with a smile. Any suggestion Hope had made of getting Doc some help was stubbornly rebuffed. Doc might be the most obstinate and pigheaded man in town. He was also old, arthritic and seemed to be slowing down more each year.

"Hit me again," the doctor said.

"I thought we had a deal," Jack said.

"Half, then. This goddamn rain is killing me. My bones are cold." He looked up at Jack. "I did pull that little strumpet out of the ditch in the freezing rain."

"She's probably not a strumpet," Jack said. "I could never be that lucky." Jack tipped the bottle of bourbon over the old man's glass and gave him a shot. But then he put the bottle on the shelf. It was his habit to look out for Doc and, left unchecked, he might have a bit too much. He didn't feel like going out in the rain to be sure Doc got across the street all right. Doc didn't keep a supply at home, doing his drinking only at Jack's, which kept it under control.

Couldn't blame the old boy—he was overworked and lonely. Not to mention prickly.

"You could've offered the girl a warm place to sleep," Jack said. "It's pretty clear Hope didn't get that old cabin straight for her."

"Don't feel up to company," he said. Then Doc lifted his gaze to Jack's face. "Seems you're more interested than me, anyway."

"Didn't really look like she'd trust anyone around here at the moment," Jack said. "Cute little thing, though, huh?"

"Can't say I noticed," he said. He took a sip and then

said, "Didn't look like she had the muscle for the job, anyway."

Jack laughed. "Thought you didn't notice?" But he had noticed. She was maybe five-three. Hundred and ten pounds. Soft, curling blond hair that, when damp, curled even more. Eyes that could go from kind of sad to feisty in an instant. He enjoyed that little spark when she had snapped at him that she didn't feel particularly humorous. And when she took on Doc, there was a light that suggested she could handle all kinds of things just fine. But the best part was that mouth—that little pink heart-shaped mouth. Or maybe it was the fanny.

"Yeah," Jack said. "You could've cut a guy a break and been a little friendlier. Improve the scenery around here."

Two

When Mel and Mrs. McCrea returned to the cabin, it had warmed up inside. Of course, it hadn't gotten any cleaner. Mel shuddered at the filth and Mrs. McCrea said, "I had no idea, when I talked to you, that you were so prissy."

"Well, I'm not. A labor-and-delivery unit in a big hospital like the one I came from is pretty unglamorous." And it struck Mel as curious that she had felt more in control in that chaotic, sometimes horrific environment than in this far simpler one. She decided it was the apparent deception that was throwing her for a loop. That and the fact that however gritty things got in L&D, she always had a comfortable and clean house to go home to.

Hope left her in possession of pillows, blankets, quilts and towels, and Mel decided it made more sense to brave the dirt than the cold. Retrieving only one suitcase from her car, she put on a sweat suit, heavy socks, and made herself a bed on the dusty old couch. The mattress, stained and sagging, looked too frightening. She rolled herself up in the quilts like a burrito and huddled down into the soft, musty cushions. The bathroom light was left on with the door pulled slightly closed, in case she had to get up in the night. And thanks to two brandies, the long drive and the stress of spoiled expectations, she fell into a deep sleep, for once not disturbed by anxiety or nightmares. The softly drumming rain on the roof was like a lullaby, rocking her to sleep. With the dim light of morning on her face, she woke to find she hadn't moved a muscle all night, but lay swaddled and still. Rested. Her head empty.

It was a rare thing.

Disbelieving, she lay there for a while. *Yes,* she thought. *Though it doesn't seem possible under the circumstances, I feel good.* Then Mark's face swam before her eyes and she thought, *What do you expect? You summoned it!*

She further thought, *There's nowhere you can go to escape grief. Why try?*

There was a time she had been so content, especially waking up in the morning. She had this weird and funny gift —music in her head. Every morning, the first thing she noticed was a song, clear as if the radio was on. Always a different one. Although in the bright light of day Mel couldn't play an instrument or carry a tune in a bucket, she awoke each morning humming along with a melody. Awakened by her off-key humming, Mark would rise up on an elbow, lean over her, grinning, and wait for her eyes to pop open. He would say, "What is it today?"

"'Begin the Beguine,'" she'd answer. Or, "'Deep Purple.'" And he'd laugh and laugh.

The music in her head went away with his death.

She sat up, quilts wrapped around her, and the morn-

ing light emphasized the dirty cabin that surrounded
her. The sound of chirping birds brought her to her feet
and to the cabin's front door. She opened it and greeted
a morning that was bright and clear. She stepped out
onto the porch, still wrapped in her quilts, and looked
up—the pines, firs and ponderosas were so tall in daylight—rising fifty to sixty feet above the cabin, some
considerably taller. They were still dripping from a rain
that had washed them clean. Green pinecones were
hanging from branches—pinecones so large that if a
green one fell on your head, it might cause a concussion. Beneath them, thick, lush green fern—she counted
four different types from wide-branched floppy fans to
those as delicate as lace. Everything looked fresh and
healthy. Birds sang and danced from limb to limb, and
she looked into a sky that was an azure blue the likes
of which she hadn't seen in Los Angeles in ten years.
A puffy white cloud floated aimlessly above and an
eagle, wings spread wide, soared overhead and disappeared behind the trees.

She inhaled a deep breath of the crisp spring morning. Ah, she thought. Too bad the cabin, town and old
doctor didn't work out, because the land was lovely.
Unspoiled. Invigorating.

She heard a crack and furrowed her brow. Without
warning the end of the porch that had been sagging
gave out completely, collapsing at the weak end which
created a big slide, knocking her off her feet and splat!
Right into a deep, wet, muddy hole. There she lay, a
filthy, wet, ice cold burrito in her quilt. "Crap," she
said, rolling out of the quilt to crawl back up the porch,
still attached at the starboard end. And into the house.

She packed up her suitcase. It was over.

At least the roads were now passable, and in the light of day she was safe from hitting a soft shoulder and sinking out of sight. Reasoning she wouldn't get far without at least coffee, she headed back toward the town, even though her instincts told her to run for her life, get coffee somewhere down the road. She didn't expect that bar to be open early in the morning, but her options seemed few. She might be desperate enough to bang on the old doctor's door and beg a cup of coffee from him, though facing his grimace again wasn't an inviting thought. But the doc's house looked closed up tighter than a tick. There didn't seem to be any action around Jack's or the store across the street, but a complete caffeine junkie, she tried the door at the bar and it swung open.

The fire was lit. The room, though brighter than the night before, was just as welcoming. It was large and comfortable—even with the animal trophies on the walls. Then she was startled to see a huge bald man with an earring glittering in one ear come from the back to stand behind the bar. He wore a black T-shirt stretched tight over his massive chest, the bottom of a big blue tattoo peeking out beneath one of the snug sleeves. If she hadn't gasped from the sheer size of him, she might've from the unpleasant expression on his face. His dark bushy brows were drawn together and he braced two hands on the bar. "Help you?" he asked.

"Um… Coffee?" she asked.

He turned around to grab a mug. He put it on the bar and poured from a handy pot. She thought about grabbing it and fleeing to a table, but she frankly didn't like the look of him, didn't want to insult him, so she went to the bar and sat up on the stool where her coffee waited. "Thanks," she said meekly.

He just gave a nod and backed away from the bar a bit, leaning against the counter behind him with his huge arms crossed over his chest. He reminded her of a nightclub bouncer or bodyguard. Jesse Ventura with attitude.

She took a sip of the rich, hot brew. Her appreciation for a dynamite cup of coffee surpassed any other comfort in her life and she said, "Ah. Delicious." No comment from the big man. Just as well, she thought. She didn't feel like talking anyway.

A few minutes passed in what seemed like oddly companionable silence when the side door to the bar opened and in came Jack, his arms laden with firewood. When he saw her, he grinned, showing a nice batch of even, white teeth. Under the weight of the wood his biceps strained against his blue denim shirt, the width of his shoulders accentuated a narrow waist. A little light brown chest hair peeked out of the opened collar and his clean-shaven face made her realize that the night before his cheeks and chin had been slightly shadowed by the day's growth of beard.

"Well, now," he said. "Good morning." He took the firewood to the hearth and when he stooped to stack it there, she couldn't help but notice a broad, muscular back and a perfect male butt. Men around here must get a pretty good workout just getting through the rugged days of rural living.

The big bald man lifted the pot to refill her cup when Jack said, "I got that, Preacher."

Jack came behind the bar and "Preacher" went through the door to the kitchen. Jack filled her cup.

"Preacher?" she asked in a near whisper.

"His name is actually John Middleton, but he got that nickname way back. If you called out to John, he wouldn't even turn around."

"Why do you call him that?" she asked.

"Ah, he's pretty straight-laced. Hardly ever swears, never see him drunk, doesn't bother women."

"He's a little frightening looking," she said, still keeping her voice low.

"Nah. He's a pussycat," Jack said. "How was your night?"

"Passable," she said with a shrug. "I didn't think I could make it out of town without a cup of coffee."

"You must be ready to kill Hope. She didn't even have coffee for you?"

"'Fraid not."

"I'm sorry about this, Miss Monroe. You should've had a better welcome than this. I don't blame you for thinking the worst of this place. How about some eggs?" He gestured over his shoulder. "He's a fine cook."

"I won't say no," she said. She felt that odd sensation of a smile on her lips. "And call me Mel."

"Short for Melinda," he said.

Jack hollered through the door to the kitchen. "Preacher. How about some breakfast for the lady?" Back at the bar, he said, "Well, the least we can do is send you off with a good meal—if you can't be convinced to stay a couple of days."

"Sorry," she said. "That cabin. It's uninhabitable. Mrs. McCrea said something about someone who was supposed to clean it—but she's drinking? I think I got that right."

"That would be Cheryl. Has a bit of a problem that

way, I'm afraid. She should've called someone else. Plenty of women around here who'd take a little work."

"Well, it's irrelevant now," Mel said, sipping again. "Jack, this is the best coffee I've ever had. Either that, or I had a bad couple of days and am easily impressed by some creature comforts."

"No, it's really that good." He frowned and reached out, lifting a lock of her hair off her shoulder. "Do you have mud in your hair?"

"Probably," she said. "I was standing on the porch, appreciating the beauty of this nice spring morning when one end gave way and spilled me right into a big, nasty mud puddle. And I wasn't brave enough to try out the shower—it's beyond filthy. But I thought I got it all off."

"Oh, man," he said, surprising her with a big laugh. "Could you have had a worse day? If you'd like, I have a shower in my quarters—clean as a whistle." He grinned again. "Towels even smell like Downy."

"Thanks, but I think I'll just move on. When I get closer to the coast, I'm going to get a hotel room and have a quiet, warm, clean evening. Maybe rent a movie."

"Sounds nice," he said. "Then back to Los Angeles?"

She shrugged. "No," she said. She couldn't do that. Everything from the hospital to the house would conjure sweet memories and bring her grief to the surface. She just couldn't move on as long as she stayed in L.A. Besides, now there was nothing there for her anymore. "It's time for a change. But it turns out this was too big a change. Have you lived here all your life?"

"Me? No. Only a little while. I grew up in Sacramento. I was looking for a good place to fish and stayed on. I converted this cabin into a bar and grill and built on an addition to live in. Small, but comfortable. Preacher has a room upstairs, over the kitchen."

"What in the world made you stay on? I'm not trying to be flip—there doesn't seem to be that much of a town here."

"If you had the time, I'd show you. This is incredible country. Over six hundred people live in and around town. Lots of people from the cities have cabins up and down the Virgin River—it's peaceful and the fishing is excellent. We don't have much tourist traffic through town, but fishermen come in here pretty regularly and some hunters pass through during the season. Preacher is known for his cooking, and it's the only place in town to get a beer. We're right up against some redwoods—awesome. Majestic. Lots of campers and hikers around the national forests all through the summer. And the sky and air out here— you just can't find anything like it in a city."

"And your son works here with you?"

"Son? Oh," he laughed. "Ricky? He's a kid from town. He works around the bar after school most days. Good kid."

"You have family?" she asked.

"Sisters and nieces in Sacramento. My dad is still there, but I lost my mother a few years back."

Preacher came out of the kitchen holding a steaming plate with a napkin. As he sat it before Mel, Jack reached beneath the bar and produced silverware and a napkin. On the plate was a luscious-looking cheese omelet with peppers, sausage patties, fruit, home fries, wheat toast. Ice water appeared; her coffee was refilled.

Mel dipped into the omelet and brought it to her mouth. It melted there, rich and delicious. "Mmm," she said, letting her eyes close. After she swallowed she said, "I've eaten here twice, and I have to say the food is some of the best I've ever had."

"Me and Preacher—we can whip up some good food, sometimes. Preacher has a real gift. And he wasn't a cook until he got up here."

She took another bite. Apparently Jack was going to stand there through her meal and watch her devour every bite. "So," she said, "what's the story on the doctor and Mrs. McCrea?"

"Well, let's see," he said, leaning his back on the counter behind the bar, his arms wide, big hands braced on either side of him. "They tend to bicker. Two opinionated, stubborn old farts who can't agree on anything. The fact of the matter is, I think Doc could use help—but I imagine you gathered he's a bit on the obstinate side."

She made an affirmative noise, her mouth full of the most wonderful eggs she'd ever eaten.

"The thing about this little town is—sometimes days go by without anyone needing medical attention. Then there will be weeks when everyone needs to see Doc—a flu going around while three women are about to give birth, and right then someone will fall off a horse or roof. So it goes. And although he doesn't like to admit it, he is seventy." Jack gave a shrug. "Next town doctor is at least a half hour away and for rural people out on farms and ranches, over an hour. The hospital is farther yet. Then, we have to think about what will happen when Doc dies, which hopefully won't be too soon."

She swallowed and took a drink of water. "Why has Mrs. McCrea taken on this project?" she asked. "Is she really trying to replace him, as he says?"

"Nah. But because of his age, it's about time for some kind of protégé, I would think. Hope's husband left her enough so she'll be comfortable—she's been widowed a long time now, I gather. And she seems to do whatever she can to keep the town together. She's also looking for a preacher, a town cop and a schoolteacher, grades one through eight, so the little ones don't have to bus two towns over. She hasn't had much success."

"Doctor Mullins doesn't seem to appreciate her efforts," Mel said, blotting her lips with the napkin.

"He's territorial. He's in no way ready for retirement. Maybe he's worried that someone will show up and take over, leaving him with nothing to do. Man like Doc, never married and in service to a town all his life, would balk at that. But…see… There was an incident a few years ago, just before I got here. Two emergencies at the same time. A truck went off the road and the driver was critically injured, and a kid with a bad case of flu that turned to pneumonia stopped breathing. Doc stopped the bleeding on the truck driver, but by the time he got across the river to the kid, he was too late."

"God," she said. "Bet that leaves some hard feelings."

"I don't think anyone really blames him. He's saved some lives in his time here. But the feeling he could use some help gets more support." He smiled. "You're the first one to show up."

"Hmm," she said, taking a last sip of coffee. She heard the door open behind her and a couple of men walked in.

"Harv. Ron," Jack said. The men said hello and sat at a table by the window. Jack looked back at Mel. "What made you come up here?" he asked.

"Burnout," she said. "I got sick of being on a first-name basis with cops and homicide detectives."

"Jesus, just what kind of work did you do?"

"Ever been to war?" she asked.

"As a matter of fact," he replied with a nod.

"Well, big-city hospitals and trauma centers get like that. I spent years in the emergency room in downtown L.A. while I was doing my postgrad work to become a family nurse practitioner, and there were days it felt like a battle zone. Felons transported to E.R. after incurring injuries during arrest—people who were still so out of control and impossible to subdue that three or four cops had to hold them down while one of the nurses tried to start an IV. Addicts with so much junk in them, three hits with an officer's Taser wouldn't even slow 'em down, much less a dose of Narcan. O.D.s, victims of violent crimes and, given it was the biggest trauma center in L.A., some of the ugliest MVAs and GSWs... Sorry. Motor vehicle accidents and gunshot wounds. And crazy people with no supervision, nowhere to go, off their meds and... Don't get me wrong, we did some good work. Excellent work. I'm real proud of what we got done. Best staff in, maybe, America."

She gazed off for a second, thinking. The environment was wild and chaotic, yet while she was working with and falling in love with her husband, it was exciting and fulfilling. She gave her head a little shake and went on.

"I transferred out of E.R. to women's health, which I found was what I'd been looking for. Labor and delivery. I went to work on my certification in midwifery. That turned out to be my true calling, but it wasn't always a sweeter experience." She laughed sadly and shook her head. "My first patient was brought in by the police and I had to fight them like a bulldog to get the cuffs off. They wanted me to deliver her while she was handcuffed to the bed."

He smiled. "Well, you're in luck. I don't think there's a pair of handcuffs in town."

"It wasn't like that every day, but it was like that often. I supervised the nurses on the L&D ward for a couple of years. The excitement and unpredictability zooped me up for a long time, but I finally hit a wall. I love women's health, but I can't do city medicine like that anymore. God, I need a slower pace. I'm wiped out."

"That's an awful lot of adrenaline to leave behind," he said.

"Yeah, I've been accused of being an adrenaline junkie. Emergency nurses often are." She smiled at him. "I'm trying to quit."

"Ever live in a small town?" he asked, refilling her coffee.

She shook her head. "Smallest town I've ever lived in had at least a million people in it. I grew up in Seattle and went to Southern California for college."

"Small towns can be nice. And they can have their own brand of drama. And danger."

"Like?" she asked, sipping.

"Flood. Fire. Wildlife. Hunters who don't follow the rules. The occasional criminal. Lotta pot growers out here, but not in Virgin River that I know of. Humboldt Homegrown, it's called around here. They're a tight-knit group and usually keep to themselves—don't want to draw attention. Once in a while, though, there'll be crime associated with drugs." He grinned. "But you never had any of that in the city, right?"

"When I was looking for change, I shouldn't have made such a drastic one. This is kind of like going cold turkey. I might have to downsize a little more gradually. Maybe try out a town with a couple hundred thousand people and a Starbucks."

"You aren't going to tell me Starbucks can beat that coffee you're drinking," he said, nodding at her cup.

She gave a short laugh. "Coffee's great." She favored him with a pleasant smile, deciding that this guy was okay. "I should've considered the roads. To think I left the terror of Los Angeles freeways for the heart-stopping curves and cliffs in these hills… Whew." A tremor ran through her. "If I did stay in a place like this, it would be for your food."

He leaned toward her, bracing hands on the bar. Rich brown eyes glowed warm under serious hooded brows. "I can get that cabin put right for you in no time," he said.

"Yeah, I've heard that before." She put out a hand and he took it. She felt his calluses as he gently squeezed her hand; he was a man who did hard, physical work. "Thanks, Jack. Your bar was the only part of this experiment I enjoyed." She stood and began fishing for her wallet in her purse. "What do I owe you?"

"On the house. The least I could do."

"Come on, Jack—none of this was your doing."

"Fine. I'll send Hope a bill."

At that moment Preacher came out of the kitchen with a covered dish wrapped in a towel. He handed it to Jack.

"Doc's breakfast. I'll walk out with you."

"All right," she said.

At her car, he said, "No kidding. I wish you'd think about it."

"Sorry, Jack. This isn't for me."

"Well, damn. There's a real dearth of beautiful young women around here. Have a safe drive." He gave her elbow a little squeeze, balancing the covered dish in his other hand. And all she could think was, what a peach of a guy. Lots of sex appeal in his dark eyes, strong jaw, small cleft in his chin and the gracious, laid-back manner that suggested he didn't know he was good-looking. Someone should snap him up before he figured it out. Probably someone had.

Mel watched him walk across the street to the doctor's house, then got into her car. She made a wide U-turn on the deserted street and headed back the way she had come. As she drove by Doc's house, she slowed. Jack was crouched on the porch, looking at something. The covered dish was still balanced on one hand and he lifted the other, signaling her to stop. As he looked toward her car, his expression was one of shock. Disbelief.

Mel stopped the car and got out. "You okay?" she asked.

He stood up. "No," he said. "Can you come here a sec?"

She left the car running, the door open, and went up on the porch. It was a box, sitting there in front of the doctor's door, and the look on Jack's face remained stunned. She crouched down and looked within and there, swaddled and squirming around, was a baby. "Jesus," she said.

"Nah," Jack said. "I don't think it's Jesus."

"This baby was not here when I passed his house earlier."

Mel lifted the box and asked Jack to park and turn off her car. She rang the doctor's bell and after a few tense moments, he opened it wearing a plaid flannel bathrobe, loosely tied over his big belly and barely covering a nightshirt, his skinny legs sticking out of the bottom.

"Ah, it's you. Never know when to quit, do you? You bring my breakfast?"

"More than breakfast," she said. "This was left on your doorstep. Have any idea who would do that?"

He pulled at the receiving blanket and revealed the baby. "It's a newborn," he said. "Probably only hours old. Bring it in. Ain't yours, is it?"

"Come on," she said in aggravation, as though the doctor hadn't even noticed that she was not only too thin to have been pregnant, but also too lively to have just given birth. "Believe me, if it were mine, I wouldn't have left it here."

She walked past him into his house. She found herself not in a home, but a clinic—waiting room on her right, reception area complete with computer and filing cabinets behind a counter on her left. She went straight back on instinct and when she found an exam room, turned into it. Her only concern at the moment was making sure the infant wasn't ill or in need of emergency medical assistance. She put the box on the exam table, shed her coat and washed her hands. There was a stethoscope on the counter, so she found cotton and rubbing alcohol. She cleaned the earpieces with the alcohol—her own stethoscope was packed in the car. She listened to the baby's heart. Further inspection revealed it was a little girl, her umbilicus tied off with string.

Gently, tenderly, she lifted the baby from the box and cooing, laid her on the baby scale.

By this time the doctor was in the room. "Six pounds, nine ounces," she reported. "Full term. Heartbeat and respirations normal. Color is good." The baby started to wail "Strong lungs. Somebody threw away a perfectly good baby. You need to get Social Services right out here."

Doc gave a short laugh just as Jack came up behind him, looking into the room. "Yup, I'm sure they'll be right out."

"Well, what are you going to do?" she asked.

"I guess I'm going to rustle up some formula," he said. "Sounds hungry." He turned around and left the exam room.

"For the love of God," Mel said, rewrapping and jiggling the baby in her arms.

"Don't be too hard on him," Jack said. "This isn't L.A. We don't put in a call to Social Services and get an immediate house call. We're kind of on our own out here."

"What about the police?" she asked.

"There's no local police. County sheriff's department is pretty good," he said. "Not exactly what you're looking for, either, I bet."

"Why is that?"

"If there's not a serious crime, they would probably take their time," he said. "They have an awful lot of ground to cover. The deputy might just come out and write a report and put their own call in to Social Services, which will get a response when they're not overworked, underpaid, and can rustle up a social worker or foster family to take over this little…" He cleared his throat. "Problem."

"God," she said. "Don't call her a problem," she admonished. She started opening cupboard doors, unsatisfied. "Where's the kitchen?" she asked him.

"That way," he said, pointing left.

"Find me towels," she instructed. "Preferably soft towels."

"What are you going to do?"

"I'm going to wash her." She left the exam room with the baby in her arms.

Mel found the kitchen, which was large and clean. If Jack was delivering the doctor's meals, it probably wasn't used that much. She tossed the dish rack onto the floor in the corner and gently laid the baby on the drain board. Under the sink she found cleanser and gave the sink a quick scrub and rinse. Then she tested the temperature and filled the sink with water while the baby, most annoyed at the moment, filled the kitchen with the noise of her unhappiness. Fortuitously, there was a bar of Ivory soap on the sink, which Mel rinsed off as thoroughly as possible.

Rolling up her sleeves, she lifted the naked little creature into her arms and lowered her into the warm water. The cries stopped. "Aw," she said. "You like the bath? Does it feel like home?"

Doc Mullins came into the kitchen, dressed now, with a canister of powdered formula. Behind him trailed Jack, bearing the towels he was asked to fetch.

Mel gently rubbed the soap over the baby, rinsing off the muck of birth, the warmth of the water hopefully bringing the baby's temperature up. "This umbilicus is going to need some attention," she said. "Any idea who gave birth?"

"None whatsoever," Doc said, pouring bottled water into a measuring bowl.

"Who's pregnant? That would be a logical place to start."

"The pregnant women in Virgin River who have been coming here for prenatal visits wouldn't give birth alone. Maybe someone came from another town. Maybe I've got a patient out there who gave birth without the benefit of medical assistance, and that could be the second crisis of the day. As I'm sure you know," he added, somewhat smugly.

"As I'm sure I do," she returned, with equal smugness. "So, what's your plan?"

"I imagine I will diaper and feed and become irritable."

"I think you mean *more* irritable."

"I don't see many options," he said.

"Aren't there any women in town who could help out?"

"Perhaps on a limited basis." He filled a bottle and popped it in the microwave. "I'll manage, don't you worry." Then he added, somewhat absently, "Might not hear her in the night, but she'll live through it."

"You have to find a home for this baby," she said.

"You came here looking for work. Why don't you offer to help?"

She took a deep breath and, lifting the baby from the sink, laid her in the towel being held by Jack. She cocked her head in appreciation as Jack took the infant confidently, wrapping her snugly and cuddling her close. "You're pretty good at that," she said.

"The nieces," he said, jiggling the baby against his broad chest. "I've held a baby or two. You going to stay on a bit?" he asked.

"Well, there are problems with that idea. I have nowhere to stay. That cabin is not only unacceptable for me, it's more unacceptable for this infant. The porch collapsed, remember? And there are no steps to the back door. The only way in is to literally crawl."

"There's a room upstairs," Doc said. "If you stay and help out, you'll be paid." Then he looked at her over the rims of his reading glasses and sternly added, "Don't get attached to her. Her mother will turn up and want her back."

Jack went back to the bar and placed a call from the kitchen. A groggy, thick voice answered. "Hello?"

"Cheryl? You up?"

"Jack," the woman said. "That you?"

"It's me. I need a favor. Right away."

"What is it, Jack?"

"Weren't you asked to clean that McCrea cabin for the nurse coming to town?"

"Uh… Yeah. Didn't get to it though. I had… I think it was the flu."

It was the Smirnoff flu, he thought. Or even more likely, the Everclear flu—that really evil 190-proof pure grain alcohol. "Can you do it today? I'm going out there to repair the porch and I need that place cleaned. I mean, really cleaned. She's here and is staying with Doc for now—but that place has to be whipped into shape. So?"

"You're going to be there?"

"Most of the day. I can call someone else. I thought I'd give you a crack at it first, but you have to be sober."

"I'm sober," she insisted. "Totally."

He doubted it. He expected she would have a flask with her as she cleaned. But the risk he was taking, and it was not a pleasant risk, was that she would do it for him, and do it very well if it was for him. Cheryl had had a crush on him since he hit town and found excuses to be around him. He tried very hard never to give her any encouragement. But despite her struggle with alcohol, she was a strong woman and good at cleaning when she put her mind to it.

"The door's open. Get started and I'll be out later."

He hung up the phone and Preacher said, "Need a hand, man?"

"I do," he said. "Let's close up and get the cabin fixed up. She might be persuaded to stay."

"If that's what you want."

"It's what the town needs," he said

"Yeah," Preacher said. "Sure."

If Mel practiced any other kind of medicine, she might've put the baby in the old doctor's arthritic hands and gotten in her car to leave. But a midwife would never do that—couldn't turn her back on an abandoned newborn. For that matter, she couldn't shake a profound concern for the baby's mother. It was settled within seconds; she couldn't leave the baby to an old doctor who might not hear her cry in the night. And she had to be close by if the mother sought medical attention because women in childbirth and postpartum were her specialty.

During the rest of the day, Mel had ample opportunity to check out the rest of Doc's house. The spare room he provided turned out to be more than something for overnight guests—it was furnished with two hospital beds, an IV stand, tray table, bedside bureau and oxygen canister. The only chair in the room happened to be a rocking chair, and Mel was sure that was by design, for the use of a new mother and baby. The baby was provided with a Plexiglas incubator from the downstairs exam room.

The doctor's house was completely functional as a clinic and hospital. The downstairs living room was a waiting room, the dining room was fronted by a counter for check-in. There was an exam room, treatment room, both small, and the doctor's office. In the kitchen there was a small table where he no doubt ate his meals when he wasn't at Jack's. No ordinary kitchen, this one had an autoclave for sterilizing and a locked medicine chest for narcotic drugs kept on hand. In the refrigerator, a few units of blood and plasma, as well as food. More blood than food.

The upstairs had two bedrooms only—the one with the hospital beds and Doc Mullins's. Her accommodations were not the most comfortable, though better than the filthy cabin. But the room was cold and stark; hardwood floors, small rug, rough sheets with a plastic mattress protector that crinkled noisily. She already missed her down comforter, four-hundred-count sheets, soft Egyptian towels and thick, plush carpet. It had occurred to her that she would be leaving behind creature comforts, but she thought it might be good for her, thought she was ready for a big change.

Mel's friends and sister had tried to talk her out of this, but unfortunately they had failed. She had barely gotten over the traumatic experience of giving away all of Mark's clothes and personal items. She'd kept his picture, his watch, the cuff links she had given him on his last birthday—platinum—and his wedding ring. When the job in Virgin River came available, she'd sold all the furniture in their house then put it on the market. There was an offer in three days, even at those ridiculous L.A. prices. She'd packed three boxes of little treasures—favorite books, CDs, pictures, bric-a-brac. The desktop computer was given away to a friend, but she'd brought the laptop and her digital camera. As far as clothes, she'd filled three suitcases and an overnight and gave the rest away. No more strapless dresses for fancy charity events; no more sexy nighties for those nights that Mark didn't have to work late.

Mel was going to be starting over no matter what. She had nothing to go back to; she hadn't wanted anything to tie her to L.A. Now that things in Virgin River were not going as planned, Mel decided to stay and help out for a couple of days and then head out to Colorado. *Well,* she thought, *it'll be good to be near Joey, Bill and the kids. I can start over there as well as anywhere.*

It had been just Mel and Joey for a long time now. Joey was four years her senior and had been married to Bill for fifteen years. Their mother had died when Mel was only four—she could barely remember her. And their father, considerably older than their mother had been, had passed peacefully in his La-Z-Boy at the age of seventy, ten years ago.

Mark's parents were still alive and well in L.A., but she had never warmed to them. They had always been stuffy and cool toward her. Mark's death had brought them briefly closer, but it took only a few months for her to realize that they never called her. She checked on them, asked after their grief, but it seemed they'd let her drift out of sight. She was not surprised to note that she didn't miss them. She hadn't even told them she was leaving town.

She had wonderful friends, true. Girlfriends from nursing school and from the hospital. They called with regularity. Got her out of the house. Let her talk about him and cry about him. But after a while, though she loved them, she began to associate them with Mark's death. Every time she saw them, the pitying looks in their eyes were enough to bring out her pain. It was as if everything had been rolled up into one big miserable ball. She just wanted to start over so badly. Someplace where no one knew how empty her life had become.

Late in the day, Mel handed off the baby to Doc while she took a badly needed shower, scrubbing from head to toe. After she had bathed and dried her hair and donned her long flannel nightgown and big furry slippers, she went downstairs to Doc's office to collect the infant and a bottle. He gave her such a look, seeing her like that. It startled his eyes open. "I'll feed her, rock her and put her down," she said. "Unless you have something else in mind for her."

"By all means," he said, handing the baby over.

Up in her room, Mel rocked and fed the baby. And of course, the tears began to well in her eyes.

The other thing no one in this town knew was that she couldn't have children. She and Mark had been seeking help for their infertility. Because she was twenty-eight and he thirty-four when they married, and they'd already been together for two years, they didn't want to wait. She had never used birth control and after one year of no results they went to see the specialists.

Nothing appeared to be wrong with Mark, but she'd had to have her tubes blown out and her endometriosis scraped off the outside of her uterus. But still, nothing. She'd taken hormones and stood on her head after intercourse. She took her temperature every day to see when she was ovulating. She went through so many home pregnancy tests, she should have bought stock in the company. Nothing. They had just completed their first fifteen-thousand-dollar attempt at in vitro fertilization when Mark was killed. Somewhere in a freezer in L.A. were more fertilized ovum—if she ever became desperate enough to try to go it alone.

Alone. That was the operative word. She had wanted a baby so badly. And now she held in her arms an abandoned little girl. A beautiful baby girl with pink skin and a sheer cap of brown hair. It made her literally weep with longing.

The baby was healthy and strong, eating with gusto, belching with strength. She slept soundly despite the crying that went on in the bed right beside her.

That night Doc Mullins sat up in bed, book in his lap, listening. So—she was in pain. Desperate pain. And she covered it with that flip wit and sarcasm.

Nothing is ever what it seems, he thought, flicking off his light.

Three

Mel woke to the ringing of the phone. She checked the baby; she had only awoken twice in the night and still slept soundly. She found her slippers and went downstairs to see if she could rustle up some coffee. Doc Mullins was already in the kitchen, dressed.

"Going out to the Driscolls'—sounds like Jeananne might be having an asthma attack. There's the key to the drug box. I wrote down the number for my pager—cell phones aren't worth a damn out here. If any patients wander in while I'm gone, you can take care of them."

"I thought you just wanted me to babysit," she said.

"You came here to work, didn't you?"

"You said you didn't want me," she pointed out to him.

"You said you didn't want us, either, but here we are. Let's see what you got." He shrugged on his jacket and picked up his bag. Then jutted his chin toward her, lifted his eyebrows as if to say, *Well?*

"Do you have appointments today?"

"I only make appointments on Wednesdays—the rest are walk-ins. Or call-outs, like this one."

"I wouldn't even know what to charge," she argued.

"Neither do I," he said. "Hardly matters—these people aren't made of money and damn few have insurance. Just make sure you keep good records and I'll work it out. It's probably beyond you, anyway. You don't look all that bright."

"You know," she said, "I've worked with some legendary assholes, but you're competing for first place here."

"I'll take that as a compliment," he said gruffly.

"That figures," she answered tiredly. "Incidentally, the night was fine."

No comment from the old goat. He started for the door and on his way out, grabbed a cane. "Are you limping?" Mel asked him.

"Arthritis," he said. He dug an antacid out of his pocket and popped it in his mouth. "And heartburn. Got any more questions?"

"God, no!"

"Good."

Mel got a bottle ready and while it was in the microwave, she went upstairs to dress. By the time that was accomplished, the baby started to stir. She changed her and picked her up and found herself saying, "Sweet Chloe, sweet baby…" If she and Mark had had a girl, she was to be Chloe. A boy would be Adam. What was she doing?

"But you have to be someone, don't you?" she told the baby.

When she was coming down the stairs, the baby swaddled and held against her shoulder, Jack was opening the front door. He was balancing a covered dish on his hand, a thermos tucked under his arm. "Sorry, Jack—you just missed him."

"This is for you. Doc stopped by the bar and said

I'd better get you some breakfast, that you were pretty cranky."

She laughed in spite of herself. "I'm cranky, huh? He's a giant pain in the ass! How do you put up with him?"

"He reminds me of my grandfather. How'd it go last night? She sleep?"

"She did very well. Only woke up a couple of times. I'm just about to feed her."

"Why don't I give her a bottle while you eat. I brought coffee."

"Really, I didn't know they made men like you," she said, letting him follow her into the kitchen. When he put down the plate and thermos, she handed over the baby and tested the bottle. "You seem very comfortable with a newborn. For a man. A man with some nieces in Sacramento." He just smiled at her. She passed him the bottle and got out two coffee mugs. "Ever married?" she asked him, then instantly regretted it. It was going to lead to him asking her.

"I was married to the Marine Corps," he said. "And she was a real bitch."

"How many years?" she asked, pouring coffee.

"Just over twenty years. I went in as a kid. How about you?"

"I was never in the marines," she said with a smile.

He grinned at her. "Married?"

She couldn't meet his eyes and lie, so she concentrated on the coffee mug. "I was married to a hospital, and my bitch was as mean as your bitch." That wasn't a total lie. Mark used to complain about the schedules they kept—grueling. He was in emergency medicine. He'd just finished a thirty-six-hour shift when he stopped at the convenience store, interrupting the robbery. She shuddered involuntarily. She pushed a mug toward him. "Did you see a lot of combat?" she asked.

"A lot of combat," he answered, directing the bottle into the baby's mouth expertly. "Somalia, Bosnia, Afghanistan, Iraq. Twice."

"No wonder you just want to fish."

"Twenty years in the marines will make a fisherman out of just about anyone."

"You seem too young to have retired."

"I'm forty. I decided it was time to get out when I got shot in the butt."

"Ouch. Complete recovery?" she asked, then surprised herself by feeling her cheeks grow warm.

He lifted a corner of his mouth. "Except for the dimple. Wanna see?"

"Thanks, no. So, Doc left me in charge and I have no idea what to expect. Maybe you should tell me where the nearest hospital is—and do they provide ambulance service to the town?"

"That would be Valley Hospital—and they have ambulance service, but it takes so long to get here, Doc usually fires up his old truck and makes the run himself. If you're desperate and have about an hour to spare, the Grace Valley doctors have an ambulance, but I don't think I've seen an ambulance in this town since I've been here. I heard the helicopter came for the guy who almost died in the truck accident. I think the helicopter got as much notice as the accident."

"God, I hope these people are healthy until he gets back," she said. Mel dug into the eggs. This seemed to be a Spanish omelet, and it was just as delicious as the one she'd eaten the day before. "Mmm," she said appreciatively. "Here's another thing—I can't get any cell phone reception here. I should let my family know I'm here safely. More or less."

"The pines are too tall, the mountains too steep. Use the landline—and don't worry about the long distance cost. You have to be in touch with your family. Who is your family?"

"Just an older married sister in Colorado Springs. She and her husband put up a collective and huge fuss about this—as if I was going into the Peace Corps or something. I should've listened."

"There will be a lot of people around here glad you didn't," he said.

"I'm stubborn that way."

He smiled appreciatively.

It made her instantly think, *Don't get any ideas, buster. I'm married to someone. Just because he isn't here, doesn't mean it's over.*

However, there was something about a guy—at least six foot two and two hundred pounds of rock-hard muscle—holding a newborn with gentle deftness and skill. Then she saw him lower his lips to the baby's head and inhale her scent, and some of the ice around Mel's broken heart started to melt.

"I'm going into Eureka today for supplies," he said. "Need anything?"

"Disposable diapers. Newborn. And since you know everyone, could you ask around if anyone can help out with the baby? Either full-time, part-time, whatever. It would be better for her to be in a family home than here at Doc's with me."

"Besides," he said, "you want to get out of here."

"I'll help out with the baby for a couple of days, but I don't want to stretch it out. I can't stay here, Jack."

"I'll ask around," he said. And decided he might just forget to do that. Because, yes, she could.

Little baby Chloe had only been asleep thirty minutes after her morning bottle when the first patient of the day arrived. A healthy and scrubbed-looking young farm girl wearing overalls in the middle of which protruded a very large pregnant tummy, carrying two large jars of what appeared to be preserved blackberries. She put the berries on the floor just inside the door. "I heard there was a new lady doctor in town," she said.

"Not exactly," Mel said. "I'm a nurse practitioner."

Her face fell in disappointment. "Oh," she said. "I thought it would be so nice to have a woman doctor around when it's time."

"Time?" Mel asked. "To deliver?"

"Uh-huh. I like Doc, don't get me wrong. But—"

"When are you due?" Mel asked.

She rubbed her swollen belly. "I think about a month, but I'm not really sure," she said. She wore laced-up work boots, a yellow sweater underneath the overalls and her brown hair was pulled back in a ponytail. She looked twenty years old, at most. "It's my first."

"I'm a midwife, as well," Mel said, and the young woman's face lit up in a beautiful smile. "But I have to warn you—I'm only here temporarily. I'm planning to leave as soon as—" She thought about what she should say. Then, instead of explaining about the baby, she said, "Have you had a checkup recently? Blood pressure, weight, et cetera?"

"It's been a few weeks," she said. "I guess I'm about due."

"Why don't we do that since you're here, if I can find what I need," Mel said. "What's your name?"

"Polly Fishburn."

"I bet you have a chart around here somewhere," Mel said. She went behind the counter and started opening file drawers. A brief search turned up a chart. She went in search of litmus, and other obstetric supplies in the exam room. "Come on back, Polly," she called. "When was the last time you had an internal exam?"

"Not since the very first," she said. She made a face. "I was dreading the next one."

Mel smiled, thinking about Doc's bent and arthritic fingers. That couldn't be pleasant. "Want me to have a look? See if you're doing anything, like dilating or effacing? It might save you having Doc do it later. Just get undressed, put on this little gown, and I'll be right back."

Mel checked on the baby, who was napping in the kitchen, then went back to her patient. Polly appeared to be in excellent health with normal weight gain, good blood pressure, and… "Oh, boy, Polly. Baby's head is down." Mel stood and pressed down on her tummy while her fingers stretched toward the young woman's cervix. "And… You're just barely dilated and effaced about fifty percent. You're having a small contraction right now. Can you feel that tightening? Braxton Hicks contractions." She smiled at her patient. "Where are you having the baby?"

"Here—I think."

Mel laughed. "If you do that anytime soon, we're going to be roommates. I'm staying upstairs."

"When do you think it'll come?" Polly asked.

"One to four weeks, and that's just a guess," she said. She stepped back and snapped off her gloves.

"Will you deliver the baby?" Polly asked.

"I'll be honest with you, Polly—I'm planning to

leave as soon as it's reasonable. But if I'm still here when you go into labor, and if Doc says it's okay, I'd be more than happy to." She put out a hand to help Polly sit up. "Get dressed. I'll see you out front."

When she walked out of the exam room and back toward the front of the house, she found the waiting room was full of people.

By the end of the day Mel had seen over thirty patients, at least twenty-eight of whom just wanted a look at "the new lady doctor." They wanted to visit, ask her questions about herself, bring her welcome gifts.

It was at once a huge surprise to her, and also what she had secretly expected when she took the job.

By six o'clock, Mel was exhausted, but the day had flown. She held the baby on her shoulder, gently jiggling her. "Have you had anything to eat?" she asked Doc Mullins.

"When, during our open house, would I have eaten?" he shot back. But it was not nearly as sarcastic as Mel imagined he wished it to be.

"Would you like to walk across the street while I feed the baby?" she asked. "Because after you and little Chloe have eaten, I really need some fresh air. No, make that—I'm desperate for a change of scenery. And I haven't eaten since breakfast."

He put out his old, gnarled hands. "Chloe?" he asked.

She shrugged. "She has to be called something."

"Go," he said. "I'll see that she's fed. Then I'll poke around here for something."

She handed over the baby with a smile. "I know you're trying to act miserable and just can't pull it off," she said. "But thank you—I'd really like to get out of here for an hour."

She grabbed her jacket off the peg by the front door and stepped out into the spring night. Out here, away from the smog and industry of city life, there were at least a million more stars. She took a deep breath. She wondered if a person actually got used to air like this— so much cleaner than the smog of L.A., it shocked the lungs.

There were quite a few people at Jack's—unlike that stormy night when she'd arrived. Two women she'd met earlier in the day were there with their husbands— Connie and Ron of the corner store, and Connie's best friend, Joy, and husband, Bruce. Bruce, she learned, delivered the mail and was also the person who would take any specimens to the lab at Valley Hospital, if needed. They introduced her to Carrie and Fish Bristol and Doug and Sue Carpenter. There were a couple of guys at the bar and another two at a table playing cribbage—by their canvas vests she took them for fishermen.

Mel hung up her jacket, gave her sweater a little tug to bring it over the waist of her jeans, and popped up on a bar stool. She did not realize she was wearing a smile. That her eyes shone. They had all come out to see her, welcome her, tell her about themselves, ask her for advice. When the day was full of people who needed her—even those who weren't necessarily sick— it filled her up inside. Passed for happiness, if she dared go that far.

"Lot of action across the street today, I hear," Jack said, giving the bar a wipe at her place.

"You were closed," she said.

"I had things to do—and so did Preacher. We stay open most of the time, but if something comes up, we put up a sign and try to get back by dinner."

"If something comes up?" she asked.

"Like fishing," Preacher said, putting a rack of glasses under the bar, then he went back to the kitchen. Out of the back came the kid, Ricky, busing tables. When he spied Mel he grinned hugely and came over to the bar with his tray of dishes. "Miss Monroe—you still here? Awesome." Then he went to the kitchen.

"He is too cute."

"Don't let him hear you say that," Jack advised. "He's at the crush age. A very dangerous sixteen. What do you feel like?"

"You know—I wouldn't mind a cold beer," she said. And it instantly appeared before her. "What's for dinner?" she asked.

"Meat loaf," he said. "And the best mashed potatoes you'll ever experience."

"You don't have anything like a menu, do you?"

"Nope. We get whatever Preacher's in the mood to fix. You wanna enjoy that beer for a minute? Or, you want your supper fast?"

She took a pull. "Give me a minute." She took another sip and said, "Ahhh." It made Jack smile. "I think I met half the town today."

"Not even close. But the ones who came out today will spread the word about you. Have any real patients, or were they all just checking you out?"

"I had a couple. You know, I really didn't have to come over here—the house is full of food. When they come, they bring food, whether they're really sick or not. Pies, cakes, sliced meat, fresh bread. It's very… country."

He laughed. "Careful," he said. "We'll grow on you."

"You have any use for a couple of jars of canned berries? I think it was a patient fee."

"You bet. Preacher makes the best pies in the county. Any news about the baby's mother?"

"I call the baby Chloe," she said, expecting a sting of tears that, remarkably, didn't come. "No. Nothing. I hope the woman who gave birth isn't sick somewhere."

"With the way everyone around here knows everyone's business, if there were a sick woman out there, word would get out."

"Maybe she did come from another town."

"You look almost happy," he said.

"I almost am," she returned. "The young woman who brought the berries asked me to deliver her baby. That was nice. The only problem seems to be that she's going to be having her baby in my bedroom. And she could be doing that pretty soon, too."

"Ah," he said. "Polly. She looks like that baby's ready to fall out of her."

"How did you know? Oh, never mind—everyone knows everything."

"There aren't that many pregnant women around," he laughed.

She turned on her stool and looked around. Two old women were eating meat loaf at a table by the fire and the couples she had met, all in their forties or fifties, seemed to be socializing; laughing and gossiping. There were perhaps a dozen patrons. "Business is pretty good tonight, huh?"

"They don't come out in the rain so much. Busy putting buckets under the leaks, I suppose. So—still feel like getting the hell out of here?"

She drank a little of her beer, noting that on an empty stomach the effects were instantaneous. And, actually, delightful. "I'm going to have to leave, if for no other reason than there's nowhere around here to get highlights put in my hair."

"There are beauty shops around here. In Virgin River, Dot Schuman does hair in her garage."

"That sounds intriguing." She lifted her eyes to his face and said, "I'm getting a buzz. Maybe I better do that meat loaf." She hiccupped and they both laughed.

By seven, Hope McCrea had wandered in and took the stool next to her. "Heard you had a lot of company today," she said. She pulled her cigarettes out of her purse and as she was going to shake one out, Mel grabbed her wrist.

"You have to wait until I'm done with dinner, at least."

"Oh, foo—you're a killjoy." She put the pack down. "The usual," she ordered. And to Mel, "So—how was it? Your first real day? Doc scare you off yet?"

"He was absolutely manageable. He even let me put in a couple of stitches. Of course, he didn't compliment my work, but he didn't tell me it was bad, either." She leaned closer to Hope and said, "I think he's taking credit for me. You might want to stand up for yourself."

"You're staying now?"

"I'm staying a few days, at least. Until we get a couple of things that need attention ironed out."

"I heard. Newborn, they say."

Jack put a drink down in front of Hope. "Jack Daniel's, neat," he said.

"Have any ideas on the mother?" Mel asked Hope.

"No. But everyone is looking at everyone else strangely. If she's around here, she'll turn up. You done pushing food around that plate yet? Because I'm ready for a smoke."

"You shouldn't, you know."

Hope McCrea looked at Mel in impatience, grimacing. She pushed her too-big glasses up on her nose. "What the hell do I care now? I've already lived longer than I expected to."

"That's nonsense. You have many good years left."

"Oh, God. I hope not!"

Jack laughed and in spite of herself, so did Mel.

Hope, acting like a woman with a million things to do, had her drink and cigarette, put money on the bar, hopped off the stool and said, "I'll be in touch. I can help out with the little one, if you need me."

"You can't smoke around the baby," Mel informed her.

"I didn't say I could help out for hours and hours," she answered. "Keep that in mind." And off she went, stopping at a couple of tables to pass the time on her way out.

"How late do you stay open?" Mel asked Jack.

"Why? You thinking about a nightcap?"

"Not tonight. I'm bushed. For future reference."

"I usually close around nine—but if someone asks me to stay open, I will."

"This is the most accommodating restaurant I've ever frequented," she laughed. She looked at her watch. "I better spell Doc. I don't know how patient he is with an infant. I'll see you at breakfast, unless Doc's out on a house call."

"We'll be here," he offered.

Mel said goodbye and on her way to her coat, stopped at a couple of the tables to say good-night to people she had just met. "Think she'll stay on awhile?" Preacher quietly asked Jack.

Jack was frowning. "I think what she does to a pair of jeans ought to be against the law." He looked at

Preacher. "You okay here? I'm thinking of having a beer in Clear River."

It was code. There was a woman in Clear River. "I'm okay here," Preacher said.

As Jack drove the half hour to Clear River, he wasn't thinking about Charmaine, which gave him a twinge of guilt. Tonight he was thinking about another woman. A very beautiful young blonde woman who could just about bring a man to his knees with what she looked like in boots and jeans.

Jack had gone to a tavern in Clear River for a beer a couple of years ago and struck up a conversation with the waitress there—Charmaine. She was the divorced mother of a couple of grown kids. A good woman; hardworking. Fun-loving and flirtatious. After several visits and as many beers, she took him home with her and he fell into her as if she were a feather bed. Then he told her what he always made sure women understood about him—that he was not the kind of man who could ever be tied down to a woman, and if she began to have those designs, he'd be gone.

"What makes you think all women want to be run by some man?" she had asked. "I just got rid of one. Not about to get myself hooked up to another one." Then she smiled and said, "Just the same, everyone gets a little lonely sometimes."

They started an affair that had sustained Jack for a couple of years now. Jack didn't see her that often— every week, maybe couple of weeks. Sometimes a month would go by. He wasn't sure what she did when he wasn't around—maybe there were other men— though he'd never seen any evidence of that. He never caught her making time in the bar with anyone else;

never saw any men's things around her house. He kept a box of condoms in her bedside drawer that didn't disappear on him, and he'd let it slip that he liked being the only man she entertained.

As for Jack—he had a personal ethic about one woman at a time. Sometimes that woman could last a year, sometimes a night—but he didn't have a collection he roved between. Although he wasn't exactly breaking that rule tonight, he wasn't quite sticking to it, either.

He never spent the night in Clear River and Charmaine was not invited to Virgin River. She had only called him and asked him to come to her twice—and it seemed a small thing to ask. After all, he wasn't the only one who needed to be with someone once in a while.

He liked that when he walked in the tavern and she saw him, it showed all over her that she was happy he'd come. He suspected she had stronger feelings for him than she let show. He owed her—she'd been a real sport about it—but he knew he'd have to leave the relationship before it got any more entangled. So sometimes, to demonstrate he had a few gentlemanly skills, he'd drop in for just a beer. Sometimes he'd bring her something, like a scarf or earrings.

He sat down at the bar and she brought him a beer. She fluffed her hair; she was a big blonde. Bleached blonde. At about five foot eight, she'd kept her figure, mostly. He didn't know her exact age, but he suspected late forties, early fifties. She always wore very tight-fitting clothes and tops that accentuated her full breasts. At first sight you'd think—cheap. Not so much tawdry or low-class as simple. Unrefined. But once you got to know Charmaine and how kind and deep down earnest she was, those thoughts fled. Jack imagined that in younger years she was quite the looker with her ample chest and full lips. She hadn't really lost those good looks, but she had a little extra weight around the hips and there were wrinkles at the corners of her eyes.

"Hiya, bub," she said. "Haven't seen you in a while."

"It's only been a couple of weeks, I think."

"More like four."

"How've you been?" he asked.

"Busy. Working. Went over to Eureka to see my daughter last week. She's having herself a lousy marriage—but what should we expect? I raised her in one."

"She getting divorced?" he asked politely, though in truth he didn't care that much. He didn't know her kids.

"No. But she should. Let me get this table. I'll be back."

She left him to make sure the other customers were served. There were only a few and once Jack showed up the owner, Butch, knew that Charmaine would want to leave a little early. He saw her take a tray of glasses back behind the bar and talk quietly with her boss, who nodded. Then Charmaine was back.

"I just wanted to have a beer and say hello," Jack said. "Then I have to get back. I have a big project going on."

"Oh, yeah? What's that?"

"I'm fixing up a cabin for one of the women in town. I put on a new porch today and tomorrow I'm going to paint it and build back steps."

"That so? Pretty woman?"

"I guess you could say she's pretty. For seventy-six years old."

She laughed loudly. Charmaine had a big laugh. It was a good laugh that came from deep inside her. "Well, then, I guess I won't bother being jealous. But do you think you can spare the time to walk me home?"

"I can," he said, draining his beer. "But I'm not coming in tonight."

"That's fine," she said. "I'll get my coat."

When they were outside, she looped her arm through his and began to talk about her last couple of weeks, as she always did. He liked the sound of her voice, deep and a little raspy, what they called a whiskey voice though she wasn't much of a drinker. She could go on and on about next to nothing but in a pleasant way, not an irritating way. She would talk about the bar, the people in the town, her kids, what she'd bought lately, what she'd read. News items fascinated her—she would spend the mornings before work watching CNN, and she liked to tell him her opinion of breaking stories. She always had some project going on in her little house— wallpaper or paint or new appliances. The house was paid for; an inheritance of some kind. So the money she made, she spent on herself and her kids.

When they got to the door he said, "I'll shove off, Charmaine. But I'll see you before long."

"Okay, Jack," she said. She tilted her head up for a kiss and he obliged. "That wasn't much of a kiss," she said.

"I don't want to come in tonight," he said.

"You must be awful tired," she said. "Think you have enough energy to give me a kiss that I'll remember for an hour or two?"

He tried again. This time he covered her mouth with his, allowed his tongue to do a little exploring, held her close against him. And she grabbed his butt. Damn! he thought. She ground against him a little bit, sucked on his tongue. Then she hooked her hand into the front of his jeans and pulled him forward, letting her fingers drift lower against his belly.

"Okay," he said weakly, a little vulnerable, stirred up. "I'll come in for a few minutes."

"That's my boy," she said, smiling at him. She pushed open the door and he followed her inside. "Just think of it as a little sleeping pill."

He dropped his jacket on the chair. Charmaine wasn't even out of hers when he grabbed her around the waist, pulled her against him and devoured her with a kiss that was sudden, hot and needy. He pushed her jacket off her shoulders and walked her backwards toward the bedroom and dropped with her onto the bed. He pulled at her top and freed her breasts, filling his mouth with one and then the other. Then off came her pants, and down came his. He ran his hands over her lush body, down over her shoulders, hips, thighs. He reached over to the bedside table, retrieved one of the condoms kept there for him, and ripped the package open. He put it on and was inside her so quickly, it startled even him. He thrust and plunged and drove and she said, "Oh! Oh! Oh, my God!"

He was ready to explode, but held himself back while her legs came around his waist and she bucked. Something happened to him—he went a little out of his mind. Didn't know where he was or with whom. When she finally tightened around him, he let himself go with a loud groan. She panted beneath him, the sound that told him she was completely satisfied.

"My God," she said when she finally caught her breath. "What's got you so hot?"

"Huh?"

"Jack, you don't even have your boots off!"

He was shocked for a moment, then rolled off her. *Jesus,* he thought. *You can't treat a woman like that.* He might not have been thinking, but at least he wasn't thinking about anyone else, he consoled himself. He had no brain power involved in that at all—it was all visceral. His body, reaching out.

"I'm sorry, Charmaine. You okay?"

"I'm way more than okay. But please, take your boots off and hold me."

It was on his mind to say he had to go, he wanted to go, but he couldn't do that to her after this. He sat up and got rid of the boots and pants and shirt, everything hitting the floor. After a quick visit to the bathroom he was back, scooped her up in his arms and held her. Her heavy, soft body was cushiony against his.

He stroked her, kissed her and eventually made love to her again, as opposed to what he'd done before. This time sanely, but no less satisfactorily. At one in the morning he was searching around the floor for his pants.

"I thought you might be staying the night this time," she said from the bed.

He pulled on his pants and sat on the bed to put on his boots. He twisted around and gave her a kiss on the cheek. "I can't," he said. "But you'll be fine now." He smiled at her. "Think of it as a little sleeping pill."

As he drove back to Virgin River he thought, *It's over now. I have to end it. I can't do that anymore, not with a clear conscience. Not when something else has my attention.*

Four

Jack drove out to the cabin, the truck bed loaded with supplies. It was his third day in a row. When he pulled up, Cheryl came out of the house, onto the new porch. "Hey, Cheryl," he called. "How's it going? Almost done in there?"

She had a rag in her hands. "I need the rest of the day. It was a real pigsty. Will you be here tomorrow, too?"

He would. But he said, "Nah. I'm about done. I want to paint the porch this morning—can you get out the back door? I haven't built steps yet."

"I can jump down. Whatcha got?" She came down the porch steps.

"Just stuff for the cabin," he said, unloading a big Adirondack chair for the porch, its twin in the truck bed.

"Wow. You really went all out," she said.

"It has to be done."

"She must be some nurse."

"She says she's not staying, but the place has to be fixed up anyway. I told Hope I'd make sure it was taken care of."

"Not everyone would go to so much trouble. You're really a good guy, Jack," she said. She peeked into the truck. He had a new double-size mattress inside a large plastic bag lying flat in the bed. On top of that, a large rolled-up rug for the living room, bags from Target full of linens and towels that were new as opposed to the graying, used ones borrowed from Hope's linen closet, potted geraniums for the front porch, lumber for the back step, paint, a box full of new kitchen things. "This is a lot more than repair stuff," she said. She tucked a strand of hair that had escaped her clip around her ear. When he chanced a glance at her, he saw those sad eyes filled with longing. He looked away quickly.

"Why go halfway?" he said. "It ought to be nice. When she leaves, maybe Hope can rent it out to summer people."

"Yeah," she said.

Jack continued unloading while Cheryl just stood around. He tried to ignore her; he didn't even make small talk.

Cheryl was a tall, big-boned woman of just thirty, but she didn't look so good—she'd been drinking pretty hard since she was a teenager. Her complexion was ruddy, her hair thin and listless, her eyes red-rimmed and droopy. She had a lot of extra weight around the middle from the booze. Every now and then she'd sober up for a couple of weeks or months, but invariably she'd fall back into the bottle. She still lived with her parents, who were at their wits' end with her drinking. But what to do? She'd get her hands on booze regardless. Jack never served her, but every time he happened upon her, like now, there was usually a telltale odor and half-mast eyes. She was holding it together pretty good today. She must not have had much.

There had been a bad incident a couple of years ago that Cheryl and Jack had had to get beyond. She had a little too much one night and went to his living quarters behind the bar, banging on his door in the middle of the night. When he opened the door, she flung herself on him, groping him and declaring her tragic love for him. Sadly for her, she remembered every bit of it. He caught her sober a few days later and said, "Never. It is never going to happen. Get over it and don't do that again." And it made her cry.

He moved on as best he could and was grateful that she did her drinking at home, not in his bar and grill. She liked straight vodka, probably right out of the bottle and, if she could get her hands on it, Everclear—that really mean, potent stuff. It was illegal in most states, but liquor store owners usually had a little under the counter.

"I wish I could be a nurse," Cheryl said.

"Have you ever thought about going back to school?" he asked as he worked. He was careful not to give her the impression he was too interested. He hauled the rug out of the back of the truck, hefted it over his shoulder and carried it to the house.

To his back she said, "I couldn't afford it."

"You could if you got a job. You need a bigger town. Throw your net a little wider. Stop relying on odd jobs."

"Yeah, I know," she said, following him. "But I like it here."

"Do you? You don't seem that happy."

"Oh, I'm happy sometimes."

"That's good," he said. He threw the rolled rug down in the living room. He'd spread it out later. "If you have the time, could you wash up those new linens I bought and put them away? Fix up the bed when I get the new mattress on it?"

"Sure. Let me help you with the mattress."

"Thanks," he said, and together they hauled it into the house. He leaned it against the wall and grabbed the old one off the bed. "I'll go by the dump on the way home."

"I heard there was a baby at Doc's. Like a baby that was just left there."

Jack froze. Oh, man, he thought. Cheryl? Could it be Cheryl's? Without meaning to, he looked her up and down. She was big, but not obese. Yet fat around the middle and her shirt loose and baggy. But she'd been out here cleaning that very day—she couldn't do that, could she? Maybe it wasn't the Smirnoff flu. Wouldn't she be bleeding and leaking milk? Weak and tired?

"Yeah," he finally said. "You hear of anyone who could have done that?"

"No. Is it an Indian baby? Because there's reservations around here—women on hard times. You know."

"White," he answered.

"You know, when I'm done here, I could help out with the baby."

"Uh, I think that's covered, Cheryl. But thanks. I'll tell Doc." He carried the old mattress out and leaned it against the truck bed. God, that was an awful-looking thing. Mel was completely right—that cabin was horrific. What had Hope been thinking? She'd been thinking it would be cleaned up—but had she expected the new nurse to sleep on that thing? Sometimes Hope could be oblivious to details like these. She was pretty much just a crusty old broad.

He reached into the truck and hauled out the bags of linens. "Here you go," he said to Cheryl. "Now get inside—I have to start painting. I want to get back to the bar by dinner."

"Okay," she said, accepting the bags. "Let me know if Doc needs me. Okay?"

"Sure, Cheryl." Never, he thought. Too risky.

Jack was back at the bar by midafternoon with time enough to do an inventory of bar stock before people started turning out for dinner. The bar was empty, as it often was at this time of day. Preacher was in the back getting started on his evening meal and Ricky wasn't due for another hour at least.

A man came into the bar alone. He wasn't dressed as a fisherman; he wore jeans, a tan T-shirt under a denim vest, his hair was on the long side and he had a ball cap on his head. He was a big guy with a stubble of beard about a week old. He sat several stools down from where Jack stood with his clipboard and inventory paperwork, a good indication he didn't want to talk.

Jack walked down to him. "Hi. Passing through?" he asked, slapping a napkin down in front of him.

"Hmm," the man answered. "How about a beer and a shot. Heineken and Beam."

"You got it," Jack said, setting him up.

The man threw back the shot right away, then lifted the beer, all without making any eye contact with Jack. *Fine, we won't talk,* Jack thought. *I have things to do anyway.* So Jack went back to counting bottles.

About ten minutes had passed when he heard, "Hey, buddy. Once more, huh?"

"You bet," Jack said, serving him another round. Again silence prevailed. The man took a little longer on his beer, time enough for Jack to get a good bit of his inventory done. While he was crouched behind the bar, a shadow fell over him and he looked up to see the man standing right on the other side of the bar, ready to settle up.

Jack stood just as the man was reaching into his pocket. He noticed a bit of tattoo sneaking out from the sleeve of his shirt—the recognizable feet of a bulldog—the Devil Dog. Jack was close to remarking on it—the man wore an unmistakable United States Marine Corps tattoo. But then the man pulled a thick wad of bills out, peeled off a hundred and said, "Can you change this?"

Jack didn't even have to touch the bill; the skunk-like odor of green cannabis wafted toward him. The man had just done some cutting—pruning or harvesting and, from the stinky cash, had made a sale. Jack could change the bill, but he didn't want to advertise how much cash he kept on hand and he didn't want that money on the premises. There were plenty of growers out there—some with prescriptions for legal use, conscious of the medical benefits. There were those who thought of marijuana as just any old plant, like corn. Agriculture. A way to make money. And some who dealt drugs because the drugs would offer a big profit. This part of the country was often referred to as the Emerald Triangle for the three counties most known for the cannabis trade. Lots of nice, new, half-ton trucks being driven by people on a busboy's salary.

Some of the towns around these parts catered to them, selling supplies illegal growers needed—irrigation tubing, grow lights, camouflage tarps, plastic sheeting, shears in various sizes for harvesting and pruning. Scales, generators, ATVs for getting off-road and back into secretive hideaways buried in the forest. There were merchants around who displayed signs in their windows that said, CAMP Not Served Here. CAMP being the Campaign Against Marijuana Planting that was a joint operation between the county sheriff's department and the state of California. Clear River was a town that didn't like CAMP and didn't mind taking the growers' money, of which there was a lot. Charmaine didn't approve of the illegal growing, but Dutch wouldn't turn down a stinky bill.

Virgin River was not that kind of town.

Growers usually maintained low profiles and didn't cause problems, not wanting to be raided. But sometimes there were territorial conflicts between them or booby-trapped grows, either one of which could hurt an innocent citizen. There were drug-related crimes ranging from burglary or robbery to murder. Not so long ago they found the body of a grower's partner buried in the woods near Garberville; he'd been missing for over two years and the grower himself had always been a suspect.

You couldn't find anything in Virgin River that would encourage an illegal crop, one means of keeping them away. If there were any growers in town, they were real, real secret. Virgin River tended to push this sort away. But this wasn't the first one to pass by.

"Tell you what," Jack said to the man, making long and serious eye contact. "On the house this time."

"Thanks," he said, folding his bill back onto the wad and stuffing it in his pocket. He turned to go.

"And buddy?" Jack called as the man reached the door to leave. He turned and Jack said, "Sheriff's deputy and California Highway Patrol eat and drink on the house in my place."

The man's shoulders rose once with a silent huff of laughter. He was on notice. He touched the brim of his hat and left.

Jack walked around the bar and looked out the window to see the man get into a black late model Range

Rover, supercharged, big wheels jacked up real high, windows tinted, lights on the roof. That model would go for nearly a hundred grand. This guy was no hobbyist. He memorized the license plate.

Preacher was rolling out pie dough when Jack went into the kitchen. "I just served a guy who tried to pay for his drinks with a wad of stinky Bens as big as my fist," Jack told him.

"Crap."

"He's driving a new Range Rover, loaded, jacked up and lit up. Big guy."

"You think he's growing around town here?"

"Have no idea," Jack said. "We better pay attention. Next time the deputy's in town, I'll mention it. But it's not against the law to have stinky money or drive a big truck."

"If he's rich, it's probably not a small operation," Preacher said.

"He's got a bulldog tattoo on his upper right arm."

Preacher frowned. "You kind of hate to see a brother go that way."

"Yeah, tell me about it. Maybe he's not in business around here. He could have been just scoping out the town to see if this is a good place to set up. I think I sent the message that it's not. I told him law enforcement eats and drinks on the house."

Preacher smiled. "We should start doing that, then," he said.

"How about a discount, to start? We don't want to get crazy."

Mel got her sister, Joey, on the phone.

"Oh, Jesus, Mel! You scared me to death! Where have you been? Why didn't you call sooner?"

"I've been in Virgin River where I have no phone and my cell doesn't work. And I've been pretty busy."

"I was about to call out the National Guard!"

"Yeah? Well, don't bother. They'd never be able to find the place."

"You're all right?"

"Well… This will probably make you perversely happy," Mel told her. "You were right. I shouldn't have done this. I was nuts. As usual."

"Is it terrible?"

"Well, it definitely started out terrible—the free housing turned out to be a falling-down hovel and the doctor is a mean old coot who doesn't want any help in his practice. I was on my way out of town when—you'll never believe this—someone left an abandoned newborn on the doctor's porch. But things have improved, if slightly. I'm staying for at least a few more days to help with the baby. The old doc wouldn't wake up to those middle-of-the-night hunger cries. Oh, Joey, my first impression of him is that he was the poorest excuse for a town doctor I'd ever met. Mean as a snake, rude as sour milk. Fortunately, working with those L.A. medical residents, especially those dicky surgeons, prepared me nicely."

"Okay, that was your first impression. How has it changed?"

"He proves tractable. Since my housing was uninhabitable, I'm staying in the guest room in his house. It's actually set up to be the only hospital room in town. This house is fine—clean and functional. There could be a slight inconvenience at any moment—a young woman who asked me to deliver her first baby will be having it here—in my bedroom, which I share with the abandoned baby. Picture this—a postpartum patient and a full nursery."

"And you will sleep where?"

"I'll probably hang myself up in a corner and sleep standing up. But that's only if she delivers within the next week, while I'm still here. Surely a family will turn up to foster this baby soon. Although, I wouldn't mind a birth. A sweet, happy birth to loving, excited, healthy parents…"

"You don't have to stay for that," Joey said firmly. "It's not as though they don't have a doctor."

"I know—but she's so young. And she was so happy, thinking there was a woman doctor here who could deliver her rather than this ornery old man."

"Mel, I want you to get in your car and drive. Come to us. Where we can look after you for a while."

"I don't need looking after," she said with a laugh. "Work helps. I need to work. Whole hours go by without thinking about Mark."

"How are you doing with that?"

She sighed deeply. "That's another thing. No one here knows, so no one looks at me with those sad, pitying eyes. And since they don't look at me that way, I don't crumble so often. At least, not where anyone can see."

"Oh, Mel, I wish I could comfort you somehow…"

"But, Joey, I have to grieve this, it's the only way. And I have to live with the fact that I might never be over it."

"I hope that's not true, Mel. I know widows. I know widows who have remarried and are happy."

"We're not going there," she said. Then Mel told Joey about what she knew of the town, about all the people who'd been drifting into Doc's house just to get a look at her, about Jack and Preacher. And about how many more stars there were out here. The mountains; the air, so clean and sharp it almost took you by surprise. About the people who came to the doctor bringing things, like tons of food, a lot of which went right across the street to the bar where Preacher used it in his creations; about how Jack refused to take a dime from either Doc or Mel for food or drink. Anyone who cared for the town had a free meal ticket over there.

"But it's very rural. Doc put in a call to the county social services agency, but I gather we're on a waiting list—they may not figure out foster care for who knows how long. Frankly, I don't know how the old doc made it without any help all these years."

"People nice?" Joey asked. "Other than the doctor?"

"The ones I've met—very. But the main reason I called, besides letting you know that I'm safe, is to tell you I'm on the old doc's phone—the cell just isn't going to work out here. I'll give you the number."

"Well," Joey said, "at least you sound okay. In fact, you sound better than you have in a long time."

"Like I said, there are patients. Challenges. I'm a little keyed up. The very first day, I was left alone here with the baby and the key to the drug cabinet and told to see any patients who wandered in. No training, nothing. About thirty people came—just to say hello and visit. That's what you hear in my voice. Adrenaline."

"Adrenaline again. I thought you swore off."

Mel laughed. "It's a completely different brand."

"So—when you wrap it up there, you'll come to Colorado Springs?"

"I don't have any better ideas," Mel said.

"When?"

"Not sure. In a few days, hopefully. Couple of weeks

at the outside. But I'll call you and let you know when I'm on my way. Okay?"

"Okay. But you really do sound…up."

"There's nowhere around here to get highlights. Some woman in town does hair in her garage, and that's it," Mel said.

"Oh, my God," Joey said. "You'd better wrap it up before you get some ugly roots."

"Yeah, that's what I was thinking."

Wednesday, Appointment Day, came and Mel watched the baby and saw a few patients with only minor complaints. One sprained ankle, a bad cold, another prenatal exam, a well-baby check and immunizations. After that there were a couple of walk-ins—she stitched up a laceration on a ten-year-old's head and Doc said, "Not bad." Doc made two house calls. They traded off babysitting to walk across the street to Jack's to eat. The people she met at the bar and those who came into the doctor's office were pleasant and welcoming. "But this is just temporary," she was careful to explain. "Doc doesn't really need any help."

Mel put in an order for more diapers with Connie at the corner store. The store was no bigger than a minimart and Mel learned that the locals usually went to the nearest large town for their staples and feed for animals, using the store merely to grab those occasional missing items. There were sometimes hunters or fishermen looking for something. They had a little of everything—from bottled water to socks. But only a few items of each.

"I heard no one's turned up for that baby yet," Connie said. "I can't think of anyone around here who'd have a baby and give it up."

"Can you think of anyone who'd have a baby without any medical intervention of any kind? Especially since there's a doctor in town?"

Connie, a cute little woman probably in her fifties, shrugged. "Women have their babies at home all the time, but Doc's usually there. We have some isolated families out in the woods—hardly ever show their faces for anything." She leaned close and whispered, "Strange people. But I've lived here all my life and have never heard of them giving up their children."

"How long do you expect the social services intervention to take?"

Connie laughed. "I wouldn't have the first idea. We run into a problem, we usually all pitch in. It's not like we ask for a lot of outside help."

"Okay, then, how long before you get in a new supply of disposable diapers?"

"Ron makes his supply run once a week, and he'll do that tomorrow morning. So, by tomorrow afternoon, you should be fixed up."

A teenage girl came into the store carrying her book bag—the school bus must have just dropped off. "Ah, my Lizzie," Connie said. "Mel, this is my niece, Liz. She just got here—she's going to stay with me for a while."

"How do you do?" Mel said.

"Hey," Liz said, smiling. Her full, long brown hair was teased up high and falling seductively to her shoulders, eyebrows beautifully arched over bright blue eyes, eye makeup thick, her glossy lips full and pouty. Little sex queen, Mel found herself thinking, in her short denim skirt, leather knee-high boots with heels, sweater tugged over full breasts and not meeting her waist.

Belly-button ring, hmm. "Need me to work awhile?" Liz asked Connie.

"No, honey. Go to the back and start your homework. Your first day was good?"

"Okay, I guess." She shrugged. "Nice to meet you," she said, disappearing into the store's back room.

"She's beautiful," Mel said.

Connie was frowning slightly. "She's fourteen."

Mel's eyes grew wide as she mouthed the words silently. Fourteen? "Wow," she whispered to Connie. The girl looked at least sixteen or even seventeen. She could pass for eighteen.

"Yeah. That's why she's here. Her mother, my sister, is at the end of her rope with the little hot bottom. She's a wild one. But that was in Eureka. Not so many places to go wild around here." She smiled. "If I could just get her to cover her naked body, I would feel so much better."

"I hear ya," Mel laughed. "May the force be with you." *But I'd consider birth control,* Mel thought.

When Mel had her meals at the bar, if there was no one around she knew, like Connie or her best friend Joy, or Ron or Hope, she would sit up at the bar and talk to Jack while she ate. Sometimes he ate with her. During these meals she learned more about the town, about summer visitors who came for hiking and camping, the hunters and fishermen who passed through during the season—the Virgin was great for fly-fishing, a comment that made her giggle. And there was kayaking, which sounded like fun to her.

Ricky introduced her to his grandmother who made a rare dinner appearance. Lydie Sudder was over seventy and had that uncomfortable gait of one who suffered arthritis. "You have a very nice grandson," Mel observed. "Is it just the two of you?"

"Yes," she said. "I lost my son and daughter-in-law in an accident when he was just a little thing. I'd sure worry about him if it weren't for Jack. He's been looking out for Ricky since he came to town. He looks after a lot of people."

"I can sense that about him," Mel said.

The March sun had warmed the land and brought out the buds. Mel had a fleeting thought that seeing this place in full bloom would be glorious, but then reminded herself that she would miss it. The baby—little Chloe—was thriving and several different women from town had stopped by to offer babysitting services.

She realized that she'd been here over a week—and it had passed like minutes. Of course, never getting more than four hours of sleep at a stretch tended to speed up time. She'd found living with Doc Mullins to be more bearable than she would've thought. He could be a cantankerous old goat, but she could give it back to him just as well, something he seemed to secretly enjoy.

One day, when the baby was asleep and there were no patients or calls, Doc got out a deck of cards. He shuffled them in his hand and said, "Come on. Let's see what you got." He sat down at the kitchen table and dealt the cards. "Gin," he said.

"All I know about gin is that you mix it with tonic," she told him.

"Good. We'll play for money," he said.

She sat down at the table. "You plan to take advantage of me," she said.

"Oh, yes," he confirmed. And then with a smile so rare, he began to tell her how to play. Pennies for points, he told her. And within an hour she was laughing, win-ning, and Doc's expression was getting more sour by the minute, which only made her laugh harder. "Come on," she said, dealing. "Let's see what you got."

The sound of someone coming through the front door temporarily stopped the game and Mel said, "Sit tight, I'll see who it is." She patted his hand. "Give you time to stack the deck."

Standing just inside the front door was a skinny man with a long graying beard. His overalls were dirty and the bottoms frayed around filthy boots. The edge of his shirtsleeves and collar were also frayed, as though he'd been in these particular clothes a very long time. He didn't come into the house, probably because of the mud he tracked, but stood just inside the door twisting a very worn felt hat.

"Can I help you?" she asked him.

"Doc here?"

"Uh-huh. Sure. Let me get him for you."

She fetched Doc to the front door and while he was chatting with the man, she checked on Chloe. When Doc finally came back to the kitchen, he was wearing a very unpleasant expression. "We have to make a call. See if you can rustle up someone to keep an eye on the baby."

"You need my assistance?" she asked, perhaps more hopefully than she wished.

"No," he said, "but I think you should tag along. See what's on the other side of the tree line."

Chloe stirred in her bed and Mel picked her up. "Who was that man?"

"Clifford Paulis. Lives out in the woods with some people. His daughter and her man joined them a while back. They have regular problems. I'd rather you just see."

"Okay," she said, perplexed.

After a few phone calls had been placed with no success, the best they could do for the baby was take her across the street to Jack's with a few diapers and a bottle. Mel carried her little bed while Doc managed the baby in one arm and his cane in the other hand, though Mel had offered to make two trips.

"Are you sure you'll be all right?" she asked Jack. "You might have to change her and everything."

"Nieces," he said again. "I'm all checked out."

"How many nieces, exactly?" she asked.

"Eight, at last count. Four sisters and eight nieces. Apparently they can't breed sons. Where are you off to?"

"I'm not sure."

"Paulises'," Doc said. And Jack whistled.

As they drove out of town, Mel said, "I don't have a good feeling about this. Seems everyone knows about this family except me."

"I guess you deserve to be prepared. The Paulises live in a small compound of shacks and trailers with a few others—a camp. They stay out of sight and drink a lot, wander into town very rarely. They keep a supply of pure grain alcohol on hand. They're dirt-poor, miserable folk, but they haven't given Virgin River any trouble. Clifford says there was a fight last night and there's some patching up to do."

"What kind of fight?"

"They're pretty gritty folk. If they sent for me, it must've been a good one."

They drove a long way into the woods, the dirt road a narrow, bumpy, one lane before it finally broke open into a clearing around which were, as Doc had said, two shacks and a couple of trailers. Not mobile homes,

but camper shells and an itty-bitty trailer that had seen
better days, along with an old wheelless pickup truck
up on blocks. They circled an open area in the middle
of which was a crude brick oven of sorts. There were
tarps stretched out from the campers and shacks with
actual furniture under them. Not outdoor furniture but
household—tables and chairs, old sofas with the stuffing popping out. Plus old tires, a couple of small trucks,
unidentifiable junk, a wringer washer lying on its side.
Mel peered into the trees and blinked to clear her vision. There appeared to be a semitrailer, half buried in
the ground with camouflage tarps over the top. Beside
it was, unmistakably, a gas-powered generator.

Mel said, "Holy shit."

"Help if you can," Doc said. "But try not to talk." He
peered at her. "That'll be hard for you."

Doc got out of the truck, hefting his bag. People
started to drift into the clearing—not from within their
homes, such as they were, but more like from behind
them. There were just a few men. It was impossible
to tell their ages; they all looked like vagrants with
their dirty and worn dungarees and overalls. They were
bearded, their hair long and matted, like real sad hill-
billies. Everyone was thin with sallow complexions;
they were not enjoying good health out here. There was
a very bad smell and Mel thought about bathroom facilities. They would be using the forest; and it smelled
as if they didn't get far enough from the camp. Their
facilities were minimal. It was like a little third-world
country.

Doc nodded to people as he pressed forward, getting nods back. He'd obviously been here before. Mel
followed more slowly. Doc ended up in front of a shack

outside of which Clifford Paulis stood. Doc turned to make sure Mel was with him, then entered.

She felt their eyes on her, but they kept their distance. She wasn't exactly afraid, but she was nervous and unsure and hurried behind Doc to enter the shack with him.

There was a small table inside with a lantern on it. Sitting on short stools at the table were a man and a woman. Mel had to stifle a gasp. Their faces were swollen, cut and bruised. The man was perhaps thirty, his dirty blond hair short and spiky, and he twitched and jittered, unable to sit still. The woman, maybe the same age, was holding her arm at an odd angle. Broken.

Doc put his bag on the table and opened it. He pulled out and put on his latex gloves. Mel followed suit, but slowly, her pulse picking up. She had never worked as a visiting nurse, but knew a few who had. There were nasty hovels all around the poorer sections of L.A. where paramedics might be called, but in the city if you had a situation like this, you'd notify the police. The patients would be brought to the emergency room. And in the event of domestic violence, which this clearly was, these two would both be booked into jail right out of the E.R. When there's an injury in a domestic, no one has to press charges besides the police.

"Whatcha got, Maxine?" he said, reaching out for her arm, which she extended toward him. He examined it briefly. "Clifford," he called. "I'm gonna need a bucket of water." Then to Mel he said, "Get to work on cleaning up Calvin's face, see if sutures are required, and I'll attempt to set this ulna."

"Do you want a hypo?" she asked.

"I don't think we'll need that," he said.

Mel got out some peroxide and cotton and approached the young man warily. He lifted his eyes to her face and grinned at her with a mouth full of dirty teeth, some of which appeared to be rotting. In his eyes she saw that his pupils were very small—he was full of amphetamine, higher than a kite. He kept grinning at her and she tried not to make eye contact with him. She cleaned some of the cuts on his face and finally said, "Wipe that look off your face or I'll let Doc do this." It made him giggle stupidly.

"I'm going to need something for the pain," he said.

"You already had something for the pain," she told him. And he giggled again. But in his eyes there was menace and she decided not to make any more eye contact.

Doc made a sudden movement that slammed Calvin's arm onto the table, hard, gripped by Doc's arthritic hand. "You never do that, you hear me?" Doc said in a voice more threatening than Mel had heard before, then slowly released Calvin's forearm while boring through him with angry eyes. Then Doc immediately turned his attention back to Maxine. "I'm going to have to put this bone right, Maxine. Then I'll cast it for you."

Mel had no idea what had just happened. "You don't want an X-ray?" she heard herself ask Doc. And her answer was a glare from the doctor who'd asked her to try not to talk. She went back to the man's face.

There was a cut over his eye that she could repair with tape, no stitches required. Standing above him as she was, she noticed a huge purple bump through the thinning hair on the top of his head. Maxine must have hit him over the head with something, right before he broke her arm. She glanced at his shoulders and arms through the thin fabric of his shirt and saw that he had some heft to him—he was probably strong. Strong enough at least to break a bone.

The bucket of water arrived—the bucket rusty and dirty—and momentarily she heard Maxine give out a yelp of pain as Doc used sudden and powerful force to put her ulna back into place.

Old Doc Mullins worked silently, wrapping an Ace bandage around her arm, then dipping casting material into the bucket, soaking it, and applying it to the broken arm. Finished with her assignment, Mel moved away from Calvin and watched Doc. He was strong and fast for his age, skilled for a man with hands twisted by arthritis, but then this had been his life's work. Casting done, he pulled a sling out of his bag.

Job done, he snapped off his gloves, threw them in his bag, closed it, picked it up and, looking down, went back to the truck. Again, Mel followed.

When they were out of the compound she said, "All right—what's going on there?"

"What do you think's going on?" he asked. "It isn't complicated."

"Looks pretty awful to me," she said.

"It is awful. But not complicated. Just a few dirt-poor alcoholics. Homeless, living in the woods. Clifford wandered away from his family to live out here years ago and over time a few others joined his camp. Then Calvin Thompson and Maxine showed up not so long ago, and added weed to the agenda—they're growing in that semitrailer. Biggest mystery to me is how they got it back in here. You can bet Calvin couldn't get that done. I figure Calvin's connected to someone, told 'em he could sit back here and watch over a grow. Calvin's a caretaker. That's what the generator is about—grow lights. They irrigate out of the river. Calvin's jitters don't come from pot—pot would level him out and slow him down. He's gotta be on something like meth. Maybe he skims a little marijuana, cheats the boss, and trades it for something else. Thing is, I don't think Clifford and those old men have anything to do with the pot. They never had a grow out there before that I know of. But I could be wrong."

"Amazing," she said.

"There are lots of little marijuana camps hidden back in these woods—some of 'em pretty good size—but you can't grow it outside in winter months. It's still the biggest cash crop in California. But even if you gave Clifford and those old boys a million dollars, that's how they're going to live." He took a breath. "Not all local growers look like vagrants. A lot of 'em look like millionaires."

"What happened when you grabbed his arm like that?" she asked.

"You didn't see? He was raising it like he was going to touch you. Familiarly."

She shuddered. "Thanks. I guess. Why'd you want me to see that?"

"Two reasons—so you'd know what some of this country medicine is about. Some places where they're growing are booby-trapped, but not this one. You should never go out to one of those places alone. Not even if a baby's coming. You better hear me on that."

"Don't worry," she said with a shudder. "You should tell someone, Doc. You should tell the sheriff or someone."

He laughed. "For all I know, the sheriff's department's aware—there are growers all over this part of the world. For the most part, they stay invisible—it's not like they want to be found out. More to the point,

I'm in medicine, not law enforcement. I don't talk about the patients. I assume that's your ethic, as well."

"They live in filth! They're hungry and probably sick! Their water is undoubtedly contaminated by the awful, dirty containers they keep it in. They're beating each other up and dying of drink and…whatever."

"Yeah," he said. "Doesn't make my day, either."

She found it devastating, the acceptance of such hopelessness. "How do you do it?" she asked him, her voice quiet.

"I just do the best I can," he said. "I help where I can. That's all anyone can do."

She shook her head. "This really isn't for me," she said. "I can handle stuff like this when it comes into the hospital, but I'm no country practitioner. It's like the Peace Corps."

"There are bright spots in my doctoring, too," he said. "Just happens that isn't one of them."

She was completely down in the dumps when she went back to the grill to collect the baby. "Not pretty out there, is it?" Jack said.

"Horrid. Have you ever been out there?"

"I stumbled across them a couple years ago when I was hunting."

"You didn't want to tell anyone?" she asked. "Like the police?"

"It isn't against the law to be a bum," he said with a shrug.

So, she thought—he didn't know about the semi-trailer. Doc had said it showed up not long ago. "I can't imagine living like that. Can I use your bathroom? I want to wash up before I touch the baby."

"Right back off the kitchen," he said.

When she got back she picked up Chloe and held her close, breathing in the clean, powdery scent.

"Fortunately, you don't have to live like they do," he said.

"Neither do they. Someone should do an intervention out there, get them some help. Food and clean water, anyway."

He picked up the baby bed to carry it across the street for her. "I think they've killed too many brain cells for that to work," he said. "Concentrate on the good you can do and don't gnaw on the hopeless cases. It'll just make you sad."

By early evening, Mel was coming around. She took her dinner at the bar, laughed with Jack and even Preacher cracked the occasional smile. Finally, she put her small hand over Jack's and said, "I apologize for earlier, Jack. I never even thanked you for watching the baby."

"You were kind of upset," he said.

"Yeah. I surprised myself. It's not as though I haven't seen plenty of bums and street people. They were frequent clientele at the hospital. I didn't realize before today that in the city we'd clean 'em up, straighten 'em out and hand 'em off to some agency or another. In the back of my mind I probably always knew they'd be back picking out of trash cans before long, but I didn't have to see it. This was very different. They're not going anywhere and they're not getting any help. It's been down to Doc. Alone. Takes a lot of courage to do what Doc does."

"He does more than a lot of people would do," Jack said.

She smiled. "This is rough country."

"It can be," he said.

"Not a lot of resources out here."

"We do pretty well with what we've got. But you have to remember, the old boys in that little camp don't seem to want resources so much as to be left alone," he said. "I know that's hard to stomach, but most of this area is the opposite—thriving and healthy. Did that trip out into the woods make your desire to get out of here even more desperate?"

"It sure opened my eyes. I thought small-town medicine would be peaceful and sweet. I never thought it had that other side—as hopeless as some of our worst inner city problems."

"Don't know that it is," he argued. "The sweet and peaceful will far outnumber the hopeless. I swear on it. You're welcome to see for yourself and call me a liar. But you'd have to hang around."

"I made a commitment to stay till the baby is placed," she said. "I'm sorry I can't promise more."

"No promises necessary. Just pointing out the options."

"But thank you, for taking care of the baby for me."

"She's a good baby," he said. "I didn't mind at all."

After she'd gone back to Doc's, Jack said to Preacher, "You okay here? I'm thinking about a beer."

Preacher's bushy black brows shot up in surprise, but he didn't say it. Didn't say, "Another beer? So soon?" He finally said, "I'm okay here."

Jack knew that if he didn't say anything at all to Charmaine for a few weeks, she wouldn't know there was anything to be said. He also knew that despite the fact Mel had captured his thoughts, it didn't mean anything would ever happen, didn't mean she'd make it even another week in Virgin River. That wasn't really the point. The issue was that it was wrong to go to Charmaine at all, ever, if he wasn't into Charmaine. It was a point of honor with him. Even though he never thought in terms of commitment, he certainly didn't think in terms of using someone.

Then there was another matter. A fear that he'd be having sex with Charmaine and behind his closed eyes, see another face. That couldn't happen. That would insult both women.

When she saw him walk into her tavern, her first reaction was one of pleased surprise and she smiled at him. Then she immediately realized how unprecedented this visit was and her smile vanished.

"Beer?" she asked him.

"Talk?" he answered. "Can Butch cover for you for ten minutes?"

She actually took a step back. She knew what was coming and sadness seeped into her brown eyes. Her face actually fell. "Is that all it's going to take?" she asked. "Ten minutes?"

"I think so. There isn't too much to say."

"There's someone else," she said at once.

"No. There isn't. Let's take a table." He looked over his shoulder. "That one over there. Ask Butch."

She nodded and turned from him. While she spoke to Butch, Jack moved to the table. Butch took the bar and Charmaine joined Jack. He reached across and took her hands. "You've been a wonderful friend to me, Charmaine. I never for one second took that for granted."

"But…"

"My mind is on other things," he said. "I won't be coming to Clear River for a beer anymore."

"There can only be one thing," she said. "Because I know you. And you have needs."

He'd thought about this long and hard on the way over, and it wasn't in his mind to lie to her. But there wasn't anyone else. Mel wasn't someone else—and might never be. Just because she'd taken over his consciousness didn't mean it would ever materialize into something more. She might stick to her word and leave Virgin River at the first opportunity, and even if she didn't, you don't show your hand this early in the game. His reason for breaking this off wasn't just about having Mel, but about not misleading Charmaine. She was a good woman; she had been good to him. She didn't deserve to be strung along while he waited to see what the other woman was going to do.

The cabin in Virgin River might be ready, but Mel sure wasn't. The baby at Doc's was keeping her in town for now, but it was impractical to think of her caring for Chloe out at the cabin—there was only the one Plexiglas incubator, no car seat for traveling back and forth, no phone. Of course, it was no punishment to have her living right across the street. But he wanted her in the cabin he'd renovated, he wanted that real bad.

Charmaine was so right—he had needs. But somehow when he looked at this young Mel, he knew it would never be like this—an arrangement for sex every couple of weeks. Jack had absolutely no idea what it might become, but he already knew it was going to be more than that. He had a very long history of not getting hooked up, so this disturbed him. The chances were real good he was casting adrift in a sea of sheer loneliness. Because Mel had complications. He had no idea what they were, but that occasional sadness in her eyes came out of the past, something she was trying to get over.

But he wanted her. He wanted all of her; he wanted everything with her.

"That's the thing," he said. "I have needs. And right now I think what I need is completely different from what I've needed in the past. I could easily keep coming here, Charmaine. I sure don't suffer, you're awful good to me. But the past two years when I've been here, I've been here completely. It shouldn't be any other way."

"The last time was different," she said. "I knew something was wrong."

"Yeah, I'm sorry. It's really the first time my head wasn't connected to my body. You deserve better than that."

She lifted her chin and gave her hair a toss. "What if I said I didn't care?"

God, he felt so bad doing this. "I do," was all he could say.

She got teary. "Okay, then," she said bravely. "Okay, then."

When he left he knew it was going to be a while before he felt all right about what he'd just done. That business about playing it fast and loose, about having no ties or commitments, that wasn't really how it was. All that no commitment bullshit meant was that you didn't talk about it, you never took it to the next level. He had had a contract of sorts with Charmaine, even if it wasn't a formal one, a legal one, even if it was pretty casual in the give-and-take department. She had stuck to the contract; he had just broken it. And let her down.

Five

In the mornings, after the baby had that first really early feeding and was settled back to sleep, Mel liked to take her coffee out to Doc's front porch and sit on the steps. She found she enjoyed watching this little town wake up. First the sun would create a kind of golden path through the tall pine trees onto the street, slowly lighting it. The sound of doors opening and closing could be heard. A Ford truck drove slowly from the east to the west down the street, tossing out papers— the *Humboldt News*. She liked getting the paper early— though it was hardly akin to the *L.A. Times*.

Soon the kids started to emerge. The bus picked them up at the far west end of the main street. Those in town would walk or ride their bikes down the street and gather there, chaining their bikes to trees in someone's front yard. That would never happen in the city— someone just allowing their yard to be used as a bike lot while the kids were in school. She saw Liz come out of Connie's house right next to the store; Liz sashayed across the street, book bag slung over one shoulder, fanny swaying seductively. Boy howdy, Mel was thinking. That girl's advertising like mad.

Cars and trucks began to drop off the more rural kids. It was not yet seven—a long day for these country kids—driven to the bus stop, ride the bus for who knows how long since there was no school in Virgin River, then back to town, back to the farm or ranch. The kids who gathered there, probably thirty, ranged in age from five to seventeen and the mothers of the younger ones stood around chatting while they waited for the bus. Some of them held their coffee cups and laughed together like old, old friends.

Then it would come, the bus, driven by a big happy woman who got off, said hello to the parents, herding each one of the kids on board.

Jack came out of the bar, fishing rod in one hand, tackle box in the other. He put his gear in the back of his truck and lifted a hand to her. She waved back. Out to the river for some fishing. Not long after, Preacher was sweeping off the front porch. When he looked up, he lifted a hand, as well.

What had she said about this little town? That it didn't resemble the pictures she'd seen? In the early morning the town was lovely. Rather than looking old and tired, the homes looked sweet and uncomplicated. They were unfussy clapboards in a variety of colors— blue, light green, beige with brown trim. Connie and Ron's house, right next to the corner store, was the same yellow with white trim as their store. Only one house on the street had been painted recently, a white house with dark green shutters and trim. She saw Rick come out of that house, sprint across the porch, jump down to the street and into his little white truck. It was a safe-looking street. Friendly homes. No one walked out of their homes to see another person and fail to greet, wave, stop and talk.

A woman came out from behind the boarded-up church down the street and seemed to be walking unevenly toward her. As she neared, Mel stood up. "Hello," she said, holding her coffee cup in both hands. "You the nurse?" she asked.

"Nurse practitioner and midwife, yes. Can I help you with something?"

"No," she said. "I heard about you is all."

The woman's eyes were drawn down sleepily, as though she had trouble staying awake, with dark circles under them. She was a large woman, maybe five-ten, and rather plain, her greasy hair pulled back. It was possible she was sick. Mel stuck out a hand. "Mel Monroe," she said.

The woman hesitated a minute before accepting a handshake. She wiped her palm down her pant leg first, then reached out. Her grip was strong and clumsy, her nails dirty. "Cheryl," she said in response. "Creighton." She pulled her hand back and put both her hands in the pockets of baggy pants. Men's pants, it looked like.

Mel stopped herself before saying, *Ahh. That would be the Cheryl who was supposed to clean the cabin; the Cheryl Hope suspected was drinking again.* Which would explain her sallow complexion and weary eyes, not to mention all the little broken blood vessels in her cheeks. "Sure I can't do anything for you?"

"No. They say you're leaving right away."

"Do they now," she said with a smile. "Well, I have a few things I made a commitment to see through first."

"That baby," she said.

Mel tipped her head to one side. "Hardly anything goes unnoticed around here. Do you know anything about the baby, or her mother? I'd like to find the woman w—"

"So you could go sooner? Because if you want to go—I could take care of the baby…"

"You have an interest in the baby?" she asked. "May I ask why?"

"I just mean to help. I like to help out."

"I really don't need much help—but I sure would like to find the baby's mother. She could be sick, giving birth alone like that."

Mel chanced a glance toward the bar and noticed that Preacher had stopped sweeping and watched. At that same moment, Doc came out of the house. "Cheryl," Doc said.

"Hey, Doc. Just telling the nurse here—I could help out with that baby. Watch her for you and stuff."

"Why'd you want to do that, Cheryl?"

She shrugged. "Jack told me about it."

"Thanks. We'll sure keep you in mind," Doc said.

"'Kay," she said with another shrug. She looked at Mel. "Nice meetin' you. Explains a lot, now I see you." And she turned and walked back the way she'd come.

Mel looked up at Doc and found him frowning. "What was that all about?" she asked him.

"Seems like she wanted to see what you look like. She tends to follow Jack around like a lovesick puppy."

"He shouldn't serve her."

"He doesn't," Doc said. "Jack's a generous guy, but not a foolish one. Giving Cheryl booze would be like throwing kerosene on a fire. Besides, she can't afford Jack's place. I think she gets some of that rotgut they keep out in the woods."

"That's going to kill her."

"Unfortunately."

"Can't somebody help her?"

"She look to you like she wants help?"

"Has anyone tried? Has Jack—"

"Jack can't do anything for her," Doc said. "That would put an awful lot of useless ideas in her head."

He turned around and went back into the house. Mel followed him and said, "Do you think it's possible she gave birth?"

"Anything's possible. But I doubt it."

"What if we checked her? It would be obvious."

Doc looked down at her and lifted one snowy brow. "Think I should call the sheriff? Get a warrant?" And he walked off toward the kitchen.

What an odd little town, Mel found herself thinking.

While the baby napped, Mel took a break and wandered down to the store. Connie poked her head out of the back and said, "Hey, Mel. Can I get you something?"

"I just thought I'd look at your magazines, Connie. I'm bored."

"Help yourself. We're watching our soap, if you want to come back here with us."

"Thanks," she said, going to the very small book rack. There were a few paperbacks and five magazines. Guns, trucks, fishing, hunting and *Playboy*. She picked up a paperback novel and the *Playboy* and went to the back where she'd seen Connie.

A parted curtain hung in the doorway to the back room. Inside, Connie and Joy sat in old canvas lawn chairs in front of the small desk, coffee cups in hand, their eyes focused on a small TV that sat on a shelf. The women were complete physical opposites—Connie being small and trim with short hair dyed fire-engine-red, and Joy must be easily five-nine and two-fifty, very plain with her long, graying hair pulled back into a ponytail, her face round and cheerful. They were an odd pair and it was said they'd been best friends since they were kids. "Come on back," Joy said. "Help yourself to coffee if you want."

On the television a very pretty woman looked into the eyes of a very handsome man and said, "Brent, I never loved anyone but you! Ever!"

"Oh, she is such a liar!" Connie said.

"No, she's not—she didn't love any of them. She just screwed 'em all," Joy said.

On the TV: "Belinda, the bab—"

"Brent, the baby is yours!"

"The baby is Donovan's," Joy told the TV.

Mel leaned a hip against the desk. "What is this?"

"Riverside Falls," Connie said. "Brent and the slut Belinda."

"This is what Lizzie is going to be doing if Connie can't get her out of those slutty clothes."

"I have a plan," Connie said. "As she grows out of her clothes and I replace them, we're going to get a more conservative wardrobe."

Joy laughed loudly. "Connie, it looks like she already grew out of them!"

The camera pulled back and Mel saw that the couple on screen were in bed together, their naked bodies barely concealed by a sheet. "Whew," she said. "Soaps have come a long way."

"You ever watch any soaps, honey?" Connie asked.

"Not since college. We watched *General Hospital.*" Mel put down her magazine and book on the desk and helped herself to a cup of coffee. "We used to get our patients to keep an eye on it for us. I had one long-term care patient—an old guy—and I used to give him his bath at two every afternoon and we'd watch it together."

"There is only one man left on this show that Belinda

hasn't done—and he's seventy. The patriarch." Connie sighed. "They're going to have to bring in some new talent for Belinda."

Back on TV, Belinda bit at Brent's lip, then his chin, then slipped lower in the bed and disappeared under the sheet. All three women in the back room leaned toward the TV. The lump in the sheet that was Belinda's head went lower and momentarily Brent threw back his head and let a delicious moan escape.

"My God," Mel said.

Connie fanned her face.

"I think that's her secret weapon," Joy said. And the program cut to commercial.

Connie and Joy looked at each other, giggled and got up out of their chairs. "Well, not much has changed since yesterday. That baby's gonna be in college before it gets out who the daddy is."

"I'm not even sure it is Donovan's. She was with Carter, too."

"That was a long time ago—it couldn't be his."

"How long have you two been watching this soap?" Mel asked.

"Oh, God, fifteen years?" Connie answered by way of a question.

"At least."

"You find a magazine, honey?"

Mel made a face and held up the *Playboy*.

"My, my," Connie said.

"I'm not too interested in trucks, fish, guns or game," she said. "Don't you ever get any others in?"

"If you tell me what you want, I'll have Ron pick 'em up on his next run. We only carry what we sell."

"Makes sense," she said. "I hope I haven't just

snatched up some poor guy's *Playboy* that he's looking forward to."

"Don't you worry about it," Connie said. "Hey,
there's a little potluck at the bar tonight for Joy's birthday. Why don't you come on over?"

"Aw, I don't have a present!"

"We don't do presents, honey," Joy said. "Just come
and party."

"Well, happy birthday anyway, Joy. I'll check with
Doc," she said. "What time? If I can come, should I
bring something for the potluck?"

"We'll get over there about six, and no, don't you
worry about bringing anything. I don't guess you do
any cooking at Doc's and we have the food covered.
Nothing new on that baby, huh?"

"Not a peep."

"Damnedest thing," Joy said. "Bet whoever's it is
came from another one of the towns."

"I'm starting to think that, too," Mel said. She pulled
some bills out of her pocket to pay for her stuff. "Maybe
I'll see you later, then."

On her way back to Doc's she passed the bar. Jack
was sitting on the porch with his feet up on the rail. She
wandered over. Sitting beside him was a fishing tackle
box full of beautiful feathery flies. Small pliers, scissors and a razor blade were sticking out of the tackle
box, as well as little plastic envelopes that contained
colorful feathers, silver hooks and other paraphernalia.

"Break time?" he asked her.

"I've been on break all day, except for a little diaper
changing and feeding. The baby's asleep, there aren't
any patients and Doc is afraid to play gin with me. It
turns out I can beat his socks off."

Jack laughed. He leaned forward and peered at the

book and magazine. He looked at her face and raised an eyebrow. "Little light reading?" he asked.

She lifted the magazine. "It was either this or guns, trucks, hunting or fishing. You want to borrow it when I'm through?"

"No, thanks," he laughed.

"You don't like naked women?"

"I love naked women—I just don't feel like looking at pictures of them. It seems like you'd get enough of that in your line of work," he said.

"Like I said, the choices were pretty limited. I haven't seen one of these in years, but when I was in college my roommates and I used to laugh ourselves stupid at the advice column. And they used to have some interesting stories. Does *Playboy* still run fiction?"

"I have absolutely no idea, Melinda," he said, grinning.

"You know what I've noticed about this town? Everyone has a satellite dish and at least one gun."

"A couple of items that seem to be necessary. No cable TV out here. You shoot?" he asked.

"I hate guns," she said with a shudder. "Try to imagine the number of gunshot deaths in a trauma center in L.A." She shivered again. *He has no idea,* she thought.

"The guns around here aren't the kind people use on each other. Hardly a handgun in the town, although I have a couple, just because I've had them for a long time. This is rifle and shotgun country—used for hunting, euthanizing a sick or wounded animal, protection from wildlife. I could teach you to shoot, so you'd be more comfortable with guns."

"No way. I hate to even be around them. All these guns I see in the gun racks in the trucks—are they loaded?"

"You bet. You don't take a minute to load your rifle if a bear is charging you. Bear fish in the same rivers we do."

"Whew, fishing just took on a whole new meaning. Who shot all the animals on the walls in the bar?" she asked.

"Preacher got the buck. I caught the fish and shot the bear."

She was shaking her head. "How can you get any satisfaction out of killing innocent animals?"

"The buck and fish were innocent," he admitted. "But that bear wasn't. I didn't want to shoot her, but I was working on the bar and she was poking around right back there, maybe looking for trash. Bear are scavengers—they'll eat anything. It was a real dry summer. Her cub wandered too close to me and riled her up. Pissed her off. She must have gotten the idea I was going to interfere with the cub. So...?"

"Aw. What happened to the cub?"

"I locked him in the bar until Fish and Game could come out for him. They relocated him."

"That's too bad. For her. She was just being a mother."

"I didn't want to shoot that bear," he said. "I don't even hunt bear. I carry repellent—sort of a pepper spray. That day the repellent was in the truck, but the rifle was handy. I wouldn't have shot her, but it kind of got down to her or me." He grinned at her. "City girl," he said.

"Yeah, I'm just a city girl. With no dead animals on my walls. Think I'll keep it that way."

Friday night, big night in Virgin River. There were more than the usual number of cars parked around the bar, though the people Mel knew best would have walked over. Mel had said to Doc, "There's a potluck for Joy's birthday at Jack's tonight. I assume you're going over. Maybe later, if you could spell me for a half hour, I can just drop in and wish her a happy birthday."

Doc scoffed at that idea. All he wanted was to go collect his one whiskey of the day, have a bite to eat and turn in. So Mel fed and settled the baby while he was across the street. She fluffed her hair and put on a little lipstick, ready for what she expected to be a fairly dull evening, but an evening with a few friendly faces nonetheless. It was seven-thirty before Chloe slept and she was able to leave. "I won't be long," she told Doc.

"I'm not going anywhere," he said. "Dance till dawn for all I care."

"Will you call me if you need me?" she asked Doc.

"Hardly ever have a party in this town," he said. "You should take advantage of it. I know how to change and feed. Been doing it a lot longer than you."

When she walked in, she found the place nearly full of people. The jukebox, which was hardly ever playing, provided background music. Country. Jack and Preacher were behind the bar, Ricky was busy busing tables. She looked around until she found Joy.

"Sorry to be showing up so late, Joy. The baby didn't really want to settle down tonight." She plucked her sweater away from herself and gave a little sniff. "I think I might smell like cheese."

"You're fine—and there's still plenty of food left so grab yourself a plate."

A few tables had been pushed together to line a wall and upon them, dish after casserole dish of delicious-looking food. Right in the center was a sheet cake practically covered with candles. After she'd put some food on her plate, people started wandering over to say hello and chat. She greeted Fish Bristol, noted fisherman in these parts, and his wife, Carrie. Harv, who was found in the bar almost every morning, was a lineman for the telephone company, but before getting out on the road he had his breakfast at Jack's. "My wife can't be bothered to get out of bed just to cook breakfast," he said with a laugh. She noticed that Liz was tucked away in the corner, looking miserably bored, her long, shapely legs crossed, her short skirt just barely covering her privates. Mel gave her a wave, coaxing a very small smile out of Liz. Mel was introduced to a sheep rancher and his wife, Buck and Lilly Anderson—Buck, tall and skinny and balding and Lilly, short and round and rosy cheeked. "Any news on that baby?" Lilly asked.

"Nothing," she said.

"Is she a good baby?"

"Oh, God, she's perfect. An angel."

"And no one's asked if they can take her? Adopt her?"

"I haven't even heard from Social Services yet," Mel said.

Connie brought a friend over to introduce. "Mel, this is Jo Fitch. She and her husband live on the end of the street—the biggest house there."

"I'm so glad to finally meet you," Jo said. "No one expected such a young, pretty girl. We—"

Before Jo could finish she was joined by a man who slipped an arm about Jo's waist and, while swirling a drink in his glass, boldly looked Mel up and down and said, "Well, well, well…so this is our little nurse? Ohh, nurse, I'm not feeling so good!" And then he treated himself to a great big laugh.

"My husband, Nick," Jo said. If Mel wasn't mistaken, she said it somewhat nervously.

"How do you do," Mel said politely, deciding that he'd had a bit too much to drink. She turned to Connie and said, "Everything is so delicious."

"So, nurse Melinda—how do you like our little town?" he asked her.

"Please, just call me Mel," she said. "It's great. You're very lucky."

"Yep," he said, looking her over again. "We really got lucky. Where do I sign up for an examination?" And he laughed at himself some more.

It came back to her then—Jo Ellen and that husband of hers. This was the guy. He'd been slapped down by more than one woman, Hope had said. He couldn't possibly be more obvious. "Gosh, excuse me just a second, I'll be right back. I need something to drink."

He grabbed her arm and said, "Let me—"

She shook him off firmly, smiling all the while. "No, no. You wait right here," and she scooted away as fast as she could. On her way to the bar she stopped to say hello to Doug and Sue Carpenter, frequent visitors at Jack's. She met the elder Fishburns —Polly's mother- and father-in-law. When she got to the bar and hopped up on a stool in front of Jack, setting her plate down, she didn't have his attention right away. He was looking into the crowded room, frowning.

Finally he looked at her. "Could I have a beer?" she asked him.

"Sure," he said.

"You don't look too happy," she observed.

His expression relaxed. "Just keeping an eye on things," he said. "Having fun?"

"Hmm." She nodded, taking a sip. "Have you eaten this stuff? It's almost as good as Preacher's. These country women can cook!"

"That's why most of them are—how should I put it? Robust?"

She laughed at him. Leaving her beer for a moment, she ate a little more off her plate. "Yet another reason for me to get back to civilization."

She stayed there for a moment longer, then he was beside her again. Nick. "I waited," he said.

"Oh, Nick. Sorry—but I have to mingle. I'm new in town you know." And off the stool she leaped, beer in her hand, leaving the plate behind.

As Nick made to follow, he found his wrist clamped down on the bar. Jack looked into his eyes darkly. "Your wife is waiting for you over there."

"Be a sport, Jack," Nick said, laughing.

"You'd better behave yourself," Jack warned.

Nick laughed heartily. "Now, Jack—you can't have all the pretty girls to yourself. I mean, come on, man! All our wives are hot for you—cut a guy some slack." And he made his escape.

Jack watched closely from behind the bar. He was able to serve drinks and draw drafts without taking his eyes off the room. Nick seemed to follow Mel around like a smitten puppy, sidling up as close as possible, but Mel was quick. She'd go around to the far sides of tables to crouch to speak to people, get other men between her and Nick, slip across the room as if there was someone she just had to see, always leaving Nick in her dust. Preacher was behind the bar with him and at a point said, "Want me to give him a little advice before he gets his nose broken?"

"No," Jack said flatly. Jack was thinking that breaking his nose was going to feel very good. If Nick put one hand on her, he was going to come apart.

"Good," Preacher said. "I haven't been to a good bar fight in years."

In keeping an eye on things, he saw Connie's young niece stand up and walk over to the buffet, stick her finger into the icing on the cake and then into her mouth, slowly, so slowly pulling her finger back out while glancing over her shoulder at Rick—and his boy Ricky froze at one of the tables where he was picking up glasses. Jack saw him see her; saw Ricky almost tremble for a moment, mouth open slightly, eyes wide, taking her in—those long legs, full breasts. Oh, boy, Jack thought.

Someone lit the candles on the cake and everyone got up from their tables and came from the edges of the room to gather round, sing and watch Joy knock herself out trying to blow out fifty-three of them.

Mel stood at the rear of the crowd; Jack's eyes were back on her. Jack scowled blackly as Nick came up behind her. He couldn't see what was happening through the crowd, but he noted that a smile grew on Nick's face just as Mel's chin rose up, her eyes grew round and startled and she threw a panicked look in Jack's direction. Jack pushed himself off the bar and was making fast tracks to the other side when Mel reacted.

Mel felt a hand run over her bottom and inch between her legs. She was stunned for a moment, disbelieving. Then her instincts kicked in and shifted her beer to her other hand, threw an elbow back into his gut, brought that same elbow up under his chin, swept his legs out from under him with one booted foot, lifting him off his feet to send him crashing to the floor, flat on his back. She put her foot on his chest and glared into his eyes. "Don't you *ever* try anything like that again!" All this without spilling a drop of her beer.

Jack froze at the end of the bar. Whoa, he thought. Damn.

A second passed. Then Mel looked around the now silent room in some embarrassment. Everyone was shocked and staring. "Oh!" she said, but her foot still held Nick on his back. Nick who, it seemed, couldn't draw a breath, just lay there, stunned. She removed her foot. "Oh…" she said.

A laugh broke out of the crowd. Someone clapped. A woman yelped approvingly. Mel backed away somewhat sheepishly. She ended up at the bar, right in front of Jack. Right where she felt safest. Jack put a hand on her shoulder and glared in Nick's direction.

Mel felt awfully sorry for Jo Ellen. What's a woman from a town this size supposed to do with an obnoxious husband like that? Once Jo peeled him off the floor and took him home, the party became much more fun, and the jokes were fabulous. Several men asked her to arm wrestle and she had clearly become a hero to the women.

The stories of Nick's antics were both shocking and entertaining. Once, when he was feeling invincible and couldn't resist a breast, he'd been coldcocked by a woman. Up till tonight that was the most legendary put down he'd suffered. He'd collected a number of slaps, but by some miracle had not yet been beat to a pulp by an angry husband; he was apparently regarded as a pathetic joke. It seemed that when there was some kind of community or neighborhood party, like tonight, he'd have a couple of pops and get frisky, take chances that, by the light of day, he managed to keep under control. His reputation was firmly established.

"And yet you keep inviting him," Mel observed to Connie.

"It's just us here, kiddo. We're kind of stuck with each other."

"He should be told that if he can't mind his manners, he won't be included anymore."

"The problem with that is it would leave Jo out—and she's good people. I feel a whole lot sorrier for Jo than any of the women he pesters," Connie said. "Makes her look like a damn fool. We can pretty much take care of ourselves." She patted Mel's arm. "And you, girl—I doubt he's going to give you any more trouble."

At nine o'clock the party abruptly ended. It was as though someone had rung a bell—all the women gathered up their dishes, men stacked up plates and picked up trash, goodbyes were being said and people were filing out the door. Mel was at the back of the group, following, when Jack called her. "Hold up," he said. So she went back and jumped up on the stool. He put a cup of coffee in front of her. "Did I call you a city girl?" he asked with a smile.

"I didn't even know I could still do that," she said, accepting the coffee.

"Mind if I ask how you learned that?"

"It was a long time ago—when I was in my last year of college. There had been some rapes around the campus and a bunch of us went to a self-defense instructor together. To tell you the truth, I was never sure that would work in a real situation. I mean, with an instructor, mats on the floor, everything rehearsed and knowing exactly what to expect—that's one thing. But I wasn't sure I could react the same way if a real rapist jumped out from behind a parked car."

"Now you know. He never saw it coming."

"Yeah, that worked to my advantage, too." She sipped her coffee.

"I didn't see what he did," he said. "I could tell by the stupid grin on his face and the shocked look on yours that something happened."

She put her cup on the bar. "Major butt grope," she said. And she noted that Jack's expression went instantly dark; mean, narrowed eyes, deep frown. "Whew, easy, buddy, it wasn't your butt. I saw you making a move— what were you about to do?"

"Way too much," he said. "I don't like seeing something like that in my bar. I was watching him all night. The second he saw you, it was a target lock-on."

"He was a giant nuisance, but I'm pretty sure he'll leave me alone now," she said. "It was kind of funny the way the party just suddenly stopped like that. Did someone look at their watch or something?"

"Livestock don't give days off," he said.

"Neither do babies," she said, getting off the stool.

"I'll walk you," Jack said.

"You don't have to, Jack. I'm okay."

He came around the bar anyway. "Indulge me. It's been an interesting night." He took her arm, telling himself he was just being gentlemanly but, in fact, if he saw the chance, he was going to get his lips on hers. He'd been wanting to kiss her for days.

They walked across the porch and down the steps, out into the street. There were no streetlights, but the moon was high and full and cast a soft glow over the town. There was a light on in the upstairs bedroom at Doc's. Jack stopped right in the middle of the street. "Look, Mel. Look at that sky. You can't find that anywhere else on earth. All those stars, that moon—the clear black sky. That belongs to us."

She looked up at the most gorgeous sky imaginable, with more stars than she thought existed. He stepped behind her and with his hands on both of her upper arms, he gently squeezed.

"You just can't see this in the city. In any city."

"It is beautiful," she said softly. "I admit, this is beautiful country."

"It's majestic. One of these days, before you pack it in and run for your life, I'd like to show you some things. The redwoods, the rivers, the coast. It's almost time for whale watching." She leaned back against him and couldn't deny it felt pretty good to be shored up by Jack. "I'm sorry about what happened tonight." He leaned down and inhaled the scent of her hair. "I was really impressed with how well you handled it—but I'm sorry he… I hate that he touched you like that. I thought I had an eye on him."

"Too quick for me. Too quick for you," she said.

He turned her around and looked into her eyes. He thought he saw an invitation there in her upturned face and he lowered his.

She put a hand on his chest. "I have to go in now," she said, a little breathless.

He straightened.

"We both know I couldn't throw you," she said, smiling weakly.

"You'll never have to," he said. But he still held her arms, so reluctant to let go.

"Good night, Jack. And thanks for everything. Despite Nick—I had a good time."

"Glad to hear it," he said. And he let go.

She turned, and with her head down, went the rest of the way alone.

He stood in the street until she was inside, then

headed back to the bar. On his way, he saw Ricky's truck parked right in front of Connie's house. Well, damn—the boy sure didn't waste any time. Ricky didn't have a mom or dad and his grandmother wasn't well. Jack had been looking out for him for a long time and he knew this day would come eventually—they'd have to have *the* talk. But not tonight. Tonight Jack would have that talk with himself.

Preacher had the chairs upside down on the tables and was sweeping up. Jack walked right by him at a good clip. "Where you going in such a hurry?" Preacher asked.

"Shower," he said miserably.

It was because Connie and Ron liked Ricky so much that they had no problem with him staying out in front of the house talking with Liz for a few minutes. They trusted him, he knew this. But maybe they shouldn't because if they knew what one look at Liz had done to him, they'd lock her up.

She leaned against the porch, crossed her legs in front of her, pulled a cigarette out of her purse and lit it.

"What are you doing that for?" he asked her.

"Got a problem with it?" she said, blowing out smoke.

He shrugged. "Makes your mouth taste like shit," he said. "No one's going to want to kiss you if you smoke."

She smiled at him. "Someone wants to kiss me?" she asked.

He took the cigarette out of her hand and tossed it. Then he grabbed her around the waist and brought her onto his lips. *Yeah,* he thought. *Makes your mouth taste bad, but not bad enough.*

She curved right to him and of course it happened

to him. Happened all the time these days. When she opened her mouth and pressed harder against him, it happened even more. Holy God, he was dying. He could feel her full, hard breasts against his chest and right now all he wanted was to palm one. Against her lips he said, "You shouldn't smoke."

"Yeah."

"It'll cut your life short."

"We wouldn't want that."

"You're beautiful," he said. "Really beautiful."

"So are you."

"Guys aren't beautiful. You want a ride to school Monday?"

"Sure. What time?"

"Pick you up at seven. What class are you?"

"Freshman," she said.

It stopped happening to him real fast. "Four...four teen?" he asked her.

"Yeah. And you're...?"

"Ah... A junior. Sixteen." He backed away a little. "Damn. Holy God."

"Did I just lose my ride?" she asked, tugging her sweater down a little bit, which only made her boobs pop out more.

He smiled at her. "Nah. What the heck, huh? See you Monday morning." He started to walk away, then turned back abruptly and decided on another kiss. Deep and strong. Long. And then another, still longer. Maybe deeper. She sure didn't feel fourteen.

Six

One morning, Doc left the house early, before breakfast, to make a call. He hadn't been gone long when Lilly Anderson came to the office to see Mel. Lilly was in the same general age group with Connie and Joy and most of the other women Mel had met—late forties to early fifties. She was pleasantly round with a soft, kind face and lots of short, curly brown hair strung with gray. She wore no makeup and her skin was perfect, blemish-free ivory with pink cheeks and a sweet dimpled smile. The moment Mel met her at the potluck, she'd sensed a safe, nurturing way about her. Mel instantly liked her, trusted her. "You still have that little one, that baby?" Lilly asked.

"I do," Mel said.

"I'm surprised no one has come forward, wanting to take her in, adopt her."

"I'm kind of surprised by that, too," Mel said.

"Perfect healthy little baby," she said. "What about all those people who want to adopt healthy babies? Where are they?"

Mel shrugged. "Maybe it's just a matter of Social Services getting their ducks in a row—I understand they're busy and small towns like this get put on the back burner."

"I haven't been able to stop thinking about her. I thought, well, maybe I could help out," Lilly said.

"That's nice of you," Mel said. "Do you live nearby? Because sometimes it's nice for me and Doc to get a break for a few hours. Especially if we have patients."

"We're ranchers—I'm on the other side of the river, but it's not so far. Thing is, I already raised six youngsters—had my first at only nineteen and my baby is eighteen now and already married. But I have room at the house, what with the kids gone off on their own. I could take in the baby until something permanent is arranged for her. I even have those old baby things stored in the barn. Maybe I could be a foster parent. Buck, my husband, he says it would be okay."

"That's very generous, Lilly, but I'm afraid we couldn't pay you anything."

"I wouldn't need pay," she said. "It's just a neighborly thing. We help out when we can. And I do love babies."

"Let me ask you something—have you any idea who might've had this baby?"

She shook her head and looked terribly pained. "You have to ask yourself, what kind of woman would give up her baby? Maybe some young girl in trouble, no one to help her. I raised three daughters and by the grace of God, none had to pass that way. I have seven grandchildren already."

"That's the beauty of starting early," Mel said. "Your grandchildren come along while you're still young enough to enjoy them."

"I'm blessed," she said. "I know this. I can only imagine that whoever left her must have been desperate, so desperate." Mel thought Lilly might have even briefly had tears in her eyes.

"Well, I'll take your offer to Doc and see what he says. You're sure? Because I can give you some formula and diapers, and that's all."

"I'm sure. And please tell Doc I'd be more than happy to do it."

When Doc returned an hour later, Mel told him the story. His white eyebrows shot up in surprise and he rubbed a hand over his head. "Lilly Anderson?" he asked. He seemed to be considering this idea with some consternation.

"Does something about that worry you, because we can make do here a while longer..."

"Worry me? No." He collected himself. "Surprises me, is all." And he shuffled off to his office.

She followed him. "Well? You didn't have an answer."

He turned back toward her. "Can't think of a better place for that infant than Lilly's," he said. "Lilly and Buck are good people. And they know what to do with a baby, that's for sure."

"You don't need time to think about this?" she asked.

"I don't," he said. "I was hoping a family would turn up." He peered at her over his glasses. "Seems like maybe you need some time to think about it."

"No," she said, somewhat tremulously. "If you're okay, I'm okay."

"Think it over, just the same. I'll walk across the street and see if anyone's willing to play cribbage. Then, if you're of a mind, we'll take her out to the Anderson ranch."

"Okay," she said. But she said it very quietly.

Jack was painfully, embarrassingly aware that Mel had only been in town three weeks, and he could think of little else. Fact was, from the moment he looked at her in the dim light of the bar that first night, he wanted to sit right down at that table with her and get to know her.

He saw her every day, and given their meals together and long conversations, he knew himself to be her closest friend at the moment. And yet there was much about herself she was concealing. She was open about having lost her parents young, her close relationship with her sister and sister's family, her nursing career, the crazy and chaotic life at the hospital, but it was as though there was a block of time missing. Him, Jack thought. The one who devastated her and left her hurt and lonely. Jack would drive him away, given half a chance.

He wished he knew what it was that had hooked him so quickly, so thoroughly. It wasn't just her beauty, though that was evident. True, there weren't any pretty, single women around town, but he hadn't been lonely. And Mel hadn't been the only sexy woman he'd laid eyes on in the past few years. He was hardly a hermit; he'd been to lots of the other towns, the coastal towns, to night spots. There'd been Clear River.

But Mel had some aura that had him all worked up. That tight little body, full breasts, compact fanny, rosy lips, not to mention some real sexy brains—it was all he could do to keep from breathing heavy in her presence. When she had those moments when whatever plagued her was forgotten, and she smiled or laughed, her whole face brightened up. Her blue eyes danced. He'd already dreamed of her; felt her hands all over his body, felt her beneath him, felt himself inside of her, heard her soft moans of pleasure and bam! He awoke to find himself as alone as ever, bathed in sweat.

Jack was already turned on before Mel dropped Nick on his ass, but if he hadn't been, that sure would have sealed the deal. She was a dynamo. Gorgeous, feminine little thing with one helluva punch. Whoa. Damn.

The vulnerability in her eyes warned him he'd better be very, very careful. One wrong move and she'd jump in that little BMW and shake the dust of Virgin River off the soles of her shoes, the town's medical needs notwithstanding. He reminded himself constantly that this was one reason he hadn't sprung the cabin on her yet. Walking away from her last week after Joy's party had been one of the hardest things he'd ever done. He had wanted nothing so much as to crush her to him and say, *It's going to be all right—I can make it all right, all good. Give me a chance.*

Doc and Preacher sat at a table in the bar, playing cribbage. Jack put a slice of Preacher's apple pie on a plate, covered it with Saran wrap and left the bar to walk across the street. No cars or trucks at Doc's except Doc's truck and that little BMW parked on the side. All clear, he thought, his pulse picking up. He opened the front door and looked around; no one. He thought to go tap on the office door, but a sound from the kitchen led him there instead.

The baby in her little Plexiglas bed on wheels sat near the warm stove and Mel was at the table, her head down, resting on her folded arms. And she sobbed. He rushed to her; he put the pie on the table and was down on one knee at the side of her chair, all in one movement. "Mel," he said.

She lifted her head, her cheeks chafed and pink. "Dammit," she said through her tears. "You caught me."

His hand was on her back. "What is it?" he asked gently. *Now,* he thought. *Now she'll tell me about it, let me help her through it.*

"I've found a home for the baby. Someone came in and offered to take her and Doc endorses it."

"Who?" he asked.

"Lilly Anderson," she said, large tears spilling over. "Oh, Jack. I let it happen. I got attached." And she leaned against his shoulder and wept.

Jack forgot everything. "Come here," he said, pulling her out of the chair. He traded places with her and pulled her down on his lap. She encircled his neck with her arms, her face buried in his shoulder, crying, and he gently stroked her back. His lips were on her soft hair. "It's okay," he whispered. "It's okay."

"I let it happen," she said into his shirt. "Stupid. I knew better. I even named her. What was I thinking?"

"You gave her affection," he said. "You were so good to her. I'm sorry it hurts." But he wasn't sorry, because he had his arms around her and it felt as he knew it would, her little body, warm and solid, against his. She was light as a feather on his lap, her arms around his neck like ribbons, and the sweet, fragrant smell of her hair coiled around his brain and tightened, addling his thoughts.

She lifted her head and looked into his eyes. "I thought about taking her," she said. "Running away with her. That's how crazy I am. Jack, you should know—I'm totally nuts."

He wiped the tears from her cheeks. "If you want her, Mel, you can try to adopt her."

"The Andersons," she said. "Doc says they're good people. A good family."

"They are. Salt of the earth."

"And that would be better for her than a single mother who works all the time," she said. "She needs a real bed, not this incubator. A real family, not a mid-wife and an old doctor."

"There are lots of different kinds of families."

"Oh, I know what's best." Then the tears began to flow again. "It's just so hard." And she laid her head back on his shoulder. His arms tightened around her and hers tightened around his neck. He closed his eyes and just rested his cheek against her hair.

Feeling these strong arms around her, Mel let herself sink into a good, heartfelt cry. She was fully aware of him, but what really mattered to her at the moment was that for the first time in almost a year of crying, she wasn't alone. Someone was holding her and she felt protected. There was the comfort of strength and warmth, and she welcomed it. His chambray shirt was soft against her cheek and his thighs hard beneath her. He had a wonderful scent of cologne and the outdoors and she felt safe with him. His hand stroked her back and she was aware that he softly kissed her hair.

He rocked her gently as she continued to dampen his shirt. Minutes passed and her weeping slowed to a sniffle, then a murmur. She lifted her head and looked at him, though she said nothing. His brain went numb. He touched her lips softly with his, gently, tentatively. Her eyes closed as she allowed this and his arms tightened around her as he pressed more firmly against her lips. Hers opened and his breath caught as he opened his own and felt her small tongue dart into his mouth. His world reeled and he was lost in a kiss that deepened, that moved him, that shook him.

"Don't," she whispered against his mouth. "Don't get mixed up with me, Jack."

He kissed her again, holding her against him as

though he would never let her go. "Don't worry about me," he said against her lips.

"You don't understand. I have nothing to give. Nothing."

"I haven't asked you for a thing," he said. But in his mind he was saying, *You're mistaken. You are giving, and taking—and it feels damn good.*

All Mel could think, in the abstract, was that her body for once wasn't hollow and so empty she ached. She drank it in, the feeling of being connected to something. To someone. Anchored. So wonderful to have that human contact again. In her soul she had forgotten how, but her body remembered. "You're a good man, Jack," she said against his lips. "I don't want you to be hurt. Because I can't love anyone."

All he said was, "I can take care of myself."

She kissed him again. Deeply. Passionately. For a long minute, two minutes, moving under his mouth with heat.

And the baby fussed.

She pulled away from him. "Oh, man, why'd I do *that?*" she asked. "That's a mistake."

He shrugged. "Mistake? Nah. We're friends," he said. "We're close. You needed some comfort and—and here I am."

"That just can't happen," she said, sounding a little desperate.

He took charge, feeling his own sense of desperation. "Mel, stop it. You were crying. That's all."

"I was kissing," she said. "And so were you!"

He smiled at her. "You are so hard on yourself sometimes. It's okay to feel something that doesn't hurt once in a while."

"Promise me that won't happen again!"

"It won't if you don't want it to. But let me tell you something—if you do want it to, I'm going to let you. You know why? Because I like kissing. And I don't beat myself up about it."

"I'm not doing that," she said. "I just don't want to be stupid."

"You're punishing yourself. I can't figure out why. But," he said, lifting her off his lap and putting her on her feet, "you get to call the shots. Personally, I think you secretly like me. Trust me. And I think for a minute there, you also liked kissing me." He grinned at her. "I could tell. I'm so smart that way."

"You're just desperate for a little female companionship," she said.

"Oh, there are females around. That has nothing to do with anything."

"Still—you have to promise."

"Sure," he said. "If that's what you want."

"It's what I need."

He stood up and looked down at her. He had warned himself of this and stupidly ignored his own warnings. He had to renew that trust. Fast. He lifted her chin with a finger and looked into her pretty, sad eyes. "Would you like me to take you and Chloe to the Anderson ranch? If I promise not to kiss you anymore?"

"Would you?" she said. "I want to take her, to see where she'll live. And I don't think I want to be alone."

Jack knew it was imperative that Mel regain her sense of control. He went back to the bar to get his truck and poked his head in. "Doc, I'm going to drive Mel and the baby out to the Andersons'. You okay with that?"

"Sure," the old boy said, not looking up from his game. When Mel had the few amassed baby things packed up, he took her. They had no car seat, so she held the baby—and she got a little teary. But once they had traversed the long road up into the hills and were passing through the fenced pastures of grazing sheep, he could see that she was pulling herself together.

Lilly Anderson brought them into her home—a simple house that spoke of the abundance of life. The floors and windows were shining from the housekeeping attention they received; there were folded quilts on the ends of sofas and draped over chairs, crewel pictures on the walls, the smell of freshly baked bread, a pie cooling on the counter and dozens of pictures of children, of family, a collection that spanned many years. A wicker bassinet stood ready for Chloe. Lilly made Mel tea and they sat at the kitchen table and talked while Jack went with Buck to the corral where his grown sons had begun the spring shearing.

"I'll be honest with you, Lilly. I got pretty attached to her."

Lilly reached across the table for her hand. "It's perfectly understandable. You should come out here often, hold her, rock her. You should stay close."

"I don't want you to go through that—when someone finally comes for her."

Lilly got tears in her eyes in sympathy with the tears Mel was showing. "You must be such a tender heart," Lilly said. "Don't worry, Mel—now that I'm a grandma, lots of little ones pass through here and don't stay. But while she's here, promise you won't be a stranger."

"Thank you, Lilly. For understanding. My women and their babies—it's what I live for."

"It shows. We're so lucky to have you with us."

"But I'm not staying, you know...."

"You should think about that. This isn't a bad place."

"I'll hang around long enough to be sure things are working out for Chloe. And I'll try to make it a few days before I'm back to cuddle her," Mel said.

"You come every day if you like. Twice a day."

It wasn't long before Mel joined Jack at the fence and stood watching the shearing. "You'll have to come back for the lambing in a few weeks," Buck said. "We like to shear before the lambing—it's easier on the sheep."

When they left the ranch, Jack drove around the hills of Virgin River. He didn't say anything—he just let her see the beauty of the green fields, the high hills, grazing livestock. He took her for a little stretch along Highway 299 through a piece of the redwoods that, despite her morose mood, caused her to gasp in awe. The sky was still and blue, the breeze light and cool, but in the tallest trees it was dark except for those blinding flashes of bright sun that broke through. He could tell she was getting better, if slowly, quietly.

It was like this place was divided into two worlds—the dank and dark world of the deep forest where life was bleak and poor, the people desperate. And this world, the national forest of redwoods, the first-rate campgrounds, the hills and valleys where the fields were lush and plentiful, where health and contentment abounded.

Jack drove down a tree-canopied road toward the widest curve in the Virgin River, pulled the truck up to the edge and parked. There were two men in the river, waders held by suspenders, wearing tan fishing vests with many pockets and wicker creels held by shoulder straps, casting out into the water. The arcs of their lines were like a ballet, so graceful, so rhythmic.

"What are we doing?" she asked.

"I wanted you to see a few things before you cut and

run. This is where a lot of the town and visitors like to fish, where I mostly fish. When the winter rains come, we come out here to watch the salmon leap up over the natural waterfalls to return to their home creeks to spawn. It's really something to see. Now that the baby is at the Andersons', I'll take you to the coast if you like. Pretty soon the whales will be migrating north to cooler waters for the summer. They'll travel close to the coastline with their new calves and it's incredible."

She watched the fishermen cast and reel in, then there was a catch. A good-size brown trout.

"During a good season, fish is the main staple on the menu at the bar," he said.

"Most of it you catch yourself?" she asked.

"Me and Preacher and Ricky. The best way to make work into play. Mel," he said, his voice soft. "Look downstream. There…"

She squinted and then sat back with a gasp. Poking their heads out of the brush at the side of the river on the other side was a mother bear and her cub.

"You were asking about the bear. Black bear. The cub looks young. They're just giving birth and coming out of hibernation. Have you ever seen anything like that?"

"Only on the Discovery Channel. The fishermen don't see her?" she asked.

"I'm sure they see her. She won't bother them and they won't bother her. But they carry bear repellent just in case. And they'll have a rifle in the truck—but if she gets too close they'll just reel in their lines and sit in their trucks until she leaves." He chuckled. "Watch while she eats their fish."

She watched in fascination for a moment, then said, "Why'd you bring me here?"

"Sometimes, if something's eating me up—I can

come out here, or drive into the redwoods, or go up on the knoll where the sheep are grazing, or maybe out to a pasture where the cows roam, and just sit awhile. Just connect with the earth. Sometimes that's all I have to do."

One elbow sticking out of the window, wrist of the other hand balanced on the top of the steering wheel, Jack just watched the fishing—the men and the bear. The men were so intent on their sport that they had never even turned around at the sound of the truck pulling into the clearing.

They were quiet. Jack had no idea what she might be thinking, but he thought, *Don't turn and run just because you got kissed. Things could be worse.*

After about twenty minutes, he started the truck. "I have something to show you. You're in no hurry, are you?"

"Doc's in town," she said. "I guess not."

Jack eventually pulled into the clearing where Hope McCrea's cabin sat. It was perfectly obvious he'd like her to reconsider leaving. But she never expected him to do what he had done. As they pulled up to the cabin and parked, she looked at him in surprise.

"My God," she said. "How did you do this?"

"Soap," he said. "Wood. Paint. Nails."

"You shouldn't have, Jack. Because—"

"I know—because you're not staying. I've heard that at least a hundred times over the past couple of weeks. That's fine. You'll do what you have to do. But this is what you were promised and I thought you ought to have the option."

Straight ahead of her was the little A-frame cabin with a new, strong, wide porch, painted red. Two white Adirondack chairs sat on the deck and four white pots holding red geraniums sat on the porch rails in the corners. It was beautiful. She was afraid to go inside. Did this mean that if it were lovely, she'd be forced to stay? Because she knew it was going to be lovely.

Wordlessly, Mel got out of the truck. She slowly walked up the steps to the house, aware that Jack had not gotten out of the truck behind her. He was letting her go alone. She pushed open the door, which no longer stuck. Inside, the wood floors gleamed, the countertops sparkled. The windows, previously so grimy you couldn't see out, were so clean it seemed possible there was no glass. The window that had been boarded up was replaced. The appliances were spotless, the furniture had been so vigorously vacuumed or shampooed that the colors were now bright because there was no dust. There was a new area rug on the floor.

She wandered into the bedroom. A new comforter replaced the old and she could tell without even checking under the covers that a fat, firm mattress had been purchased and that the nasty soiled one was gone. The brightness of the sheets indicated these were not Hope's hand-me-downs, but newly purchased linen. On the floor beside the bed, a wide, thick rug. In the bathroom, new towels and accessories. The shower glass had been completely replaced and the tiles had been scrubbed to such a high sheen that even the grout was immaculate. There was the faintest smell of bleach; not a spot or stain remained. She loved the bright towels, alternating red and white. The rugs were white; the trash can, glass and tissue dispenser were red.

There were two bedrooms downstairs and a small, open loft upstairs at the peak of the A-frame—only large enough for a bed and maybe a small dresser. Both of them had been scoured clean, but they were empty of furniture. Back in the living room, she saw the fire had been laid and a fresh pile of wood sat at the side of the hearth. The books in the bookcases were dust free, the trunk that could be used as a coffee table had been polished with lemon oil. The cupboards shone with oil, as well. She opened one of them and saw there were new ceramic dishes to replace the dingy Melmac that had been there before. Graying old plastic was replaced with glass. A wine rack on the counter held four bottles.

Inside the refrigerator, which also gleamed, there were a few staples. A bottle of white wine was chilling, a six-pack of good beer. There was milk, orange juice, butter, bread, lettuce and other salad items. Bacon and eggs. Sandwich items—lunch meat, cheese, mayo, mustard. On the kitchen table, which wore a pretty new tablecloth, sat a festive ceramic bowl holding fresh fruit. In the corner of the counter, a set of four thick, round white candles. She lowered her face and sniffed. Vanilla.

She left the house, pulling the door closed behind her and went back to the truck. It made her melancholy, all that he'd done. This was not what she'd expected, either. Mel had come to terms with the fact that she'd made a mistake. Now that she'd accepted that, she was ready to move on. As soon as they could spare her.

"Why did you do this?"

"It was promised to you," he said. "You're under no obligation."

"But what did you hope?" she asked.

"The town needs you. Doc needs help, you can see that. I hoped you'd give it a chance. A few more weeks, maybe. Just to see if it worked for you. I think the Virgin River folks have already made it clear—it works for them."

"Did you do this hoping it would force me to the terms of Hope's one-year contract?" she asked him. "Because as the place was, we were at an impasse. She couldn't hold me to it—she hadn't met the terms."

"She will not force that contract," he said flatly.

"But yes, she will."

"No. She will not hold you to that contract. Guaranteed. I'll see to it. This is just for you—not leverage for Hope."

She shook her head sadly. "You can see I don't belong here," she said softly.

"Aw. I don't know, Mel. People belong wherever they feel good. It can be a lot of different places. For a lot of different reasons."

"No, Jack, look. Look at me. I'm not a camper—I'm a shopper. I'm really not one of those homespun country midwives. I'm so citified, it's scary. I feel so out of place here. It's as if I'm not like anyone. They don't make me feel that way, but I can't help it. I shouldn't be here, I should be at Nordstrom's."

"Come on," he laughed.

She lowered her face into her hands and massaged her eyes. "You just don't understand. It's complicated, Jack. There's more to this than you realize."

"Tell me. You can trust me."

"That's just it—one of the reasons I agreed to come here is so I wouldn't have to talk about it anymore. Let's say I made a crazy decision. An insane decision. The *wrong* decision. This isn't for me."

"It wasn't just burnout, was it?" he asked her.

"I got rid of everything that tied me to L.A. and ran for my life. It was a panicked, crazy, irrational decision," she said. "I was hurting all over."

"I assumed as much. A man, maybe. A heartache or something."

"Close enough," she said.

"Believe me, Mel. This is as good a place as any to work through a heartache."

"You?" she asked him.

"Yeah, in a manner of speaking. But I didn't come here in a panic. I was looking for a place like this. Good fishing and hunting. Remote. Uncomplicated. Clean air, decent values, hardworking people who help each other out. It serves."

She took a deep breath. "I don't think it's going to work for me in the long term."

"That's okay—no one asked you to make a long-term commitment. Well, no one except Hope, but no one really takes her seriously. But you shouldn't rush out of here with the same panic as you rushed in. It's a healthy place. It's a loving place. Who knows? You might find it helps you get through…whatever."

"I'm sorry. I'm such a downer sometimes. I should be so thankful. Grateful. And instead—"

"Hey, easy," he said, throwing the truck into gear to take her back to town. "I blindsided you. You had it in your head that you could use the excuse of having no decent housing. And now Chloe isn't holding you here. But I figured, you don't have to stay at Doc's now, and if someone's going to give birth in your bedroom there, maybe it's time you have your own place. If you want it, that is."

"Are there bears out here?" she asked.

"It might be best if you kept your trash indoors, and drive it into town to put in the Dumpster. Bears so like garbage."

"Oh, for the love of God!"

"We haven't had a bad bear scare in ages." He reached across the console and squeezed her hand. "Just give yourself a break. Work on your particular heartache. And while you do, take the occasional temperature. Give a pill now and then. No one's holding you hostage."

She watched him as he drove. That strong profile. He had a solid square face, straight nose, high cheekbones, bristle of stubble on his cheeks. He was a hairy guy; she noticed that he shaved his neck down to the top of his chest and she found herself wondering what was under his shirt. She remembered Mark's complaints of his receding hairline, which did nothing to detract from his boyish good looks. But this man, Jack, wasn't boyish. He had the hard good looks of a woodsman. And, though his hair was cropped short in that military buzz, it was so thick that it looked as if it should be thinned. The big hands on the steering wheel were calloused—he worked hard. The guy was dripping in testosterone.

What was this magnificent man doing locked away in a little town of six hundred, where there were no women for him? She wondered if he had the faintest clue about her—that she had no heart. He had just given so much and she had absolutely nothing to give. Nothing. She was hollow inside. If she weren't, a man like Jack would appeal to her.

This was the worst thing about grief, she thought as she walked back to Doc's house. It emptied you. She should be flattered and pleased with what had been done for her in the renovating of the cabin. She should be thrilled that a man like Jack was interested in her, because clearly he was. But instead she was sad. She had lost the ability to be moved by these acts of kindness. Instead, it made her feel depressed and alone, because

she didn't feel up to the task of receiving gifts and kind-
nesses graciously. She couldn't respond to a handsome
man's interest. She couldn't be happy. Sometimes she
asked herself if she was paying some tribute to Mark's
memory by hanging on to the sadness of losing him.

Ricky worked at the bar after school every day
and some weekends, whenever Jack wanted him. He
dropped Liz at the store after school, then parked behind the bar next to Jack's and Preacher's trucks. As he
was going in, Jack was coming out. "Grab your gear,"
Jack said. "We're going to run out to the river, see if
we can make a catch."

"There isn't anything out there now," Ricky said.
The good catch was in the fall and winter, dwindling
by spring, starting to pick up again in summer.

"We'll cast a while," Jack said. "See what you got."

"Preacher coming?" Ricky asked, going to the store-
room in the kitchen to get his rod, reel and waders.

"Nah. He's busy."

Jack remembered the first day he'd met Ricky. The
kid had been thirteen and had ridden his bike up to the
cabin that would become the bar. Skinny and freckle-
faced with the most engaging grin and sweetest dispo-
sition. He let him hang around, help with the carpentry
during the renovation if he could pay attention. When
he found out it was just Ricky and his grandma, Lydie,
he kind of took him under his wing. He'd watched the
boy grow tall and strong; Jack taught him to fish, shoot.
Now he was damn near a man. Physically, he didn't
have far to go, but mentally and emotionally, sixteen
was still just sixteen.

At the river's edge, they cast their lines a few times
and then it came. The real reason for fishing when there

were few fish. "You and I should have a little talk, I think," Jack said.

"About?"

Jack didn't look at him. He just cast in long beautiful arcs. And said, "About all the places you can put your dick that aren't statutory."

Ricky snapped his head around and looked at Jack's profile. Jack turned his head and met the boy's eyes.

"She's fourteen," Jack said.

Ricky looked back at the river, silent.

"I know she doesn't look fourteen. She's fourteen."

"I haven't done anything," Ricky said.

Jack laughed. "Oh, gimme a break. I saw your truck over at Connie's the first Friday night she was in town—you moved on her fast. You want to stick with that story?" He reeled in and turned toward Ricky. "Listen, son, you have to keep your head. You hear me, Rick? Because this is dangerous ground you're on. She's a little hottie—"

"She's a sweet girl," Rick said defensively.

"You're already hooked," Jack said, hoping they weren't already doomed. "How hooked?"

Ricky shrugged. "I like her. I know she's young, but she doesn't seem that young, and I like her."

"Okay," Jack said, taking a breath. "Okay, maybe we should talk about the things you can do to avoid putting your sixteen-year-old swimmers in contact with her fourteen-year-old eggs. Hmm?"

"You don't have to," Ricky said, casting. And casting pretty badly.

"Aw, Jesus. You're already involved. Physically, huh?" Rick didn't answer and Jack thought, who knew what they were up to. Jack remembered only too well the things experimental kids could do to get a little satisfaction without going all the way. It was a frickin' art form. Problem was, it just didn't last, and the closer you got, the greater potential for slipups. Sometimes it made more sense to decide you were going all the way with good birth control in place, rather than risk an accident. But man, you should be older. Older. "Aw, Jesus." Jack took a breath. He dug down into his waders, down into the pocket of his jeans. He pulled out a fist full of condoms. "This is tough, Rick, because I don't want you to use these on her, and I don't want you not to. I'm stuck here. Help me out, will you?"

"It's okay, Jack. I'm not going to do her. She's fourteen."

Jack reached out and tousled his hair. Those freckles had given way to the stubble of a young beard; he wasn't skinny anymore. The work he did at the bar plus the pastimes of hunting and fishing, not to mention chores for his grandma, had bulked the kid up and his shoulders and arms were muscled. Handsome kid, he thought. Real grown-up. He had a lot of responsibility—he worked hard, maintained his grades, did every physical thing around his grandma's house that needed doing. With Jack's supervision, Rick had painted her house. All that built toward creating a solid, reliable man—one who shouldn't get shot in the foot by a teenage pregnancy.

"So, how old were you?" Ricky asked him.

"'Bout your age. But the girl was much older."

"Much?"

"Way older than Lizzie. Older than me. Smarter than me." He handed Rick the condoms and although Rick's cheeks took on a dark stain, he accepted them. "I know you're at that age—I was that age once. You know what the problem is. She might not look so young, but she's got a long way to go yet. Huh?"

A shiver went through Ricky and Jack caught it. Well, it's not as though he had been oblivious to Lizzie's rather overmatured charms. Thus the talk. "Yeah," Ricky said, a little breathless.

"Let's be sure you know some things," Jack said. "You know that old business about pulling out in time—you know that doesn't work. Right? And trying to not put it all the way in? Useless. First of all, if you can do that, you're a stronger man than I am, and even if you can, it's not good enough—you can still get her pregnant. You know these things, right?"

"Of course I know that."

"Rick, you understand, if there's no backing out of this relationship with her and if there's a strong potential for it to get more serious rather than less, you might have to be the one to take charge. Draw a line in the sand—insist on birth control at least. You got a midwife in town—there's help available. For Liz. I think she's too young to be having sex, personally. But I *know* she's too young to be pregnant. You with me here, buddy?"

"I told you, I have it under control. But thanks, Jack. I know you just want me to do the right thing."

"Which includes not getting caught off guard. If it's getting close, you get her fixed up. Double protection—hers and yours. You have to use the head with the brain in it. Believe me, I've seen more than one good man go down because he was thinking with his dick." He watched Ricky's chin lower as he looked down and he knew. Liz was irresistible to him. He was fighting for his life. His pants were on fire.

"Yeah," Ricky said. "I hear ya."

"You make sure you always have a condom, okay?

It's your responsibility to keep her safe, son. If you use even one condom, Rick, you get her to Mel. Right away."

"Do we have to talk about this anymore?"

Jack grabbed the boy's arm and felt solid biceps in his grasp. Damn, Ricky was nearly six feet and still growing. "You wanna be a man, son? You have to think like one. It's not enough to just feel like one."

"Yeah," he said. Then, "By the way, it's not statutory unless I'm over eighteen."

Jack laughed in spite of himself. "Too smart for your own goddamn good, aren't you?"

"I hope so, Jack. Holy God, I hope so."

Seven

Mel talked to Joey at least every other day, sometimes every day. She would place the call from Doc's when she had a free minute and Joey would call her back so it wasn't on his nickel. She sent her digital pictures of the renovation of the cabin from Doc's computer and Joey, being an interior decorator, was fascinated by all the building and refinishing Jack had done. Then Mel told Joey that she was going to stay a little longer. A few weeks. At least long enough to be sure Chloe was doing well with Lilly. She loved the little cabin and wanted to see Polly through her delivery.

She didn't tell Jack. But by her daily presence at the grill, he came to realize that she was giving it a chance, and he couldn't hide the fact that it pleased him.

She and Doc played gin, Mel walked down to the store in time to watch the soap with Connie and Joy, and spent a large amount of time at the bar. Joy, who was not a librarian, was the person who opened up the little library on Tuesdays—and Mel was always there. It was about ten by twelve feet, crammed with books, mostly paperbacks with the stamps from secondhand stores inside the covers. It was the only entertainment Mel had when she went home at night.

Mel learned that Lydie Sudder had poor general health when Doc sent her down to the Sudder house to deliver diabetic testing supplies, insulin and syringes. Lydie, beside being diabetic and arthritic, had a weak heart, but Mel was surprised to find that the little house she shared with Ricky was very well kept and nicely furnished; Lydie somehow managed to keep up with things. She got around slowly, but her smile was kind and her manners delightful. Of course, she wouldn't let Mel out of the house without tea and cookies. She was still there, visiting with Lydie on the front porch, when Ricky came home from school, driving up in his little white truck.

"Hey, Mel," he said. He leaned down and kissed his grandmother's cheek. "Hi, Gram. I'm going to work if you don't need anything."

"I'm just fine, Ricky," she said, patting his hand.

"Call me if you need me," he said. "I'll bring you something of Preacher's later."

"That would be nice, honey."

The boy went inside to drop off his books, then out again, jumping off the porch steps and back into his truck to drive the whole block to the bar. "I guess a man can't be separated from his wheels," Mel observed.

"That appears to be the case." Lydie laughed.

The next day she sat at the grill at lunchtime with Connie. "I haven't heard you say you're leaving for days now," Connie said. "Something change on that score?"

"Not a great deal," Mel said. "But since Jack went to such a lot of trouble to work on that cabin, I thought I owed it to him to give it a few weeks. I can deliver Polly's baby."

Connie glanced at the bar where Jack was setting up lunch in front of a couple of fishermen. She gave a nod in his direction. "Bet that makes Jack real happy."

"He seems to think the town can use me, even if Doc doesn't think so."

Connie laughed at her. "Girl, you need glasses. The way Jack looks at you, I don't think it's about Doc. Or the town."

"You don't see me looking back in any particular way, do you?"

"You should. There isn't a woman within a hundred square miles wouldn't leave her husband for him."

"Even you?" Mel asked with a laugh.

"I'm different," she said, drinking her coffee. "I married Ron when I was about seven." She took a drink of her coffee. "But okay—if he begged me, I'd leave Ron for him."

Mel laughed at her. "It is pretty strange that no one's latched on to him."

"I heard he was seeing a woman in Clear River. Don't know how serious it is. Might be nothing."

"Do you know her? The woman he's seeing?"

She shook her head, but lifted one curious brow at Mel's obvious interest. "He's private, isn't he? Doesn't let anything slip. But he can't hide those looks he sends your way."

"He shouldn't waste his time," she said. *I'm not available,* she didn't add.

In her new abode, Mel had put her own favorite books on the shelves—all of which she had already read and reread—and Mark's picture on the table beside the bed. Each night she told him how much she missed him. But she cried less. Maybe because of the way Jack looked at her. The soothing way he talked to her.

The house Mel sold in L.A. was almost four thousand square feet and it had never seemed too big; she had loved the spaciousness of the rooms. Yet the cabin, maybe twelve hundred square feet total, felt right. Like a cocoon. It hugged her.

One of her favorite parts of the day was at the end, before she drove out to her new cabin. She would go to the bar for a cold beer and some chips or cheese and crackers. Once in a while she had dinner, but she didn't mind being by herself at her cabin where there was now food in the cupboard.

Jack put her cold beer in front of her. "We have macaroni and cheese tonight," he said. "I can talk Preacher into putting a slice of ham with that."

"Thanks, but I'm going home for dinner tonight."

"You're cooking?" he asked.

"Not exactly," she said. "I cook things like sandwiches. Coffee. The occasional fried egg. And takeout."

"A modern woman." He laughed. "But that place is working out for you?"

"It's wonderful, thanks. And I need the quiet. Did you know Doc snores like a freight train?"

He chuckled. "Doesn't surprise me."

"I picked up a little gossip about you. That you're seeing a woman in Clear River?"

He didn't look all that surprised. He lifted his brows and his coffee mug. "Seeing? That sounds a little delicate for this crowd."

"I was glad to hear you have someone in your life."

"I don't," he said. "Ancient history. And I wasn't exactly seeing her. It was a lot more basic than that."

Somehow, that made her smile. "Sounds like maybe you had some kind of arrangement."

He sipped from his mug and gave a shrug. "It was—"

"Wait," she said, laughing. "You don't owe me any explanation."

He put both hands on the bar and leaned toward her. "We had an understanding. I went to her place once in a while. For an evening. Nothing deep. No love affair. Casual sex, Mel, between consenting adults. When I realized it didn't work for me, we parted as friends. I'm not with a woman."

"Well, that's kind of too bad," she said.

"It's not necessarily a permanent condition," he said. "That's just how it is right now. Want a slice of pie to take home?"

"Yeah," she said. "Sure."

Mel had been in Virgin River four weeks. In that time, patients and friends dropped by frequently. Some had a little cash for medical services, a few had insurance, but the majority had produce from their farms, ranches, orchards, vineyards or kitchens. The latter, knowing that a single loaf of bread or pie probably didn't cover the cost of an exam and treatment or medication, tended to stop by with a little something even when they were well. The unprepared food—a bushel of apples or nuts, canned or fresh fruit, vegetables, berries, lamb shank or veal, would go right over to Preacher, who could make good use of it, later feeding some of it to Mel and Doc. In some ways, it was like a commune.

That usually left Doc and Mel with more food than they could use, especially since they were getting most of their meals at Jack's. Mel packed up a box of some stuff that was likely to go bad soon—some eggs, bread, sliced ham and a brick of cheese, a pie, apples and nuts. A carton of orange juice she'd picked up from Connie. She put the box in the passenger seat of Doc's old truck before she asked him, "Could I borrow your truck for a couple hours? I want to drive around some and I don't really trust the BMW. I promise, I'll be real careful with it."

"My truck? I can't see you in my truck," he said doubtfully.

"Why not? I'll gas it up, if that's what you're worried about."

"I'm worried about you driving it off a cliff and leaving me with that piece of shit you call a car."

She pursed her lips. "Some days, you're more than I can take. Really."

He picked up his keys and flipped them at her. She caught them. "Don't hurt the truck. As God is my witness, I will never be caught driving that foreign job."

She drove his truck out of town and the minute she was on the winding mountain roads, in the trees, driving up up up and then down down down over the mountain, her heart started to beat a little wildly. She was afraid, plain and simple. But she'd been haunted for two weeks and couldn't live with the feeling. And that brought a plan into focus.

She surprised herself by remembering where Clifford Paulis's camp was. She wondered if she was driven by some psychic energy. Her sense of direction in the hills, through the trees, was perfectly lousy. But—before long she was there, recognizing the nearly invisible old logging road that led to their compound. She drove in, made a big turn inside the opening so that she was pointed toward the way out, and then got out of the truck. She stood right beside the driver's door and yelled, "Clifford!"

No one appeared immediately, but in a few moments a bearded man came out from around a camper shell that had been pulled off a pickup and she recognized him as one of the men she'd seen on her last visit. She crooked her finger at him, beckoning him to her. He shuffled slowly toward her and as he neared, she reached back into the truck and pulled out the box. "I thought maybe you guys could use this," she said. "It was going to waste at the clinic."

He looked at her dumbly.

"Go ahead," she said, pushing the box toward him. "No strings. Just a little neighborly gesture."

He seemed to take the box reluctantly. He looked inside.

She dazzled him with her prettiest smile. When he smiled back, his teeth were god-awful, but she didn't react. After all, she'd seen people like him before. But before, she'd call one agency or another, hand them off, clear her charts. It was different out here.

She got in the truck and put it in gear to leave. In the rearview mirror she saw him hurrying toward that camper shell, and a couple of guys had come out from behind and joined him. It made her heart feel better. Good.

When she got back to town, she returned the keys to Doc, who sat behind his desk in his cramped office. "I guess you think I don't know what you did," he said. She lifted her chin in some defiance. "I thought I told you—stay away from there. It isn't an innocent place and no one knows what might happen."

"You go," she said.

"And I told you not to."

"Did we have some understanding? That I was going to follow your nonmedical orders? Because I don't recall that in my personal life, I'm obligated to do everything you tell me."

"Guess you're not obligated to use your brain in your personal life, either."

"I filled your truck up with gas, you old pain in the ass."

"I didn't get caught in that piece of shit foreign job of yours, you obstinate little strumpet."

And she laughed at him so hard, tears came to her eyes and she had to leave, laughing all the way back to her cabin.

It was a bright and sunny afternoon when Mel went to Doc's office. She tapped lightly and stuck her head in. "Do you have any idea what's taking Social Services so long to do something about Chloe?" she asked him.

"Certainly don't," he said.

"Maybe I should do a follow-up—give them a call."

"I said I'd take care of it," he answered, not looking up.

"It's just that—you know—I got attached. I didn't mean to, didn't intend to, but there it is. I'd hate for Lilly Anderson to go through that withdrawal. It doesn't feel good."

"She's raised a passel of kids. She knows the score."

"I know, but…" She stopped talking as she heard the front door open. She leaned out of his office and looked down the hall. Right inside the door stood Polly. She seemed to be holding her belly up with her hands and instead of that usual glow on her cheeks, she looked just a bit pale. Nervous. Right behind her was a young man in almost identical overalls, holding a small, worn suitcase. Mel looked back at Doc and said, "Showtime."

Polly wasn't even sure how far apart the pains were. "It feels like one big one," she said. "Mostly down real low."

"Okay, let's just go upstairs and get settled."

"Can Darryl come?"

Mel reached over and took the suitcase from Darryl. "Of course. That would help a lot. I'm going to concentrate on you." She took Polly's hand. "Come on."

Once upstairs, she had Polly sit in the rocker while she went about the business of getting a bed ready with the plastic mattress protector and clean sheets. "Good timing, Polly. My cottage was ready at the same time my littlest patient went out to Lilly Anderson's ranch to stay. I'm all moved out and you, Darryl and the baby can have the whole room."

"Arrrgggghhhh," Polly answered, grabbing her belly and leaning forward. There was a slightly muffled sound that preceded the soft dripping of amniotic fluids onto the floor.

"Oh, Polly!" Darryl exclaimed. He looked suddenly stricken. Embarrassed.

"Well," Mel said, looking over her shoulder. "That should speed things up. Just stay put until the bed's ready and I can help you change."

A half hour later Polly sat up in the hospital bed, not terribly comfortable on a couple of towels, her green hospital gown stretched over her belly. Mel had changed into a pair of scrubs and Nikes she'd packed for just such an event. If this were L.A., the anesthesiologist would be on his way to check her and discuss the epidural, but this was the country, no anesthesia here. Doc came around right after Mel had given Polly a pelvic to see how far she had dilated, and then upon noting Darryl's pallor, he said, "Young man—let's you and me wander across the street and have a drop of courage."

"Darryl, don't leave me!" Polly begged.

"He'll be right back, and I won't leave you," Mel

promised. "But, sweetheart, you're only at four centi-meters—it's going to be a while."

Good to her word, Mel stayed at her side. She wasn't sure what she had expected the situation to be like, but was admittedly surprised by a few things. One—Doc Mullins stayed out of her way and let her have the case even though Polly had been his patient. Two, he took on the job of watching Darryl in case it became neces-sary to take the lad out of the room. Doc was staying up long after his usual bedtime. And, the few times Mel wandered out of the patient's room through the night to fetch supplies or a fresh cup of coffee, she looked across the street to see the lights were on and the Open sign lit at Jack's. He kept the bar open all night.

Polly's labor intensified slowly as the hours ticked by, but she remained stable and progressed normally. Mel had her up walking, squatting, getting gravity on their side. She had Darryl hold her forward while she rocked her hips side to side and at three-thirty in the morning, Polly began to push. The girl was most comfortable on her side, so Darryl and Mel joined forces to help her deliver in that position. Mel had Polly lie on her side in the fetal position, the leg beneath her tucked up and under while Polly and Darryl together lifted the upper leg to clear the field of birth. It was a big first baby and Polly couldn't have managed that position, pushing for so long, without a good assistant. It was important that the mother have whatever control she could, trusting her body; it made the whole experience so much more beautiful. Darryl held up pretty well despite the fact that it was difficult to watch his young wife in pain, and the sight of blood, even though he'd slaughtered his share of pigs, was clearly tough on him.

At four-thirty Polly's baby emerged after an hour of

pushing. Mel cut the cord, wrapped the baby and passed him to his father. "Mr. Fishburn," she said to Darryl, "there is another Mr. Fishburn in the family. Please help Polly get your son situated on her breast—it'll help her deliver the placenta and slow the bleeding."

This was so much more like a scene from *Gone with the Wind* than the type of midwifery Mel had known in a large, well-equipped city hospital. While Doc checked over the newborn, Mel cleaned up the mother with soap and water and changed her sheets and bedclothes.

By six-thirty in the morning, physically exhausted but wired on caffeine, Mel's work was done. The baby would reside in the room with Polly, and Darryl could have the other bed if he wanted it. It took them both about sixty seconds to fall into a deep sleep. Mel washed her face, rinsed her mouth with a little mouthwash, let her hair out of the clip that had held it on top of her head and went looking for Doc.

"Go to bed, Doc," she said. "It was a long night. I'll keep the office open."

"No, sir," he said. "I don't sleep in daylight, and you did all the work. I'll keep an eye on the Fishburns. Go to your place."

"I'll make a deal with you. I'll go take a nap and come back in early afternoon to spell you."

"That'll do," he said. Then, peering over his glasses, added, "Not bad. For a city girl."

The sun was just peeking over the mountains, bathing the little town in pinkish beige rays. The April air was cold. She pulled her wool jacket around herself and sat on Doc's front porch, feeling exhilarated, and perhaps a little too wound up for sleep right away.

Polly had done well, for a mere girl. No Lamaze training for those two, and no drugs. There had been some powerful grunting, groaning and straining; Darryl had grunted along with his wife with such sincerity, it was lucky he didn't mess his pants. Nice, big, eight-pound country baby. There was nothing in this world like pulling a squalling infant from its mother's womb; no panacea for a breaking heart could do more. This didn't throw Mel into a stupor of longing or depression because this was her life's work—what she loved. And she loved it so much more when the couple was happy and excited, the baby robust and healthy. Holding the baby she had just delivered, handing it to its mother and watching it suckle hungrily—it was like seeing God before you.

She heard a loud thwack. And another. She had no idea what time Jack's usually opened. It was only six-thirty. Another loud thwack, coming from his place.

She went down the porch stairs and across the street. Behind the bar there was a big brick barbecue. Wearing boots, jeans and a flannel shirt, and hefting a heavy ax, Jack was splitting logs on a tree stump. She just stood there watching him for a moment. *Thwack, thwack, thwack.*

He looked up from his chore to see her leaning against the side of the building, pulling her jacket tight over turquoise scrubs. She had no idea that what made him grin at her was the huge toothy smile she wore. "Well?" he said, leaning the ax against the tree stump.

"Baby boy. Big baby boy."

"Congratulations," he said. "Everyone is okay?"

She walked toward him. "They're better than okay. Polly did great, the baby is strong, healthy, and Darryl is expected to recover." And then she laughed, throwing her head back. Nothing, nothing was more satisfying than coming out of a delivery with one-hundred-percent success. "My first country birth. Harder on Mom than on me. In the city, it's always an option to just roll over, bare your spine, and labor in comfort from an epidural. Women out here are made of steel."

"I've heard that," he said with a laugh

"Know what Doc said? 'Not bad for a city girl.'" She reached for his hand. "Did you stay open all night?"

He shrugged. "I nodded off by the fire a couple of times. But you never know when someone might need something. Boiling water. Ice. A stiff drink. You want some coffee?"

"God, I think it would make me barf. I've had enough coffee to jangle even the nerves of a caffeine junkie." Uncharacteristically, she wrapped her arms around his waist and hugged him. This man had become her closest friend. "Jack, it was wonderful. I had forgotten how wonderful. I haven't delivered a baby in, gee, almost a year, I think." She looked up into his eyes. "Damn, we did a good piece of work. Me, Mom and Dad. Damn."

He smoothed a little hair off her forehead. "I'm proud of you."

"It was so awesome."

"See? I knew you'd find something here to sink your teeth into." He reached down, crossed his arms under her bottom and lifted her straight up so that her face was even with his.

"Nowwww, what did we decide?" she asked, but her tone was teasing. Her smile was playful.

"We decided that I would not kiss you."

"That's right."

"I haven't," he said.

"Maybe we should have talked about this," she added, but she certainly didn't struggle. In fact, this seemed oddly right. Celebratory. Like being picked up and swung around after the win of a big game. And that was how she felt—as though she'd just scored a touchdown. Arms resting on his shoulders, she clasped her hands behind his head.

"We further decided that if you kissed me, I would let you," he said.

"You're fishing."

"Does this look like fishing to you?"

"Begging?"

"Doing exactly as I've been told. *Waiting.*"

What the hell, she thought. Absolutely nothing could feel better after the night she'd just spent than to plant a big wet one on this guy—a guy who'd keep his business open all night just in case they needed something. So she laid one on him. She slid her lips over his, opening them, moving over his with wicked and delicious intent, getting her tongue involved. And he did nothing but hold her there, allowing this.

"Did you not like that?" she asked.

"Oh," he said. "Am I allowed to respond?"

She whacked him softly in the head, making him laugh. She tried it again, and this time it was much more interesting. It made her heart beat faster, made her breathe hard. *Yes,* she thought. *It is okay to feel something that doesn't hurt sometimes.* This wasn't because she was grief-stricken or needy, this was because she was victorious. And all she could think about at the moment was his delicious mouth.

When their mouths came apart, she said, "I feel like a total champ."

"You are," he said, enjoying her mood more than she would ever guess. "God, you taste good."

"You don't taste that bad," she said, laughing. "Put me down now," she instructed.

"No. Do it again."

"Okay, but only one more, then you have to behave."

She planted another one on him, thoroughly enjoying his lips and tongue, the strength of the arms that held her. She refused to worry about whether this was a mistake. She was here, she was happy for once, and his mouth felt as natural to hers as if she'd been kissing him for years. She let the kiss be a little longer and deeper than she thought prudent, and even that made her smile.

When it was over, he put her on her feet. "Whew," she said.

"We don't have nearly enough births in this town."

"We have another one in about six weeks. And if you're very, very good…"

Ah, he thought. *That gives me six weeks.* He touched the end of her nose. "Nothing wrong with a little kissing, Mel."

"And you won't get ideas?"

He bellowed. "You can make me behave, it turns out. But you can't keep me from getting ideas."

April waned and May brought out the early spring flowers; foxgloves and Queen Anne's lace grew wild along the roads. Australian Fern blanketed the earth beneath the big trees. Every week or ten days, Mel borrowed Doc's truck, took a little lip from him, and delivered a box of food to the Paulis camp that would otherwise go to waste. Doc would have no part of it and scolded her. She ignored him indignantly and that alone made her feel good. It made her heart pound wildly as she went, and beat with satisfaction as she returned to Virgin River.

The cabin was turning out to be a haven for Mel. She purchased a small TV on which she got terrible reception. If she were staying, she'd get a satellite dish, but she was only committed to a few more weeks. And one day she came home from the clinic to find she had a telephone in her kitchen and bedroom. Jack spoke to Harv, telephone lineman for the county, and had stressed Mel's occupation as midwife to get her phone installed ahead of schedule. He got another kiss for that—behind the bar where no one could see. Okay, two or three kisses. Deep and long. Strong and delicious.

Living and sleeping in the cabin in the woods was as restful and peaceful as anything Mel had known in almost a year. She woke in the early mornings, in time to see the sun slowly creeping over the tall pines, to hear the birds singing. She liked to get a cup of coffee and go out on that new, strong porch and enjoy the clean morning air, still cold on early spring mornings.

It wasn't yet 6:00 a.m. when she opened her front door and there, before her, were at least a dozen deer, grazing contentedly on the grass, bushes and ferns at the edges of her clearing. She took note of the freckled fawns—it was spring and time for birthing of all sorts.

She went for her digital camera and snapped a few sneaky shots. Then she loaded the pictures onto her laptop and dialed up the internet, which took forever, but there was nothing faster out here. After she had sent the pictures to Joey, she called her.

"Go online," she told her sister. "I've sent you something amazing."

"What is it?" she asked.

"Just hurry," Mel said. "You're going to love it."

There was only a short wait as Joey could get online and download in seconds as opposed to the length of time it took Mel. She heard her sister gasp. "Deer!" she said.

"In my front yard," Mel said. "Look at the babies. Aren't they adorable?"

"Are they still there?"

"I'm looking out my kitchen window at them right now," she said. "I'm not leaving the house until they're done with breakfast. Isn't that the most wonderful thing you've ever seen? Joey, I'm staying a little longer."

"Oh, Mel—no! I want you to come here! Why are you staying?"

"Joey, I'm delivering another baby pretty soon. After that last one, I can't resist. It just isn't like in the hospital where everything's so sterile and artificial and there's a surgeon and anesthesiologist right down the hall. It's just me and her, getting the job done. So pristine and wonderful and natural. So country—like Doc taking Mom's twenty-year-old husband across the street to the bar for a shot of courage so he can be a less nervous assistant."

"Oh, lovely," Joey said sarcastically, causing Mel to laugh.

"It was fantastic," Mel said. "There's another pregnant woman in town and I'm thinking of staying for her, too. The cabin is just great—you saw the pictures."

"I saw. Mel, are you dressed for the day?"

"Yeah…?"

"Look at your feet. Tell me what's on your feet."

She sighed. "My Cole Haan boots. I love these boots."

"They cost over four hundred dollars!"

"And they're starting to look like crap, too," she said. "If you only knew where I've been…"

"Mel, you're not one of them. Don't get them depending on you. Come to Colorado. We can accommodate your shoe fetish and you can find a good job here—close to us."

"I sleep so well here," she said. "I was afraid I'd never sleep well again—it's probably the air. It's so unbelievable, it almost wears you out—by the end of the day the bed feels so good. The pace is slower. I've needed a slower pace."

"Are you that busy? With patients?" Joey asked.

"Not that much. They're very sparse, actually. We only make well-visit appointments on Wednesdays and the rest of the week they either wander in with one complaint or another, or Doc goes to them. I go along most of the time. Or people wander in to talk, or drop off a pie, or some fresh baked dinner rolls. But the women—the pregnant ones—are so relieved after one look at my hands, compared to Doc's."

"What do you do with yourself?"

"Well," she said, laughing, "every day I walk down to the corner store to watch a soap with Connie and Joy, two middle-aged best friends who have been watching televised adultery on *Riverside Falls* for about fifteen years. The side comments are more interesting than the show."

"Gawd," she said.

"I go out to the Anderson ranch and hold the baby—Chloe. She's thriving there, and so is Lilly. More and more I know that was the right thing to do, and it just fell in my lap. Sometimes I take some of our leftover food out to this bunch of bums in the forest—they look so thin and hungry, but Doc says they'll probably bury us all. I stop by the bar to see if anyone's playing cribbage. If I can reel him in, Doc and I play gin—but it's hard to catch him in the mood. He taught me to play and now he can't beat me. Penny a point—I'm funding my retirement."

"So—when do you think you're going to get over this break from sanity?"

"Oh, I don't know. Just let me think about it. I've only been here a couple of months—it's not an eternity."

"But I hate to think of you rotting away in some dinky town, watching the soaps and growing bad roots."

"I could visit Dot in that garage where she does hair…"

"Ugh. Aren't you lonely, honey?"

"Not so much. At the end of the day, if nothing's going on, we go to the bar—Doc has his one whiskey of the day and I get a cold beer. There are always people around. We eat dinner—someone usually says, come over and sit with us. There's great gossip, that's the cool part about small towns where everyone knows everyone's business. Except, apparently, who gave birth to little Chloe. I just count it lucky that no woman who suffered postpartum hemorrhage or infection turned up. And also—no word from Social Services."

"I miss you so much. This is about the longest we've been apart in years… Why do you sound happy?"

"Do I? Maybe because everyone around me is happy. They let me know they're glad I'm here, even if my presence isn't medically saving this town." She took a breath. "I still feel out of place a lot, but I think I'm more content than I've been in eleven months and three days. I might finally be detoxing from the adrenaline."

"Promise me you're not going to stay in that godforsaken place, alone, watching soaps and drinking beer."

Mel's voice became soft. "It's not godforsaken, Joey. It's…" She struggled for a word. "It's breathtaking. Oh, the architecture leaves something to be desired—most of the houses and buildings are small and old and could use paint. But the countryside is wondrous. And I'm not lonely—I have a town. I've never had a town before."

Ricky and Liz were going to the spring dance at the high school. Except they didn't. It gave Rick a twinge of guilt because he knew in his heart that Connie and Ron trusted him. And probably they shouldn't.

The thing about living in a small town in the midst of dozens of small towns separated by forests was there were a million secluded places to park and make out. He always had a condom in his pocket, one that he was determined not to have to use, but he had it just the same. He hadn't even needed Jack to supply him—he was on top of that. He felt protective toward Liz; he didn't want to get her into trouble. What they were doing was working, even if it was getting them pretty worked up.

And they were doing plenty. It got off to a roaring start. Lots of deep kissing, heavy petting, incredible rubbing. They'd done a lot of bumping and grinding on the outside of clothes, but now they were getting right down to the skin, deeper than skin, but not going all the way. They were catching on real fast. It hadn't taken them long to figure out how to have orgasms without penetration, for which Rick was sublimely grateful. Even so, he wanted more. Wanted it real bad, and so did she. He was about ready to have the big talk with her, but he knew he had to save it for the clear light of day, not the dark of night while they were pawing each other in the cab of his little truck.

He loved making her feel good; she really wanted to please him. He hadn't imagined it could be this wonderful—holding someone, loving them, touching them, giving these feelings, receiving them. Nothing had prepared him for how you could be swept away by it all; it was as though the sheer pleasure had a life of its own.

He had moved over to the passenger seat and held her on his lap, kissing her, hard and hot while she squirmed around deliciously.

His hand wandered under her short skirt and met with... *Nothing.*

"Oh my Jesus," he whispered.

"Surprise," she said, grinding on his lap. Then her hand went there, feeling him through his clothes, making him nearly cry out.

She scooted forward on his lap a little. He slid back in the seat slightly, knowing that she would now take him in her small hand. He lived for that. As she opened his pants to free him, he massaged her with his fingers of one hand, fondling her breast with the other, drowning in her mouth, holding her tight against him. She was moving roughly against his hand, wriggling, reaching desperately for her special moment, when suddenly she shifted her weight slightly. She was straining toward him, he was straining toward her, her hands went to his shoulders, his hands grabbed her fanny, her knee went across his lap and she was over him. She moved down, he moved up and they were suddenly disastrously, wondrously, exquisitely merged. She came right down on him. He lifted right up into her; she was all around him. It was a whole new world, a lot better than a hand. He couldn't breathe.

"Holy God, Liz," he whispered. "Oh my Jesus."

She was oblivious, pressing furiously into his lap, on a mission.

"Liz. Lizzie. No. Lizzie. Holy God. Holy Jesus."

He was half trying, half hoping to fail to lift her off him, to get out of her, when it happened for her and the sensation of her body squeezing around him, clenching in hot spasms as she moaned her ecstasy, caused him to lose his mind. He thought he might have been momentarily unconscious. He lost all will. And that wasn't all he lost. He blew it—erupted inside of her with the force of a volcano. Right after he thought *Ahhhh,* he thought *Oh, fuck. Way to go, genius.*

She collapsed into his arms and he held her, stroking her back as she calmed. As he calmed. As they caught their collective breath. Finally he said, "That could have been a huge mistake."

"Oh-oh," she said. "Oh-oh. Now what?"

"Well, I sure as hell can't reel it back in," he told her. "If I'd known that was going to happen… Liz, I have a condom, for Christ's sake."

"I didn't know that."

"Well, I didn't know we were going to do that."

"I didn't know, either." She sniffed. "I'm sorry." She dropped her head to his shoulder and cried. "I'm sorry, Rick."

"No. I'm sorry. Okay, baby, take it easy. Can't do anything about it now. Shh." He held her and she rested against him, close in his arms. He kissed her cheeks and lips until her tears stopped. Then he took her open mouth again. God, her mouth was hot. And after a little while, as he held her, he began to grow firm again, and he was still there, inside. Without meaning to, without planning to, he began to pump his hips up and down again, driving himself into her. And she pushed into his lap. What the hell—the damage was done, he thought. And he said, "Can't do anything about it now…"

Eight

There were no patients in the morning and Mel took the opportunity to drive over to Clear River for gas, there being no service station in Virgin River. She took the pager with her so that Doc could call her back if something happened, but hardly anything ever happened.

Every time she went to one of the little surrounding towns she looked in particular at the women, wondering where Jack might have gone once in a while for "something a little basic." It didn't take her long to realize that he probably had his pick, and that there were plenty of attractive women around these towns.

She thought she might like to get something like a salt lick or some kind of feed for the edge of her property to draw the deer, so went to the very small strip mall on the main drag. As she passed the hardware store, she saw a window display of shears mounted on pegboard. They ranged in size from tiny scissors to clippers with six-inch, thick, curved blades. She stared at them, frowning, for a long time.

"Help you?" a young woman in a green store apron asked.

"Hmm. What do you do with those?"

"Roses," she said, smiling.

"Roses? I haven't seen that many roses around."

"Oh, you're not looking hard enough," she said, grinning.

"Hmm. Well, I'm looking for something that would draw deer," Mel said.

"Like a doe call? But hunting season is months away."

"God, I wouldn't shoot at them! I like seeing them in my yard in the early morning. Can you tell me where to find that?"

"Um, if you want deer in your yard, you're the only one. Just plant some lettuce or a couple of apple trees. With deer, if you don't want them in your produce, you can hardly keep them away."

"Oh. If I throw some lettuce out there, will that work? Because I don't garden."

The woman tilted her head and smiled with eyes that frowned. "Where you from?"

"Los Angeles. Concrete jungle."

"I mean, now."

"Up in Virgin River. Kind of back in the woods, you know…"

"Listen, don't try the lettuce, okay. Because there are also bear. Just keep your food indoors and don't press your luck. If you get deer, you get deer." Then she looked down and said, "Nice boots. Where can I get a pair like that?"

Mel thought a second, then said, "Can't really remember. Target, I think."

Rather than going back to Doc's, she drove out to the river. She saw that there were six anglers in the river, and that one of them was Jack. She pulled up, parked, and got out to lean against the front of her car to watch. He looked over his shoulder at her, smiled a hello, but went back to his sport. He'd pull out some line and let it slack, then gracefully cast out, the line reaching behind him in a large S before sailing smoothly out over the river, touching down on the top of the water as lightly as a leaf floating lazily down from a tree. And again, and again.

She loved to watch the arc of the lines, the whir of them going out, the clicking of them reeling in. They seemed almost synchronized, choreographed, the air above the water filled with flying lines. The men, in waders and vests, would walk around the swirling shallow waters while fish jumped now and then in the river. If there was a catch, the fish would either be released or go in the creel dangling from a shoulder strap.

After a peaceful interlude, Jack came out of the river with his rod and reel in hand. "What are you doing out here?"

"Just watching."

"Want to try?"

"I don't know how," she said.

"It's not very hard—let's see if I can scrounge some boots or waders." He went to his truck and dug around in the back. He came up with some huge rubber hip boots. "This'll keep you dry—but you won't be able to wade too far out."

She stepped into them. His legs were so much longer than hers that he had to fold them down twice at the top of her thighs, not an unpleasant sensation. They were so big that she had to shuffle rather than walk, dragging them along. "I won't be able to run for my life, either," she said. "Okay, what do I do?"

"It's all in the wrist," he said. "Don't worry about

aim so much as a nice clean arc and a little distance—
getting you into the deeper part of the river where the
fish are more plentiful." He took her hand, led her to
the water's edge, and showed her his casting. "Don't
snap it hard, just roll it off nice and easy. Give it a little
arm, but don't throw your body into it."

He handed her the rod, showed her where to unlock
the reel. She gave it a try and the fly plunked down right
in front of her. "How's that for distance?"

"We're going to have to work on that," he said. He
stepped behind her and guiding her hand, helped her
cast. Twenty-five feet, maybe. Probably a fourth of the
distance he could achieve, and her fly came down hard,
making a splash. "Hmm, better," he said. "Reel her in,
slowly."

She brought it back and repeated the process, this
time without his hand guiding hers. "Good," he said.
"Watch your footing—there are spots where you can
drop, trip, slip off a rock. You wouldn't want to fall in."

"I wouldn't want to," she said, casting again. That
time she flicked her wrist too hard and the hook flew
back behind them, whooshing past their heads. "Oops,"
she said. "Sorry."

"It's okay, but be careful. I'd hate to have that thing
pulled out of the back of my head. Here," he said. He
stood behind her and put a hand on her hip. "Don't
throw your body into it—just use your arm and wrist—
and go easy. You'll get the distance. Eventually."

She did it again, and it was good. A nice, graceful
arc, a respectable distance into the river. A fish jumped
out where her fly had landed. "Oh, he's a big one."

"Brown trout—a beauty. You get him today and
you'll show up all of us."

Something slithered past her feet and she jumped

with a gasp. "Lamprey eel," he said. "They like to suck the roe and fluids out of the salmon."

"Ew. Charming." She cast again. And again. This was fun. Now and then Jack would take her wrist and cast with her, reminding her of the wrist action. The other hand stayed on her hip, holding her still. "I like this," she said. Then she had a hit and reeled in a fish. It wasn't a very big fish, but it was a fish. And she'd caught him by herself.

"Not bad," he said. "Take it off the hook carefully."

"I don't know how," she said.

"I'll show you, but then you have to do it. If you're going to fish, you're going to take the fish off the hook. Like this." He demonstrated, sliding his hand from the fish's head to his wriggling body, holding it firmly, disengaging the hook cautiously. "His mouth is okay. We're going to let him grow into a civilized meal," he said, tossing the fish back.

"Aw," she said.

"You got lucky. Come on," he said, turning her back to the river. He stood behind her, holding her body straight and still with that large hand on her hip, his other hand guiding her wrist. She cast again, reeled in again.

"Jack, are there an awful lot of roses around here in summer?" she asked.

"Hmm? I don't know. Sure, some."

"I stopped by the hardware store this morning and they had this huge display of rose clippers. All sizes. I guess I've never noticed anything like that before…"

When she brought in her line, he turned her around slightly. He frowned. "Rose clippers?"

"Uh-huh. From little tiny ones to great big ones with curved blades and leather grips."

"Where?"

"Clear River. I went over for gas and—"

"Mel, those aren't rose clippers. Well, I guess you could use 'em for that. More likely, they're for marijuana harvests. Little ones for manicuring buds, big ones for cutting down plants."

"Naw. Come on."

He turned her back toward the river. "There are towns around here that stock a lot of the stuff illegal growers need. Clear River's one. What were you doing at the hardware store?"

"I thought I'd pick up something that would invite the deer to my yard, like a salt lick or feed or something, but—"

He turned her back to face him again. "Salt lick?"

"Well, cows like that, right? So I thought…"

He was shaking his head. "Mel, listen—don't do anything to invite wildlife to your yard. You might get some unfriendlies. Okay? Like maybe a buck who's more interested in rutting than having his picture taken. Or a bear. Understand?"

"Rutting?" She frowned.

He smiled patiently and touched the end of her nose. "Making love."

"Oh. Sure. Okay," she said, turning back to the river. Casting again.

"Rose clippers." He laughed. "I think you're getting the hang of this," he said.

"I like it. I'm not sure about that getting the fish off the hook part."

"Come on, don't be a sissy."

"Well…"

"You have to catch one first," he said.

"You just watch. I'm precocious."

Mel lost all track of time as she worked the rod, sending the colorful fly out across the water, bringing it back slowly. Again and again she cast, noting, too, that Jack kept his hand on her hip and now and then ran his other hand down her arm to her hand to guide her. "Come on," she kept telling the fly. "I'm ready!"

"Keep your voice down," he said softly. "This is a peaceful sport."

Again and again she would cast her line. She wasn't skilled by any means, but she was getting it out there, and doing so prettily. At least, she thought so.

She felt that hand that had been on her hip slide stealthily around her, holding her at her waist, pulling her just slightly back against him. "You're distracting me," she said, casting again.

"Good," he said, lowering his lips to her head, inhaling.

"Jack, there are *people!*"

"They could care less," he said, holding her against him.

She looked around and saw that what he said was true—the other fishermen didn't even glance their way. Their lines were flying around in gentle, beautiful arcs. They didn't even look at each other. *Okay,* she thought. *This feels good. I like the hand, the arm around me. I can manage this.*

Then she felt his lips on her neck. "Jack! I'm fishing!"

"Okay," he said hoarsely. "I'll try not to bother you too much."

He pulled her just a little harder against him and began to nibble at her neck. "What *are* you doing?" she asked, laughter in her voice.

"Mel, please… Can't we go somewhere and just make out for a while?"

"No!" she laughed. "I'm *fishing!*"

"If I promise to take you fishing after…?"

"No! Now behave yourself!" But she was smiling because it was pretty heady having this big tough guy turn weak and desperate just from the taste of her neck. She concentrated on her casting while he concentrated on her neck, his arm tight around her waist. Ahh… Nice. Very nice.

After a few more minutes passed, he let go of her with a tortured moan, walked back to his truck and laid himself over the front, arms outstretched wide, head lying on the hood. She looked over her shoulder at him and chuckled. Brought him to his knees, she thought. Big tough marine. Ha!

She treated herself to a few more casts, then turned and shuffled in those great big boots back to Jack. She leaned the rod against the truck and pulled her feet out of the rubber boots. He lifted his head and looked at her through narrowed eyes. "Thanks, Jack. I have to go. It's time for my soap." She treated him to a conciliatory peck on the cheek. "Maybe we can do this again sometime."

As she drove back to town, she got to thinking—a few weeks ago, she was absolutely certain there was nothing in her that allowed her to respond to a man. To Jack. Now she wasn't so sure. A little contact, a little kissing—deep kissing—it felt good. It made her forget sometimes that she had nothing to give. In fact, it made her wonder if maybe she was wrong about that. Going somewhere to make out for a while didn't sound like a bad idea. She was going to give that more thought.

She poked her head into Doc's and found him on the computer and said, "Anything?"

"Nope," he said.

"Okay, I'm going to the store. Need anything?"

"Nope," he said again.

She checked her watch, found herself hoping she hadn't missed the beginning. When she walked into the store, Joy stood in the curtained doorway and said, "Mel! Thank God!"

The panicked look on her face sent Mel rushing to the back room. Leaning forward in the lawn chair, her hand gripping the front of her sweatshirt and breathing shallowly was Connie. Mel kneeled down. "What is it?" she asked.

"I don't know," she said weakly. "I can hardly breathe."

"Joy, get me a bottle of aspirin. Pain?" she asked Connie.

"My back," she said.

Mel put a hand between her shoulder blades. "There?"

"Yeah."

Joy handed her a brand-new aspirin bottle off the shelf and Mel ripped it open, shaking one out into her palm. "Swallow this quickly." Connie did so and Mel asked, "Pressure in the chest?"

"Yeah. Oh, yeah."

Mel got up, grabbed Joy's hand and pulled her out of the back room. "Run for Doc. Tell him it might be her heart. Hurry."

Mel went back to Connie. She took her pulse and found it fast and irregular. She had grown clammy and her respirations were rapid and shallow. "Try to relax and breathe slowly. Joy has gone for Doc."

"What is it?" she asked. "What's happening?"

Mel noticed that Connie's left arm dangled at her side, probably in pain, while she gripped her shirt with her right hand and tried to pull it away from her body, as though to relieve the pressure in her chest. If Mel had speculated on a heart attack for one of these two women, she'd have bet on Joy who was overweight and probably had high cholesterol. Not Connie who was petite and didn't even smoke.

"I'm not sure," Mel said. "Let's wait for Doc. Don't talk, just stay calm. I'm not going to let anything happen to you."

A tense couple of minutes passed before Joy, breathless, came flying through the door with Doc's medical bag and rushed to Mel's side. "Here," she said. "He said try the nitro and get an IV started. He'll be right here."

"Okay, then." She dug around in the bag, found the nitro tablets and shook one out of the bottle. "Connie, hold this under your tongue."

She did as she was told while Mel got the blood pressure cuff and stethoscope out of the bag. Connie's pressure was high, but within seconds some of the pain was easing. The nitro might be working. "That better?"

"A little. My arm. I can hardly move my arm."

"Okay, we'll take care of that." She snapped on a pair of gloves. She pulled the rubber strap around Connie's upper arm and started searching for a good vein, slapping her inner arm with two fingers. She tore open the package containing the IV needle and inserted it slowly. Blood eased up the clear tube and dripped on the floor. Mel then capped it off because she had no tubing or bag of fluid.

A moment later she heard a sound she didn't recognize and looked out of the back room to see old Doc wheeling a squeaky old gurney into the store. He left it in the store aisle and picked up a bag of Ringer's solution from its bed, handing it to Mel, while he toted a small portable oxygen canister. He put the cannula around Connie's neck and into her nostrils while he asked, "What've we got?"

As Mel hooked up the tubing to the needle and the Ringer's to the tube, she said, "Elevated pressure, diaphoretic, chest, back and arm pain... I gave her an aspirin, and the nitro."

"Good. How's that pill working, Connie?"

"A little," she said.

"Here's what we're going to do. Put her on the gurney in the back of the truck, you beside her holding the Ringer's and monitoring her pressure, and if you think we have to stop for any reason, you bang on the window. The black bag goes with you—you have oxygen, a portable defibrillator in the truck bed, and I want you to draw an eppie and atropine right away, to have ready." He went back to the gurney, pushed it into the very narrow space in the back room, and lowered it. He shook out and spread a large, heavy wool blanket over the sheet and said, "Okay, Connie."

Managing the IV bag and tubing, Mel supported Connie under the arm so that she could be transferred from her chair to the lowered gurney. Doc lifted the back slightly so that she wouldn't be lying flat, then wrapped the blanket around her and strapped her in. He put the oxygen canister on the gurney between Connie's legs, then said to Mel, "Have Joy hold up the bag of Ringer's while we get her out of here."

"Shouldn't we wait for an ambulance?"

"Not the best idea," he said while together they lifted the gurney to its former upright position. As they rolled out of the store, Mel once again in control of the IV bag, Doc said, "Joy, as soon as we get out of here I want you to call Valley Hospital and ask them to get a cardiologist to meet us in E.R. Tell Ron to meet us at Valley." Doc and Mel released the legs on the gurney and slid it in the back of the truck. Doc took off his heavy wool coat and draped it over Connie. As he would have headed for the driver's door of the truck, Mel grabbed his sleeve.

"Doc, what the hell are we doing?"

"Getting her there as fast as possible," he said. "In you go. You're going to be cold."

"I'll manage," she said, climbing into the truck bed beside Connie.

"Don't bounce out," Doc said. "I don't have time to stop and pick you up."

"Just drive carefully," she said, already dreading those narrow, curving roads and sheer drops, squeaking by big logging trucks, not to mention the darkness and drop in temperature as they passed through the towering trees.

He jumped in, pretty spry for seventy, and put the truck in gear. He made a wide turn in the street, Mel in the back of the truck, holding the Ringer's above Connie's head because there was no IV stand on this old gurney. As they drove out of town, Jack was just returning. But Mel's attention was focused on Connie. She balanced the bag of Ringer's on the gurney above Connie's head, and dug around in Doc's black bag for syringes and vials, drawing her drugs quickly despite the hectic driving and bouncing. She capped the syringes and took up the IV bag again.

Just don't arrest, Mel kept thinking. Just to be safe, she used one hand to open the portable defibrillator case, having it handy to be switched on if necessary. It was the kind used on commercial airlines; rather than paddles, there were patches that adhered to the chest. Rather than bare Connie to the cold before it became necessary, she decided not to attach the patches to her chest. Then, with one hand over her head, she leaned her body close across Connie's to keep her warm.

She had to give Doc a lot of credit for fancy driving. He managed to move down the mountain at a pretty fast clip, braking suddenly for the sharp curves and picking up speed for the straightaways while avoiding potholes and bumps. Mel was freezing, but Connie was taking steady breaths and her pulse was even and slower, when from the sheer fright and the ride in the back of the truck, it should probably be racing.

"That Doc," she said breathlessly into Mel's ear. "He sure is bossy."

"Yeah," Mel said. "Try to rest."

"Oh, sure," she whispered.

Mel had to switch the arm that held the Ringer's several times, she got so sore. And even when she stayed low in the bed of the truck, the wind was chilling her to the bone. May in the mountains, under the shade of huge, towering trees, was not warm. She tried to imagine doing this in winter, and she got colder. Her cheeks were numb, her fingers nearly without feeling.

After just over an hour ride, they pulled into a parking lot in front of a small hospital where two med techs and a nurse stood ready in the parking lot, waiting with their own gurney.

Doc jumped out of the truck. "Take her on my gurney—I'll get it later."

"Good," one said, pulling the gurney holding Connie out of the back of the truck. "She have any meds?"

"Just an aspirin and a nitro tab. Ringer's TKO."

"Gotcha," he said. "Emergency staff standing by," and off they went, running with the gurney across the parking lot.

"Let's go, Melinda," he said, moving a little more slowly now.

Mel began to realize that waiting for emergency transport could have been a tragic mistake—it could have turned that trip into three hours. As she waited with Doc in the emergency room, she learned that Valley Hospital was small but efficient, serving the needs of many small towns. They were capable of labor and delivery, C-sections when the infant and mother were not at major risk, X-rays, ultrasounds, some general surgeries, lab work and outpatient clinic, but if something as serious as emergency heart surgery or major surgery were required, a larger hospital was needed. It was a while before the doctor finally came out. "We're going to run an angiogram—I think we're looking at blockages. She's stable for the moment, but they may be considering bypass surgery as soon as possible. We'll transport her by helicopter to Redding for that. Has her next of kin been notified?"

"He should be here any minute. We'll wait for him here."

Within ten minutes, Connie was wheeled past them and down the hall. Another ten minutes brought Ron with Joy into the emergency room doors. "Where is she? Is she all right?" Right behind them were Ricky and Liz, straight from school.

"They've taken her for an angiogram—it's like an X-ray of blood vessels. Based on what that test tells them, they'll decide whether or not she needs surgery. Let's go to the cafeteria and get a cup of coffee and I'll try to explain it to you—then we'll go see how they're doing on that test."

"God, Doc, thank you," Ron said. "Thank you for getting her help."

"Don't thank me," he said. "Thank Melinda. She saved Connie's life."

Mel's head jerked toward him in surprise.

"It was her fast action—that aspirin and calling for help—not to mention her ride in the back of my pickup, that I believe allowed us to get her to the hospital so fast."

It was nine o'clock before Mel and Doc got back to town, and of necessity they both headed for Jack's, more than a little grateful he had stayed open. And she knew he'd stayed open for them. Doc asked for his whiskey and Mel said, "I think I better have one, too. Maybe something a little smoother than that."

Jack poured her a Crown Royal. "Long day?" he asked.

"Shew," Doc said. "We spent most of it waiting for a decision. Connie's going to have bypass surgery in the morning. We waited around until they transported her to Redding."

"Why didn't we just take her to Redding?" Mel asked. Both men laughed. "What? I looked at the map before I even came up here. It's just over a hundred miles of highway."

"It's about a hundred forty, Mel," Jack said. "Narrow, two-lane, over the mountains. Would take about three hours to cross at best from Eureka. Probably closer to four. Coming from Virgin River—five."

"Jesus," she moaned.

"I think Ricky is taking Liz to her mother's for the

night while Ron and Joy will make the long drive to Redding to spend the night at Connie's bedside. They're a little on the nervous side," Doc said.

"No doubt," Jack said. "I saw you flying out of town. I couldn't tell who you had in the back—I just saw Mel hanging on for dear life."

Doc took a sip. "She came in kinda handy."

"What would you have done without a little help?" she asked him.

"I probably would've thrown Joy back there. But who knows if we'd have gotten that far. You know how great one little aspirin is for a heart attack?"

"Hmm." Mel took a sip of her drink and let her eyes slowly drift closed appreciatively.

"Connie's going to be all right?"

"Oh, better than all right," Doc said. "People go into that surgery a little gray around the gills and they give them nice fresh, clear arteries to float their oxygen through and they come out rosy cheeked and brand-new."

Mel took another sip. "Oh, God, I didn't think I'd ever be warm again."

"You want me to light the fire?" Jack asked her.

"No, just let me drink this. Tell Doc I caught a fish today."

"She did," he said. "Wasn't much of a fish, but she caught it herself. Even if she couldn't take it off the hook without help."

Doc peered at her over his specs and she lifted her chin a bit defiantly. "Careful, Melinda," he said. "You could become one of us."

"Not likely," she said. "Not until you at least get a camper shell. We'd have been better off in the back of my BMW."

"You'd have been better off," Doc said. "That piece of shit isn't big enough for a patient having a heart attack and a practitioner trying to keep her alive."

"I'm not going to fight with you for saying that," she said. "Because you at least called me a practitioner and not a nurse. You seem to be coming around, you old fart." She looked up at Jack. "We keeping you up?"

"Nah," he said, chuckling. "Take your time. In fact, I'll join you." He reached behind him and selected a bottle, tipping it over a glass. He lifted it in a toast to both of them. "Good team work, amazingly. Glad everything's okay."

Mel was exhausted, most of which came from the ride and long afternoon of tensely waiting at the hospital. Connie, she realized without much surprise, was more than a patient to her—she was a friend. And when you do this kind of work in this kind of place, your patients are almost always your friends. Must be hard to maintain objectivity. On the other hand, success was that much more gratifying. Fulfilling.

It wasn't like this in L.A.

Doc finished his whiskey and got up. "Nicely done, Melinda. We'll try to have a dull day tomorrow."

"Thank you, Doc."

After the doctor left, Jack said, "Sounds like maybe the two of you have started to bond or something."

"Or something," she said, sipping.

"How was that trip to Valley Hospital?"

"Like Mr. Toad's wild ride," she said, making him laugh a little. She pushed her glass toward him and he gave her another splash of Crown.

"You want ice or water with that?" he asked her.

"No, this is good. Very good, in fact."

She sipped her drink rather too quickly. She looked

up at him, tilted her head to one side, then inclined it toward the glass.

"You sure? Because I think maybe that's enough. Your cheeks are flushed and I can tell, you're not cold anymore."

"Just a tish."

A tish was what she got—a couple of swallows.

"Thanks for taking me fishing," she said. "Sorry you didn't get in my pants again."

A large surprised laugh escaped him. She was getting a little tiddly. "That's okay, Melinda. Whenever you're ready."

"Aha! I knew it!"

"Like it's been hard to tell."

"You're so transparent." She downed the rest of her drink. "I'd better get going. I'm completely shot." She stood up and nearly fell down. She grabbed at the bar to right herself and Jack came around to her side. He put an arm around her waist. She looked up at him with watery eyes and said, "Damn. I forgot to eat."

"Let me make you some coffee," he suggested.

"And ruin this perfectly good buzz? Hell, I've earned it." She took a step and wavered. "Besides, I don't think it'll make me sober. Probably just wide-awake drunk."

Jack tightened his hold around her and laughed in spite of himself. "All right, Mel. I can put you in my bed and take the couch…"

"But sometimes I have deer in my yard in the morning," she said, a little whiny. "I want to go home. They might come back."

Home. That sounded good to Jack, that she thought of that cabin as her home. "All right, Mel. I'll take you home."

"That's a relief," she said. "Because I'm pretty sure

I already can't drive. Even on a straight and undangerous road."

"You're a lightweight," he said.

They took a couple of steps and her legs buckled a second time. He gave a sigh and bent to lift her into his arms. She patted his chest. "It's good that you're strong," she said. "You're good to have around. It's like having my own personal valet."

He chuckled under his breath. Preacher had gone upstairs for the night so he turned off the Open sign and managed to get his keys out of his pocket without dropping her. He locked the front door and took her down the steps and around to the back of the bar where he kept his truck. He put her in and she managed, though with some difficulty, to buckle her seat belt. When he got in and started the truck she said, "You know something, Jack? You've turned out to be my very good friend."

"That's nice, Mel."

"I really appreciate this. Boy, whew. I'm sure not much of a drinker. I think I'm a one-beer girl. Two if I've had a side of beef and an apple pie."

"I think you've assessed the situation correctly."

"If I ask for the good stuff again, be sure to ask me if I've had food."

"Sure will," he said.

She laid her head back on the seat. Within five minutes, it lolled. And Jack spent the rest of the drive wondering a couple of things. One—what if she roused enough as he was taking her inside to invite him to stay? That would be okay, wouldn't it? Even though she was just a "tish" disadvantaged? Or—what if she didn't rouse and he just lay down beside her to be there in case she woke and decided it was time? That would be okay. Or maybe he could just wait on her couch, in case she needed anything…like sex. Then if she woke up during the night he'd be there. He'd be ready. He'd *been* ready.

He played a dozen scenarios in his mind. He would carry her to her room and she would wake and say, "Stay with me tonight." He really didn't have the strength to say no. Or, she would wake and he would kiss her and then she would say, "Okay." Or morning would come, he would already be there and she would say, "Now, Jack." Whoo boy. He was getting a little warm.

But she was still asleep when he pulled up in front of her cabin. He unbuckled her and lifted her out of the truck. He whacked her head on the door frame. "Ow!" she yelled, her hand going to her head.

"Sorry," he said. And thought to himself, *Foreplay that was* not.

"S'okay." She laid her head back on his shoulder.

Now, he thought, *I should stay to be sure she doesn't have a concussion. And that she doesn't need sex for it. Or just to be there in case she did…*

He carried her across the porch, through the door to her room and, flipping on the light, laid her on the bed. Without opening her eyes she said, "Thank you, Jack."

"You're welcome, Melinda," he said. "Your head okay?"

"What head?"

"Okay. Let's get your boots off."

"Boots. Off." She lifted a leg, making him laugh. He pulled the boot off. The leg dropped and the other one came up. He pulled that one off and the leg dropped. Then she curled into a cute little package, pulling the quilt around her. He looked down at her and saw that it was lights out for Melinda. Then he saw the picture.

Something hit him, and it didn't feel particularly good. He picked up the picture and looked at the man's face. *So, you're the guy,* he thought. He didn't look like a bad guy—but clearly he had done something to Mel. Something she was having trouble getting beyond. Maybe he'd left her for another woman—but that seemed impossible to imagine. Maybe he left her for a man. *Oh, please let it be so—I can make that better— just give me five minutes.* Or maybe he looked harmless but had been an impossible asshole and she'd broken off with him, but still loved him helplessly. And here she had his picture right there, to be the last face she saw before falling asleep at night.

At some point she was going to give Jack a chance to make that picture go away, but it wasn't going to be tonight. Probably just as well. If she woke to find him there, either in her bed or ready to be, she would put the blame on Crown Royal. He wanted it to come from desire—and he wanted it to be real.

He scribbled a note. *I'll be back for you at 8:00 a.m. Jack.* He left it by the coffeepot. Then he went to his truck to get something he'd purchased earlier in the day. He brought the leather case holding the dismantled fly-fishing rod and reel and the waders into the house and left them by the front door. And went home.

At 8:00 a.m. he was back in front of her cabin and what he saw made him smile. All the disappointing thoughts that had plagued him the night before vanished. She was sitting in her Adirondack chair in her new waders, idly casting her fly into the yard. A steaming cup of coffee rested on the wide chair arm beside her.

He got out of the truck, grinning. "You found it," he said, walking to the porch.

"I *love* it! Did you get this for me?"

"I did."

"But why?"

"When we go fishing, I need to stand beside you. Not in back of you, smelling your hair and feeling you against me. You need your own stuff. How do they fit?"

She stood up and turned around for him. "Perfect. I've been practicing."

"Getting any better?"

"I am. I'm sorry about last night, Jack. I had been tense and hungry and freezing all day and it really hit me."

"Yeah. It's okay."

"I should keep this in my trunk, huh? In case we have a light day at Doc's and can just sneak off and fish."

"Good idea, Mel."

"Let me put my gear away," she said happily.

And he thought—*Just give me time. I'm going to get that picture put in storage.*

Ricky hadn't been around the bar the week right after Connie's heart attack, hanging close to the family in case they needed him for anything. When he did come into the bar, it was late and there were only two men at a table and Preacher behind the bar. Ricky sat up at the bar, his eyes downcast.

"How's everybody doing?" Preacher asked.

He shrugged. "Connie's doing pretty good I guess. They sent Liz back to her mom's in Eureka."

"Eureka isn't the end of the world, man. You can visit her."

Ricky looked down. "Yeah, but…probably shouldn't," he said. "She was…she was the first girl I felt that way about." He looked up. "You know. *That* way."

The two men at the table stood and wandered out of the bar. "Close call?" Preacher asked him.

"I wish. Holy God," Rick said, shaking his head. "I thought I had it under control."

Preacher did something he'd never done before. He drew a couple of cold drafts and put one in front of Rick, one in front of himself. "Tough call, that control thing."

"Tell me about it. This for me?"

Preacher lifted an eyebrow. "I thought maybe you might need it right about now."

"Thanks," he said, lifting the glass. "She doesn't look like a kid, but she's just a kid. She's way too young."

"Way," Preacher agreed. "You got a handle on it now?"

"Oh, yeah," he said. "Now that it's too late."

"Welcome to the world." Preacher drank half his draft.

Rick just looked into his. "It's just that I'd die if anyone got hurt, you know. If I hurt her. If I let you and Jack down."

Preacher put his big hands on the bar and leaned toward Rick. "Hey, Ricky, don't worry about letting us down. Some things are just nature, you know? You're a human being. You do the best you can. Try to think ahead next time, if you get my drift."

"I do now."

Jack came into the bar from the back. He noticed right away that Ricky and Preacher had beers and that Ricky wore a troubled expression. "Do I need to toast anything?" He poured himself a glass of beer.

"I'm pretty sure that's a no," Ricky said.

"Ricky here, if I'm reading him right, has entered the world of men. And wishes a little bit he hadn't."

"Instead of giving me a handful of rubbers, you should've had me laminated," he said to Jack.

"Oh, boy. You gonna be okay, buddy?" Jack asked. "She gonna be okay?"

"I don't know. When am I gonna know? How am I gonna know?"

"A month," Jack said. "Maybe less. Depends on her cycle. You're going to have to ask her, Rick. If she got her period."

"I'm gonna die," Ricky said miserably.

"Okay then. Let's toast to your continued good luck. Since you got, you know, lucky."

"Right now I gotta wonder why they call it that," Ricky said.

Nine

The grass grew tall in the pastures, the ewes fat with lambing imminent. The cows were ready to calve and Sondra Patterson was almost to term.

Sondra was expecting her third child, and the first two had come to her quickly and easily, so she and Doc claimed. She had decided to have this one at home, as she had the first two. This would be the first home birth for Mel, and she looked forward to it with nervous delight.

May aged bright and sunny—and brought with it a bunch of men in pickups and campers. There was a great deal of horn-honking at the bar in the afternoon and Mel looked out to see this gathering descend on Jack's. She watched as he came out on his porch and greeted them with bear hugs and shouts and whistles.

"What's going on?" she asked Doc Mullins.

"Hmm. I think it's another Semper Fi reunion. Jack's old buddies from the Marine Corps. They come up here to hunt, fish, play poker, drink and yell into the night."

"Really? He never mentioned that." *And,* she thought, *is this my cue to be scarce?* Because that after-work beer, the occasional kiss, had become the best part of her day. She was further bewildered by the fact that he hadn't tried anything more. And yet, if he had, she would have worried about the consequences. She shouldn't be involved with anyone, even Jack. Not until she was sure she could handle it. Thing was, she just couldn't bring herself to give up that little bit of kissing. She was sure that Mark would understand. If their situations had been reversed, she told herself, she would.

But with the marines in town, there would be none of that.

Doc seemed to have no inclination to stay away, and at the end of the day he took himself over to the bar. "Coming?" he asked her.

"I don't know… I don't want to distract anyone from their reunion…"

"I wouldn't worry about that," he said. "The whole town looks forward to seeing these boys."

She went with him and found that of course Doc was greeted by these visiting men as if they were old friends. Jack dropped a possessive arm around Mel's shoulders and said, "Boys, meet Mel Monroe, new nurse midwife in town. She's been working with Doc. Mel, meet Zeke, Mike Valenzuela, Cornhusker—Corny for short, Josh Phillips, Joe Benson, Tom Stephens and Paul Haggerty. There will be a test later—no name tags."

"Doc, you are a fine and smart gentleman," Zeke said, grinning, reaching for her hand, obviously under the impression Doc had hired her rather than resisted her. "Miss Monroe, it's an honor. An honor."

"Call me Mel," she said.

The noise with which they descended on her was invigorating. The next surprise for her, and perhaps it shouldn't have been, was that Preacher was one of them.

And of course they drew Rick in as though he were a younger brother.

Mel learned that Preacher had served under Jack when he was just a kid of eighteen in the first conflict in Iraq—Desert Storm—it turned out he was much younger than he looked. During that same time a cop from L.A. by the name of Mike Valenzuela and a builder from Oregon by the name of Paul Haggerty also served with them, but the two latter marines, being reservists, were called up for the latest Iraq conflict, again with Preacher and Jack, who were still on active duty at that time. The others, all reservists, were called up for Iraq where they were united in Baghdad and Fallujah. Zeke was a fireman from Fresno; Josh Phillips, a paramedic, and Tom Stephens, a news helicopter pilot—were both from the Reno area. Joe Benson was an architect from the same Oregon town as Paul Haggerty—Paul often built Joe's houses. And Corny, another firefighter, came the farthest, from Washington state, but he was born and raised in Nebraska, thus the nickname.

Jack was older than these men by four years or more, the next oldest in the crowd being Mike at thirty-six. Four of them were married with kids—Zeke, Josh, Tom and Corny. Mel was fascinated by the way they talked about their women with lusty smiles and glittering eyes. No jokes about the old ball and chain here. Rather, they sounded as though they couldn't wait to get home to them.

"How's Patti doing?" someone asked Josh.

He curved his hands over his flat belly to indicate a pregnant tummy and grinning boastfully, said, "She's ripe as a tomato. I can hardly keep my hands off her."

"If she's ripe as a tomato, I bet you get slapped

down like crazy," Zeke laughed. "I got another one on Christa."

"No way! I thought she said you were through!"

"She said that two kids ago—but I snuck one more by her. She's cooking number four. What can I say— that girl's been lightin' my fire since high school. You should see her, man. She's lit up like a beacon. Nobody cooks 'em like Christa. Whew."

"Hey, buddy, congratulations, man! But I don't think you know when to quit."

"I don't. It's like I can't quit. But Christa says she's all done with me. She said after this one, snip snip."

"I think I can go one more," Corny said. "Got my girls. I feel a boy coming on."

No one could better appreciate this kind of enthusiasm for pregnant women than a midwife. Mel was loving it. Loving them.

"Yeah, I've heard that a lot," Jack said. "Eight nieces later, no one got their boy. My brothers-in-law have run through all their chances, I think."

"Maybe you're packin' a boy, Jack."

"I don't even kid myself about that," he laughed.

Jack was among the five single men with Preacher, Mike, Paul and Joe. Confirmed bachelors, Mel was warned. They loved women, but couldn't be caught. "Except Mike," Zeke said. "He gets caught regular." Mel learned that Mike was twice divorced and had a girlfriend back in L.A. who was trying to be wife number three.

The camaraderie was engaging, electrifying. These guys were tight, it was real easy to see. Mel didn't exactly rush away—she had fun. Other folks from town who frequented the bar seemed, like Doc, to be acquainted with this band of brothers and dropped in to partake of the reunion, every bit as welcoming of them as Jack and Preacher had been.

As she left that evening, Jack broke away from his buddies to walk her to her car. "Oh, now there will be talk," she said.

"There's already talk, but around here, what do you expect? Listen, Mel, you shouldn't stay away on account of them—they're a good bunch of guys. But let me tell you what the agenda will be. There will be lots of beer and poker, fishing all day. They'll stay in their campers, make too much noise, and fill the place up with cigar smoke. Preacher will have something on the stove every day. And I sense a lot of fish coming our way. Preacher's got a stuffed trout that will knock you down, it's so good."

She put a hand against his chest. "Don't worry about it, Jack. You just enjoy yourself."

"You're not going to ignore me for five days, are you?"

"I'll come by after work for a beer, but you know I like my cabin, my peace and quiet. Have fun. That's the important thing."

"These are great guys," he said. "But I have a feeling they're going to get in the way of my love life."

She laughed at him. "Your love life is pretty bleak, as a matter of fact."

"I know. I keep trying to spool it up. And now them," he said, giving his head a jerk in the direction of his bar, which seemed to be throbbing from the noise and laughter within. He put his hands on her waist. "Kiss me," he said.

"No," she said.

"Come on. Haven't I been perfect? Haven't I followed all your rules? How can you be so selfish? There's no one around—they're busy drinking."

"I think you should go back to your reunion," she said, but she laughed at him again.

Boldly, he picked her up under her arms and lifted her high, holding her above him, slowly lowering her mouth to his. "You're shameless," she told him.

"Kiss me," he begged. "Come on. Gimme a little taste."

It was simply irresistible. He was irresistible. She grabbed his head in her hands and met his lips. She opened hers, moving over his mouth. When he did this to her, she thought of nothing but the kiss. It consumed her deliciously. She allowed his tongue, he allowed hers, and she reached that moment when she wanted it to never end. It was so easy to become lost in his tenderness, his strength.

And then, inevitably, it had to end. They were standing in the street, after all, though it was almost dark. "Thank you," he said. He put her on her feet and behind them, a raucous cheer erupted. There, on the porch at Jack's, stood eight marines and Rick, their tankards raised, shouting, cheering, whistling, catcalling.

"Oh, brother," she said.

"I'm going to kill them."

"Is this some kind of marine tradition?" she asked him.

"I'm going to kill them," he said again, but he kept his arm around her shoulders.

"You realize what this means," she said. "These little kisses are no longer our little secret."

He looked down into her eyes. The shouts had subsided into a low rumble of laughter. "Mel, they are not little. And since it's leaked," he said, grabbing her up in his arms, lifting her up to him again, her feet clear of the ground, and planted another one on her, to the excited shouts of the old 192nd. Even with that riot in the background, she found herself responding. She was growing addicted to the perfect flavor of his mouth.

When it was done she said, "I knew it was a mistake to let you get to first base."

"Ha, I haven't even thrown out the first pitch yet. You're invited to go fishing with us, if you like."

"Thanks, but I have things to do. I'll see you tomorrow night for a beer. And I'll get myself to my car. I'm not going to make out in front of them for the next week."

A little local research revealed to Mel that there was an ultrasound machine in Grace Valley, about thirty minutes away in northern Mendocino County. She had a long chat with one of the town doctors, June Hudson, and they worked out a deal for the use of the ultrasound—the deal was that June would provide this service out of the goodness of her heart. "The ultrasound was donated," she said. "Women from at least a half dozen surrounding towns make use of it."

Mel arranged to bring Sondra in for a screening that day but Sondra insisted on baking six dozen cookies that she would leave at the Grace Valley clinic. "Are you sure your husband can't come along? It's really something to see," Mel said.

"It would have to be him and the kids," Sondra said. "And I'm really looking forward to getting away for a few hours."

The two of them set out for Grace Valley, driving down through the foothills and along back roads that led them past farms, pastures, vineyards, ranches, flower

fields and through a few towns that were not even specs
on a map. Sondra, having lived in this part of the country all her life, was able to give Mel a running com-
mentary on where they were, whose ranch was whose,
what kind of crops were being grown—mostly alfalfa
and silage for the cattle—orchards of fruit and nuts,
and the inevitable lumber harvesting. It was a gorgeous
day, a beautiful drive, and when they entered the town,
Mel was instantly impressed by the shiny clean appearance of the place.

"It's kind of brand-new," Sondra said. "A flood
nearly wiped them out not long ago and they did a lot
of rebuilding and painting. You can still see the high
water marks on some of the big old trees."

There was a café, a service station, a big church, the
clinic and lots of well-kept little houses. Mel pulled up
to the clinic and got out. Inside she was immediately
faced with Dr. Hudson, a trim woman in her late thirties, dressed much like Mel. She was clad in jeans and
boots, chambray shirt with a stethoscope around her
neck. She smiled and stuck out her hand. "It's such a
pleasure, Ms. Monroe," she said. "I'm delighted you're
working with Doc Mullins—he's due a little assistance."

"Please, call me Mel. You know the doctor?"

"Sure. Everybody knows everybody."

"How long have you been in Grace Valley?" Mel
asked.

June laughed. "I've been here all my life. Except for
medical school." June stuck her hand out toward Sondra. "This must be Mrs. Patterson."

"I've brought you cookies," she said. "It's really generous of you to do this for me. I never had one with the
other two kids."

"It's a very convenient precaution," June said, gladly

taking the box of cookies. She opened it up, inhaled deeply and said, "Oh, these are sinful looking." Then looking back at Sondra and Mel she said, "If you knew how many people from the neighboring towns helped us rebuild after the flood, then you'd know generosity. Come on, let's see what we've got. Then if you have time, we can go grab a bite to eat at the café."

Over the course of the next hour, they determined that Sondra would give birth to a baby boy, the baby was already in position and there was nothing to indicate there would be complications. They met Dr. Stone, a drop-dead gorgeous blond man June referred to as a city-boy transplant. At the café, they met June's father, the town doctor before her, and he asked after Old Mullins, who couldn't be any older than Doc Hudson. "He still as ornery as ever?" Doc Hudson wanted to know.

"I'm softening him up," Mel said.

"So, what's your story?" June asked over lunch. "How long have you been in Virgin River?"

"Just a couple of months. I came up here from L.A., looking for a change, but I admit, I wasn't prepared for country medicine. I took all of our resources and hospital technology for granted."

"How do you like it so far?"

"It has its challenges. There are aspects of rural living that I think might be growing on me," Mel said. "But I'm not sure how long it's going to work out for me. My sister is in Colorado Springs, married with three children, and she really wants Aunt Mel nearby." She took a bite of a delicious hamburger and said, "I don't want to completely miss out on her kids' childhoods."

"Oh, don't say that," Sondra said.

"Not to worry," she said, patting her hand. "I'm not

going anywhere before you deliver, which from the look of things is going to be real soon." She laughed and added, "I just hope we don't have to pull off to the side of the road on our way home today."

"I hope you'll stay on," June said. "It'll be nice to have you so close by."

"Close by? It took us over a half hour of twisting, turning and inching past logging trucks, just to go one way! And I bet it's not twenty miles!"

"I know," June said. "It's just over fifteen miles. Isn't it great that we're neighbors?"

Before they were done with lunch a man came into the café carrying a baby. He reminded Mel just slightly of Jack—equal in height, muscled, rugged-looking in his jeans and plaid shirt, fortyish, and handling a baby with ease. He bent, gave Dr. Hudson a kiss on the cheek and handed over the baby. "Meet Jim, my house husband. And our son, Jamie."

All the way back to Virgin River Mel was thinking, I *didn't feel so out of place today.* She loved June and John Stone. Even old Doc Hudson was a kick. After she dropped Sondra off at her farm and drove back into town, it seemed as though the town was cuter somehow. Not quite the falling-down little burg she'd first thought. It seemed oddly like home.

She pulled up in front of Doc's house and noticed as she did so that the men were just getting back to Jack's from fishing all day. She went into the house to find Doc in the kitchen assembling something at the kitchen table. It looked as though he'd gotten himself a new bag. "Doc Hudson sends his regards, as do June and John. What are you up to?"

He put a couple of things in the bag and pushed it toward her. "Time you had one of your own," he said.

* * *

It was fun to watch the marines load up their gear and head for the river in the early morning. Mel waved to them from her spot on Doc's front steps where she took her morning coffee, and though they'd been up half the night playing poker and drinking, they seemed full of energy and enthusiasm. They'd shout and wave, and whistle at her. Flirt. "Oh, baby, you are so beautiful in the morning," Corny yelled across the street. His reward was a playful whap on the back of the head from Jack.

They were barely gone when a large, dark SUV pulled into town, driving slowly down the street. To Mel's surprise, the driver stopped in front of Doc's. The door opened, but the engine continued to run. A man got out and stood in the street next to the open door, half-hidden. He was a tall guy, broad-shouldered. He wore a black ball cap and his hair curled out beneath it. "This doctor make house calls?" he asked.

Mel stood up. "Someone's sick?" she asked.

He shook his head. "Someone's pregnant," he answered.

She felt a smile reach her lips. "We can make house calls, if necessary. But it's a lot more convenient to do prenatal checks here in the clinic. We see well patients on Wednesdays."

"You Doc Mullins?" he asked, his eyes crinkling doubtfully.

"Mel Monroe," she said with a chuckle. "Family nurse practitioner and midwife. Doc hasn't been doing much women's health since I got here. Where does your wife plan to have the baby?"

He shrugged. "That's up in the air."

"Well, where do you live?"

He tilted his head. "She's on the other side of Clear River. Almost an hour from here."

"We have a hospital room here. Is it a first baby?"

"I think so, yeah."

She laughed. "You think so?"

"It's the first one I've been around for," he said. "She's not my wife."

"Sorry," Mel said. "I made an assumption. Bring the lady in for a prenatal checkup," Mel said. "I can show her our room and talk to her about her options."

"How about if she has it at home?" he asked.

"Well, that's an option, too," Mel said. "But really, Mr....?" The man didn't respond as he should, with his name. He just stood there, big in his denim jacket, tall in his boots. Serious. "Really, the person having the baby needs to be involved in the discussion. Want to make an appointment?"

"I'll call," he said. "Thanks." And he got in the SUV and proceeded out of town.

She found herself chuckling; she'd never had a consultation go quite like that. She hoped the man would confer with the pregnant woman about where she'd like to give birth.

The marines left at the end of the week and the town quieted down, but after getting to know them, she was actually sorry to see them go. While the boys were in town, Preacher was a lot more animated, laughing easily, scowling so much less. And each one of them grabbed her and hugged her goodbye, like she was part of their family.

Mel found herself looking forward to having Jack to herself again, but it was not to be. Jack was oddly morose and somewhat distant. He didn't lift her off the ground or pester her for kisses, and for someone who had resisted and complained of the inadvisability of same, she was disappointed. Bereft. When she questioned his strange mood, he said, "I'm sorry, Mel. I think the boys wore me out."

When she went to the bar for lunch, Preacher reported that Jack was fishing. "Fishing?" she said. "Didn't he get enough of that last week?" To which Preacher merely shrugged.

Preacher didn't seem particularly worn-out. He presided over the bar with the help of Ricky, polishing glasses, serving food, busing tables and partaking of the occasional game of cribbage. "What's the matter with Jack?" Mel asked.

"Marines. They take their toll," he replied.

Four days later, a week ahead of schedule, Mel got the call from the Patterson farm that it was time. Given the fact that Sondra reported easy, quick births and had already been experiencing contractions through the night, Mel went immediately.

Babies are odd— they do as they please. Having a history of short labors didn't necessarily mean they would all be that way. With the support of her mother, mother-in-law and husband, Sondra labored hard through the day. Finally in the early evening, the little boy arrived. He didn't emerge with a lusty cry and Mel had to suction, stroke and cajole him into the world. Sondra bled a little too much and the baby wasn't interested in nursing right away. Even Sondra quickly knew the difference between this and her previous two experiences.

Getting a slower than usual start in the world doesn't necessarily mean trouble, and the baby's heart, respirations, coloring and cry caught up right away. Still, Mel stayed a bit longer than she ordinarily might have. She rocked the baby for three hours past the time she felt everything was fine, playing it extra safe.

It was ten at night by the time Mel finally decided to give them back their lives, their family, that it was perfectly safe to leave them. "And I'm wearing my pager," she said. "Don't hesitate, if you think anything is amiss."

Instead of going right back to her cabin, she went into town. If Jack's was dark and closed up, she'd go home. But the light was on in the bar, though the Open sign was not lit.

When she pushed open the door, she was greeted by a most unexpected sight. Preacher was behind the bar, a steaming cup of coffee in front of him, but Jack sat at a table with his head down on his arms. In front of him was a bottle of Scotch and a shot glass.

When Preacher saw her enter, he said, "Throw the latch on that door, Mel. I think this is enough company."

She did so, but the look on her face was completely nonplussed. She walked over to Jack and put a hand on his back. "Jack?" she asked. His eyes briefly opened and then rolled back in their sockets and closed again. His head lolled and one arm fell off the table and dangled at his side.

Mel went to the bar, hopped up on a stool in front of Preacher and said, "What's the matter with him?" Preacher shrugged and made a move to reach for his coffee mug, but before he could connect with it, Mel virtually lunged across the bar, grabbed the front of his shirt in her fist and said, hotly, "What's the *matter* with him?!"

Preacher's black brows shot up in surprise and he put up his hands as if being arrested. Mel slowly let go of his shirt and sat back on the stool. "He's drunk," Preacher said.

"Well, no kidding. But there's something wrong with him. He's been different all week."

Again the shrug. "Sometimes when the boys are here, it dredges things up. You know? I think he's having some remembering of things not so good."

"Marine things?" she asked. Preacher nodded. "Come on, Preacher. He's the best friend I have in this town."

"I don't think he'd like me talking."

"Whatever this is, he shouldn't go through it alone."

"I'll take care of him," Preacher said. "He'll snap out of it. He always does."

"Please," she implored. "Can't you guess how much he means to me? I want to help, if there's any way I can."

"I could tell you some things, but they're very ugly things. Not for a lady to hear."

She laughed a little. "You can't imagine the things I've seen, much less heard. I worked in a trauma center for almost ten years. It could get pretty ugly at times."

"Not like this."

"Try me."

Preacher took a deep breath. "Those boys that come up every year? They come to make sure he's okay. He was their sergeant. My sergeant. Best sergeant in the marines. He's been in five combat zones. The last one, Iraq. He was leading a platoon into interior Fallujah and one of the boys stepped on a truck mine. Blew him in half. Right away we were pinned down by sniper fire. Our boy who stepped on the mine, he didn't die right away. Something about the heat of the explosion—it must've cauterized arteries and vessels and he didn't bleed out. Didn't have pain, either—it must have done something to his spine. But he was fully conscious."

"My God."

"Jack ordered everyone to take cover in the buildings, which we did. But he sat with his man. He wouldn't leave him. Under sniper fire, leaning against a fat tire on an overturned truck, he held him and talked to him for a half hour before he died. Kid kept telling Jack to go, take cover, that it was okay. You know he didn't go. He'd never leave one of his men behind." He took a drink of coffee. "We saw a lot of stuff back there that will give you nightmares, but that's the one that sometimes gets to him. I don't know what hits him harder—the kid's slow death or the visit he paid his parents to tell them all the things he said before he went."

"And he gets drunk?"

"Fishes a lot. Maybe goes into the woods and camps awhile to get his stability back. Sometimes he'll try to drink it away, but that's pretty rare. First, it doesn't work too well and second, he feels like crap afterward. But it'll be okay, Mel. He always comes out of it."

"Jesus," she said. "I guess everyone has baggage. Gimme a beer."

He poured one from the tap and put it before her. "So maybe the thing to do is just let him be awhile."

"Is he going to wake up soon?"

"No. He's tanked. I was just about to carry him to bed when you walked in. I'll sleep in the chair in his room, just in case."

"In case of what?"

"In case he's not just drunk. In case he gets sick or something. He carried me down a road in Iraq—about a mile. I'm not letting anything happen to him now."

She drank some of her beer. "He's carried me a little, too," she said. "I don't think he knows it, though."

They sat in silence for a little while. She drank about half her beer. "I'm trying to get a picture of him carrying you," she said. "Must've looked like the ant and the rubber tree."

He surprised her with a chuckle.

"How'd he get you to come here? To this little town?"

"He didn't have to talk me into it. I kept in touch with him when he got out, and when I got out, I came up. He said I could stay and help around the bar if I wanted to. I wanted to."

A noise behind her made her turn. Jack fell off the chair and crashed to the floor, sprawling there.

"Nightie-night time," Preacher said, coming around the bar.

"Preacher, if you'll get him to his room, I'll stay with him."

"You don't have to do that, Mel. Could be unpleasant. You know?"

"Not a problem," she said. "I've held many a bucket, if it comes to that."

"Sometimes he cries out."

"Sometimes, so do I."

"Is it what you want?"

"It is. I want to."

"You really do care about him, then?" he asked.

"I said so, didn't I?"

"Well, okay. If you're sure."

Preacher crouched and pulled Jack upright. Hands under his armpits, he got him to a limp standing position, then putting a shoulder to his midsection, hoisted him over his shoulder in a fireman's carry. Mel followed him to Jack's bedroom.

She'd never been in Jack's quarters. It was set up like a little efficiency apartment with two means of entry—either through the kitchen behind the bar or the back door that led out to the yard. It was L-shaped, the bedroom being in the short end of the L and the living area larger. There was a table with two chairs by the window and while there was no kitchen, there was a small refrigerator.

Preacher put Jack on the bed and unlaced and removed his boots. "Let's get the jeans off," she said. To Preacher's dubious look, she said, "I assure you, I've seen it all." She undid the leather belt and unsnapped the jeans. Mel took the right pant leg, Preacher took the left and they pulled, leaving him in his boxers. Mel unbuttoned his shirt and rolling him from side to side, removed it. She took the clothes to his closet. Hanging on a peg just inside the door was a holster with a handgun in it and it made her gasp. She hung the pants and shirt over the gun.

Preacher was staring down at Jack, clad only in boxers. "He's gonna kill me for this," Preacher said.

"Or thank you," she supplied, giving him a small smile. "If my pager goes off, I'll come for you." She pulled the comforter over Jack.

"Or if you have any problems," the big man said.

When Preacher had gone, Mel pulled off her boots and in stocking feet, she poked around a little. He had a roomy bathroom with cupboards and drawers. She opened one and found that he kept underwear and socks in there. Towels were stored there, as well, and remembering that first day in Virgin River, she sniffed one. Downy, like he had said.

The closet was a medium-size walk-in. There was a small laundry room with cabinets in addition to the washer and dryer. The bathroom and laundry room had doors that closed, but the bedroom was in full view of the living room.

Looking around, it was so obviously Jack. Very masculine; very functional. He had a leather couch and big leather chair. There was a television on the facing wall and beside it, a glass-and-wood gun case filled with rifles, the key dangling from the lock. There was a heavy wood coffee table and a side table between the sofa and chair with a lamp on it. The walls were of rough-hewn wood and there were only two framed pictures on the side table. A family photo showing all of them, Jack, four sisters, four brothers-in-law, eight nieces, one silver-haired father as large as Jack. Beside it, a rather older portrait of his mother and father.

She picked up the family photo. This was a family of strong good looks, the men all tall and handsome, the women trim and pretty, the girls adorable—the youngest just little, like three or four, the oldest a teen. She thought Jack the best looking of them all, and he stood in the middle of the group, an arm around a sister on each side.

She took the throw off the couch, wrapped it around herself, and curled up in the large chair. Jack hadn't moved a muscle. Eventually she, too, nodded off.

Somewhere in the night, sounds came from Jack's bed. He was fitful, rolling around, muttering in his sleep. Mel went to the bed, sat on the edge and touched his brow. He grumbled something unintelligible and curled toward her, grabbing her and pulling her into the bed. He rested his head against her. She took his head in the crook of her arm and lay down beside him. "It's okay," she said to him. And he quieted at once, draping an arm over her.

She pulled the comforter over them both and snuggled up to him. She sniffed the pillow—Downy. Who was this guy? she found herself asking. Looks like Paul Bunyan, runs a bar, has all these guns, and cleans and launders like Martha Stewart.

In his sleep, he pulled her closer. His breath smelled of Scotch. Whew, she thought. She put her face against his hair, which smelled of his musk combined with the wind and trees. She inhaled deeply; she'd already begun to love his particular scent and the taste of his mouth. She had wondered what was under the shirt—a nice mat of brown hair on his chest and a couple of tattoos. On his upper left arm an eagle, globe and anchor, almost as big as her hand. On the upper right, over a ribbon, the words:

SAEPE EXPERTUS,
SEMPER FIDELIS,
FRATRES AETERNI

She couldn't resist, she rubbed her hands over the mat of hair on his chest and over his smooth shoulders. She pulled him close. Within minutes, she had fallen back to sleep, cradling Jack in her arms, his arm comfortably embracing her.

In the dim light of early morning, Jack awakened with a pounding head. He turned his face to the side and the first thing he saw were Mel's golden curls against the pillow next to him. She clutched the covers under her chin, sleeping soundly. He raised himself up on an elbow and looked down at her face. Her pink lips were parted in sleep; sooty lashes lay against her cheek. He lifted a soft curl off the pillow and held it to his face, inhaling. Then he leaned toward her and lowered his lips to gently touch hers.

Her eyes came open. "Morning," she whispered sleepily.

"Did we do it?" he asked.

"No," she said.

"Good," he said.

She smiled at him. "I didn't expect you to say that."

"When we do it, I want to remember it. I don't even know why you're here."

"I stopped by the bar for a beer just about the time Preacher was scraping you off the floor. Headache?"

"It went away the minute I saw you. I must have had one too many."

"Did it work? Did you scare away all the demons?"

He shrugged. "It got you in my bed. If I'd known it was that easy, I'd have gotten plastered weeks ago."

"Lift the covers, Jack," she said.

He did so. There he was, boxer clad and sporting quite a healthy morning erection. And there she was, fully clothed. "Don't look down," he said, dropping the comforter. "You have me at a *huge* disadvantage." She laughed at him. "We could do it now," he suggested. He felt the texture of her hair between his thumb and finger. "I'll treat you real, real good." He grinned.

"No, thank you," she declined.

"Did I try anything?" he wanted to know.

"No." She laughed. "Why?"

"I drank enough so that could have been really humiliating. Assault with a dead weapon."

She ran her fingers over the tattoo. "I sort of expected this," she said.

"Rite of passage. I bet every young marine wakes

up with a splitting head and a little remembrance of the Corps."

"What does this mean?" she asked, running her fingers over the words on the other arm.

"Often tested, always faithful, brothers forever." He touched her cheek. "What did Preacher tell you?" he asked her.

"That the boys come up here and stir up some of your roughest memories of the wars you've been in. But I suspect that now and then you'd have those memories anyway, whether they came or not."

"I love those boys," he said.

"And they're devoted to you. So—maybe it's worth a little discomfort now and then. Friendships like that don't come cheap."

Ten

Jack was back to his old self. It was either the Scotch or the fact that he woke up to a pretty blonde in his bed. He bet on the blonde.

He never did ask Preacher precisely what he had told Mel. And he didn't ask Mel to be more specific. It didn't really matter. What did matter was that he had bonded with Mel on a new level that night without planning to. That she knew he was tortured over something terrible from his past and instead of shying away, stayed with him, willing to take it on   it had meant something. She had held him while he tossed and turned against a mean-spirited ghost. After that, she yielded more willingly to those kisses. He was definitely ready to move ahead with her.

They were the current talk in Virgin River, which gave Jack a strange satisfaction. For a man who didn't want to be tied down to a woman, a man who tended to keep his woman in the shadows, he found himself wanting everyone to know they were a couple. And he worried that she would make good on her threats to leave before he could convince her to stay forever.

Jack took Mel to the coast to whale watch and they

talked all the way there and back, but on the high cliffs above the ocean, they held hands, quiet, while the great fleet of behemoth mammals swam by, jumping out of the water and landing with an enormous splash. Their own guard of dolphins escorted them to the north. She let him kiss her for a long time that day. Many times. Then if his hand wandered she said, "No. Not yet." And that gave him hope. Not yet meant it was on the agenda.

He was completely smitten. Jack was forty and this was the first time that he had a woman in his life he couldn't imagine giving up.

Mel called her sister. "Joey," she said quietly, in almost a whisper. "I think I have a man in my life."

"You found a man in that place?"

"Uh-huh. I think so."

"Why do you sound so…strange?"

"I have to know something. Is it okay? Because I'm not even close to being over Mark. I still love Mark more than anything. Anyone."

Joey let out her breath slowly. "Mel, it's all right to get on with your life. Maybe you'll never love anyone as much as you loved Mark—but then maybe there will be someone else. Someone next. You don't have to compare them, honey, because Mark is gone and we can't get him back."

"Love," she corrected. "Not past tense. I still *love* Mark."

"It's all right, Mel," Joey said. "You can go on living. You might as well have someone to pass the time with. Who is he?"

"The man who owns the bar across from Doc's clinic—the one who fixed up the cabin, bought me the fishing pole, got my phone installed. Jack. He's a good man, Joey. And he cares about me."

"Mel... Have you...? Are you...?"

There was no answer.

"Mel? Are you sleeping with him?"

"No. But I let him kiss me."

Joey laughed sadly. "It's okay, Mel. Can you really think otherwise? Would Mark want you to wither away, lonely? Mark was one of the finest men I've ever known—generous, kind, loving, genuine. He'd want you to remember him sweetly, but to get on with your life and be happy."

Melinda started to cry. "He would," she said through her tears. "But what if I can't be happy with anyone except Mark?"

"Baby sis, after what you've been through, would you settle for some marginal happiness? And a few good kisses?"

"I don't know. I just don't know."

"Give it a go. Worst case—it takes your mind off your loneliness."

"Is that wrong? To use someone to take your mind off your dead husband?"

"What if you put that another way? What if you *enjoyed* someone who took your mind off your dead husband? That could pass for happiness, couldn't it?"

"I probably shouldn't be kissing him," she said. And she cried. "Because I just can't stay here. I don't belong here. I belong in L.A. with Mark."

Joey sighed heavily. "It's only kissing, Mel. Just take it one kiss at a time."

When they hung up the phone, Joey said to her husband, Bill, "I have to go to her. I think she might be heading for a crisis."

* * *

Mel had started thinking about the past more—that morning that the police came to the door to tell her that Mark was dead. They had worked the swing shift together at the hospital the night before. They'd taken their lunch hour together in the cafeteria. But Mark was on call and the E.R. was busy, so he stayed through the night. It happened when he was on his way home.

She had gone to the morgue to view him. Left alone with him for a little while, she took his cold, lifeless body into her arms, his chest riddled with three perfect holes, and wept until they dragged her away.

She had a video in her mind—one that ran from the pictures of Mark lying on the floor at the convenience store, the police at her door at dawn, through the funeral, those nights that she cried literally through the entire night, right up to the long days of packing up his things and the long months of not being able to part with them. She saw the film in her head as if from above, curled into a fetal position in her bed, grabbing herself around the gut as though she'd been run through by a knife, crying hard, loud tears. Cries so loud that she thought the neighbors would hear and call for help.

Rather than just telling his picture that she loved him, she began carrying on long, one-sided conversations with his flat, lifeless face. She would tell him everything she'd done all day and it would inevitably end with, "I still love you, damn you," she would exclaim harshly. And urgently, "I still love you. I can't stop loving you and missing you and wanting you back."

Mel had always thought that Mark was the kind of lover, the kind of husband, who would find a way to contact her from beyond, because he was so devoted. But there had never been any evidence that he'd crossed back. When he went, he went all the way. He was so gone, it left her feeling desolate inside.

She woke up crying three days running. Jack had asked her if anything was wrong, if there was anything she wanted to talk about. "PMS," she told him. "It'll pass."

"Mel, have I done anything?" He wanted to know.

"Of course not. Hormones. I swear."

But she was starting to think that the brief reprieve she seemed to have experienced lately was now officially over and she was on her way back to the darkness of grief and longing. Back to the stark loneliness.

Then something happened to jar her out of it. She returned from her short walk to the corner store to watch her soap with Joy and a recovering Connie to see a rented car in front of Doc's. When she went inside she was face-to-face with her sister's bright smile. Mel gasped, dropped her bag and they swooped together, lifting each other off the ground, laughing and crying at once. When the crazy moments had passed, still holding Joey's hand, Mel turned toward Doc to make a formal introduction. But before she could, Doc said, "Kind of scary, there being two of you."

Mel ran her hand over Joey's shiny and smooth brown hair. "Why are you here?" she asked.

"You know. I thought you might need me."

"I'm okay," she lied.

"Just in case, then."

"That's so sweet. Do you want to see the town? Where I live? Everything?"

"I want to see the man," Joey whispered in Mel's ear.

"We'll do that last. Doc? Can I have the afternoon?"

"I certainly wouldn't be able to stand having the two of you yakking and giggling around here all day."

Mel rushed on Doc and gave him a kiss on his withered cheek, which the old boy quickly wiped off with a grimace.

Mel's spirits were high and she didn't think about Mark for a little while. She took Joey to all her favorite places, beginning with her cabin in the woods, which Joey thought was charming, if a little in need of her professional decorator's touch. "You should have seen it when I arrived," Mel laughed. "There was a bird's nest in the oven!"

"God!"

Then they went to the river where there were at least ten men in waders and vests, angling. A couple of them turned and waved to her. "The first time I was here, Jack brought me and we saw a mama bear and her cub, right downriver, fishing. First and last bear I've ever seen. I think I'd like to keep it that way. The next time I came, I fished. I fly-fished—not as good as what they're doing, but I actually caught a fish. I have my own gear in the trunk."

"No way!"

"Way!"

Next, to the Anderson ranch to visit little baby Chloe and see the new lambs. Buck Anderson lifted a couple of little lambs out of the pen and handed one to each woman.

Mel stuck her finger in a lamb's mouth and he closed his little eyes and sucked, making the women say, "Aww...."

"I raised six kids—three boys and three girls—and each and every one of them smuggled a lamb into their bedroom to sleep in their beds. Keeping the livestock out of the house was a lifetime chore," he told them.

Mel drove her sister down Highway 299 through

the redwoods and took great pleasure in her oohs and aahs. They got out and walked through Fern Canyon, one of the filming sites of Spielberg's *The Lost World*. She showed her the back roads of Virgin River, the green pastures, fields of crops, craggy knolls, towering pines, grazing livestock, vineyards in the valley. "If you're going to stay awhile and I can pry myself away from Doc, I'll take you to Grace Valley to meet some of my newer friends. They have a larger clinic there, complete with EKG, a small surgery and ultrasound."

Then, as the dinner hour approached, so did a heavy and cool summer shower and they ended up at Jack's, where the drop in temperature had prompted the laying of a friendly fire. Word had apparently gotten out, because the bar was busier than usual—so untypical of a rainy night. Some of her favorite people were present. There was Doc, of course, and Hope McCrea. Ron brought Connie for a little while and where Connie went these days, Joy was nearby with her husband, Bruce. Darryl Fishburn and his parents stopped by and she introduced Darryl as the daddy of her first Virgin River baby. Anne Givens and her husband were there, a couple from out on a big orchard—their first baby was due in August. Preacher treated Joey to his rare smiles, Rick was his usual grinning, adorable self, joking about how the whole family must be gorgeous, and Jack charmed her thoroughly. When he went to the kitchen to get their dinners, Joey leaned close to Mel and said, "Holy crap, is he a hunk or what?"

"Hunk," Mel confirmed.

They were served a delicious salmon-in-dill-sauce dinner, which Jack ate with them, and Mel regaled her sister with tales of country doctoring, including the two births she had attended on her own.

It was a little after seven when Doc's pager sent him to the phone in Jack's kitchen. Then he dropped by Mel's table. "Pattersons called. The baby seems to be having trouble breathing and is getting a little pale and blue around the gills."

"I'm going with you," Mel said. She stood and told Joey, "I delivered that baby and he had a slow start. If I'm late, can you find the cabin?"

"Sure. Want to give me a key?"

Mel smiled at her sister. She kissed her cheek. "We don't use too many keys around here, sugar. It's open."

Mel rode with Doc in his truck, just in case some of the dirt roads had gotten soft from the rain. She didn't want her BMW stuck in the mud.

They found Sondra and her husband in a state of panic, for the baby did seem to be wheezing. His respirations were accelerated and shallow, but he had no temperature. After a little oxygen, he cleared right up, which did nothing to tell them what was wrong. Mel rocked him for a good long while. Doc sat at the kitchen table and talked to the Pattersons, drinking coffee. "He's too young for something like asthma. Might be some kind of allergic reaction, a symptom of an infection, or it could be more serious—a problem with his heart or lungs. Tomorrow you're going to have to take him over to Valley Hospital to the outpatient clinic for tests. I'll write down the name of a good pediatrician."

"Is he going to be all right through the night?" Sondra asked tearfully.

"I expect so, but I'll leave the oxygen. You can drop it off tomorrow. It wouldn't hurt to spell each other and stay awake, just in case. If you have any problems or you're worried about him, call me. That little foreign thing of Mel's isn't worth a crap on these roads in the rain. Besides, Melinda has company from out of town."

Two hours later, Doc was ready to take Mel back to her sister.

By eight o'clock, all the patrons had left Jack's except Joey. Jack had sent Ricky home, Preacher was cleaning up the kitchen, and he brought Joey a cup of coffee and sat down with her again. He asked about her kids, what her husband did, how she liked living in Colorado Springs, and then, "She didn't know you were coming."

"No, it was a complete surprise. Though it shouldn't have been."

"Your timing couldn't be better. Something's been eating at her."

"Oh," Joey said. "I guess I thought you knew what was going on. Because she said that you and she…" She stopped and looked into her coffee cup.

"We what?" he asked.

Joey raised her eyes and smiled sheepishly. "She said you kiss."

"Every time she'll give in a little."

"In a place like Virgin River, does that make you a couple?" she asked.

He sat back in his chair, willing the bar to stay empty. "Yeah, something like that," he said. "With a big hunk of something missing."

"Look, I don't know that I have the right…"

"To tell me who ripped her heart out and crushed it under the heel of his boot?" he finished for her.

"Her husband," Joey said bravely, lifting her chin.

That caused Jack to sit up straighter. Joey hadn't said *ex*-husband. "What did he do to her?" he asked, a definite angry edge to his voice.

Joey sighed. In for a penny, in for a pound, she thought. If Mel hadn't told him, she didn't want him to know. She was going to be pissed. "He got himself murdered in an armed robbery that he happened into by accident."

"Murdered," Jack said weakly.

"He was an emergency room doc. He'd worked an all-nighter and stopped into a convenience store for milk on his way home in the morning. The robber panicked and shot him. Three times. He died instantly."

"God," Jack said. "When?"

"A year ago. Today."

"God," he said again. He leaned an elbow on the table and rested his head in his hand. He massaged his eyes. "She knows it was today?"

"Of course she knows. She's been heading for it. Painfully."

"In L.A.," he said. It wasn't a question. "And to think I wanted to punch him in the face a few times for hurting her."

"Look, I feel kind of funny about this. Disloyal. One of the things that drew her here was that no one knows. No one looks at her with pity. No one asks her fifteen times a day how she's doing, if she's lost more weight, if she's sleeping yet... I guess I thought she'd have told you, since..."

"She's holding back," he said. "Now I know why."

"And I let it out. I don't know whether to be guilty or relieved. Someone who cares about her out here should know what she's been through. What she's going through." She took a breath. "I didn't think she'd make it a week here."

"Neither did she." Jack was quiet for a minute and then said, "Can you imagine what kind of courage it took for her to chuck her big job in L.A. and come to this little town, to work with a man like Doc Mullins? She told me a little about what it was like there—city medicine, she called it. A battle zone, she said. She thought it was going to be real dull and boring here. Then she ends up riding to the hospital with a patient in the back of an old pickup, over these roads, holding an IV bag over her head, freezing. Christ, I could've used her in combat."

"Mel has always been tough, but Mark's death really derailed her. That's why she did this—she started being afraid to go to the bank, the store."

"And she hates guns," he supplied. "In a little town where everyone has a gun because they have to."

"Oh, jeez. Look, it's no secret—I begged her not to do this— I thought it was crazy and way too drastic a change," Joey said. "But something about this seems to be working for her. What she calls country doctoring. Or maybe it's you."

"She has these spells," he said. "When she's so sad. But it passes and there is such a brightness inside her. You should have seen her the morning after she delivered her first baby at Doc's. She said she felt like a champ. I've never seen anyone so lit up." He chuckled at the memory, but there was a morose tone to his laugh.

"You know what—I think I'm going to call it a night. Go back to Mel's and hang out until she gets home, so I can be there for her."

"Let Preacher drive you," he said. "These roads at night, in the rain, can be treacherous if you don't know them. The first night Mel drove out to the cabin, she slid off a soft shoulder and had to be towed out."

"What about Mel?" she asked.

"Doc might just take her straight home—he has no

respect for that little car of hers. Or she could come here for her car—she's pretty good on these roads now, but if she has any worries about it, I'll drive her out. Fact is, it wouldn't surprise me if she was out at Patterson's half the night, so don't worry. She hates leaving a sick patient. But I'll wait up." He went to the bar and got a piece of paper. "Call me if she shows up at the cabin. Or if you need anything," he said, writing down his number.

It was nearly ten by the time Mel walked into the bar. She saw Jack at the table by the fire, but frowned when she looked around and didn't see Joey. "Where's my sister?" she asked. "Her car's out front."

"I had Preacher take her home in the truck. Her first night in town she shouldn't have to deal with those roads in the rain."

"Oh. Thanks," she said. "I'll see you sometime tomorrow, then."

"Mel?" he called. "Sit with me a minute."

"I should go to Joey. She came all this way…"

"Maybe we should talk. About what's been going on with you."

She had been on this precipice for days, teetering on the fine edge of losing it. The only thing that seemed to take her mind off the violent event that changed her life was work. If she had a patient or an emergency, she could lose herself in it. Even the day with her sister, showing Joey the town, the lambs, the beauty, took her away a little bit. But it just kept coming back, haunting her. A picture of him lying on the floor bleeding out could float in front of her eyes and she'd have to pinch them closed, praying she wouldn't break down. There was no way she could sit down and talk about it.

What she needed right now was to get out of here, go home and have a good hard cry. With her sister, who understood.

"I can't," she said, her words little more than a breath.

Jack stood up. "Then let me drive you home," he said.

"No," she said, holding up a hand. "Please. I need to just go."

"Why don't you just let me hold you. Maybe you shouldn't be alone."

So, Mel thought. She *told* him! She closed her eyes and held up a hand as if to ward him off. Her nose became red, her lips pink around the edges. "I really want to be alone. *Please,* Jack."

He gave his head a nod and watched her leave.

Mel went down the porch steps to her car, but she didn't make it. It hit her before she could get there. She was nearly doubled over by the sudden crushing pain of memory, of loss. The emptiness came back, draining her of all good feelings and filling her up with the horrific unanswerable questions. *Why, why, why? How can this happen to a person? Even if I'm not good enough to deserve better, Mark was! He should have lived to be an old man, to save lives and treat people with the brilliance and compassion that made him one of the best emergency room doctors in the city!*

She had made it all day without falling apart, but now in the dark, in the cold night rain, she felt as though she was going to collapse to the ground and just lie there in the mud long enough to perish, to be with him. She stumbled toward a tree and grabbed the trunk, embracing it, holding herself up and holding on at the same time. The cries that came out of her were loud and wrenching.

Why couldn't we at least have had a baby? Why

couldn't even that small thing have worked in our favor? Just to have a piece of him to live for...

Inside, Jack paced back and forth in the bar, feeling his own helplessness because he couldn't do anything for her. He knew all about the crushing pain of loss; even more about the difficulty of getting beyond it. He hated that she'd left without at least letting him try to comfort her.

Frustrated, he opened the door to go after her. There sat her BMW, right in front of the porch, but she wasn't in it. He squinted to look into the car, but then he heard her. Sobbing. Wailing. He couldn't see her. He stepped out onto the porch, went down the steps into the rain. And then he saw her—holding on to the tree, the rain drenching her.

He ran to her, embracing her from behind, holding the tree with her, holding her against the tree. Her back heaved with her cries, her cheek pressed against the rough bark. The sound of her anguish broke his heart; no way could he let her go, no matter what she said about being alone. This crying made her weeping over baby Chloe look like a mere rehearsal. She was racked. She started to crumble to the ground and he put his arms under hers and held her upright as the rain soaked them.

"Oh God, oh God, oh God," she howled. "Oh God, oh God, oh God!"

"Okay," he whispered. "Let it go, let it out."

"Why, why, why?" she cried in the night, her breath coming in jagged gasps. Her whole body jerked and shook as she cried. "Oh, God, *why?*"

"Let it all out," he whispered, his lips against her wet hair.

She screamed. She opened up her mouth, tipped her head back against him and screamed at the top of her lungs. He hoped she wouldn't wake the dead, the sound was so powerful. But he only hoped she wasn't heard so that no one would disturb them and stop this purging. He wanted to do this with her. He wanted to be there for her. The scream subsided into hard sobbing. Then more quietly, "Oh, God, I can't. I can't, I can't."

"It's okay, baby," he whispered. "I've got you. I won't let anything happen to you."

Her legs didn't seem to hold her up anymore; he was keeping her upright. He had the passing thought that no amount of emotion he had ever expelled in his lifetime could match this. It was almost phenomenal in its strength, this pain that gripped her. What had he thought? That his few days of brooding, a good drunk, had been demonstrative of his pain? Ha! He held in his arms a woman who knew more about gut-wrenching pain than he did. His eyes stung. He kissed her cheek. "Let it go," he whispered. "Get it out. It's okay."

It was a long time before she began to cry more softly. Fifteen minutes, maybe. Twenty. Jack knew you don't stop something like this until it's over. Till it's all bled out. They were both soaked to the skin when her breath started coming in little gasps and hiccups. It was a long time before she pushed herself away from the tree and turned toward him. She looked up at his rain soaked face, hers twisted with pain, and said, "I loved him so much."

He touched her wet cheek, unable to tell the tears from the rain. "I know," he said.

"It was so unfair."

"It was."

"How do I live with it?"

"I don't know," he answered honestly.

She let her head drop against his chest. "God, it hurt so much."

"I know," he said again. Then he lifted her in his arms and carried her back into the bar, kicking the door closed behind him. He took her to his room in the back, her arms looped around his neck. He put her down on the big chair in the sitting room. She sat there, shivering, her hands tucked between her knees, her head down, her hair dripping. He went for a clean, dry T-shirt and towels and came back to her, kneeling in front of her. "Come on, Mel. Let's get you dry."

She lifted her head and looked at him with eyes that were both terribly sad and exhausted. She was listless. Spent. And her lips were blue with cold.

He peeled off her jacket, tossing it on the floor. Then her blouse. He was undressing her like one might a baby, and she didn't resist. He wrapped a towel around her and keeping her covered, reached beneath and undid her bra, slipping it off without exposing her. He pulled the T-shirt over her head, holding it for her arms, and once it covered her to her thighs, he yanked out the towel. "Come on," he said, pulling her upright. She stood on shaky legs and he unbuttoned and pulled down her trousers before sitting her back down. He removed her boots, socks and pants; he dried her legs and feet with the towel.

Though still drenched himself, he used the towel to attempt to dry her curling hair, blotting the locks between folds of the towel. He wrapped the throw from the couch around her shoulders, then went to his bureau and found a pair of clean, warm socks. He rubbed her cold feet vigorously, warming them, and put on the socks. When she looked up at him, some sanity had seeped into her eyes, and this made him smile a small smile. "Better," he said softly.

He went to the cupboard in his laundry and brought out a decanter of Remy Martin and two glasses. He poured her a small amount of the brandy, neat, and took it to her, kneeling in front of her. She took a sip and then in a voice both weak and strained, she said, "You're still wet."

"I am," he said. "Be right back."

He went to his closet and quickly stripped off his clothes, pulling on only a pair of sweatpants, leaving his chest bare and his wet clothes in a pile on the floor. He poured himself a little brandy and went to her. He sat forward on the sofa at a right angle to her, putting the palm of his hand against her cheek and was pleased to note that she had already warmed. She turned her face against his hand and kissed the palm. "I've never been taken care of like this," she said.

"I've never taken care of anyone like this," he said.

"It seemed like you knew exactly what to do."

"I guessed," he said.

"I crashed," she said.

"It was a helluva crash. If you're going to go down, go down big. You should be proud." And then he smiled.

He held her hand as it lay on her lap while she lifted her brandy to her lips with the other hand, trembling a bit. When it was gone, he said, "Come on. I'm putting you to bed."

"What if I cry all night?"

"I'll be right here," he said. He pulled her hand and led her to his bed, holding up the covers so that she could slip in. He tucked her in as if she were a little girl.

Jack dealt with the wet clothes, spinning the water out of them and putting them in the dryer. When he checked on Mel, she was asleep, so he went back into the little laundry and behind closed doors, called Joey. "Hi," he said. "I didn't want you to worry. Mel is with me."

"Is she okay?" Joey asked.

"She is now. She had a meltdown. Out in the rain, it was awful. I don't think she has another tear in her, at least for tonight."

"Oh, God," she said. "That's why I came! I should be with her now…"

"I got her in some clean, dry clothes and put her to bed, Joey. She's asleep and I—I'll watch over her. If she wakes up and wants to go home, I'll take her, no matter what time it is. But for now, let's let her sleep." He inhaled deeply. "She's had it."

"Oh, Jack," Joey said, "were you with her?"

"I was. She wasn't alone. I was able to… I held her. Kept her safe."

"Thank you," Joey said, her voice small and shaky.

"There's nothing more to do right now but let her rest. Have a glass of wine, get some sleep and try not to worry about Mel. I'm not going to let anything happen to her."

With only a dim night-light in the room, Jack pulled a chair from his table near to the bed. His feet planted on the floor, his elbows resting on his knees and the rest of his Remy clutched in his hands, he watched her sleep. Her hair curled across his pillow and her pink lips were parted slightly. She made little noises in her sleep—little hums and purrs.

I have a high-school education, he thought. *She was married to a medical doctor. A brilliant, educated man. An emergency room hero, made even more perfect in death. How do I compete with that?* He reached out and lightly touched her hair. *There's no way,* he thought. *I'm sunk. And my heart hasn't beat the same since she walked into town.*

He was in love with her. This man who had never been in love in his life. Not once. As a kid, a young man, he'd thought himself in love a couple of times, but it hadn't felt like this. Lust, he was familiar with that. Wanting a woman was something he knew quite well—but wanting to take care of a woman so that she would never hurt, never want, never be afraid or lonely—he had no experience with that. There had been beautiful women in his past; intelligent women, clever women, women with wit and courage and passion, but as far as he could remember, never one like Mel; never before a woman who had everything he'd ever wanted. *And it just figures,* he thought. *I'm stupid in love with a woman who isn't available to me. She's still in a relationship, albeit a relationship that was no longer viable.*

Didn't matter. He'd held her while she was racked with the pain of losing someone else. She had a lot to get over, to get past. Even if he stood by her and waited for that to happen, it didn't mean she could fall in love with him. Still, he had no choice. He was into her all the way.

He finished the brandy, putting aside the glass, but he didn't leave her. He watched her, occasionally succumbing to the temptation to softly, carefully, touch the silkiness of her hair. When she sighed contentedly in her sleep, he found himself smiling, pleased that she had found some peace. At some point he realized that he knew how she felt—once you know how much you love someone, no one else would do.

He looked down at the floor. *I'll be here for you, Mel,* he thought. *It's the only place I want to be.* When he raised his head, her eyes were open and she was looking at him. He stole a glance at the bedside clock and was surprised to see that two hours had passed.

"Jack," she said in a whisper. "You're here."

He smoothed her hair back from her face. "Of course I am."

"Kiss me, Jack. When you kiss me, I can't think of anything else."

He leaned toward her and touched her lips with his for a soft kiss. Then more firmly, moving over her mouth, feeling her lips open and her small tongue enter. Her hand crept around to the back of his neck to pull him closer, and his kiss became hungrier, deeper.

"Come in here with me," she whispered. "Hold me. Kiss me."

He pulled back slightly, but she wouldn't let go of his neck. "I'd better not."

"Why?"

He laughed a little. "I can't just kiss you, Mel. I'm not a machine. I won't want to stop."

She pulled the covers back for him. "I know," she said in a breath. "I'm ready, Jack. I don't want to hurt anymore."

He hesitated. What if she called out another man's name? What if the morning came and she was sorry? He had fantasized about this, but he wanted it to be the beginning of something, not the end.

Then you better make it good for her, he told himself. *You'd better leave her wanting more.* He slipped in beside her, pulling her into his arms, devouring her mouth with a kiss so hot and powerful she melted to him with a whimper. Her arms went around him, holding him as she yielded to his lips, his tongue. His sweatpants, so loose and soft, left nothing to the imagination and he was instantly hard against her. She moved against him, rubbed against him, inviting him. With a large hand on her bum, he held her there.

Jack rolled with her, bringing her on top of him. He grabbed the bottom of the T-shirt that covered her and raised it, pulling it over her head. When he felt her breasts against his bare chest, he said, "Ahh." Her breasts were soft and full in his big hands, her nipples hard. Running his hands along her ribs to her hips, he found that she still wore her thong panties; he slid them lower and she wiggled out of them. Her skin was so delicate, so smooth, he worried that his hands were too rough for her, but by her soft and eager moans, she was not unhappy with the sensation.

Holding her lips with his, he rolled with her again, so that they lay on their sides, and he took a moment to free himself from those sweats. Her hand wrapped around him, causing his breath to catch in his throat, and he thought, *Better not leave your boots on this time, buddy. You better do it for her.* And he concentrated, because he'd never wanted to please a woman more than tonight.

Feeling her against him like this made it very difficult to slow down, to wait, but by sheer dint of will he managed. He took his leisure of her, employing a slow hand that fondled her breasts. His mouth followed, drawing on one nipple then the other. She arched toward him greedily, spreading her legs, throwing one over his hip, urging him closer. He slipped a hand down and touched her in her soft center, bringing a passionate moan from her. He touched her deeply, and learned that he wasn't the only one feeling a little desperate. She was ready for him. Starving. "Mel," he said in a throaty whisper.

"Yes," she answered. "Yes."

He turned her onto her back and held himself over her. He captured her mouth with his and entered her in one long, slow, deep, powerful stroke that caused her to gasp and rise against him urgently. With one hand under her bottom and the other still caressing a place that turned her sighs to moans, he began to move within her. The heat of her nearly drove him out of his mind, but he held on. He was determined that her needs would come before his own. He moved steadily, pushing and pulling, and within moments her breathing came harder and faster, her body straining toward his, reaching for satisfaction. He was more than happy to deliver it, pushing into her, rubbing against her. And then he felt those hot spasms of fulfillment, heard her cry out in ecstasy and he held her fast, pressing himself into her. In that moment of blinding pleasure, she bit down on his shoulder; sweet, welcome pain. And he hung on with all the strength he could muster, saving himself, and finally she weakened beneath him and the clenching spasms that surrounded him slowly subsided. Her body relaxed and her breathing began to slow. Her pants became sighs and her kisses came soft and sweet against his lips.

Mel stroked his back, tasted his mouth, her body still quivering from a thundering climax. She felt the muscles of his shoulders and back at work as he held himself up enough to keep from crushing her with his weight. When he released her mouth and looked into her eyes, she saw in his a smoldering fire that was not even close to being extinguished. She put her palm against his cheek. "Oh, Jack," she said, breathless.

His name on her lips brought him such pleasure, he felt himself expand somewhere inside his chest, as if his heart grew just a little bit. He lowered his lips and sucked gently at hers. "Are you all right?" he asked softly.

"You were right there. You know exactly how all right I am," she said. "It's been a long, long time."

"It's never going to be that long again," he whispered. "Not ever again."

He began to move down her body with his lips and tongue, kissing and nibbling, tasting in slow, delicate strokes. He ran a tongue around each nipple until they were hard little pebbles, perfect for his mouth. He slid lower, until he had moved down over her flat belly. He gently parted her legs and buried his face in her, hearing her gasp above him. No longer delicate, he went to work on that prominent, erogenous knot in her center. He felt her moving her hips against his mouth and when her breathing became rapid and labored once more he rose, slowly kissing his way up her body. "God, you're sweet," he whispered against her lips. "You taste like heaven." He slid into her again, filling her, moving in long deep strokes that became powerful thrusts that brought her to yet another shattering climax. Again she cried out and he covered her open mouth with his. Swept away, she couldn't be quiet, and that thrilled him. Every sound, every wild cry gave him joy. He held her as she collapsed beneath him, spent.

Jack felt her small hands on his back, her lips on his neck, and her breathing inevitably slowed and came under control. To his surprise he heard the sound of her soft laughter. He rose above her and looked at her smile. "You lied to me," she said. "You are a machine."

"I just wanted to make you happy," he said. "Are you happy?"

"I've been happy a couple of times. What can I do so that you can join me?"

He laced his fingers through hers and holding her hands, stretched her arms up above her head, holding them there. "Baby, you don't have to do anything but be present."

He lowered his mouth to hers, kissed her deeply and began to move inside her once more, pumping his hips. She lifted her knees and tilted beneath him, bringing him deeper, and he could feel her begin to move in concert with him. She wrapped her legs around his waist and he followed the rhythm she set in place. He rocked with her, slow and steady, deep and long, hanging on to control until he heard her moaning and sighing rise again, her tempo increased, and finally the noises she made, already familiar to him, already beautiful to him, told him she was reaching for yet another orgasm. He had expected her to be passionate, but the heat and power of her passion amazed him, and it filled a need in him. And this time, when she clenched around him and pleasure stole her breath away, he let himself go and matched her. Surpassed her. For a moment, through the powerful pulsing, he felt light-headed. His eyes watered. And he heard it again. "Jack!"

"Ah, Mel… Ah, baby," he whispered, kissing her, loving her.

He gently caressed her as she calmed. "Jack," she whispered. "I'm sorry…"

"What do you have to be sorry about?" he asked in a whisper.

"I think I bit you."

He laughed, a deep throaty sound. "I think you did. Is that a habit of yours?"

"I must have been a little out of control…"

He laughed again. "I take the blame," he said. "That was all part of the plan."

"Ohh," she said. "I might've lost my mind there for a while."

"Yeah," he whispered. "I love it when that happens."

"You were taking a big chance, driving an already crazy woman out of her mind like that."

"Nah, you were in good hands. You were always safe." He kissed her softly. "Would you like to rest now?"

"Maybe for a little while," she answered, her hands gentle on his face.

He gathered her close to him, holding her. Their naked bodies entwined, they spooned. He kissed the back of her neck as she lay on his arm. His face rested against her soft, fragrant hair, one arm over her and cupping her breast. Very soon he could hear the sounds of her even breathing, her sleep. He closed his eyes and relaxed with her in his arms, finding sleep himself.

Sometime in the dark of night he opened his eyes to find she had rolled over to face him, her hands boldly caressing him. He kissed her and asked, "Have you slept?"

"I did," she said. "And woke up wanting you. Again."

"I guess it's pretty obvious, the feeling is mutual."

Mel woke in the early morning and to her surprise, there was a song in her head. She was humming along with Johnny Mathis in her sleep. "Deep Purple." Her music was back.

She rolled over to find the bed beside her empty. She could hear the sound of Jack splitting logs in the backyard. She rinsed her mouth and rubbed his toothpaste against her teeth. A light blue, long-sleeved denim shirt hung on a hook in his closet and she put it on, sniffing the collar, smiling at his scent on it. It more than cov-

ered her; she was drowning in it. She went to the back
door and stood watching him heft the ax and bring it
down. Thwack. The air was clear and sharp; the rain
was gone and the huge trees were washed clean. She
watched him heft the ax again, and bring it down. His
shirtsleeves were rolled up to the elbows and his biceps
rippled under the weight and force of the ax.

Then he looked in her direction. She lifted a hand
toward him and smiled.

He dropped the ax at once and came to her. As he
stood before her, she put her hand on his chest. He ran
the back of a knuckle against her pink cheek. "I think
I roughed you up a little with whiskers."

"Yeah. Don't worry about it. I like it. It feels right.
Natural. Good."

"I love the way you look in my shirt," he said. "I love
the way you look out of my shirt."

"I think we have a little time," she said.

He swooped her up into his arms, kicking the door
closed behind him, and bore her gently to the bed.

Eleven

The morning air was cool and foggy as Mel drove to her cabin. The front door was open, letting in the crisp June morning air. She kicked off her muddy boots on the porch and when she went inside found Joey sitting on the sofa, a quilt wrapped around her, a steaming cup of freshly brewed coffee on the table beside her.

Joey lifted a side of the quilt for Mel and Mel went to her, cuddling beside her, resting her head on Joey's shoulder. Joey pulled the quilt snugly around them both. "You okay, baby sis?" Joey asked.

"I'm okay. I lost it last night." She turned her head and looked up at her older sister. "Why didn't I see that coming? You did."

"The anniversary of deaths has a reputation," she said. "Even if you don't remember the exact date— it'll sneak up on you and knock the wind out of you."

"It sure did," she said, laying her head back down on Joey's shoulder. "I knew what day it was. I just didn't expect such a dramatic event."

Joey stroked Mel's hair. "You weren't alone, at least."

"You just wouldn't have believed it, even if you'd seen it. I was completely out of control, standing in the rain, screaming. I screamed for a long time. He just held me and let me. He kept telling me to let it out. Then he took care of me like you would a stroke victim. Undressed me, got me into dry clothes, gave me a brandy and put me to bed."

"I think Jack must be a very good man…"

"Then I invited him into bed with me," Mel said. Joey said nothing. "We made love all night long. I've never had so much sex in my life. I mean—never."

"But you're all right," she said, and it was not a question.

"When I lifted the blanket for him, all I could think was, this will numb me. Rub out the pain, give me escape."

"It's okay, sweetie."

Mel looked at Joey again. "It didn't exactly work that way," she said. "Maybe if he'd been average, I could've closed my eyes and just gone to a happy place. But he's not average. Holy shit, he's astonishing."

Joey laughed a little, sentimentally. Sisters. They had talked about sex since they were teenagers. Laughed about it, told dark secrets about it. With Mark's death, Joey had feared these kind of talks would never happen again.

"All he wanted was for me to have pleasure. Wild, blinding, crazed pleasure."

Again Joey laughed. "Did it work?"

"Oh, yeah," she said in a breath. Then she turned and looked at her sister. "Do you think he just felt sorry for me?"

"Well, you were there. Do you think that?"

Mel smiled. "I don't care," she said. "I just hope he feels sorry for me again, real soon."

Joey smoothed the curly hair away from her sister's

pretty brow. "I'm glad you have this in your life again." And then she giggled, and so did Mel.

"How did this happen, Joey? That I went from wanting to die, to wanting Jack? Wanting him so much I was almost a maniac? Wouldn't you think that would be impossible? That I wouldn't be able to even think like that?"

Joey took a breath. "I think when your emotions reach a pitch like that, it follows suit. You just feel everything more intensely. I think it makes stupid sense, actually. Haven't you ever noticed that some of the best sex seems to follow a big fight? I'm pretty sure I conceived Ashley on the same night I told Bill that if I didn't just leave him, I'd at least never speak to him again."

Giggles.

"I haven't even asked you how long you can stay," Mel said.

"I can stay as long as you want me to, but a truly kind sister would pack up and get out of your hair right now."

"No," she said, shaking her head. "I've missed you so much." She smiled. "It's a sacrifice I'm willing to make for you."

Joey hugged her close. "A few days, then. If you're sure."

"I'm sure."

"Mel?"

"Huh?"

Joey revisited a topic from their earliest discussions on this subject, reaching back to their high-school and college days. "Do you think there's any truth to that old wives' tale that you can tell from the size of a man's foot?"

"Uh-huh."

"So. What size boot do you think Jack wears?"
Giggles.
"Twenty-seven," Mel said.

Mel took Joey with her to Doc's that very morning. Joey cozied up in the kitchen with a book while Mel and Doc saw a few patients. The three of them had lunch together at the house, then the girls went to Grace Valley where they visited June and John at the clinic. There were no patients scheduled for the next day and Doc wore his pager while he went to the river to fish, so Joey and Mel drove all the way to the coast, having lunch in the adorable little Victorian town of Ferndale.

They visited the shops—there were things that Joey thought would be perfect for Mel's cabin—a throw for the sofa, some accent pillows, a wall clock, colorful place mats. They stopped off and bought a small barbecue for the yard and wooden salad bowls. A vase that would complement the table. On the way home they went to the market and bought some groceries and fresh flowers.

It seemed like a quick beer at Jack's was in order and they went into the bar arm in arm, laughing because Mel had whispered, "If I catch you looking at his crotch, I will slap you." Which almost guaranteed Joey was going to find the temptation irresistible. Then they invited him to come out to the cabin for dinner, and he not only eagerly accepted, he brought a six-pack.

They told stories from their childhood and teenage years that had him laughing right along with them till almost midnight.

When Jack was getting ready to leave, Joey slipped discreetly away so Mel could say good-night to him in private. Outside, on the porch, with only the filtered light from inside the cabin, Jack stepped down a step so that he could be eye-to-eye with Mel. She draped her arms over his shoulders while he encircled her waist with his large hands. She leaned toward him and teasingly nibbled at his lower lip.

"You told her everything," he said.

"Nah," she said, shaking her head.

"She keeps looking at my crotch," he said.

Giggles. "Not everything," she said. "I kept the more delicious stuff to myself."

"Have you been all right?" he asked, drawing his brows together in concern. "Any more tears?"

"Completely all right." She smiled.

"I miss you already, Mel."

"It's only been a couple of days…"

"I missed you after a couple of hours."

"You're going to be a lot of trouble, aren't you? Demanding, imposing, insatiable…"

He covered her mouth in a searing kiss that answered the question. She yielded happily, holding him closely. *Ah,* she thought. *This is such a wonderful, powerful, sexy man.* She never wanted it to end, but at length it had to. "I have to go," he said in a husky voice. "Either that, or carry you into the woods."

"You know, Sheridan… This place is growing on me."

He gave her a little peck on the lips. "Your sister is great, Mel." He gave her another. "Get rid of her," he said. Then with a whack on the butt, he turned and left her.

When he got to his truck and opened his door, he turned to look at her. He stood there for a long time. Then he slowly lifted his hand. And she did the same.

* * *

Jack was sweeping off the porch at the bar the next morning when he saw Joey and Mel walk out of Doc's house and embrace at Joey's car. Then Mel walked back inside and to his surprise, Joey came over to the bar.

"I'm going to shove off," she said to him. "I thought I'd beg a cup of coffee from you on my way out of town. Mel has a couple of patients this morning, or she'd have come with me. So we said our goodbyes."

"I'd be glad to buy you breakfast," he said.

"Thanks, I've had a little something already. But I'm not going to pass up your coffee. And I wanted a moment. To talk. To say goodbye."

"Coming up," he said. He leaned the broom against the wall and held the door for her. She jumped up on a stool and he went behind the bar to serve her coffee. "It was great meeting you, Joey. And spending a little time."

"Thanks. You, too. But mostly, thanks for what you've done for Mel. For taking care of her, looking out for her…"

He poured himself a mug. "I think you know—you don't have to thank me. I'm not doing anybody any favors."

"I know. Still… Just so you know, it's easier for me to leave her here, knowing that she isn't all alone."

It was on his mind to tell her that he hadn't felt like this since he was sixteen. All steamed up, crazy in love, willing to take a lot of chances for just one chance. But what he said was, "She won't be alone. I'll keep an eye on things."

She sipped her coffee. She seemed to struggle with something. "Jack, there's something you should keep in mind. Just because the crisis seems to have passed doesn't mean… Well, there could still be some struggles ahead for her."

"Tell me about him," Jack said.

Joey was startled. "Why?"

"Because it might be a long time before I can ask Mel. And because I'd like to know."

She took a deep breath. "Well, you have every right to ask. I'll do my best. But the only thing that allows the rest of us to hold it together as well as we do is because Mel has been so fragile. It *was* like losing a brother. It *was* losing a brother. We all loved Mark."

"He must have been one helluva guy."

"You have no idea." She sipped more of her coffee. "Let's see—Mark was thirty-eight when he died, so that made him thirty-two when he met Mel. They met at the hospital. He was the senior resident in the emergency room and she was charge nurse on the swing shift. They fell in love right away, moved in together a year later, married a year after that and had been married four years. I think the most characteristic things about Mark were his compassion and sense of humor. He could make anyone laugh.

"And he was the one doctor you wanted in Emergency when there was a crisis that required the family be handled with kindness, with sensitivity. Our whole family loved him right off. His entire staff adored him."

Jack didn't realize that he chewed absently on his lower lip.

"It's hard to remember that he wasn't perfect," she said.

"You'd be doing a guy a big favor by telling me one or two things that made him less than perfect," he said.

She laughed at him. "Well, let's see. He clearly loved Mel very much and he was a good husband, but she used to say that his first wife was the E.R. It's that way with doctors anyway, and I don't think it was much more than an irritation—she was a nurse and knew the score. But they fought about his long hours, about him going into the hospital even when he wasn't on call. There were lots of times they had plans and he didn't show up. Or he'd leave early and she'd take a cab home."

"But that's how it is," Jack said. Marines left their families behind to do the country's work abroad. While a part of him wished that Mel had hated her husband for frequently abandoning her for work, there was another part that held a grudging respect for a woman who knew the ways of the world and held strong through them.

"Yeah. I don't think it threatened their marriage, not really. He'd get absorbed in his work and miss entire conversations. She said she sometimes thought she was talking to a wall. But of course, Mark being Mark, he'd apologize and try to make it up to her. I'm sure if he hadn't died, they'd have stayed married for fifty years."

"Come on, Joey," he said. "Didn't he drink too much, smack her around, cheat on her?" he asked hopefully. So hopefully that it made Joey laugh.

She dug around in her purse, pulled out her wallet and flipped through the pictures until she came to one of Mel and Mark. "This was taken about a year before he died," she said.

It was a studio portrait, husband and wife. Mark had his arm around her and they were both smiling— carefree. Her eyes twinkled; so did his. A doctor and a nurse midwife—brilliant, successful people—they had the world by the balls. Mark's face was familiar to Jack, having seen the picture beside her bed. But he looked at this with new eyes, knowing what he knew. Mark was not bad looking—and this was the only context under which Jack would allow himself to make such an assessment of another man. Short, neat brown hair, oval face, straight teeth. He would have been thirty-seven in the picture, but he looked much younger—he had a baby face. He did not look unlike many of the young marines Jack had taken into battle with him.

"A doctor," Jack said absently, staring at the picture.

"Hell, don't be intimidated by that," Joey said. "Mel could easily have been a doctor. She holds a bachelor's in nursing and postgrad degree in family nurse practitioner with a certification in midwifery. She's got a brain bigger than my butt."

"Yeah," he said. That Joey's butt wasn't big was not the point she was making.

"They had as many arguments as any couple," Joey said. "Vacations brought out the worst in them—they never wanted to do the same things. If he wanted to golf, she wanted to go to the beach. They usually ended up going somewhere he could golf while she lay on the beach, which might sound like a reasonable compromise, except for one thing—they weren't spending the vacation together. That used to piss her off," she added. "And Mel, pissed off, is unbearable.

"And," Joey went on, "he was lousy with money. Paid absolutely no attention. His focus had been purely on medicine for so long, he'd forget to pay bills. Mel took over that job right away to keep the lights from being turned off. And he was pretty anal about tidiness—I'd eat off the floor of his garage in a second."

Such urban, upper-class problems, Jack found himself thinking.

"Not an outdoorsman, I guess," Jack said. "No camping?"

"Shit in the woods?" she laughed. "Not our man, Mark."

"Funny that Mel would come here," he said. "It's rugged country. Not too refined. Never fancy."

"Um, yeah," Joey said, looking into her coffee cup. "She loves the mountains, loves nature—but Jack, you need to know something…this was an experiment. She was a little crazy and decided she wanted everything different. But it isn't her. Before Mark died, she must have had subscriptions to a dozen fashion and decorating magazines. She loves to travel—first class. She knows the names of at least twenty five-star chefs." She took a breath and looked into his kind eyes. "She might have a fishing pole in her trunk right now, but she's not going to stay here."

"Rod and reel," he said.

"Huh?" Joey asked.

"Rod and reel, not a fishing pole. She really likes it."

"Take care of your heart, Jack. You're a real nice guy."

"I'll be okay, Joey," he said, smiling. "She'll be okay, too. That's the important thing, isn't it?"

"You're amazing. Just tell me you understand what I'm telling you. She might have run from that old life, but it's still inside her somewhere."

"Sure. Don't worry. She was good enough to warn me."

"Hmm," Joey said. "So, what do you do for vacation?" she asked him.

"I'm on vacation every day," he said, smiling.

"Mel said you were in the Marine Corps—what did you do then? When you had leave?"

Well, he wanted to say, *if I wasn't recovering from some wound and we were in country, I'd get drunk with the boys and find a woman. A far cry from flying first-class to the islands to tan on the sandy beach or snorkel in the bay.* But he didn't say that; it was another life. One he left behind. People do that, he thought briefly and hopefully, leave another life behind and move on to something new. Different. "If I had a long leave, I'd visit the family. I have four married sisters in Sacramento and they live for the opportunity to boss me around."

"How nice for you," she said with a grin. "Well, you have any more questions? About Mel? Mark?"

He didn't dare. More information about the sainted Mark might do him in. "No. Thanks."

"Well, then, I'm going to get going—I have a long drive and a plane to catch."

She jumped off the stool and he came around the bar. He opened his arms to her and she happily gave him a robust hug. "Thanks again," she said.

"Thank you," he returned. "And Joey, I'm sorry for your loss."

"Jack. You don't have to compete with him, you know."

He put an arm around her and walked her out onto the porch. "I can't," he said simply.

"You don't have to," she said again.

He gave her shoulders a final squeeze and watched as she walked across the street to where her car sat at Doc's. She gave one last wave as she drove out of town.

Jack couldn't help but spend way too much time trying to picture Mel's life as it had been with Mark. He saw an upscale home and expensive cars. Diamonds as birthday gifts and country club memberships. Trips to Europe; to the Caribbean to unwind and relax from the high stress of city medicine. Dinner dances and charity events. The kind of lifestyle that even if Jack could fit into it, he wouldn't want to.

The upscale life wasn't alien to him—his sisters lived in that world very well. They and their husbands were educated, successful people; they had grappled with finding the best schools so their girls would be likewise. Donna, the oldest at forty-five, was a college professor, married to a professor. Jeannie, the next at forty-three, was a CPA married to a developer. Then there was Mary, thirty-seven, a commercial airline pilot married to a real estate broker—they were the country clubbers. His baby sister and the most bossy—and his favorite—was Brie, almost thirty, a county D.A. married to a police detective. He was the only one in the family who had gone into the military as an enlisted man—as a mere boy—educated only through high school. And found that what he had a gift for was physical challenge and military strategy.

He wondered if Joey was right, that Mel couldn't possibly be happy here for long in this dinky little town full of ranchers and blue-collar types, without a five-star chef within three hundred miles. Maybe she was just too classy for this backwoods life. But then an image of the Melinda he'd fallen in love with would float into his mind—she was natural and unspoiled, tough and sassy, uninhibited and passionate, stubborn. Perhaps it was a premature worry—he'd hardly given her a chance. It was always possible she'd find things here to love.

He didn't see her all that day. He never left the bar, just in case she came by for a sandwich or cup of coffee, but she didn't. It wasn't until almost six that she showed her face. As she walked in, he felt that sensation that had become so common for him lately—desire. One look at her in those tight jeans and he was in agony. It took willpower to keep himself from responding physically.

There were people present—the dinner crowd and about six fishermen from out of town—so she said hello to everyone she knew on her way to the bar. She jumped up on a stool and, smiling, said, "I wouldn't mind a cold beer."

"You got it." He fixed her up a draft. Now this woman, looking like a mere girl really, asking for a beer and not a champagne cocktail, this did not fit the picture he'd had earlier of the country club set, the diamonds, the charity dinner dances. Still, seeing her in a fitted, strapless black dress—he could manage that. It made him smile.

"Something's funny?" she asked.

"Just happy to see you, Mel. Going to have dinner tonight?"

"No, thanks. We were busier than I thought we'd be all morning, so I fixed Doc and I something to eat at around three. I'm not hungry. I'll just enjoy this."

The door opened and Doc Mullins came in. A couple of months ago he'd have sat at the other end of the bar, but no more. He was still as grouchy as he could manage, but he took the stool next to Mel and Jack poured him a short bourbon. "Dinner?" he asked the doctor.

"In a minute," he answered.

The door opened again and in came Hope. She had finally discarded the rubber boots in favor of tennis shoes—just as muddy. She sat on Mel's other side. "Oh, good, you're not eating," she said, pulling a pack of cigarettes out of her pocket. "Jack?" she asked, requesting her usual Jack Daniel's.

"Jack coming up, neat," he said, pouring.

Hope puffed and asked, "So, how'd your sister like your little town?"

"She had a good time, thanks. Though she expressed some concern about the state of my roots."

"Get that old codger to give you a day off and go over to Garberville or Fortuna and get a do."

"You have nothing but days off anymore," Doc grumbled.

"That's an interesting statement coming from someone who didn't want any help around here," Mel teased. Then to Hope she said, "You know big sisters. She just wanted to make sure I hadn't gotten myself into anything that held the potential for disaster, and now that she's convinced I'll live, she can go back to her family with a clear conscience. What have you been doing with yourself, Hope?" Mel asked. "I haven't seen much of you."

"Just the garden, from morning till night. I plant and grow, the deer come in and eat it. I need to round up Jack's marines and get 'em all out there to pee a border around the property."

Mel sat back. "That works?"

"Hell, yeah. Better than anything."

"Well, live and learn," she said. Mel finished her beer. "I'm going home," she stated flatly, getting off her stool.

Mel was barely out the door when she felt Jack come up behind her. He took her arm and walked with her to her car. Once there she turned to him and said, "Think you can find your way out to that little cabin?"

He leaned down to kiss her and groaned. It was happening to him again. "I'll be right there," he said.

"Take your time. Give me a head start so I can wash

Hope's cigarette out of my hair. Go finish serving dinner."

He lowered his lips to her neck. "I'm going to walk back in there and yell 'Fire!'"

She laughed at him and pulled away. "I'll see you later," she said. And got in her car to leave.

Mel drove home knowing that he was starving and wouldn't be long. He was the most sexually driven man she'd ever known. But there were a couple of things she wanted to do. When she got home, she put her medical bag by the front door and went to the bedroom. She sat on the bed, picked up Mark's picture and held it. She looked into his kind eyes and mentally said to him, "You know I love you, and I know you understand." And then she slipped it into the drawer.

Then she went to the shower to freshen up.

Jack went back behind the bar and made sure everyone was taken care of. He brought Doc his dinner, said good-night to Hope as she left, then went for Preacher. "It's thinning out," he said. "I'm going out to Mel's," he added, knowing Preacher would have his tongue cut out before he'd tell anyone. As if anyone needed telling. When Jack and Mel were in the same room, the air warmed up. People glanced at them knowingly. "You can reach me there if you need me. Don't need me."

"I'm good," Preacher said. "Ricky and I can handle things."

Jack might've driven a little too fast down the curving, tree-canopied road, but he was dying for her. He parked and went to the porch, sitting in one of the Adirondack chairs to pull off his boots. Inside, he heard the shower running and called out so he wouldn't frighten her. "Mel?"

"I'll be out in a minute," she called back.

But he was already out of his shirt, his hands on his belt buckle. He left a trail of clothes through the living room to the bathroom. The glass of the shower was steamed and inside was her small naked form in the mist. He slowly opened the door and stood there looking at her in all her glistening beauty. God, she was so perfect. She reached a small, inviting hand in his direction and he stepped in with her.

"You didn't take your time," she said against his lips.

"I tried," he admitted.

"I wanted to freshen up for you."

He covered her mouth with his, but his hands were all over her, running up and down her smooth, soft back, over her bottom, caressing her breasts, digging into her wet hair, down her neck and over her shoulders, down her arms to entwine his fingers with hers. He trembled, he wanted her so badly. And her hands were on him, running over his chest, around to his back, filling her hands with the hard muscles on his butt, and finally over his flat belly and down to his swollen erection, causing him to say, "Ohh... Mel..." before capturing her lips anew.

His fingers wandered lower to examine her, gently probing. It made him swell with some kind of erotic pride to find that she was slick and as anxious as he. This woman didn't need much warming up. This mutual need, this had become the best part of his life. He lifted her up. Her arms went around his neck, her legs around his waist and he settled her upon him, entering her slowly, firmly. He turned with her in his arms, bracing a shoulder against the shower wall. Then he began to move her upon him, lifting her up and down.

Her sighs became quickened breaths, her legs tightened around him.

Mel hung on to his shoulders and neck, her mouth on his, their tongues hot and desperate as they devoured each other. The sensation of his arms and shoulders at work as he held her caused her blood to boil and she felt her desire rising and rising to a wonderful pitch that soon erupted into bliss.

Jack loved nothing so much as bringing her that crazy moment and feeling her tighten around him. When she cried out, he held her closer, if possible. He reached himself as far inside her as humanly possible and the storm of his own wild climax shook him to his core.

She held on to him, he on to her, while they calmed, their breathing slowly returning to normal. She nibbled at his lip and said, a little breathlessly, "I didn't know that was even possible. Being with you… It's an adventure."

"You do something to me. You drive me out of my mind."

"Good. You do good work, brainless." And then she laughed and touched his shoulder. "You have a little bruise…"

"I love that little bruise…"

"Let's dry off and meet in the bed."

"You don't have to ask me twice. But please, don't move just yet. This part is dicey." He held her a moment longer and then, carefully and slowly, lifted her up and away from him, setting her down on her feet in the shower. They showered off, dried off. Mel needed a little extra time to dry that golden mane of hers— emerging roots and all. Jack went to the bedroom and sat on the bed. It was gone—the picture. He wasn't an idiot, he knew that only the picture was gone, not the memories. Still, it made him smile to himself. He settled himself in her bed and waited impatiently.

When she came to the bedroom, she reached for the light and he said, "Leave it on, Mel." Without questioning him, she slid into the bed beside him. Lying on his side, he rose up, his head braced on his hand. "There are a couple of things we should talk about. The other night wasn't about talking."

"Oh-oh," she said, suddenly on edge. "Is this the part where you explain about casual sex and consenting adults?"

"No," he said. "Not at all. Just details. I want you to know something—there have been…women. You know? Mel, I'm forty. I've never been celibate. I always wore a condom. Always. Plus, the marines were ridiculous about medicals, including tests for STDs. But if you'd like me to be tested…"

"I tend to be cautious…"

"Done. And then, we didn't talk about birth control, and I don't want to be irresponsible. This comes a little after the fact—I'm sorry."

"You're okay," she said. "I've got that covered. But, if you're so used to putting on the condom, what happened the other night?"

He shrugged. "I didn't have anything handy, and the only thing on my mind was making sure everything was good. It started out as such a bad night for you and Jesus, I didn't want you to regret it. I guess I went a little crazy. But I can be prepared in the future. Just say the word."

"And tonight?" she asked.

"I apologize—in the pocket of those jeans on the living room floor, there's… Sorry. I was so ready to be with you. I was out of my head, Mel. It doesn't have to be like that every—"

She put a finger on his lips, smiled and whispered, "I like it like it is. When you're a little crazy." She looked up into his eyes. "Ordinarily, I would have thought of the condom, but I guess the state I was in…well. If you'll just take care of that screening, I'm sure we'll be all right. Have there been an awful lot of women?"

He made a face. A frown. "More than I like."

"Any really special ones?" she asked.

"You're going to think I'm lying. No."

"What about the woman in Clear River?" she asked.

"Mel, we were only sleeping together. No, not true— I never spent a night. She didn't come to Virgin River. I never thought I'd be embarrassed about that."

"You don't have to be embarrassed. You're a grown-up."

"It wasn't like this. This feel casual to you?" he asked her.

"Actually, it feels a little intense."

"Good," he said. "Everything about this is different. I hope you understand that."

"You're not just sleeping with me?" she asked, teasingly.

"I *am* sleeping with you," he said, running his hand over her smooth shoulder and down her arm. He gave her a sweet, short kiss. "It's not just sex. It's everything. It's special."

She laughed at him. "Are you *seeing* me?" she teased.

"Yeah," he said. "It's a first for me."

"So, in some ways, you're just a virgin from Virgin River."

"In this, I am."

"That's very sweet."

"This is madness, I want you all the time. I feel like a kid."

"You don't act like a kid," she said.

"Melinda—I have had more erections in the last week than I've had in the last decade. Every time you walk by, I have to concentrate on something else. This hasn't happened to me since I was sixteen, when anything from a beer commercial to a geography assignment could put me in agony. It was almost laughable, if it wasn't just so ridiculous."

"Raging hormones," she said with a laugh. "You are an amazing lover."

"I'm not doing this alone," he said. "You're pretty amazing yourself. Damn, baby. We fit together real nice."

"Jack—does everyone in town know?"

"They'd be guessing. I haven't said anything."

"Somehow, I don't think you have to."

"We could try to keep it quiet, if that works better for you. I could manage to not look at you like I'm going to have you for dessert, if that's what you want."

"It's just that…well, you know. I have these issues."

"I know. I held you through some major issues. And I do understand that it's going to take more than a little sex to resolve all that." He grinned. "Good sex."

"*Very* good sex."

"Oh, yeah…" he agreed breathlessly.

"Just so you know. I'm still all screwed up. I don't want to disappoint you. Jack, I don't want to hurt you."

He ran a hand down her body, lightly brushing her soft, warm skin. "Mel, this doesn't hurt." He smiled. "It feels real, real good. Don't worry about me." He gave her a light kiss. "You want to try to keep this… us…quiet? Private?"

"Think it would work?"

"There's probably no point in pretending," he said. "It's your call."

"Oh, what the hell," she said. "It isn't against the law, is it?"

He leaned over her and kissed her more deeply. "It probably should be." He kissed her again.

In the early morning as dawn was just beginning to streak through the cabin windows, Jack was stirred awake by the soft sound of slightly off-key humming. He found Mel nestled into the crook of his arm, her breath tickling his chest. She was purring, humming, her lips moving slightly, as though singing. It might've troubled him if her expression had been sad or disturbed. But she was smiling. She snuggled closer, throwing a leg over his. And this sleepy little music, contented, drifted out of her.

He could count on one hand the number of times he'd spent the entire night in bed with a woman. And already, he couldn't imagine waking up alone. He pulled her closer knowing he'd never been happier in his life.

Twelve

Rick called Liz every couple of days, although he wanted to call her seven times a day. His pulse always picked up when he dialed, then the sound of her voice made it race.

"Lizzie, how you doing?" he'd ask.

"I miss you," she would always say. "You said you'd come over."

"I'm going to. I'm trying. But with school and work… So, how are…things?"

"I just wish I was there, instead of here." Then she'd laugh. "Funny, I hated my mother for making me go to Aunt Connie's, and now I hate her for making me stay here."

"Don't hate your mom, Liz. Don't."

Then they'd talk for a while, about kids, about school, about Virgin River and Eureka, just mundane stuff. She never volunteered any information about the feared pregnancy.

Rick was dying a million deaths. He was terrified something had gone wrong and she was caught with a baby on that one and only night. But almost worse than that, he wasn't sure what was happening to him, in his head, in his body. He dreamt about her, wanted to feel his arms around her, wanted to smell her hair and kiss her lips. He wanted her breast in one hand, but he also wanted to have her riding beside him in that little truck on the way to and from school, cracking jokes, laughing, holding hands.

This phone call was no different than the others had been. Then she asked, "Why don't you come to Eureka?"

He drew a heavy breath. "I'll tell you the truth, Liz—I'm afraid to. You and me, we get pretty worked up."

"But you have those rubbers..."

"I told you before, that's not enough. You have to get something, too. Pills or something."

"How'm I gonna do that? I don't even drive. You think I should say to my mom, 'Hey, I have to get some birth control—me and Ricky want to do it'?"

"If you were here, you could see Mel. Maybe you can talk your mom into a visit to Virgin River." But even as he said that, he cringed. And flushed so hot he thought he might faint. Was he really suggesting to a fourteen-year-old that she get herself fixed up so they could have sex? In the cab of a truck?

"I don't know," she said softly. "I think I would hate that. I don't think I could tell someone who's like, grown-up. Could you?"

He already had; Preacher and Jack both knew. But he said, "I could if it was this important."

"I don't know," she said. "I'll think about it."

If you couldn't stop dreaming about a girl, if you constantly thought about the way her hair felt against your cheek, if you couldn't get the softness of her skin out of your mind, did that mean you loved her? If you felt a little better after every time you talked to her, heard her laugh, did that mean anything, or were you just this horny sixteen-year-old boy? He knew he was that—the thought of getting inside her again almost made steam come out of his ears. But there was other stuff. He could talk to Liz; he could listen to her. *Wanted* to listen to her. He could almost go into a trance when she told him about something as boring as algebra. If he had one drop of courage, he'd ask Jack—what is love and what is sex? When are they the same thing?

Finally he asked, "Any news about being pregnant, Lizzie?"

"You mean...?"

"Yeah, I mean that." Silence answered him. She was going to make him say it, once again. Every time he asked, his gut clenched just from forming the words, words alien to a boy. "Did you get your period?" he asked, grateful she couldn't see the color of his cheeks.

"That's all you really care about."

"No, but I care about it a lot. Liz, baby, if I got you in trouble, I'm gonna want to die, okay? I just want the scare over, that's all. For both of us."

"Not yet—but that's okay. I told you—I'm not regular. And I feel fine. I don't feel like anything's different."

"I guess that's something," he said.

"Ricky, I miss you. Do you miss me?"

"Ohh, Liz," he said in an exhausted breath. "I miss you so much it scares the hell out of me."

Mel made a few phone calls the following week, then asked Jack if he could pry himself away from the bar for a full day to run some errands with her. She wanted to drive into Eureka, she said. And she didn't want to go alone. Of course he said he could—he did anything she asked of him. He offered to drive, but she told him she'd like to take her car, put the top down and enjoy the sunny June weather.

When they were under way, she said, "I hope this wasn't too presumptuous of me, Jack. I made myself an appointment at the beauty shop and one for you at the clinic—that testing you offered."

"I was going to run over to the coast, to the Naval Air Station there, but this is just as convenient. I meant it when I offered. I want you to feel safe."

"I'm not worried, really. It's just a precaution. And if anything turns up, I'll get screened. I wouldn't put you at risk, you understand. But the last seven years, it was only…" She stopped.

"Your husband," he finished for her. "You can say it. That was your life. That *is* your life. We have to be able to talk about it."

"Well," she said, gathering herself up again. "Then, I've made arrangements to test-drive a vehicle and I'd like your opinion. A vehicle that doesn't get stuck in the mud."

"Really?" he said, surprised. "What kind of vehicle?"

She stole a glance at him, so neatly folded up in the front of her BMW, his knees sticking up so high it almost made her laugh. "A Hummer," she said.

He was speechless. Finally he said, "I guess you know what they cost."

"I know," she said.

"Hope's paying you better than I would've guessed."

"Hope's paying me practically nothing—but it also costs me practically nothing to live. Especially with that end-of-the-day cold beer on the house every night. No, this is my own investment."

He whistled.

"I have a little money," she said. "There were...there was..."

He reached across the console and put a hand on her thigh. "It's all right, Mel. I didn't mean to pry."

"You didn't pry!" she exclaimed. "You don't even ask, which is amazing to me. Here it is—there were investments. Retirement. Insurance. I sold the house at a ridiculous profit. And then there was a wrongful death suit—pending. It'll settle. The little scumbag came from money. Jack, I have plenty of money. More than I really need." She glanced over at him. "I'd appreciate it if that went no further."

"No one even knows you're widowed," he told her.

She took a deep breath. "So—I had a long talk with June Hudson, the doctor in Grace Valley. I asked her what she'd do to turn an all-wheel-drive vehicle into a makeshift ambulance, and I have quite a shopping list. If it works out I'll have a vehicle that can not only get me and Doc all over valley and into the hills, but get our patients to the hospital when we need to, without me sitting in the back of a pickup, holding an IV bag up in the air."

"That's a lot to do for a little town like Virgin River," he said, and he said it very quietly.

He'd done a lot for the little town, too, she thought. He renovated a cabin into a bar and grill, served meals at low prices all day long. Drinks were cheap and it served more as a gathering place than a profit-making establishment. He probably didn't need Ricky in there, but clearly he was a surrogate father. And Preacher— there was no question he was looking out for him, as well. But then, it probably didn't take much for Jack to get by, either—he'd done most of the renovation work himself, collected a retirement from the military, and surely eked out a modest but completely adequate income from the place. And at the same time, enjoyed his life.

Mainly what Jack did for the town was sit at the center of it, helping anyone who needed anything. Anyone who served the needs of the town, like Doc or Mel, and lately the occasional sheriff's deputy or highway patrol officer ate free. He'd do repairs, babysit, deliver meals and absolutely never went for supplies without phoning up little old ladies like Frannie and Maud, to ask if they needed anything. He'd done that with her, too. Behaved as though it was his mission to serve her needs.

"That little town has accidentally done a few things for me, too," she said. "I'm starting to feel like I might live after all. A lot of that is because of you, Jack."

Jack couldn't help himself. He said, "You're staying."

"For the time being," she said. "Another baby is coming at the end of summer. I live for those babies."

One of these days, he said to himself, *I'm going to tell her. Tell her I love her more than I thought I could love a woman. Tell her that my life started when she walked into town. But not yet.* He didn't want to back her into a corner and make her feel she had to either say she loved him, too, or run.

"Well, Mel, as it happens, I've driven a ton of Hummers."

She glanced at him with surprise, for she hadn't even thought of that. "Of course you have!" she said. "I had forgotten that!"

"I'm also a passably good mechanic. Born of necessity."

"Good then," she said. "You'll be a bigger help than I realized."

The first items on the agenda were her hair and his

blood tests. Mel was very appreciative of the fact that her seventy-five-dollar cut and highlights seemed to be more than adequate. Either she'd been countrified or ripped off in L.A.

After that they went to a used car lot where there was one ridiculously high-priced used Hummer. It was a repo, had only twenty thousand miles on it, and seemed to be in good condition. Jack looked at the engine and had them put it up on the lift so he could examine the axle, frame, shocks, brakes and whatever else he could see. They took it out and it drove well, but the price was out-of-sight. Sixty thousand and it wasn't loaded.

Except—Mel had a sweet little BMW convertible trade-in and cash. It took only a couple of hours to bring that price into range and Jack was able to pridefully explore another aspect of Mel's character—she was a hardheaded, master negotiator.

Next they went to the hospital supply where they had the back of the Hummer outfitted with some emergency equipment, from a defibrillator to an oxygen tank. Some medical supplies had to be ordered and would be delivered to Virgin River within a couple of weeks. Then they drove it back down the highway and up the mountain pass to Virgin River. "You don't want anyone to know where this came from," Jack said to Mel. "How are you going to explain it?"

"I'm going to say that I used to work with a lot of rich, bored doctors in L.A. and hit them all up for donations for the town."

"Ah," he said. "If you leave?" He just couldn't make himself say "when."

"Maybe I'll actually call some of those rich, bored doctors I really do know, and hit them up for a donation," she said. "But let's not put the cart before the Hummer."

He laughed. "Let's not."

Mel and Jack took the Hummer back to the bar where they did a little show-and-tell with the dinner crowd who would waste no time spreading the word to the rest of the town. Doc Mullins, as if he was annoyed by this unnecessary addition to the town, grumbled that his old truck had worked just fine. But Mel countered his comments by telling him that he would have to get checked out in the new vehicle the very next morning. It soon became apparent that his fit of pique was obviously contrived and he was even caught smiling once or twice as he looked it over. Ricky talked her out of a spin and Preacher stood on the porch, arms crossed over his massive chest, grinning like a schoolgirl.

When Mel called June Hudson the next morning to tell her about the new vehicle, June suggested they get together at her home the next Sunday for a casual dinner of burgers and hot dogs. "If I bring some potato salad and beer, may I bring a friend?" Mel asked. She told herself she asked because this little picnic was comprised of couples, except for June's dad, old Doc Hudson, and she didn't want to feel oddly alone. But really it was because she had found she didn't much like being away from Jack.

"So," Jack said, grinning, "are you bringing me out of the closet?"

"Just for the day," she answered. "Because you've been very good."

June had the kind of adorable country house that Mel had fantasized about when planning her escape from the city—wide porch, bright paint, cozy furnishings, right up on a knoll from which she had a view of the valley. Part of her decor was comprised of needlepoint pillows and quilts—June was a master stitcher. She seemed to have the perfect country doctor life—her husband, Jim, to back her up and help with the baby; an ornery father butting in all the time and supportive and delightful friends in John and Susan Stone.

Susan was a nurse, so she and Mel compared notes. Plus, Susan and John were transplants from the city and she was candid about how it took her a while to appreciate the slower pace and get used to the absence of amenities in Grace Valley. "I used to go to the day spa down the street for a facial and eyebrow wax," she said. "Now it's a major undertaking just to buy groceries." Susan was also very, very pregnant. She was continually pressing on her lower back, pushing her belly forward.

The women sat on the porch. June rocked in the porch swing and nursed her baby, Susan fidgeted, trying to get a throw pillow to sit right against her lower back, while out in the yard the men stood around the Hummer, each one with a beer, occasionally looking inside or under the hood.

"That's quite an attractive man you brought along," June observed.

Mel glanced out at them. Jim and Jack were about the same height and weight and both wore their uniforms of jeans, plaid or denim shirts and boots. John, just a bit shorter at a very respectable six feet, was not quite as casually dressed in his khakis and polo, but a damn fine specimen. "Look at them," Mel said. "They look like an ad for *Virility Magazine*. Mother Nature's best work."

"Mother Nature is twisted," Susan said, squirming. "If she had any compassion, we'd have six-week pregnancies." She winced. "I bet it's really Father Nature. The creep."

"Uncomfortable, huh?" Mel asked.

"I'm going to have back labor again, I just know it. It's such a nice day to be so pregnant."

"This is nice, June. Thank you," Mel said. "It's so relaxing, low stress, for me if not poor Susan. Does everybody in the valley have such simple, uncomplicated lives?"

June surprised her by laughing, after which Susan joined in. Sydney, Susan's seven-year-old, burst through the door, blond curls flying, and ran down the steps with Sadie, June's collie chasing her into the yard. She ran to her dad and hung on his leg for a minute, then continued racing around the yard with the dog in pursuit, the collie trying to herd her back to the group.

"Something's funny?" Mel asked.

"Things haven't exactly been uncomplicated around here. A couple of years ago I was pretty sure I'd never get married, much less have a baby."

This caused Mel to scoot to the edge of her chair. "It seems like you and Jim have been together forever."

"He came into my clinic late at night a little over a year ago, looking for help with a comrade's gunshot wound. Jim's now a retired law enforcement officer. When I met him, though, he was skulking around the countryside, working some case—and in the dark of night he'd sneak into my bedroom. I kept him my little secret for quite a while—until my tummy started to grow."

"No way."

"Oh, yeah. No one in town knew I even had a man in my life, and then suddenly I'm pregnant. And not a little pregnant—by the time I realized it, I was already pretty far along. We've only been married a few months. We didn't get it done before the baby came."

"In a small town like this?" Mel was flabbergasted.

"People were decent about it. I mean, we did have a flood, lost our preacher for a while, there was a huge drug raid out in the woods, one thing after another. And probably because they all took to Jim so quickly. But my dad almost had a stroke."

"And maybe because Jim moved right into your house and wouldn't let you out of his sight until you agreed to marry him," Susan added.

"I had been single a long time," June said. "I was a little nervous about the whole thing. I mean, we hadn't even been together all that long—and my God, not very often. I don't know how it happened," June said. "But it sure happened fast."

"No—you know how it happened," Susan said. "This," she said, petting the giant mound that would soon be screaming to be changed, "is the great mystery. We had to try for a long time to get Sydney. We needed a little help, in fact. I just don't get pregnant."

Maybe in time Mel would join in, share her secrets. For now, though, she just wanted to hear theirs.

"John and I were having a big fight," Susan said. "We were barely speaking. I had him sleeping on the couch—he was such an ass. By the time I forgave him and let him back in bed with me, he was packing quite a punch." She giggled. Her eyes twinkled.

"At least you're married," June put in.

"Tell us about your man," Susan said.

"Oh, Jack's not my man," she said automatically. "He is the first friend I made in Virgin River, however. He runs a little bar and grill across the street from Doc's— as much a meeting place as a restaurant. They don't even have a menu—his partner, a big scary-looking guy named Preacher who turns out to be an angel—cooks up one breakfast item, one lunch item and one dinner item every day. On an ambitious day, they might have two items—maybe something left from the day before. They run it on the cheap, fish a lot, and help out around town wherever needed. He fixed up the cabin I was given to stay in while I'm there."

The women didn't say anything for a moment. Then Susan said, "Honey, I have a feeling he doesn't think of you as a friend. Have you seen the way he looks at you?"

She glanced at him and as if he could feel her gaze, he turned his eyes on her. Soft and hard all at once. "Yeah," Mel said. "He promised to stop doing that."

"Girl, I'd never make a man stop doing that to me! You can't possibly not know how much he—"

"Susan," June said. "We don't mean to pry, Mel."

"June doesn't mean to pry, but I do. You mean to say he hasn't…?"

Mel felt her cheeks flame. "Well, it isn't what you think," she said.

June and Susan burst out laughing, loud enough to cause the men to turn away from their conversation and look up at the porch. Mel laughed in spite of herself. Ah, she had missed this—girlfriends. Talking about the secret stuff, the private stuff. Laughing at their weaknesses and strengths.

"That's what I thought," Susan said. "He looks like he can't wait to get you alone. And do unspeakable things to you."

Mel sighed in spite of herself, her cheeks growing hotter. *He can't,* she almost said. *And ohh…*

June took the baby off her breast and put him on her shoulder to burp him. The group of men seemed to turn as one and head for the porch, Jim first. "Sounds like trouble up here," he said. He reached for the baby and took over the burping.

John lowered his lips to Susan's forehead and gave her a kiss. His other hand ran smoothly over her belly. "How are you doing, honey?" he asked solicitously.

"Great. Right after dinner, I want you to get it out of me."

He handed her his beer. "Here, have a slug and mellow out."

Jack stood behind Mel and put his hand on her shoulder. Without even realizing it, she reached up and stroked his hand.

"I'll start the grill," old Doc Hudson said, going through the house.

They all sat around a picnic table in the backyard, talking about their towns, their cases. Mel got some tips from John on home births—he explained that he was an OB before doing a second residency in family practice. He'd never done a home birth in Sausalito, but once he'd arrived in Grace Valley he'd become the local midwife. He liked the hospital but couldn't convince all the women to leave their homes to deliver. Small-town stories were told, laughter was shared, and too soon it was growing dark.

As Jack and Mel were leaving, Mel took an opportunity to speak with June about the baby—Chloe. She expressed her concern that they still hadn't heard anything from Social Services.

June was frowning. "It's true that the county has a lot of ground to cover, but they're usually pretty good. One of my closest friends is a social worker, although she's in Mendocino County. I could run this by her—get her impression."

"Maybe you should. Especially if you think this is irregular," Mel said.

"I'll do it, and give you a call. Meanwhile, if you consider the baby your patient, you can assess the situation. See if you can find out anything. Doc Mullins is smarter than he lets on," June said. "He's a crafty old devil. Find out if he's got something up his sleeve."

Mel hugged June while Jack waited at the car. "Thank you. For everything. It was a perfect day."

Driving back to Virgin River, Mel was lost in one of the most serene moods she'd felt in a long time. Her connection to this place had deepened with the new friendships, and no small part of that was their acceptance of Jack.

"You're awfully quiet," Jack observed.

"I had such a good time," she said dreamily.

"Me, too. Nice people, your friends."

"They liked you, too. Did you know that Jim is a former cop?"

"I got that, yeah."

"And John and Susan came up here from the city a couple of years ago. And Elmer—the old doc—he's a riot. I'm so glad we did that."

They drove in companionable silence until they neared Virgin River. Jack said, "What do you want to do tonight? My place?"

"Would you be terribly hurt if we took a night off?"

"Whatever you need, Mel. Just so long as nothing's wrong."

"Nothing's wrong. In fact, I've never felt more right with the world. I just thought I'd go home, shower off the picnic and get a good night's sleep."

"It's up to you." He reached across the front seat and

grabbed her hand. "It's always up to you." He drew her hand to his lips and pressed a soft kiss into her palm.

He pulled up to the bar and they traded places so she could drive home. After a kiss good-night, she left him there and went out to the cabin.

As she entered the clearing in front of her home, the first thing she noticed was a big, dark SUV parked in front of her cabin. The driver, the big nameless man with the ball cap and hair that curled beneath it was leaning against the passenger door. When she pulled up, he straightened and slipped his thumbs in his front pockets. She recognized him and the vehicle at once. This was the big guy who'd stopped by Doc's several weeks ago, and what flashed through her mind was "someone's pregnant." Then she took note of his side-arm—a big gun, with straps holding the holster to his thigh. But his hands stayed away from it.

In a place like this, she was never sure how to feel about a person toting weapons. If she'd seen this in the city, she'd have ducked for cover. But out here, it didn't necessarily mean anything. She could play it safe and make a run for it, though she didn't handle the Hummer so well yet. Besides, the man had already approached her in the clear light of day to ask about a delivery. She pulled up, keeping her headlights on him, and he seemed to straighten expectantly, stepping away from the SUV. She opened her door and stepped out. "What are you doing out here?"

"That baby's coming," he said.

No matter what the circumstances, the same thing seemed to happen to her when she heard that—she stopped thinking of herself and began to concentrate on the work at hand, the mother and child. "That was pretty quick," she said.

"No. I was pretty slow," he said. "She kept it to herself for a long time and I didn't realize she was this ready, this—look, I need you to come. To help."

"But why are you here? Why didn't you go into town, to the doctor's office? I almost didn't come home tonight…"

"Lucky for me you did. I couldn't go to town, couldn't run the risk of someone wanting to come with you, or someone telling you not to come with me. Please, let's go."

"Where?"

"I'll take you," he said.

"No. I'll follow you. I'll just go inside, make a call and—"

He took a step toward her. "We can't do it that way. It'll be better for all of us if you don't know exactly where you are. And really, it has to be just you."

"Oh, gimme a break," she said with a short laugh. "You expect me to get in that car with you? Without knowing you or where we're going?"

"That's the general idea, yeah," he said. "She thinks she's doing this alone, having the baby. But I'd rather you come with me, in case… What if there's a problem? Huh?"

"I can call Doc Mullins, maybe he'll go with you. I don't make a habit of getting in a vehicle with a stranger to be driven to some mysterious birthing…"

"Yeah, I wish it was mysterious. I wish it wasn't happening, but it is. I don't want to have to do this at all—but I also don't want anything stupid to go wrong that we could prevent. I don't want any unnecessary trouble. You should probably be there. In case."

"This your baby?" she asked him.

He shrugged. "Yeah, could be. Probably."

"I don't even know there *is* a baby coming. I've never seen the mother," Mel said. "What if there is no baby?" she said.

He took a tentative step toward her. "What if there is?" he asked.

She looked around her. It was obvious if he wanted to hurt her, he wouldn't need to take her anywhere. He wouldn't even need to draw that weapon. They were completely isolated. He could take ten short steps toward her, whack her across the jaw and it would be done.

He spread his arms wide. "I just have to keep the place covered. It's a place of business, all right? Could we please go get that baby born? I'm not kidding, it freaks me out. She says she's been hurting all day. And there's blood."

"A lot of blood?"

"What's a lot? Not puddles, but enough to make me get in the truck and come for you. Pronto."

"You have a gun," she pointed out to him. "I hate guns."

He rubbed a hand along the back of his neck. "Protection for you," he said. "I'm just a businessman, but there's some crazy people stuck out there in the woods. I'm not going to let anything happen to you—that would make my life way too complicated. I don't want any attention from the sheriff. We really gotta go. There's a baby coming. Real soon."

"Oh, shit," she said. "Don't do this to me."

"I'm doing something to you? I'm asking. That's all. I want to get a baby born without anything stupid and wrong happening to the baby or the mother. Get me?"

"Why didn't you just take her to the hospital?" she asked him.

"She works for me, okay? And she has warrants. They ID her at a hospital and she's going to jail. You can't take care of a baby from jail. That's why it's gotta be this way."

"Look, go get her and take her to town, to Doc's. We'll do it there and no one will ask any questions about—"

"I'm telling you, there isn't *time!*" he shouted. The look on his face was desperate and he took a pleading step toward her, arms wide, palms out. "It's gonna happen soon, and we're almost an hour from her! We might not make it as it is!"

She took a deep breath. "We should take the Hummer..."

"Can't," he said. "Can't leave my vehicle here in case someone comes looking for you and finds only my truck. Sorry."

"I'll get my bag," Mel said reluctantly.

She grabbed her bag out of the Hummer and got in his SUV. He held a black sash in his hand. "You should blindfold," he said.

"Get real," she answered. "I'm not doing that. Hurry up. If she's been hurting all day, just hurry up."

"Put it on. Come on."

"So I won't see what? Where we're headed? I'm from L.A., buddy. I've been here three months and I can hardly get myself to town in the daylight along these mountain roads. It's pitch-black. Just move it—I'm never going to be able to tell anyone where we went." And more softly, "Besides, I wouldn't. The only thing that would make me do that is if I needed to find you, or her, to save a life."

"This some kind of trick?" he asked.

"Oh, please. Now stop scaring me. I might panic

and throw myself out of the car, and then where would you be?"

He put the SUV in gear and peeled out of the drive and headed east. "I hope you're not lying to me, setting me up. Because after this is taken care of, you don't have to see me again. Unless...?"

"Setting you up?" She laughed. "Did I come to *your* house? You want to just get this baby born on your own?" she asked him.

"I never did anything like this before," he said, his voice solemn and serious. "If I'd known there was a baby coming, I would've taken her somewhere. Somewhere out of this county. But I didn't know. Just do your thing, I'll pay you, and we'll be done. Okay?"

"We'll be done?" she asked. "These babies that no one expects? Sometimes they last about ninety years! After labor and delivery, there's stuff to do! Children to raise!"

"Yeah," he said tiredly. Focused on the road he whirled the SUV around the tight turns, gunned the engine when the road was straight. But the straight-aways were short, always followed by more tight turns. Most of the time the speedometer read about twenty miles per hour. He used not only his headlights, but the lights mounted on his roof. It was a long, silent spell before he said, "I'll take care of what they need. After the baby's here, when she's up to it, there's a sister she can go to in Nevada."

"Why's this all so secret?" Mel asked. She looked at his profile and saw him grin largely. He had a slight bump in his nose. Under the bill of his ball cap his eyes crinkled when he smiled like that, and she noted that while he was rugged and scruffy, he was not un-attractive.

"Jesus, you're something, you know that? Just go with it, little girl."

"How'd you know where I live?" she asked him.

He laughed. "I hope you don't think you're hiding out there, miss. Because everyone knows where the new midwife lives."

"Oh, great," she said under her breath. "That's just great."

"It'll be okay. Nobody wants you hurt or anything. That would just bring a whole heap of trouble on a whole lot of people." He stole a glance at her. "Someone like you goes missing, three counties go tearing up the hills. That's bad for business."

"Well," she said softly, "I guess I should be honored." She looked over at him. "Why am I not feeling so honored yet?"

He shrugged. "I guess this is all new to you."

"Yeah," she said. "Boy howdy."

They rode silently for a while, twisting around the mountain roads, up and over, down and around. "How'd you get yourself into this mess?" she asked him.

He shrugged. "Just one of those things. Let's not talk about this anymore."

"She better be okay," Mel said.

"That's what I'm thinking. Jesus, she better be okay."

Mel thought again about all the help available in a big city—lots of people. Not the least of whom was law enforcement—real handy. Cops parked right inside the hospital all the time. Right now, it was just her. Before her, it had been just Doc. If a woman was having a baby out in the middle of nowhere and there was only one midwife in the area, what were the options?

Mel began to tremble. What if they were too late and something wasn't right—what if things turned nasty?

She wasn't sure how long they'd been on the road. Definitely over a half hour. Maybe forty-five minutes. The man took a left turn down a one-lane dirt road that seemed to stop at a dead end. He got out and pushed open what appeared to be a gate made entirely of bushes and they drove through, down a potholed, washboard road thickly enshrouded by big trees. At the end, the powerful lights on the roof of his SUV illuminated a small building and an even smaller trailer. There were lights on inside the trailer.

"This it is. She's in there," he said, pointing at the small trailer.

That's when she knew, and was amazed that she hadn't understood sooner. She—who was so cynical about the crusty side of big city medicine—was totally naive about the pretty mountains and what she had thought was benign small-town life. The house and trailer were buried beneath the trees, camouflaged by the tall pines, and right between the two was a generator. This was why everything was so secret, why there was a gun for protection—he was a grower. Further, this was the reason he'd hire someone to work for him who had felony warrants, the only kind that could get you sent straight to jail—because that's who you could get to sit out in the woods and watch over a crop like this.

"Is she alone in there?" Mel asked.

"Yeah," he said.

"Then I need your help. I'll need you to get me some things."

"I don't want any part of—"

"You better just do as I say, if we're going to salvage this situation," she said, her voice sounding more authoritative than she felt inside. She rushed to the trailer, opened the door, stepped up and in. Five steps took her through a little galley and into what passed for a bedroom, a berth, upon which a young woman writhed beneath a sheet soiled with blood and fluids.

Mel put a knee on the bed, placed her bag beside her knee and opened it, dropped her jacket off her shoulders onto the floor behind her, and there was a transformation within her, taking her from scared and uncertain to driven and focused. Confident. "Easy does it," she said gently. "Let's have a look." Over her shoulder she said, "I need a large, empty pan or bowl, some towels or blankets—soft as possible—for the baby. A pan of warm water for cleanup. Ah…" she said, lifting the sheet. "All right, sweetheart, you have to help me. Pant like this," she instructed, demonstrating while she put on her gloves. "No pushing. More light!" she yelled over her shoulder.

The baby was crowning; another five minutes and Mel would have missed the whole thing. She heard the man moving around behind her and suddenly a saucepan appeared beside her bag. Then there were a couple of towels and an overhead light flicked on. Mel made a mental note to add a flashlight to the articles in her bag.

The woman grunted weakly and the baby's head emerged. "Pant," Mel instructed. "Do *not* push—we have a cord situation. Easy, easy…" She gently tugged on the ropey, purplish cord, pulling it from around the neck, freeing the baby. She hadn't been in the trailer for five minutes, but it was the most critical few minutes of this infant's life. She slipped a gloved finger into the birth canal and gently eased the baby toward her. Cries filled the room before the baby was completely born; the strong, healthy cries of a newborn. Her heart lifted in relief; this was a strong baby. Suction was not even necessary.

"You have a son," she said softly. "He looks beautiful." She looked over the raised knees of her patient and saw a young woman of perhaps twenty-five years at most, her long, dark hair damp from perspiration, her black eyes tired but glowing, and a very small smile on her lips. Mel clamped and cut the cord, wrapped the baby and made her way around the narrow space to the woman's head. "Let's put this baby on the breast," she said softly. "Then I can deal with the placenta." The woman reached for her baby. Mel noticed that sitting beside her on the bed was a large basket, ready to receive the baby. "This is not your first," Mel said.

She shook her head and a large tear spilled down her cheek as she took her son. "Third," she said in a whisper. "I don't have the other ones."

Mel brushed the damp hair back from her brow. "Have you been out here alone?"

"Just the last month or so. I was here with someone, and he left."

"Left you, out in the woods in a trailer, in advanced pregnancy?" Mel asked softly, running a finger over the baby's perfect head. "You must have been so scared. Come on," she said, giving the woman's T-shirt a tug. "Let the baby nurse. It'll make a lot of things feel better." The infant rooted a little bit, then found the nipple and suckled.

Mel went back to her position, donned fresh gloves from her bag and began to massage the uterus. She heard the trailer door close behind her and glanced over her shoulder. On the short counter in the galley she saw a dishpan of water.

Mel's patient was able to direct her to supplies from newborn diapers to sterile wipes. She found clean sheets and peri-pads, washed up the baby and mother, then sat on the edge of the bed for a long while, holding the baby. Her patient reached over and held Mel's hand a couple of times, giving a grateful squeeze, but they didn't talk. An hour after the birth, Mel looked in the refrigerator. She rummaged around for a glass and poured the woman some juice. Then she brought a plastic container of water near the bed. She checked her patient's bleeding, which was normal. She got her stethoscope out of the bag and listened to the baby's heart, then the mother's. Coloring was good, respirations normal, mother exhausted and the baby, sleeping contentedly. All was complete.

"Tell me something," Mel said. "Is the baby going to have drug issues?" The woman just shook her head, letting her eyes close. "All right—there's a small clinic in Virgin River. I work with the doctor there. He won't ask you about yourself or the baby, so you have nothing to worry about. He likes to say he's in medicine, not law enforcement. But you both should be looked at to be sure everything is okay."

Mel picked up her jacket off the floor. "Is there anything else I can get for you?" she asked her patient. The woman shook her head. "Plenty of fluids tonight, for the breast milk." Then she went around the narrow space to the head of the bed and leaned down, placing a small kiss on her head. "Congratulations," she whispered. Then wiped a couple of tears gently from her patient's cheeks. "I hope everything works out for you and the baby. Be very safe and careful."

"Thank you," the woman said softly. "If you hadn't come…"

"Shh," Mel shushed. "I came. And you're fine."

Mel realized, not for the first time, that it didn't matter if her patient was a happily married Sunday-school teacher who'd been waiting years for her first baby, or a felon handcuffed to the bed—a birth was the great equalizer. In this vulnerable state, mothers were mothers, and it was her passion to serve them. Helping a baby safely into the world, its mother accomplishing the experience with health and dignity, was the only thing that mattered. Even if it meant putting herself at some risk, she was bound to do what she could. She couldn't control what became of a mother and child after she left them, but when called upon for this, she was unable to refuse.

Her chauffeur was waiting at the SUV as she came out. He opened the passenger door for her. "They're okay?" he asked anxiously.

"They seem to have come through very well, considering. I guess you don't live there with them?"

He shook his head. "That's why I didn't see she was pregnant. I only come around sometimes and I dealt mostly with her man. I guess he left her when—"

"When he realized you'd dealt with her a little, too?" Mel finished for him. She shook her head and got into the car. When he was in beside her she said, "I want two things from you, and the way I see it, you owe me. I want you to go back there tonight, stay with them, so you can get them to the hospital if anything goes south in the night. If there's any real heavy bleeding, or if the baby has problems. Don't panic—they seem good— but if you don't want to take any unnecessary chances, that's what you do. Then, in a couple of days, two to four days, bring them to the clinic to be checked over. Doctor Mullins in Virgin River won't ask any questions, and all I care about right now is that they stay healthy." She looked over at him. "You'll do that?"

"I'll get it done," he said.

She leaned her head back against the seat and let her eyes close. The hard and fast beating of her heart now was not from fear, but from the rapid decompression of adrenaline that always followed an emergency. It left her feeling weak, a little shaky, slightly nauseous. If the conditions had been different, she might have felt even more alive than before the birth. This one, however, had been rife with complications.

When he pulled up in front of her cabin, he held out a wad of bills toward her. "I don't want your money," she said. "It's drug money."

"Suit yourself," he said, putting it in the front pocket of his jacket.

She stared at him for a second. "If you'd left her to deliver herself, if I hadn't gone with you, that baby wouldn't have— You understand about the cord, right? Wrapped around his neck?"

"Yeah, I get that. Thanks."

"I almost didn't go with you. Really, there's no reason I should have trusted you."

"Yeah. You're a brave little girl. Try to forget my face. For your own sake."

"Listen, I'm in medicine, I'm not a cop," she said. Then she gave a weak huff of laughter. She'd been used to having the backup of LAPD, but tonight it had been down to her. There was no backup. And if she hadn't been there, it could have been down to Doc, who was seventy. What was going to happen five years from now? To her chauffeur she said, "Now keep it in your pants or use protection—I don't really feel like doing business with you again."

He grinned at her. "Tough little broad, aren'tcha? Don't worry. I'm not looking to have that kind of trouble again."

She got out of the SUV without comment and walked toward her porch. By the time she neared her front door, he had turned around and driven out of the clearing. She sank into the porch chair and sat in the dark. The night sounds echoed around her; crickets, an occasional owl, wind whirring through the tall pines.

She wished she could just go inside, undress and go to bed alone, but she was wired and out of courage for the night. After a moment, when she could no longer hear the engine of his big SUV, she went down the stairs to the Hummer. She drove into town and parked behind the bar, next to Jack's truck. The sound of the engine and car door must have awakened him, because a light went on and the back door to his quarters opened. He stood in the frame, a dim light behind him, wearing a pair of hastily pulled on jeans. She walked right into his arms.

"What are you doing here?" he asked softly, pulling her inside and closing the door.

"I went out on a call. A baby. And I didn't want to go home. Didn't want to be alone after that. It was a close one, Jack."

He slipped his hands inside her jacket to hold her closer. "Did everything work out okay?"

"Yes," she said. "But there wasn't very much time. If I'd been five minutes longer getting there… The cord was around his neck." She shook her head. "But I did get there. And he's a beautiful baby."

"Where?" he asked, smoothing her hair over her ear.

"The other side of Clear River," she said, remembering what the man had said when he pulled up to the front of Doc's clinic. In truth, she had no idea where they'd gone. He could've driven around in circles for all she knew.

"You're trembling," he said, pressing his lips to her brow.

"Yeah, a little. Coming down from the experience." She tilted her head to look up at him. "Is it okay that I'm here?"

"Of course it is. Mel, what's wrong?"

"The mother was going to deliver herself, but the father got nervous and came for me." She shivered. "I thought I had some wild experiences in L.A.," she said with a weak laugh. "If you'd told me a year ago that I'd go out to some poor trailer in the woods, in the middle of the night to deliver a baby, I would have said, never gonna happen."

He rubbed a knuckle along her cheek. "Who was it?"

She shook her head. If she told him she didn't have the first idea, he'd flip. "They're not from around here, Jack. He dropped by Doc's a while ago, looking for someone who could handle a birth. I can't talk about patients unless they say it's okay, but these patients, I didn't even ask. They weren't married or anything. She lives in a crappy little trailer by herself. It's a pretty horrid situation for her." And she thought, *I'm doing things out here in the mountains that I never, in a million years, thought I could do. Terrifying, impossible, dangerous things. Exhilarating things that no one else would do. And if no one had, there'd be a dead baby. Possibly a critical mother.* She leaned her head against Jack's chest and took a deep, steadying breath.

"He called you?" Jack asked.

Damn. Bold-faced lies to straight questions were so hard for her. "He was waiting at the cabin. If I'd stayed the night here with you, I'd have missed him and that baby wouldn't have made it."

"Did you tell him where to find you after hours?"

She shook her head before she thought about her answer. "He must have asked someone," she said. "Everyone in Virgin River knows where I live. And probably
half the people in Clear River."

"God," he said, tightening his arms around her. "Did
it ever occur to you that you could have been at risk?"
he asked her.

"For a minute or two," she said. She looked up at him
and smiled. "I don't expect you to understand this—but
there was a baby coming. And I'm glad I went. Besides,
I wasn't in trouble. The mother was."

He let out a slow, relieved breath. "Jesus. I'm going
to have to keep a much closer eye on you." He kissed
her brow. "Something happened tonight. Something
you're not telling me. Whatever it was—never, never
let that happen again."

"Could we get in bed, please? I really need you to
hold me."

Jack was sitting on the porch of the bar, tying off
flies, when a familiar black Range Rover pulled slowly
into town and parked right in front of Doc's. He sat forward on the porch chair and watched as the driver got
out, went around to the passenger door and opened it.
A woman carrying a small bundle got out of the car,
walked up the porch steps to enter the clinic and Jack's
heart began to pound.

When the woman entered Doc's, the man went back
to his SUV and leaned against the hood, his back to
Jack. He took out a small penknife and began to idly
clean under his nails. Because of the kind of guy this
was, Jack knew he had seen him sitting there, on the
porch. He would have observed everything worth seeing
when he came into town; he'd know every escape route,

any threat. Today, coming into town with a woman and new baby, Jack would bet there wouldn't be contraband of any kind in that vehicle and if he had weapons, they'd be registered. And...his license plate was splattered with mud so it couldn't be read. Lame trick. But Jack remembered it; he'd memorized it the first time this guy had come to town.

So, he hadn't come to Virgin River for a couple of drinks a while back. He'd come to see if there was medical assistance here. Mel had said that the delivery that shook her up had occurred on the other side of Clear River and there was no doctor or clinic in that town. Grace Valley and Garberville were just a little farther away, but there were more people around.

It was a little over a half hour before the woman came out, Mel walking behind her. The woman turned and shook Mel's hand; Mel squeezed her upper arm The man helped her into the car and drove slowly out of town.

Jack stood and Mel met his eyes across the street. They were on their respective porches and, even from the distance, she could see the deepening frown gather on his face. Then he walked over to her.

She slipped her hands into the pockets of her jeans as he approached. When he was near, he put one foot up on the porch steps and leaned his forearms on his bent knee, looking up at her. The frown was not angry, but definitely unhappy. "Doc know what you did?" he asked her.

She gave a nod. "He knows I delivered a baby, if that's what you mean. It's what I do, Jack."

"You have to promise me, you're not going to do that again. Not for someone like him."

"You know him?" she asked.

"No. But he's been in the bar and I know what he is. The problem isn't him bringing a woman to the doctor, you know. It's you being on his turf. It's you going with him in the middle of the night. Alone. Just because he says—"

"I wasn't threatened," she said. "I was asked. And he had been by the clinic before, looking for a doctor, so he wasn't a complete stranger."

"Listen to me," Jack said firmly. "People like that aren't going to threaten you in your clinic or my bar. They like to keep a real low profile. They don't want their crops raided. But out there," he said, giving his chin a jerk toward the mountains to their east, "things can happen. He could've decided you were a threat to his business and—"

"No," she said, shaking her head. "He wouldn't let anything happen to me. *That* would be a threat to his business—"

"Is that what he told you? Because I wouldn't take his word for that." He shook his head. "You can't do that, Melinda. You can't go alone to some illegal grower's camp."

"I doubt there will be a situation like that again," she answered.

"Promise you won't," he said.

She shook her head. "I have a job to do, Jack. If I hadn't gone—"

"Mel, do you understand what I'm telling you? I'm not going to lose you because you're willing to take stupid chances. Promise me."

She pursed her lips and merely lifted her chin defiantly. "Never…never suggest I'm stupid."

"I wouldn't do that. But you have to understand—"

"It was down to me. There was a baby coming, there

really was, and I had to go because if I hadn't it could've been disastrous. There wasn't time to think about it."

"Have you always been this stubborn?" he asked.

"There was a baby coming. And it doesn't matter to me who the woman is or what she does for a living."

"Would you have done something like that in L.A.?" he asked, lifting an eyebrow.

She thought for just a moment about how life had changed since leaving L.A. After being picked up by a gun-carrying illegal grower and delivering a baby back in the woods, shouldn't she be packing? Running for her life? Unwilling to ever be put in a position like that again? Instead, she was doing a mental inventory of what was in Doc's refrigerator, wondering if it wasn't about time to take a few things out to Paulis's camp. It had been a couple of weeks since she'd last done that.

Although she really didn't want a repeat of the scenario with the grower, something about the experience got her attention. When she'd left L.A., they didn't have any trouble filling her job. There were ten people who could do what she did, and do it just as well. In Virgin River, and the surrounding area, it was her and Doc. There just wasn't anyone else. There was no day off or week off. And if she had hesitated even long enough to fetch Doc to go with her, that baby wouldn't have made it.

I came here because I thought life would be simpler, easier, quieter, she thought. *That there would be fewer challenges, and certainly nothing to fear. I thought I'd feel safer, not that I'd have to grow stronger. Braver.*

She smiled at him. "In L.A. we send the paramedics. You see any paramedics? I'm in this little town that you said was uncomplicated. You're a big liar, that's what you are…"

"I told you, we have our own kind of drama. Mel, you should listen to me—"

"This is a real complicated place sometimes. I'm just going to do my job the best I can."

He stepped up onto the porch, put a finger under her chin and lifted it, gazing into her eyes. "Melinda, you're getting to be a real handful."

"Yeah?" she asked, smiling. "So are you."

Thirteen

Mel didn't tell Doc where she was going, just that there were a couple of people she wanted to look in on. He asked her, since she was out, to stop and check on Frannie Butler, an elderly woman who lived alone and had high blood pressure. "Make sure she has plenty of medicine and that she's actually taking it," he said. He popped an antacid.

"Should you be having so much heartburn?" she asked him.

"Everyone my age has this much heartburn," he answered, brushing her off.

Mel got Frannie's blood pressure out of the way first, though it wasn't quick. The thing about house calls in little towns like this was it involved tea and cookies and conversation. It was as much a social event as medical care. Then she drove out to the Anderson ranch. When she pulled up, Buck came out of the shed with a shovel in his hand and an astonished look on his face when he saw the Hummer. "Who-ee," he said. "When did that thing turn up?"

"Just last week," she said. "Better for getting around the back roads than my little foreign job, as Doc calls it."

"Mind if I have a look?" he asked, peering into the window.

"Help yourself. I'd like to check on Chloe. Lilly inside?"

"Yup. In the kitchen. Go on in—door's open." And he immediately stuck his head in the driver's door, taken with the vehicle.

Mel went around back. Through the kitchen window she could see Lilly's profile as she sat at the kitchen table. The door was open and only the screen door was closed. She gave a couple of quick raps, called out, "Hey, Lilly," and opened the door. And was stopped dead in her tracks.

Lilly, too late, pulled the baby blanket over her exposed breast. She was nursing Chloe.

Mel was frozen in place. "Lilly?" she said, confused.

Tears sprang to the woman's eyes. "Mel," she said, her voice a mere whisper. The baby immediately started to whimper and Lilly tried to comfort her, but Chloe wasn't done nursing. Lilly's cheeks were instantly red and damp; the hands that fussed with her shirt and held the baby were shaking.

"How is this possible?" Mel asked, completely confused. Lilly's youngest child was grown—she couldn't possibly have breast milk. But then she realized what had happened. "Oh, my God!" Chloe was Lilly's baby! Mel walked slowly to the kitchen table and pulled out a chair to sit down because her knees were shaking. "Does everyone in the family know?"

Lilly shook her head, her eyes pinched closed. "Just me and Buck," she finally said. "I wasn't in my right mind."

Mel shook her head, baffled. "Lilly. What in the world happened?"

"I thought they'd come for her—the county. And that someone would want her right off. Some nice young couple who couldn't have a baby. Then she'd have young parents and I —" She shook her head pitifully. "I just didn't think I could do it again," she said, dissolving into sobs.

Mel got out of her chair and went to her, taking the fussing baby, trying to comfort her. Lilly laid her head down on the tabletop and wept hard tears.

"I'm so ashamed," she cried. When she looked up at Mel again she said, "I raised six kids. I spent thirty years raising kids and we got seven grandkids. I couldn't imagine another one. So late in my life."

"Wasn't there anyone you could talk to about this?" Mel asked.

She shook her head. "Mel," she wept. "Country people… Small-town country people know that once you talk about it… No," she said, shaking her head. "I was sick when I realized I was pregnant and forty-eight years old. I was sick and a little crazy."

"Did you ever consider terminating the pregnancy?"

"I did, but I couldn't. I just couldn't. I make no judgment, but it isn't in me."

"What about arranging an adoption?" Mel asked.

"No one in this family, in this town for that matter, would ever understand that. They'd have looked at me like I killed her. Even my friends—good women my age who would understand how I felt, could never accept it if I said I didn't want to raise another child, my own child. I didn't know what else to do."

"And now what do you intend to do?" Mel asked.

"I don't know," she wailed. "I just don't know."

"What if they come now—Social Services? Lilly, can you give her up?"

She was shaking her head. "I don't know. I don't think so. Oh, God, I wish I had a chance to do it over."

"Lilly—how did you conceal your pregnancy? How did you give birth alone?"

"No one pays much attention—I'm overweight. Buck helped. Poor Buck—he didn't even know till it was almost time—I kept it from him, too. Maybe we can adopt her now?"

Mel sat down again, still jiggling the baby. She looked down at Chloe, who was burying her fist in her mouth, squirming and fussing. "You don't have to adopt her, you gave birth to her. But I'm awful worried about you. You abandoned her. That must have almost killed you."

"I watched the whole time. Till you and Jack came to the porch. I wouldn't let anything happen to her. It was terrible hard, but I felt like I had to. I just didn't know what else to do."

"Oh, Lilly," Mel said. "I'm not sure you're okay yet. This is just too crazy." She passed the baby back to Lilly. "Here, nurse your baby. She's hungry."

"I don't know that I can," she said, but she took the baby. "I might be too upset."

"Just hook her up—she'll do the work," Mel said. When the baby was again at the breast, Mel put her arms around Lilly and just held them both for a few minutes.

"What are you going to do?" Lilly asked, her voice a quivering mess.

"God, Lilly, I don't know. Do you understand that doctors and midwives protect your confidentiality? If I'd been here when you'd discovered your pregnancy, you could have trusted me with your secret. You could have trusted Doc, or Dr. Stone in Grace Valley. The people in the family planning clinic keep confidential records—they would have helped. But…" She took a breath. "We're also bound by laws."

"I just didn't know where to turn."

Mel shook her head sadly. "You must have been so scared."

"I haven't ever been through anything as difficult in my life, Mel. And me and Buck, we've had some real hard times holding this family and ranch together."

"How did you keep the breast-feeding from your kids? I assume they're around quite a bit—and don't your boys work the ranch with Buck?"

"I give her a bottle if anyone's around, and I nurse her when we're alone."

"Even though you planned to let her go, you nursed her? You didn't have to do that."

Lilly shrugged. "It seemed like the least I could give her, after what I did. I'm sorry. I'm so, so sorry. You just don't understand what it's like—spending your whole life raising kids—and then having another one on the way when you're a grandmother. Me and Buck—we've struggled with money our entire marriage! You just don't understand."

"Oh, Lilly, I know you were terrified and desperate. I can imagine. But I'm not going to kid you, this is complicated."

"But will you help us? Will you help Chloe?"

"I'll do what I can—but those laws…" She sighed. "I'll do whatever I can," she said gently. "We'll find a way to sort this out. Just let me think."

Not long after, when Mel was sure that Lilly was calmed down and safe, Mel left her. She'd been with her about forty minutes, but Buck was still combing the Hummer with envious eyes. "Helluva ride, Mel," he said, grinning.

"Buck, go in the house and comfort your wife. I just walked in on her nursing your daughter."

"Oh, boy," he said.

It was on the ride back to town that Mel realized Doc Mullins was onto this. In fact, he might've given birth to it, so to speak. He'd always said the mother would turn up, and she had. Weeks ago when Mel had told him that Lilly had offered to take in the baby, his eyebrows had shot up in surprise. He hadn't expected it to be Lilly. He had *never* called social services. And yet, he never brought her into the conspiracy.

By the time she got back to his house it was after four and she was steamed up pretty good. Doc was seeing a patient who was coughing and hacking like a dying man. She had to wait. And while she waited, she began to seethe. When the man finally left with a butt full of penicillin and a pocket full of pills, she faced him down. "Your office," she said flatly, preceding him in that direction.

"What's got your dander up?" he asked.

"I went to the Andersons'. I walked in on Lilly nursing the baby."

"Ah," he said simply, limping around her to sit behind his desk, his arthritis obviously kicking up again.

She leaned her hands on the desk and got in his face. "You never called social services."

"Couldn't see the need. Her mother came for her."

"What do you plan to do about the birth certificate?"

"Well, when we get this straightened out a little better, I'll sign and date it."

"Doc, you can't pull this shit! That baby was abandoned! Even though her mother came back for her, it might still be considered a crime!"

"Settle down. Lilly was a little overwrought is all. She's fine now—I've been keeping an eye on it."

"At the very least, you could have told me!"

"And have you go off half-cocked like this? Snatch up that baby and turn her in? That woman was at the end of her rope—and turned out all she needed was a little time to cool down, come to her senses."

"She should've seen a doctor."

"Aw, Lilly had all her kids at home. She'd have come in if she was sick. Fact is, if Lilly had turned up any sooner—I'd have insisted on examining her, just to be safe. By the time she came around, it was obvious she was in good health."

Mel fumed. "I can't work like this," she said. "I'm here to give good, sound medical care, not run around in circles trying to guess what you're dreaming up!"

"Who asked ya?" he threw back.

She was stunned quiet for a moment. Then she said, "Shit!" And she turned to leave his office.

"We're not done here," he bellowed. "Where are you going?"

"For a beer!" she yelled back.

When she got to Jack's it was impossible for her to hide the fact that she was all riled up, but she couldn't talk about it. She went straight to the bar without saying hello to anyone.

Jack took one look at her and said, "Whoa, boy."

"Beer," she said.

He served her up and said, "Wanna talk about it?"

"Sorry. Can't." She took a drink of the icy brew. "Business."

"Must be sticky business. You're pissed."

"Boy howdy."

"Anything I can do?"

"Just don't ask me about it, because I'm bound by confidentiality."

"Must be a doozie," he said.

Yeah, a doozie, she thought.

Jack slid an envelope across the bar to her. She looked at the return address—it was from the clinic in Eureka he had visited. "Maybe this will brighten your mood a little. I'm clear."

She smiled a small smile. "That's good, Jack," she said. "I thought it would come out like that."

"Aren't you going to look?" he asked.

"No," she said, shaking her head. "I trust you."

He leaned forward and put a light kiss on her brow. "Thanks, that's nice," he said. "You go ahead and sulk in your beer. Let me know if you need anything."

She began to calm down with her beer. It was probably a half hour later that Doc Mullins came into the bar and sat on the stool beside her. She glared at him, then focused again on her glass.

Doc raised a finger to Jack and he set up a whiskey. Then wisely, left the two of them alone.

Doc had a sip, then another, then said, "You're right. I can't leave you out of the loop like that if you're going to help take care of the town."

She turned and looked at him, one eyebrow lifted. "Did you just apologize to me?"

"Not quite, I didn't. But in this one instance, you're right. I'm just used to acting on my own, is all. Meant no disrespect."

"What are we going to do?" she asked him.

"You're not going to do anything at all. This is on me. If there's any malpractice involved, I don't want it on you. You were always prepared to do the right thing.

I wanted to do the right thing, too—but I had a different right thing in mind."

"I think she should be examined. I can do it or we can make her an appointment with John Stone."

"I'll call John," Doc said, taking another sip of his whiskey. "I want you away from this for now."

"And this time, you'll actually make the call?"

He turned and regarded her, glare for glare. "I'll call him."

Mel just concentrated on her beer, which had gone warm and dull.

"You do a good job, missy," he said. "I'm getting too old for some things, especially the babies." He looked down at his hands, some fingers bent, knuckles swollen. "I can still get things done, but these old hands aren't good on the women. Better you take care of women's health."

She turned toward him. "First a partial apology. Then a partial compliment."

"I apologize," he said without looking at her. "I think you're needed here."

She let out her breath slowly. She knew how hard that was for him. She took another deep breath and put her arm around his shoulders. She leaned her head against him.

"Don't go soft on me," she said.

"Not a chance," he returned.

Jack had no idea what had passed between Mel and Doc, but she said they were going back to the clinic and would have a bite to eat together there. He assumed they had issues to work out. Then she promised to come back to the bar before going home.

He served quite a few people at six. By seven the

crowd was thinning and there were only a few people there when the door opened. Charmaine. She'd never come to Virgin River before; he'd let her know that he wanted to keep those two parts of his life separate. She wasn't wearing waitress clothes tonight, so her intention was pretty obvious. She wore a nice pair of creased slacks, a crisp white blouse with the collar folded on the outside of a dark blue blazer. Her hair was down and full, makeup thick but perfect, heels. It pleased him to be reminded that she was a handsome woman, especially so when she didn't wear those tight clothes that drew attention to her large breasts. She looked classy. Mature.

She sat up at the bar and smiled at him. "I thought I'd drop by and see how you've been," she said.

"Good, Char. You?"

"Great."

"How about a drink?" he asked.

"Sure. Yes. How about a Johnny Walker, ice. Make it a good Johnny."

"You got it." He set her up with a black label—he didn't have any blue. Too pricey for his usual crowd. In fact, he didn't move much of the black label. "So, what brings you to my neighborhood?"

"I wanted to check in. See if things are the same with you."

He looked down for a second, disappointed. He had hoped not to have to do this again, and certainly not here. This was no place to discuss their relationship, such as it had been. He looked back into her eyes and simply nodded.

"No change, then?"

He shook his head, hoping he could leave it at that.

"Well," she said, taking a sip of her drink, "I'm sorry

to hear that. I was hoping that maybe we could… Never mind. I can tell by the look on your face—"

"Char, please. This isn't the right time or place."

"Take it easy, Jack, I'm not going to push. Can't blame a girl for checking it out. After all, what we had was pretty special. To me, anyway."

"It was special to me, too. I'm sorry, but I had to move on."

"So—you still insist there's no one else?"

"There wasn't at the time. I didn't lie to you. I've never lied to you. But now—"

Just as he said that, the door swung open and Mel came in. Her expression earlier had been angry, but now it was subdued. Tired. And she did something she had never previously done. Rather than jumping up on a stool and asking for a beer, she came around the bar. To Charmaine he said, "Excuse me just one second." He met Mel at the end of the bar.

Mel immediately put her arms around his waist and hugged him, laying her head on his chest. His arms went around her, as well, returning the gesture, painfully aware that Charmaine was burning a hole in his back with her eyes.

"Today was trying," Mel said softly. "Doc and I had a come-to-Jesus meeting about how we're going to work together, if we're going to work together. It was harder than I thought. Emotionally draining."

"Are you all right?" he asked.

"I'm fine. Might I have one of those nifty little Crowns? I've eaten and I promise to only have one, with ice, and you're welcome to take me home tonight. If you want to."

"You're kidding, right? I'm scared to death to let you go home alone. Who knows what you'll do, who you'll take a ride with." He put a small kiss on her brow and turned her around so she could go to the front of the bar. He didn't make eye contact with Charmaine, but rather fixed the drink and put it before Mel. By now she was on a stool at the very end of the bar. "You'll have to give me a minute."

"Sure," she said. "Take your time. I just want to unwind."

"Unwind away." He went back to Char.

The expression in Charmaine's eyes was one of hurt, but at least there was clarity.

"I think I understand," she said, taking another sip of her drink.

He reached for her hand and held it. "Charmaine, I wasn't lying. Doesn't really matter now, I guess, but I'd like it if you believed I was telling the truth. There wasn't anyone else."

"But you wanted there to be."

He nodded, helplessly. He glanced at Mel. She was watching them. Her expression was perplexed and unhappy.

"Well. Now I understand," Charmaine said, pulling her hand away from his. "I'm going to take off. Leave you to your business."

She plunked down a twenty-dollar bill, insulting a former lover who would buy her a drink. She whirled off the bar stool and headed for the door. Jack grabbed that twenty and went down to the end of the bar. "Mel, I'll be right back. Stay put."

"Take all the time you need," she said, but she didn't say it happily.

Just the same he followed Charmaine outside. He called to her and she stopped once she got to her car.

He caught up with her and said, "I'm sorry it worked out like this. I wish you'd just called."

"I'm sure you do." She had moist eyes, as though any minute there might be tears. "I see now," she said.

"I'm not sure you do. This is... It's very recent," he said.

"But she was on your mind?"

He took a breath. "Yeah."

"You love her," she said.

He nodded. "Oh, yeah. Big-time."

She laughed hollowly. "Well, who'd guess. Mr. No-Attachments."

"I didn't mean to mislead you, Char. That's why I broke it off, because I knew if Mel gave me half a chance, I'd find myself with two women, and I wouldn't do that to either one of you. I'd never deliberately..."

"Aw, take it easy, bub. She's young, she's pretty—and you're a goner. Now I know. I just wanted to be sure."

He grabbed her hands, pressing that twenty into one. "You can't believe I'd let you buy a drink in my bar."

"Old lovers drink on the house?" she asked sarcastically.

"No," he said. "Good friends drink on the house." He leaned toward her and kissed her forehead. "I'm sorry if I hurt you. I didn't mean to." He took a deep breath. "I never saw it coming."

She sighed. "I understand, Jack. I miss you, is all. I hope it all works out for you, but if it doesn't..."

"Char, if this doesn't work, I won't be worth a damn."

She chuckled. "Okay, then. I'll take off. Good luck,

Jack." She got in her car, backed out and drove away. He watched until she was gone, then went back inside.

He stood behind the bar, facing Mel. "I'm sorry about that."

"What was that?"

"An old friend."

"Clear River?"

"Yeah. Just checking up."

"Wanting another run at you?"

He nodded. "I made it clear…"

"What did you make clear? Huh, Jack?"

"That I'm off the market. I tried to do that kindly."

Her expression softened somewhat. She smiled a little and put the palm of her hand against his cheek. "Well, I guess I can't bitch about that. Your kindness is one of your best features. But tell me something, cowboy. Is she going to keep showing up here?"

"No."

"Good. I don't like competition."

"There isn't any, Melinda. There never was."

"There better not be. Turns out I'm a very selfish woman."

"I broke it off with her before I even held your hand."

She lifted an amused eyebrow. "That was optimistic of you. You could have ended up with no one."

"A chance I was willing to take. The other way—I didn't want to take that kind of chance. It could have seriously messed up what I wanted. And I wanted you." He smiled at her. "You're being a pretty good sport about this," he said.

"Hey. I know why she was here. I wouldn't give you up at the point of a gun. Wanna take me home? Spend the night?"

"Yeah," he said with a smile. "I always want to."

"Get permission from your bald guy then. I want you to prove yourself to me tonight. Again." Then she grinned.

July came in sunny and warm with a bit of occasional rain. Jack was sitting out on the porch when Rick showed up for work. He came in earlier in the day during summer when there was no school—sometime between breakfast and lunch. It was the peculiar look on his face that caused Jack to say, "Hold up, pardner. How you doing?"

"Good, Jack," he said.

"Pull up a chair. I haven't wanted to ask, but it's been on my mind. You and Liz."

"Yeah," Ricky said, leaning against the porch rail rather than sitting. "Must show all over me, huh?"

"Something's showing. Everything okay?"

"Yeah, I guess." He took a breath. "I kept after her to let me know if we were all clear, you know? And when she finally said it was okay, she wasn't pregnant or anything, I told her that I thought maybe we should cool it. It killed her."

"Whooo," Jack said. "Rough."

"I feel like the biggest dog."

"I guess you had your reasons."

"I tried to explain—it's not that I don't like her. A lot. I really like her a lot. I'm not just saying that. And it's not just because of what we did. You know."

"I get that, yeah," Jack said.

"Can I tell you something?"

"It's all up to you, bud."

"I really like the girl a lot. I maybe even love her, if that doesn't sound too stupid. But it turns out it's a little too hot for me to handle, and I don't want to screw up

my life and her life because of that. That one time—
Jack, I did *not* see that coming. I think it's best for her
and me to put some miles between us. Does that make
me a wimp?"

Jack felt a slow smile spread across his lips. "Nah.
That makes you a person with a brain."

"I feel like a damn dog. But Jack, that girl—she just
does it to me. Holy God. I get close to that girl and I
have no brain at all."

Jack sat forward in his chair, leaning toward Rick.
"There will be times when too hot to handle will work
right into your plans, Rick. But you won't be sixteen
anymore. You need to be smart. Sounds like you're
being smart. I'm sorry you and the girl are having a
hard time with this."

"I hope you're right about this. Because I feel like
shit. Plus, I miss her like mad. And not just that… I
miss *her*."

"Ricky, buddy, you are too young to be a daddy. I'm
sorry this hurts, but sometimes you have to do the difficult thing. And she's just too frickin' young to be put
in that position. Someone has to be a grown-up. You're
doing the right thing. If she's the right girl, it'll keep."

"I don't know," he said, shaking his head sadly.

"Let the girl get a little older, pal. Maybe you can
check back with her later."

"Or maybe not, Jack. I think I hurt her real bad. I
might not get another shot."

"Do yourself a favor. Don't keep going back to the
scene of the crime. It'll just buy you trouble."

Mel began to glow in the brightness of summer. She
had a patient in her last trimester with a first baby and
first babies were so much fun. This couple, unlike Polly

and Darryl, unlike the sad and anonymous couple in the woods, had been trying for a baby for quite a while, so they were filled with anxiety and excitement. Anne and Jeremy Givens were in their late twenties and had been married eight years. Jeremy's dad owned a large orchard, and Jeremy and Anne lived on the land with the extended family. The baby would come before the apple crop.

Jack and Mel had solidified a couples' friendship with June and Jim, and John and Susan. They spent more time in Grace Valley and the other couples came to Virgin River twice—once to Mel's little cabin for dinner, once to Jack's bar. On the last visit Susan announced that she wouldn't be leaving town again, unless she could use the twisting, bumpy, thirty-minute drive to start labor. She was about to pop. Jack invited Jim, Elmer Hudson and a friend of Elmer's, Judge Forrest, to fish with him and Preacher in the Virgin, and their catch was good. It made her almost as happy that the men were friends as it did that she had these women friends in her life.

Given the time she was spending with her girlfriends, Mel had opened up a little, but just a little. She admitted she was in a relationship with Jack and that he was the best thing that had happened to her in Virgin River. "It looks like you were made for each other," Susan said. "Kind of like June and Jim—barely acquainted and like old soul mates."

To Joey she reported, "I never sleep by myself anymore. It feels more natural to have him near. And Joey—it's so nice not to be alone anymore." She didn't dare tell her sister that after going out to a marijuana grow to deliver a baby, Jack would hardly let her out of his sight. She smiled secretly; there was always a bright spot to everything.

"Do you get any sleep?" Joey asked.

Mel laughed. "I sleep very well, every night. But Joey," she said, shivering, "I've never known anything like this. Every time I look at him, I just want to get undressed."

"You deserve it, Mel."

"He asked me to do something that has me a little tense—he's going to Sacramento for his youngest sister's birthday—a gathering of the whole family. And he wants me to go."

"Why would that make you tense? You sprung me on him and it went very well. He's crazy about me," she added with a laugh.

"I'm not worried that they won't like me. I'm worried they might make more of this than there is."

"Ah," Joey said. "Holding back a little?"

"Not on purpose," she answered. "For some reason I just can't stop feeling that I'm married to someone else."

"Oh, Mel—go! That other guy—the one you still feel married to? He's not going to get in the way of this. In fact, if he's watching, he's probably glad you have someone special to warm up your nights."

"If he's watching," she said, "I'm blushing."

Jack convinced her. All the way to Sacramento, she was nervous as a cat. "I just don't want your family to think we're in a serious relationship."

"Aren't we?" he asked her. "Aren't you?"

"You know there's no one else in my life," she said. "I'm completely monogamous. I just need time… You know…"

"Man," he said, laughing. "This figures."

"What?"

"All those years I made sure the woman I was seeing at the time knew I couldn't be tied down... There are women out there, Mel, who would think I'm getting just what I deserve right now."

"You know what I mean. It's just my issues..."

"I'm waiting out the issues. And I'm serious about that."

"You're very patient with me, Jack. And I appreciate it. I just don't want them to get the wrong idea. And we will sleep in separate bedrooms at your dad's."

"No," he said firmly. "I'm over forty years old. I sleep with you every night. I told my dad that one bedroom would be just fine."

She sighed heavily. Nervously. "Okay then. But we're not doing it at your dad's." And he laughed at her.

It was so much hotter in Sacramento in July than in Virgin River. Hotter even than L.A. in July—Sacramento was located on an inland valley and had no ocean breezes to cool the land.

Sam Sheridan still lived in the house where he'd raised his five children—a spacious ranch-style home in the suburbs with a lush yard, pool and a big kitchen. When Mel met him, she looked into the eyes of an older version of Jack—a man of the same height and girth with thick, steel-gray hair, a big smile and a powerful handshake. Jack and Sam embraced like brothers, so happy to be together.

The three of them had a nice evening with steak cooked on the backyard barbecue and red wine. The men insisted on cleaning up the dishes, so Mel took her glass of wine and wandered around the house a little bit. She found herself in what passed as Sam's study, or office or bragging room. There was a desk, a TV, com-

puter, bookshelves and wall upon wall of pictures and
awards. All his daughters in their wedding dresses, all
his granddaughters, ranging in age from five to eighteen, but the thing she hadn't given any thought to at
all were the pictures she would see of Jack. Pictures she
had never seen around Jack's room—a marine wearing
rows of ribbons. Jack and his various squads and pla-
toons, Jack and his parents, Jack and generals. Jack and
the guys who came to Virgin River for their Semper Fi
reunions. And cases of medals. She didn't know much
about military awards, but there was no mistaking three
purple hearts and silver and bronze stars.

She reached out and gently ran her fingers over the
glass case that held the medals. Sam came up behind
her and put his hands on her shoulders. "He's a hero,"
he said softly. "Many times over."

She looked over her shoulder at Sam. "You'd never
know that from talking to him," she said.

"Oh, I know." He laughed. "He's modest."

"Dad," Jack said, coming into the room, drying a
wineglass with a dish towel. "I told you to put all that
shit away."

"Ha," Sam said, just ignoring his son, turning his
back on him. "This one is from Desert Storm," he told
Mel. "And this—Bosnia. There were downed fighter pi-
lots—Jack and his unit went into a hot zone and pulled
them out. He got shot in Afghanistan, but still managed
to get his squad out of danger. And this one—the latest
Iraq conflict—he saved six men."

"Dad…"

"Your dishes done, son?" he asked without turning
around, dismissing Jack.

Mel looked up at Sam. "Do you think this bothers
him? The memories?"

"Oh, I'm sure some of them do. But it never bothered him enough to keep him from going back, time and again. They might've sent him anyway, but every bit of training and fighting—he volunteered. This boy has been awarded medals by many generals and one president. He was the marines' best—and I'm damn proud of him. He won't keep the medals with him. He'd put 'em in storage or something. I have to keep them here to keep them safe."

"He's not proud of this?" she asked.

Sam looked down at Mel. "Not the medals so much as the men. He was committed to his men, not military awards. You didn't know this about my son?"

"I knew he was in the marines. I met some of his friends. These guys," she said, pointing at a picture.

"He's a leader of men, Melinda," Sam said. He glanced over his shoulder and seeing that his son was gone, said, "He tends to act embarrassed that he was only a high-school graduate when his sisters—and their husbands for that matter—all hold college degrees, and even some postgraduate degrees among them. But I think the man has accomplished more, done more good and saved more lives, than many a man or woman with more education. And if you know him, you know he's very intelligent. If he'd gone to college, he'd have excelled there, as well, but this was his path."

"He's so gentle," she heard herself say.

"He is that. I've seen him with each one of my granddaughters, handling them like they're nitro and might blow up if he makes a wrong move. But he is not gentle when he's in the fight. This man is not just a marine. He's a highly decorated hero. His sisters and I stand in awe."

"It must have been hard for you, when he was in combat."

"Yes." He looked at the pictures and medals with a wistful expression on his face. "You can't imagine how much his mother and I missed him. Worried about him. But he did what he was driven to do. And he did it well." Sam smiled. "We'd better get back to the kitchen. He gets surly when I brag."

When Mel got up the next morning, Jack was not beside her. She heard him talking with his dad in another room; she heard them laughing, so she showered and dressed before joining them. She found them in the dining room, paperwork spread out all over the table.

"Board meeting?" she asked.

"Something like that," Sam said. "So, son, everything look okay to you?"

"Great. As usual." He stuck out his hand and shook his father's. "Thanks, Dad. Appreciate it."

Sam gathered up the papers, clutched them in a stack atop an accordion file and left the room.

"My dad was an agent for a brokerage firm before he retired. While I was in the marines, I'd send him money from time to time. He's been investing for me for twenty years."

"I didn't think a marine made a lot of money," she said.

"Not really." He shrugged. "But if you're single and you keep re-upping and going to war, there are bonuses, incentives, combat pay, promotions. My buddies—most of them—had those benefits eaten up by housing, braces on kids' teeth, the usual. I always lived cheap and saved. My dad," he said, "he always made that such an issue while I was growing up."

"Smart man," she said, and she wasn't speaking of Sam.

Jack grinned. "You thought I was making a killing on that little Virgin River bar?"

"I figured you didn't need to. With a military retirement and low cost of living..."

"Nah. That aside, I'm set," he said. "If the bar burns to the ground, all I have to do is support Preach for the rest of his life. And I'd like to make sure Ricky gets an education. That's about it." He reached for her hand. "Otherwise, I have everything I need."

That afternoon the rest of the family descended on the Sheridan home—four sisters and their husbands, eight nieces. As they came, one family at a time, they flung themselves on Jack. His sisters ran to him, hugging and kissing him. His brothers-in-law embraced him fondly. He picked up each one of his nieces and hugged them like they were his daughters, spun them around, laughed into their pretty faces.

Mel wasn't sure what she had expected them to be like. Having seen the family picture in his room and those around the house, she knew they were a good looking family; good genes. His sisters were very different from each other, but each was svelte, lovely, smart. Donna, the oldest, was very tall, probably five-ten, with short, frosted hair, Jeannie was nearly as tall, quite thin and chic, Mary was next tallest at perhaps five-five, but so trim and fragile-looking it was hard to imagine her handling a big commercial jet. Donna and Jeannie each had three daughters, Mary had two. And then there was Brie, the baby, celebrating her thirtieth birthday. She was the only sister who did not yet have children. She was just about the same size as Mel with long light

brown hair that fell down her back almost to her waist—
a little bitty thing who put away hardened criminals for
a living. And their men, like Jack and Sam, were big
guys, the nieces, each one beautiful.

Jack's sisters brought some of Mel's closest friends
with them—Ralph Lauren, Lilly Pulitzer, Michael Kors
and Coach. Each one of them had a strong sense of style,
but what was more obvious than their collective taste in
fashion was their warmth and humor. They all met Mel
with delight, eschewing the offered handshake and immediately embracing her. It was a very physical, affectionate family. Every time Mel stole a look at Jack he
had his arms around a sister or niece, frequently dropping kisses on their heads or cheeks. Just as frequently
he would seek out Mel and put a possessive arm about
her shoulders or waist. And to her surprise, so would
Sam, as though they'd been close for years.

All Brie had wanted for her birthday was to have the
family together and her brother home. "He's not so very
far away," Mel said. "Don't you get to see him often?"

"Not nearly often enough," Brie said. "Jack has been
essentially gone for twenty-three years. Since he was
seventeen."

It was a loud day, filled with laughter and good food.
Sam took care of the meat while the sisters brought
delicious side dishes. After dinner, the kids took off
to watch DVDs on the big screen or jump in the backyard pool or play video games on Grandpa's computer.
It was just the adults sitting around the patio tables and
they told stories about Jack that almost made him blush.

"Remember, Dad, when you were giving away Jack's
bed and were going to surprise him with a new bigger
one because he'd gotten so tall? So heavy?" Immediate laughter from everyone—Mel was the only one not

intimate with this story. "A friend of the family wanted the bed for one of his younger kids. He was a respected member of the PTA…"

"Aw, you act like he was the frickin' preacher or something," Jack protested.

"And when they pulled off the mattress, Jack's private library was exposed for all eyes to see," Donna said, and everyone howled.

"I'd been raising girls," Sam said. "I completely forgot what boys were doing when they were supposed to be doing homework."

"At least it was good, solid, decent girlie magazines and not pictures of women in bras from Sears catalogs," Jack said in his defense. "Fine, upstanding, naked women!"

"Hear, hear," the brothers-in-law intoned.

"You know," Mel said, "I've noticed there's only one bathroom besides the master bath in this house…"

Immediate noise erupted—shouts, laughter, whistles, jeering. "We used to have the biggest fights over the bathroom," one of the women said.

"I wasn't in that," Jack insisted.

"You were the *worst!*" it was accused.

"Plus, when he got the bathroom, he'd stay in there for hours! He wouldn't give it up until all the hot water was gone!"

"Mom had to give him a timer for his shower—so the rest of us could get clean, too. Of course, he just ignored it. And Mom would say, now, now, I know Jack's trying. Because Jack was her little precious."

"I started showering at night—it was the only way," Donna said.

"Speaking of nights—do you know what he used to do to us at night? Mary and I had the same bedroom, and it was crammed to the ceiling with our stuff. Jack and one of his friends used to sneak in when we were asleep and tie strings to our fingers and toes and connect the strings to stuff around the room, so when we turned over in our sleep—everything came crashing down around us!"

"That's nothing," Jeannie said. "I used to come home from school and find all my stuffed animals with nooses around their necks, hanging from my bed canopy!"

"They act like they never did anything to me," Jack said.

"Do you remember the time we were all in the family room, all five of us, and Mom came into the room with a bunch of condoms in her hand and said, 'Guess what I found floating in the washer? Jack, I imagine these must belong to you.'"

Wild laughter erupted and Jack got all stirred up. "Yeah, but they weren't mine, were they? Because mine were right where I'd left them! I suspect Donna!"

"I was a feminist," Donna declared.

"Mom would never have believed it—Donna was her pride and joy!"

"Donna was screwing around!"

"I can't take these stories," Sam said, standing up and going for a beer, making them all laugh.

"It's okay, Dad," Donna yelled. "I don't need birth control anymore!"

When it was time to clean up and the sun had set, the men went off somewhere and three of the sisters insisted that the birthday girl and the guest relax while they did the work. Mel was left with Brie. They sat at the patio table by candlelight.

"My brother has never brought a woman home before," Brie said.

"After watching him with his family—all these females—it's so hard to imagine. He's completely comfortable with women. He should have been married years ago. He should have a big family of his own," Mel said.

"It just never happened," Brie put in. "I blame it on the marines."

"When I first met him, I asked him if he'd ever been married and he said, 'I was married to the marines, and she was a real bitch.'" Brie laughed. "Have you visited him in Virgin River?" Mel asked.

"Not en masse," she said. "But we've all gotten up there at one time or another. The guys like to fish with Jack and Preacher. Dad will go up there for as long as a couple of weeks at a time—he loves that little bar of Jack's."

"Jack seems to have found his niche, his happy place," Mel said. "I've only been there a little over four months, and my adjustment hasn't been that easy. I'm used to big-city medicine where you can get anything you want, and fast. This is a whole new game. And I had to drive for two hours to get a decent haircut and frost job."

"What made you choose Virgin River?" Brie asked her.

"Hmm. The flip side of big-city medicine—I'd had it with the chaos and crime. As I told Jack, I left the E.R. not just because I felt drawn to midwifery, but I thought I could get away from having half my patients brought in by the police. And guess what? The first woman I ever delivered had multiple felony warrants and was being arrested when she went into labor. She was handcuffed to the bed when I examined her prior to delivery." She chuckled. "I was looking for something smaller and simpler." She laughed. "I got smaller, but simpler? Little towns like Virgin River have their own challenges."

"Like?"

"Like how about loading a critical patient in the back of a pickup truck and speeding down the mountain, hanging on for dear life, trying to get her to the hospital before she goes into cardiac arrest. Man, did I ever lust after that big, chaotic emergency room that day. And there's always the adventure of having your services requested by a big, gun-toting drug farmer in the middle of the night… Um, if you tell Jack that version of the story, there's going to be a scene."

Brie laughed. "He doesn't know?"

"Not some of the details. He was very pissed that I went alone to an unknown location with a man who was basically a stranger."

"Holy smoke."

"Yeah, well, it's a good thing I did. There were complications with the delivery. But I don't think that will cheer up Jack too much." She shrugged. "Jack's protective. Of everyone."

"Have you found your niche?" Brie asked.

"I kind of crave a trip to Nordstrom's," Mel said. "I wouldn't mind a facial and leg wax, either. On the other hand, I didn't realize I could get by on so little. So simply. There's something about that… It's freeing, in a way. And there's no question, it's beautiful. Sometimes it's so quiet, your ears ring. But when I first got there, I thought I'd really screwed up big—it was so much more rugged and isolated than I expected. The mountain roads terrified me, and Doc and I manage in that clinic with the most rudimentary equipment. The cabin I was promised, rent free for a year, was horrible. In fact, my first morning there the porch collapsed and dumped me into a deep, freezing mud puddle. The cabin was so filthy, I was on my way out of town—running for my life—when a medical emergency stopped me and I reluctantly stayed a few days that turned into a couple of weeks."

"That turned into a few months…" Brie observed.

"Jack renovated the cabin without being asked, while I stayed at Doc's house," Mel said. "About the time I was going to make a break for it, he showed it to me. I said I'd give it a few more days. Then my first delivery occurred and I realized I should give the place a chance. There's something about a successful delivery in a place like Virgin River where there's no backup, no anesthesia… Just me and Mom… It's indescribable."

"Then there's Jack," Brie said.

"Jack," Mel repeated. "I don't know when I've met a kinder, stronger, more generous man. Your brother is wonderful, Brie. He's amazing. Everyone in Virgin River loves him."

"My brother is in love with *you*," Brie said.

Mel shouldn't have been shocked. Although he hadn't said the words, she already knew it. Felt it. At first she thought he was just a remarkable lover, but soon she realized that he couldn't touch her that way without an emotional investment, as well as a physical one. He gave her everything he had—and not just in the bedroom. It was in her mind to tell Brie—*I'm a recent widow! I need time to digest this! I don't feel free yet—free to accept another man's love!* Her cheeks grew warm and she said nothing.

"I realize I'm biased, but when a man like Jack loves a woman, it's a great honor."

"I agree," Mel said quietly.

* * *

Late, in the dark of night, as he held her in his arms in the bed in his father's house, she said, "You have the most wonderful family."

"They love you, too."

"It was such fun watching you all together. They're ruthless—you don't have a secret left!" And she laughed.

"I told you. No slack here."

"But what fun, to have all that history, all those hysterical stories."

"Oh—I listened to you and Joey for a few days. You didn't grow up deprived." He kissed her neck. "I'm just glad you had fun. I knew you would." He kissed her neck again, nuzzling closer.

"Your sisters are all so put together," she said. "Very classy, very sharp. I used to dress like that, before I moved to a place where you're overdressed in good jeans. You should have seen my closet in L.A.—it was huge, and bulging."

He pulled the T-shirt she wore up and over her head. "I like what you're wearing right now. In fact, I find you overdressed in this thong."

"Jack, I thought we decided, we're not going to do it in your father's house…"

"No, you said you weren't going to." He slipped the thong down. "I'm thinking of going after that G-spot again…"

"Oh, God," she said, weakening. "We shouldn't. You know how we get…"

He rose above her and grinned into her eyes. "Want me to get a sock for your mouth?"

Susan Stone delivered her son in August—a robust eight-pounder. She went to Valley Hospital, had a stunning delivery and was home in Grace Valley in forty-eight hours. It was in Mel's mind to give her some time alone with her baby, but both John and June called and urged her to come the next Sunday afternoon, the baby not yet a week old.

Jack would not be left behind. He brought the beer and cigars.

Susan was very fit for a woman who had just delivered, but still she stayed on the couch, bassinet nearby, and let her friends fuss over her. In typical country fashion, women brought food so that the new parents wouldn't have to be bothered with cooking. Mel was surprised to see such an air of celebration and atmosphere of an open house so soon after bringing a baby home.

There was another couple present, a very pregnant Julianna Dickson and her husband, Mike. John dropped an arm around Julianna's shoulders and said to Mel, "This one is legendary—she could never seem to wait for the doctor. June and I finally got to attend one of her births—it was the last baby, and it was sheer luck. She delivers with about fifteen minutes' notice. This is number six. We're going to admit her tomorrow and induce."

"Don't let the baby hear you say that," Julianna said. "You know what always happens."

"Maybe we should go over there right now?"

"Maybe you should strap yourself to me and keep one hand on my stomach."

The women gathered in the living room around Susan with cups of coffee and cake. John plucked the baby out of his bassinet to show him off. As Jim already had baby Jamie in his arms, John offered the baby to Jack. And he willingly, happily took him into his arms. He cooed at the little bundle.

Mel's eyes warmed as she watched him.

"You're pretty good at that for a bachelor," John said appreciatively.

"Nieces," he said.

"Eight of them," Mel added.

Jack jiggled and the baby sent up a loud wail. "I guess you're not that good," John said.

"Jack did fine. He's hungry," Susan said, reaching for the baby.

"Okay—there's going to be breast-feeding," John said. "We should find something to do."

Jack pulled cigars out of his breast pocket and immediately a very grateful hum of approval sounded. Jim handed Jamie off to June and left the women and babies in the house to go outside and indulge.

"They're going to stink," Julianna said.

"To high heaven," June agreed.

"At least they're out of our hair." Susan settled the newborn onto her breast and Mel watched with longing. "Mel," she said, "how'd it go in Sacramento? With Jack's family?"

"Oh, they're fantastic," she said, coming back to herself again. "Four sisters who tell every secret he'd ever dream of keeping, and eight nieces, all beautiful, all in love with their uncle Jack. It was delightful. So, Susan—how was your labor? Back labor, like you predicted?"

"Epidural," she said with a grin. "Piece of cake."

"I've never had time for one of those," Julianna said somewhat wistfully, smoothing a hand over her round tummy.

"You and Julianna are awful close to the same due date," Mel observed.

They all laughed. "I might've neglected to mention—

the big fight John and I had before this little conception? It happened at a night of cards with Julianna and Mike."

"We were both so furious with our husbands—they had both been banished. Apparently we let them both into bed at about the same time." More laughter. Julianna rubbed her swollen tummy. "I meant to stop doing this…"

"What in the world happened?" Mel wanted to know.

"Long story short—they had a couple of beers and started in on working women. I wanted to work along-side John and June in the clinic, but John wanted me to stay home, mind my own business and clean house. And make sure he had one of those solid country meals in front of him when he got home. Now, I come from the part of the world where a salad with some chicken strips is a dining delight."

"Mike, on the other hand, thought it was wonderful that I *didn't* work. With five kids and a farmhouse to run," Julianna said.

"Oh, brother," Mel said.

"They were made to suffer very appropriately," June put in. "No conversation, no sex. Perfect discipline for idiots."

"How'd it turn out?" Mel asked.

"Well, when I'm not nine months pregnant or post-partum and nursing, I run the clinic."

"And very well, at that."

"But a side effect was… Well, as you can plainly see—we had been knocked up. You might not want to drink the water around here," Susan advised.

"No kidding," said June, propping Jamie on her shoulder.

I drank the water, Mel almost said.

Nursing done, Susan passed the baby to Mel. She

smiled gratefully and took the little guy. His rosy round face was contented in sleep; little baby noises escaped him.

The women talked about their labors, about their men, and they brought Mel into the conversation very well with questions about her midwifery experiences. June went to the kitchen for the coffeepot and refilled them all while Mel happily cuddled with the newborn. Her breasts actually ached as she held him. *Hormones are amazing,* she found herself thinking.

On the way back to Virgin River, Jack said, "Your friends throw a nice little party."

"Don't they?" she replied, reaching across the truck's front seat to hold his hand.

"All these babies," Jack said. "Everywhere you look."

"Everywhere."

He pulled up in front of her cabin. "I'll shower off the cigars," he said.

"Thanks," she answered. "It actually makes me a little nauseous."

"I'm sorry, honey. I didn't realize."

"No big deal. But I'll be glad to loan you the shower. And meet you in the bed. I'm suddenly exhausted."

Mel was just pulling up to the clinic in the morning when beside her an old pickup was pulling into the next parking spot. She recognized the man at once—Calvin. She hadn't seen him since that first time, when she treated his facial wounds. He jumped out of the truck as she got out of the Hummer. His hands were plunged into his pockets and he seemed to nearly vibrate with the jitters. She suddenly realized something—the man who took her to deliver his baby in the backwoods, also a grower, didn't seem to be on anything. This guy was wired. High. She'd never have gotten in a truck, in the middle of the night, with Calvin—baby or no baby. She further realized that without a plan of any kind, she could get hurt if she refused such a request from Calvin. He was pretty scary, and clearly unstable.

Before she could even address him, he said, "I need something. Back pain."

"What do you need?" she asked calmly, very practiced in handling his type back in the city.

"Pain medicine. I need something for pain. Fentanyl, maybe. OxyContin. Morphine. Something."

"Did you hurt your back?" she asked, trying to avoid his eyes as she proceeded to Doc's front porch. He was jerking and tweaking, and upright rather than sitting on a low stool, she became aware of his size. He was almost six feet and broad-shouldered. It was clear he'd gotten his hands on something not depressive. Maybe methamphetamine, as Doc had earlier suspected. He wanted a narcotic to bring him down. The pot from his garden must not be doing it for him.

"Fell off a ledge out there. Might've broke it. It'll be okay, but I need a little medicine."

"Fine. You'll have to see Doc," she said.

His feet moved nervously. He pulled a hand out of his pocket and grabbed at her sleeve and she jerked out of his reach.

Jack, coming from her cabin arrived behind her and was just pulling into town as Calvin made that move and for a split second she almost felt sorry for him. Jack accelerated, screeched to a stop within inches of Doc's porch and was out of the truck in one second. "Get away from her!" he shouted.

The guy backed away, but just a little bit. He looked

at Mel. "I just need something for the pain in my back," he said.

Jack reached into his truck and had his hand on his rifle. The look in his eyes was frightening. "I'm okay," she said to Jack. Then to the twitchy young man, "I don't prescribe the kind of drugs you're looking for. We leave that to the doctor. And he'll want an X-ray, undoubtedly."

The guy stared at her, then grinned stupidly. "You ain't got no X-ray."

"There's one at Valley Hospital," she said.

Jack pulled the rifle off the rack and held it at his side for a moment. Then he kicked the truck door closed and came up onto the porch to stand beside Mel. He put an arm around Mel and pulled her against him. "Want to see the doctor?" he asked Calvin, rifle in hand.

"Hey, man," he laughed nervously. "What's your deal, man?" He backed away with his hands up, palms facing Jack. "Take it easy. I'll go to the valley," he said. He jumped off the porch, not bothering with the steps. Must be some back pain, she thought. He got in the old pickup, started it, put it in gear and drove away. But he didn't go toward the valley—he went toward the woods.

"You know him?" Jack asked.

"He was at that camp Doc and I went to a few months ago. When you watched the baby for us. You remember…"

"Paulis's?"

"Uh-huh. Did you have to do that?" Mel asked. "He really hadn't done anything threatening."

Jack glared after the departing truck. "Yeah," he said. "I had to. He's wrong. He's just wrong."

Fourteen

Every August before school started, the Andersons played host to a huge late-summer picnic at their ranch. Everyone they knew in Virgin River and even some folks from surrounding towns showed up. Buck had a huge canvas tent he erected in the pasture outside the corral, barbecues were set up, people provided tables and chairs. The Bristols brought their miniature horses and set up pony rides. Jack always donated a couple of kegs while Preacher whipped up some of his best potato salad in a tub so big it looked as if it would feed a third-world nation. There were barrels of lemonade and iced tea, ice chests full of sodas and, in the afternoon, homemade ice-cream makers were brought out of trucks and SUVs, and the hand cranking began.

The barn floor was swept clean and a small band was set up for country dancing. There were children everywhere, running from one end of the ranch to the other, from corral to hayloft.

Mel had looked forward to the picnic as a chance to hold Chloe for a while, and also to do something she hadn't done before—meet the rest of the Anderson family. She had a passing acquaintance with two of the three sons who worked the ranch with Buck, and one of the daughters had come to Doc's for a prenatal exam, but otherwise, they were strangers to her.

But not strangers for very long. Each one of them, the sons, the daughters, their spouses and children, greeted her as the person who had given them Chloe. The baby was passed around from Anderson to Anderson, cuddled, swept up in the air, kissed, tickled. Even the little ones—Lilly and Buck's seven grandchildren—ran to Chloe to snuggle her as if she were their newest sweet puppy. Buck was pretty busy around the barn and barbecues, but from time to time he was near the picnic tables or food tables and she would catch a glimpse of him holding Chloe comfortably on his hip.

The Andersons were wonderful, homespun, authentic people with nothing but tons of love in their hearts. Just like Lilly; sweet, nurturing and tender. The sun was beginning to lower in the late afternoon sky when Jack found Mel sitting on the porch swing with the baby, giving her a bottle. He sat beside her and played idly with Chloe's dark curls. "She seems to be doing well here," he said.

"She should," Mel said. "She's home." And it gave her deep satisfaction to know that this was true in all ways.

"I'd like to spin you around the barn a little bit," he said, leaning over the baby's head to give her a kiss.

"Another surprise. You dance?"

"I think that might be overly optimistic," he said. "I do something. I'll try not to hurt you."

Lilly came out of the house, wiping her hands on her apron. "Here, Mel, let me take her off your hands. I'll put her to bed."

Mel stood with the baby in her arms and walked into

the house, Lilly right behind her. She turned and placed the baby in Lilly's arms. Then she leaned toward Lilly and gave her a kiss on the cheek. "You have a wonderful family," Mel said. "I think you'll find just the right time to tell them."

Mel made an appointment at the Grace Valley clinic. She was surprised to learn that both doctors were available, so she requested the OB. Prenatal consult, she said. "We'll go ahead and put your patient with Dr. Stone," the receptionist said, and Mel did not correct her. After all, she'd been there before with a couple of pregnant women for ultrasounds and they knew her as the midwife upriver. After seeing a few patients, Mel headed for Grace Valley in the afternoon.

It had only been a short time since the gathering at the Stones' house and she could no longer deny the truth. She was pregnant. She already knew it. They had plenty of pregnancy tests on hand at Doc's and she'd used one. Then another one. And another. Half of her hoped it was wrong, the other half was afraid it was.

When she got to the clinic, June was hanging around the reception desk. "Hey, there." She leaned as if looking around Mel. "I thought you were bringing in a prenatal consult?"

"Yeah," Mel said. "Me."

June's eyes grew momentarily round, surprised.

"It must be the water," Mel said with a shrug.

"Come on back. You're with John, and as you know, our nurse is on maternity leave. Want me to stand in or keep out of your business?"

Mel felt a shudder of nervous emotion. "Please, come with me. I think I need to explain a few things," she said.

"Oh, boy," June said, draping an arm around her shoulders. "Sounds like it might be a little complicated."

"Not a little," Mel answered.

John came out of the back and said, "Hey, Melinda. You bring me a prenatal consult?" Before she could answer, June inclined her head toward Mel. "Oh," John said. "Well, first things first—June, set her up in there. Let's get the facts."

"Okay," Mel said, suddenly meek and nervous. "But I already know."

"Don't try to make my job so easy," he said with a laugh. "There's no challenge in that."

Mel went into the exam room where she found a gown and sheet. She undressed and sat up on the table, waiting. How was she supposed to feel about this? She'd been desperate for a baby, and now she was having one. Why did it feel so damn confusing? As though something had gone wrong, when in reality it had finally gone right.

But this wasn't what she had planned. And she knew it wasn't what Jack had planned—he'd offered to take care of their birth control needs. Oh, brother, was he going to be surprised.

John came in, June on his heels. "How are you feeling, Mel?"

"Besides terribly confused? A little nauseous in the morning."

"Damnest thing, isn't it? But you're keeping food down?"

"Yep."

June set up the instruments and pap slide while John got her blood pressure. "Want to talk first or second?" he asked her.

"Second."

"Okay. June—can you fire up the ultrasound? Thanks. Mel, lie back and slide down for me, okay?" He guided her feet into the stirrups and kept hands on her legs in case she slid too far and accidentally fell. When her position was solid, he took his place on his stool and snapped on the rubber gloves. He inserted the speculum. "You know how far along?"

"Three months," she said, her voice quieter than usual. "Approximately."

"Congratulations," he said. Beside her the ultrasound bleeped as it warmed up. He pulled out the speculum after the pap slide was complete and gently palpated the uterus, measuring for size. "You're almost as good at this as I am, Mel," he said. "You have reached the right approximate diagnosis. Good. Everything's good." He pulled the wand from the ultrasound; because this was an early pregnancy he would do an internal probe for a better reading as opposed to running the probe over her still flat belly. "Turn your head, Mel," he said. "Beautiful," he added.

She looked at the monitor. Tears slid out of her eyes and into the hair at her temples. There it was, a small mass, limbs just visible to the practiced eye, moving around inside of her. They watched the new life for a little while and she gave a hiccup of emotion, moving a trembling hand to cover her mouth.

"Just about twelve weeks," John said. "Out of the miscarriage woods. We'll print you out a picture, though the view is going to be lots better in another few weeks."

He removed the probe and helped her to sit up. June leaned a hip on the counter and John returned to his stool.

"You're in perfect health," her doctor said.

June handed Mel a tissue. "I've been there, Mel," June said. "Believe me."

Finally John said, "What's the matter, Mel? How can we help?"

She blotted her eyes. "I'm sorry to do this to you, but it's just so complicated."

John reached out to her and gave her knee a squeeze. "It probably isn't as complicated as you think."

"Oh, wait," she said with a weak, embarrassed laugh. "How about I start by telling you I'm hopelessly infertile."

He gave a little laugh. "Let's see—you have a uterus, ovaries, fallopian tubes… And I've heard this business of not being able to get pregnant from pregnant women before."

"And I went through three years of infertility treatment, including surgery, without success. We even had one very expensive, very failed attempt at in vitro."

"Well, that puts an interesting spin on things. Maybe you should back up a little. You don't have to talk to us, Mel. It's up to you."

"No, I want to. I need advice. I'm a mess. See—before moving up here from L.A., I was married. My husband was a doctor—we often worked together. We tried desperately to have a baby. He was killed when he happened into a robbery in progress. That was a year and three months ago. Almost exactly. I came up here looking for a simpler life, a safer life. I just wanted to start over."

John shrugged. "Kind of looks like you found what you were looking for."

She laughed. "Virgin River isn't all that simple. But yes, in some important ways, I found what I was looking for," she agreed. "Of course, this wasn't planned. I didn't think it was possible for me to get pregnant."

"Is the problem Jack?" June asked.

"Yes, but he doesn't know it. He's so wonderful, but he knew from the beginning that I wasn't quite over my husband. I adore Jack—you can't imagine—but I still haven't gotten to that point where I feel free to move on to—" She took a breath. "To another man." They gave her a moment and another tissue. "This is supposed to be my baby with my husband. The one we tried so hard to have." She blew her nose.

June stepped forward and took her hand. "It seems apparent that Jack loves you. And that he's a good man."

"Good with children," John put in.

"Whether you planned to or not," June said with a shrug, "it appears you have moved on. At least in some ways."

"The last time I gave my heart and soul to a man, he died," she said with a sniffle. Then she lowered her head and a couple of tears fell on the hands folded in her lap. "I don't think I could survive something like that again."

June stepped forward and took her into her arms and John was quick to join her. They comforted her for a minute. Then John gave her shoulders a squeeze and said, "Mel, I like Jack's chances. Five wars couldn't kill him."

"Five *wars?*" June asked.

John shrugged. "You didn't know that?"

"I knew he was in the marines!"

"Men actually do talk," John said.

"That husband of mine," she groused. "He's so badly trained!"

"I'm so confused," Mel said. "I don't really know what to do!"

"Naw, that's not true. It's a done deal, Mel," John said. "Now you just have to be a little kind to yourself and work through it. You wanted a baby real bad, and you're having one. Jack—he doesn't know?"

"No. He knows I'm widowed—he's the only one who knows in Virgin River. But he doesn't know how hard I tried for a baby. He's been so supportive of me in my grieving moments—he hasn't said a word to anyone, because I asked him not to. It's easier, you know—when people don't look at you that way. Like you might be in constant pain. But," she said, "he also offered to take care of our birth control concerns, and of course I told him I had it covered. I was absolutely sure I couldn't get pregnant. God, I'd never do this to a man!"

"He's a good man, Jack. He's going to understand."

"He's going to think I tricked him, isn't he? I mean, he's forty!"

"Yeah, lot of that going around, too," June said. "I remember dealing with some of these same issues when I found out I was pregnant. Jim was over forty when I broke it to him that he was going to be a father. I was afraid he'd bolt."

"I had surgery to remove endometriosis, had my tubes blown out, took hormones, took my temperature every day for two years..." She hiccupped. "We tried everything. Mark wanted a baby as badly as I did. I'm telling you—I'm completely sterile!"

"Welll...." they both said.

"It's the funniest thing," John said. "Nature suffers to fill a void. I can't believe how many miraculous pregnancies I've seen..."

"What if Jack is furious? Who would blame him?

I mean, he hasn't even been in a serious relationship, and here I come. Bouncing into town, telling him I have the birth control issue covered. What if he just says, no, thank you?"

"Something tells me he's not going to say that," John said. "But there's only one way to find out. And—at three months—I'd recommend you not wait much longer."

"I'm afraid," she said quietly.

"Of Jack?" June asked, shocked.

"Jesus, of everything! I'm not even sure I should be here! From the beginning, I thought it was a mistake, making such a big change. I'm a city girl."

"You'd never know it," June said. "You seem to fit in just fine."

"Some days I think this place was just what I needed. Other days I ask myself what I'm doing here. Not only that, do you know how scary it is to think of being committed again and opening myself up to the pain that follows when something goes terribly, terribly wrong? I'm afraid to move on—even though you're right—I already have. I still cry sometimes—over my dead husband. How can I ask another man to put up with that?" She drew in a jagged breath. "At the very least, we should have been able to plan for a possible baby before…"

June held her hand. "Hardly any of us manages to work things out that neatly," she said. June lifted Mel's chin with a finger and looked into her eyes. "I think you should try to remember two things—you have a baby inside you now, a baby you longed for. And a good man back in Virgin River. Go with it, Mel. You'll know what to do."

Mel knew John and June were right. It was important to face this head-on and tell Jack as soon as possible. Let him have time to react. Respond. When she got back to Virgin River, she intended to go straight to the bar. But there, in front of Doc's, was a car she recognized. Anne and Jeremy Givens. It was her time.

When she got inside she found the Givenses with Doc, waiting in the kitchen with a cup of tea. "So this is it?" Mel asked.

"I think so," Anne said. "I've been in labor all day, and now I'm having contractions less than five minutes apart and some spotting. That's when you said to call, right?"

"That's what we decided. Would you like to come upstairs, settle in and let me check you?"

"I'm scared," Anne said. "I didn't think I would be."

"Darling, there is nothing in the world to be afraid of. You're going to sail through this. Jeremy, why don't you let me get Anne comfortable and then you can come upstairs."

"But I want to be there for everything!" he said.

Mel laughed in amusement. "She's just going to get undressed, Jeremy. I bet you've been there for that about a million times." She took Anne's suitcase and her arm. "Come on, sweetheart. Let's go have a baby."

Once settled in, Anne proved to be only four centimeters dilated. Back at the hospital in L.A. they would call that the price of admission—anything less than four centimeters and you were sent home to labor a little longer. Mel observed a couple of contractions and they were coming strong and long. That business about sailing through was perhaps overly optimistic.

Jeremy was at his wife's side as soon as he was invited and, unlike Darryl, he was completely prepared for the rigors of labor. This couple actually had had some birthing training. Mel told Jeremy to walk his wife up and down the upstairs hallway and left Anne in his able hands to go downstairs to use the phone to call Jack.

"Hi," she said. "I have a delivery, so I'm not coming to the bar,"

"You think it'll be long?" he asked.

"There's no telling. She hasn't progressed very far yet."

"Can I bring you anything? Something to eat?"

"No, Jack, not for me. Doc can walk across the street if he wants to. But listen—my instinct tells me maybe he shouldn't have a whiskey tonight."

"Don't worry about Doc—his instincts are pretty good, too. Mel? My door will be unlocked."

"Thank you," she said. "If we finish up before morning, I'll sneak into your room. Would that be all right?"

He laughed his low, sexy laugh. "It's always all right, Melinda. I might not be able to sleep for hoping."

"I'll hope, too—but for Anne's sake, not yours or mine."

Anne's blood pressure was stable and her labor was difficult. Three hours later, in spite of walking, squatting and laboring, she was still only at four centimeters. At midnight she was at a possible five. Doc suggested a Pitocin drip and breaking her water, which Mel had just been considering. Her contractions were coming every two minutes. Near midnight Mel checked her and with great relief, found that she had progressed to eight centimeters. But then, just thirty minutes later, she was back at five. Mel had been down this road before—the cervix had swollen and appeared as though it was shrinking. That indicated they might not be able to have a vaginal birth. She examined Anne during a contraction when her cervix widened and literally tried to hold her cervix open to the great discomfort of the patient, but it just wasn't working. Anne was wet with sweat and growing more exhausted by the minute.

It was three-thirty in the morning when Mel made the call to John Stone. "God, I'm sorry to do this to you," she said. "I have a delivery that might be going south. I've got a patient who's been laboring for hours, stuck at five. Her cervix advanced to eight and swelled back to five. She's not progressing. We could ride this out, but mother is wilting and I have no indication that... I think it's very possible the baby's not going to fit. I suspect I'm going to need a cesarean."

"Did you pit her?"

"Yeah. Pitocin running and I broke her water."

"Okay, stop the pit, turn her on her left side. How long has she been laboring, stuck at four or five?"

"Ten hours with me. She labored at home for about eight."

"Have you tried stretching the cervix?"

"Unsuccessfully," she said. "Our ultrasound at your clinic showed a competent pelvis and average-size baby."

"Things change," he said. "Any fetal distress?"

"Not yet. The doptone shows a strong, regular, even heart rate, but mother's pressure is up a bit."

"You could ride this out awhile, but if she's exhausted, I vote for not waiting. I'll meet you at Valley. Can you make the drive or do you need helicopter transport?"

"We've got some real good shocks on that Hummer," she said. "Either way, she's an hour or more from the hospital. I'll wake Jack. Get his help."

Mel checked Anne once more; she had finally made six centimeters, but she was weakening. Anne's heart rate was increasing and the baby's had dropped just slightly. Jeremy was growing nervous and pale despite the number of times Mel reassured him that this wasn't unusual. It was starting to look like even if the baby was going to fit, Anne might not have the energy to push him out.

It was 4:00 a.m. when Mel called Jack. He didn't sound as though he'd been asleep. "Jack, I'm going to have to transport my patient to Valley Hospital for a cesarean. John's going to meet us there. I could use some help."

"Be right there," he said.

"I'll try to get her downstairs and then if you'll—"

"No, Mel," Jack said. "Leave her where she is. I'll get her downstairs. I wouldn't want both of you to fall."

"Okay, sure. Thanks."

Then she went back to her patient. Although Doc was standing by, this was Mel's case and a decision like this was entirely hers. "Anne," she said, gently brushing the hair away from her soaking brow. "We're going to transport you to Valley Hospital for a C-section...."

"Nooo," she cried. "I want to have the baby normally."

"Nothing abnormal about a C-section," she said. "It's a good operation, and it keeps you and the baby out of distress. Fortunately, we have the time so you're not at major risk. But with the distance to the hospital, we shouldn't wait until you are. It's going to be fine, Anne."

"Oh, God," she cried.

Then she was gripped by another hard contraction and fear gave way to pain. Her husband tried the breathing with her, but after all these hours of hard labor, it was futile. She had very little space between contractions and some residual pain that made it feel, to her, as if her contractions were continual, back to back.

Mel had had tough deliveries before, but it was different in the hospital, when you could just wheel your patient down the hall to surgery and let the surgeons and anesthesiologist take over; in a hospital she would give the mother every chance to make it through, if she wanted to try. It was different for her here, when the hospital was so far away, staffed and equipped for only routine procedures and surgeries. She couldn't help but feel very disappointed for Anne, who had so looked forward to a natural childbirth with her husband.

"Anne, it's just one of those things. Sometimes a C-section is the best answer," Mel said. "You're not going to have this baby here, but we want you to have as many healthy births as you desire."

"Of course you're right," she answered breathlessly.

Mel heard the front door open, Jack's feet on the stairs and then his voice outside the door. "Mel?"

She pushed the door open.

"Let me take her down for you. I'll drive you to the hospital in the Hummer."

"Thanks. Come in. Just let her get through this next contraction."

Jack stepped into the room and nodded at Jeremy. "How you doing, man?" he asked. "I'm going to carry your wife downstairs for you—you look pretty exhausted. You and Mel can ride in back with her and I'll drive." As soon as Anne seemed to relax a bit, Jack bent over the bed and lifted her easily into his arms. "Hang on, kiddo," he said. "I'll get you down before the next one hits, how's that?"

Mel grabbed her bag and said, "Jeremy, please get Anne's suitcase." She followed Jack downstairs, grabbed her coat and while Jack held Anne, she opened up the back of the Hummer and slid out the gurney. "Anne, I want you on your left side, please." Once she was situated, Mel and Jeremy climbed in on either side of her, kneeling, while Jack got behind the wheel and took off in the direction of Valley Hospital.

Mel kept the fetoscope handy and blood pressure cuff on Anne's upper arm. She checked her pressure and the fetal heartbeat every few minutes. They were nearly halfway when she reached forward and put a thankful hand on Jack's shoulder. His hand automatically came up to cover hers. "You were still awake," she said softly.

"In case you needed anything," he answered.

She gently squeezed his shoulder, but what she really wanted to do was throw her arms around him. She so appreciated the way he instinctively supported her in her work.

When they got to the hospital they entered the emergency room and, once inside, Mel handed Jack her coat and said, "You should move the SUV. Jeremy and I will take her up to labor and delivery. John's meeting us. I hate to ask you, but…"

"Of course I'll wait. I'll be right here. Don't worry about me."

"Am I going to be allowed in?" Jeremy asked while they were in the elevator.

"That's going to be up to Dr. Stone," she said. "If it were up to me, I wouldn't have a problem with it."

Mel pushed the gurney through the swinging doors and was very happy to see John standing at the sink, finishing his scrub. Hands held up, he turned toward her and gave a nod and a smile. "Number two is set up, Mel. The anesthesiologist is here."

Beside him at the adjoining sink, pumping the faucet pedal with her foot, was a nurse in scrubs, her mask tied around her neck. She looked over at Mel and with a sarcastic twist of her lips, said, "Another botched home birth?"

Mel's mouth dropped open and her eyes widened as if slapped. John whirled on the nurse, glaring at her. Then John turned back to Mel and said, "Can you scrub in with me, Mel?"

"I'm prepared to assist, Dr. Stone," the nurse said from behind him.

"Thank you, Juliette, but I'm leaning toward someone more professional. You and I will talk later." And to Mel, "You have less than fifteen minutes."

"Certainly. Jeremy wants to be there," she said.

"Of course. Juliette, find the father some scrubs. Mel, you'll find some in the locker room. Shake a leg."

Mel pushed the gurney to operating room number two and let the circulating nurse pull Anne into the room. She donned green scrubs in the locker room and joined Jeremy at the sink, saying, "If you scrub in, the doctor might be inclined to let you hold your son when he's born. Just like this," she said, demonstrating the scrubbing technique. "No guarantees on that, so no pouting. And you'll have to stay at Anne's head."

"Have you done this before?" he asked her. "Assisted in a C-section?"

"Many times," she said.

"Mel?" he asked. "It wasn't botched, was it?"

"Of course not. What Anne experienced wasn't all that unusual. You were there, Jeremy. You see anything happen that bothered you? I trust you would've said something or at least asked a question or two." She smiled at him. "You have one stubborn little boy to raise. Fortunately, we have a very good surgeon at our disposal."

By the time they entered the operating room, Anne had received her spinal from the anesthesiologist and was much more comfortable. John was ready to begin and Mel took her place next to him, her instruments lying out on the mayo stand.

"Scalpel," he said.

She slapped it into his hand. "Thank you," she said. "For what you did out there."

"She's a good nurse, but I never figured her for jealous. I apologize for her. We're ready to retract," he said. He chuckled. "You do a damn fine job, Mel. I'd let you deliver my wife in a second."

The ride back to Virgin River wasn't exactly quiet—Jeremy was a literal motormouth. Jack heard the details of the surgery several times. While Jeremy's wife was in recovery and his son in the nursery, he needed a lift home to fetch his own vehicle so he could go back. He chattered while Jack drove, and Mel's head lolled on the seat beside him.

"Exhausted, baby?" he asked her.

"I'll be fine after a nap," she said.

"Mel assisted Dr. Stone," Jeremy sounded from the back. "He asked her to. It was incredible. The things she knows how to do."

Jack glanced over at her and smiled. "You know what's incredible, Jeremy?" Jack said. He reached over and squeezed her thigh. "She never surprises me."

It was 9:00 a.m. before they got back to Virgin River. Mel checked in with Doc. "Mother and baby came through very well. John Stone is a wonderful, fast surgeon."

"Good call," he said. "For a city girl." And then he treated her to a rare smile.

She found there were only three people scheduled for morning appointments and Doc was more than capable. She had asked Jack to give her a call in five or six hours—she didn't want to sleep all day or she wouldn't sleep that night. But the labor and delivery had been taxing and she was spent.

Jack helped Preacher serve lunch, then he went to the river to fish for a couple of hours. He had a lot on his mind. It hadn't escaped him that Mel had been moody lately. He'd seen suspicious evidence of tears. And she wasn't drinking that end-of-the-day beer—she played with it for a little while before pushing it aside and asking for ice water.

At about three in the afternoon, while Preacher worked on preparing the evening meal, he went out to the cabin. He took off his boots on the front porch and tiptoed into the house. He stripped down to his boxers and slipped into the bed beside her, gently kissing her neck. She stirred slightly, turned her head and smiled at him.

"Now this is a good way to wake up," she murmured, closing her eyes again and snuggling closer to him.

He held her for a long while, then his hands began to move. Softly and sweetly. Before even seconds passed, her hands began to move, as well, and she pressed herself against him. When she began to strain against him, he got rid of the T-shirt she slept in and the boxers he still wore. He made gentle love to her, careful to keep her comfortable and safe, even as she picked up that eager pace, that frenetic yearning that drove him wild.

He knew her body as well as she did herself by now, and he knew exactly what gave her the most pleasure.

She settled back to earth slowly. "I thought you were going to call," she said.

"Isn't this better?"

"You always know what to do," she said.

"Not always," he said, holding her close. "Right now, for example. I'm not sure what to do."

"Why?" she asked, her eyes still closed, her face buried in his chest.

"When are you going to tell me?"

She lifted her head. "Tell you?"

"About the baby."

"But Jack, you know the baby and mother are—"

"The baby inside of you," he said, placing a large hand over her flat tummy.

A startled look crossed her features. She pushed him away a little bit "Did someone say something to you?" she asked.

"No one had to say anything. Please tell me I'm not the last to know."

"I just saw John yesterday—and how in the world would you know?"

"Mel," he said, running the back of one knuckle along her cheek, "your body's changing. You haven't had a period. For a while, I thought maybe you'd had a hysterectomy or something because I haven't noticed a period since the first time we made love, but there's a blue box under the bathroom sink. You don't drink your beer, and you get nauseous from time to time. Not to mention being more tired than usual."

"Lord," she said. "You never think a man will notice. Not things like that."

"Well?"

She sighed. "I went to see John yesterday to confirm what I already suspected. I'm pregnant. Three months."

"You're a midwife. How could you not know at three weeks?"

"Because I assumed I was sterile. Infertile. Mark and I did everything to try to get a baby—even in vitro fertilization. To no avail. This was the last thing I ever expected."

"Ah," he said, finally clear on why she might keep it from him. "So, here we are," he said.

"I'm sorry, Jack. You must think I'm an idiot."

He kissed her. "Of course not. Mel, I'm in love with you."

She was frozen for a second. "Oh, God," she finally said, plummeted into tears. "Oh, God, Jack!" She buried her face in his chest and wept.

"Hey, no reason to cry, baby. You a little surprised? No more than me," he laughed. "I never thought this could happen to me. It hit me so hard, I damn near fell down. But I love you." She continued to softly cry. "It's okay, honey. It'll be okay." He stroked her hair. "You want to have a baby, obviously."

She lifted her head. "I wanted a baby so badly, I ached. But do you?" she asked. "I mean, you're forty."

"I want everything with you. Everything. Besides, I like babies. And I'm wild about pregnant women."

"When did you decide you knew for sure?" she asked him.

"At least a month ago." He put a hand over her breast. "Sore? Haven't you noticed the changes? Your nipples have darkened."

"I was in denial," she said, wiping at her tears. "I was so desperate for a baby—but I had accepted that it couldn't happen. I wouldn't have done it this way."

"And how would you have done it, exactly?"

"If I thought it even remotely possible I could get pregnant, I would have at least been sure you wanted a family, so that we could make a decision like this together. Fully informed. So if it happened, it would be okay. I hate that you've had this thrust on you. With no warning."

"That wasn't going to happen, not under the circumstances. It never would have occurred to you to try for a baby—convinced it was impossible. So—maybe it's a good thing it just happened like this."

"And what if it had gone the other way? What if I told you the thing I wanted most in the world was a baby, asked you to try for one with me?"

He pulled her a little closer. "I'd have been happy to help out." Then he smiled into her eyes.

"I don't know what to say. You just accept everything. You're amazing. I thought you might be very pissed."

"Nah. The only thing that disappoints me is that it took me this long to find you."

"Even with all my baggage?" she asked.

"I don't consider this baggage." He leaned over and kissed her belly. "I consider this the grand prize."

"You want it?" she asked.

"I told you," he said. "I want it. It makes me happy."

"God," she said in a breath. "I was afraid."

"Of?"

"Of you saying, 'Holy shit—I'm forty! What do I want with a baby?'"

He laughed at her. "I didn't say that, did I? Nah, I'm ready. A family sounds good."

"Jack," she said, "I'm still afraid."

"Of?"

"Of believing in us. My last stab at something like this ended so, so badly. I thought I'd never get over it. I'm not sure I am yet."

"Well, you're just going to have to take a leap of faith," he said.

"I think I can do that," she said. "If you're there to catch me."

"I'm here," he said. "I haven't let you down yet, have I?"

She put her hand against his face. "No, Jack. You sure haven't."

Jack had seen his brothers-in-law, all puffed up with testosterone pride when they'd gotten their wives pregnant, when the babies came. He never pretended to really understand it. He was too busy with his career, with his troops, when it seemed to him a woman getting pregnant was probably the worst career suicide a man could suffer. He didn't get their male egos; he thought his sisters were just getting fat and mean.

He got it now. He felt as though his chest might explode. There was a fire in his belly and it was all he could do to keep from running up a flag. He couldn't wait until he and Mel could make some plans, get married, tell the world they were lifetime partners and bringing a baby on board.

She shooed him out of the cabin, told him to go take care of the dinner crowd while she showered off that long night with a patient. She promised to drive into town to have a diet cola at the bar and tell those present that Anne and Jeremy and their baby boy were doing fine. Then later, they'd go back home together.

He was almost to town when he turned around to go back. Preacher might get testy, being stuck with the bar and cooking, too, but he just had to hold her for a minute more. He tiptoed up the porch steps, took off his boots, and silently opened the door. He expected to hear the shower running, but instead he heard her weeping.

"I'm sorry," she was saying through her tears. "I'm so, so sorry." Then she sobbed briefly. "I never planned this. Oh, Mark, please understand…"

He stole a peek into the bedroom and saw Mel sitting on the edge of her bed, talking to the picture of her dead husband. It cut through him like a knife; damn near ripped his heart out.

"Please understand—this was the last thing I expected," she cried. "It's just the way it happened, and it took me by surprise. Total surprise. I promise I'll never forget you!"

He cleared his throat and she jumped. She looked at him, tears running down her cheeks. "Jack!" she gasped.

He held up a hand. "I'll go," he said. "You can work this out with Mark. I'll see you later."

He turned to leave and she ran after him, tugging on his shirt. "Jack, please…"

"It's okay, Mel," he said, profound sadness showing in his eyes. He forced a smile. "It's not as if I didn't know what I was up against."

"No! You don't understand!"

"Sure I do," he said, tenderly touching her cheek. "Take your time. I'm not going anywhere. Except back to the bar. I think I need a drink."

Jack walked out of the cabin, collected his boots on her porch and got back into his truck. *So,* he thought, *probably the best day of my life, turned to total shit. She's still back there, with him. She can love you like she's yours, but she's not. Not yet.*

Hadn't he always known this was the risk he was taking, as long as he loved her? That she might not be able to let go of him? Ever?

What the hell, he told himself. *She might never really belong to me; good thing he can't come back from the grave and snatch her away. But that baby is mine. And I want it. I want her. Whatever she has to spare...*

Fifteen

Mel showered, put on clean clothes and prepared to go to the bar to take her medicine. She felt terrible; her heart ached when she thought of the look in Jack's eyes. He never should have witnessed that performance. It must have shattered him. She could only hope he would forgive her.

She brought a change of clothes and her makeup for work the next day. If Jack didn't want to come back to her cabin with her, she would force her company on him. They had to get beyond this. This was her fault. It wasn't just the two of them anymore. He wanted this baby. He wanted her *and* the baby. She was going to find a way to make this right.

There were only about a dozen customers in the bar when she got there—the Bristols and Carpenters sitting at a table for four, Hope and Doc at the bar, a couple of men playing cribbage with a pitcher of beer, and a young family. Jack stood behind the bar and lifted his chin slightly in greeting as she entered. It was a very subdued gesture; there was going to be penance to pay.

She stopped and chatted briefly with the Bristols and Carpenters, filling them in on the Givens baby, before going to the bar. She got onto the stool next to Doc. "Did you get any rest today?" she asked him.

"I don't sleep in daylight," he grumbled. He popped an antacid and Jack put a whiskey in front of him.

"Long night?" Hope asked her.

"Long night for the Givenses," she said. "But they're going to be fine."

"Good work, Mel," she said. "I knew I was smart to get you up here." She stubbed out her cigarette and left, chatting her way out the door.

Without being asked, Jack put a cola in front of her. She mouthed the words, *I'm sorry.* His lips curved just slightly, hurt in his eyes, but he leaned toward her and placed a gentle kiss on her brow. *Ow,* she thought. *This is bad.*

And it just got worse. They had only the most superficial conversation while Mel picked at her dinner, but determined, she waited out the emptying of the bar. It was eight o'clock by the time Preacher was sweeping the floor and Jack was putting up clean glasses. "Are we going to talk about it?" she quietly asked Jack.

"How about we let it go and move forward," he said.

"Jack," she whispered so that Preacher wouldn't hear. "I love you."

"You don't have to say that."

"But it's true. Please believe me."

He lifted her chin and put a light kiss on her lips. "Okay," he said. "I believe you."

"Oh, God," she said, tears gathering in her eyes.

"Don't, Mel," he said. "Don't start crying again. I'm afraid I won't understand why—and it'll make things worse."

She sucked it back, forced herself to still the nerves that were tightening inside her. Her fleeting thought was, *God, what will I do if he's through with me on account of that?* "I'm going to your room," she told him. "I'm going to stay there until you come to me and I'm going to convince you, somehow, that we belong to each other. Especially now."

He gave a nod that was so slight, it was almost imperceptible, so she got off her stool and walked through the back of the bar to his quarters. Once alone, she couldn't suppress the tears. They flowed freely down her cheeks. *He thinks I'm going to spend the rest of my life explaining myself to my dead husband, apologizing for how I feel about Jack. Well, that's what I was doing—what's he to think? He won't believe me if I tell him that's not true, not how it's going to be. It was just a one-time thing—the shock, the exhaustion, the high emotional state I'm in.*

Mel sat in the big chair in his room, revisiting in her mind that night she sat in this spot, drenched from the rain, and he gently undressed her, dried her and put her to bed. That was when she knew, without a doubt, there was a partner here for her, even if she couldn't admit it to herself for quite a while. Since the ultrasound, she was pretty convinced she had conceived that night. Jack opened her up, showed her passion she didn't know existed, and put his baby in her. It was nothing short of a miracle—the love, the passion, the baby. She just didn't know how difficult it would be to make that transition into a new life. A second life. A completely different life.

She sat in that chair for an hour. Waiting.

Jack put up all his clean glasses and dishes, wiped down the bar and poured himself a drink. There was a particular, old single malt, an aged Glenlivet, that he saved for special occasions. Or emergencies.

Preacher put away his broom and went to the bar. "Everything okay, man?" he asked.

Jack pulled down a glass and poured a shot for his friend. He lifted his toward Preacher in something of a toast and said solemnly, "Mel's pregnant." Then Jack took the shot in one swallow.

"Aw, man," Preacher said. "What are you gonna do?"

"I'm going to be a father," he said. "I'm going to marry her."

Preacher picked up his glass and lifted it tentatively, taking a drink. "You sure about that?"

"Yeah, I'm sure."

"That what you want, man?"

"Absolutely."

Preacher grinned. "Sarge. A family man. Who'd think?"

Jack tipped the bottle once more, over both glasses. "Yeah," Jack said.

"Seems like, maybe, things aren't so hot right now," Preacher said.

"Nah," he lied. "Just found out," he further lied. "It's gonna work out great. It's gonna be perfect." Then he smiled. "You know I never do anything I don't want to do. Uncle Preacher." He threw back the second shot and put his glass on the bar. "Good night."

Jack felt bad about leaving Mel in his room for so long, but they both needed some time to compose themselves. If there were going to be more tears, this one time he wanted her to get that out of the way on her own. There's only so much one man could do, so he didn't rush to her. She was going to be feeling a little desperate—pregnant, just caught apologizing for it to the picture of Mark, afraid Jack wouldn't be able to deal with that. There was nothing either of them could do about it—Jack had known from the beginning that Mark was still there, in her life, in her heart. He would never have all of her. Well, then, he'd make the most of what he did have. He wasn't going to make her grovel; he was just going to love the heck out of her. He could manage this, even if it wasn't the most ideal situation. In time, maybe she'd come around. Mark's memory could fade enough so that even if Jack wasn't the only man in her life, he would come to feel like the most important one. Maybe when she held their child, she would realize life was for the living.

He walked in, looked across the room at her, and leaned down to pull off his boots. He yanked his shirt out of his pants and took it off, hanging it on the peg in his closet. He removed his belt and tossed it aside. Then he approached her and put out a hand to her.

She put her hand in his and let him draw her to her feet. She leaned her head against his chest and said again, "I'm sorry. I love you. I want to be with you."

His arms went around her and he answered, "That's good enough for me."

Jack kissed her tenderly.

"You've had a couple of drinks," she said. "Scotch."

"It seemed like the thing to do," he said. He slowly began to undress her, leaving her clothes in a pile on the floor, because when words failed him he had never failed to be able to speak to her body. There was no confusion about this—when he touched her, she was all his. When she responded to him, she held nothing back. There might be a glitch in her heart, some of it stuck in the past. But her body came alive under his lips, his hands.

He carried her to his bed, laid her sweetly on the sheets and went to work on her. He touched her, kissed and caressed her in the ways he knew filled her up, pleased her, gave her joy, released her. She rose to him, hot and ready, wrapping herself around him, giving. Taking. Crying out.

God, he didn't know he could want this much. Love this much.

Okay, he thought—*here's the reality. He would always have this.* He would make her body sing just as she sent him reeling into the most incredible madness a man can feel. He would hold her every night and wake up with her every morning and there would be many times, like this, when they would come together in this incomparable passion and no matter what else was going on, this mutual joy belonged only to them. Just the two of them. There were no ghosts present in these moments.

Sufficient compensation. Sweet consolation.

"Jack," she said, snuggled up against him. "I hate that I hurt you."

He buried his face in her hair and inhaled the sweet scent. "Let's not talk about that anymore. It's behind us. We have a lot in front of us."

"Would it be a good idea for me to go to Joey for a little while? Give you some space? Try to get my head together?"

He rose over her and looked into her eyes. "Don't, Mel. Don't run just because we hit a rough patch. We'll work through this."

"You sure?"

"Mel," he said hoarsely, his voice a mere whisper, "you have my baby inside you. I have to be a part of that. Come on…"

She fought the tears that threatened. "I know it must be hard to deal with an emotional basket case like me."

He smiled at her and said, "I've heard that pregnant women get like that."

"I think I'm just like that, period."

"Marry me," he said.

She touched his beautiful face. "You don't have to."

"Melinda, six months ago we were two people without attachments. Two people who had accepted we would never have any—and that we'd never have families. Now we have it all. We have each other and a baby. A baby we both want. Let's not screw this up."

"Are you sure?"

"I've never been more sure about anything. I want this. If you can't stay here, I'll go anywhere you want to go."

"But Jack, you love it here!"

"Don't you realize I love you more? I need you in my life. You and our baby. God, Mel—I don't care where that happens. As long as it happens."

"Jack," she said in a whisper. "What if you change your mind? What if something happens? You have to remember, I never thought anything terrible would happen to—"

He put a finger on her lips, stopping her. He didn't want to hear his name. Not now. "Shh," he said. "I want you to trust me. You know you're safe with me."

Mel awoke humming. The song this morning was "Mamma Mia" by ABBA, of all things. It made her smile. She got out of bed and showered. When she came out of the shower and put on one of Jack's shirts, she found a steaming cup of coffee on the bathroom counter. There was a note under it. *Half-caf. Daddy.* Jack was already up and in the bar, taking care of breakfast. Taking care of her. Robbing her of caffeine.

She dressed for the day; she had been so out of focus lately, she had no idea what kind of schedule lay ahead. She couldn't remember making any appointments for the morning. Still, she wasn't rushing to Doc's. It was early and she had a very important phone call to make.

"I wish I could see the look on your face when I tell you this, Joey," Mel said. "I hope you're sitting down. I'm pregnant."

There was a gasp, then silence.

"Pregnant," she said again. "Totally knocked up."

"Are you *sure?*"

"Three months," she said.

"Oh, my God! Mel!"

"I know. Kind of blew my mind, too."

"Three months? Let's see…"

"Don't bother trying to do the math. I haven't had a period since he touched me for the first time. I guess he's potent enough for both of us. At first, I thought it so impossible, an absurd fantasy. I figured I was late because of stress, change, how weird my life is. But it's real. I had an ultrasound."

"Mel! How is this possible?"

"Don't ask me—stranger things have happened. But not around here, apparently. I'm surrounded by women who were pretty sure they couldn't get pregnant and voilà! There's a rumor about the water… I'm thinking of calling my L.A. infertility specialist to tell him about this place."

"What are you going to do?"

"I'm going to marry Jack."

"Mel—do you love him?" Joey asked, her voice subdued. Cautious.

Mel drew in a breath, trying to calm her voice, which she knew would be tremulous and emotional. "I do," she said. "Joey, I love him so much, I almost ache with it. I never thought I could love this much. I was in denial about that for a while, too."

"Mel," Joey said, then began to cry. "Oh, my sweet baby."

"It made me feel guilty, like I was doing something wrong I was so committed to the idea that I'd lost my one true love and would never feel anything even close to that again in my life. I never considered the possibility that I might find something even more powerful. It seemed, briefly, like a betrayal. Jack even caught me crying to Mark's picture that I was sorry, that I didn't expect it to happen, and promising never to forget him. God. It was an awful moment."

"Baby girl, you haven't done anything wrong. You've been through such a lot."

"Well, in my sane state, I know that. Jack knew about my problems, and he just hung in there, just kept loving me and loving me, putting all my needs ahead of his own, promising me I'd be safe with him, that I could trust him. Oh, God," she said, tears coming in spite of the fact that she was so, so happy. "God, he's wonderful. Joey," she said in a near whisper, "he wants the baby as much as I do."

"This is just unbelievable. When are you getting married? Because we're going to be there."

"We haven't had a chance to even talk about it—I just broke it to him yesterday and he asked me last night. I'll let you know when I know."

"But does this mean you're staying there?"

Mel laughed. "You were right, you know—coming here was completely crazy. It was irrational. To think

I'd choose to go to a town where there's no mall, much less a day spa, and one restaurant that doesn't have a menu? Please. No medical technology, ambulance service or local police—how is it I thought that would be easier, less stressful? I almost slid off the mountain on my way into town!"

"Ah… Mel…"

"We don't even have cable, no cell phone signal most of the time. And there's not a single person here who can admire my Cole Haan boots which, by the way, are starting to look like crap from traipsing around forests and farms. Did you know that any critical illness or injury has to be airlifted out of here? A person would be crazy to find this relaxing. Renewing." She laughed. "The state I was in, when I was leaving L.A., I thought I absolutely had to escape all the challenges. It never occurred to me that challenge would be good for me. A completely new challenge."

"Mel…"

"When I told Jack I was pregnant, after promising him I had the birth control taken care of, he should have said, 'I'm outta here, babe.' But you know what he said? He said, 'I have to have you and the baby in my life, and if you can't stay here, I'll go anywhere.'" She sniffed a little and a tear rolled down her cheek. "When I wake up in the morning, the first thing I do is check to see if there are deer in the yard. Then I wonder what Preacher's in the mood to fix for dinner. Jack's usually already gone back to town—he likes splitting logs in the early morning—half the town wakes up to the sound of his ax striking wood. I see him five or ten times through the day and he always looks at me like we've been apart for a year. If I have a patient in labor, he stays up all night, just in case I need something. And when there are no patients at night, when he holds me before I fall asleep, bad TV reception is the last thing on my mind.

"Am I staying here? I came here because I believed I'd lost everything that mattered, and ended up finding everything I've ever wanted in the world. Yeah, Joey. I'm staying. Jack's here. Besides, I belong here now. I belong to them. They belong to me."

Right after a light breakfast, she headed for Doc's. She supposed it was in order to tell him right away, but when she walked into the house, she was greeted by quiet. Good, she thought. No patients yet. She went to Doc's office and tapped lightly on the door, then pushed it open. He was sitting in the chair at his desk, leaning back, his eyes closed. *Hmm. Doesn't sleep in daylight, huh?* She stood over him. It was good to see Doc docile for once.

Mel was about to leave and wait for a better time, but something made her take a closer look at Doc. His eyes were pinched closed, his face in a grimace and his coloring wasn't right. He was gray. She reached down and squeezed his wrist with the forefingers of one hand. His pulse was racing. Mel felt Doc's brow and found his skin clammy. His eyes opened into slits. "What is it?" she asked him.

"Nothing," he said. "Heartburn."

Heartburn does not make your pulse race and your skin clammy, she thought. She ran for the stethoscope and blood pressure cuff in the exam room, returning to him. "You going to tell me what it is—or make me guess?"

"I told you… Nothing. I'll be fine in a few minutes."

She took his blood pressure, though she had to struggle with him for cooperation. "Did you have breakfast?" she asked him.

"A while ago."

"What did you have? Bacon and eggs? Sausage?"

"It wasn't that great. Preacher's a little off on the cooking…"

His blood pressure was elevated. "Any chest pains?" she asked.

"No."

She palpated his abdomen, although excess lipid tissue on his pot belly made it impossible to feel his internal organs while he was sitting upright. And he slapped at her hand, trying to push her away. But as she palpated, he grunted in pain. "How many of them have you had?" she asked him.

"How many what?"

"Attacks. Like this."

"One or two," he said.

"Don't lie to the nice little nurse," she chastised. "How long has this been going on?" She pulled the lids back on his eyes and they had begun to yellow. He was jaundicing. "You waiting for your liver to blow?"

"It'll pass."

He was having a major league gallbladder attack, and she wasn't sure that was all. She didn't even think about it—she picked up the phone and called the bar. "Jack," she said, "come over, please. I have to get Doc to the hospital." And she hung up.

"No," Doc said.

"Yes," she said. "If you argue with me now, I'll get Jack and Preacher to put you in a fireman's carry and dump you in the Hummer. That should make your belly feel good." She looked at his face. "How's your back?"

"Terrible. This one is kind of bad."

"You're getting jaundiced, Doc," she said. "We can't wait. I suspect you're in a biliary crisis. I'm going to start an IV and I don't want any lip."

Before she could get the needle in, both Jack and Preacher arrived. "We'll get him in the car and I'll drive you," Jack said. "What's the matter with him?"

"I think it's a gallbladder attack, but he's not talking. It's serious. His blood pressure is up and he's in terrible pain."

"Waste of time," Doc said. "It'll pass."

"Please be still," she implored. "I don't want to have to ask these big boys to hold you down."

Once the IV was in, she made a mad dash to the drug cabinet while Jack and Preacher each got on either side of him, walking him slowly out the door, Jack holding the Ringer's over his head. When they got to the Hummer she joined them. Doc said, "I'm not lying down."

"I think you should—"

"I can't," he said. "Bad enough sitting up."

"All right then, we'll take out the gurney and put up the backseat. I'll pull the IV bag hook forward and sit beside you. Have you taken anything for the pain yet?"

"I was just starting to have very kind thoughts toward morphine," he said. Jack adjusted the backseat, leaving the gurney on Doc's porch. Doc climbed clumsily into the backseat. "We just don't have good enough drugs," he muttered.

"Can you make it to the hospital without drugs? Give the doctor a clean slate?"

"Arrrgggghhh," he grumbled.

"If you insist, I'll give you something—but it would be better to let the E.R. decide what's best." She took a breath. "I grabbed some morphine."

He peered at her through slits. "Hit me," he said. "It's just god-awful."

She sighed and drew up a syringe from the vial in her bag, putting it right into the IV. It took only moments for him to say, "Ahhh…"

"Have you seen anyone about this?" she asked him.

"I'm a doctor, young woman. I can take care of myself."

"Oh, brother," she said.

"There's a clinic in Garberville," Jack said as he started the car. "It's closer than Valley Hospital."

"We're going to need a surgeon," Mel informed him.

"I'm not going to need surgery," the old boy argued.

"You a betting man?" was all she said.

Doc Mullins rested a bit easier with the narcotic in him, which was good since it was over an hour, even with Jack's fast and skillful driving. It wasn't the distance so much as the roads—just getting to the county road that connected with the highway twisted and turned and was slow going. Mel watched out the window, remembering that first night she came here, terrified of these sharp twists and turns, the sheer drops, steep climbs. Now, with Jack managing the Hummer, she was comfortable. Before long they were out of the hills and speeding through the valley. With her attention focused on Doc, she couldn't fully appreciate the landscape. It did occur to her, however, that every time she traveled anywhere around this county, she was amazed by the beauty as if seeing it for the first time.

She had a fleeting thought that if anything bad happened to Doc, it would be down to only her. How was she going to have a baby and take care of a town?

She thought about Joey's question—are you staying

there? It made her smile. It would hardly seem a punishment to live out her life in this glorious place.

This was only Mel's second visit to the emergency room—the first was with Connie. She had taken Jeremy and Anne to labor and delivery the night the baby came, so she didn't really know the staff in E.R. They all knew Doc, however. He'd been putting in regular appearances there for upwards of forty years. And they greeted Mel very enthusiastically, as if she were an old friend.

Doc was not one to allow fussing; he made it plain he didn't think he needed to be there. Mel and Jack were seated outside the exam room while the emergency room doctor checked him over. Then another doctor went into the exam room and Doc was heard to bellow, "Aw, for Christ's sake! Can't I get a better surgeon than you? I don't want to die on the goddamn table!"

Mel blanched, but she saw that some of the staff was chuckling. After a bit the surgeon came out to them. He had a smile on his face. He held out his hand. "Dr. Simon, Miss...?"

She stood and took his hand. "Monroe," she said. "Mel Monroe. I work with Doc. Is he going to be all right?"

"Oh, I think so. Doctors. Great patients, aren't we? I'm going to admit him and that gallbladder has to come out, but we can't take him into surgery until we get him out of this biliary crisis. That could take a day or week. Good call, Miss Monroe. I assume he didn't assist you a bit."

"He tried not to. May I see him?"

"Of course."

She found Doc in a raised position in the bed while the nurse was fiddling with the IV. The E.R. doctor was writing in the chart and when he saw her, gave a nod of hello. And on Doc's face was the unhappy expression she had come to view with fondness.

Mel looked around the E.R.—far smaller and less crowded than the one she was used to in L.A. Still, memories flooded back to her—the days and nights she had spent working in that environment. The adrenaline rush of emergencies; the edgy environment that had excited and stimulated her. At the nurses' station a young doctor was bent over a nurse, reading over her shoulder, making her laugh at some whispered remark. That could have been Mel and Mark a few years ago. She let her eyes slowly close as she realized that she had moved completely beyond that. That familiar pang of longing did not plague her anymore. Now the only man she longed for waited for her just outside this room, prepared to go through anything with her. Her hand crept absently to her tummy, resting there. *It was all right,* she realized. *What I suffered was very bad; what I have is very good.*

"Young woman," Doc snapped. "You gonna be sick?"

"Hmm?" she said, coming out of the haze. "No. Of course not."

"For a minute there you looked like you were going to cry. Or puke."

She just smiled at him. "Sorry. I was on another planet there for a second. Are you feeling better?"

"I'll live. You'd better go. There might be patients back at the house."

"I'll come back for your surgery," she said.

"No! I'm probably going to die in surgery anyway with that young pup cutting me up—you're needed back in Virgin River. Someone has to look after things. I guess you're in charge. God help us all."

"I'll call to see how you're doing, and I will come back when you have surgery. And Doc? Try to behave yourself. Try not to get thrown out of here."

"Ach," he scoffed.

She put her small cool hand on his wizened brow. "Feel better. I'll watch your practice."

In an uncharacteristically soft voice, she heard him say, "Thank you."

On the drive back to Virgin River Mel said, "He's going to need time to recover before he can start seeing patients again. I suppose I'll be staying at his house for a while after he gets home."

Doc's age, weight and blood pressure put him at a disadvantage in both surgery and recovery. It was a week before the surgeon could operate, and while the normal hospital stay for a cholesystectomy was brief—couple of days at most—they kept Doc for another week.

For those two weeks, Mel drove back and forth to Valley Hospital to check on him, plus managed the meager amount of patient care in Virgin River. June and John offered assistance, should she need it, but she was holding up fine. She stayed at the clinic during the days, spent her nights with Jack across the street, and the only huge inconvenience was planning and executing a wedding.

Jack told his dad and sisters that he and Mel were marrying, news which was met with much approval and excitement. He saved the news about the baby; he wanted to see the looks on their faces when they found out. Since there were no inns or motels in Virgin River, the couple decided they'd have a small, family-only wedding in Sacramento as soon as possible—at the Sheridan house. Jack told his sisters to plan something simple, quiet and quick for three weeks from the date Doc had gone into the hospital. He and Mel would drive down, tie the knot, and hurry home. "What about a honeymoon?" Sam asked.

"Don't worry about that," Jack said. And what he thought was, *I'm going to be on a honeymoon for the rest of my life.*

Rick took the news of the pregnancy and fast approaching marriage with a bit of shock. "You okay with this?" he asked Jack.

"Oh, yeah. Big-time. I'm ready for a family, Rick." He put his hand around the back of the boy's neck and pulled him against his shoulder. "In addition to you and Preach, that is. You okay with it?"

"Hey, man. You're not too young, that's for sure." Then he grinned. "I really thought she was out of your league."

"She is, buddy. But what the heck."

The evening before Mel was due to pick up Doc at Valley Hospital and bring him home, Jack asked, "Do you have to spend the nights at Doc's?"

"Probably just for a few days—long enough to make sure he's getting around all right. He's ambulatory at the hospital, but he's miserable. His grimace isn't just from being ornery at the moment. He'll need pain medication—and I don't want him administering his own. He could get confused and overdose."

Jack sat in the big chair in his room and said, "Come here," to Mel. She went to him and he pulled her down onto his lap. "I have something for you." He pulled a small box out of his pocket, shocking her into silence. It was definitely a ring box. "I don't know how practical this is in a place like Virgin River. It might be a little fussy. But I couldn't help myself. I want to give you everything—but this will have to do."

She opened the box to find a diamond ring so beautiful it brought tears to her eyes. It was a wide gold band with three large diamonds set in; classy and understated, yet very rich and unique. "Jack, what were you thinking? This is beautiful! The diamonds are huge!"

"I understand if you can't wear it often, given your work. And if you don't like the design—"

"Are you kidding? It's gorgeous!"

"I went ahead and got a band like it, no diamonds. Is that okay?"

"Only perfect. Where in the world did you find this thing?"

"Not the Virgin River jewelry store, that's for sure. I had to drive over to the coast. Are you sure you like it?"

She threw her arms around his neck. "You gave me a baby," she said. "I wasn't expecting this, too!"

"I didn't know I was giving you a baby," he said, grinning. "This, I did on purpose."

She laughed at him and said, "People will think we're uppity."

"Mel—I got it a while ago. When I first thought you might be pregnant. Probably before you did. Even if it had turned out you weren't, I was set on this. This idea to marry you, to have my life with you… It's not something I feel like I have to do. It's what I want."

"God, how did this happen?"

"I don't care how," he said.

He went with her the next day to pick up Doc and bring him home. Mel got him settled in his bed at home where he proved to be a very annoying patient; however, it seemed he would make a full recovery and be back to his old schedule in no time. He might not be seeing patients by the time Mel and Jack slipped down to Sacramento for a couple of days, but he'd be able to look after himself.

Meanwhile, with all Mel had to do, running the clinic and looking after Doc, Jack, Preacher or Ricky were bringing his meals, and Mel was able to escape to the bar for an hour here and there, just for a change of scenery. Nights she spent in the hospital bed down the hall from Doc. Alone.

After just a few such nights, she was startled awake by noise downstairs. She sat up sleepily and listened. It was unusual, but not unheard-of, for someone to come pounding at the doctor's door after hours, so when Mel heard the knocking, she rolled over and looked at the clock. It was 1:00 a.m., which implied an emergency and as she was shrugging into her robe, she began to form contingency plans if she had to go out on a call. Jack could come to the house to look after Doc—or maybe go with her, leaving Doc to sleep through till morning without her.

She remembered hearing about that near-fatal truck accident some years ago and thought, *What if I'm not enough help? Who could I call?*

When she opened the front door, no one was there. Then the pounding came again and she realized that whoever it was had come to the back, to the kitchen door. She looked through the glass to see the face of that man from the compound. Calvin. If he was coming to fetch her out to that camp, she wouldn't go. She'd have to send him away. If he'd come to ask her for drugs, she thought she might have to call Jack.

She opened the door with an excuse on her lips when he rushed her, the back of his forearm against her neck. He shoved her backward with enough force that she knocked over a chair, crashed into the countertop and sent coffee cups that were drying in the dish rack hurtling to the floor. He had a snarl on his lips, a glazed look in his eyes, and a big hunting knife in his hand. She screamed, a noise that was quickly cut off as he grabbed her by the hair and put the knife to her throat.

"Drugs," he said simply. "Just gimme what you got, then I'm getting the hell out of these mountains."

"They're in there… I have to get the key," she said, indicating the drug cabinet.

"Forget it," he said. As he held her, he tried kicking the wooden door. The whole cabinet shook and wobbled; she could hear the contents bouncing around.

"Don't!" she cried. "You'll break the vials! You want the drugs or not?"

He stopped. "Where's the key?" he said.

"In the office."

He pulled her backward, flipped the lock on the back door and said, "Come on. Let's move it." With one arm around her waist and the knife at her throat, he walked her out of the kitchen. She had no option but to lead him to the office.

He held her in front of him, hostage style, as they slowly shuffled down the hall to the office. As she opened the drawer to reach for the key, he started to laugh. He grabbed her hand. "I'll take this," he said, pulling at her ring.

"Oh, God," she cried, retreating. But he easily pulled her back by the hair and threatened her with the knife right in front of her face. She froze and let him pull off the ring.

He shoved it in his pocket and said, "Hurry up. I ain't got all night."

"Don't hurt me," she said. "You can have anything you want."

He laughed. "And what if I want you, too?"

She thought she might vomit on the spot. She willed herself to be brave, to be strong, to let this ordeal end.

But he was going to kill her. She knew who he was, what he'd done, and suddenly she knew—he was going to kill her. As soon as he had what he wanted, that knife would slice across her throat.

Lying on top of the desk were the Hummer keys, obvious by the trademark and remote. He scooped them up, put them in his pocket with the ring and steered her out of the office back toward the kitchen. And he muttered, "Asshole doesn't pay me enough to sit in the woods with Maxine and a bunch of old bums. But this should catch me up." And then he laughed.

Jack rolled out of bed to answer the ringing phone. "Mel's in trouble," came Doc's gravelly voice. "Someone's trying to get in the back of the house. Downstairs. She's down there. Glass broke."

Jack dropped the phone and grabbed his jeans off the chair. No time for a shirt or shoes, he took his 9 mm handgun out of the holster that hung on a hook in the closet, checked to be sure it was loaded and that he had one in the chamber and bolted out the door. He crossed the street at a dead run. He didn't think—he was on automatic. His jaw ground, his temples pulsed and his blood was roaring in his ears.

There was an old truck at the clinic beside Doc's truck and Mel's Hummer. He knew exactly who was in there.

He looked into the front door window in time to see Calvin pushing Mel into the office, and they had come from the direction of the kitchen where the drug cabinet sat. He ran around to the back of the house and looked into the kitchen door window; they were still out of sight. Then they came back into view from down the hall and Jack ducked—but not before he saw that Calvin had a big, serrated knife against her neck. He waited; he wasn't going to give him the time or opportunity to flee or to do any damage to Mel before fleeing. It was a long few seconds as he waited for them to get back into the kitchen. He could hear their movements, the man's hostile voice as he held Mel.

They were almost to the drug cabinet when Jack kicked the door. It crashed open and bounced off the opposite wall, but he was already inside. Legs braced apart, arms raised, pistol pointed at the man who held his woman, he said, "Put down the knife. Carefully."

"You're gonna let me out of here, and she'll come with me to be sure," Calvin said.

Knife against her throat, Mel looked at Jack and saw a man she had never seen before. The expression on his face should be enough to terrify the man who held her. Bare chested, barefoot, his jeans zipped but not buttoned, his shoulders and arms frighteningly huge, big tattoos on his swollen biceps, he looked like a wild man. He looked over the barrel of the gun, his eyes narrow, and a set to his jaw told her he was going to act. There was no question. He did not look at Mel, but at Calvin. And for a woman terrified of guns, she was unafraid. She believed in him. She knew, in that instant, that he would risk his life for her, but he would never put her at risk. Never. If he was going to make a move, she wouldn't be in danger. Her expression went from frightened to trusting.

Jack had less than a four-inch target—the left side

of the man's head. Right next to that was Mel's head, Mel's beautiful face. At her throat, the blade. He didn't even have to think about it—he wasn't going to lose her like this.

"You have one second."

Out of the corner of his eye, Jack saw her cast a look his way, a look that in that split second told him she loved him, believed in him. Then her eyes dropped closed and her head dipped ever so slightly to the right.

"Back off, man—"

Jack took his shot, blowing the man backward, the knife flying out of his hand.

Mel ran to Jack. The arm that held the gun was dangling at Jack's side and his other arm went around her. Jack held her close as she let out a long slow breath against his bare chest, clinging to him. He never took his eyes off the offender. A nice, neat hole was bored right into his head, a growing pool of blood spreading under him as he lay motionless.

They stood like that for a while, Mel trying to catch her breath and Jack watching. Ready. She pulled away enough to look up at him and was nearly startled anew by an expression so fierce, so angry. "He was going to kill me," she said in a whisper.

His eyes remained on the man as he said, "I will never let anything happen to you."

The sound of running footfalls came up behind them, but Jack didn't turn.

Preacher stopped suddenly in the doorway, a hand braced on each side as he leaned in, panting. He looked into the kitchen, saw the man on the floor, Mel in Jack's protective embrace, the gun dangling at Jack's side. And Preacher's expression went dark, his brows drawn close, his mouth turned down in a scowl. He walked into the kitchen, kicked the knife across the floor and bent to the man. He felt the man's neck for a carotid pulse. He looked over his shoulder at Jack and shook his head. "It's okay, Jack. It's done."

Jack put the gun on the table and, with Mel still protected against him, turned to the wall phone. He lifted the receiver, punched a few numbers and said, "This is Jack Sheridan in Virgin River. I'm at Doc Mullins's— I just killed a man."

Sixteen

It took the sheriff's deputy, Henry Depardeau, longer to arrive in Virgin River than it took him to determine that Jack had acted in defense of Mel, whose life was in danger. Just the same, Jack's second call that night had been to Jim Post, June Hudson's husband. That background in law enforcement could come in handy. Jim was there faster than Henry. And, Jack learned that night, Jim was a former DEA agent who had actually worked in the area prior to retirement.

"We better have a little look at Calvin's camp," Jim said. "If it's just a little compound of vagrants, I don't see that as a problem. But I suspect it might be more than that. If so—we'll want to tell the sheriff."

Jack was invited to spend what was left of the night with Mel at Doc's. She saw a side of him she didn't know existed. This gentle, tender giant was gripped with fury, and it was a silent and impressive fury. He held her through the night, both of them in one small hospital bed. Sleep was difficult for her and she was fitful, but every time she opened her eyes and looked at him, she found him awake, watching over her. She would look up at his face, his tense jaw and eyes narrowed in anger, but when she put her hand against his cheek, he would relax his features and turn soft eyes on her. "It's all right, baby," he said. "Try to get some sleep. Don't be afraid."

"I'm not afraid while I'm with you," she whispered, and this was the truth.

The next morning, early, June and Jim arrived in town. June came over to the clinic while Jim went to Jack's. "I just wanted to make sure you aren't having any stress-related problems with your pregnancy," June said. "Any cramping, spotting?"

"Everything seems to be fine. Except for those frequent shudders I feel when I think about what might have happened."

"I'm just going to spend a couple of hours in town," June said. "If you have patients, I'll help. Do you need to rest?"

"Jack was here last night. I don't think he slept, but I got a little rest. Where's the baby?" Mel asked.

"Susan has Jamie, and John and my dad have the clinic." She smiled. "We country folk have to be flexible."

"What's Jim doing?" Mel asked.

"He's with Jack and Preacher. They won't be long. They're going to have to take a look at that place the man came from, Mel. Be sure there's no one else out there that will come into town and threaten a life."

"Oh, God," she said.

"I think they can handle it," June said. "I guess it has to be done."

"That's not it, June. I've been out to that camp a dozen times. I didn't see Calvin Thompson there except the very first time, when I went with Doc to help him treat some injuries. But I went, though I'd been told not to. And I was a little nervous and scared, but it never once occurred to me that someone from there might hold a knife to my throat and—" She stopped, unable to go on.

"Good Lord," June said. "What were you doing?"

Mel shrugged. Her voice was small when she answered. "They looked hungry."

A slow smile grew on June Hudson's face. "And you thought you weren't one of us. What hooey."

Jack, Preacher and Jim piled into Jack's truck and drove back into the woods. The compound was less than twenty miles away, but traversed by so many old logging roads and concealed roads, it took almost an hour to get there. They were so buried, one would never be inclined to worry that these people would pose a dangerous threat.

The young man with the knife, Calvin Thompson, hadn't been with them long. He wasn't just a vagrant, but a violent felon. It hadn't taken Henry Depardeau long to learn he had a long drug-related criminal record from other California cities and had been hiding in the forest to dodge felony warrants for his arrest. It was likely that Maxine had brought him to her father's hideaway in the forest.

When they got to the camp, Jim Post said, "Yeah, that's what I figured." He pointed to the camouflaged semitrailer, a generator beside it. The three men from Virgin River got out of the truck, brandishing rifles of the caliber that would kill a black bear with one shot. Rifles that would cut a man in half. Of course there was no one in evidence. "Paulis!" Jack called.

A skinny, wasted-looking, bearded man came out of a hut. A shack. Behind him was a stringy-haired, skinny young woman. Slowly a few more men came around from the back of dilapidated trailers. This small crowd didn't display arms, but they stayed back, having knowledge of the firearms Jack, Jim and Preacher carried.

Jack approached Paulis. "Are you growing?" Jack asked.

The man shook his head.

"Did Thompson bring that operation in here?"

The girl made a sound and covered her mouth with her hand. Paulis gave a nod.

"He tried to kill a woman last night. For drugs and property. He's dead. Who brought in the trailer?"

Paulis shook his head. "We don't exchange names around here."

"What'd he look like?" Jim asked.

Paulis just shrugged.

"Come on, man. You want to go to jail for him? What'd he drive?"

Paulis shrugged again, but Maxine stepped around her father, tears on her pale cheeks. "A big black Range Rover. Lights up top. You know the kind. He paid Calvin to watch the grow."

"I know who he is," Jack said quietly to Jim. "Don't know where he is, but I have a good idea this isn't his only grow. And I happen to know the license number on that big SUV."

"Well, that could come in handy."

Then to Clifford Paulis, Jack said, "You have twenty-four hours to clear this camp and move out. The sheriff's deputy will be out here to close down this spot real quick, and if you're here, you'll be arrested—that shit's in your possession now. You have to move on now. I don't want you around. You hear me?"

Paulis just nodded.

"That woman was my woman," Jack said more quietly. "I'm going to look for you, and if I can find you, you haven't moved far enough, you understand me?"

Paulis dipped his chin once more.

The differences in the men—those from the camp and Jack, Jim and Preacher, left no doubt as to who would be the winners in any kind of conflict. Just to drive the point home, Jack raised his 30-06 caliber, bolt action rifle, aimed it at the generator beside the half-buried trailer in the compound, and fired, decimating it. The report was loud enough to shake the trees. The men in view flinched, raised their hands to cover their faces or cowered back.

"I'm coming back tomorrow," Jack said. "Early."

When they were back in the truck, Jack asked Jim, "What do you make of them?"

"Vagrants. Just living in the forest. They didn't have the means to put that trailer in there—that was arranged by whoever Calvin was working for. They'll go, most likely. Deeper in the forest, where they can set up camp again and be left alone. We'll let Henry know where to find it. But you should make good on your advice just the same. They can't be here anymore. If they're not dangerous, they're willing to be taken advantage of by dangerous people."

"I didn't see any guns. They have to be armed."

"Oh, sure—but they're not armed with much. They saw what we're carrying—none of these old boys are going to be shooting at us. The ones to worry about are guys like Calvin's boss, and his boss's boss. DEA cleared out a whole town in the Trinity Alps several years ago while I was an agent—and now those boys had 'em some guns." Jim gave Jack a shot in the arm. "I'm for staying out of their business. If Forestry runs

across them, they'll report them to the sheriff's department or maybe to the DEA."

The spirit of the town was tense and worried. Jack
had become their favorite son, and his chosen woman—
the woman who had come here to help people—had had
a brush with death.

Throughout the day, neighbors came to Doc's bearing food and offering conversation. There were no patients, only friends. Doc got out of bed and dressed,
coming downstairs to visit. With the exception of a
short nap in the afternoon, he stayed up the entire day.

Jim and June only stayed a couple of hours, but Jack
was a presence on and off throughout the day, which
worked well because people who came by the house to
check on Mel were anxious to talk to him. "Shot him
while he held her at knifepoint, they're saying." Jack
merely nodded and reached for her hand. "How'd you
dare? How'd you know you wouldn't be off by a half
inch?"

"I didn't have that much to spare," he said. "I
wouldn't have pulled the trigger if I thought there was
any chance I'd be off my mark."

Another matter of great interest was the shining ring
that graced Mel's finger. The engagement was met with
happiness and affection, though not surprise. There
were many questions about the wedding, and a serious
protest when it was learned that there would be a small
ceremony in a few days for family only in Sacramento.

Jack, Doc and Mel ate a dinner made up of the food
brought by well-wishers and when it was done and the
dishes cleaned up, Doc said, "I'm going to bed, Melinda.
You should go back to your man's bed. Those hospital

beds are no place for the two of you." And up the stairs he slowly trudged.

"Yes, you should," Jack confirmed, taking her with him across the street.

Having slept so little the night before, once she was in Jack's bed, curled up against his warmth, she nearly passed out from exhaustion.

Before the sun was even up the next morning, she was awakened by the sound of amassing vehicles. She looked at the clock and saw that it was barely 5:00 a.m. She rummaged around for clothes and went through the bar onto the porch to see what all the commotion was about. There in the street were trucks, campers, AWD vehicles, SUVs, cars. Men were standing around in the street, checking their rifles, even putting on flak jackets and bulletproof vests. Some wore jeans and work shirts, some wore fatigues. She recognized faces among them—Mike Valenzuela from L.A., Zeke from Fresno, Paul Haggerty and Joe Benson from Grants Pass, Oregon. There were also neighbors and ranchers and farmers from Virgin River. She saw that Ricky was with them, looking for all the world like a grown man.

She watched them for a while before Jack noticed her standing there, her hair all mussed from sleep, her feet bare. He handed his rifle off to Paul and went to her. "You look like a girl," he said. "A little pregnant girl, but I know better." He grinned. "I thought maybe you could sleep awhile longer."

"Through this? What's going on?"

"Scavenger hunt," he said. "Nothing for you to worry about."

"Come on, Jack."

"We're going to check, see if the woods need to be cleaned out," he said.

"With weapons? Vests? My God, Jack."

He pulled her against him briefly and said, "I doubt we'll have any trouble, Mel. But we should be prepared for whatever we run into. We're just going to cut a wide circle around the town—be certain there are no drug farmers or criminals close by. No camps like the one Thompson came from. No camps for people like Thompson to hide out in."

"How will you know whether there are dangerous people in ordinary camps? I'm told there are plenty of those kind of camps scattered around. Squatters, vagrants, mountain people."

He shrugged. "Then we should know who's out there. Look for what's in their camps, check their weapons so we know what they have. Pot's pretty easy to spot—it has a real distinctive green color and it almost always comes with camouflage and a generator."

She put a hand on the vest he wore. "And you need this because—"

"Because I'm going to be a father soon, and I don't take foolish chances. One of these idiots could misfire."

"You're taking Ricky with you?"

"I look out for Ricky. We'll all be looking out for him, but believe me—he's up to this. I taught him to shoot myself. He wouldn't be left out, because it's about you."

"Is this absolutely necessary?"

"Yes," he said, and looked down at her with the expression she had learned meant he was all about business.

Jim Post was beside Jack, grinning. "Morning," he said.

"Does June know you're doing this?" she asked.

"Yes, ma'am."

"And what did she say?"

"Something like, 'You better be careful.' The hard part was convincing old Doc Hudson he couldn't come."

"Isn't this better left to the police? The sheriff?"

Jim put a foot up on the porch step. He shrugged. "We've already told Henry about Paulis's camp and gave him the description of the vehicle being driven by the man who probably had it set up. Hopefully, the Paulis camp is deserted and their plants left behind. We saw 'em, Mel—and there's no question—those old squatters didn't bring a semi in, bury it, camouflage it and set up a grow. But someone did—and there could be more of those. There's real trouble way back in there— on federal land. We're not going that far back. We'll stay out of their business. We'll leave that up to the professionals."

"It just seems so vigilante-like," she said.

"Naw, we're not going to do anything illegal, Mel. We're just going to send a little message. You don't want to give our women, our towns, any reason to feel they have to fight back. Understand?" She didn't answer. "If there's anything like that near enough to threaten Virgin River, we'll give them a chance to run for their lives before we disclose their location to authorities. It'll be fine. We'll be home by dark."

She said to Jack, "I'm going to be scared to death all day."

"Do I have to stay here with you, so you won't be scared?" he asked her. "Or can you believe in me one more time?"

She bit her lip, but nodded. He slipped an arm around her waist and lifted her up to his mouth, kissing her deeply. "You taste so good in the morning," he said, smiling down at her. "Is that normal?" he teased.

"You'd better be careful," she said. "Remember that I love you."

"I don't need any more than that," he said, putting her back on her feet.

Preacher came to the porch. He nodded at her, bushy brows drawn together in a frown that made her almost shudder. "Just send him in," Mel said. "That'll scare them all away." And to her surprise, Preacher smiled so big, for a moment she didn't recognize him.

When they had finally left in a grand parade, Mel called June. "Do you know what your husband is doing?" she asked.

"Yes," June said, sounding annoyed. "Not babysitting."

"Are you worried?"

"Only that one of them will shoot off a toe. Why? Are you?"

"Well… Yes! You should have seen them—in their vests and with those big guns. I mean, big guns!"

"Well, there are bear out there, you know. You don't want a peashooter," June said. "You don't have to worry about Jack, honey. I think it's been established he's a good shot, if he needs to be."

"What about Jim?"

"Jim?" She laughed. "Mel, Jim used to do this for a living. He won't admit he misses it just a little bit. But I swear I heard him giggle."

All day long she had visions of gun battles in the forest. The unfortunate lack of work couldn't keep her from pacing. With the bar closed and so many of the men out on the scavenger hunt, the town was impossibly quiet.

Mel spent most of the day on Doc's porch, sitting on the steps. It was about noon when the black Range

Rover pulled slowly into town. He drove up alongside the clinic and lowered his tinted window. "I heard what happened to you," he said.

"You did? I didn't know we had any mutual friends."

"I wanted to tell you a couple of things, because you did me a favor. Number one—I know about Thompson and he's a loose cannon. I know a lot of what goes on back there and there aren't any others like him, that I know of. People like Vickie—that's the woman who had the baby—she's been in some trouble, but she's not dangerous to anybody. She just flies under the radar, has had some tough breaks, doesn't know a lot of ways to make money. By the way—she's gone. Took that baby and went to a sister's in Arizona. I got her on a bus."

"You said Nevada before," Mel said.

"Did I now?" he asked, a small smile. "Well, I could be mistaken."

"I just hope you know where to send the check, since it's yours."

"I said, they'll have what they need. Didn't I say that?"

She was silent a moment, thinking. The check he was going to send would come from the sale of marijuana. There were people who thought it was no worse than a few beers, and she was about to pledge her life and love to a man who owned a bar, thought nothing of serving up a few beers. Then there were others who recognized its medical benefits. And a third faction saw it as a dangerous drug—one that, in the wrong hands, perhaps young hands, could lead to more dangerous addictions. Mel only knew two things: it was still illegal without a prescription and, because it was illegal, crime was often associated with it.

"You said you wanted to tell me a couple of things," she said.

"I'm leaving the area. There's been a death. Doesn't really matter that Thompson won't be any great loss to society," he said with a shrug. "He's associated with a couple of the operations here, so there's going to be an investigation, warrants, arrests. I'll be moving on." He smiled at her. "You get your wish. You won't be doing business with me anymore."

She leaned forward on the porch steps. "Have you done violence?"

"Not really," he said with a shrug. "Not so far. We've had our little misunderstandings. But I'm just a businessman."

"You couldn't find a more legal business?"

"Oh, sure," he answered, smiling. "I just couldn't find a more profitable one."

The window went up and he moved down the street and out of sight. She memorized the license plate, knowing that if he was any good at his profession, it wouldn't matter.

At dusk, she sat out on Doc's porch and waited. As darkness began to descend, she heard the vehicles return. As they drove slowly into town and pulled up to the bar, she tried to assess the mood of the group. Everyone seemed solemn and tired as they got out of trucks and Jeeps, stretching their backs and arms. Vests were gone, guns stowed in their racks and sleeves rolled up. But shortly they were clapping each other on the back, laughing and gathering around Jack's porch. She was so relieved to see Ricky, laughing with the men, one of the brothers, completely safe. The last truck to pull up was Preacher's, in which Jack rode, as well, and they had something large in the bed, something hanging out. When he parked, all the men gathered around, and the tempo of the group seemed to pick up. There was laughter and loud voices.

Almost afraid to know what was going on, she walked across the street. Jack was coming for her and met her halfway.

"Well? You find anything?"

"Not bad guys," he said. "Paulis's camp was busted up and what junk they left behind, we destroyed. Henry and a couple of deputies showed up to confiscate their plants. I just don't want them back in the neighborhood if they're going to let a drug operation in. Truthfully, they don't have the strength to keep them out, so we will."

"Haven't you ever thought—it's only a little pot?"

"I don't have an opinion about that," he said with a shrug. "But if it's legalized and pharmaceutical companies grow it, we won't have to be afraid for our women and children."

"What have you got in the truck? What's that awful smell?"

"A bear. Wanna see?" he asked, smiling.

"A bear? Why on earth…?"

"He was really pissed," Jack said. "Come and see—he's huge."

"Who shot him?" she asked.

"Who's taking credit or who actually shot him? Because I think everyone is taking credit." He slipped an arm around her waist and walked her the rest of the way.

She began to pick up the voices. "I swear, I heard Preacher scream," someone said.

"I didn't scream, jag-off. That was a battle cry."

"Sounded like a little girl."

"More holes in that bear than in my head."

"He didn't like that repellant so much, did he?"

"I never saw one go through that stuff before. They usually just rub their little punkin eyes and run back in the woods."

"I'm telling you, Preacher screamed. Thought he was gonna cry like a baby."

"You wanna eat, jag-off?"

There was laughter all around. A carnival-like atmosphere ensued. The serious group that had left town in the morning had come back like soldiers from war, elated, victorious. Except this war turned out to be with a bear.

Mel glanced in the back of the truck and jumped back. The bear not only filled the bed, he hung out the end. The claws on his paws were terrifying. He was tied in, tied down, even though he was dead. His eyes were open but sightless and his tongue hung out of his mouth. And he stunk to high heaven.

"Who's calling Fish and Game?"

"Aw, do we have to call them? You know they're gonna take the frickin' bear. That's my bear!"

"It ain't your bear, jag-off. I shot the bear," Preacher insisted loudly.

"You screamed like a girl and the rest of us shot the bear."

"Who really shot the bear?" Mel asked Jack.

"I think Preacher shot the bear when he came at him. Then so did everybody else. And yeah, I think he screamed. I would have. That bear got so damn close." But as he said this, he grinned like a boy who had just made a touchdown.

Preacher stomped over to Jack and Mel. He bent down and whispered to Mel, "I did *not* scream." He turned and stomped off.

"Honey," Jack said softly, "we found one other thing today." She looked up at him expectantly. "We found the black Range Rover. Ran off the road and went down a couple hundred feet..."

"Is he dead?" she asked fearfully, surprised that she even cared.

"There wasn't any body."

She gave a short, startled laugh. "God," she said. "He came by here today at about noon. All he did was roll down the window and said that because I did him a favor he wanted me to know there was no one else out there in the cannabis trade like Thompson that he knew of, and he was leaving the area. Jack, he must have ditched the truck."

"Probably," he said. "Which means he might be getting a new vehicle, new look and be back. Never go with him again, Mel. Promise me."

She was thinking, insanely, that he was one person who treated her okay and seemed to have something of a conscience. If he came to her and said someone needed medical help, it would be hard to refuse him. "Just how many children do you think he can father?" she asked with a laugh.

"Men have lapses in judgment."

"Do they? Hopefully you haven't had too many," she said.

"I haven't had any," he said with a smile.

"So. That's all you got? A wrecked SUV and a bear? Must be a little anticlimactic for you," she said.

"You calling that bear anticlimactic? Baby, that is a huge frickin' bear!"

There must have been about twenty-five men, they all smelled bad, and they were filing into the bar. Mel sniffed Jack's shirt. "Whew," she said. "You smell almost as bad as the bear."

"It's going to get worse before it gets better," he said. "Now we'll have beer, food and cigars. I have to get in there and start serving beer while Preacher and Ricky fire up the barbecue pit."

"I'll help," she said, taking his hand. "It was a waste of time, wasn't it?"

"Not in my mind. Our forest is nice and tidy, we're turning a trailer full of plants over to the sheriff and we got a mean old bear."

"You had fun," she accused.

"Not on purpose," he said. But his smile was very large.

"Is it over, Jack?" she asked him.

"I hope so, baby. God, I hope so."

For once Mel was behind the bar. She helped serve beer and drinks, tossed a great big salad while Preacher turned steaks on the grill. Plates and utensils were put out for a buffet-style service. The men poked fun at each other, their laughter getting louder and wilder as the night wore on. Although Ricky was officially working, when he'd pass one of the men, he'd be pulled into a strong-armed embrace and praised as though he was a comrade. Doc wandered across the street for a whiskey, visited with the men for a while before going back to his house. Most of the locals left before the meal was served, home to claim to their wives that they shot the bear.

It was about nine when the cards and cigars came out. Jack grabbed Mel's hand and said, "Let's get out of here. You must be exhausted."

"Hmm," she said, leaning against him. "My feelings won't be hurt if you want to hang out with your boys."

"They'll probably be around a day or two. Since they came all this way, they'll want to fish and stink up my bar. Fishing's starting to get good." He put an arm around Mel and walked her through the back of the bar. "We need to give the baby a nap."

"We need to give the baby's father a shower," she said, wrinkling her nose.

While Jack showered, Mel put on one of his shirts, her favorite soft chambray. She curled up on the sofa with one of Jack's magazines in her lap, flipping through the pages. She would have to find something better than *Field and Stream,* she decided.

She could hear the raucous laughter from the bar; she could almost smell the cigar smoke, but it made her smile. These were good people—people who came running when they thought there was a possible danger. Jack's friends, the people in town—they knew the meaning of being neighbors.

She had only known the neighbors on each side of her in L.A. With Mark's long hours, they didn't socialize as much as she'd have liked. And big cities can be less friendly. Everyone was so focused on work, on making money, on buying things. Mel used to concentrate on that, as well. Besides that Hummer, which she'd needed for work and was as much for the town as herself, she'd hardly bought a thing in six months. She patted her tummy—she would have to buy clothes soon—she couldn't get her jeans closed. As she thought about it, she didn't crave any particular label. It made her smile. Lately, she didn't recognize herself. She was not the same woman who nearly slid off the mountain six months ago.

Jack came out of the shower, a towel around his waist, rubbing dry his short hair with another one. He tossed the second towel and went to his bed, lifting the covers and inclining his head toward her. She put aside the magazine and went to him. As she slipped in, she said, "You're sure you don't want to play poker and make yourself smell disgusting? They're going to keep us up all night anyway."

He dropped his towel and got in beside her. "You're kidding, right?" He scooped her up next to him and she snuggled close.

"Have I told you how much I like sleeping with you?" she asked him. "You sleep very well. And you don't snore. But I think maybe you wake up too early."

"I like the mornings."

"I can't fit in my pants already," she said. She lifted herself up and with her elbows resting on his chest said, "You call them and they just come."

"I only called one of them—Mike in L.A.—he called the others. They're just like that. And if any of them called—I'd go." He smiled at her. "I never expected a posse like that to turn out. Says something about the way people feel about you."

"But you didn't actually find anyone scary out there."

"I liked what I found. I wasn't willing to take any chances, and neither was anyone else. The same thing would happen for any other crisis—like a bear mauling or a forest fire or someone lost in the woods. People band up, go out and take care of the problem if they can. What else are you going to do?"

She played idly with his damp chest hair. "That look you get when you're facing off with someone or something, do you have any idea how dark it is? You might want to keep that look in the closet—it's disturbing."

"I want to tell you something," he said. "I asked your sister all about your husband. Mark."

"You did?"

"Yep. I understand he was a great man. A brilliant man—and kind. He did a lot of good in the world, and he was good to you. I have a lot of respect for him."

"She didn't tell me this."

"I've been trying to figure out how to say this to you. I might muck it up, but you have to listen. A couple of weeks ago I let you cry alone, because I was pissed. I caught you talking to his picture and I got threatened. Threatened by a dead man, which makes me a true candy-ass." He touched her hair. "I won't ever do that again, Mel. I understand why you love him, why you'll always—"

"Jack—"

"No, I'm going to do this, and you're going to listen. I know you didn't want your life to change the way it did, and you couldn't control it. Just like you can't control what you feel. You don't have to pretend you don't think about him, or miss him. And if you have those moments when you're sad, when you wish you could have him back in your life, you can be honest with me. You don't have to pretend it's PMS." He smiled. "We both know you don't have PMS anymore."

"Jack, what are you talking about?"

"I just want one thing. If I can be a sport about the fact that he'll always be an important part of your life, can you try to not be sorry that we're together, having this baby? Because I have to tell you, I've never been more ready for anything. I'll do my best not to be jealous. I realize I'm not your first choice, but your next choice. That's good enough for me, and I'm sorry someone died. I'm sorry for your loss, Mel."

"Why are you saying this? It's such nonsense."

"It's what I heard," he said. "I heard you saying you were sorry you were pregnant, that it just happened, and you promised not to forget him."

Mel gave him a look of disbelief. "I thought you were hurt by what you heard me say—but you were hurt because of what you *didn't* hear!"

"Huh?"

"Jack, I'm not sorry I'm pregnant. I'm thrilled! I got myself all worked up because I realized that I was more in love with you than I thought possible. Maybe more in love than I've ever been in my life. I had a short insane moment of feeling that I'd betrayed his memory somehow. As though I'd been unfaithful or something. It's true—I didn't mean for it to happen, but it did. I know I resisted, but you just got to me. I promised Mark I wouldn't forget him. And I won't because you're right, he was a good man. And I respect him, too."

"Huh?" he said again.

"Look," she said, playing with his thick, damp hair. "I was upset and a little confused. I loved Mark very much. I didn't think I'd get to feel that again, much less for someone new. Imagine how it threw me when I realized I felt something even stronger. Something even more powerful. Jack, I was telling Mark I had moved on. I was saying goodbye—it was difficult. I'm not going to be a widow anymore, darling. I'm going to be a wife. This thing I have with you—it's amazing."

"Seriously?"

"I was in this high, emotional state," she said with a shrug. "I was tired and pregnant. Jack, I love you so much. Can't you tell?"

"Well…yeah," he said, sitting up in the bed a little. "But I thought it was mostly physical. I mean—damn,

Mel. We're really good together. The way we come together, it almost makes me weak to think about it."

"I don't mind the physical part one bit," she said with a mischievous grin. "But I love more about you than that. Your character, for one thing. Your generosity and how about your courage. Oh, there are about a million things, but I'm done talking now." She kissed him. "Now I want you to say something wonderful to me right before you tear this shirt off my body."

He rolled her over onto her back and, looking into her eyes, said, "Mel, you're the best thing that's ever happened to me. I'm going to make you so happy, you won't be able to stand it. You're going to wake up singing every morning."

"I already do, Jack."

* * * * *

Be sure to pick up the next novel in the new
SULLIVAN'S CROSSING *series from*
#1 New York Times *bestselling author Robyn Carr,*
ANY DAY NOW
A story of one woman reconnecting with family
and rediscovering herself.
Available April 4, 2017
from MIRA Books

Acknowledgments

Thanks to Pamela SF Glenn, CNM, MS—without whose expertise in midwifery, this story would not have been possible. My deepest gratitude for poring over manuscript after manuscript with sharp eyes and a ruthless pen, keeping me straight. And to Sharon Lampert, RN, WHNP, for sharing her expertise as a women's health nurse practitioner, but mostly for picking up your cell phone no matter where you were and answering delicate questions about female anatomy and function with directness and honesty. I'm sure there are people out there still talking about what they overheard in the grocery store, beauty parlor and Department of Motor Vehicles. The passion and devotion with which you two professionals serve your women patients is inspiring, and was an enormous help in shaping the character of a dedicated nurse practitioner and certified nurse midwife.

Thanks to Paul Wojcik for sharing your experiences in the United States Marine Corps, and to Richard Gustavson, RN, with twenty-three years in the Navy Reserves. I thank each of you for reading the manuscripts and for offering your invaluable technical input.

Kris Kitna, Chief of Police, Fortuna, California, thanks for valuable information on local law enforcement, not to mention help with details about hunting, fishing and firearms.

Kate Bandy, the best assistant a writer can possibly have, my dear friend of many years, thanks not only for reading copy and offering suggestions, but especially for accompanying me on an exciting research trip to Humboldt County. Without you there I would have floundered...or slipped off a mountain.

Denise and Jeff Nicholl—thanks for reading first drafts, taking exhaustive notes and answering a million questions. Your friendship and support during the whole process mean the world to me.

Many thanks to Nellie Valdez-Hathorn for her help with my Spanish. Other early readers whose input was critical included Jamie Carr, Laurie Fait, Karen Garris, Martha Gould, Pat Hagee, Goldiene Jones and Lori Stoveken—I'm deeply in debt to you for your comments and suggestions.

Huge thanks to Clive Cussler, Debbie Macomber and Carla Neggers for reading and commenting on *Virgin River*. To take the time, with your busy schedules, is a monumental compliment.

Huge thanks to Valerie Gray, my editor, and Liza Dawson, my agent, for your commitment to helping me craft the best series possible. Your hard work and dedication made all the difference—I'm so grateful.

To Trudy Casey, Tom Fay, Michelle Mazzanti, Kristy Price and the entire staff of Henderson Public Libraries, thank you for the monumental support and encouragement. I've never known a more hardworking and motivated group of public servants.

And finally, thanks to Jim Carr for your loving support. And my God, thank you for cooking! I wish I'd known years ago that you could!

WHEN LIGHTNING STRIKES

Brenda Novak

To Pierce Rohrmann.

Your many talents and drive never cease to amaze me. Thanks for your hard work on my behalf, your brilliant ideas, your endless support, your wit and generosity— and last but not least, thanks for picking me up, dusting me off and shoving me back into the fight whenever I try to escape. LOL.
You make one heck of a BFF!

One

She was ruined. She'd become anathema—the Jerry Maguire of the Los Angeles public-relations biz. And it'd happened almost overnight.

"You don't look so good."

Gail DeMarco turned away from the phone she'd just hung up to focus on Joshua Blaylock. Dressed in a pair of skinny black jeans with long-toed shoes, a designer jacket and rectangular-shaped glasses, her personal assistant hovered at the corner of her desk, a hopeful yet worried expression on his face. Like her, he'd been hoping they could pull out of the nosedive she'd caused by making one impetuous call, and then a number of thoughtless statements, three weeks earlier. But she could tell Joshua had overheard enough to understand what her other employees didn't grasp quite yet. They hadn't just lost a few important clients, like Maddox Gill and Emery Villere; they'd lost them all. Big Hit Public Relations had fallen from its lofty perch at the top of the PR food chain to crash and burn at the bottom. And it was all thanks to one man. Simon O'Neal, the hottest male lead in the movie business, had flexed his superstar muscles and brought down her company so quickly and easily Gail could hardly believe it. She kept thinking she'd wake up to find that their feud was all a bad dream—or that others would see Simon as the train wreck she knew him to be and side with her instead. But America loved him. He was their new James Dean. He was screwing up right and left, but he had the most loyal fans in the world, fans who were as fascinated by his self-destruction as his talent.

She should never have told him she'd no longer work for him. One client after another had deserted her ever since.

But any self-respecting public-relations professional would've grown tired of Simon's antics. He'd done everything she'd specifically asked him *not* to, created so many media nightmares, and that made her, as his personal publicist, look as bad as he did. How was she supposed to represent someone like that?

"Hello?" His smile gone, Joshua snapped his fingers in front of her eyes.

Gail forced back her tears. For more than a decade, ever since she'd graduated with a degree in advertising and public relations, then interned for Rodger Brown and Associates, she'd devoted herself to building her company. She had no husband, no kids and very few friends, at least in the L.A. area. Her ambition hadn't allowed time for that. There was only the group of childhood friends in Whiskey Creek six hours north. She saw them every couple of months. But by and large she'd left both family and friends to make her mark in the big city. Here, her employees were closer to her than anyone else. And now she'd have to let them all go. Even Joshua.

"That was Clint Pierleoni." She groomed her voice into a careful monotone to keep it from cracking.

He blinked rapidly, as if he was tempted to cry himself. It wouldn't be the first time he'd broken down in her office. He was always getting upset over one man or another. She usually consoled him, actually enjoyed living vicariously through him since it'd been so long since *she'd* had a love life. But today she had no words of comfort because his pain was her pain, too.

"Don't tell me—" he started.

She broke in before he could get the words out. "He said it's time for him to find another PR company."

"But... Clint's been with us from the beginning. I've *slept* with Clint—after signing that form agreeing not to reveal he's gay, of course."

Gail ignored the last part of what Joshua had said. She didn't condone her employees having sex with the firm's clients. But she'd already written Josh up for his inappropriate relationship with Clint. It seemed pointless to go over her objections again, especially at this late date. What Joshua said about Clint was true. He'd been the first up-and-coming actor to take a risk on her. And she'd done a hell of a job for him at a steal of a price.

She'd expected more loyalty. They'd come so far together. He was bigger now than he'd ever been, and she'd helped make that happen. "He tried to explain—"

Joshua broke in. "Explain what? That he was caving in to the pressure of the Hollywood heavyweights who've joined Simon O'Neal and turned against us?"

"He's afraid staying with us will adversely affect his career. Simon promised him a part in his next movie, and he's positive it will disappear if he doesn't kowtow."

"Simon's a bastard! An *alcoholic* bastard!"

She narrowed her eyes. "You haven't slept with *him,* have you?" For just a moment, she allowed herself to imagine what it would do to the almighty Simon's career to leak *that* information. He'd never be able to play a romantic male lead again. But she knew what Joshua was going to say before he said it.

"He's yummy enough that I'd sleep with him if I had the chance. I don't know many people who wouldn't, except you," he added as an afterthought. "But...he's not gay."

"Right." She attempted a shrug, even though she'd had her fantasies about Simon, too. Who hadn't? "Too bad."

He leaned on his knuckles as if he was planning to reveal a big secret. "He *is* a womanizer, though. I bet we could come up with all kinds of dirt—"

She waved him to silence. "Not the kind that'll surprise anyone. His wife left him because he couldn't keep his pants zipped. His exploits in *that* area are second only to Tiger Woods's." Even if she had the goods, she doubted she could bring herself to destroy him. She was hurt and angry, but she didn't believe in creating bad karma.

"So what do we do?" Josh asked.

"What *can* we do?" Drawing a deep breath, she tried to sit tall in her chair, like she was used to doing when barking out orders and handling calls in rapid succession. She thrived on the adrenaline that sustained her on any given day. But her groove was gone, along with her clients.

Sagging against her expensive leather chair, she thought about calling the actors who'd fired her. If only she could talk them into coming back...

But it was no use. She'd already tried that. No one would cross Simon, except a few inconsequential clients who didn't care enough about him to follow his lead, and three of them were charities she repped *pro bono.*

"He's going with Chelsea Seagate at Pierce Mattie," she added dully.

"No!" Joshua punched the air. "That bitch has everyone!"

Also thanks to Simon. He'd been with Big Hit for three years, knew they were rivals, so he'd gone to Chelsea and taken almost fifty of Gail's sixty-four other clients there, too. "Pierce will regret letting Chelsea sign him. Simon will ruin them. There isn't a PR firm in America, or anywhere else, that can protect the image of a client so bent on self-destruction. Since his wife left, he's worse than Charlie Sheen ever was."

"At least PM will die a slow death," Joshua said, dropping into the chair across from her. "How long before we have to close our doors?"

She pursed her lips as she glanced around her swanky office. There'd been days when she'd been unable to believe her own success. Now it all seemed to have been an illusion. "Two months?" Could she even hold out that long?

He rocked forward. "That's it?"

"Our overhead is huge, Josh. Rent alone is fifteen thousand. Together with salaries for twenty people… the money will dry up fast."

His next words were muffled; he'd buried his face in the stylish scarf he wore under the collar of his too-cool jacket. "When do we tell the others?"

She couldn't bear to see him slumped over like that. He'd told her not to cast Simon aside but she'd done it, anyway. Simon had deserved to be cut from her client roster—he'd been asking for it—but he wasn't anyone to mess with, and he'd proven that.

Struggling under the weight of her responsibility, she got up and walked to the interior window overlooking the expansive lobby designed to impress visitors. The staff cubicles and three other offices branched off to the right. They couldn't be seen from where she stood, but she could make out the back of Savannah Barton's dark head as she lounged in the doorway of Serge Trusso's office. Savannah was a single mom with two kids. Where would she go? Serge would land on his feet. He saved money, never took anything for granted. But what about Vince Shroeder, one cubicle over? He had a disabled wife. Then there was Constance Moreno, barely twenty years old. She'd come from New York two months ago and signed a year's lease on her apartment. How would she pay the rent?

These people depended on her. Why had she been so determined to punish Simon, to see that he received some type of backlash?

Gail tapped her forehead on the cool glass. "You'd better call a meeting. I'm sure they already know trouble's brewing. It's been dead around here. They're out there throwing spitballs at one another."

"You want me to get them now?"

She thought of Simon's movie premiere tonight and the fact that he'd be at the after-party, probably roaring drunk but enjoying the fame and fortune that followed him everywhere. He shouldn't get away with what he'd done. She'd been in the right, damn it. But... if she wanted to save her employees, she was going to have to humble herself and apologize, maybe even *beg*.

She'd rather throw herself in front of a bus, but there was more at stake here than pride. She had a good team; they didn't deserve to lose their jobs. "No, wait."

"You think something's going to change?" he said with a telltale sniff.

She didn't dare hope. But she had to make one last-ditch effort to save the firm, just in case it was still possible. "Give me until tomorrow."

He toyed with the expensive pen set he and the rest of her staff had bought her for Christmas. "For what?"

She turned to face him. "A Hail Mary."

Two

Simon spotted Gail immediately. In a sea of silicone, Botox and spray tans, she stood out. Maybe it was her chest, flat by L.A. standards, the severe cut of her business suit with its starched white shirt or the stubborn set to her jaw. Or maybe it was her general disdain for Hollywood parties and the licentious behavior that went on, and her unwillingness to dress up and join the fun.

Regardless, Simon had always liked the fact that she wasn't an adoring fan—almost as much as he hated it. One would think she'd at least *try* to blend in if she was going to crash the party. He was fairly certain she hadn't received an invitation.

"What's wrong?"

He jerked his gaze back to the stunning blonde sitting in the booth next to him. A "hot yoga" instructor he'd met about twenty minutes earlier, her name was Sunny Something, and she was smarter than the stereotype her short skirt and low-cut blouse brought to mind. She was a nice person, too. But he was bored. These days the women he socialized with seemed virtually interchangeable.

"Nothing." He tossed back the rest of his drink. "Why?"

She angled her head to see where he'd been looking but skimmed right over Gail. She probably couldn't imagine such a nondescript woman being of any consequence to him. If not for the guilt that plagued him, he might not have given Gail a second thought. When he'd told Ian Callister, his business manager, that he wished she'd go broke and return to the small town she called home, he hadn't meant it literally. He'd been drunk when he made that statement. But Ian had decided to take revenge for her defection, and Simon had been preoccupied and angry enough to turn a blind eye. He hadn't even asked what Ian was up to. Part of him figured Gail DeMarco deserved whatever she got. The other part didn't see why Ian would go to *too* much trouble.

But just yesterday he'd learned that Ian had called all her clients and "suggested" they might like it better with Chelsea Seagate at Pierce Mattie. Almost every one of them had promptly switched.

"You were frowning," Sunny said. "Is there someone here you're not happy to see?"

"No," he lied.

"What did you say?"

She couldn't hear him for the music. He raised his voice. "Just getting tired, that's all."

"Tired? Already?" She offered him a pout. "It's barely ten."

His lack of interest was an insult to such an attractive woman. He understood that. If he were a better man he'd pretend to be entertained, but he simply couldn't fake it. Not tonight. He did enough acting when the cameras were rolling. Besides, he didn't care if she moved on to someone more attentive. He'd been telling the truth when he said he was tired. He'd been tired since before he came, hadn't slept in days. Every time his mind grew quiet, the regrets that tortured him returned.

"Would you like another drink?" he asked.

She didn't get a chance to answer. When Gail started making her way over, he couldn't help shifting his attention again. She'd located him, as he knew she would. She was nothing if not focused. And it wasn't as if he could disappear into the crowd. He was always the center of attention whether he wanted to be or not.

What would happen from here on, however, was anyone's guess. He'd never dreamed his ex-PR agent would have the moxie to show up at an event like this, where he'd be surrounded by friends and supporters, not to mention the regular contingent of hangers-on—people who were willing to kiss his ass regardless of what he did.

The girl had guts. He had to give her that.

"Simon?"

He looked up at her from beneath his eyelashes, as if he was too lazy or intoxicated to move. Maybe his temper, and what he'd said to Ian, had sparked the conflagration that had consumed her business, but he hadn't intended for Ian to be quite so vindictive and didn't want to take responsibility for it. Barring a few minor faults, Ian was a good manager. He'd certainly never done anything like this before. She could call Ian if she wanted to discuss the problem. It wasn't as if she was entirely innocent; she'd vented her fury by making a series of unflattering statements that had wound up in the press.

Maybe when Simon O'Neal grows up, he'll realize that women are good for more than just one thing.

Simon O'Neal is his own worst enemy. He hates himself in direct proportion to everyone else's admiration. Why is anyone's guess. The guy's had it all. As far as I'm concerned, there's no excuse for his behavior....

Maybe some people find him attractive. But I wouldn't sleep with him if he were the last man on earth. There's no telling what kind of disease he's carrying....

There were other comments he couldn't remember verbatim. Something about how he needed more therapy than even a fortune like his could support. And another about his being a waste of God-given talent, a man without decency, a charming Dr. Jekyll on-screen and an evil Mr. Hyde off...

"What can I do for you?" he replied, using the same overly polite tone with which she'd addressed him.

She lifted her chin. "Could I have a word with you, please?"

Was she crazy? He had no interest in walking off with her. "'Fraid not. Maybe you don't remember, but we don't have anything to discuss these days. And in case you haven't noticed, I'm with someone." He could feel Sunny's interest in their exchange; she watched them but didn't say anything.

Gail ignored her completely. "It'll just take a minute."

He flicked his hand, hoping she'd interpret the gesture for what it was—an indication that she should take herself off. "I'm busy."

Unfortunately, she didn't go anywhere. With a decisive tug on her tailored jacket, she cleared her throat.

"Fine. We'll talk here. I—I'd like to offer you an apology."

He didn't want an apology. People were beginning to stare, to realize she was the PR woman who'd dissed him. Everyone would want to hear what she had to say. He should get rid of her as soon as possible. But she'd just given him an opportunity to challenge the integrity she clung to like a battle shield, and he couldn't resist.

"Are you saying you didn't mean all the terrible things you said about me?" he drawled.

She hesitated while searching for words, eventually coming up with a response designed to placate him without being overtly untruthful. "I shouldn't have said them."

Damn right she shouldn't have said them! She'd drawn first blood. She'd been so sanctimonious while sitting on the throne of her PR empire that Ian had shown her just how vulnerable she was. It'd been tit for tat, no big deal. And as far as Simon was concerned, their little…*disagreement* was over.

"No problem. I'm willing to let bygones be bygones if you are," he said. "Have a nice night."

"That's it?" Her blue eyes widened.

He slung an arm around Sunny, slouching into her so he'd look comfortable and cozy and unlikely to go anywhere. "Were you hoping for more?"

Her bottom lip quivered as tears filled her eyes.

Ah, shit.

"I was hoping that you might—"

Jerry Russell, the director of his latest project, interrupted by walking up and bending to look in her face. "What's going on here? You making the ladies cry already, Simon?"

"You got trouble, Simon?" someone else piped up,

and that was all it took to send a murmur through the crowd that made everyone turn toward him.

Tears rolled down Gail's cheeks. He could tell she was trying to hold them back but that only seemed to make matters worse. She was emotionally strung out and under scrutiny.

He had to get her out of here before he wound up on the front page of the tabloids again. One picture of her sorrowful face and some stupid paparazzi would report that he'd purposely and vengefully acted to destroy her: Box Office Hit Simon O'Neal Sends Small-Town PR Girl Packing. Which, thanks to Ian, was close enough to the truth that he wouldn't even be able to fight it.

He couldn't afford to give his ex-wife any more ammunition for the bitter war she was waging. If he didn't clean up his act he'd never gain even partial custody of his son. The judge had been very firm about that.

People were starting to converge on them. He had to act now to avoid a spectacle.

"No trouble," he said with a reassuring smile and, telling Sunny he'd be right back, slid out of the booth. "It's damn hot in here. I think we'll get some air."

Taking Gail's hand, to throw any curious onlookers off the scent of another disagreement, he led her at a measured pace, nodding and exchanging greetings as they passed through the other guests to an expensively appointed back room, one that'd been designated for his use. No one ever specified what such a room was for because it was for anything he wanted. He could do drugs in here, have sex, throw a private party…whatever.

He'd never been more grateful for it than now.

"What were you thinking coming here?" he growled as soon as he closed the door securely behind them. "And for the love of God would you stop crying?"

She dashed a hand across her face. "I'm sorry. I... I'm embarrassed, but... I can't seem to help it."

Tears made him feel inadequate. Especially coming from her. In the three years they'd worked together, throughout all the bookings and events and movie releases and good and bad publicity, she'd always been so composed. "Try harder."

"Thanks for the empathy," she muttered.

Partially so he wouldn't have to look at her, he crossed the room and poured a glass of champagne from the bottle that had been put on ice, then pressed it into her hands. "Here, maybe this will help."

"I don't drink."

He grimaced. "One of the many reasons I don't like you. Drink it, anyway."

She downed it as though it was water and the subsequent coughing fit distracted her enough that she was able to shut off the waterworks.

"So what is it you want from me?" he asked. "How do I make this...go away?"

The shrewdness in her eyes returned. "You mean me? How do you make *me* go away?"

After taking a second to think about it, he shrugged. "Basically, yeah."

"You can say that so nonchalantly after destroying my business?"

He considered explaining that he hadn't been as actively involved as she might imagine, but didn't bother. He doubted she'd believe him, anyway. "You need money, is that it?"

"No! I want my former clients back. And not for my sake—well, not entirely. The way things sit right now, I'll have to let my employees go, and...they need their jobs."

Her situation was that dire? *Already?* He was going to kill Ian. Why'd he have to take it so damn far? "Fine. I'll contact a few people, see what I can do to reverse the damage. Call me next week. Good enough? Will you go home now and…watch TV or reorganize your cupboards or whatever exciting thing you do in your spare time? Maybe you can go online and look for a dress that would be appropriate for a party like this."

He could tell she was tempted to land a good jab of her own. He knew she was capable of it. But she held her tongue. With a sniff and a nod, she handed him the champagne flute and started to leave.

"And, Gail?"

She glanced over her shoulder.

"I don't have a disease, sexually transmitted or otherwise. I can provide the test results if you're interested."

At least she had the decency to blush. "No. Sorry," she said, and slipped out.

Three

Joshua jumped to his feet the moment Gail breezed into her office. "Did you see it?"

She wasn't surprised to find him waiting for her. Not after what they'd discussed yesterday. Looking forward to being able to put his fears to rest, to reassure all of her employees, she smiled. It hadn't been easy eating crow at the party last night—breaking into tears had been downright humiliating—but as agonizing as those few minutes had been, they'd also been worth it. Simon had promised to right what he'd done and she trusted he'd follow through. He wouldn't want her bothering him again, especially in public; he'd made that clear.

She'd slept soundly for the first time since dropping Simon O'Neal from her client roster. After spending an hour at the gym, she'd stopped off at a different coffeehouse than her usual one, just for a change, and was really enjoying the new blend. It was a good morning.

"See what?" She handed Josh her coffee while she removed her jacket and hung it on the rack.

His own smile a bit smug, he held up the folded tabloid he carried in his other hand. *"Hollywood Secrets Revealed."*

"No." She hadn't even signed on to her computer yet. She'd skipped that part of her morning ritual because she hadn't been worried she might find some damaging anecdote or tell-all about one of her clients in the gossip blogs or Hollywood e-zines. She wouldn't have to worry about *that* until she'd recovered some of her list. "Did Simon do something stupid after I left last night?"

This seemed to take Josh aback. "What do you mean?"

"At the premiere party."

"You went there? You saw him?"

She sent him a conspirator's smile. "I sure did."

His mouth hung open in surprise as she took her coffee. "What for?"

"To apologize. Why else would I go? He's agreed to do what he can to help us get back on our feet. We're going to be fine." *Hallelujah!* What a weight had been lifted from her shoulders. She felt so light, as if she could walk on air—until she noticed that Joshua wasn't reacting to this news as favorably as she'd expected. "What's wrong? Aren't you relieved?"

Stumbling back, he reached behind him to locate a seat and sank into it, clasping *Hollywood Secrets Revealed* to his chest. "Heaven help me…"

She felt her eyebrows go up. "Heaven help you *what*? I said we *wouldn't* be filing for bankruptcy. I fixed things. We'll be okay." She gave his arm a reassuring squeeze and sipped her coffee while waiting for him to absorb the good news. "So…what's in *HSR* this morning? A mess for Chelsea Seagate to clean up?"

With a chuckle for poor Chelsea, she started to round her desk, then stopped. "Why do you look like you just swallowed a marble?" she asked as her assistant's horrified expression finally dispelled the euphoria that had carried her to work this morning.

"I—I didn't know you planned to make up with Simon. You didn't say that. Not exactly. You said you were going to throw a Hail Mary. I thought that meant you'd try and beg Clint to come back, or…or apply for a loan…or go after Chelsea's old clients…or consider branching into fashion and beauty PR. I never dreamed he'd accept your apology even if you offered him one."

She remembered the argument she and Simon had had when he'd been charged with public drunkenness. "Neither did I. He's been a bear lately, angry all the time. I must've caught him in a benevolent mood." She gestured for Josh to give her the paper. "Let me have a look at what's got you so worked up."

Closing his eyes, he dropped his head back as if his neck could no longer hold it up.

"What's wrong with you?" She laughed because she couldn't take him seriously. He tended to be overly dramatic. And whatever was upsetting him couldn't be worse than the problem she'd just solved. Absolute disaster had a way of putting lesser setbacks in proportion. "Josh? The paper?" she prompted when he made no move to hand it over.

At last, he held it out. But he didn't look at her. He acted as though he couldn't bear to see her reaction.

Frowning, Gail opened the paper, read the headline—and felt her coffee cup slip out of her fingers. "Oh…my… God!"

He covered his face and groaned.

Clutching the paper, she jabbed it with a finger. "How did this happen?"

"It's all my fault," he mumbled from beneath his hands. "I… I met a friend at the paper for drinks. I thought Big Hit should go out with a bang instead of scuttling off like a dog with its tail between its legs. I told her she had to be careful how she wrote the story—to protect the magazine and to protect us. And she was. There's nothing directly attributed to you. It's all hearsay."

Gail wasn't even listening anymore. The ringing in her ears drowned out all other sound as she read and reread the opening paragraph. This had to be a joke. It couldn't be happening, not now. But she could tell from Josh's body language that it was most definitely for real.

> Simon O'Neal Accused of Sexual Assault
> An unnamed source from Big Hit PR, the firm that recently slammed its doors on Hollywood's biggest bad boy when he started a fight on the set of his latest movie, has revealed that the trouble between Simon and the owner of the firm, PR princess Gail DeMarco, stems from an evening the two spent together almost a month ago. Although details remain murky, and both sides are rushing to cover it up, there has been talk about a sexual assault....

Ignoring the coffee fanning out on the expensive carpet, Gail leaned on her desk so she wouldn't fall. "I've never accused Simon of assaulting me," she gasped.

"The article doesn't claim to have proof," Josh said.

"But the media will be calling day and night, hounding me for details. If this was true, it'd be the biggest story of the year. And—" She reached into her purse for her cell phone. No doubt she already had dozens of messages. She'd turned it off when she went to the gym to save battery power and hadn't yet turned it back on. "I'm going to be sick."

"I know the feeling," Josh said.

"What made you think I'd ever condone such a lie?" She pressed the button on her phone that would start the power-up sequence. "Simon is trying to get custody of his five-year-old son." She held the paper in front of her. "Even though none of this is true it'll give his ex-wife one more stone to throw at him in court."

Wearing a sheepish expression, Josh lowered his hands and sat up. "I wasn't thinking straight. I was so…angry. And she says *talk*."

He'd already pointed that out. It didn't help. "She says I was Simon's victim! And now I *will* be his victim. He's going to strangle me! He'll destroy the company, and then he'll come after me. And I can't blame him. Don't you understand? All he cares about is regaining contact with Ty. It's the divorce and what he did to cause it that's eating him up inside. This will… Oh, God. I'll refute it. Of course I'll refute it, but that won't help."

"He deserved to have his wife leave him. He was cheating on her with half a dozen other women—"

"I know. It doesn't make much sense. But he loved her. A lot. Even I could tell that much."

Josh got up and began to pace. "I admit, now that I'm sober, what I did seems…reckless. And impetuous. And foolhardy. But…he gets away with whatever he does, and I didn't want to let him get away with what he did to us. I wanted him to pay a price."

The phone rang, the sound jangling Gail's nerves. It was eight o'clock, the time the answering service transferred all calls back to the office.

She glanced across her desk but didn't reach for the handset. She remained rooted to the spot until Ashley poked her head into the room. "A reporter from *The Star* is on the phone. They're offering loads of money for the exclusive. But… I'm not sure you're going to be interested in that."

"I'm definitely *not* interested. Tell him so." She needed to get her bearings, make a plan to stop the spread of this story. She could do that, couldn't she? Avoiding this type of disaster, or minimizing it, was what she did for a living. She'd just never had to do it for herself.

"Got it." Ashley lowered her voice. "I know this can't be easy for you. I have to admit I didn't agree with refusing Simon's business. But now I don't blame you one bit. I'm sorry I've been complaining behind your back about what a stupid decision it was."

"You might try thinking before you open your mouth next time," Gail muttered.

Ashley winced. "Not exactly behind your back. Yeah, I guess I'll shut up. But… I am sorry. Are you okay?"

No. She wasn't okay. She was in the middle of the worst nightmare of her life and couldn't figure out how she'd gotten there. She was always the one in the right, the problem-solver, the first with good advice. She'd made a living out of these strengths, only to have Josh shove her firmly into the wrong.

Ashley stepped closer. "What can I do to help?"

She curled her nails into her palms. "Get Josh out of here before I start yelling."

"Excuse me?"

"I'm sorry." Josh was distraught, but Gail wasn't ready to hear his apology. Not yet. Maybe he'd done what he'd done in some misguided attempt to defend her, to defend them all, or at least get in a good swing at the Goliath in their lives. Considering the situation, that was understandable, especially if he'd been drinking. But there was no escaping the fact that he'd crossed the line, and she was going to pay dearly for it. They all were.

"Josh?" Ashley said uncertainly. "You coming?"

"I'm sorry," he said again, and burst into a full-blown wail.

Gail breathed deeply as he ran out. "Let him cry."

"So…what should I do when other reporters begin to call?" Ashley was still waiting for direction, and not about how to handle Josh.

"Tell everyone that I'm unavailable. Whatever you do, don't even hint that I'm here or put anyone through. Not until I give the word."

"Does that go for the police? Because they left a message with the answering service."

Oh, no…

Ashley wrung her hands. "You're so white. You're not going to faint, are you?"

"Maybe." Was it just last night she'd gone home and congratulated herself on having a second chance?

"Should I get you something? A glass of water or— Oh, you've dropped your coffee. Look at the mess."

A stain couldn't compare to everything else that was going on. Gail pointed to the door. "The other line's ringing. Someone has to answer."

"Right. Of course. No one will get through. You can count on me," she said, and snatched up Gail's cup before scurrying out.

Bracing herself for what she might find, Gail checked the call log on her cell phone. Sure enough, she had thirty missed calls. All of which had been left in the past two hours.

Almost every one of them came from Simon or Ian. What was she going to do?

She had no chance to decide. A second later, the outside door banged open and everyone started screaming while trying to stop the man who'd stalked inside. It was Simon. And he had his eye on her office as he shoved one person after another out of his way.

Four

Gail jumped to her feet and put her desk between them. She had no idea what else to do. She'd never seen Simon this angry, not even when he'd punched out his costar for calling him "Tiger Woods" after news of his divorce, and the reason behind it, broke.

"What the hell kind of game are you playing?" he yelled. "I told you I'd reverse whatever Ian did to your business. We agreed last night. Didn't you believe me?"

The veins that stood out in his neck made Gail as uncomfortable as his bloodshot eyes. If she had her guess, he hadn't been to bed since she'd seen him. Unshaven, with his thick black hair mussed and his clothes wrinkled, he had lines of fatigue bracketing his eyes and mouth. But he still looked gorgeous.

Gail considered that more than a little unfair. At six feet tall, he wasn't even short like so many other male actors.

"I'm not playing games," she said. "I believed you, and I can…explain. If you'll just give me a chance."

He pulled *Hollywood Secrets Revealed* out of his back pocket and slapped it down. "This is bullshit! All of it. And you know it."

Her knuckles ached with tension as she clasped her hands in front of her. "I do. And I'll admit it. I promise. We just need to brainstorm how…how to proceed from here, figure out the best way to neutralize the damage."

He tilted his head as if a new thought had occurred to him. "Is that why you did it? To get me back in here? So we could work together again?"

"What?" Losing some of her fear, she stood taller. "Absolutely not. I'm the one who kicked you out to begin with."

His lips, so sensuous-looking in the movies, thinned. "But now you regret losing the income."

"I regret that it cost me my other clients. I don't regret that it cost me *you*. You're a mess and it's time someone had the guts to tell you."

"I'm a mess?" he repeated. "At least I'm not falsely accusing anyone of a felony!"

She cringed. "Right. That's bad."

"If you agree, then *why?* I've never laid a hand on you—and I've had plenty of opportunities. How many times have we been alone in the back of a limousine, coming or leaving an event, or meeting after hours right here in this office?"

Not many. And certainly never for very long. Ian, his business manager, was usually with them, or Serge, who worked for her and helped with the bigger accounts. Sometimes one of Simon's bodyguards came along. But she wasn't going to quibble over such a small detail. Especially when he added, "Not that I wouldn't like to wring your neck this very second."

"You wouldn't want to make matters any worse." She edged away when he took a few steps to the left, always keeping the same distance between them. She doubted he'd really hurt her. He'd never been known to strike a woman. But he'd been unraveling pretty fast since the breakdown of his marriage. She wasn't taking any chances.

"Matters *can't* get any worse," he ranted. "I've been accused of a lot of things, but never *rape!* Don't you realize what this is going to do to me? My ex-wife's lawyers have already called. They're going to use this to delay my next custody hearing. It could slow the process for months, make it impossible for me to get my little boy back...." When his voice broke, his muscles bunched as if he'd rather slug the wall than show her his softer side, the side that actually cared about something. "If that happens, if I lose him, I'll make you sorry you were ever born."

Gail couldn't help cringing again. He meant it. "I apologize. Sincerely. Please, calm down and—"

The door swung open and Ian Callister charged in. Face mottled with emotion, blond hair standing on end as if he'd just rolled out of bed, he was obviously in a hurry. But he didn't seem to be looking for her. At least, not yet. He had eyes only for his frazzled client. "Simon, let me handle this. You don't need to be here, okay? This is dangerous. You touch one hair on her head and it'll just exacerbate the problem. Why don't you go home and try to get some sleep? I'll call as soon as I have this resolved. We'll work it out. I swear."

"Like you worked out taking away her clients?" Simon asked. "Why do you think she did this?"

"*I* wasn't trying to get revenge," Gail said. But the men weren't listening.

"She was too full of herself," Ian replied. "I was just giving little miss prim and proper a much-deserved wake-up call."

Full of herself? Was that how she came off? Gail

opened her mouth to offer some sort of defense; she wasn't the one who'd acted badly when she'd represented him. But Simon was already responding.

"What the hell am I even doing here?" He threw up his hands. "What's done is done. There's nothing we can do to take it back. As far as I'm concerned, you can both go to hell. Good luck saving your business," he said to her. "Because I won't lift a finger to help you, and you'd better be prepared to defend yourself against a slander suit. And you." He pointed at Ian. "You're fired."

With that, he left, but not before slamming every door he encountered.

In the wake of his noisy departure, Gail could see her employees creeping toward her interior window. They gazed in at her with wide eyes and mouths hanging open.

She ignored them. Ian was still in her office, breathing heavily and eyeing her as if *he'd* like to wring her neck on Simon's behalf.

"Thanks for that," he snapped.

She swallowed hard. "You deserved it. If you really went after my business the way he said, you don't deserve to work for him. Or anyone else in Hollywood."

"Like *you* deserve to work here after the little stunt you pulled? Accusing an innocent man of rape?"

"I didn't leak that bogus story!"

"Then where'd it come from?"

She felt too much loyalty to Josh to reveal his complicity. Since he worked for her, she was responsible for what he'd done, anyway. Caught between her disapproval of his actions and her understanding of the frustration that had fueled them, she shook her head to avoid answering. "Regardless, it's become public. Now we have to decide what to do about it."

He paced to her credenza and back. "What, exactly, do you suggest?"

The sarcasm that dripped from those words implied that there was no way out. But there had to be.

She pressed her fingers to her temples. "First of all, we have to calm down so we can think." Her employees, all except Ashley, who was busy with the phones, were still gaping at them, trying to figure out what was going on. Irritated by the lack of privacy, she waved them away.

"Easier said than done when we're all facing the end of our careers," Ian grumbled, frowning as their audience reluctantly dispersed.

"This article is just the latest in a series of bad developments," she said. "The real problem started long before now. Simon's been rolling downhill for months, drinking too much, fighting, acting belligerent, walking out on jobs and getting sued for breach of contract. He was already in trouble."

"That's no excuse for what you've done. Chelsea Seagate and I have been trying to get things turned around, but you've just made his situation exponentially worse."

She wondered what Chelsea was going to say about this, how she'd try to contain the damage, and was actually grateful that she might have some help. "I agree. I'm saying this isn't a *new* problem. It's more of the old problem. Simon needs a fresh image. We've got to pull him out of circulation until he can decompress and get hold of himself."

Ian shoved a hand through his thick, unruly hair. "How do we pull him out of circulation? He has a new movie coming out. He's contractually obligated to promote it. That puts him on every major talk show in America."

He'd probably show up drunk at those appearances because he couldn't bear to do them sober anymore. She'd never seen anyone so burned out. "What if he had a good reason to change things up? What if we gave the movie's producer such a great PR angle he'd be thrilled *without* the usual dog-and-pony show?"

"I'm not following you," he said, but he seemed somewhat mollified and encouraged by her tone.

"It's been six months since Simon's divorce."

"And he's still not over it."

She threw him a dirty look. "We're talking about *solutions*. He's available again. That's the bright spot."

He stood by the window and peered out through the blinds. "What are you saying?"

"That what we should do is—" her mind scrambled to focus the idea that was coming to her "—find a nice girl for him to marry."

The blinds snapped as he let go of them and swung around to face her. "*Marry?* After what Bella the Bitch has done, I don't think he'll ever marry again."

"But consider what a new relationship would do to distract from, and counteract, all the bad press. *If* we could find the right person."

He prowled around, examining the awards she'd won, tossing her paperweight from hand to hand. "And who would the right person be?"

"Someone sweet enough to soften his rough edges. Someone whose character is sterling, above question, so there won't be any shocking revelations down the road."

He sighed. "Too dangerous. Anyone could end up being unpredictable."

"Not necessarily. This will be a business deal. The

woman will sign a prenup as well as a contract outlining exactly what she can and can't do. If she fulfills her obligations, she'll be generously compensated. But she'll get paid only if she abides by the terms. We'll make sure she says nothing that isn't nice about him and acts with proper adoration in public. He'll have total control."

Ian still seemed skeptical. "There's no such thing as total control. How do you know that whoever we get won't turn out to be a psycho? Or cause bigger problems? It's not like you're going to find someone who doesn't know who he is. Any woman would smell money."

"You have so much confidence in the female gender," she said with a grimace.

He shrugged at her sarcasm. "I'm just sayin'. What if she gets tired of putting in the time and sells her story to the tabloids to make a quick buck instead? Reveals that she's a plant? Tries to blackmail him or take him to the cleaners?"

"That would be breach of contract."

"So?" he said, exasperated. "People break contracts all the time. And once the truth is out there—"

"The wife would have to be someone we trust," she conceded, "someone who has no appetite for fame and no interest in pursuing the Hollywood crowd."

"Someone who appears dutiful and devoted," he added.

He was starting to see the potential, which ignited a flame of excitement in Gail. What she was picturing could work, even for someone as far gone as Simon. "The public will eat it up. Who doesn't enjoy a good love story—especially one in which beauty tames the beast?"

He hesitated as if tempted, but ultimately shook his

head. "No. What're we thinking? That's crazy. Even if we could find the ideal lady, Simon would never agree to this. He's had enough of women—er, marriage. That ex-wife of his ran his heart through a meat grinder."

Gail propped her hands on her hips. "And he didn't do the same to her?"

"Maybe he did. But he never used their son as a weapon against her, like she's doing to him. He hasn't been able to see Ty for weeks. And there's a lot more you don't know, because Simon refuses to make her look bad. He's taking full responsibility for the breakup of the marriage, even though she's no gem."

"I'm glad to hear you think *her* actions are reprehensible, since destroying someone's business doesn't seem to bother your conscience. At least you have your limits."

He made a face at her. "You asked for what I did. You left Simon in the lurch, then compounded the problem by opening your big mouth."

"He showed up at his ex-wife's drunk and tried to bust into her house!"

"Because he wanted to see his son!"

"And accomplished just the opposite. Now she has a restraining order against him."

"What she's doing hurts Ty as much as Simon. Ty has to be wondering where the hell his daddy is, and that tears Simon up. Anyway, Simon's ex isn't the one who's paying my bill, so I'll let someone else worry about what's best for her."

"Right now *no one* is paying your bill," Gail reminded him. "If you want Simon back, you're going to have to make him an offer, show him a way out of the mess he's in."

"And you think a fake marriage is the ticket?" Suspicion entered his eyes. "Or are you setting me up for failure?"

Gail spread her hands wide. At this point, she wanted them all to regain their footing, even Ian, so they could move on. "I'm not setting you up. To prove it, I'll handle all the PR for this myself, free of charge."

"Which includes…"

"I'll get the information into the hands of key people, position it as one of the best-kept secrets in town that Simon has a new love interest. Everyone will be salivating to learn who the lucky girl is. Meanwhile, you can find the best candidate. Once that happens, I'll sell the exclusive to *People,* and he can use those funds to pay her if he wants." Satisfied that she'd come up with the perfect fix, she raised her hands palms up. "Or Chelsea could take my idea and run with it."

"No way," he said, shaking his head. "Why would Pierce Mattie be willing to get involved in this, to put their reputation on the line?"

"The money? Or the challenge—"

"No way. They'd never go along with it." He cracked his knuckles.

"Then I'll do it, like I said."

"That's better. But how am I supposed to find an innocent woman in the circles Simon's been hanging out with lately? He's so afraid he'll actually be tempted to trust someone he's sworn off all women except the most jaded and easy. You're the only one he knows who—" His head jerked up. "That's it!"

Gail wasn't sure why, but she took a step back. "What's it?"

"*You'll* be his wife. That way even Chelsea won't have to know. It'll stay between us. The three of us."

"You're not serious…."

"Of course I am. It's got to be someone he knows or people will see this as the ruse it is. Besides, you owe us, and you need the money a lot more than Chelsea Seagate. She has all your old clients, remember?" he added with a devilish grin.

"How could I forget? But I'm not cut out for the part of Simon's wife!"

"Sure you are. You're perfect. No one will pay attention to the rape claim because they'll know that if you're marrying him, it couldn't possibly be true. Everything will be tied up with a neat bow."

Was she really the one who'd come up with this idea? She was beginning to feel faint again. "But Simon and I aren't the least bit compatible. Seeing us together, the way we interact, will be a dead giveaway."

"He's an actor, and a damn good one. He can pretend to love even you. And you're a PR agent, which requires no small amount of stretching the truth."

She considered what his suggestion would entail and gulped. "Wait a minute…"

"For what?"

For the room to stop spinning. "What about my business? I'm needed here."

"You said you don't have any business left."

"I don't, but I was…hoping that—"

"We'll send your staff on vacation until we have everything set up and ready for you to return."

"That won't work. My employees can't survive without a paycheck, even for two weeks."

"Then they can stay and work. Simon will cover your payroll."

He was overcoming every argument. "And the rent until we can make a comeback?"

"Simon will cover that, too."

Her knees buckled, and she sank into a chair. She had to admit she'd had her fantasies about Simon. What woman in America hadn't imagined his mouth on hers? She'd imagined a little more than that. But those were silly daydreams about characters who didn't exist, not the flesh and blood and very fallible man who played those larger-than-life parts. At least, that was what she'd always told herself....

"I'm not sure I can do this."

Shoving his hands in his pockets, Ian came closer. "Why not? Who better than a PR pro to stay at Simon's side night and day? If that won't keep him out of trouble, what will? Besides, you'll know exactly what to say when someone shoves a microphone in your face."

Gail grabbed for the one remaining argument she could think of. "How can you promise that Simon will pay my employees and my rent or anything else on his behalf? Last I heard you were fired."

He winked at her. "Simon needs us. He'll understand that once I've had a chance to talk to him."

Maybe he'd refuse. He wouldn't like this idea. No question about that.

But if he thought it would give him Ty he'd do it in a heartbeat.

Five

"Seriously? This is what my life has come to? A fake marriage?"

Suddenly finding it too much of a distraction, Simon put the football game he'd recorded on his DVR on pause. Ian was hoping to retain his job, so it was understandable that he'd come here with some crazy idea that was supposed to save the day. But even if it had been a *good* idea, Simon doubted he'd take him back. In his opinion, Ian had revealed some disturbing character flaws.

Then again, Simon knew he probably wasn't anyone who should be pointing a finger.

Ian sat on the edge of his chair. Showered and ready for the rest of the day, his sunglasses dangling from one hand, he looked refreshed and energetic, which counted for more than anything he'd had to say so far. His manner made him convincing. Simon needed *someone* who felt ready to tackle the world. *He* felt as if he'd just been hit by a truck.

"It wouldn't be fake," Ian said. "It would be real."

"That makes it worse. I'd be acting my own life." Simon brought his recliner upright. He spent a lot of time in this room. It had no windows, so it was completely dark if he wanted it to be, and that helped whenever he had a headache. It was comfortable, too. After barging into Gail's office and ranting like a madman early this morning, he'd come here to calm down and recover from a raging hangover. But he wasn't succeeding, at calming down *or* feeling better. Every time he thought of Gail and that rape charge, he wanted to put his fist through a wall. And although beer sometimes helped with a hangover, it didn't seem to be doing much today. His head pounded as though it might explode.

What he needed was sleep. He hadn't slept well in weeks. But nothing he did, short of pills, made sleep possible.

"This is what you come to me with?" he asked Ian. "*This* is how you plan to prove your worth?"

Surprisingly, his manager—possibly ex-manager; Simon was still trying to decide—didn't back down. He was completely convinced he had the answer to all of Simon's problems. "Yes. It's brilliant."

"It's crazy!" He winced. Raising his voice had been a mistake. "There's got to be another way out of the mess I'm in," he added more calmly. "I've got more money than I know what to do with. Let's put it to good use."

Ian shook his head. "Money's not enough this time, Simon. You need a more drastic solution."

"This is drastic, all right," he responded with a humorless chuckle. "Are you listening to yourself? You're suggesting I pay Gail DeMarco, a woman I don't even like, to be my wife."

"She's a PR professional, the best in the business. We can't expect her to give up two years of her life for free."

"Two *years?*" The sour taste of the beer was making his stomach queasy. He should've eaten something.

"You've got to create a track record of stability, give her time to build the illusion of peace and happiness, a life in control."

Simon said nothing. He was too busy trying to subdue his nausea. Maybe he didn't want to admit it to Ian, but he knew one thing—he couldn't go on like this. He'd known that for a while.

"Think about it," Ian said. "You won't have much to do with her. It's mainly for appearances. You get married, you lie low, you get Ty back and then you part amicably. This is a PR campaign, not a marriage in the normal sense. You're taking it way too seriously."

"Then *you* marry her."

"I would if it'd help."

Simon tried to picture Gail as his wife and couldn't. They'd worked together too long in carefully defined roles that rarely crossed into their personal lives. And what he'd seen of her on a personal basis hadn't impressed him. Talk about a straight arrow. Could he tolerate having this person in his life on a day-to-day basis? "Who picked the length of time?"

"She did. But it's a worst-case scenario. If our plan works sooner than expected, we can make adjustments."

He sure as hell hoped it wouldn't take two years. At the moment, Bella had full custody of their son and, thanks to a hard-ass judge who'd ranted on about his "moral corruption," she'd managed to deny him visitation rights. Yet she was leaving Ty with one nanny after another while she had surgery to fix cosmetic flaws that didn't exist, took expensive trips with men she'd barely met and tried too hard to be seen, to be part of the Hollywood "in" crowd, as if she wanted to be famous herself. After his mother died, Simon had been raised by nannies. He didn't want that for his son.

"It beats rehab," Ian murmured when Simon didn't respond. "Something has to be done."

Surely marriage would do more for public perception than a rehab program. But it would only work if he could get his drinking under control.

He turned his beer around and around in its holder. "How much is she charging?"

"The price of the wedding photos. Whatever we sell them for, that's what she'll get. She'll even negotiate the sale and handpick the placement so we get maximum publicity."

"*People* magazine will want them. And they'll pay a couple mil, at least."

"That's a lot, but it's money you wouldn't have without her, so she's essentially paying for herself, right?"

He didn't care about the money. He just wanted to understand the setup. "Apparently you two have thought of everything."

Ian smiled. "This will work, Simon. If you'll let her take charge for a while, do everything she tells you, you'll get Ty back. I fully believe that. Will you meet with her?"

"Not today." He wasn't sure he could trust himself not to lay into her again. Every time he remembered that whole assault thing, he wanted to go ape shit.

"Tomorrow, then?"

Why not? It was worth a shot. Gail DeMarco wasn't the most appealing woman in the world, but she was better than the alternative. "Fine."

Ian slapped his knees and stood. "Fantastic. So…are we good? Are we back in business?"

Simon hated to give in so easily, but in his current condition he didn't have the wherewithal to do much else. "Yeah, I guess so. For now," he added grudgingly.

"You'll be glad you hired me back. I promise. But…"

"What?" Simon said when he hesitated.

"No drinking tonight, okay? I don't want Gail to see you like this."

Simon gave him a wry smile. "You think she'll walk out on two million dollars?"

"I know she will. Her reputation will be on the line. She'll only do it if she believes we can succeed."

He was probably right. That was partly why Gail had always made him a little defensive and uneasy. His money didn't matter to her. Neither did his fame. And he wasn't too strong in any of the categories that did.

It was a beautiful Saturday afternoon. Pale October sunlight drifted into the living room of Simon's Beverly Hills mansion through a series of large front windows, but Gail barely noticed. They'd just come in from outside, where Ian had taken pictures of her and Simon wrapped in each other's arms, their mouths only millimeters apart as if they'd just kissed or were about to. They planned to kick off the campaign by leaking those suggestive photographs to the press. It was all calculated and arranged. It meant nothing. And yet…standing so close to Simon had left Gail a bit breathless.

She tried to pretend otherwise, but Simon immediately threw her off balance again.

"What about sex?" he asked, taking a seat on the sofa, while she stood closer to Ian, who had his laptop on a table and was downloading the pictures.

Gail had been planning to cover this herself. She just hadn't found the nerve. "What do you mean?" she asked, stalling while she formulated her response.

He held the club soda he'd poured himself. "You've told me that from this minute on I can't drink a drop of alcohol. You've negotiated your price. And you've covered how we'll make the marriage look real by leaking information and photographs to the press. You've even had Ian take the pictures you plan to start with." He motioned to his manager. "He'll be emailing them to you any minute. Don't you think it's time to address how we're going to handle our marriage on the *inside?* I'm assuming I can't cheat—"

"Of course not. That would endanger the whole campaign!" she broke in.

"So what am I supposed to do?" He slid one hand down his thigh as he shifted, adjusting the fit of the faded jeans he wore with a simple T-shirt and expensive-looking house shoes. "If we were talking about two months it might be different. But we're talking about *two years.*"

Dressed in a standard business suit, since she considered this a business meeting, she fiddled with one of her buttons. "I realize that sounds like a long time."

"Damn right," he said. "An eternity. You're not suggesting I go without, are you?"

Hoping he'd explain why her answer had to be what it was, Gail looked at Ian. But he merely glanced up from his computer and arched his eyebrows, implying that this one was all hers.

"Thanks for jumping in to break the bad news," she grumbled.

He grinned for the first time. "It's kind of funny to watch you flounder. I've never seen a grown woman turn so red."

She grimaced. "With my coloring, it doesn't take much." Which hardly seemed fair, since the two of them were tanned to a perfect café au lait despite the fact that summer had ended two months ago.

Ian's grin stretched wider. "I'm starting to like you, you know that? For someone who's so uptight and controlling, you're not bad."

God, he made her sound like her father. She cringed at the militant image that presented. But she was her father's daughter. She'd heard that before. She'd even inherited his freckles and strawberry-blond hair, both of which she hated as much as his intensity.

"I don't care if you like me or not," she said. But it wasn't true. She was the worst kind of type A, worse than her father, because she was also a pleaser, which meant she'd work herself to death to meet everyone's expectations, no matter how unreasonable they might be.

"Is there an answer in my near future?" Simon shook his drink, causing the ice to clink against the glass.

Lifting her chin, she addressed him herself. "Yes."

"Yes, what?"

"Yes, I expect you to go two years without sex. That's what the job requires."

He took another drink of his club soda as if this didn't bother him, but a subtle tightening around the mouth and eyes said otherwise. "So you'll be my wife in name and pocketbook only."

"Basically. Although I'll be signing a prenup, so I'll have enough to make you look generous and in love, but no access to your millions. You'll pay for our wedding rings and the kind of wardrobe your wife should have. The sale of the pictures will cover my contract."

She got the impression he was circling, searching for vulnerability, like a buzzard.

"A rock on your finger and a few clothes. That's all you'll need from me to get you through the next two years?"

"That and some privacy. Once I'm Mrs. O'Neal, my

business should recover on its own. I say we go our separate ways behind closed doors, don't you?" How else
would they survive suddenly being shackled to each
other, two people who were so opposite and ill-suited?

"For the most part...yes."

She'd expected him to be more adamant that she keep
her distance whenever possible. He'd had no interest in
her on a personal level before. In the past year, neither
had he listened to anything she'd told him profession-
ally, despite paying a hefty monthly retainer for her
guidance and advice. He was only listening now because he'd bottomed out.

"We'll need personal space and time alone," she went
on. "Considering the number of mansions you own, having our own space shouldn't be a problem." There was
definitely room enough for two at his twenty-five-thou-
sand-square-foot home in Belize, for instance. Room
enough for her to handle her business remotely, with
Serge's and Josh's help; it would grow by leaps and
bounds as soon as word of their union got out. Simon
could...read scripts or whatever he did when he wasn't
shooting a movie. "We should live a few weeks here
and a few weeks there—preferably out of the country
as much as possible. That'll help us keep ahead of the
paparazzi, control which details get out."

He pursed his lips. "You won't miss sex? It won't be
hard for you to sleep alone for two years?"

She gestured carelessly. "I'll *miss* it, but...my world
doesn't *revolve* around getting lucky. I'm a mature adult.
I can delay gratification until our marriage is over."

If he got her hint that he should be able to do the
same, he didn't let it deter him, didn't act the least bit
chastised or embarrassed. "And if I feel more strongly
about not having to go so long?"

She curled her fingernails into her palms. "I'm afraid you—you don't have any choice. It's the only way this will work."

"You could change your mind."

That was what he'd been getting at all along. Gail's anxiety rose until the muscles in her back felt like rubber bands twisted to maximum torque. "I'm sorry. That's not going to happen."

He jiggled one knee, an obvious sign of agitation. She'd seen him do it before when he was on edge or growing impatient—or anytime he had to sit still for too long. "What if I let you keep the ring? A big diamond. One of your choosing."

Of course he'd think he could buy anything he wanted. He was richer than God. And every decision they'd arrived at so far had been reached through negotiation. But he had to understand that this was different. She had her limits. "I won't trade sex for money."

"Oh, quit being such a prude," he said with a roll of his eyes. "We'll be married. It's not like you'd be standing on a street corner. And if you won't let me get it anywhere else, I need to know we have some sort of... arrangement, in case I get desperate."

"Desperate?"

He didn't bother to apologize. He'd been cross all morning, supremely unhappy with the problem as well as the solution. But Simon was always cross these days. The only thing that mattered right now was procuring a commitment to the no-sex rule, just as she had with the no-alcohol rule, so they'd both be going into this with the same expectations.

"I understand that you're trying to be practical," she said. "And I realize two years is a long time for...a man of your age and, uh, limitations." She smiled, knowing she'd just jabbed him back. "But our relationship isn't real, so we won't be sleeping together no matter how desperate you become."

"Why the hell not?" he demanded, finally losing the battle with his temper.

"Because I'm not an object! And we don't even respect each other!"

There was more to it. For one thing, after the sex goddesses he'd been with, he was certain to find her lacking. And what could she possibly gain? Nothing. Sleeping with Simon would only set her up for future disappointment. It wasn't as if she could expect the relationship to last, even if she wanted it to.

Fortunately, she could stand on principle and wouldn't have to explain the more embarrassing reasons behind her refusal. "Look, don't make a big deal out of this, okay? This is acting. You don't *really* get to sleep with the female leads you pretend to make love to in the movies, do you?"

Too late, she realized that might not be true off-set and couldn't believe she'd let her tongue get so far ahead of her brain.

"Only eighty or ninety percent of them," he responded, and Ian began to laugh.

When she shot Simon's manager a dirty look, he laughed even harder but tried to speak through it. "Come on, we all know the number of women who fall at his feet. Why pretend otherwise? In any case, you can't expect him to give up the good life—"

"You were with me on this!" she complained. "We talked about it last night."

Obviously sensing how easily their deal could fall apart, Ian sobered. "I agreed that he couldn't have any extramarital affairs. I *didn't* agree that he couldn't screw his own wife."

She'd said no sex, right after no alcohol, and he hadn't corrected her. "But I won't really be his wife!"

"You'll be legally married."

"That doesn't mean anything."

Finished emailing her the photos, he closed his computer. "It means he should be able to sleep with you if he wants."

"No, it doesn't."

"Then what else is he supposed to do?"

"He could try exercising a little self-restraint!"

"Like you?" Ian asked. "Someone who wouldn't know how to have fun if it came up and bit her on the ass?"

Fun had never been her top priority. Her mother had walked out when Gail was eight. Since then, she'd had too much to prove to her father and brother. "That won't change my answer."

Ian expelled a loud sigh. "He *will* be exercising some restraint. If he gives up booze and refuses the women who hit on him, he'll be exercising a lot of it. But you have to be realistic. If you take other women away, you have to provide *something* else instead."

Gail dropped her purse to the floor. "No matter how undesirable."

She'd imbued her voice with enough sarcasm to wither them both on the spot, but it didn't seem to make an impact. If anything, her words had the opposite effect. It was almost as if she could see them mentally offering each other a high five for scoring a direct hit. They respected her professional ability—she knew that much—but they'd never been particularly fond of her. She and Simon had too often been at cross-purposes, with him trying to do what he wanted regardless of the consequences and her trying to protect his image.

"It's a fair question," Ian insisted.

"A sabbatical might be good for him," she argued, "give him a chance to pull his life together."

Simon came to his feet. "This is bullshit! You'll have my name, my ring and two years of my life, and I can't even climb into bed with you?"

Suddenly Gail realized that this conversation had nothing to do with the topic. He wasn't attracted to her; he'd made that clear. He was responding to being nudged out of the power position and wanted to get back on top in some way. So he was demanding she make a difficult concession, one that couldn't be overruled simply by pointing to the fact that it would compromise the campaign.

"Sleeping together is *not* part of the deal," she reiterated.

Jaw set, he slammed his glass down on the coffee table. "Fine. I'll make some sort of discreet arrangement with a third party."

"No, you won't! We've been over that."

"It won't matter if no one knows."

"Isn't that the kind of thinking that got you into this mess? Word *would* get out, eventually. Your bed partners are too anxious to brag about their good fortune." Besides, she wouldn't want to lie awake night after night imagining what he might be doing in another part of the house. "Can't you look at this as a job? Pretend you're preparing to play a monk and celibacy is key to getting into character? If you can stay focused and put in the time, we'll all get what we need in the end. Then you can have a whole harem if you want."

Pivoting, he spoke to Ian as if she was no longer in

the room. "This won't work. I'm already going without alcohol. I'll be cut off from my friends, in case they see through this…sham of a marriage or—" he made quotation marks with his fingers "—lead me astray. And I'll be connected at the hip to someone who'll be monitoring my every move and, no doubt, criticizing it."

"Stop it," she told Simon before Ian could respond. Simon whirled on her. "Stop *what?*"

"Stop looking for a way out. If you don't want to do this, fine. But don't justify blowing up the deal by acting like you would've jumped in with both feet if only I'd been reasonable."

"You're *not* being reasonable! It'll be hard enough giving up alcohol."

"You said you could do it. I said maybe you should go into rehab instead. We'll just make matters worse if we attempt this and fail. And *you* said you weren't addicted."

"I'm *not* addicted, but… God, I could use a little help. A shoulder to cry on, if nothing else."

She folded her arms. "I'll lend you my shoulder, if you've got to have one, but nothing else. And I won't be criticizing everything you do," she added. "If it has no impact on the campaign, I won't say a word."

"You won't *have* to," he said. "I'll be able to see it in your face, which happens to reveal every thought you have. In any event, I have *no* intention of going without sex for two years on top of everything else. The way I see it, getting lucky every once in a while might be the only enjoyment I'll experience in two hellish years. Why would I give that up?"

Gail held her ground even though her high heels were beginning to pinch her toes and she was dying to sit.

"Because you've let your son down and this is the only way to make it up to him, that's why!"

His hands curled into fists as if he wanted to strike her, or strike something. Maybe it was only verbal, but she'd slugged him where it hurt. She'd had to. If they didn't stay focused, keep their goals in sight, they'd fail before they ever got started. And she had a lot riding on this, too.

"How hard can it be?" She went on more calmly, hoping to placate him. "You've already made it abundantly clear that I don't appeal to you."

His eyes, now glittery, roamed over her, making her want to cover herself even though she was fully dressed. "I assumed you'd be better than nothing. But maybe I was wrong."

"Oh, stop acting like a—" She caught herself before she could call him any names. He was looking for a fight. Why accommodate him? "Never mind. Forget it. No sex. Do I have your agreement?"

"I wouldn't touch you if you stood in front of me naked and begged," he grumbled.

Fabulous. She had what she wanted. But somehow it didn't make her feel any better. His capitulation, and the sentiment behind it, stung enough that she couldn't resist a final salvo. "Fine, because I have some standards myself, you know, and dissolute movie stars aren't high on my list of must-have men."

"That's the best you've got? *Dissolute?*" Wearing a pained expression, he turned to Ian. "Does anyone in the real world even use that word these days?"

"I've seen it in books," Ian said, his voice speculative.

She rolled her eyes. "I doubt you've ever picked up a book. It means—"

"You're not the only one here with a brain," Simon interrupted. "I know what it means. And as far as comebacks go, it sucks. Do you think I haven't heard it all before? That you're the only person with an opinion on how I live my life?"

All the things she'd wanted to tell him in the past but hadn't seemed to rise in her throat and propel her forward, until she stood almost nose to nose with him. At six feet, he still had her by a few inches, but the heels helped. "You probably haven't heard the half of it," she said, "because I'm the only one who'll state it plainly, the only one who's not out to get something from you. Who else will tell you that you need to pull your head out of your ass? The people who depend on you for a paycheck?" She motioned at Ian. "Him? Mr. Suck-up?"

Ian pressed a hand to his chest as if she'd just shot him. "Ouch! I take back what I said. I don't like you at all."

Simon ignored him. "Seriously? I hear how rotten I am all the time. My ex has said much worse than you could ever come up with—and she's said it to the papers so I have the print version in case I forget."

She'd made some comments that'd been printed, too, but she didn't want to remind him. "Yeah, well, you can't trust Bella, either. She's hurt and she's angry, and she's determined to have her revenge. I'm honest, not vindictive. If *I* tell you something, it's true. And I'm telling you this—you need to pull your head out!"

"Maybe she's not so bad at comebacks." Ian was obviously trying to break the tension, but it didn't work.

Sending his manager a dirty look, Simon returned to the couch. "You're not some sort of oracle, Ms. DeMarco, so quit pretending. I won't take advice from a repressed PR failure with her jacket buttoned up to her neck. And you *are* hoping for something from me. You want me to save your business and cut you a hefty check when this is all over."

She put her hands on her hips. "If you'd like to marry someone else, I'll do the PR for free. But two years of *my* life doesn't come cheap. And you're the one who destroyed my business in the first place. You *owe* me."

She thought he'd come right back at her, tell her it was Ian who'd gone after her and not him. But without his name Ian wouldn't have had the power to pull off what he'd done.

Simon didn't attempt to argue, however. A sigh hinted at how tired he was. Had he even been to bed last night? He looked like he'd been up for days. "Maybe I do," he relented, "but you don't have to make this so hard."

She got the feeling that they weren't talking strictly about sex anymore, but it was more comfortable to respond as if they were. "I'll be going without, too."

"You don't seem to have a problem with it, which doesn't say much for your love life."

He'd hit a little too close to the truth. She wasn't sure whom she'd sleep with even if she wanted a bed partner. Her last relationship ended three years ago; she hadn't been with anyone since. But she wasn't about to admit that to him. "Let's leave my love life out of it."

In an effort to turn the conversation around, Ian abandoned his seat by the computer and came forward. "Look—" he touched her elbow to get her to face him "—this'll be a piece of cake for you. What's so terrible about a couple of years spent eating at the best restaurants, shopping at the most expensive stores and flying around the world?"

Besides the fact that it meant she'd have to endure

two years of knowing Simon found her completely un-
attractive and, worse, unlikable? Could her self-esteem
survive such a constant beating?

Simon jumped to his feet, suddenly decisive. "I'm
calling it off. She's not up to the task."

Gail felt her jaw drop. "That's it? We just wasted the
past two hours?"

"I guess so."

"Fine. I'm out of here." Grabbing her purse, she
headed for the door.

Six

"Wait!" Ian caught her arm. "Don't leave. He's upset, not thinking clearly."

"He can't control his emotions and appetites long enough to implement a simple plan, let alone one that'll be as tricky as this," she said. "That's all we need to know."

"I can do whatever I have to," Simon said.

"Then why do you need me?" she asked.

With a grimace, he dropped onto the couch, leaned back and draped an arm over his face. "I don't know. You haven't helped matters so far."

Gail told herself to leave, as she'd intended to a moment earlier, but she couldn't seem to convince her feet. She wouldn't let him purposely destroy this opportunity to get his life back on track the way he'd destroyed all the others since he started acting out a year ago. He had *so* much potential. It drove her crazy to watch him self-destruct, especially in the public eye. Regardless of her opinion of him these days, he'd once been her favorite actor. His performances still captivated her.

"You don't get it, do you?" she said. "No one can do

this for you. If you want to see your life improve, you need to stand up and fight."

"What do you think I've been doing?" he mumbled into the crook of his arm.

Fighting the wrong kind of battles. And if he didn't change that soon, he'd learn how much worse his life could become. "Lashing out randomly in anger isn't what I'm talking about."

When he didn't respond, Ian's alarm seemed to grow. "Simon, we talked about this. When you hired me back, you said you could do it. You said you *would* do it."

"I know." Deadpan. Resigned.

"So…are you backing out or not?" Ian asked.

Simon muttered something Gail couldn't decipher; it sounded like a curse. But then he said, "I'm in if she is. I'd walk through fire for Ty. Do anything."

That didn't mean he had to be happy about it, and he wasn't, which would make her job that much harder. "Give me one reason I should trust you to pull this off," she said.

He lifted his arm so could look at her. "I can pull it off. I'll pour it on so thick there'll be times when even *you'll* think I'm in love with you."

More than a little fatigued herself, Gail slumped into a chair. "There's no danger of that."

The fact that she'd cracked, shown some exhaustion and weakness, seemed to surprise him. The tension in his body eased. "What about you? You don't particularly admire me, and you've had no experience with acting. Can *you* be convincing?"

Self-conscious about her clothing ever since he'd made the repressed-PR-failure comment, she unbuttoned the top of her jacket. "I won't have to be. No one will bother to question how I feel. They'll take it for granted. Average-looking no-name lands big movie star. Why wouldn't a girl be happy about that?"

He sat up so he could study her with that intense expression she'd seen him wear so often in the movies. She'd said something that made him think or caused him to reevaluate. After all the bickering and chafing at their new roles, she couldn't imagine what it was. But acute interest transformed his face from dark and brooding to arresting, and she found it impossible to look away.

"Even if we do everything we can, it'll take some luck for this to work," he said at length.

"Yes," she agreed.

A frown tugged at his lips. "These days I'm not sure I can depend on luck."

She tucked the fine hairs that'd fallen around her face behind her ears. "Feel free to hire a real actress, if you think it'll help." She hoped he would. Then she could have him return as merely a client, which would be enough to protect her business, and life would go on as usual.

Ian jumped back into the conversation. "Simon, no. We don't want anything to do with a woman who might be interested in using you to get famous. You never know what someone like that will do. I say we stick with what we've got. Gail's a known entity."

"She's inflexible." He spoke in the third person even though his gaze never wavered from her face.

"She's trustworthy." Ian shifted his gaze to her, too. "That's more important than flexible. Two years will go by quicker than you think."

Gail held her tongue. She got the impression Simon was testing her to see how she'd respond. But despite what he said about her, criticizing him further wouldn't help. She had a feeling he already thought the worst of himself. At least *she* gave him credit for his talent.

"There's just one more thing," she said.

Stretching out his legs, Simon crossed one ankle over the other—another deceptively casual pose. "What's that?"

"My father."

Lines formed on his forehead. "What about him?"

When she'd agreed to be Simon's "wife," she'd been thinking of it primarily in the context of PR advantages. She'd been so focused on how to pull it off, she hadn't considered the impact it would have on her other relationships—probably because, until now, L.A. and what she did here had always felt so removed from Whiskey Creek. Despite being a small town of barely two thousand, it was a world unto itself. But news of her marriage would travel everywhere. There'd be no way to keep it from getting back to her family and friends. She had to allow for that, prepare for it. Which meant she had to include them in the process.

"Before the wedding, we'll need to take a trip to my hometown so I can introduce you to everyone."

He didn't consider that for even a second. "Absolutely not. I'm not going to some Podunk town to be judged by your family."

Her friends would be just as hard on him, maybe harder. She'd hung out with the same crew since grade school. But she wasn't about to mention that. "If we don't enlist their support, my father or brother will drive to L.A. to convince me that I'm making a mistake marrying someone with…shall we say…such a tarnished reputation."

Ian spoke up. "So go to your mother. Tell her you're in love, get her to intercede."

Gail straightened in her seat. "I don't have a mother."

Simon was still watching her. "Why not? Is she dead?"

"No, but she might as well be." Gail hadn't seen her in twenty years. "We don't have a relationship."

Ian raked his fingers through his hair. "We've got everything else worked out. This can't be *that* hard. Tell your father he has nothing to worry about. You'll get a big settlement even if your marriage turns out to be the worst thing you ever did."

"News of the prenup will be in the press," she said. "We have to make sure it is. It has to look like love and only love is the reason we're getting together."

"So?" he argued. "You'll be receiving other money."

"But I can't tell anyone about that, not without letting them in on our little secret." To Martin, having her marry someone he'd consider morally bankrupt would be bad enough. Getting paid for it would be worse. "Anyway, he doesn't care about money. That's not what matters to him."

"What does?" It was Simon who asked. She could tell he was leery of the answer. Knowing her father, he had reason to be.

"Me." Martin DeMarco also cared about character. But a list of Simon's faults had come from her own lips as recently as a few days ago, when she'd last spoken to her dad. In retrospect, what she'd said during that phone call was unfortunate; telling Martin she was marrying Simon O'Neal would be no better than announcing she was marrying Charlie Sheen or Tiger Woods. "That means we'll *have* to visit, show him you're a changed man."

"Forget it," Simon said. "I'm a good actor but even I'm not *that* good, or I wouldn't need to be doing this in the first place. If your dad is such a stickler, he won't accept me even if I grovel."

"So what do you suggest?" she asked.

"You'll just have to cut ties with him for a while," he replied.

"What?" She tightened her grip on her purse. "I can't disappear from my network of family and friends for *two years.*"

Finished with his drink, Simon set it aside. "That's what you're asking from me, isn't it?"

"It's *your* image that needs improving! Your associates are the ones who threaten that, not mine."

"I don't care. Considering everything I'm giving up, you can make a sacrifice, too. I have enough to deal with. Why should I put up with people who are convinced I'm the devil out to drag you off to hell?"

"Because you're the one who has to face down what you've done." Why did her sacrifice have to be equivalent to his? She hadn't screwed up her life the way he had.

"Not with your father looking on I don't. I just have to survive the next two years without doing anything stupid. The rest is up to you."

"Why are you making this so difficult?" she demanded.

"You started it."

"Going without sex isn't the same as giving up my family and friends!"

"I think it's pretty equal," Ian inserted, but both she and Simon ignored him. They were locked in battle.

"I make some concessions. You make some concessions," he said. "How's what I'm doing so unfair?"

He was attempting to punish her, but she wouldn't let him. "You'd know if you had a family to bother with!"

When a muscle jumped in his cheek, she realized what she'd just said and had no idea how she'd allowed herself to be so callous, even to someone who provoked her as much as he did. His father, a dissolute movie star himself, had conceived Simon with his wife's sister. For obvious reasons, the relationship between father and son had always been strained. His father's wife refused to have Simon anywhere near her. And his mother, who'd been disowned by the rest of the family for sleeping with her sister's husband, had died of breast cancer when Simon was ten. After she was gone, he'd been moved from the small house he'd lived in until that time to his father's estate, where he'd been raised by the hired help that slipped in and out of Tex O'Neal's life, not all of whom were particularly reliable. Rumor had it that the one nanny Simon had loved most had gone to prison for embezzlement.

"I'm sorry." Her cheeks burned as she gaped at him.

He glared back. "I'm not going anywhere close to your family," he said, and got up and walked out.

"Simon, you okay?" Ian's expression filled with so much concern that Gail was tempted to believe he really cared about his employer, beyond just the paycheck, but Simon didn't respond.

"Did you have to go that far?" He turned to face her once it was clear that Simon wasn't coming back.

She was so busy kicking herself she didn't need him to pile on, too, but she couldn't blame him. "I didn't mean it. I—I'm overwrought. Couldn't sleep a wink last night. Other than that, I have no excuse."

"You're in the public-relations business, damn it!"

"I wish I could take it back." She honestly hadn't meant to hurt Simon, hadn't realized she could. He seemed so…impervious. Still, she prided herself on using restraint and diplomacy especially in difficult situations. What had gotten into her?

Sinking onto the sofa, she tilted some of the ice left in Simon's glass into her mouth. She'd turned him down when he'd offered her a drink, but she shouldn't have. She needed something to relieve her dry throat, and she was rattled enough not to care where she got it.

"For what it's worth, he's going through hell," Ian said.

She set the glass, now empty, back on the table. "You've mentioned that. But he's not the only one, okay? I don't like this any more than he does."

"Of course you don't." He made a noticeable effort to calm down. "You're out of your comfort zone, and that's understandable. But…can't you… I don't know… put out for him once in a while? Just to help him stay on the straight and narrow? I bet he'd agree to meet your dad if you do."

She smacked her forehead with the palm of her hand. "Tell me you're kidding."

"No! Come on, what would it hurt? You'll be married so it won't be illegal *or* immoral. Even Mother Teresa couldn't object."

When she didn't respond, he seemed encouraged.

"It might be something you'd enjoy," he added. "He could loosen you up. Teach you a few things. If this marriage is going to work, he'll need an outlet."

"I am *not* going to become his blow-up doll." Something to be used and tossed away when he was done, something that would never mean anything to him. She had to live with herself when this was over.

"Forget it. I shouldn't have brought the subject up again." He shrugged. "Time will take care of it."

"What are you talking about?"

"You'll see. You're going to want it as bad as he does. I mean, you've got to have *some* physical desires of your own. You're what, thirtyish? And not bad-looking. A bit pale, maybe, but if you were to forget the business suits, let your hair down and laugh once in a while, you could get laid."

She held up a hand in the classic stop position. "Please, don't try to cheer me up."

"Just my two cents," he said with an attitude that indicated he was as obtuse on this as he sounded.

"Could you shut up for a second, please? I need to think."

He shoved his hands in his pockets while she tried to sort out her thoughts and feelings, but silence didn't offer the clarity she'd hoped for. She kept coming back to two things. She couldn't bear to cast her employees aside. And she couldn't return home in defeat. Whether she liked it or not, that left her with only one option—to ignore her frustration and unhappiness and marry Simon.

But the second she said, "I do," she'd step into the spotlight that followed him mercilessly and attract far more attention than she'd ever feel comfortable with. And if Simon refused to make an appearance in Whiskey Creek, her father would be positive that she'd turned out as disloyal as her mother, and her friends would feel snubbed and betrayed that she hadn't included them in the "courtship."

"Don't." Ian broke into her thoughts.

She lifted her head. "Don't what?"

"Back out. You're Simon's only hope for getting even partial custody of his kid. He's counting on you."

But what about her family? "What if something goes

wrong—we can't get along or…whatever? I don't want to make matters worse."

"This marriage won't be easy, but if anyone can do it, you can. I've never met a more talented publicist."

"Really?" His confidence in her actually made her feel a bit better. She eyed him, wondering what he was about to add that would twist the compliment into something less flattering, but he seemed to be in earnest.

He lowered his voice as if he thought their host might be standing outside the door. "This will give Simon a second chance. I think he deserves one, if that makes any difference."

Someone as shallow as Ian probably wasn't the best judge of character. But it would give Big Hit PR a second chance, too. Considering the money she stood to make, she'd have her payroll covered for a long time, even if things turned bad again. But could she really do this? Could she placate her family and friends with calls and emails for a few months by pleading Simon's busy schedule?

If so, maybe she could convince her "husband" to visit Whiskey Creek for Christmas. Or at least let *her* return for a visit. "This is going to require such a commitment," she said, feeling the weight of it. "And for so long."

"Not *that* long, not as far as marriages go. Think of it as a job, like you told Simon to do." He bent at the waist to catch her eye. "Okay?"

The years she'd toiled to get on top came to mind. So did the fact that she had nowhere to go if this didn't work out. She couldn't bear the thought of moving back home; she'd done everything she could to escape Whiskey Creek the first time. "Okay."

"You're making the commitment?"

She stood. "I'm making the commitment."

He crossed to the minibar and brought the prenup they'd painstakingly devised on the phone last night. "So when should we have the wedding?"

She glanced over the legalese Simon's attorneys had thrown together on short notice, made sure everything was in order and signed before panic could overtake her. "A month from now is the earliest we could have the ceremony and make the relationship seem credible. Check Simon's schedule. See if he's free the first Saturday in November."

"I'll clear off whatever else he has going."

"What are you going to tell Chelsea Seagate?"

"Nothing. I've already called her to say we're canceling our contract with Pierce Mattie and returning to you."

She wished she could take some small pleasure in that. "Fine."

When she handed him the contract, he smiled in apparent relief. "Thanks. First Saturday, private ceremony in Vegas. The two of you will take his jet, of course. But that doesn't give us much time to prepare."

"Then we'd better get to work." She left the house but stopped in the drive, her finger hovering over the send button on the pictures he'd emailed her. Once she forwarded them to Josh and he leaked them to his friend at *Hollywood Secrets Revealed,* there'd be no turning back.

A creeping sensation gave her the feeling that she was being watched. Twisting around, she spotted movement in a second-story window. It was Simon, looking out at her. They stared at each other for a few seconds.

Then she held up her phone to let him know they were at the point of no return.

After a slight hesitation, he nodded, and she pressed Send.

Seven

Gail hadn't expected her other life, the life she'd known in Whiskey Creek, to intrude quite so quickly. But as she walked into the office, which was closed up and dark on a Saturday afternoon, Callie Vanetta, a member of the clique she'd grown up with, tried to reach her on her cell phone. Gail let it go to voice mail because she wasn't sure she wanted to talk to anyone from Whiskey Creek at the moment. She'd just left Simon's and hardly felt prepared.

"You okay?"

She was standing in the middle of her office, staring at her phone and feeling guilty about avoiding Callie when she heard Josh's voice. She glanced over her shoulder, surprised to see him in the doorway. Her employees typically took weekends off, unless they were working on a big project. When she'd sent Josh the pictures, she'd assumed he was home and would forward them from there. But he knew she spent most weekends in her office, catching up on what she hadn't been able to finish during the week. Considering what was going on, he'd probably made a special trip to see her.

"I'm fine, why?"

"You need me to explain?"

She turned to face him. "No." She knew perfectly well why he'd asked.

"So?" Eyes wide with curiosity, he closed the door. She wasn't sure why, since they were alone. Just more of his sense of drama, she supposed. "Give me the low down. How'd it go?"

Could she classify the meeting she'd had with Simon and Ian as *good?* They'd worked out a lot of details, launched "The Plan." But whether or not they'd regret what they'd started remained to be seen. "Simon's in." That was about all she could say, all that was certain.

"I figured, when you sent me those pictures. It's the dirty details I'm after." His voice took on a husky undertone. "Were you two really kissing in that photo? Or did it just look that way?"

They hadn't kissed. But they'd stood awfully close. Close enough so she could smell the toothpaste on Simon's breath. Close enough to feel the warmth radiating from his body. When her breasts accidentally grazed Simon's arm as Ian pressed them into ever more compromising positions, she'd jumped back as if he'd burned her, and Simon had scowled.

Maybe she *had* overreacted. But that brief contact had sent a jolt through her.

"It was all staged," she assured Joshua. "We weren't kissing."

He flopped into a seat. "How disappointing."

It *had* been a little anticlimactic to continue their discussion while her heart was pounding like a jackhammer. Thanks to her line of work, she associated with the rich and famous quite often, but she'd never gotten so worked up over anyone else. In an effort to fight the effect Simon was having on her, she'd searched his face, only inches above her own, for one significant flaw, something to convince her that he wasn't as attractive as she'd originally thought—and found nothing.

His eyes were especially distinctive. An unusual sea-green color contrasted with thick black lashes and even thicker eyebrows, they reflected too much cynicism. That wasn't attractive, but there was a hint of the lost little boy in there, too. His fine build, combined with those eyes and that sense of hidden vulnerability, packed a punch that had left her reeling.

She'd been pleased to find his bottom teeth slightly crowded.

Not that such a small imperfection really mattered. Thanks to *Shiver,* his last suspense thriller, she'd seen what he could do to a woman with his lips and tongue.

"You should've made out with him," Joshua said.

She pulled a skeptical face. "Right. In front of Ian?"

"Why not? He was *hoping* to get a steamy pic. You could've blamed it on the PR campaign. I can't believe you missed the opportunity to indulge. *I* would've made out with him to my heart's content."

Instead, she'd been clinging to her control, trying not to get swept up in the lust surging through her veins. "Simon's too feminine for my taste."

"Are you *kidding?*"

Kidding herself, maybe. High cheekbones and a prominent jaw, not to mention the perennial shadow of beard growth, added more than enough of the masculine to compensate for his pretty eyes and pouty lips. But she had to create some kind of defense. There were moments when she was afraid the hero worship she'd once felt would reassert itself and undermine what she knew of the real Simon. "I'm just saying he looks like his mother more than he does his father."

"Doesn't make him *feminine*."

"Did you get those pictures off?" she asked instead of responding.

"As soon as they hit my in-box."

Rounding her desk, she straightened her blotter. "And…did you get confirmation that they've been received?"

"Immediately. Sarah's ecstatic about breaking the story—and avoiding any heat from that other mess we created."

"Good."

"So." He crossed his legs. "You're sure you'll be able to make yourself go through with it? You'll marry him?"

"I don't see that I have any choice. I've already signed the contract."

Hanging his head, Joshua peered at her through the hair, dyed a stark black instead of his usual brown, falling into his eyes. "I feel so bad about what I did."

"I know."

"I endangered Sarah's job, too."

"Yes." Gail drummed her fingers on the desk. "What'd her boss say?"

"He's every bit as excited as you'd expect. Anything Simon does is big news."

That picture they'd taken in the backyard would soon be online. Other magazines and bloggers would jump on the publicity bandwagon before she could blink.

Sick at the thought of all the calls that would pour in, how *she'd* become the focus of the paparazzi who'd harried her biggest clients, Gail propped her chin on one fist. "Do you think this is a disaster waiting to happen?"

"Could go either way, but you're saving my ass by doing it, so I can't tell you how grateful I am." He gave her a childlike smile. "Makes me love you all the more, if that helps."

"It doesn't," she said, but smiled back.

He sobered. "I deserve to be fired."

"Except that you've been great at your job and I can't judge your entire performance by one stupid, drunken mistake."

"I appreciate that. I really do." His mood brightened. "Tell you what—*I'll* marry Simon."

She pictured the fury in Simon's face when she'd said what she had about his family, or lack thereof. At this point, he'd probably prefer *anyone* to her—maybe even Josh. "I wish you could."

She prided herself on being able to handle anything, but she was out of her element here. Maybe she was better at running other people's lives than her own. "What if he won't stop drinking?" she asked. "Or he secretly bites his toenails? Or sleeps in a coffin? Or burns incense and offers up prayers to his own picture?"

"All movie stars are eccentric—or get that way if they go unchecked for too long. Just roll with it. The marriage is only temporary."

Two years didn't feel as short as he made it sound. "But he might be more insufferable than I'm expecting. Maybe he's…abusive."

Josh grimaced. "He's not abusive, not physically, anyway. With his ex running her mouth to anyone who'll listen, we would've heard about it if he'd ever even threatened to hit her or the kid."

"He's hit a few guys," she mused. "He got in that fight on-set, remember?"

"I'm not likely to forget. That's the reason you refused to work for him anymore."

Ignoring the censure in his voice, she proceeded to

prove it wasn't the *only* reason. "What about that time a few months ago when he tried to force his way into his ex-wife's house and got in a shoving match with her brother?"

"Maybe he had a good reason for what he did."

"On *both* counts?"

"That's how we tried to spin it," he said with a shrug.

"He could've walked away."

"We both know he's not the type. Too short a fuse."

"That's no excuse." She searched for other examples to support her "Simon's unstable" theory. "And those bikers?"

Joshua adjusted the scarf he wore with his pink button-down shirt. "I think he *wanted* to get his ass kicked that night. Why else would he drive to the shitty side of town and confront so many dangerous gangbangers? He was all alone, had no chance from the beginning."

That was what she thought, too. Nothing else made sense. After the judge signed the restraining order that would keep Simon from his wife and son, he found a seedy bar he later admitted he'd never been to before, one with a row of motorcycles out front, and picked a fight with three Hells Angels. They would've destroyed his face, maybe a lot more, if not for one of their own. Fortunately, a member of the club happened to be a big fan. He saved Simon an extended hospital stay by pulling the others off and pushing him out of the joint while he could still walk—but the biker later confessed he was disappointed that Simon didn't really know kung fu. He'd expected more from him after watching *Take It or Leave It,* Simon's most violent movie.

"Honestly? I think the worst he's done is cheat," Joshua said.

"You say that like it's nothing."

"It's nothing to you."

She cocked her head in challenge. "I'm only his future wife!"

He cocked his head right back at her, exaggerating the movement. "But you don't love him. Cheating on you would be more of a...breach of contract."

"It'll be adultery to the rest of the world! And he might have other problems, ones we haven't discovered yet. Maybe he's a sex addict." He'd certainly made a big enough deal about her refusal to service him....

"You should ask."

"I did. Ian and I talked about the possibility last night. He says no. Claims there were extenuating circumstances to Simon's extramarital affairs."

"Like...he got bored and horny?" Josh said with a laugh.

"Ian doesn't know for sure. He thinks she may have cheated first, but he can't substantiate that and it doesn't really make sense. Wouldn't Simon have said so if it meant keeping custody of Ty?"

"No doubt." Josh swung his foot. "You didn't confront Simon himself?"

"I'd already called him an alcoholic. I didn't think it would go over too well if I accused him of being a sex addict, too."

"So what do you want me to say, Gail? Don't do it?"

The anger drained out of her. "More or less."

"Then don't do it. We'll...go into promoting beauty products or something."

If that happened, she'd have to start over alone. "What about Sonya? And Serge? And you and everyone else? I *have* to do this."

"Then keep Simon in bed."

"*Excuse* me?"

Eager to convey his point, he leaned forward. "If you're so worried he might stray, keep him in bed, darling. Don't give him time for anyone else."

Sometimes Gail wished she could be as sexually unfettered as her assistant. She was beginning to feel a lot older than she was.

What are you doing this weekend?
Working.
Any plans for Friday night?
Catching up on some paperwork.
Tell me you have a hot date for Valentine's Day.
With my television.

She'd fallen to a new low when she went to a movie alone on her birthday. She was still mad at herself for not heading back to Whiskey Creek, but she'd been so slammed with new clients she hadn't wanted to take the time off.

"Thanks for that piece of advice, but I don't want to talk about what I should do to keep Simon interested on a sexual level." He wasn't interested to begin with.

"Why not? You can do it. So what if you're a late starter?"

"I'm not a late starter. I'm *selective*."

Josh formed a steeple with his fingers. "You didn't lose your virginity until you were twenty-six. That definitely qualifies as a late start."

She should never have admitted that. Josh had a way of getting personal information out of anyone.

"I was twenty-*five*," she corrected. "But who's keeping track?"

"Just me."

"Thanks for that."

"Maybe it's good you're tying the knot. Maybe this is the only way you'll ever say 'I do,' seeing as you cross every guy off your list before you even give him a chance."

"Before I sleep with him, you mean."

"Same thing."

She arched an eyebrow. "Not quite."

A soft knock interrupted them, which surprised her. She'd figured they were alone.

Bracing herself in case it was the beginning of the media onslaught—some reporter who'd somehow gotten in—Gail called out, "Yes?"

It wasn't a reporter. It was Ashley, her receptionist, who poked her head into the room. "Thought I might catch you here."

"What brings you to the office on your day off?" Gail asked.

"The answering service contacted me. They're being inundated with calls from a guy with *The Star,* who claims he has to talk to someone in the office right away." Barely five feet, Ashley looked more like a child than a twenty-one-year-old woman. Her large-framed glasses added to the effect; they always gave Gail the impression she was playing dress-up. "I thought maybe it was important, that someone should get back to him."

Joshua's eyes latched on to Gail's. "You know what this means."

"I do. Word is getting out." It was time to quit fighting what she'd agreed to do and throw herself into her role. If they had any hope of pulling off this campaign, there could be no halfway measures. She had to play the part even for her own employees.

But when it came right down to it, she couldn't lie, bald-faced, to Ashley. She knew she'd feel ridiculous saying that one of the most famous men in America had fallen in love with her, especially when he'd never so much as given her an appreciative glance.

She couldn't bear lying to the rest of the people who worked for her, either. Which meant Josh had to do it. "Josh will explain the situation to you and everyone else."

Josh blinked at her. "I will?"

"Yes." Maybe it'd be more believable if everyone heard it secondhand while she went underground, anyway. She'd take the phone off the hook and hole up in her house for two or three days. That would go far toward convincing everyone that her "relationship" with Simon was real. If she suddenly went quiet instead of going on the record with an admission *or* a denial, the press would chase after the story that much harder and break it that much bigger.

The paparazzi would be waiting for her when she emerged, of course. She wouldn't be able to avoid them altogether. But hiding out until Wednesday would save her a lot of acting, which she feared wasn't her strong suit despite the misplaced confidence she'd exhibited at Simon's.

Josh cleared his throat. "Right, I will. And you…"

"Will be at home for a couple of days," she finished while packing up her briefcase.

"Right again. Not coming in is probably a good idea. We'll do what we can without you."

"Thanks." In a moment of clarity, Gail realized she'd set a match to a trail of gunpowder by making that agreement with Simon. But it was too late to put out the fire.

All she could do was try to survive the explosion.

Eight

Relieved to be safe in her little beach house, Gail lowered the blinds in her bedroom, curled up on her bed and stared at Callie's picture and contact information on her cell phone. She'd never purposely ducked a friend's call before. At least not one of her friends from Whiskey Creek.

"Oh, what the heck," she mumbled. "Get it over with." Once the news that she was seeing Simon O'Neal broke, she'd have to worry about her phones being tapped or her house being bugged—laughable considering she was no head of state or criminal informant. Her only claim to fame would be that she was "dating" a box office hit.

But tabloids were big business, hence the worry that someone could stoop to such means to get inside information. She might as well use this time to prepare her friends and family, before sightings of her and Simon began to appear in the media.

Her father should've been her first call, but Gail preferred to break into this easily. It was the weekend. She had that going for her. With so many people out doing other things, word wouldn't spread quite as fast as it would on a weekday.

Callie picked up on the second ring. "Jeez, there you are. I've been trying to reach you all day."

"Sorry. Been working."

"On a Saturday?"

Gail pictured her curvaceous bombshell of a friend. She used to wish she looked like Callie, who resembled Marilyn Monroe. "Always."

"You should really take a day off here and there."

"You've mentioned that before. What's up?"

"I've been *dying* to tell you something."

"What?"

"You're not going to believe it."

Callie wouldn't believe what Gail had to say, either. "Try me."

"Matt's moving back to town!" she announced with a "ta da" flourish.

Sure she must've heard wrong, Gail gripped her chest.

"Hello?" Callie said. "Did I lose you?"

She'd forgotten to breathe. Air. She needed air. Taking a big gulp, she sat up and forced words out as she exhaled. "No... I'm... I haven't gone anywhere."

"Did you hear what I said?"

This had to be a mistake. Matt wouldn't leave Wisconsin in the middle of football season. "What happened? He didn't get injured again, did he?"

"Not a new injury, no. Just more of the same old stuff. Knee's acting up."

Gail wasn't sure how to react. She'd been in love with Matt since she was in middle school. They'd finally gone out in July and nearly wound up in bed together. But, to her severe disappointment, he hadn't called since. "So…is he out of the NFL for good?"

"I don't think so. They had to do a second surgery, and he's in therapy, but he's planning to return to Green Bay next season."

Too agitated to remain on her bed, Gail got up and began to pace. "How did you find out? You talked to him?"

"No. My mother heard the news while she was having her hair done. You know what this town is like."

Gail had been hoping Matt would come home eventually, had dreamed of it. Given the opportunity, she thought he might ask her out again. But she found herself cringing at the possibility that he wouldn't be able to continue playing football. He loved the sport like nothing else. "Do you know how long he'll be staying?"

"Months. Until he's recovered."

"Wow." She pivoted near the French doors that opened onto her postage stamp of a backyard. "I hope… I hope it heals well."

"You mean you hope it heals *slowly*," Callie said with a laugh. "I thought of you as soon as I heard. He'll be here when you come home for Thanksgiving in a few weeks." She put some innuendo into her voice. "With you two in the same town for a few days, you never know what might happen."

Nothing would happen now because Gail wasn't going home. And even if she did, she'd be married. She'd been waiting years for this news—and it had to come on the day she'd made a business arrangement to marry someone else. "He's probably got a girlfriend," she said. Maybe that was why he hadn't called her after their date last summer. Maybe there'd been someone else all along.…

"Nope. Word has it he's as single as he's ever been."

So they would've had a chance?

Suddenly claustrophobic, Gail went out onto the patio where she liked to read or answer email. Normally, she loved it out here, but her piece of heaven didn't hold the same magic for her today. Her heart had been yanked back to the Sierra Nevada foothills, to the historic gold-mining town where she'd grown up and so many of her friends still lived.

The sound of laughter and voices from the beach, only ten feet or so from her fence, engulfed her. So did the cool, moist air of autumn and the briny scent of the ocean. She closed her eyes as she considered backing out of the deal with Simon. But the practical side of her wouldn't allow it. What did she think—that she and Matt would bump into each other and he'd suddenly regret not pursuing the relationship? Why would that happen now when he'd gone back to Wisconsin and basically forgotten about her after they'd all but had sex?

It wouldn't. For the sake of her future and her employees, she needed to live up to the commitment she'd made to Simon. "There's just one problem," she heard herself say.

"What's that?"

She felt she sounded wooden, mechanical, but soldiered on. "I can't come home next month."

"Why not?"

"I'm...sort of involved with someone else, someone who lives here." She figured she'd be better off not mentioning the "M" word. She could always justify her marriage by saying it was an impulsive act, something they'd done while visiting Vegas. Otherwise, she'd send the whole town of Whiskey Creek into an uproar.

There was a slight pause. "Since when?"

"It's been a few months."

"You've never mentioned anyone."

Gail slipped past two trellises to gaze over the fence at the inline skaters rocketing down the walkway, the athletes playing sand volleyball beyond that and the waders at the water's edge. "I didn't think it would go anywhere."

"If you're willing to miss seeing Matt, it must be serious."

The scent of damp wood and seaweed filled her nostrils. It didn't matter that L.A. and Whiskey Creek were in the same state. They were as different as two places could be. No wonder she hadn't thought of all the complications she'd bring to her personal relationships when she'd decided to save Simon's image—and her business—with a temporary marriage. "More serious than it was before."

"Are you in love, G.?"

"I...might be." She was waffling, but her response shocked her friend enough that Callie didn't seem to notice.

"Oh, my gosh! Who's the lucky guy?"

Wincing at the reaction she'd receive when she uttered the name, Gail made her way back toward the bedroom. "Simon O'Neal."

Callie's pause extended into awkward silence. No doubt she'd expected Gail to add, "Not the Simon you're thinking of." When she didn't, Callie said it for her.

"You're not talking about *the* Simon O'Neal, are you? The actor? I know he was your client before you fired him. But you said he was an asshole."

Gail was going to get this a lot. She'd complained far too much to her friends. "I was frustrated when I said that."

"So it *is* Simon."

The wind chimes on her porch tinkled softly. "Yes."

"You're dating him even though you told him you wouldn't work for him anymore?"

Her bedroom seemed far cooler and darker than before her excursion into the afternoon sunshine. But she went inside and closed the door. "The stress of trying to have a professional relationship while seeing each other caused everything to blow up. You can imagine how difficult it would be to date someone so famous. We were sneaking around, and he was…acting out because of…you know, the divorce, and I was wondering how I could continue to represent him if I was emotionally involved with him. I swore I'd never date one of my clients. You've heard me say that. It's just not wise." She was talking too fast and too much and throwing in too many justifications. She needed to be careful but couldn't seem to catch herself until Callie interrupted.

"Speaking of the divorce, it's only been a few months since he and his wife split."

Gail kicked off her flip-flops and smoothed her bare feet against the plush rug near her bed. "Actually, she took Ty and moved out over a year ago. The divorce has been final for six months."

"Okay. About a year, then. He could still be on the rebound, Gail. If he ever loved Bella to begin with. You can't tell me his behavior doesn't spook you. It would have to. What about all the things he's done?"

He spooked her, all right. But she'd never be able to do business in L.A. again if she didn't come through. "The divorce was an acrimonious one. I'll be the first to admit that. But you have to understand it's been really, really hard on him."

"I don't think it's been any easier on his ex-wife. Last

I heard, he showed up at her house drunk and got into a fight with her brother. You shouldn't be dating someone who...who's spinning out of control, G."

Gail laughed uncomfortably. "Come on, Callie. He'll get turned around. It's not easy living under a microscope."

"I understand. But...you're the most stable, level-headed girl I know. Why would you get involved with someone who needs so much therapy? He cheated on his wife with *six* different women."

At last count. Gail was pretty sure he'd been shooting for Tiger's record. "He screwed up, ah, literally." She managed a weak chuckle at her bad pun. "But it's killing him to be kept from his little boy."

"I'd like to believe you, but most people who feel bad about losing their kids resist jumping from one bed to the next because they know it won't help their case."

Gail squeezed her forehead. "He was depressed, fatalistic, going through a rough time. That's not who he really is."

"The pictures in the tabloids, showing him with one woman after another, sure don't make him look depressed and fatalistic. He's living the high life."

Gail suspected that appearing so happy in public was a purposeful cover, a way to save face, but she couldn't use that in her argument. And if this was how it was going with Callie, she cringed to think of the conversation she'd have with her father.

Suddenly Gail was glad Simon had refused to go to Whiskey Creek. She needed to keep him away at all costs. "The tabloids make up a lot of that stuff."

"You once told me there's a kernel of truth behind most of those stories."

She'd been so transparent about everything that she

had no wiggle room left. "It's more complicated than it seems. He had a horrible childhood."

"So...you feel sorry for him? For a rich, spoiled, self-indulgent movie star?"

"You don't even know him. How can you judge?"

"His mistakes are public knowledge!"

"I see a different side, okay? He's a good man." She cringed because she had no confidence in that statement. She'd fantasized about him as much as anyone, but she'd known in her heart that the real Simon couldn't live up to the man in her dreams. "Can you give him a break? Please? For me?"

"I'm just saying...before you get too committed to Simon, maybe you should come home and see if there's anything between you and Matt. Matt's a great guy."

Callie would know. He'd been her neighbor growing up. But Gail had too much on the line to risk it all on the hope that Matt Stinson would finally return her interest. Dropping onto the bed, she watched the fan rotate overhead. "My relationship with Matt has been completely one-sided."

"You kissed last summer."

"He hasn't called since."

"Because he's too focused on his career. He doesn't want to risk getting involved with someone like you, someone who's marriage material. He's not ready for that kind of commitment. He's said as much."

"He has?"

"Not in so many words," she hedged. "But I know he thinks you're amazing."

Torn, Gail rubbed her face. "He could've followed up, come to see me."

"At the moment football is his whole life. But at least he's not some hotheaded philanderer who's using his power and money to destroy everyone around him. Where can you expect your relationship with Simon to go? If even one-tenth of what I've read about him is true—"

"Have some faith in me, Callie. I don't fall in love easily. There's...something inside him that's worth fighting for." She believed that much. Occasionally she caught a glimpse of Simon's good side, saw how warm and generous he could be. If she could figure out a way to avoid his rougher edges, they might be able to establish an equilibrium of sorts—build a friendship over the course of their marriage. "Besides, people can change."

That was the classic line used by every woman who'd ever dated the wrong guy, but it couldn't be refuted so she had to go with it. People *could* change. But they seldom did, and Callie latched on to that immediately.

"And if he doesn't? Why take the risk? His last wife was heartbroken and publicly humiliated—"

"You don't know what caused the breakup of his marriage."

"I think six affairs would do it, don't you?" Obviously Callie thought being with Simon was a huge mistake. The other people who cared about Gail would, too. But they didn't know she already understood how the whole thing would play out, that she wasn't in love with Simon and never would be, because she knew too much about him.

"You're being really hard on him. You'd like him if you gave him half a chance." Simon had to be the most charismatic person on the planet—but only if he cared enough to bother pouring on the charm.

"When will we get to meet him?" Callie asked.

"Maybe I'll bring him home for Christmas," she said,

but just talking to Callie had convinced her that she'd never contest his decision not to visit her hometown.

"Okay, but… I wish you were coming next month. Everyone was looking forward to it." Callie's voice reflected her disappointment. No doubt she thought a few days with the old gang would set Gail straight.

"I'll reschedule soon." The buzzer that indicated someone was at her front gate sounded, so Gail got back on her feet. She wasn't expecting anyone. Would the paparazzi be bold enough to come to her house and ring the doorbell?

Some would. Her gate faced the narrow street leading down to the beach, which meant it was accessible to anyone passing by. And the value of taking the right photographs made the paparazzi unbelievably intrusive.

"I've got company," she said. "I have to go. Don't tell anyone about Simon, okay? Not yet. First, I need to break the news to my dad."

"I won't say a word, but…good luck with Martin." Callie knew he wouldn't take the news well.

"Thanks. I'll call you in a few days." Gail disconnected as the buzzer went off again.

Setting the phone aside, she hurried out of her small cottage and down the flagstone path dividing the abundance of plants in her front yard. There was a man at her gate. Despite the foliage that provided her with a modicum of privacy, she could see part of his dark head above the tall stone fence and arch of the gate. He appeared to be wearing a uniform, one typical of a courier service, but that could be a trick.

"Who is it?" she called.

He tried to look over at her, so she flattened herself against the gate and peered through the crack.

Unfortunately, he was standing too close for her to see more than a four-inch square of his chest.

"Courier," he said. "I have a package for you."

"Go ahead and leave it."

"Can't. Requires a signature."

Really? She opened the gate by a wary inch, just enough to see a little more of the guy.

He seemed legit. He wasn't holding a camera, he seemed to be alone and an ID badge hung from the collar of his shirt.

"Are you going to sign for this or not?" he asked impatiently. "I've got other deliveries to make."

When she spotted a small truck with his company logo double-parked on the street, she finally released her death grip on the gate and swung it wide. "Yes. Sorry."

He handed her his clipboard. "Right here."

She scribbled her name, and he gave her the small box he'd been holding.

"Thank you," she murmured.

He walked off without responding; a moment later, she heard the rumble of his delivery truck. No doubt he thought she was some kind of paranoid hermit. But she didn't care. She had reason to be skittish.

After shutting and locking the gate, she examined what the courier had given her. The return address indicated it had come from O'Neal Productions—Simon's company.

Ian had said he'd mail her a copy of the contract once Simon had signed it, but this wasn't flat. The size and shape resembled a jeweler's box.

Most likely the wedding ring, she supposed. But that wasn't it at all. Once she opened the package, she saw that Ian—she assumed it was Ian—had sent her a pendant, one with a giant ruby and two diamond baguettes.

Classy, solid and probably expensive, it was exactly what she might've chosen herself if she'd had a cool ten or twenty grand to drop on a necklace.

"Nice," she breathed. But…why the unexpected gift?

She guessed it was Ian's way of keeping her moving in the right direction—a sample of the finer things she'd enjoy while married to someone so rich. But when she read the accompanying handwritten note, she realized the pendant hadn't come from Ian at all. It was more personal than that.

"I'll make it up to you where I can. Simon."

Nine

It was late evening by the time Gail summoned the nerve to call her father. She would've called him a little earlier, but she'd been on the phone with the police. They wanted to get a statement from her, make sure that no crime—no assault, sexual or otherwise—had been committed.

Taking responsibility for a lie she hadn't uttered was embarrassing, but she'd managed to assure them that it was just a lovers' quarrel and they took the news pretty well. They'd probably heard crazier stories. The officer on the phone was very professional, and because there was no evidence to support any charges, none were going to be filed.

She was relieved to have that out of the way, but now she had another hurdle to clear. The photographs of her and Simon were already posted online. She'd checked. That meant the fervor was starting and she risked having her father find out before she could tell him. Fortunately, Martin DeMarco wasn't fond of the internet. He didn't watch a lot of TV, either.

Still, sooner or later—and probably sooner—someone in Whiskey Creek would see the pictures of her "kissing" Simon. Then her father would hear about it from everyone in town. Back home, in "the heart of the Gold Country" as the town slogan went, it only took one person to start a social epidemic.

As she sat in the dark of her living room, blinds drawn and clock ticking closer and closer to ten, she imagined how it would go when the news did get out. *Have you heard? Gail is dating that no-good bastard, Simon O'Neal. Yes, that Gail—and that Simon!*

She almost felt sorry for her soon-to-be husband. If he thought his name had been maligned before, he hadn't seen what they could do in her conservative hometown. The people who lived there had deep roots and strong values. They prided themselves on living circumspect lives. In Whiskey Creek, his celebrity could not outweigh his notoriety. Not anymore. He'd passed that point six months ago.

As Gail pictured the Old West boardwalk and historic architecture of Sutter's Antiquities, Black Gold Coffee and Whiskey Creek Five and Dime, she realized that she would, for once, supplant Matt Stinson in the gossip arena—even with all the speculation about his knee injury and the possibility of early retirement. She was Whiskey Creek's hometown girl made good: valedictorian of her high school, a Stanford grad and, to all appearances, a successful entrepreneur. They'd see Simon as using her, and them by extension, and it wouldn't go over well.

Too bad she'd helped shape their hard feelings when she visited last month. Their prejudice would only make things more difficult. But back then, she and Simon had been in the heat of battle. She'd had no clue she'd wind up *marrying* him.

Steeling herself against her family's reaction, she

picked up the phone. All things considered, the evening had been a quiet one. But it felt rather ominous, like the calm before a storm.

She had a feeling that storm was about to break.

"'Lo?" Her brother, Joe, had answered. Not only did he and her father own the gas station and towing service at the edge of town, they shared the same house, at least since Joe's divorce four years ago.

Gail attempted to put a smile in her voice. "Hey, big brother. How are you?"

"Hangin' in. You?" Although he was more connected to the world outside Whiskey Creek than her father was, he didn't seem to have heard anything that upset him. He was treating her like he always did.

She breathed a sigh of relief. She'd called in time. "Fine. Busy, as usual."

"How's the biz?"

"Getting better all the time." Or it would soon....

"So it didn't hurt you to cut Simon O'Neal from your list? I know you were worried about that."

She'd been far too vocal about *everything*. "Um, not so much. It's going to work out in the end. Dad around?"

"Right here."

"Who's at the station tonight?"

"Sandra Morton."

"I thought she only worked days during the weekend."

"She's asked for some extra hours. Robbie's getting married. You might've heard about that."

"No." When she'd spoken with Callie earlier, that detail must've gotten lost in the news of Matt's return. "Robbie's just...what, seventeen?"

"Yep. A senior in high school. Knocked up his girlfriend."

Maybe she wasn't the *only* one Whiskey Creek would be gossiping about. Matt's return and Robbie's shotgun wedding would also be hot topics. She would've been relieved to have competition for the best scandal in town, except this wasn't good news for Robbie or his mother, whom she liked. "I'm sorry to hear that, for everyone concerned."

"They claim they're in love, want to get married and keep the baby."

"What does Sandra say?"

"She's determined to let them." He didn't sound like he thought the marriage had a snowball's chance in hell, but that was probably because he blamed the failure of his own marriage on settling down too early.

"They'll be living with her?"

"Until they finish high school, anyway."

Sandra was a widow, mostly dependent on social security. "How will she afford to feed them?"

"He's working at the station now, too. He does nights. She's training him."

For all his exacting ways, her father had a soft heart. He just didn't want anyone to know it—and could be darn good at hiding his secret. "Do you and Dad really need that much help?"

"Can't hurt, I guess. Dad's grabbing the phone," he said, and passed it off.

"'Bout time you checked in." Her father's voice was as commanding as ever.

She stayed in close touch, but he was never satisfied. He wanted her back in Whiskey Creek, like Joe. "Sorry, Dad, my life's been crazy."

"What's going on?"

Hesitant to launch into what she had to say about

Simon, she searched for other things they could talk about. "Just...work. You know how it is."

She asked about the station and Sandra and Robbie. He confirmed what Joe had told her. Then he mentioned that Matt Stinson was coming back to town and assured her Matt's knee would heal. How he knew anything about it wasn't clear. Matt and her father spoke only if they bumped into each other on the street. But her father was the last word on everything, regardless of his lack of firsthand knowledge. Ironic though it was, he was usually right, too.

"That boy's not done playing football," he said.

"I hope not. He loves it."

"And we love watching him. You know what it's like around here when the Packers have a game." She did. Forget the San Francisco 49ers. As long as Matt played for the Packers, Whiskey Creek would be wearing green and gold.

Eventually her father said it was getting late and he had to be up early. At that point, Gail knew she'd waited too long to broach the subject of Simon. With Martin about to hang up, it would be even more awkward to give him her news. But she had no choice.

She cleared her throat. "Before you go I, uh, there's something I want to tell you."

This met with silence. No doubt he'd heard the nervousness in her voice.

"Everything okay, Gabby?"

Where he'd gotten that nickname, she had no idea, but he'd used it like an endearment ever since she was a child. "Yeah, of course. I'm fine. It's just—"

"What the hell?" Joe spoke so loudly in the background that he interrupted their conversation. "Give me the phone."

"What's the matter with you?" her father responded, but the phone changed hands, and Joe's voice came back on the line.

"Tell me it's not true, Gail! Tell me Simon O'Neal didn't rape you."

She bit back a groan. "No, he didn't. That was... Well, it doesn't matter. The important thing is that it didn't happen and I never said it did."

"You're sure? You'd tell us if you'd been hurt...."

And have them attempt to punish Simon? Probably not. She'd let the police handle something like that so her father and brother wouldn't end up in jail. But she didn't say so. "Of course. I'd speak up if I had anything to tell. That claim is one hundred percent false."

He wasn't completely mollified. "That's what it says on AOL. But you wouldn't lie about something like that. If you said it, it's true."

"I *didn't* say it. One of my employees got drunk and started that rumor."

There was a slight pause while Joe considered what she'd told him. "You've got to be kidding me."

"No."

"Which employee?"

"It's been taken care of."

"Whoever it is should be fired."

"It's been handled, like I said."

"Is the same person responsible for the rest of it, too? Because Dad's reading the article right now, and it says you and Simon have been secretly seeing each other for several weeks."

Saying a silent prayer that this would go better than she feared, Gail changed her phone to the other ear. "My employee has nothing to do with that part of it."

"Which means...what? It can't be true! I can't believe you'd go out with a man like Simon O'Neal. Any woman who got involved with him after all his bad press would be asking for trouble."

"I... He... We're not... I mean, I've been out with him a few times, but it's not serious." She told herself to calm down so she could at least speak coherently. "The media is making more of our relationship than it is."

"There's a picture with the caption Simon O'Neal's Love Life Heats Up Again—with PR Maven Who Cried Rape."

"Like I said, we went on a few dates, that's all."

Her father took over again. "Gail? What's this all about?"

"I mentioned to Joe that Simon and I have gone out a couple of times, Dad. But it's no big deal."

"There's no truth to the rape stuff?"

"None. I didn't say it, and it didn't happen. The rumors about Simon are crazy. He can't do anything without the press making an issue of it."

He didn't let her comment about media exposure distract him. "Your brother's right. Getting involved with someone like Simon is asking for trouble. You don't want to screw up your life, do you?"

Imagining what he'd have to say when he learned about the marriage, she wrung her hands. "No, of course not. But...he—he's not as bad as I thought."

"Don't you believe it, Gabby," he warned. "If you have any doubts, all you have to do is ask his ex-wife."

"It's not like Bella and I are friends, Dad. Besides, I don't get the impression that the divorce was entirely his fault." In reality, she had no idea, but she had to use what she could.

"She's got a restraining order against him, doesn't she? That tells you all you need to know right there."

It looked pretty cut-and-dried from the outside. Simon had been convicted in the court of public opinion. At one time—not long ago—she'd convicted him in her own mind, too. But Ian had suggested there was more to the story, and that made her a bit defensive. America only knew so much—Bella's side. Not only that but Gail was *Simon's* publicist. She was wearing his ruby necklace. And she'd agreed to become his wife. If she didn't stand up for him, who would? "Does that mean he's not worth helping through a rough time? That he should never get another chance to straighten out his life?"

"He's had plenty of chances. You've told me that yourself. You don't want to risk your heart on someone who's sure to break it."

She'd expected that response, and yet it bothered her. "I'm thirty-one, Dad. I'm quite capable of deciding who I want to date."

"Not if you're talking about a guy who can't keep his pants zipped, Gail."

The endearments were gone; she was Gail now. "He's trying to change his life. Have I not communicated that part?"

Her father snorted. "If he wants to change, more power to him, but keep your distance or you'll be sorry."

"He's fighting to gain custody of his son. That means he cares."

"If he cared he never would've lost custody to begin with. A court doesn't take your children away unless you deserve it." The way her mother had deserved it. But Simon wasn't her mother.

"You're coming on really strong, Dad. Could you just…back off a little?"

The sudden chill told her she'd offended him. And

he didn't forgive easily, even small slights. He'd probably withhold his love and approval for weeks over this call. But she didn't have the opportunity to apologize or try to make amends.

"You're making a mistake, Gail," he said, and hung up.

Gail stared at the phone in her hand. Part of her was inclined to call her father back. She'd always fallen in with his wishes before, and she certainly couldn't deny the wisdom of his words. But firemen couldn't avoid a burning building just because it was dangerous. *Someone* had to rush in and look for survivors.

Simon was standing in a burning building and, as belligerent, sarcastic and aloof as he could be, he didn't know how to get himself out. He had too much anger and self-loathing working against him. Did she try to help? Risk getting burned herself? Or did she turn a blind eye, walk on and leave the job to someone else?

Who would do it if she didn't? He had everyone he trusted cowed. And he wouldn't cooperate with anyone he didn't trust.

Why was it always someone else's responsibility, anyway?

It wasn't. This time she was holding the fire hose and she was going to use it whether her father approved or not. She might live to regret her actions—whenever she crossed her father she usually did—but if she were Simon, she'd want someone to brave the flames.

Taking a deep breath, she redialed.

Her father didn't answer. He had to teach her a lesson for disrespecting him. But she wasn't going to succumb to his emotional blackmail. Not today. She had a date with a burning building.

Joe answered. "Hey, Gail. I don't know if Dad wants to talk—"

"I'm not asking him to speak to me. I just called to tell you both that I'm going to marry Simon," she said, and disconnected.

Ten

Simon had had every drop of alcohol removed from his house, including the cooking sherry. He'd canceled all outings and appearances, lest he be tempted. And he'd agreed to have his chef administer random Breathalyzer tests every day for the first week, as a fail-safe to keep him honest. If he screwed up, Ian and Gail would be notified and it would all be over.

Those were extreme measures, and yet he was beginning to wonder if they'd be enough. It was only day three of Operation Desperation, as he secretly referred to it, and already he was having fantasies about gulping down the rubbing alcohol under his bathroom sink—anything to give him a few moments' peace from the constant craving. He'd let drinking become such a big part of his life, had used it to create a buffer from all the things he'd rather avoid. When he was too bored, he drank. When he was too angry, he drank. When he was too frustrated or disillusioned, he drank. Alcohol even helped him sleep, if he consumed enough of it. Now he had to deal with all the emotions he'd purposely dulled, and he'd never felt more exposed to his enemies, more...*raw*.

As he glanced around his son's old bedroom, he suffered a tremendous sense of loss. That was what he'd really been hiding from—his own inadequacies and what they'd cost him.

"Simon? Where the hell are you?"

Hearing his manager in the hallway, Simon stepped up to the window as if he was interested in what was going on outside. He didn't want Ian to know he'd been sitting here for an hour or more, just missing his kid. "In here."

The thump of footsteps stopped as Ian came to the open doorway and leaned against the frame. If he thought it was strange to find Simon in Ty's old room, he didn't say. His eyes swept over the stuffed animals in the hammock, the portrait of father and son taken a few days after Ty was born, the alligator-shaped rug on the floor and the extensive bug collection hanging on the wall, but he said only, "Holy shit, man. You scared me. Why haven't you been answering your phone?"

Simon turned back to the spectacle of a woman with a camera attempting to scale his back fence. "Don't know where it is."

"Might be wise to keep track of it for the next couple of weeks, make yourself accessible to Gail and me, don't you think?"

No, he didn't. Keeping his phone close by would also make him accessible to his other friends, and he wasn't supposed to see them, didn't even want to hear their voices. Although he'd promised himself he'd get control of his life many times in the past few months, now he had no choice. He had to hold the line without a single mistake. Gail had been right when she'd said he was on his last chance. His attorney had called this morning to tell him that Bella's side had been successful in convincing the judge to postpone the next hearing. He no longer saw that as a bad thing, since it gave him a chance to prove he'd changed. But it was absolutely imperative that the next several months go by "without incident."

There won't be anything I can do, his lawyer had emphasized, *unless you make this reprieve work to your benefit....*

He got that. He was trying.

"Figured you'd find me if you needed me," he said.

"You could make it easier. Takes twenty minutes just to go through this damn house."

Simon preferred not to talk about why he'd been so hard to find. He didn't want Ian to realize he was hanging on by such a slim thread. Somehow, despite the fact that he'd broken every promise he'd ever made to himself or anyone else since the real problems with Bella began, he'd managed to convince Ian and Gail that he could play the part of a sober, doting husband. Why erode their confidence? Their expectations, their willingness to trust him, were all that kept him going right now. That was why he'd sent Gail the necklace. In his better moments, he could acknowledge that his publicist's life had been doing just fine until he'd come crashing into it.

He had a habit of bringing people down, whether he intended to or not. The least he could do was compensate her with a nice gift. "How's the campaign coming along?"

Ian rubbed his hands. "Now that the weekend is over, the news is spreading fast."

Simon was glad *someone* was excited about this. He was filled with trepidation and a sense of dread that he'd screw up again. "Good."

"You haven't heard anything?"

"No." He'd avoided the computer and the TV, had spent his time in the woodshop, building a playhouse and jungle gym. He liked working with wood, enjoyed the physicality of sanding, sawing and hammering. And constructing something so elaborate for Ty helped him have faith that one day his son would be back to use it.

"Hollywood's in an uproar," Ian said. "*Hollywood Secrets Revealed* put the pics online right away. I guess they didn't want to get scooped. Then everyone ran with the story. Facebook, Twitter, celebrity blogs. They're all buzzing about it."

Simon had witnessed some added activity outside. He knew that his security personnel were having more of a fight than usual keeping people off the premises. "What are they saying about the rape accusation?"

"That it's bogus, just like we wanted. Have you heard from your attorney on that yet?"

Yes. Harold J. Coolridge, attorney at law, had used the false accusation as his excuse for supporting a postponement of the hearing. He'd told the judge that there were too many issues that needed to be resolved before the court could make a fair decision, so he agreed with Bella's motion. But Simon didn't want to go into that with his manager. The more intricate details of his personal life weren't any of Ian's business. "No."

"Then you will, and I'm sure he'll be relieved." He gestured at the window. "What's so interesting out there?"

"Some chick's sitting on the fence. She just flashed my security guys."

"No kidding?" Ian hurried over to see for himself. "Hey, look at that." He whistled long and low. "Nice tits. God, it must be great to be you."

Simon rubbed his neck. "This place is crawling with crazy people and paparazzi."

Ian didn't take his eyes off the spectacle unfolding outside. "It hasn't been this bad since Bella called the cops on you. How's security holding up?"

"They're managing, I guess. Godzilla—" also known as Lance Pratt, Simon's best bodyguard "—had to knock some fat guy on his ass when he slipped through the front gate along with the delivery truck that brings my groceries, but…that's been the worst of it."

Ian shook his head. "I wouldn't want to tangle with Godzilla. He's a bruiser."

He was also a loyal friend. Simon knew Lance would get him a fifth of vodka if he asked for it and not tell a soul, but that wasn't the kind of friend he needed at the moment. He needed more people like his hard-hitting publicist. Maybe she wasn't a barrel of laughs, or even particularly good for his ego, but she demanded he follow the rules—more so than anyone else.

"How's Gail handling the onslaught?" he asked. The paparazzi had to be all over her; she'd never had to protect her privacy so was therefore much easier to reach.

"Haven't talked to her. She's shut herself in her house like you have and won't come out." Pointing outside, he clicked his tongue. "Aw, they got her."

Simon didn't care about the girl with the camera. He had too many other things to worry about. Besides, women acted in zany ways to get his attention all the time. "Will Gail be able to handle the pressure when she does come out?"

Now that there was nothing exciting going on, Ian turned from the window. "Of course. She's tough. You know that."

Truer words were never spoken. Gail had such control of herself, her life. Simon envied that. When he'd married Bella, he'd been so sure he was doing the right thing, so sure he'd do a better job of being a husband than his father had.

"When does she plan on surfacing?"

Ian clipped his sunglasses to his shirt. "Don't know. I checked in with Joshua this morning. He said Gail won't pick up, even for him. I guess the news that she was seeing you got her in some kind of fight with her family."

Simon felt his muscles tense. "They don't think I'm good enough for her?"

"You know how judgmental people can be. Give her father a Ferrari and everything will be fine."

Simon didn't get the impression Gail's father was that easy to placate. "She's old enough to make her own decisions. It's none of their business."

"Doesn't matter. They don't want her with someone who has a reputation for sleeping around."

Ian's words cut, but Simon had gotten damn good at pretending nothing could hurt him. He was actually surprised that something this small *could* bother him. It was the lack of alcohol, the new vulnerability. He had to figure out how to shield himself some other way.

"On top of that she's afraid her phones are bugged," Ian went on. "She won't trust her cell, either. Even Josh insisted on calling me from somewhere other than the office." He chuckled. "She's militant, man. That's what makes her so great at her job. I'm being straight up with you. I wouldn't want to go into this with anyone else."

Simon agreed and—suddenly—wanted to see her. His manager meant well but often did more harm than good. Maybe he could draw some strength from Gail's no-nonsense, do-or-die approach to life's tougher choices. Maybe spending a few minutes with her would give him a fresh shot of determination. "When are we supposed to get together for that romantic dinner?"

"The one where we leak your location to the press but pretend we're shocked when they show up? We talked about next week sometime, right?"

"Let's do it tonight."

Ian straightened. "It's already after noon. How will I get a message to her if she won't answer her phone? I guess I could text, but who knows if—"

"Go over there."

"And if the paparazzi follow me?"

"That's what they're supposed to do, isn't it? That's what this whole thing is about."

Simon wasn't looking his best, but the restaurant was so dimly lit Gail couldn't discern any one reason. He was well-groomed, well-dressed—more so than when she'd sat with him in the living room and plotted out their marriage. So…maybe it wasn't his looks that were off; it was something else. The bravado that was normally such a part of him was gone. The way he kept shifting, he seemed tired, stressed, restless. She would've assumed he was bored, except that he'd drawn out the meal as long as possible, even though he had no apparent interest in eating. He'd downed five Cokes while barely touching the oysters on the half shell he'd ordered or the salmon and Italian sausage pasta he professed to love. When she asked him why he wasn't eating, he said he wasn't hungry.

"You okay?" This was the second time she'd asked, but she didn't dare say more. Not in public. Although a gaggle of people holding cameras had thronged them at the entrance, the restaurant had done a good job of keeping out the paparazzi. That didn't mean she and Simon could forget the roles they were playing until they had to emerge onto the street, however. The other patrons and the restaurant staff were watching them carefully and could report what they saw, especially if there was any money to be made.

To keep up the illusion of intimacy they'd come here to create, she reached across the table for his hand, and he threaded his fingers through hers. She'd expected him to be receptive. They were here to canoodle in public. But she hadn't expected the little hitch in her chest at his touch, or the relief that came over his face when they joined hands.

There was more of the lost little boy in him tonight than ever before. Usually, he hid it quite well; at times, she wasn't even sure it existed.

She cleared her throat. "Are you going to answer me?"

His chest rose as if he'd just taken a deep breath, but then a smile broke across his face. It looked so natural she was tempted to believe it was—but he was acting. She could already read him more deeply than even a few days ago. "I'm fine."

In case someone was using a device that amplified their voices in an attempt to pick up on their conversation, she didn't push for more. "My dinner was delicious. Too bad you weren't very hungry."

"How do you like the pendant?"

Although she could tell he hadn't been too invested in any of their other chitchat, he seemed genuinely curious about this. The look on his face gave her the impression that he'd truly meant to please her, which was something new.

"It's lovely." She was wearing it; the solid weight of it rested just above her cleavage. "But... I'm not sure why you sent such an expensive gift. That really wasn't necessary."

"You're worth it."

More acting. Lies, false compliments and fake smiles were easy to combat on an emotional level. But his touch seemed so honest it confused her. It also set her on edge because she liked it. The movement of his thumb, rubbing lightly back and forth on hers, put butterflies in her stomach.

"I knew it would look good on you," he said.

For the sake of anyone who might be watching, she gave him a smile to match the one he'd bestowed on her and resisted the urge to withdraw her hand. "It was very sweet of you."

"Finished with your meal?"

"I am." She used the fact that they were about to leave as an excuse to let go of him. But after he tossed a couple of large bills on the table, he put an arm around her shoulders, which kept them in close contact. At first, she thought it was part of the show but his sense of purpose soon told her he was preparing for the crowd that awaited them outside.

"Are you ready for this?" he murmured as he guided her through the restaurant.

"This?"

"The paparazzi."

They wanted her picture as badly as his, and that was an experience she'd never had before. "As ready as I can be. I don't know how you put up with the loss of privacy."

"Part of the territory," he said. But she knew it bothered him more than he was letting on. She'd heard him make statements about "being hunted." He might have elaborated, but the restaurant manager darted into their path to thank Simon for his patronage.

"I hope you found each dish to your liking," he said, all but bowing in deference.

Simon gave him a stiff nod. "Everything was delicious."

Knowing the man must have noticed that Simon had eaten very little, Gail jumped in. "It was wonderful," she gushed. "The best!"

Relieved, he thanked her profusely and begged them to come again.

"What I said wasn't enough?" Simon muttered as they moved on.

Had she irritated him? "He was so…hopeful."

"That's how they all are."

The constant attention would get tiresome. She could see that. She could also see that being a celebrity was exhausting. Tonight that was more obvious than ever. Simon could never give enough to the people he encountered because there was only one of him and so many of them. He never got to feel he'd met others' expectations.

"There's no break," she said as they stepped out of the restaurant and into a sea of flashing lights.

Gail had told herself she'd smile and hold her head high whenever she encountered the paparazzi, just as she advised her clients to do. *Make them think you enjoy it, that you have nothing to hide.* After all, what were a few pictures? It was better to pose and get good ones. That was her classic line.

But because of the crush, there was a much greater sense of urgency than she'd ever seen or experienced before. And acting as if this was an unwelcome surprise was part of the campaign. She turned her face into Simon's chest to avoid being blinded by the strobelike effect and felt his arm tighten as he sheltered her from the most aggressive of the cameramen.

"Car's right here," he said.

One of Simon's bodyguards, who'd been waiting with their driver, had created a path. Relieved to have a safe resort, Gail slipped inside the same limousine that had picked her up at her house. Simon rarely traveled in vehicles like this, unless it was Oscar night, a premiere or some other special event where it was expected, but there hadn't been any point in holding back on the accoutrements for this date. Tonight he'd *planned* to dive into the shark-infested pool of celebrity obsession—and he'd taken her with him.

The silence that met them as soon as the door was shut felt odd, oppressive. But it didn't last long. The stereo went on, playing classical music, as the driver inched through the crowd, most of whom were still vying for photographs—from the curb, the street, anywhere they might gain advantage.

"Wow," Gail breathed. This was what she had to look forward to. Could she keep up the charade?

She thought Simon might be as talkative on the drive as he'd been in the restaurant, but he didn't say a word. Back to his laconic self, he stared out the window.

"So? How do you think it went?" she asked as they glided around the corner like a slow-moving parade float.

"Good." His response was clipped, perfunctory. Apparently he'd been acting a lot more than she'd realized. Maybe that vulnerability that appealed to her was part of the character he'd decided to play. She hoped so. It made her too eager to defend him, whether he deserved it or not. She'd always been an "underdog" kind of girl.

But a movie star of Simon's caliber and success could

hardly be considered an underdog; she had to remember that.

They merged into traffic, finally leaving the scrambling photographers behind. "I played my part well enough?" she pressed. "It was convincing even though I'm not an actress?"

He didn't turn to look at her. "You did fine."

"Did it come across as natural when I reached for your hand?"

This seemed to pull him out of his brooding. "That was smart. It made you appear confident of my feelings for you and suggested that we're comfortable touching each other."

"Great." Especially since nothing could be further from the truth. Although it was easier to touch Simon in public than anywhere else, even that simple gesture had given her pause.

"But surprised the hell out of me," he added.

"Why?" He'd taken her hand earlier.

"Because you think I'm the big bad wolf."

"I don't know what you're talking about."

"Yes, you do. You're afraid to make even accidental contact."

Knowing him the way she did, she should've expected his candor. He always said what he thought, regardless of whether it put her on the spot. "I'm not *afraid*." She searched for a better way to explain her reaction to him. "I'm just not groveling at your feet, dying to get a piece of you, like most people." Because she knew how superficial his attention would be, how quickly it would pass. "You should find that…refreshing."

The panel between the front and back opened before he could answer. "Boss?"

Simon's gaze cut to the rearview mirror and the reflection of his chauffeur's eyes. "What is it?"

"Where to?"

"My place."

"*Your* place?" Gail echoed. "You mean, after you drop me off, right?"

"We're being followed," he said. "Might as well let them think you're staying the night. We've already put this much into it."

She twisted around to look behind them. It made sense that the paparazzi who'd staked out the restaurant would want to know where they were going next and follow in hopes of another photo op. She couldn't pinpoint any specific driver as one of the people she'd seen outside the restaurant, but she hadn't looked at them as individuals—only as a pack. "Okay, but...won't they hang around for a while?"

Simon's gaze returned to the buildings whipping past them now that they'd picked up speed. "Some of them will probably camp out."

"How will I get home without them noticing?"

"You won't." His lips curved into a challenging smile. "I guess you'll just have to share my bed."

Eleven

Once they got inside the house, away from the photographers' prying eyes, Gail suggested she sleep in the room next to Simon's, where they'd each have some privacy. She didn't want to worry about brushing up against him during the night, and she didn't see how having her own room in such a big house would hurt. With her hair mussed and her clothes wrinkled, she'd still be able to put on a good show for any media that had the tenacity to wait until morning.

But he said he had too many domestic workers who might notice and would, no doubt, find the arrangement odd enough to mention to others. So Gail relented. They had to look like lovers, which meant she'd probably be the first woman to spend the night in Simon's bed without taking off her clothes.

Actually, she did undress—but in his expansive closet, with the door closed. She borrowed a T-shirt and a pair of boxers so she could at least be comfortable. Then she climbed into bed beside him, propped some pillows behind her back as he'd done and watched an indie film he'd been meaning to vet on his big screen.

"You've got a nice setup here," she said when the

credits began to roll. She was wondering what they'd do next. Even if he could go to sleep, she couldn't. Ever since they'd closed the door to his bedroom, she'd been trying to pretend that spending time with him was no different from hanging out with any other platonic friend. She and Joshua had shared a hotel room at various PR conventions, hadn't they?

But this didn't feel the same. Besides the obvious difference in Josh's and Simon's sexual orientation, Simon was sitting only a couple feet away from her wearing nothing but his boxers. She'd asked him to put on some pajamas, but he'd given her that look of his, the one that said he'd do as he damn well pleased.

His stubbornness on that point should've bothered her more than it did. She had a long list of complaints about his character, but she couldn't fault his looks or his sex appeal.

"It's not hard to have a nice setup when you've got money," he said, and used the remote to start flipping through channels. "It's the things you can't buy that are difficult."

Even in the dark, with only the glow of the TV screen to light the room, his bare chest drew her gaze. She knew most women in America would give anything to trade places with her, but all she wanted was to go home. Being here, feeling what she was feeling—it wasn't good. She was the one who'd insisted on the "no sex" mandate, and yet having sex with Simon was suddenly all she could think about. No doubt he'd been hoping that would be the case when he brought her home.

"Are you talking about peace of mind? Or personal relationships?" Using all the self-restraint she could muster, she shifted her attention back to the TV.

"Both."

She nodded. "You do need some help in those areas."

With a withering glance that said he didn't appreciate her comment, he switched to the Golf Channel.

"Golf? Really?"

"Wow, this *is* like being married." He kept surfing, but what he chose next didn't make her any happier

"Oh, this is perfect," she said. "I'm equally interested in basketball."

One dark eyebrow slid up. "It's *SportsCenter.* And they're talking about the Colts. They're a football team."

She hadn't really been paying attention or she would've known that from following Matt's career. "Whatever. You sure know how to entertain a woman."

He gave her a crooked smile. "You're the one who tied my hands."

"Sort of makes you appreciate all those women who'll put out, doesn't it?" She manufactured a yawn.

"Sort of makes me mad you won't," he grumbled.

She couldn't help laughing at his surliness. Their date tonight hadn't been bad. As a matter of fact, she'd enjoyed it. Despite some of his comments since, she was beginning to believe they might actually get along. "We could always watch the shopping network."

"I'd rather stick a fork in my eye."

"But it's time I started spending your money."

"Who says?"

"Isn't that what wives of movie stars do?"

"You've made it abundantly clear that you won't *really* be my wife."

"And you've made it clear that I could still have some decent pocket change."

He got up. "Fine. I don't care. Just shop on your own time."

She pulled the blankets higher. "Whose time is this?"

"Mine," he said without looking back.

"According to who—you?"

"It's part of your contract." He went into the bathroom and shut the door.

"I didn't sign anything that said I had to watch TV with you," she called after him.

He poked his head out. "You don't. You only have to share my bed and pretend to like it. So feel free to roll over and go to sleep."

She tried. But she was too aware of every move he made.

A few minutes later, he was back in bed, surfing stations again. "How long are you going to be up?" she asked.

"It's still early."

"In which country? Because here it's after one o'clock."

"One more program."

"Fine," she said with a sigh. "But I'm going to sleep."

His hair stood up as he raked a hand through it. "Does that mean I can finally watch what I want?"

"Of course," she said, and flopped over, but she'd expected him to choose something sports-related, like before. She had no idea he'd settle on a skin flick.

Male and female moans immediately drew her attention back to the screen, where a woman with obscenely large breasts was having sex with a man whose body parts were equally exaggerated. It was low-budget, down and dirty, but it was effective. Gail hadn't been with a man in so long, a sight like this couldn't fail to trigger a deluge of hormones. "What are you doing?" she gasped.

He blinked innocently at her. "Watching TV."

"That's *pornography!*"

"You just said you were going to sleep. I said, 'Does that mean I can finally watch what I want?' and you said, 'Of course.'"

"But that's cheating! You're trying to get me interested."

He raised his hands as he shook his head. "Not my plan at all."

Then he was after revenge. No doubt he thought it was funny to arouse her, since she was the one who'd taken physical satisfaction off the menu.

When the woman threw her head back and cried out in ecstasy, Gail felt her face flush. "I don't want to watch this!"

"Fine. Then choose something else." Tossing her the remote, he scooted down and closed his eyes.

Gail selected a news channel for a few minutes, then a cop show for a brief time, then an old rerun of *CHiPs*. She'd won that skirmish, she told herself, satisfied that she'd gained control of the remote. But as the minutes lengthened and Simon's breathing grew regular, she couldn't help going back to see if the show he'd chosen was still on. And then she couldn't seem to pull away from it until it was over. By the time she turned off the TV and put the remote on the nightstand, she was far from sleep. As a matter of fact, she was so hot and bothered she wanted to slug Simon.

"Something wrong?" he asked when she couldn't get comfortable.

He hadn't moved in some time. She'd assumed he was asleep. "No, why?"

"I thought you didn't want to watch *Here Comes Pussy.*"

She could hear the laughter in his voice and felt a

certain amount of embarrassment. "I didn't really watch it. I was just…surfing around."

"Sure you were."

He'd caught her and he knew it. "It was your fault!" She threw a pillow at him, which he batted away.

"You were in charge of the remote."

"I told myself not to go back to it, but…"

"But?" he challenged.

She stopped searching for an excuse he wouldn't believe, anyway. "It was sort of fascinating," she admitted. "I've never seen anything like it."

This seemed to startle him. "Seriously?"

"Seriously."

"Damn, you really are straitlaced." He didn't sound pleased.

"And you're already corrupting me," she muttered.

"Just living up to my reputation." He covered a yawn. "Anyway, if I'd known it was that great, I would've watched it with you. What was so fascinating about it?"

She couldn't find the words to explain, but having those images on TV while he was lying next to her, all but naked, had been erotic. Which went to show how poor her sex life had been so far. He hadn't even touched her and it was still the best sexual experience of her life. "It just…was." Since he'd played the male lead in her fantasy, she decided she'd be much better off to let it go at that.

"Good to know you have a libido," he said.

She shot into a sitting position. "Was that some sort of *test?*"

"It was a joke." He reached out and took hold of her chin so that she had to look him in the eye. "But since it was a little more effective than I expected, I'll do right by you if you want."

She might've gone for it. There was a small part of her that was urging her to take what she could get. But he was laughing at her again. She could feel the bed shake with his mirth.

"You are *so* bad!" she said.

Dropping his hand, he sobered instantly. "I know."

These days, Simon slept only in snatches and giving up alcohol wasn't making getting through the night any easier. His mouth was dry, his hands felt shaky and he was nauseous. It was nothing for which he needed a doctor; just his body's way of trying to demand he return to his earlier habits. Maybe it was more of a psychological craving than a physical one. Regardless, he woke up only forty minutes later and couldn't go back to sleep.

Shit... He'd hoped by giving himself a bed partner, even one who slept on her own side and wouldn't let him cross that imaginary line, he'd have better luck, some reason to stay put instead of rambling around the house. But nothing seemed to help. He figured he could take a sleeping pill, but considering his state of mind, he was afraid of where that might lead. He didn't want to toss away one crutch only to grab another. Ty deserved a better effort than that.

Rolling over, he scooted toward Gail. He was afraid to get too close for fear she'd think he was making a move. But maybe the steady sound of her breathing and the solidity of her presence would anchor him, somehow ease his insomnia. If he kept his eyes closed, he could pretend she was Bella and this was before they'd torn each other apart—that Ty was still a baby sleeping in the next room.

It might've worked, but Gail wasn't asleep.

"What's wrong?" he asked, slightly embarrassed when he realized she was watching him.

"Don't you ever sleep?"

"Not much. Not these days. What are you doing up?"

"Thinking."

He punched his pillow. "Be careful. Don't do too much of that or it'll drive you crazy."

"Is that what it does to you?"

"Unless I stop the whole process by dousing my brain with alcohol."

"Which you can't do at the moment."

"Or any moment in the next two years."

"I'm glad you're taking that seriously."

He blew out a sigh. "It's been a whole seventy-two hours." He could've given her the minutes, too. He was pretty sure she understood that.

"So...now you're looking for other distractions."

"Except there's nothing on the list of approved activities."

She adjusted the bedding. "Is that why you didn't watch the porn flick you showed me?"

"Part of the reason."

"I suppose you could start gambling, if you must have a bad habit."

"I'm willing to consider anything."

"I believe it." When she laughed, he realized she was more attractive than he'd ever given her credit for. She wasn't a beauty in the classic sense, but...there was *something* about her.

"You're a lot prettier when you laugh," he said.

She didn't respond, just stared at him with those serious gray eyes, and he could tell she'd discounted his words as soon as he'd uttered them.

"I meant that as a compliment."

"You don't have to pay me compliments." Her shrug suggested she didn't believe him, anyway. "I don't expect you to pretend to see something that's not there."

The silence stretched with only the swoop of the ceiling fan to interrupt it. "Is that why you won't let me touch you?" he asked at length. "You think, for me, it's all about the perfect body?"

She seemed to consider her answer carefully. "No, I don't think you care what I look like or that you'd even notice. For you, sex is like alcohol. You're just trying to deaden the pain."

She was right. Since the breakdown of his marriage he'd gone from one woman to the next. Some of them he'd never seen before or after, never even learned their names.

"You're going to be hard person to live with, Ms. DeMarco," he said.

Her lips curved into a wry smile. "Why's that? Because you can't bullshit me?"

"Because you see enough truth to think you know it all."

"I haven't been wrong yet."

"Yes, you have. I *do* think you're pretty," he said, and got up.

She leaned on her elbows. "Where are you going?"

"I have a project I'm working on."

"It's the middle of the night."

"I need something to do," he said, and pulled on his jeans.

Gail woke up alone in Simon's bed. After dressing in last night's clothes, she wandered out of the room and down to the kitchen, where his chef, a stout man who reminded her of Emil Villa, insisted on making her an omelet for breakfast. Once she was finished eating, Simon's driver, a handsome younger man of maybe twenty-five, came in through the French doors and announced that he'd be happy to take her home whenever she wanted to leave.

"Where's Simon?" She gazed out a wall of glass toward the pool—the direction from which the driver had come.

He set about gathering his keys. "I'm sure he's on the property. All the cars are here. But, honestly, I can't say where. He texted me earlier and asked me to drive you home whenever you're ready. That's all I know."

Arching a disbelieving eyebrow, she waited for him to look up. When he did, he acted a little embarrassed, as if he understood that she knew he was covering for his boss. From the driver's perspective, Simon had had his fun with her; now his job was to drop her off, like he'd probably done with so many women before her.

But why would Simon treat her the same as all the others when they needed to convince everyone he felt more for her?

"Or… I could text him and tell him you want to see him—if you like," the young man added reluctantly.

Mere platitudes. He didn't expect her to take him up on that offer. He was obviously skeptical it would do any good, even if she did.

Gail didn't dare risk having Simon brush her off in front of his staff. Not saying goodbye was bad enough. "No, that's fine," she said, but to compensate she fondled the ruby pendant at her throat. "I'm ready whenever you are. I just wanted to thank him for the necklace."

On learning that Simon had given her such an expensive gift, the cook and the driver exchanged a meaningful glance, but they said nothing more. The chauffeur, dressed in a polo shirt and chinos, grabbed a pair of sunglasses off the counter and led her through the house to a tunnel that ran to the garage—a garage that appeared to be detached when viewed from ground level.

"This reminds me of the Bat Cave," she said.

He opened the back door of the limousine. "Comes in handy."

"I bet." Raking her fingers through her tangled hair, she settled against the leather upholstery. She had none of her toiletries, hadn't even been able to brush her teeth. Maybe Simon had done her a favor by letting her duck out with no farewell.

I do think you're pretty....

She'd mulled over those words long after he'd left last night. They rose in her mind now, but she quickly shoved them away. She could never compete with the kind of women he usually enjoyed. There was no reason to get excited about a "you're not so bad." What he'd said didn't matter, anyway. This was a job.

The driver began to back out, but she stopped him. "Wait! Do we have to take this car?" It attracted so much attention.

Eyes hidden by his silvery lenses, he looked in the rearview mirror. "It has tinted windows. Simon said to get you home without letting anyone bother you."

So he'd done *something* to convince his staff that he might care about her well-being. She supposed she should be grateful for that small courtesy, but she was still a little put out that he hadn't bothered to see her. Had he ever come to bed?

She couldn't remember. Once she'd fallen asleep, she hadn't stirred until morning. "This is fine."

Her cell phone buzzed as they made a three-point

turn and started down the drive. She'd gotten a text. From Callie. How'd it go with your father?

Not good, she responded.

I'm sorry. But...you might want to listen to him.

Gail didn't text back. She'd crossed her father and was ignoring her friend's advice because she'd already committed herself to this course of action. But...what made her think her plan would work? Simon had just sloughed her off on his hired help like he did all the women he didn't care about, even though he understood the need to treat her as if she was special. What was going through his mind?

She had no idea, but part of her feared he might be drinking. And if he was drinking she needed to know about it. She had so much riding on this campaign. There was more at risk than her business; she had her relationship with her father to consider, too. She wouldn't let Simon prove Martin right. Simon *could* change, pull himself together and stop his downward spiral. And she was going to do everything in her power to see that he did.

"Take me back," she said.

The driver slowed in surprise. They'd just passed through the gate. "Excuse me?"

"You heard me. I want to go back to the house right now."

Twelve

Security didn't want to let her on the premises. But Gail wasn't taking no for an answer. She called Ian, told him the deal was off unless she could get onto the estate immediately, and somehow he arranged it. After fifteen minutes of haggling between him and a gigantic muscle-bound man named Lance, during which she was pretty sure Ian told Lance she was to be accommodated no matter what she wanted, the limousine rolled through the gate, down the long winding drive and into the garage.

By the time Gail got out, she'd called Simon's cell phone twice. She'd texted him, too. There'd been no response. Was he passed out somewhere? Dabbling with a maid? Or did he have enough of his wits about him to know he'd better hide?

Damn him. She'd gone out on a limb for him. If he was drinking...

"Ma'am? Ma'am, is there something I can help you with?" The driver hurried after her. He didn't like letting her have free run of the place any more than Lance, the security guard, did. But she didn't care. Avoiding the tunnel, she headed to the house by circling around to the front entrance.

The driver stuck with her, a few feet behind. "How can I help you?" he called again.

"You can find Simon," she called back, "because I'm not leaving until I talk to him." No way would she sit passively by and let her former client—her "fiancé"—ruin everything. They were all in this together now.

"Simon? Where are you?" she shouted as she entered the house. Sweeping staircases, to the right and left, a marble floor with nothing but a grand piano and a high ceiling made for perfect acoustics.

Simon didn't answer.

A maid came to the top of the stairs. Obviously surprised by the interruption, and the angry edge to Gail's voice, she stood at the railing and gaped down at her.

"Where is he?" Gail demanded when their eyes met.

The maid shook her head. "I don't know. I swear."

"Somebody here does." She marched into the living room where she'd met with Simon yesterday. Empty. She found a study, a library, a movie theater, a game room…too many rooms to count. But they were all perfectly clean and perfectly empty. When she finally reached the kitchen, she'd decided he was drinking for sure. She was going to bust him, then cut ties completely, no matter what happened afterward.

At the sound of her heels clacking on the tile floor, Simon's chef twisted around to look over his shoulder.

"Have you seen him?" she asked.

Unlike the maid, he'd been expecting her. He was sitting on a bar stool, having a cup of coffee with the driver, who'd given up following her once she started through the house. The stubborn tilt to the chef's round head indicated he wouldn't tell her anything and his words confirmed it. "No. But I rarely see him in the mornings."

"Because he's usually hungover," she muttered, afraid no one had seen him this morning for that same reason. "You're not doing him any favors, you know. I'm trying to help him."

"Looks like it," the chef said.

Suddenly she remembered the project Simon had mentioned in the middle of the night. "Where does he go when he's here but not in the house?"

They knew, of course, but were too loyal to tell her. The driver blinked at her. "I have no idea, Ms. DeMarco."

The chef spread his hands. "He could be anywhere."

She hadn't introduced herself. Either Simon had given them her name or they'd seen the pictures of her and Simon kissing and read about her online. But if that was the case, they didn't seem to be putting much store in the tales that were circulating. The press called her Simon's latest "love interest." They probably thought she was just another conquest, that she'd already passed out of favor or Simon wouldn't have foisted her on them.

"I'm talking about when he works on his project," she prompted. "Where does he go then?"

They glanced at each other but remained mute.

"Fine, I'll just have to keep looking," she said, and stalked out the French doors.

Before she could cross the patio, however, the driver came to the door and called after her. "Ms. DeMarco?"

She turned to see that he was frowning. Speaking up went against his training. But he had obviously gauged her determination and decided it was better to get what was coming over with than have her searching the property for hours, haranguing everyone she saw.

"I've texted him several times, but he's not answering. At this point, I don't know what to do, so… I guess he can tell you himself if he wants you to leave. I'll take you to his woodshop."

Woodshop? Simon didn't seem like the carpenter type, but maybe the project he'd mentioned involved wood.

"Thank you."

Hurrying to keep up, she followed as he crossed the grass and went behind the tennis courts, past the pool house, the guesthouse, a second barbecue area, this one with a koi pond, and what looked like an outdoor dancing pavilion.

At last they came upon a giant cabinlike structure at the far corner of the property. "This is it?" she asked.

He waved her ahead of him. "This is it."

Heart pounding for fear of what she'd find, and the disappointment that might go with it, she knocked on the door.

There was no response but she could hear a saw going inside. She tried the handle.

It wasn't locked. She poked her head in. "Simon?"

At first she thought the shop was empty. She spotted the saw, but there was no one near it. The motor grated as the blade whirled freely. "I don't think he's here, either—" she started to say, but then she saw the blood. "Oh, my God!"

Simon's driver stood behind her. He noticed the drops the same second she did, but he found his employer faster. Pushing past her, he dashed across the concrete floor to where Simon sat, slumped against the wall, blood covering his hands and phone and staining his clothes.

She hurried over and crouched on the other side. "Simon? What happened?"

"I don't think he can hear you," the driver said, and he was right. Simon's eyes were glassy, his skin cold and clammy.

Standing, Gail pulled her phone out of her purse. Her hands were shaking so badly she could hardly dial, but she hit 9-1-1.

"How long do you think he was bleeding?" Gail stood in a corner of the hospital waiting room, conversing quietly with Simon's doctor.

"Considering the size of the cut?" the doctor replied. "At least an hour."

She attempted to swallow, but her mouth was too dry. "So…was it a suicide attempt?"

A tall, spare man with gray hair, the doctor pursed his lips. "I don't believe he was trying to kill himself, no."

"Then why didn't he seek help?"

"Who can say? Maybe he thought he could get the bleeding under control, that he only needed to sit down and put some pressure on it. But it was much worse than he realized and he eventually went into shock. To be honest, thanks to significant sleep deprivation and the lifestyle he's been leading, I'm not sure he was in a clear frame of mind to begin with."

She could certainly confirm that. "What about alcohol? Was he drunk when this happened?"

"No. There was no alcohol in his system at all."

For some reason this helped her relax and made her tear up at the same time. It meant he was trying. "He told me it's been three days since he's had a drink."

"How much was he drinking before?"

"A lot."

"Maybe he's going through withdrawal and that figures into this somehow. It can cause depression, anxiety, myriad other things. I'm guessing this accident is a culmination of a number of factors. Including exhaustion."

"But not suicide." For some reason, she needed to hear him say that again.

"I doubt it. A saw would be an emotionally daunting way to take your own life. Besides, only one of his hands is cut and not near the wrist. This was an accident, but…the fact that he didn't immediately call for help might say something about his state of mind. Then again, it might not. It could've happened like I said."

"Gail? What's going on?"

Ian had arrived; he was hurrying toward her. Thanking the doctor for taking the time to speak with her, she turned and greeted Simon's manager. "He's going to be okay."

His eyes darted between her and the departing doctor. "What the hell happened?"

She blew out a long breath. "I'm not sure. The doctor thinks it was an accident."

"You don't?"

The image of Simon sitting on the floor of his woodshop, cradling his hand and staring off into space as if he'd just as soon slip away came to mind. Why didn't he call someone? He had all kinds of domestic help on the property. The doctor didn't feel it was an *active* attempt to take his own life, but he'd intimated that it could have been a passive one, which still gave them plenty to worry about. "I don't know what to think," she admitted. "Except… Simon needs a break, Ian."

He scowled. "What do you mean?"

"I mean he needs a break, a real break. Some time to

take care of himself, to get back on his feet emotionally and physically, to rest from all the demands on him."

"But he's under contract for promotion! I already told you that. And he's supposed to start another movie in two weeks."

She was so upset it didn't take much to set her off. "You said you could clear his schedule in early November for our wedding."

"I was talking about a weekend or maybe even a week. But he's slammed with work before *and* after."

"I don't care! Get him out of whatever obligations he's got. He shouldn't be working in this condition."

"I can't just—"

"Yes, you can." She grabbed his arm to make her point. "It's only money."

"Easy for you to say. It's not *your* money that'll be lost, not *your* career that will suffer. This film he has coming up—it's supposed to be the kind that makes or breaks a career. The producers are pressuring me to make sure he'll be at the studio and in good shape."

A couple on the couch glanced up, so she pulled Ian farther into the corner and lowered her voice. "He nearly cut off his hand. Whether that was an accident or not, he didn't seek help. He sat on the floor as if he didn't care whether he lived or died and nearly bled to death. If that isn't a cry for help, I don't know what is. Now get on the phone and call whoever you have to, but tell everyone that Simon will be unavailable for the next three months."

Agitated, Ian began to pace. "They'll think he's cracking up, that he's finally lost it. I've spent so much time trying to make them believe he'll be fine, snap back, get into it again."

She threw up her hands. "Then tell them it's because

he's fallen in love and is getting married. We'll provide plenty of pictures to prove it. Making a commitment to someone stable should be a good sign, not a bad one."

"They don't know you're stable. Anyway, you could be perfectly stable until you hook up with him."

"Well, that's how we need to sell it, because I now believe this is Simon's last chance in more ways than one."

Ian's mouth hung open for several seconds before he could find the words to respond, but at least he'd quit pacing. "So… I get him out of all his obligations, and then what?"

"We leave L.A."

"And go where?"

Gail's mind whirled. She was on to something. She could feel it. Her certainty grew as she considered the problem from all angles. Simon couldn't stay in Los Angeles. Here, he was surrounded by the same temptations, reminders, people and worries. How could he effect the changes he needed to make when he was mired in the past? When nothing else was changing?

Getting away made sense. But where should she take him? To one of his houses abroad?

No. What if the accident hadn't been an accident? She didn't want to be out of the country if something like this happened again. Or he went back to drinking. She preferred someplace she felt comfortable and safe and could get the help he would need. Someplace where he could dry out and recover without the intrusion of the paparazzi. Someplace where there were no painful memories of Bella or Ty, no friends who might encourage him to keep partying, no enticements from film-industry types to make another movie before he was ready.

She was sure he had other houses in America they could go to, but she didn't want an army of domestic workers taking note of everything that transpired, either.

They needed privacy, support, protection and a change of scenery. Given all that, the answer became obvious. "I've got it," she said.

Ian narrowed his gaze. "You've got what?"

Her father wouldn't like it. Neither would her brother and her friends. They were already convinced she was making the biggest mistake of her life. Even Simon would object. They'd all reject one another—at first. But the people who loved her were good people. They'd made her whole and happy despite her mother's defection. They'd been there when she needed them most. And they were still there for her.

Simon needed rock-solid commitment from the right sorts of friends and associates and for the right reasons. He needed to figure out what really mattered in life and what he wanted out of his own.

She couldn't think of a better place to do that than Whiskey Creek. "I'm taking him home."

Thirteen

When Simon woke up, he found Ian and Gail sitting on either side of his bed, glaring at each other.

"Why all the hostility?" he muttered.

Gail came to her feet. "What hostility?"

Whatever they'd given him made him groggy, but even then he could tell she was covering up. "You two act like you want to choke each other."

"So what's new?" She laughed, and Ian did, too, but their eyes were cold when they met and their smiles seemed brittle.

"Something. I can feel it." He glanced between them. "I thought we'd called a truce, that we were all playing on the same team again."

"We are," Gail told him. "Ask anyone—you and I are madly in love and having wild sex at your Beverly Hills mansion. Everything is fine. Right on track."

Except that she was treating him like he'd lost his mind—was probably wondering what kind of crazy man she'd gotten involved with.

Damn... Somehow, despite all his good intentions and effort, he'd screwed up again. "Wild sex, huh? That's what they think?"

"How do you feel?" Ian stood up, too.

Simon had never seen his business manager so serious. "Drugged. What happened?"

"You don't know?"

He lifted his right hand to examine the bandage that made his arm look liked it ended in a club. "Nurses told me I cut my hand. They said it wasn't too bad, but they were somber as shit and it has to be more than a scratch or I wouldn't be here, right?"

Gail bumped up against the steel rail of his bed. "You don't recall the accident?"

He honestly didn't. The last thing he remembered was getting a text from Bella—a short video of her having sex with some guy and a note that said, Ty's new daddy. "No, I was exhausted, completely out of it." He realized how that sounded and hurried to amend his words. "But I wasn't drinking. At least… I'm pretty sure I wasn't drinking." He'd considered it. Had he given in?

"No, you weren't drinking," she said.

"There's a bright spot." He grinned, but when she didn't lighten up he stopped trying to charm her. "So… what? Are you backing out? Cutting me loose?" Why wouldn't she? He knew how this looked. He could tell by some of the questions the doctor had asked that he hadn't called for help when he should have.

They wondered if he'd purposely hurt himself. And maybe he had. He wouldn't be stupid enough to attempt suicide by power saw, but subconsciously he might've been sabotaging his own efforts to reform, or trying to save himself from failing through lack of willpower. He'd always been his own worst enemy. His father told him that all the time, even though it felt more like his father was his worst enemy. Their relationship had never been a strong one, but recently they'd become completely estranged.

He let his eyes slide closed. "You're off the hook, if you want."

He expected her to jump at the chance, provided he agreed to a stipulation that saved her business, but she surprised him.

"That's not what I want."

Opening his eyes, he found her and Ian watching him a little too closely. He nearly assured them he was stable, that he could cope with whatever he had to, but he'd been saying that for too long. His actions hadn't backed it up, so why bother? "Then, what is?"

She nibbled at her bottom lip. "I want to take you to Whiskey Creek."

Had he heard her correctly? "Isn't that where your family lives?" He didn't bother hiding the skepticism in his voice.

"That's right."

"We already discussed it."

"We did, but…" She folded her arms, which told him she was anticipating a fight. "A few things have changed since then and…now I think it's imperative to the success of our marriage."

He raised his eyebrows. "Why? What difference does it make whether or not I meet your family? Are you *trying* to drive me to drink?"

He thought she could at least smile at his joke, give him credit for the effort he was putting into pretending he was okay, but Ian piped up before she could react.

"It'll mean canceling everything you've got going for the next three months."

So Ian wasn't excited about this change of plan….

Simon rubbed the beard growth on his chin. "I'll miss starting my next movie."

"Yes."

"That's a long time to be in Whiskey Creek."

Gail stood taller. "Given your injury and our wedding, you have a good excuse, a believable excuse, to clear your schedule without losing face. Take the out. It'll only make our marriage look more genuine."

He scowled at her. "How is Whiskey Creek going to do that?"

"It'll suggest you care enough to spend time with me and my family. And dropping out of public view will ultimately make it easier for you to regain custody of Ty."

The sex video Bella had sent and those taunting words—*Ty's new daddy*—floated to the forefront of Simon's brain. The images turned his stomach. But it was the idea of the man who was screwing his ex-wife replacing him as his son's father that hurt, as Bella knew it would. "You really believe it would make enough of a difference?"

"You couldn't go wrong in Whiskey Creek even if you wanted to."

He could go wrong anywhere. He'd proven it. But... she seemed so convinced and, whether he wanted to admit it or not, he was starting to trust her, certainly more than Ian. Ian had his strengths, but she was smarter, more disciplined. Just what he needed at the moment. "What would I do there?"

"Anything you want. I saw the playhouse you've been building. It's amazing! You like working with wood. Why don't we rent a house while you build us a bigger one?"

Building a house with his own two hands had always appealed to him. He felt a flutter of excitement, the first in a long, long while—but Simon refused to succumb to it. He didn't want to be disappointed. "Are you setting me up?"

"Excuse me?"

"Your dad's going to hate me."

"He already does," she said. "So does my brother. But you can win them over. You can win anyone over."

She was offering him a chance to be a regular person for a while, a chance to step out of the limelight and catch his breath.

"This'll cause damage to certain key relationships," Ian warned. "You're booked solid. And if I have to buy your way out of your next movie, it'll be pricey."

True, but his sanity was worth any amount. Simon had learned firsthand that even piles and piles of money couldn't buy happiness. That cliché was a cliché for a reason.

"The producers of *Hellion* will freak out if you postpone too long," Ian went on. "It'll put them in trouble with the rest of the cast, studio time, everything."

"If they can't wait, they'll have to find someone else," Simon said.

"Seriously?" Ian looked stupefied.

Simon couldn't imagine trying to make a movie in his current state of mind. "Seriously." He turned to Gail. "Okay, we'll go to Whiskey Creek."

"You'll do it?" She sounded skeptical, and he couldn't blame her.

He thought of all the hours he'd spent aching for his son while standing or sitting in Ty's room. Maybe it was time for a radical change. "Why not? Let your dad take his best shot."

They needed to get married before doing anything else. Only if Simon was legally bound to her and couldn't be easily relegated to the "temporary" category would Whiskey Creek even begin to accept him. Gail understood that, which meant they had to change the proposed timeline of their "courtship."

Because she'd never been engaged and had no idea of the process required to make a marriage legal, she used her smartphone while sitting at Simon's bedside to go online and figure out what they'd need to do to get a license.

Fortunately, it was going to be easy. As long as they had proper ID and proof of the dissolution of Simon's marriage, they could pay a fee, get a license on the spot and be married shortly after. No need for a blood test; no need to go to Vegas.

But they had to appear at the county clerk's office together, and Simon hadn't yet been released from the hospital so it wouldn't happen today.

Ian had stayed, too, although Simon was too drugged to do much talking. Mostly, he slept. There were moments when Gail was tempted to leave so she could prepare for their big move. But the number of hospital personnel who popped into the room bothered her. They all came in and fiddled with this or that, pretending to be on official business. However, Gail was convinced they were merely gawking at the big movie star, which felt wrong since he wasn't even aware of them.

How many times did a guy with stitches need to be checked? she wondered. It wasn't as if Simon had had a heart attack or any other problem that required such close monitoring. He just needed to catch up on his sleep, and medicating him made sure he was able to do that.

"Word is spreading," she told Ian as the door closed on yet another visitor.

Simon's business manager sat with his elbows on his knees and his head in his hands. "What are you talking about?" he asked, looking up.

"That's the fifth nurse to come in here in under an hour."

"I know. He'd probably be getting a blow job by now if you weren't here."

She could tell by the sulk in Ian's voice that he was no longer happy to be involved with her. He'd expected her to keep Simon productive so that the next two years would run smoothly. Instead, she was pulling his client out of circulation. "Simon doesn't need a blow job. He needs a break from all the celebrity worship and scrutiny."

"You're sure about that, are you? Why don't we ask him if he'd like one of these cute little nurses to—"

"Stop it." She rolled her eyes. Ian was being crude on purpose, trying to shock her. "I've got a novel concept—how about if we give Simon what he needs instead of what he wants?"

"He doesn't need you to tell him what to do. He's a grown man."

She lowered her voice just in case Simon was nearing consciousness. "Who's on the brink of total collapse! You asked me to help for a reason, remember? The fact that you're fighting what's best for him tells me you're as bad as his other so-called friends. You're all vultures, hoping to pick his bones."

Ian shot to his feet. "That's bullshit! I care more about him than you do."

She stood, too. "Then prove it."

"I don't have to prove anything to you."

"At least quit pouting. You're driving me crazy."

"Feel free to go home if you don't like it."

No way. That was exactly what he'd been hoping she'd do. Then he could try to talk Simon out of going to Whiskey Creek. "Sorry to disappoint you but I'm not leaving you alone with him."

Ian leaned toward her. "What you're doing is crap, you know that? You're changing everything."

"I'm making necessary adjustments."

He combed his fingers through his hair, hesitated, then continued in a calmer voice, one meant to sway her. "Come on, I'll go with one month, okay? One month is plenty of time for Simon to be gone. We can put the producers of his next movie off until his hand heals but that's it."

"Sorry. Simon has to be out of circulation long enough to feel it, to unwind and focus on other—"

Yet another nurse popped in, but she got only half-way through the door before the look on Gail's face stopped her dead in her tracks. Mumbling a quick "Excuse me," she ducked out as if she'd entered the room by mistake.

Ian whistled. "You're a freakin' pit bull."

"You knew what I was like before you agreed to our deal."

"I had no idea you'd talk him into quitting work!"

"He's not quitting work, he's taking a break so he'll be able to salvage his relationship with his son and his career. And call me what you will, but now that I'm committed I'm going to do whatever it takes, so get used to it."

Simon shifted in the bed but didn't open his eyes. "Hey," he said. "Could you guys argue somewhere else?"

How much had he overheard? Gail exchanged a glance with Ian that essentially asked that question.

But she got the impression that Simon hadn't been paying attention to much more than the harshness of their whispering.

"Sorry," Ian muttered. "I think I'll take off."

Simon's eyes opened. "I'm surprised you lasted this long. You must be bored stiff."

"I thought you might need me, but...you're in good hands with Attila the Hun over there."

"Attila was a man," Gail snapped.

"I know that," he snapped back.

"Sure you did."

Ian lunged forward and gnashed his teeth. "He was ruthless, right?"

Simon put up his good hand. "Whoa, what'd she do to you?"

"How can I get some of the nurses to give me their number if she's chasing them off?" He smoothed his wrinkled shirt.

"You that desperate?"

"Desperate enough."

Simon didn't press him further. "Okay. Talk to you later."

"I'll get your schedule cleared," Ian said, his tone letting them know that he still thought it was a mistake.

As the door swung shut behind Ian, Simon raised his bed and turned his attention to her. "What's up between you two?"

Stiff from sitting all day, Gail rolled her shoulders. "I made it obvious that I wouldn't let him get in my way, that's all."

"And he backed down?"

"I prefer to believe he realized I was right."

"I don't know...." He studied her with a frown. "A blow job is never a *completely* bad idea."

So he'd overheard more than she'd assumed. "If you already knew what we were arguing about, why'd you ask?"

"Honestly? That's the only part I can remember."

She could tell he thought she'd snap at him, tell him to keep his priorities straight, but why would she? He wasn't serious. She was beginning to believe he purposely painted himself as shallow and hedonistic so the people around him wouldn't realize he was so sensitive. Somehow it was easier for him to outrage everyone than to allow them to see how deeply he was hurting.

"Enjoy your painkiller," she said. "Because that's all the feel-good you'll be getting here." She offered him a facetious smile. "And after that things will really go downhill because you'll be married to me."

"Wait, *I'm* the one who's supposed to put *you* down."

"We're getting to know each other so well, I can actually predict what you're going to say."

He didn't react to her sarcasm. "So…when's the big day? I'm guessing it's changed. You'll want to be married before introducing me to Daddy, am I right?"

Of course he was right. Then Martin couldn't talk her out of it or disapprove of their living together. "How'd you know?"

"You've got to have some way to make them accept such—what'd you call me? A dissolute movie star?"

He was slurring some of his words but she could still understand them. "*You're* going to make them accept you, not me. But to answer your question, I say we marry as soon as you're up and around."

"I'll be fine tomorrow. That's when we'll get our rings." His eyes drifted shut. He seemed to be having trouble remaining lucid, but he managed to say something else. "You don't have to stay here if you don't want."

Given his strained relationship with his family, who else would come? One of his bodyguards? His driver or a maid? That seemed so impersonal. "Sorry, but I've dedicated my entire day to beating back these nurses, and I won't quit now."

As if on cue, the door opened. When a male hospital worker walked in, Simon offered her a wry look. "I'm safe with this one."

Gail was too preoccupied to respond to his joke. "Do you have some reason for being here?" she asked the young man.

A sheepish expression appeared on his face. "Actually, I'm a huge fan." He held up paper and pen as his gaze darted in Simon's direction. "I was wondering if…if maybe I could get an autograph. I've seen *Shiver* so many times."

"If you don't mind—don't mind an *X*," Simon said, but Gail knew he was too groggy to hold a pen. And it was his right hand that had been injured. This guy was probably a nurse or an X-ray tech or someone who should know better than to barge into a patient's room without a legitimate reason.

"Get out and let him rest," Gail said. "And if you don't post a sign on the door saying that only authorized personnel are allowed in, I'll file a complaint and then maybe a lawsuit."

The man's eyes rounded. "But… I didn't mean to… What kind of lawsuit?"

"I'm sure a good attorney could think of something. If you like your job, you wouldn't want to be the cause of all the trouble."

"No, ma'am," he said, and hurried out.

Simon chuckled. "Jeez, with you around who needs security?"

She sank into her chair, which felt no softer than it had before. "I'm glad you feel that way because you won't have any security in Whiskey Creek."

The humor fled his face. "I won't?"

"No. No maids or chefs or drivers, either."

He scowled. "Why the hell not?"

"It's too insular, too alienating, especially in a place as small as Whiskey Creek."

"*Somebody's* got to cook."

"I'll do it if you'll do the driving."

"Are you any good?" he asked skeptically.

"I'm not bad."

"Fine. Because I'm a hell of a driver. We'll bring the Ferrari."

She crossed her legs. "Do you want everyone to hate you even more?"

"Money's the one thing I've got left. I might as well enjoy it."

"Later. Otherwise, it'll look like a shield—or an enticement. This is about creating a humble image of reform."

He tried to adjust his pillow despite his bandaged hand. "You're making your hometown sound like a real bitch."

She'd been trying to make it sound like a second chance. That was what she believed it could be. And, unlike Ian, Simon understood, or he never would've agreed to go there. He even seemed a little excited by the opportunity, although she guessed that once the drugs wore off, he'd also be frightened by the challenge. It'd been a long time since he'd gone into any relationship on an even footing. In her estimation, that was why he had no true friends.

In Whiskey Creek, it would be different. Simon would be normal, just like everyone else, or as "normal" as someone so famous could be. She hoped that he'd engage others and develop some mutual trust and respect, self-sacrifice, deep feelings. Those were the things he needed right now.

"Most of them won't kiss your ass, but you'll survive," she said.

"I can hardly wait."

Chuckling, she called up the ESPN website on her phone. "Did you hear that the Lakers are taking on the Heat tonight?"

He rested his injured hand on his chest. "What are you talking about?"

"Basketball."

"I know *that*. I'm wondering *why*. You hate sports."

"I'm beginning to rethink my position. Anyway, you used to be a big fan of the Lakers."

"I haven't been following them in preseason."

He hadn't been keeping up with a lot of the things he normally enjoyed. She thought that should be remedied, too. "I know. So?"

"So what?"

"They'll be starting out strong if they win."

"How many have they won?"

"Eight of their first ten games." She filled him in on the details before going on to the rest of the sports news. Then she moved to other sites and shared snippets of information about Egypt, China, Sudan, anything that involved people outside the U.S. She hoped doing so would remind him that L.A. wasn't the only city in the world, that there was much more out there than fame and the movie industry and his current problems.

Hearing about people being killed and driven out of their homes seemed to put it all in perspective.

"You think you're smart, don't you," he said.

He'd caught on. She smiled innocently. "Excuse me?"

"How am I going to put up with you?"

"Pretending to love me will be the biggest challenge of your acting career."

He didn't respond for a few seconds. Then he said, "How many people live in Whiskey Creek?"

"Population 2,000, give or take a hundred."

Sleepiness no longer seemed to be an issue. "And they're *all* going to hate me?"

She dropped her phone in her purse. "Give or take a hundred," she repeated.

His eyes narrowed. "I'll have them eating out of my hand in a matter of weeks."

"Glad to hear it." She had no doubt he could do it; she just hoped she wasn't one of them.

Fourteen

Every diamond was huge, much bigger than any Gail had seen before. And the prices... The average American house didn't cost this much.

Mr. Nunes, who sat in Simon's living room with the nondescript briefcase he'd carried in, had spread his entire cache of loose diamonds out on a piece of black velvet. "This one is the finest quality you'll ever find," he boasted as he held up yet another five-carat rock. "Just look at the clarity."

It was beautiful. But so were the others. "How much?" she asked, and braced herself for another shocking figure. The last one had been four hundred and thirty-five thousand.

Nunes was starting to show some irritation at her continued insistence on knowing the price. "If it's the one you like, I'm sure Simon and I can work something out." He leaned forward to gaze deep into her eyes. "This is your engagement ring. Price is no object."

Easy for him to say. But, surprisingly, Simon didn't argue with him about that. He didn't ask for smaller or cheaper diamonds, either. He simply looked on, wiggling the fingers that dangled out of the sling on his arm.

"It's an ideal cut," Nunes added. "And it has absolutely no color. Diamonds of this size, with a D grade *and* an IF clarity, are very rare."

"Is it more money than the last one?" she asked.

He made a dismissive motion. "Not by much."

What did that mean? Five thousand? Ten? It irritated her that he wouldn't be specific. Just because Simon was rich didn't mean he shouldn't be concerned with getting a fair deal. "How long will it take you to set it?"

"I can have it ready in three days. You will be my top priority."

At that price, she should be. But... "I don't know." Overwhelmed by the prices and the selection, she frowned at the twinkling display. "Maybe...maybe Simon and I should talk about this."

Simon stared at her as if he couldn't figure out what the problem was. "Talk about what?" he asked. "There must be a hundred diamonds here. Surely you can find *one* you like."

She gave Nunes an apologetic smile. "Excuse us for a moment."

"Just pick one so we can decide on the setting," Simon insisted, but she grabbed him by the sleeve of his good arm and led him out of the room.

"What are you doing?" he asked when they were alone in the foyer.

"I think we should forget about the diamond."

His eyebrows shot up. "You need a wedding ring."

"We both do. But gold bands will be fine."

"Why would you settle for a gold band?"

She wasn't sure. There was something...hollow about choosing a big diamond when there was no meaning behind it. She felt as if they were mocking all the tra-ditional wedding symbols. She could see someone with his wealth buying a stone like that to express his devo-tion to the love of his life, but she wasn't the love of his life. So it was just…wrong. Especially when she knew that canceling his next project would cost him a fortune already. "I don't want to be responsible for such an ex-pensive piece of jewelry," she said. "What if I lose it?"

"It'll be insured."

But a diamond, particularly of this caliber, wasn't part of her contract price. At least, that wasn't what she'd meant when she said he'd have to buy the rings. Her conscience would demand she return it when they divorced, so why get attached to it? What was the point? "There's no need to invite comparisons between me and Bella. Let's keep it simple, modest, understated."

"You're serious."

"I am. I think we should sell the public on the fact that this marriage is different from the typical Holly-wood marriage. That we're about the things that really matter. No pomp or ceremony. No obvious publicity stunts. No lavish lifestyle. Just the two of us in love, liv-ing in a small house in my hometown—until we grow apart and divorce amicably, of course."

He studied her. "Does this have anything to do with the offer I made you before? Are you afraid you'll owe me sex in return?"

"No."

"Then what? You don't want to have *any* positive feelings for me?"

"That's not it, either," she said, but she couldn't quite meet his eyes and he jumped to his own conclusion.

"Wow, even my money isn't good enough," he said. "Fine. No problem."

When he headed back without her, she knew she'd offended him. He thought she wouldn't let him redeem himself even where he could, that she found him unworthy of *any* approval.

But that wasn't the problem. She found him appealing whether she approved of him or not.

And she couldn't see how adding a half-million-dollar diamond ring to his side of the equation would make him any easier to resist.

It took nearly a week to get ready for the ceremony and still the time seemed to come up fast. They'd given Simon a chance to recover a bit, gotten the marriage license, purchased the wedding bands. Ian had found some guy on the internet who could legally officiate. For an additional fee, he was willing to come to Simon's house. They'd have a small, private affair with only Josh and Ian as witnesses.

The ceremony would make their marriage legal and binding, and in less than an hour it would all be over.

This wasn't exactly the type of wedding Gail had dreamed about when she was a little girl, but she'd never imagined that her mother would abandon the family, either. She had to deal with what life handed her, just like everyone else.

She sat in Simon's bedroom, where she'd been staying most nights for the sake of appearances, and painted her fingernails. She'd just finished one hand when someone knocked on the door.

"Who is it?"

"Me. You okay?"

Josh. He'd come to find her. Thank God. Just hearing his voice steadied her nerves. "I'm alive," she said, and jumped up to let him in.

"Wow, you look beautiful," he told her as soon as she opened the door.

He seemed honestly impressed. She liked her outfit, too. Yesterday, Simon had sent her to Rodeo Drive with his credit card but, given the recent press, she'd felt too conspicuous among all those exclusive shops. Pulling on a pair of sunglasses for camouflage, she'd driven to the closest mall, where she felt more comfortable and was able to blend in with the crowd. There, she purchased yet another suit to add to her already extensive collection. She knew that probably wouldn't be a popular decision with Ian or Simon. But this one was teal in color and reminded her of the tailored fashions of the 1940s. She almost felt she should be wearing a fancy hat.

"Really?" She turned in a circle. "This is okay?"

"It's stunning on you. Simple but classy."

She released a nervous sigh. Josh was a fashionista if ever there was one. If she didn't look good he would've told her. "You prepared to be a witness?"

He whipped a small camera out of his pocket. "As well as the official photographer."

She knew he'd also help with the sale of those pictures to *People*. They'd agreed on that beforehand. "Great. Is Simon downstairs?"

"Waiting in the library. That's where they've decided to hold the ceremony."

"What's he wearing?"

"A suit and, man, does he look delicious—even with his hand all bandaged up."

"You think he looks delicious in anything."

"He does."

She couldn't argue with that. "What about the officiant? Is he here, too?"

"Officiant?"

"That's what they're called. At least, that's what I read on the internet."

"Oh, you mean the *minister.* He's not here yet, but he's on his way." He lifted the hand with the fingernails she hadn't painted. "Shouldn't you get on with this?"

"I was about to." She brushed on the pink lacquer while he talked, but when she finished, he looked at her closely.

"Oh, boy, you're not going to pass out, are you?"

"No, why?"

"You look pale."

"Pale is my usual color," she said, but her shaky laugh confirmed that she was more than a little out of her element. What they were doing invited bad karma. She and Simon would be making promises to love, honor and cherish each other for as long as they lived, with no intention of fulfilling those promises. She wasn't superstitious, but she couldn't help wondering if she was jinxing her future.

"I saw the rings," he said. His tone indicated he wasn't impressed.

"What do they look like?"

"You don't know? They're gold bands. What a cheap asshole. Why didn't he get you something expensive and gorgeous?"

"I didn't want that." She fanned herself to dry the polish. "I'm trying to keep what's happening *somewhat* real. Otherwise, it'll all feel too…outlandish."

"I have news for you, Ms. DeMarco. You're marrying one of the most famous movie stars in America. There's no way to avoid outlandish. I would've asked for the biggest diamond I could find."

"Why make him go to the expense? It wouldn't mean anything. And I'd just have to give it back."

He looked at her as if she was crazy. "Who said?"

Another knock interrupted. "Ms. DeMarco?"

"Yes?"

"They're ready for you in the library."

Simon had sent a maid up to get her. Squaring her shoulders, she offered Josh another tentative smile. "Shall we?"

"Allow me," he said and, with a gentlemanly flourish, escorted her downstairs.

As promised, Simon was in a suit. Freshly shaved, with his hair combed back, he looked every bit as good as Josh had said. Ian stood next to him, also in a suit but clearly no longer as enthusiastic about the idea of their marriage as he once was. The only other person in the room was a distinguished-looking man with silver hair who introduced himself as Reverend Bob Grady, a minister with the United Disciples of Christ Church.

Gail wasn't remotely familiar with the beliefs of that church, was pretty sure she'd never even heard of it, but she figured that didn't matter.

"It's nice to meet you," she said.

"I was just discussing with Simon the type of ceremony the two of you would like," he told her. "Some people write their own vows, but he said you'd both prefer a simple recitation of the traditional promises. Is that right?"

"Yes, that's fine." Her heart was beating so hard, she dared not look at Simon, but she could feel his gaze on her. Was he feeling hopeful? Relieved that the time had come and they'd be able to get this part over with? Hesitant to go through with what they'd planned? She didn't know and she didn't *want* to know for fear it would undermine her own resolve.

The minister bent his head. "Then that's what we'll

do. If you two will join hands—as best you can," he said in deference to Simon's injury, "and face each other in front of me, we'll get started."

Simon stepped up and did as he was asked. At that point, Gail *had* to look at him. He seemed pensive. Maybe he was as nervous as she was. And she could guess why. He'd sworn never to marry again. Even if this wasn't a regular marriage, wasn't real in the same sense, it sure *felt* real.

She almost pulled away to verify that they all believed they were doing the right thing, but Simon tightened his grip to hold her in place and she decided it was his commitment that mattered.

Sweat ran down her back as Reverend Grady began—and her fear of bad karma grew worse, especially when he reached "in sickness and in health" and then "till death do us part."

Still, she managed to repeat her vows. Simon did the same without sounding too panicked. As a matter of fact, he seemed…resolute.

They exchanged rings and the minister said, "I now pronounce you husband and wife. Simon, you may kiss the bride."

Gail knew Simon was in acting mode. He was used to such intimate contact, didn't think anything of it. But the warmth of his lips against hers made her knees weak. Hoping to play her part as well as he was playing his, she slipped her arms around his neck—until Simon's tongue entered her mouth. Then she drew back.

If she'd shocked the minister by stopping the kiss, he didn't show it. Smiling his approval, he gave her elbow a squeeze and, when Simon turned away to speak to Ian, lowered his voice. "I hope you can bring him peace."

"I do, too," she murmured.

They posed for several pictures. Then Josh swept her into a hug. "Congratulations. You'll be fine, you know that?"

"Of course I do. We both understand—" she dropped her voice to a whisper so the reverend wouldn't overhear "—what's riding on this." She forced a bright smile as she stepped away from him but felt dangerously close to tears.

"Thank God for every new day you have together," the minister said. "May you have a long and fruitful union."

When Gail heard Simon thank him, she was once again embarrassed and uncomfortable with the lies they were telling. But it wasn't until Simon went to show Josh, Ian and Reverend Grady out that she allowed herself to sink into one of the leather chairs along the wall and drop her head in her hands.

"They're gone," Simon said when he came back.

She looked up. "I can't believe we did it, that we went through with it."

He leaned against the door. "You were thinking of bailing on me?"

"No, not really. But…" She finished in a whisper so that no one else in the house could hear. "I felt like an idiot taking those vows. Didn't you?"

He stared at her for what seemed like an interminable time. "I don't know how I missed it."

She had no idea what he was talking about. "Missed what?"

"You're completely…*innocent*."

Her mind scrambled to put his comment into some sort of context. "Because I don't watch porn or—"

"No." He chuckled as if his meaning was obvious, but she couldn't imagine what he was trying to convey.

She'd never had anyone call her innocent. It wasn't a word most people associated with a business professional, especially one over thirty.

"Then what?" she asked.

He shook his head. "You're so tough and inflexible that—"

She held up a hand. "You've mentioned my lack of better qualities before."

Ignoring the interruption, he moved closer to her. "That I keep expecting you to be jaded and self-serving. But you're not. You're not that person at all."

Shifting in the giant but soft leather chair, she studied the polish on her nails to avoid looking up—but ended up looking at him anyway. "I'll probably kick myself for asking, but…according to you, who am I?"

"Someone who's honest, sincere and too tender-hearted for her own good." He frowned as if these things were terrible, the latest blow in the long series of blows he'd recently been dealt. "As I said, innocent."

"And you don't like innocent any more than you like tough and inflexible, is that it?"

He did what he could to loosen his tie with one hand. "That's where you're wrong. I *crave* innocent. It's so rare in my world that I'm immediately drawn to it. Which is why I think we might have an unexpected problem."

"Admiring some of my positive traits is a problem?"

"It could be, for you. So I'll add my voice to all the others who've tried to warn you away. If you know what's good for you, you'll walk out of here right now and petition for an annulment."

He was serious. "I can see you're feeling confident in our success. That's encouraging."

"I'm feeling guilty," he clarified.

"For taking vows you don't mean?"

"For knowing I'll probably end up destroying your innocence."

"And how do you think you'll do that?"

"You haven't been through what I've been through, haven't lost the ability to fall in love." He jerked his head toward the door. "So get out while you can. I'll still be your client, do whatever you need to help get your business back on solid ground."

And what would *he* do? Continue to battle his demons with alcohol? He'd certainly made a mess of his life. She wasn't sure he deserved the second chance she'd constructed for him, but she wanted to see him take it.

"You're reading too much into one kiss. It was nothing. I was embarrassed to have an audience, that's why I reacted the way I did."

He said nothing. But his skeptical expression goaded her on.

"Come on, you're not *that* irresistible." She merely had to remind herself of the dangers involved in falling for him and she'd be fine. It wasn't as if she was going into this with her eyes closed. Even *he'd* been up front with her about his limitations.

His gaze lingered on her body. "I give it a week."

"A week for what?"

"That's how long I think you'll last with your no-sex rule."

The awareness that had slammed into her when she was in his arms returned with a vengeance. She wanted him and he knew it. She'd wanted him ever since she'd first seen him on the silver screen.

But most women did. She wasn't stupid enough to act on it.

"Quit trying to scare me off. We've already come this far. We're going to see it through." She got to her feet. "I'm heading home to pack. I suggest you pack, too. We leave for Whiskey Creek in the morning."

"You're staying somewhere else tonight?"

"Yes."

He laughed softly. "See?"

That proved nothing. "See what?"

"You felt it."

"I felt nothing. I just have a lot to do," she said, but she had to sleep sometime, and the fact that she'd decided to stay in her own bed said something, even to her.

He stiffened as she brushed past him but didn't stop her. Neither did he try to talk her into coming back.

"We'll be taking my Lexus to Whiskey Creek, so be ready when I come by in the morning," she said, and left.

Fifteen

Simon's introduction to Gail's hometown started with a sign posted on the meandering highway they'd been traveling since leaving Interstate 5: Welcome to Whiskey Creek, the Heart of the Gold Country. They'd passed through other places, similar in size and architecture. Jackson and Sutter Creek also dated from the Gold Rush—era of the 1800s and looked it. But there was something different about Whiskey Creek. Subtle though it was, Simon noticed it right off. There was a definable unity here, a certain pride evident in the way the buildings were maintained and cared for that made him believe it should've been named Happy Valley.

"What do you think?" Gail adjusted her seat belt so she could turn toward him.

"It's...interesting." He'd insisted on driving, even though he wasn't familiar with the route. He had to retain *some* semblance of control, and she hadn't fought him on that. She seemed happy enough to play the role of navigator.

"You don't like it?"

Resting his left hand over the steering wheel, he used his injured right to slide his sunglasses down and take a better look. "The surrounding countryside is gorgeous. I've just never lived in a small town. I'm not sure how I'll adapt."

She lowered the passenger window and stuck her head out as if she couldn't wait to smell the air. "There's nowhere like the foothills, especially in the fall."

That she loved the area so much surprised him. Although they'd never really socialized when he was her client, they had spent significant time together. Other than an occasional mention of where she came from she'd never talked about Whiskey Creek. But then... she'd always been straight-up business. This was the first glimpse he'd had into her past. He'd never had any reason to take an interest before.

"Why'd you leave here?" he asked.

She lowered the volume on the radio. "For the same reasons I keep coming back. My family lives here. And I know everyone."

"Those are bad things?"

"My father can be...a bit overbearing and opinionated."

He'd already gotten that impression.

"And when you know everyone, there's no chance to break out and be anything other than what people expect," she added. "It can be...confining." She rolled her eyes. "Then there's the inevitable gossip."

"I can't imagine *you've* ever been gossiped about. You always play by the rules." He glanced over to see if she'd refute that statement.

"I've had my less-than-stellar moments."

"Name one."

"No, thanks. Those incidents were painful enough when they happened. No need to relive them." She rummaged through her purse and came up with a pack of gum. "Now that we're married, there will, of course, be more gossip."

"Unlike you, I'm used to being gossiped about." He shook his head when she offered him a piece. "I don't think I could feel at home anywhere I wasn't the center of attention," he teased.

"Then you'll feel right at home here." She tossed him a grin. "Anyway, I had to leave. There's not much opportunity in Whiskey Creek for a PR firm."

"What about in Sacramento? According to the signs I've seen, it isn't far."

"It's still an hour, which makes for a long commute. Unless you want to run one of the stores around here, or maybe a B and B, and we already have two, you're pretty much out of luck in the business world."

He nodded toward A Room with a View Bed and Breakfast, a quaint Victorian perched prominently on Main Street, where the road made a ninety-degree turn. "Tell me we can stay there," he said, but he knew it wasn't likely that she'd change her mind. She'd told him they'd be staying with her father until they could find a rental. He'd heard her confirm it on the phone earlier. He was going to be Martin DeMarco's guest even though he wasn't particularly welcome.

"We have to stay at my dad's, at least for a day or two, or he'll never forgive us," she explained.

"*Us?* He doesn't want me there."

"I can't let him reject you. We're married. We're a package."

"I'm being rescued by a girl." He sighed. "I can't believe my life has come down to this."

If he thought she'd give him a bit of sympathy, he was mistaken. "I hope it's as humbling as it should be," she said.

"Good thing my ego is all but indestructible." He let his gaze stray to the V of her tan dress, which had distracted him all day. As much as he didn't want to find his new "wife" too appealing—they both knew their relationship would best be handled as simply a business transaction—he was intrigued on a number of levels. Mostly, he liked her mind. He'd always admired her quick thinking and no-nonsense, honest approach to life, or he wouldn't have hired her as his PR agent. But there was something more, something about her that just felt...right. She inspired him.

If that was the extent of it, the next two years should progress uneventfully. But in the past few days he'd actually been wondering why he'd never noticed how flawless her skin was. Or how her lips quirked endearingly to one side when she was trying to tell him he was full of bullshit.

"Stop it," she said, nudging his shoulder.

"What?" he asked innocently.

"Just because you're wearing sunglasses, don't think I can't tell what you're looking at."

It was their wedding kiss, he decided. Ever since she'd drawn back almost as soon as their lips touched, he'd been preoccupied with kissing her again. But that wasn't a welcome realization. If he wasn't careful, he'd drag her down before she could pull him up.

"I'm happy to hang out on my own at the B and B, if I'm bothering you," he said.

"Nice try, but I'm not going to my father's without you."

The reminder of what they would soon face quashed his libido. "How difficult *is* Mr. DeMarco?" he asked, slowing for a traffic signal.

"What do you mean?"

The light turned green before he had to stop. "He's never been abusive with you...."

"No. I hope I didn't give you that impression. He's a good man, a *really* good man. It's just that he expects so much of me, and is so easily disappointed. The... force of his personality can be hard to take."

Simon considered that and grimaced. "I don't do well with authority figures."

She didn't attempt to convince him otherwise. That was another thing that made her different. If she said something he could believe it. "No kidding."

He adjusted his seat to give himself more legroom. "So...how do you think this is going to work?"

"We'll figure it out," she said. "At the very least it'll be interesting."

Besides the B and B, they passed an antiques store called Eureka Treasures, Black Gold Coffee, Whiskey Creek Five and Dime, 49er Sweets and a smattering of mom-and-pop-style restaurants, including a diner called Just Like Mom's that could've come right out of the 1960s. There wasn't one fast-food joint or chain grocery store that Simon could see, which made this town and others in the area different from most.

Farther down the street there was a post office, a bike store named Crank It Up and a barbershop, complete with the traditional pole.

"When do we get our own house?" He came to the second stoplight and glanced over to see some flyers taped in the window of Harvey's Hardware. One advertised a tour of a nearby gold mine. Another enticed visitors to go spelunking at a place called Moaning Caverns. The display behind these flyers featured Halloween decorations.

"As soon as Kathy Carmichael, down at KC's Gold Country Realty, is able to find us something suitable."

The hill to the right sported several century-old homes. Others—those along Sutter Street—had been turned into gift shops or art galleries. "Doesn't look like there's a big housing market around here. Will there be anything to choose from?"

"Not much but—" she gave him a pirate's smile "—thanks to you, money's no object, so we'll just take the best one we can get. Picking our lot and getting started on the house you'll build will take more time."

Not if he could help it. He needed to stay busy or he'd revert to his old ways before she could raise a disapproving eyebrow. She'd removed all his coping mechanisms. They hadn't been working particularly well, but they had always provided an escape. "You realize I can't build a house by myself. I've never taken on a project quite that big."

"I have a good friend who's a general contractor. I'm sure he'll be happy to provide any support and guidance you need—for a fee."

"And you think we can build a house in the time we plan to stay here?"

"Probably not, but you can always have Riley take over when we go back to L.A. Then we'll have somewhere to stay when we visit." She conjured up an expression of mock innocence. "Unless you'd like to stay with my father whenever we return."

"Point taken," he grumbled.

Her attention shifted back to her hometown as if she was making note of any subtle changes, but he broke the silence again. "So…you were serious about three months, right? I have to last here for three months and then our Whiskey Creek days are over, except for an occasional visit?"

She touched his arm. "Give it a chance, okay?" She gestured at a small side street jutting off to the right. "Turn here."

Somewhere in his late fifties, Martin DeMarco was a tall, grizzled redhead with erect posture, big shoulders and hands large enough to palm a basketball. He treated Simon with cool reserve, wouldn't address him directly, but said nothing overtly unwelcoming. He didn't say much at all. He greeted his daughter with a stiff nod and suffered through a brief introduction. Then he helped carry their luggage from the car to Gail's old bedroom in his home, which resembled a large cabin. After putting down her suitcase, he gave Simon one long, assessing look, frowned as though he wasn't happy with what he saw and turned back to his daughter.

"Dinner's in the fridge. Go ahead and heat it up if you're hungry." He didn't say it, but the intimation was there: *And feed him if you have to.* "I've got a problem at the station, but it shouldn't take long."

"Anything serious?" she asked.

"No, just Robbie. He can't figure out how to open the till to give change—the little idiot."

"Where's his mother? I thought she was training him."

"She's been trying, but she's not feeling well. This is his first night on his own."

"He'll learn," she said.

With a skeptical grunt, Mr. DeMarco left, but as far as Simon was concerned his absence did little to improve the situation. Joe, Gail's older brother, was still at home, and he was just as tall, just as imposing and just as unhappy with Gail's choice of husband. He'd spent the whole time they were coming in leaning against the counter, drinking a cup of coffee and sizing Simon up.

When they returned to the kitchen, the disapproval rolling off him was offensive, but Simon had expected to encounter disapproval. He did his best to ignore it— until the sound of the older DeMarco's engine disappeared and Joe addressed him. "So. You're the badass."

"Joe! You don't have to be rude," Gail cried, but Simon talked over her. He didn't want her sticking up for him. He'd face these people down on his own. Maybe he'd get his ass kicked by her Goliath of a brother, but he wasn't sure that would be entirely a bad thing. A bit of violence would provide an outlet for the emotions he could no longer dull with sex and alcohol. His temper had never been closer to the surface.

"That's right." He adopted the cocky air so effective in pissing people off. "How'd you know?"

"I read the papers."

Simon lowered his voice as if divulging a fact Joe should already know but was too stupid to figure out. "Do you mean the tabloids? Because in case you hadn't heard, they're quite often full of shit." He spoke at a normal volume again. "But don't let that change your mind. I'm as badass as they come."

"Funny, too. I like that." Lifting his coffee cup, Joe smiled, looking perfectly comfortable—except for the muscle flexing in his cheek, which said otherwise. "But the fact that you're a big movie star doesn't matter that much to me."

Simon felt his muscles tense. "Then why'd you bring it up?"

He set down his cup and straightened. "There's one thing you need to know."

"Joe—" Gail tried to break in. She'd been glancing between them, a worried expression on her face, but Simon pulled her behind him so she couldn't get in the way.

"What's that?"

"I don't care how rich or famous you are. All the shit you're used to getting away with? Won't fly around here. You step on someone's toes in Whiskey Creek, they're going to knock you down a peg. And if you cheat on my sister, I'll be handling that myself. Understood?"

He deserved the lack of faith, the censure, so Simon tried to take it like a man. But that wasn't easy when it came from someone who had no clue what his life had been like with Bella. "I won't embarrass you or your family. You have my word."

Joe turned to rinse his cup. "For what it's worth," he muttered under his breath.

Had he not added that, Simon would've been able to let it go. As it was, the angry words he'd been biting back rose to his tongue. "Now that we've covered what went wrong in *my* marriage, what happened to yours?"

The question took Joe off guard. No doubt thanks to his size, he'd expected to swagger around and do the big-brother routine without any backlash. "Come again?"

"You heard me."

"None of your damn business." He dried his hands and tossed the towel aside.

"Simon," Gail warned, but Simon ignored her.

"You can keep a scorecard on me but I can't keep one on you?"

Joe sneered at him. "I don't know what you're talking about."

"Sure you do. Few women walk away from a perfect husband."

When Joe's face flushed, Simon thought he'd start swinging. He had more than three inches and fifty pounds on Simon. With an injured right hand, Simon wouldn't even be able to land a decent punch. But he wasn't about to back down. Trying to change his life was hard enough without taking the crap this guy was dishing out.

Fortunately, Joe didn't start a fight. Chest rising and falling fast, he sent an accusing glare at his sister, as if she must've revealed his situation, and stormed out. A second later, his truck's engine roared to life and tires squealed as he peeled down the drive.

"Wow," Gail breathed, and crumpled into a chair at the kitchen table.

Prepared to defend himself further, Simon whirled to confront her. He thought she might be upset that he wasn't willing to tolerate her brother's abuse, but her next words surprised him.

"Good job."

"Good job?" he repeated. "I just pissed off your brother."

"He was pissed off to begin with. He's probably been waiting to do that to you ever since I told him we were getting married."

Simon gave himself a couple of seconds to process the fact that she wasn't going to turn on him. "But now he hates my guts."

"That's okay. At least he understands that he can't push you around. Respect is more important than anything else. Respect will create a foundation. But, just so you don't walk into something you aren't prepared for in the future, you need to be aware that he has his limits."

"So do I," he grumbled.

She regarded him quizzically "How did you know?"

He had no idea what she was talking about. "What?"

"That he's been married before. That Suzie left him."

"There's a picture of him with a woman and two little girls hanging in the hallway."

"Oh...right." She nodded. "Of course. But *he* could've left *her.*"

"I figured he wouldn't be living here if that was the case."

"I see." She studied him. "It's going to be tough settling in."

"I can handle it," he said. "Don't worry about me." But he was suddenly craving alcohol so badly it was all he could do not to head for the closest bar or liquor store. "Let's get out of here, go to dinner."

She hesitated. "You're sure you're okay?"

"Fine."

"There's a good Italian place around the corner."

"Great. Maybe there's a casino nearby, too."

"As a matter of fact, there is. Some of the locals work there, but I'm not sure that's the best place for you to go." She picked up her purse. "Still on the hunt for an acceptable vice?"

He pulled her car keys from his pocket. "I need some kind of distraction. And I'm guessing you don't want to provide it."

"What happened to his hand?"

Gail sat at the kitchen table, only now it was her father who stood at the sink. She'd had Simon drop her off after dinner. Although she wasn't happy about the risks involved, he'd insisted on heading to the casino. He said he needed a break, some time alone. She'd finally agreed because she knew she'd ensure the failure she was trying to avoid if she smothered him or pressed him too hard. Besides, she'd wanted some private time with her family, felt that might take the edge off their reaction to her marriage, but Joe hadn't yet returned. "He had an accident with a power saw."

The smell of the coffee her father had just put on filled the room as he eyed her skeptically. "Are you sure he didn't get in another fight? Go after his ex-wife's brother again?"

She scowled. "I'm sure," she said, and left it at that. The details wouldn't help convince Martin she'd made a good match.

With a click of his tongue, he shook his head. "What were you thinking, marrying someone like him, Gail?"

"Someone like him?" she echoed.

"Someone so shallow…and reckless…and stupid…"

Since he seemed to be searching for more adjectives, she stopped him before he could continue. "Simon is anything but stupid." The other things made Gail defensive, too. Coming into their "deal," she'd felt the same irritation and repugnance for Simon's behavior as her father did. She'd sympathized completely with Bella. But Simon's lack of action when he cut his hand had made her realize that his behavior wasn't the result of elitism or arrogance, as most people believed. He'd been so emotionally distraught he couldn't cope.

She wanted her father and everyone else to put his past in the proper context, but Simon wouldn't allow anyone to get close enough to gain any sort of understanding. If not for his meltdown, and how she'd been drawn into it, she wouldn't have come close enough to understand him, either. "He's been through a lot."

"So you've said. But if you're talking about his divorce, I don't buy it. I went through a divorce, too. And I had kids to raise and not nearly as much money."

Her mother had walked out on her father for an old high school sweetheart. They were now married and living in Phoenix. Gail knew how painful losing Linda had been for Martin. She also knew it had changed the way he behaved every bit as much as Simon's divorce had changed him. He obviously felt his situation had been harder. But Gail wasn't convinced. At least there'd been no fame to complicate matters, no media coverage to broadcast every sordid detail, which would've made everything that much worse, especially for such a proud man. Even so, Martin had become strict and controlling, especially where she and Joe were concerned. There were times Gail suspected her mother would've remained a part of her life if not for her father, who could be autocratic and difficult to deal with.

Gail wanted to tell him those things, but she knew he wouldn't take kindly to the criticism. Besides, *he* could allude to her mother, but Linda was still a taboo subject for everyone else, even after all the years that had passed.

"He's worth trying to save," she said simply.

"That's what you're doing? *Saving* him?" He shook a finger at her. "You can't save people from themselves, Gail. You're foolish to think you can."

"So… I should quit without even trying?" she challenged.

He didn't seem to have an answer for that.

"We're already married, Dad. All I'm asking is that you treat him with some respect while we're here, give him a chance."

The door opened, and they both glanced up. Gail

feared it was Simon. She wasn't quite ready for him. But it was Joe who walked in.

Her brother gazed around the kitchen, then speared her with an angry glare. "Where's pretty boy?"

Prepared to take on the two of them, if necessary, she squared her shoulders. "You started that fight, Joe."

Her father pulled out a chair and sat down across from her. "What fight?"

"After you left, he tried to belittle Simon," Gail explained.

"That couldn't have been hard," her father said wryly.

She folded her arms. "Maybe not, but he lived to regret it. Simon feels attacked on all sides. He'll snap at anything, even if he's the one who'd take the worst of any fight it might cause."

"Why'd you bring him here?" Joe demanded. "You know how we feel."

Scooting her chair away from the table, she stood. Her father and brother were so big, so…overpowering, they could be intimidating even when they weren't teaming up against her. "What are you saying, big brother? That I should've come without him? Or that *I* should've stayed away, too? Because Simon and I can head over to the B and B if you don't want us here—"

Her father raised his hand in a calming gesture. "Hold on. There's no need for that. Simon's here now. We'll make the best of it."

Joe wasn't willing to let it go quite so easily. "You don't expect this marriage to last, do you? Because I can tell you right now it won't."

For a second, Gail wished she'd be able to prove him wrong. But that was crazy. Under normal circumstances, Simon wouldn't have given her the time of day. No doubt, once he had Ty back, he'd return to Hollywood and all the women who'd throw themselves at him—and forget about her. He was with her for Ty's sake, and only for Ty's sake. He'd made that clear from the beginning.

"Maybe it won't," she admitted. "But that's okay."

"No, it's not," her father argued. "You don't want to go through a divorce, Gail."

"It's too late to worry about that! I took the risk when I married him. All I ask is that you don't make my life or my marriage any more difficult by rejecting my husband."

Her words met with silence. She'd made an impact, showed them no good could come out of how they were acting. She could tell by the sheepish expression on her brother's face and the stoic one on her father's that they suddenly understood it was too late to talk her out of being with Simon.

"He needs friendship," she went on. "I'm asking you to offer him that and see what you get in return. If you hate him, just be sure you hate him because he's earned it. Don't hate him on principle."

Joe sagged into the seat next to her father and propped his elbows on the table. "You want us to forget what we've heard about him and give him a clean slate."

Intent on her appeal, she sat down again, too. "Why not? You don't even know him! All you know is what you've read and heard in the media."

"And from you," he pointed out.

Her conscience pricked her. "I was wrong to say what I did. I was reacting to…false perceptions. Just like you're doing now. Anyway, can you imagine going to your wife's home and being treated the way he was treated tonight?"

Joe toyed with the sugar bowl sitting on the table. "I

know what that's like. My in-laws hated me because I wasn't interested in their religion."

"Exactly."

"You always did know how to make me feel like shit," he muttered.

She managed a halfhearted grin. "We're siblings. That's my job."

Her father got up to pour himself some coffee. "So tell me this, Gail. If the two of you are so in love, why are you here in Whiskey Creek and not on some extravagant honeymoon celebrating your marriage?"

She could no longer meet his eyes. "This is about something more important than that."

"Like what?"

The memory of finding Simon on the floor of his woodshop came into sharp focus. After that, a honeymoon hadn't even crossed her mind. She'd just wanted to help him recover. "This home has always been my safe harbor."

Her father's eyes widened. "But it can't be the only place someone who's *that* famous has to go."

"Anywhere else wouldn't have the support he needs. This is the best place *I* know. The one I trust. I want him to have the peace of mind you've both given me. *That's* why I brought him here."

After setting his cup on the table, her father came over to crouch in front of her. "He's not a stray dog, Gail," he said, taking her hands. "He's a wealthy movie star who'll probably break your heart—"

"If he does…he does. He's human, Dad. And he's going through hell. Sure, he's asked for a lot of it but everyone screws up now and then. He needs a way to break his fall. I'm trying to give him that."

Another silence descended as he considered her words.

"Fine." Her brother relented first. "I'll be on my best behavior from here on out. You can get us to do anything. I think you know that."

Tears filled her eyes, which surprised her. She hadn't realized this meant so much to her. "Thanks, Joe. Just give him a chance. That's all I ask."

"Okay." Her father squeezed her hands and stood as if that made it official. "Far as I'm concerned, he has a clean slate. But if he hurts you—"

"He can't hurt me, Dad. I know what to expect."

He returned to his coffee. "You just want to help him. That's it."

"That's it." She wasn't sure when her motivation had changed, when she'd become more interested in seeing Simon get back on his feet than in saving her business, but there was no doubt she was far more emotionally committed than she'd been before.

"At least it makes sense to me now," her father said. "But pity is a hell of a reason to marry someone."

It was more than pity. It was sadness over his lost potential, even a little of the hero worship she'd felt for her favorite movie star. She knew that worship was what frightened her family. It frightened her, too. Maybe she'd become disenchanted with him in certain ways, but it was hard to get on an equal footing with an idol.

"Thanks, Dad."

"You're too good for him," her father added when she came around to kiss his cheek. "But I'm willing to give him the opportunity to prove me wrong."

She offered them both a watery smile. She'd known they'd come through for her. They always did. "Thanks."

Sixteen

Gail stared at the ceiling in her old bedroom for three hours. She'd been waiting for Simon to return, but he hadn't come. She couldn't help fearing he'd driven to Sacramento, left her car in long-term parking and taken a plane to L.A. Or that he'd gone home with one of the cocktail waitresses at the casino. She'd asked her family to give him a chance, but even *she* wasn't sure she could fully trust him. If making the changes he needed to make were easy, he would've been able to do it on his own.

But she'd doubted him once before, and he hadn't been breaking his commitment to her. Not that the memory of finding him hurt made the passing time go by any faster. Surely, he hadn't gotten into a car accident or a fight....

As it neared one-thirty, she was too anxious to stay in bed. Getting a sweatshirt, she pulled it over her tank top and pajama bottoms, then went downstairs, where she made a cup of hot cocoa and sat on the front porch.

The weather was clear but cool, somewhere in the low fifties. A gentle wind whispered through the trees in the yard, causing the red and gold leaves still clinging to the branches to fall and rustle against those on the ground. This wasn't a traditional neighborhood. There was no curb or gutter. No square blocks, either. Just a narrow country road with two neighbors farther down, where it turned to dirt.

Her father had built the house shortly after he married her mother. She and Joe had both been born here.

It was good to be back. She just hoped she hadn't made a mistake in bringing Simon with her.

Because she hadn't expected it, hadn't even glanced at the driveway, it took her a moment to realize her car was parked there. Blinking several times, she tried to see inside it.

Simon was behind the wheel, looking back at her. How long had he been sitting there? And why?

When she stood, he got out and came toward her. "You okay?" she asked.

"Not too bad. At least I'm sober."

That answered one of her questions. Maybe. She wasn't sure she could take his word for it. But he walked without weaving or stumbling.

Cradling her cup to keep her fingers warm, she waited for him to draw closer before speaking again. "Did you win any money?"

He stopped a couple of feet away. "I was up at first."

"And at the end?"

"Lost about twenty grand."

His speech wasn't slurred, either, which relieved her for several reasons. A DUI would destroy what she was trying to accomplish with his image, not to mention all the worse things that could've happened if he'd been driving while intoxicated. "Gambling's an expensive vice."

"Maybe I should go back to drinking."

"That could cost you even more."

He motioned to the dark, shadowy porch behind her and the swinging chair she'd ignored. "What are you doing out here?"

"Just getting used to being home."

His eyes narrowed in disbelief. "Really?"

"And wondering when you were coming back." She figured she might as well admit it; he'd already guessed she'd been worried.

"You thought I might be breaking the terms of our agreement."

She felt bad for doubting him, but she knew the first few days and weeks were going to be the hardest. And the way her brother had treated him... That could've acted as a trigger. "Yes."

"I almost did," he said, and circumvented her to go inside.

At least he was honest.

Gail waited another fifteen or twenty minutes. She wasn't sure what to say to Simon. One part of her wanted to know which had been more of a temptation—alcohol or women. The other part was too afraid to hear his answer. As Josh had so aptly pointed out, she had no claim on him in an emotional sense. But it still wasn't easy to acknowledge that the man she'd married, for whatever reason, might've been tempted to go home with someone else.

The next two years were going to be even more of a challenge than she'd realized.

When she thought he'd had enough time to go to bed *and* to sleep, she carried her empty cup into the house, rinsed it in the sink and crept up the stairs. The house was quiet and all the lights were off. She didn't turn any on because she didn't want to wake her father or brother—or Simon, for that matter.

Simon was in bed. She could see the shape of his body in the moonlight streaming through the window. Her room faced the yard, which wasn't really a yard so much as raw land that backed up to the mountain. Without any neighbors around to worry about, she rarely bothered to lower the blinds.

Being as quiet as possible, she yanked off her sweatshirt and slipped under the covers.

But Simon wasn't asleep. When he shifted, she got the impression it was to avoid contact with her, which gave her some idea of how he was feeling. "Something wrong?" she asked.

"I'm not sure I'm going to stay," he said.

She'd been so afraid he'd give up, had felt the tension of that fear, the worry eating at her ever since she'd said, "I do." "Why? What happened tonight?"

"I almost took off, drove to L.A."

Was that what he'd been doing in the car? Thinking about leaving? "I'm sorry if it was my brother who—"

"It wasn't his fault," he broke in. "He has every right to be defensive of you. I'd be defensive, too, if you were my sister."

She fussed nervously with the blanket. "Then what caused the...flight response?"

"I don't see how my involvement in your life can be a good thing."

Releasing the blanket, she curled her arms around her pillow. "Why not?"

"Because it'll end. In two years, just like we planned."

She lifted her head, trying to see his face in the dark. "What makes you think I expect anything else?"

"I'm afraid at some point saving your business won't be enough to compensate for what you'll sacrifice."

"There's more in it for me than that. There's the money, of course. It might not seem like a large sum to you, but it's a fortune to me. Don't get me wrong. I'm earning every penny of it, so I won't feel bad taking it, but…there's that. And it'll be gratifying to see you on your feet again and in control of your life. I feel as if I'm doing America a great service by helping you salvage your career. They want to see more of you in the movies, and so do I."

"But I'm afraid you don't really understand what'll happen on a personal level."

"We spelled everything out in the contract. What else is there to understand?"

"This could get very complicated."

"It's already complicated."

"Not as bad as it will be with time." He rubbed a hand over his face. "This is just the beginning."

"What are you talking about?"

"I'm talking about met and unmet expectations and desires, our developing friendship, the obligations that'll go with it, becoming accustomed to having each other around. I'm talking about jealousy, familiarity, entitlement and all the other ways our lives will become entwined, including relationships we form along the way with the people around us. Our 'deal' sounded simple enough when we made it, even to me. But I didn't really like you then, didn't see myself as *ever* liking you. I certainly didn't anticipate coming to Whiskey Creek and getting to know the people who are closest to you."

"Sometimes you can be too blunt," she said.

"I'm trying to be fair!"

"That's the problem? That's what has you so freaked out? You *like* me?"

"Yes, and you seem to like me."

"I do, but that's good. It means our marriage won't be as miserable as we both thought."

There were a few seconds of silence. "The problem is, I will never *love* you, Gail," he said. "You understand that, right? I don't want to find myself in the same situation I was in with Bella—*ever*. I won't allow another woman to hold that kind of power over me."

She nibbled her lip. He had loved Bella. He was *still* in love with her, just as Gail had expected. "I'm not trying to keep you, Simon."

"I know that. Now. But…what if it changes? What if we make love and—"

"We're not going to make love. I've already told you that. We can keep it simple if we want to. You just worry about staying clean and sober and acting like the dutiful husband in public. I'll take care of myself."

He was staring at her; she could see the shine in his eyes. "I just hope you don't live to regret getting involved with me. I don't want to leave you worse off than when I found you. I have enough on my conscience," he said. Then he rolled over and went to sleep.

When Gail woke up, she had her face pressed to Simon's back. He was wearing a T-shirt and a pair of pajama bottoms, probably because her bed wasn't as big as his and that meant there wasn't much room to avoid each other. But she didn't care about staying on her side at this particular moment. She was too relieved he hadn't left. When she'd finally dropped off into an uneasy sleep she'd worried that he'd be gone by morning.

But he was still here, and it seemed he'd actually

stayed in bed and been able to get some rest. She was so happy about those two things that she slid an arm around his waist, gave him a squeeze and kissed his back. "You made it."

"Hmm?" His arm covered hers, holding it in place, but he seemed reluctant to wake.

"Your first night in Whiskey Creek is behind you."

Letting her go, he stretched and turned to face her. "Once I closed my eyes I didn't even stir. I can't tell you the last time that's happened to me."

She leaned over him, smiling. "It's a sign. Don't you think?"

Reaching up, he tucked her long hair behind one ear. "What kind of sign?"

"That last night you were worried for nothing. You're where you should be. I'm glad you didn't give up."

"I was too exhausted to drive, anyway."

He could never take any credit when he did something right. That would destroy his bad-boy image. But she was so proud of him she couldn't help bending her head to kiss his whisker-roughened cheek. "We can both get everything we want—as friends."

"You're becoming pretty comfortable with me," he said as she pulled away.

"We like each other now, remember?"

His gaze dipped to her braless chest. "I think I'm liking you a little too much."

"Meaning…"

"What do you have against friends with benefits?"

She made a face. "Quit pretending. Last night you acted as if sex between us would be a terrible thing."

"It would be. But that doesn't mean I don't want it."

"Sorry. We can be affectionate but not intimate. That's how we'll get through the next two years."

He covered his eyes with one arm. "Sounds safe—but boring."

Now that he wasn't watching her, she let her gaze range over him. He was so attractive—even with the imprint of the bedding on his cheek and his hair mussed. She loved the rough-hewn angles of his face, the smoothness of his golden skin, the thickness of his unruly hair.

"You like what you see?"

She felt herself blush. "So I was looking. Big deal. You're handsome. Everyone knows that."

"Don't worry. In case you haven't heard, it's only skin-deep."

She'd believed that once, but not anymore. He had plenty of good qualities. One of them was an active conscience. Who knew?

"Fine. Then I won't be tempted. *Safe* is our new buzzword," she said, and hopped out of bed.

His biceps bulged as he propped up his head with his arms. "Are you really getting up?"

"We both are."

"Why? It's early."

"We have a coffee date."

He watched as she searched through her suitcase. *"We?"*

"As in…both of us?"

"That's the 'we' I thought you meant. Who are we meeting?"

"The friends I grew up with."

"What time?" He didn't sound particularly enthusiastic.

She glanced at the clock. It was 7:10. "In twenty minutes."

Sprawling across the bed, he shoved his head under her pillow. "Can't we put it off for an hour or two?"

"I wish. There's no time to even shower. But...unlike us, they have to work."

"How many people are we talking about?" His voice was muffled, but she could understand him.

"Depends. It's a standing date for anyone who can come."

"Do your friends know you're back? Are they expecting you?"

She came up with some black jeans, a pair of gorgeous leather boots and a turquoise sweater she'd bought with Simon's credit card at the mall. It was an attractive outfit—one that made the most of a slender figure. Maybe she'd known these people for years and their opinion wasn't likely to change, but she wanted to look decent. She certainly didn't want her husband to outshine her, although that was pretty much a given.

"No. My dad's the only person I told," she said. "And he's the one person in this town you can trust to keep what you tell him quiet. Everyone except Joe is on a 'need to know' basis." Callie had tried to reach her several times, but except for a few texts saying she was happy and not to ruin it for her, she hadn't responded. She hadn't been ready to deal with Callie's reaction to the news of her marriage. But she'd be doing that this morning—with all her friends.

Checking over her shoulder to make sure Simon still had his head under the pillow, she faced the corner to change. But a second after her tank top hit the floor, the clarity of his voice indicated he was looking right at her.

"Okay, that's going too far."

She glanced at him again. He was watching her with predatory interest. The intensity of his expression lit a fire inside her, but she did her best to shrug it off. "Surely you've seen a woman's bare back before."

"I don't think I've ever seen one as tempting as yours."

"Getting desperate already?" She laughed to let him know she wasn't convinced he was remotely sincere, and he didn't argue with her. But when he spoke again, the gruff edge to his voice left no question as to how her near-nudity affected him.

"Turn around."

It was a challenge, a command. She told herself she'd be crazy to respond. They'd just gone over all the reasons they had to be careful not to let their situation get too complicated. But categorizing their relationship as affectionate friends somehow took the pressure off. It made her feel safe, as if she could relax a little now that they'd recommitted themselves to the rules.

"Just for a second," he coaxed.

He *did* sound desperate. And she *was* tempted. Especially when she considered that over the course of the next two years they'd probably see each other in various stages of undress all the time. It wouldn't be a catastrophe if he caught a glimpse of her now, would it?

Telling herself to lighten up and do something wild and exciting for a change, she hesitated. She'd always been too conservative, and she'd never felt more like a stereotypical librarian than since she'd started hanging out with Simon.

Innocent. Straitlaced. Inflexible. Those were the words Simon had used to describe her....

Determined to shake him up a bit, she turned while she had the nerve.

His expression was worth it. She'd shocked him— just as she'd intended.

"God," he whispered as his gaze latched on to her breasts.

She didn't stick around long enough to find out what he might say or do next. Suddenly willing to risk having her brother or father catch her sneaking into the bathroom to change, she put on her sweater, grabbed her bra and jeans and fled.

That was a mistake.

It took Simon all of ten minutes to get his heart rate to return to normal. He should never have baited Gail. He'd mostly been teasing when he'd thrown out that challenge, had done it to see how she might react. She was so prim and proper; it was fun just to make her blush.

Never had he expected her to turn and show him her breasts....

And now he couldn't get the vision out of his mind.

She'd certainly gotten the last laugh in that encounter.

She knocked softly, then opened the door and poked her head through. "You coming?"

"Gail..." he started.

She raised her eyebrows. "What?"

She was pretending it had never happened. Considering what they'd discussed last night, it was probably best if he did, too.

"Never mind," he said. "I'll be right there."

Seventeen

For all of Whiskey Creek's old-fashioned charm, the coffee shop felt current. It listed the menu on a chalkboard, boasted of selling only fair-trade coffee, used organic beans and offered chai and other options. Several people sat with laptops at small round tables, taking advantage of the free Wi-Fi.

"Now *this* feels like home." Simon breathed deep, enjoying the comforting scent of fresh-ground coffee as the door swept shut behind them.

Gail didn't respond. She was too busy searching the crowd.

She waved to a group sitting in one of two large booths. "There they are. Over in the corner. Looks like..." She angled her head to see them all. "Ted, Eve, Callie, Cheyenne, Riley and...oh, boy. Sophia."

"What's wrong with Sophia?" Simon asked.

She lowered her voice. "No one likes her."

"Maybe no one will like me, either."

"Don't worry." She patted his back. "This won't be as painful as you're expecting."

"Why would I expect it to be painful? Meeting your family was such fun."

She nudged him. "Stop with the sarcasm."

Her friends quickly spotted her.

"Oh, my gosh! Gail's home!"

"Where?"

"Look…and she's brought Simon!"

"Here we go," she murmured. "I hope your acting's up to par."

He wished he hadn't left his sunglasses behind. He didn't care if it was too dark inside the café to bother with them. The world he was living in since Gail had started this latest PR campaign felt so much more up close and in his face. "Hey, I'm a pro, remember?"

By that point, everyone in the coffee shop had turned to stare. But Simon was used to attracting attention. Pretending not to notice, he waited for Gail to order, then asked for an espresso. She hurried over to her friends while he paid, leaving him to approach them on his own, but she'd been right. Joining the group wasn't nearly as awkward as he'd initially feared, once the suddenness of their marriage had been handled and they moved on to other topics.

Fortunately, these people weren't as obvious in their disapproval as Gail's brother and father had been. A few of them sent Simon sidelong glances, as if they weren't sure what to make of his presence, but they smiled politely if he caught their eye and shifted their attention—to whoever was speaking or their coffee or fruit and yogurt.

As they chatted about this or that, Simon was more than happy to kick back and enjoy his espresso. He liked watching Gail, he realized, liked how animated and expressive she was, especially now that she was in her element. Of course, he also liked recalling the image of her standing in the bedroom this morning, wearing nothing but her pajama bottoms as she turned to face him—

"Ted's an author," Gail explained, cutting into his thoughts.

Simon had lost the thread of the conversation. Sitting up, he cleared his throat and attempted to pretend otherwise. "What kind of books does he write?"

"Thrillers. Already has two out."

With that enthusiastic lead-in, Simon expected Ted to ask for the usual favor. Hundreds of authors sent their work to his production company, hoping to gain interest in a movie adaption. But to Simon's relief, the conversation moved on to another guy, someone by the name of Kyle Houseman, who wasn't there. Kyle was going through a nasty divorce. It soon became apparent that everyone blamed his wife.

Simon guessed he was the only one in the group who felt sorry for the maligned soon-to-be ex. He knew how being "the problem" felt. He also knew that a divorce was never as clear-cut as it appeared.

After the talk of Kyle's divorce, a woman with black hair and a widow's peak—Eve Something—spoke up. "What would you guys think if I started a new marketing campaign for the B and B focusing on those scary stories we used to pass around as kids?"

"The ones where we claimed the inn was haunted?" This was Sophia. Simon had noticed that every time she tried to contribute, everyone else immediately stiffened.

"Last I heard, you wanted to keep a lid on the history of the place for fear of scaring off patrons," she said.

Eve shrugged in response but wouldn't quite meet her gaze. "That's true, but...times have changed. I need to try a more aggressive approach."

All of these people were attractive, Simon thought.

Sophia, with her wide blue eyes, brown hair and porcelain skin, was probably the prettiest, but he wasn't as taken with her looks as he would've expected to be. He returned his attention to Eve of the widow's peak. "You own A Room with a View?"

She blushed as if she was surprised he'd get involved in the conversation. "No. The other B and B—the Gold Nugget Inn. It's not quite as nice or as prominently situated."

"It *is* nice," Gail chimed in. "But Simon hasn't seen it." She turned to him. "Eve's parents bought it just after they were married and fixed it up, so it's been in her family for years. It's around the bend, heading out of town to the north. Cheyenne—" she motioned to her other friend "—helps run it. I'll show it to you later."

Riley entered the conversation. Gail had introduced him as her contractor friend, so Simon had made a special note of his name. "Do you think that story we used to tell is true? About the young daughter of the couple who built the Gold Nugget being murdered in the basement?"

"It is." Cheyenne contributed this remark. She'd been listening quietly, seemed to hang on every word, but she came across as the type who typically kept her thoughts to herself. "When we first moved to town my mother dragged me and my sister into the cemetery and said if we didn't take good care of her while she was sick, the same evil that got little Mary Hatfield would come after us."

"That's so out of line." This came from Callie, the only member of the group who seemed unwilling to accept Simon. She'd frowned when they were introduced and bristled whenever he looked at her. "But knowing her, it doesn't surprise me," she added.

"You were in high school when you moved here," Gail said to Cheyenne. "I hope you knew better than to believe her."

Cheyenne's somber gray eyes focused on Gail. "I absolutely believed her. There was no telling what she might do."

"That was so unnecessary," Ted put in.

"Exactly," Eve agreed. "They would've taken care of her. Look at them now that the cancer is back."

"She's my mother," Cheyenne said. "What else can I do? Anyway, I don't want to talk about Anita. We were talking about the inn."

"Tell them what you found at the library, Chey," Eve prompted.

"You tell them," she responded, but Gail joined Eve in prodding her.

"What'd you find?"

Cheyenne stirred the whipped cream into whatever drink she'd ordered—hot chocolate?—as she began to speak. "When Eve first mentioned the idea, I went down to the county library and researched the story. I found an old newspaper article dated August 1, 1898, that said the girl's father came upon her strangled in the basement."

Ted nodded. "That's the same story I heard. They never figured out who did it."

"I used to be so afraid of seeing Mary's ghost," Eve said.

"And you want to use that tragedy for marketing purposes?" Callie looked horrified. "Don't you think that's kind of…morbid?"

Eve shrugged. "It is but, like I said, I've got to do something."

"That'll be taking things in a new direction, all right," Riley said with a laugh.

It was obvious that Eve didn't appreciate his attitude.

"Will you change the name, too?" Sophia wanted to know. "All Hallows Inn would be chilling."

Slumping in her seat, Eve played with a sugar packet. "I'm willing to do anything. The place needs updating and repairs, and I don't have the money. I don't want to lose it to the bank. So I'll have to get creative. If I make the wear-and-tear part of the theme, I might be able to limp along for another year or two until I can get on my feet."

"Makes sense to me." Gail reached across the table to squeeze her hand. "When you're ready, I'll help you put together a press packet so we can get the word out."

Eve smiled her thanks.

"I don't know...." Riley wasn't convinced. "Might be too gimmicky, Eve."

"I disagree," Cheyenne piped up. "I think we should do it."

Everyone seemed surprised that she would argue with him.

"There's so much interest in the supernatural," she went on. "We should hire some good fortune-tellers and offer free tarot readings on check-in, really go with the theme."

Eve turned her attention to Simon. "What do you think?"

Simon hadn't expected to be singled out when he was the least likely to have an opinion. He searched his mind for some useful idea. "Well, if you want to go in a darker direction... I could come up with some interesting props from various films that might add an Alfred Hitchcock air to the place."

She perked up. "That's a great suggestion! But… won't real movie props be expensive?"

"They don't have to be," he said. "I happen to know some people in the industry." He heard a few chuckles at the understatement. "I'll see what I can arrange."

"That's *so* nice." Eve looked at Gail as if to say she liked him, and Gail smiled, but the atmosphere grew tense as soon as someone mentioned a guy named Matt.

"Have you seen him yet?" Ted asked Gail.

Everyone fell silent. Clearly, they'd all been dying to ask the same question.

Gail poured more cream into her coffee even though she didn't usually take very much. "No, not yet. We just got in last night."

"He's been here a couple days already," Sophia said. "I saw him at Just Like Mom's last night."

"How does he look?" someone else wondered.

Eve answered. "Better than ever."

"What about his knee?" Gail asked.

"He's wearing a brace, but he's walking on it," Ted told her.

Gail added even more cream to her coffee. "Will he ever get to play again?"

"Hard to say," Riley replied. "No one knows."

Simon's gaze circled the group. Normally he would've let this go, as he had the talk about Kyle Houseman. But there was a definite undercurrent here, and it seemed to be swirling around Gail. "Matt is…"

Gail seemed eager to answer before anyone else could. "Just another friend."

"He plays football for the Packers, when he's not injured," Eve said.

"He's part of the group?" Simon asked, trying to clarify.

"Not really." This came from Eve again. "I mean… he's not one of the original members. We all graduated the same year. Matt's three years older."

"He's a *great* guy." When Callie said this as if he was the perfect contrast to Simon, Gail made a point of checking the time.

"Whoa, don't some of you need to be at work?"

"Yeah, Chey and I are already late," Eve agreed. "Jane's there cooking breakfast, but she'll need us to help serve."

Everyone stood. As they cleared the table of plates and cups, Callie pulled Gail aside, but Simon could hear what she said.

"What the hell are you doing?"

Gail met Simon's eyes over her friend's head. "Nothing, why?"

"I can't believe you married him. Already! Didn't you think we'd want to know you were that serious before seeing it on TV?"

"I told you we were dating."

"Dating's a little different, Gail."

"We didn't plan it, Callie. We just…decided to do it. It happened very quickly."

"I'm sure it did. Let's hope you don't end up broken-hearted and divorced just as quickly." Callie whirled around to glare at Simon. "Nice of you to come and meet the family, even if it is too late for us to talk her out of ruining her life."

"I didn't realize we needed to get your approval," he responded dryly.

Callie turned back to Gail and said something else that sounded harsh, but Simon missed it because Riley had approached him. "Hey, sorry about your injury." He gestured at the bandage still protecting Simon's stitches. "That sucks."

"I certainly have a new appreciation for how often I use my right hand." Simon glanced over to see if he could catch another snippet of the Callie/Gail exchange, but Callie had left. It was Sophia who was talking to Gail now.

"What do you two have planned for today?" Riley asked, maintaining a separate conversation with him.

"We're hoping to meet up with someone named Kathy and take a look at some rental property."

"You're planning to stay *here*?" Riley spoke loudly enough that everyone still there turned toward them. "What about your acting career?"

Simon held up his injured hand. "I'm taking a couple months off."

When he saw that he also had Gail's attention, Riley directed his next question to her. "You're leaving Big Hit in the hands of someone else?"

"I am. My assistant is going to be running the show for a bit. We were actually hoping to hire you to help Simon build us a house."

"I'd be happy to do that," he said. "You know my number. Give me a call."

"Sounds like we'll get to see more of you," Sophia said to Simon as Riley moved toward the exit. "That's great! I was just going to say I'd love to have the two of you over for dinner sometime, if you're interested."

Sophia's enthusiasm created a stark contrast with Callie's anger. Simon couldn't help responding to it. "Sure. We'll come to dinner. When?"

She seemed surprised and relieved at the same time, as if she hadn't expected an acceptance. "Day after to-morrow? I mean, I don't know if my husband will be home. Skip travels a lot on business. But Alexa will be there."

"Alexa is…"

"My daughter."

Dinner sounded fine to Simon. At least he'd met someone who was eager to offer him friendship. "Fine. We'll see you then."

Gail took his arm. "Actually, we don't know our plans yet. Can we call you?"

Sophia's smile briefly wobbled but she managed to keep it in place. "Of course."

The other woman's disappointment nearly made Gail relent. She paused as if she was tempted, then seemed to think better of it. "Ready to go?" she asked, turning to him instead.

"Whenever you are." They said goodbye to those who remained. Then Simon led Gail from the shop and out into a sunny fall day. While they were within earshot of the others, they talked about the weather, their search for a rental, how nice her friends were.

But as soon as they got in the car he said, "Who's Matt?"

Eighteen

"You just met six of my friends. And you want to talk about one who wasn't even there?" she said as she put on her seat belt.

This was clearly a deflection. But Simon allowed it. For the moment. "Okay, let's talk about Sophia." He buckled his own belt. "Why did you refuse her invitation to dinner?"

"I didn't refuse it. I said I'd call."

He started the car. "Will you?"

"I don't know."

"Why?" he asked as he shifted into Reverse.

She blew out a sigh. "I'm having a hard time forgiving her."

"For?"

Facing the window as he backed out of the parking space, she waved at Ted, who was climbing into his SUV. "A lot of reasons."

"We're here for three months. I think you've got time to explain."

"It's old gossip," she said as if it didn't matter, but obviously it did, or she wouldn't be holding a grudge.

They reached the exit, where he waited for an opening in traffic. "Everyone else knows, right?"

"Of course. There are no secrets in Whiskey Creek."

"Then you might as well fill me in."

"Fine." She turned off the radio. "Back when we were in high school, her father was the mayor. She was an only child and very spoiled. She was also the most popular girl in school and dated Scott Harris, the best basketball player Eureka High has ever seen." Her voice softened. "Scott was Joe's best friend. And he was like another brother to me."

Simon merged onto Main Street: Speed Limit 25. Just as well he hadn't brought the Ferrari. "This story doesn't feel like it's going in a good direction."

"No. He lost his life in a drunk-driving accident, and most people here blame Sophia."

He winced. "Including you."

"Maybe. To a point," she said, obviously not wanting to commit herself. "It's hard *not* to blame her."

A bicyclist swerved around the corner. Simon swung wide to make room. "What happened?"

"He was expecting her to join him at a party one night, but she didn't come. When someone mentioned that she'd been seen with another guy earlier in the day, he took off to find her, even though he was far too drunk to get behind the wheel."

"No one tried to stop him?"

"Of course. He pretended to change his mind, then slipped out when the rest of us relaxed and stopped paying attention."

Simon could guess what happened next. "He crashed?"

"Wound up in a ditch. It was too late by the time the paramedics arrived."

"I'm sorry."

She seemed lost in the memory. "He would've made a wonderful husband and father, had he been given the chance."

"*Was* she with someone else?" he asked as they came to a red light. He couldn't help wondering.

"She claims she wasn't and no one's stepped up to say, 'I'm the other guy.' There have been rumors, though."

"Of course. It's a small town. But blaming her for his drinking and driving is like blaming Bella for my bad behavior. Last I checked I don't get to do that."

She studied him. "You haven't even tried."

Because it felt too much like cheating. He had his faults but blaming others for his actions wasn't one of them.

"Come to think of it, you should be commended for that," she added.

Surprised by her concession, he glanced over to make sure she was serious. When he saw that she was, he shrugged. "So I have one redeeming feature."

Her lips curved into a smile. "You've got a few others."

A dose of sexual awareness warmed his blood. "Feel free to elaborate," he said, tempting her to flirt a little more, but she backed off.

"I think you know what they are."

The light turned green. "If you're talking about my looks, I'm not particularly flattered. I had no control over the face I was given."

"You've worked hard for that body."

"All part of the job. But I'm glad you noticed."

She scowled. "I've also noticed how easy it is for you to light up a room, how fast you neutralized all the people who should've been defensive of me. They fell for your charm almost immediately."

He got stuck behind someone in an SUV who was waiting for a parking spot on the street. "Really? Because Callie seemed completely immune."

"She'll come around."

Maybe. Maybe not. She'd seemed pretty unhappy. "What was that bit about Cheyenne and her mother?"

"Anita's a piece of work. You wouldn't believe what Cheyenne has been through. When she and her sister were little, her mother dragged them from one town to the next. They lived out of cars or in cheap motels. She didn't even go to school until she moved here, and by then she was fourteen!"

The people who owned the Jetta in the parking space the SUV wanted began the process of loading up, but they had a baby and a toddler to strap in, and a stroller to contend with. "How did she fare?"

"Not as badly as you'd think. She'd taught herself a lot by then, is naturally very smart. But it took most of high school for her to catch up. And, of course, she didn't get the chance to go to college, like the rest of us."

"Her name's unusual."

"She thinks she was named after Cheyenne, Wyoming."

"One of the cities they passed through."

"You guessed it. Who knows where she'd be right now if Anita hadn't gotten sick? That's the only reason they settled down."

"A haunted B and B, someone who didn't start school until the age of fourteen, a woman blamed for the death of a local sports hero… You have an interesting group of friends."

"And everyone knows too much about everyone else, like I told you before."

"I guess that's the downside of living in such a small place," he said. "No one can forget. No one can forgive."

"Publicity has made the whole world that small for you."

That was one of his problems. The other was that he didn't seem to be the best judge of character. Had he been able to detect the deep reservoir of insecurity that lurked beneath Bella's beautiful face he would've had some inkling of what he was getting himself into. But he'd been oblivious. Or maybe Bella was right— and he'd somehow created her insecurity. To him, it seemed as if he'd tried *everything* to convince her he loved her. He *had* loved her, more than he'd ever loved anyone—other than Ty. She just couldn't believe it for any length of time, had to make him prove it over and over and over.

Finally, the Jetta pulled into the street and the SUV took its place. "Tell me this," he said.

"What?"

"If Sophia knows she's not wanted, why did she show up at the coffee shop?"

"The news that we got married has been flying around." She put a piece of gum in her mouth. "Maybe she was hoping we'd be there."

It hadn't felt as if she'd come to gawk at him. He'd gotten the impression that she was honestly trying to make friends, maybe even make amends, but who was he to say? He'd just met her. "Tell the truth. You were tempted to feel sorry for her because she looked so depressed when you waffled on dinner."

"No, I wasn't. She did a lot of other things I haven't told you about. As far as I'm concerned, if people don't want to have dinner with her it's because she deserves it," Gail said, but he could tell she was torn.

They had to stop at the next red light, too. Simon felt annoyed by the pace of life here—until he realized there was no point in hurrying. For once the world wasn't going to fall apart if he didn't make it to a certain place by a certain time. And he had nothing to fear about being out in the open. There were no paparazzi, no cameras, no Bella and no reporters with uncomfortable questions. He wasn't even afraid of being recognized, because being recognized here didn't turn into an embarrassing worship session. These people just sort of stared and murmured, then glanced at their toes if he caught them gawking.

The light turned green, so he gave the car some gas. "Okay, now tell me about Matt."

She let her head fall against the seat. "We're back to him?"

"Is there someone else you want to talk about first?"

"Not if it won't distract you."

The Jetta he'd been following turned, and he came up on a Prius that was barely creeping along, looking for a parking place—obviously more tourists out to visit the shops on Sutter Street. "He's *that* big a deal to you?" Simon said. If so, why hadn't she ever mentioned him? He would've expected that information to come out *before* they got married.

"He's a professional football player. That makes him a big deal to everyone, at least around here."

She'd taken the personal element out of his question, so he put it back in. "I want to know what he means to *you*."

"Nothing. We went out once last summer. That's it."

Although she tried to shrug it off, Simon didn't believe he'd misunderstood what he'd sensed at the coffee shop. "Then why does everyone seem so interested in your reaction to him?"

"I couldn't tell you."

The Prius found a car with some people who looked like they might be loading up, but they were only storing their packages. "You're a terrible liar," Simon said. "Has anyone ever told you that?"

"I'm not lying...exactly."

"Then what are you hiding? Did you sleep with him?"

Her hesitation told him he'd hit somewhere not far from the truth.

"You don't have to conceal any indiscretions from me," he reminded her. "I'm pretty much the poster boy for sin, remember?"

"I didn't sleep with him."

"But..."

"We went out once and came close."

"Aha! Here we go. So he's your local love interest and everyone knows it."

"No one knows anything, because nothing really happened. It was one date. So he's not a...*love* interest, per se."

At last the Prius found a spot. "You're not head over heels," Simon said.

"No."

They reached the turnoff to her father's. "Tell me where we're going."

"Home, to shower and get ready for the day. I want to check our media hits and see what Josh has arranged with *People* on our wedding pics. Then we'll contact Kathy and see when she has time to show us whatever rentals are available."

Still intrigued by her self-conscious reaction to his questions about Matt, he returned to the same subject. "Has he called you since the big night? Was he expecting to see you again?"

"What does it matter?"

"Maybe I want to be sure you'll keep your end of our marriage contract, now that *you're* the one facing temptation."

She folded her arms, which made her look even more prim than usual. "Give me a break. You have nothing to worry about. It's always been a very one-sided crush. I mean...not crush. Brief infatuation."

"*It's* is present tense," he pointed out. "And *always* isn't brief."

Her face turned red. "Can we drop it, please?"

She was getting flustered....

He pulled into the driveway, to the far left, just in case her father or brother returned. Their vehicles were gone—thank God—which meant he was going to get a reprieve from the we-hate-Simon vibes that had bombarded him yesterday. "I just want to be sure I'm not holding you back."

"You're not."

After putting the transmission in Park, he cut the engine. "You've got feelings for Matt. I can tell."

"No."

"What do you see in him?"

She opened her door. "Callie already told you—he's a nice guy."

He came around to meet her. "And I'm not. She made the distinction very clear. Which brings me back to Callie—what do you see in *her?*"

"Don't hold the way she acted at the coffee shop

against her. She'll warm up to you. She's just being protective."

"She's being judgmental. Hasn't she ever done anything wrong?"

"Most people haven't crashed and burned quite as publicly as you have. You have that going against you."

"Such is the price I pay for being rich and famous." It was a glib response, designed to cover how it felt to have his every mistake and shortcoming advertised to the public. If not for that added dimension, maybe he wouldn't have become so determined to prove he'd do exactly as he pleased, regardless of the world's shock and recrimination. To a certain extent, the worst of his behavior was simply his way of giving the world—and everyone who judged him—the finger.

"Are you sorry you didn't have sex with Matt while you had the chance?"

Clearly, she wanted to be done with this conversation, so it took him off guard when she suddenly stopped and whirled around. "Yes," she said in exasperation. "I am. Especially now that I'm getting paid *not* to have sex for the next two years."

He put a hand to his chest as if she'd just wounded him. "Who's paying you not to have sex?"

"Our marriage will fall apart the second we cross that line, and you know it."

The stubborn glint in her eyes offered an irresistible challenge. Gail was so…normal. That was one of the things he liked most about her. She kept problems in perspective and demanded he do the same. Since she'd taken charge, his life had begun to make sense again.

But she was also a bit starchy, and that made her fun to bait. "I'm willing to compromise in that area," he said. "I'll give you a night off from our deal if you'll give me one." He adopted a sultry tone. "Think about it…all that pent-up desire could be unleashed on your old crush."

Oddly enough, he didn't want her to accept, but he was curious whether or not she'd be tempted by the offer. That alone would tell him how important this Matt the Football Player was.

She didn't take the bait. Grabbing his shirtfront, she tried to yank him toward her. When she couldn't budge him, and he started chuckling at her efforts, she stood on her tiptoes so she could come nose to nose with him instead. "Don't mistake the tranquil setting here in Whiskey Creek for privacy or anonymity. *Everyone's* watching. You do one thing wrong in this town and you can say goodbye to making yourself remotely respectable." She let go and brushed the wrinkles out of his shirt. "And I'd rather you didn't make a fool of me in front of the home crowd, if you get my meaning."

He lowered his gaze to her lips. She was so close he could smell the mint of her chewing gum. If he kissed her, he'd probably taste it, too. "I guess that leaves us with only one alternative."

"And that is?"

Tilting her chin up, he brought his mouth within a hairbreadth of hers. "You can't guess?"

"Sure I can." Shoving his good hand up against his crotch, she said, "Have fun," and walked away.

Apparently she'd had enough of his teasing. But something about her reaction to her old flame triggered an unpleasant response in him.

It couldn't be jealousy, he told himself. It had to be wounded pride. He wasn't used to being upstaged.

Unwilling to let her have the last word, he called after her, "You're supposed to want *me*. *I'm* the movie star!" as if he was the egotistical ass so many of the tabloids described.

"Some women prefer professional athletes to self-absorbed movie stars," she retorted, and when she reached the stoop, she tossed a taunting smile over her shoulder. "You should see how *big* Matt is."

Simon felt his eyebrows jerk together. "You're talking about height, aren't you?"

No answer. She was trying to unlock the door.

He strode over to the porch. "You can't compare what you haven't seen. To be fair we should go into the bedroom and check it out. I'm not afraid of a little competition."

"I want a divorce," she grumbled as she finally got the door open.

Trying not to laugh, he swatted her bottom. "I seem to have that effect on women."

Bringing a movie star home to Whiskey Creek wasn't turning out like Gail had imagined. Her father and brother had reacted as defensively as she'd thought they would but, except for Callie, her friends had not. Probably because she and Simon were already married. Considering that, there wasn't much anyone could do to warn her away.

Still, she'd anticipated a bit more…concern.

At breakfast, her old school chums had looked as if they couldn't believe her situation had changed so drastically, but she'd talked about the people on her client roster enough in the past that they associated her with a lot of big names. They were more surprised to have Simon O'Neal sitting at coffee with *them*. She'd never brought anyone home before, let alone an actor of his stature, and they were understandably flustered.

But, interestingly enough, they didn't seem to blame her for marrying him. The guys took it for granted that Simon would be able to have anyone he wanted, even her, regardless of what he'd done. And her girlfriends harbored no illusions that they would've refused him had he shown interest in any of them. So there'd been no frowns, no head shaking, no "what the hell were you thinking?" when they got together this morning. Everyone had been too busy trying to acclimate to having Simon around. Gail had almost laughed out loud as all but Callie succumbed easily to his potent charm.

That grin of his was like a slow-acting poison, she decided. It wasn't lethal but it could certainly incapacitate a woman. It entered at the eyes and jammed up certain frequencies of the brain, making the victim susceptible to almost any suggestion Simon made. That had to be the reason she'd been stupid enough to flash him this morning, even though she didn't want to be compared to his many other women, didn't want to become his temporary antidote to grief, didn't want to be just another meaningless lay. She already knew her self-esteem couldn't take it.

He'd win Callie over eventually, too. Callie was only holding out because she'd cautioned Gail not to get involved with him, and had been ignored. Callie couldn't swoon at his feet the second he walked into town or she'd look ridiculous.

"Hey, what's taking so long?" Simon called up.

Apparently he was off the phone with Ian, who'd been expounding on the difficulties of getting Simon out of his next movie. She could hear the TV but Simon's conversation seemed to have ended several minutes ago, probably around the time she'd finished reading all the blogs and articles posted about them on the web.

"Just handling a few details," she called back.

"How are we looking? Am I coming off as innocent? Reformed?"

"America hasn't gotten that far yet. Everyone's in shock."

"I still have the ability to shock people?"

She couldn't help laughing, despite the fact that she was wounded by so many of the comments she'd read. Being realistic about her own limitations was one thing. Reading so many snarky reasons he should've chosen someone better was another.

"They're calling me Plain Jane," she said.

"They don't know you," he responded.

Nice try. "That comment doesn't refer to my personality."

When she heard his tread on the stairs, she was about to turn off her computer. It'd been hard enough to read these remarks when she was alone. But he'd only demand she turn it on and show him some of the press. He had a right to be interested.

"Who's been writing about us?" he asked as he entered the room.

"'Perez Hilton,' 'Hot Hollywood Gossip,' all the usual celeb sites."

"'Hollywood Hunk Marries Plain Jane,'" he read over her shoulder. "The *hunk* part is pretty accurate."

She knew he was trying to soften the blow by making it into a joke, but that didn't help. She said nothing, just clicked on the other sites she'd seen so he could continue to skim through the headings.

"'Box Office Hit Simon O'Neal Ties the Knot... What's Simon O Thinking?... Simon O'Neal's Latest

Debacle… The Real Cinderella… Big Hit PR Scores and So Does Its Owner, but for How Long?'"

"Looks like they're buying it," he said.

"Of course they're buying it. I may be plain but I'm good at what I do." She could at least take pride in that.

"Come on." He rested his hands on her shoulders and kneaded the tense muscles there. "I'll bet you anything that was written by a woman."

"John McWhorter would be an odd name for a woman."

"So a gay guy. A jealous gay guy. It's possible. I've gotten love letters from guys before."

"It doesn't matter." She really felt that way. She'd known what she'd be up against coming in to this. Known that everything would be criticized, especially her.

And yet…it wasn't pleasant to know that the world found her lacking as Simon's wife. This morning, when she'd flashed Simon, the way he'd looked at her had made her feel drop-dead gorgeous. No other man had ever made her feel so intoxicated with desire.

But Simon was out to get laid, and she'd made herself his only quarry. He was probably using all his acting skill in the hopes of achieving sexual gratification. Considering how beautiful Bella was, he couldn't have been as impressed as he seemed.

"That's what you've been doing up here this whole time?" he asked. "Reading all this negative crap about yourself?"

"I have to know what's being said or I won't know what we need to do to enhance or combat it."

He didn't seem pleased. "Why do people have to have an opinion on everything I do? Can't they just enjoy my movies and leave it at that? Close up and let's go."

"I haven't been crying over it, if that's what you think." She stopped him when he tried to shut down her browser. "I've been answering email."

That was true. She'd had to check on Big Hit, see what was going on with the new pitches and assure herself that Josh and Serge were covering for her in her absence. Josh had written, telling her not to read any of the blogs, that he'd keep track of their buzz, which should've warned her, but she'd had to look.

"Any word from *People?*" Simon asked.

"We have a two-million-dollar offer."

"Hold out for three."

"That's what I told Josh."

He kept rubbing her shoulders, but she didn't like that he was doing it because he felt sorry for her. "What about Kathy Carmichael? Have you reached her?"

"Not yet. I left her a message."

"What's happening at your office?"

"We're being deluged with calls. A lot are from media interested in getting whatever scoop they can on us, but there are others who are potential clients. Josh thinks we should hire two more publicists."

"Do you agree?"

She was surprised he'd ask. What did he care about her PR business? "We have to be able to grow quickly enough to accommodate our sudden popularity. And I don't want the quality to suffer. That would ruin my brand. So, yeah, I told him to do it. Maybe it's the news of our marriage that's bringing business to Big Hit, but only hard work will keep that business, especially after you and I split up."

"Are you okay with missing all the fun?"

Gail hated feeling so removed from what she'd created. She was too used to standing at the helm. But she had enough challenges right here, she reminded herself. One of those challenges was not moaning at the pleasure his fingers were giving her with his massage. Another was making sure her soft spot for him didn't get any larger. "I'm on assignment."

"And you'll see it through."

"Of course."

The rubbing stopped for a moment as he saluted her. "That's your brand, too."

"That's my personality."

He stared at her for several seconds.

"What?" she asked, growing self-conscious.

"You're right. It is your personality. You're responsible, dependable."

Although that sounded like it was meant as a compliment, being responsible and dependable wasn't flattering enough to counteract the negative comments she'd just read. It wasn't like being told she was gorgeous or sexy or charismatic, like he was. But she figured the world could use a few more dependable people. Lord knew she dealt with enough who weren't. "Be careful. I might get a big head—like yours," she said with a laugh.

He started to rub again. "I *like* responsible and dependable."

She watched him in the mirror of her dresser. "Sure you do. Being responsible and dependable is almost as good as being conscientious and trustworthy."

"You're not flattered."

"No."

His hands stilled. "Okay. Would you believe me if I said you have the prettiest tits I've ever seen?"

He was getting a lot closer to the things a woman

really wanted to hear—even someone as practical, responsible and conscientious as her. But he couldn't be serious. She was barely a C cup. "No."

"Now you know why I didn't bother."

She told herself to let it go at that, but couldn't. "Is it true?" she asked warily.

A sexy smile lifted one corner of his mouth as he bent to whisper in her ear, "I'd be happy to convince you of my sincerity if you'll give me the chance," he said and his hands came around to cup her breasts through her clothes.

The heat of his palms made her nipples tighten. She told herself to get up and step away, but she could only stare at the sight of his dark fingers against her turquoise sweater. "Something must be wrong with me...."

His thumbs moved back and forth, and darts of pleasure raced through her. "No, there's not," he said, his lips against her neck.

She could hardly breathe. She wanted to let those well-sculpted hands delve beneath her top and really touch her. But she was determined to be smart about Simon. "I mean, there must be something wrong with *you* if you think I'm going to fall for that," she said, and knocked his hands away.

She'd thought he'd straighten and laugh it off as if touching her hadn't meant anything to him, anyway. As if it had been some sort of test to see what she'd do. But he didn't. When their eyes met in the mirror, she could plainly read his disappointment.

God, no wonder he could get any female on the planet, she told herself. It wasn't just his celebrity and appearance. There was an emotional honesty about him she found oddly courageous. Maybe he didn't always feel the way she might like him to feel, but he didn't hide the truth.

"What would it hurt?" he murmured. "You're my wife."

He wanted the physical intimacy a regular wife would give him. But he wouldn't be happy if she wanted the emotional intimacy a regular wife would expect in return. "I know you're not used to going without, that it's been a few weeks—"

"Ah, shit. Don't patronize me," he said, and walked out.

Gail sat there for several more minutes. She was waiting for the tingling in her breasts to subside. But every time she thought of Simon touching her with that intense look in his eyes, the sensation came back.

Finally, she told herself to quit being an idiot and went downstairs.

"Should we drive around and see if we can find any for-rent signs?" she asked.

He was sitting on the couch, watching TV, and didn't even bother to look up. "I've decided a for-sale sign would work just as well."

"You want to buy a house?"

"I'm just saying I'll take what I can get."

Of course. He wouldn't want to stay with her father and brother any longer than necessary, and she couldn't blame him.

"You're mad at me."

"Frustrated," he said.

"Simon—"

"But I don't want to talk about it."

"Fine. Let's just…" She swallowed hard, feeling at a loss because she was frustrated, too, even torn. "Pretend nothing happened," she finished. "Come on."

Picking up the remote, Simon snapped off the TV and followed her through the kitchen. They were just stepping outside when Kathy called.

"Is it true?" the Realtor squealed.

Distracted by Simon, who insisted on driving even though she thought she should probably do it this time, since she knew her way around, Gail didn't immediately understand what Kathy meant. "Is what true?"

"That you married *Simon O'Neal?*"

Sometimes Gail couldn't believe it herself. "Yes."

"Oh, my God!" Kathy shouted. "Oh, my God! Oh, my God!"

"Kathy—"

"What's it like to sleep with him?" she asked.

Gail froze. This was the last question she'd expected from middle-aged, happily married Kathy Carmichael. Simon was so famous, people thought they had some sort of claim on him, which gave them the impression they had the right to ask such personal questions.

Simon had obviously overheard. He glanced up to see what her response would be.

"He's not all he's cracked up to be." She wasn't sure why she said that; she just couldn't stop herself from needling him.

Whatever Kathy said was lost on Gail, who was too focused on Simon.

"You keep saying stuff like that and you're going to *have* to give me the chance to prove you wrong," he told her.

Which was exactly what she wanted him to do. She was just afraid of what might come after. "Kidding!" she told Kathy. "He's amazing, of course. Just looking at him makes me drool." She stuck her tongue out so he wouldn't take that seriously.

"The truth at last," he murmured sarcastically.

"Lord, you and me both, honey," Kathy was saying. "I've seen *Shiver* at least half a dozen times. The way he makes love to Tomica Kansas in that movie is beyond anything I've ever seen. All I have to do is hear the musical score and…" Her voice softened. "Oh, my."

Gail didn't want to think of that movie but the images danced through her brain, anyway. "Don't hold your husband accountable if he can't duplicate that scene," she said. "I'm sure the director had a lot to do with it. And the music. And the magic of make-believe. Sex is never messy on screen."

Simon settled behind the wheel of her car. "Keep talking. You might actually believe it one day."

She couldn't respond to him. Kathy was murmuring, "You're one lucky girl, darlin'. That's all I'm saying."

Eager to change the subject before she had to hear any more, Gail cleared her throat. "Thanks. Do you know of any places we can rent for three months, Kathy?"

"Only one that's good enough for Simon."

Gail covered the phone. "Did you hear that?"

"Yeah," he said. "Sounds hopeful."

"I'd better not run into this very often," she told him. He raised a questioning eyebrow.

"The way people gush over you is so ridiculous it makes me sick."

"Is that why you're looking at me as if you'd like to tear my clothes off?"

She gaped at him. How could he see through her so easily? "You're *so* conceited!"

"What did you say?" Kathy asked while he laughed.

She removed her hand from the phone. "Sorry, I was talking to Simon. I told him you have just the place."

"I do," she said. "It's the old Doman mansion. You know it, don't you?"

"Of course. But…that's up for rent?"

"For sale. Why would someone like Simon pay rent, especially in your hometown, where you'll be coming again and again? This is pocket change for him."

That diamond guy had felt he should be able to tell Simon how to spend his money, too. "How much pocket change?"

"Two-point-five million. It's an entire compound, with ten acres and stables and everything."

"We'll take it." Simon was still listening in, but Gail had no interest in buying the old Doman place.

"I'm afraid that won't work," she told Kathy. "It's far more than we're willing to take on. Simon wants to get a piece of land and build us a house, but for now we just need something small and cozy, something temporary and a lot less work."

"Oh." Kathy seemed disappointed.

"If she doesn't have anything small and cozy, we're taking the Doman place," Simon informed Gail.

Gail gestured for him to be quiet.

"Well, in that case—" Kathy hesitated. "Meet me at the office. I can show you a couple of possibilities, but… there's not much on the market right now."

"I understand. We're on our way." With a triumphant smile, Gail hit the end button.

"What's wrong with the Doman place?" Simon asked, scowling. "Kathy seemed to think it would be perfect for me."

Gail fastened her seat belt. "You trust her more than you do me?"

"Hell, yeah," he said. "At least she recognizes a good love scene when she sees one."

"That love scene was…generic," she responded, but it was a lie, and they both knew it. That love scene was one of the best to ever hit the screen. Every time Gail climbed into bed with Simon she had to face the memory of his perfect mouth moving down Tomica Kansas's flat stomach.…

His gaze lowered to her breasts. "That's not what your body is telling me."

She resisted the urge to fold her arms over the evidence of her arousal. "I'm not Tomica Kansas." She had to keep the distinction between her, at Plain Jane status, and the femme fatales who starred in his movies clear in her mind.

"You could've been fifteen minutes ago," he said, but he was no longer looking at her. He was checking the road as he backed out of the drive.

Nineteen

"This is it?" Simon didn't seem impressed with the house Gail wanted.

"What's wrong with it?" she asked.

He waited until Kathy was out of earshot. She'd gotten a call and was heading to her car for an address. "It's a two-bedroom, one bath that was built in 1880."

"So?"

"It's functionally obsolete."

"No, it's not."

"The only bathroom is in the hall, Gail. And it has a claw-foot bathtub. There isn't even a shower."

She rolled her eyes. "There's a shower head above the tub and a curtain you can pull around."

Obviously he'd seen the makeshift shower. He just didn't think it was an acceptable arrangement. "I don't want to have to stand in one place and turn in a tight circle. The entire bathroom is half the size of a normal closet!"

"By L.A. standards, maybe. But we're not in L.A. anymore."

He gave her a pained look. "I think I'm clear on that."

"We're not going to be here long," she said, trying to convince him. "We can get by with this place, can't we?"

After glancing into both bedrooms and the bathroom again, he sighed. "There has to be something else. This is barely...what did she say? Eight hundred square feet?"

"Eight hundred and seventy-five." She shoved the flyer at him, but he didn't take it.

Crossing his arms, he leaned dejectedly against the wall. "It's the size of my bedroom back home."

"But you heard Kathy. This is our last option. There are no rentals, and we saw the only other houses on the market. Neither of them were as nice."

"That first one was bigger," he grumbled. "We could fix it up."

"It was right in town. We don't want neighbors, do we? Certainly not nosy neighbors, and there isn't any other kind in Whiskey Creek. Here, we'd have some privacy. Better yet, we'd each have our own bedroom."

He turned to face her. "Being told I'll be sleeping alone? That's supposed to convince me?"

She grinned. "Convinces me."

He lowered his voice. "Only because you're *scared*."

"Of what?" she scoffed, but immediately regretted it when he cocked his head as if he had no intention of backing down.

"Of me. Of how much you might enjoy my hands on your body. Of what it might feel like to lose control."

She swallowed hard. "I'm not scared," she lied. "I'm just...not stupid enough to..." To what? To get too comfortable in a marriage that wasn't going to last?

He shot her a sullen glance. "To get involved with me?"

"I'm already involved with you. That's not what I was about to say."

"There's another way of looking at it, you know."

"Which is…"

"My way."

"Let me guess. You think I should let you use me until you're ready to move on."

"I'm offering you two years of endless orgasms. Why reject that out of hand?" He poked her. "You need an orgasm more than any woman I've ever known."

She stepped out of reach. "Quit treating me like I'm frigid!"

He lifted his hands. "Whoa, no need to get defensive. I wasn't implying that."

"But you think it."

"I think you're too uptight. But you have nothing to worry about. I'll take care of you."

He thought she was denying them both for no good reason. But he didn't understand what was at stake. How could he? Maybe sex meant nothing more than a fun time to him, but she wasn't built that way. "I might be uptight but I'm not shortsighted."

"Typically not," he said. "So why are you renting a house with only one bathroom?"

Arguing about sex *and* the number of bathrooms in their first rental made her feel more married than she'd felt before. "We'll have to share it but…otherwise, this house is perfect."

Hands on his lean hips, he turned in a circle.

"Okay, it's quaint, but quaint is good enough." She drew him back to the living room, with its high ceiling, crown molding and hardwood floors. "Look at this place. Look at the fireplace mantel. It has so much character."

"I like the porch," he admitted, gazing through the

gigantic front windows with the diamond-shaped cut-glass inserts above them.

"I *love* the porch," she said. "It's almost as big as the living room. Imagine sitting out there with a glass of iced tea as the sun goes down. Summers in Whiskey Creek are so gorgeous. And the kitchen's got potential," she added.

He followed her around the corner. "If someone were to gut it and completely redo it, maybe." He eyed the lime-green cupboards. "These cabinets are hideous."

"It wouldn't be that hard to renovate," she said. "Maybe we should remodel instead of build."

The screen door slammed as Kathy came back in. "So? What do you think?" she asked when she found them, but she had eyes only for Simon. What Gail thought didn't matter.

Simon stared at Gail for several seconds, during which she silently pleaded with him. Then he shifted his attention to Kathy. "We'll take it."

"You want to make an offer?"

"Give them their asking price," he said. "It's not much."

Gail had begun to figure out that Simon was a pushover when it came to money and possessions. She was pretty sure she could get just about anything out of him. His willingness to buy her a half-million-dollar diamond was proof. So she wasn't surprised that he'd let her have the house even though he didn't want it and that he'd agreed to the original price. She was surprised, however, when he leaned over and brushed a kiss across her lips. It was a loving gesture manufactured for Kathy's benefit, of course. They'd been holding hands for most of the day; it was beginning to feel natural. But that kiss. It was nothing, a split second of contact, and yet it stole Gail's breath.

She glanced up to see if he was laughing at her, if he realized how much she'd liked it, but he turned away before she could ascertain what he might be thinking.

"When can we move in?" he asked.

That night Gail made a Caesar salad, pasta and garlic bread. The cream sauce for the pasta had onions and peas and bacon. Simon liked it. But sitting at the table with Martin and Joe DeMarco, who were home from work for the evening, was a silent and awkward affair.

Gail must've said something to them about how they'd treated him so far, because they were on their best behavior. Martin no longer shook his head in disgust whenever he glanced at Simon, and Joe didn't seem so hostile, either. Both men bent their heads over their plates and shoveled in their food as if they were sitting at the table alone.

"Would you like some more garlic bread?" Gail asked Simon.

He looked up from his own plate. "No, thanks."

This polite exchange aside, Simon thought they'd go the whole meal without any conversation. Which was fine with him. He didn't have a lot to say to her family, anyway.

But then Martin wiped his mouth, tossed his napkin on the table and spoke. To *him*.

"What do you think of Whiskey Creek?" he asked.

There was a bottle of Napa Valley wine sitting on the counter. Simon had been given a glass of soda. Gail had poured herself a soda, too. But he could smell the wine from where he sat. "I like it."

"Great place to raise a family."

Was he referring to *his* having raised a family here? Or was he fishing to see if Simon and Gail planned to have children?

Simon supposed it was natural that the old man might hope for another grandchild. But even if they hadn't already made provisions for their divorce, even if he could get Gail to sleep with him, Simon would insist on using some form of birth control. Never again would he hand a woman a weapon as powerful as a child. Love was far too fickle.

"I'd like to bring my son here sometime." He'd side-stepped what he suspected might be the real issue, but he couldn't be faulted for what he'd said.

Joe nodded. "I was wondering if we'd get to meet him. My daughters come every other weekend."

Simon twirled another forkful of pasta but didn't bring it to his mouth. "Where do they live the rest of the time?"

If Joe recalled Simon's earlier words about his divorce, he seemed willing to let bygones by bygones. "In Sacramento. Their mother's a nurse at UC Davis."

"How old are they?"

People with children loved to talk about them, and Joe was no different. He took a couple of pictures out of his wallet. "This is Summer. She's ten." His face split into the proudest of grins. "And this little devil's Josephine. She's only seven, but she's a spitfire."

"Like her mother," Martin added dryly.

Joe clicked his tongue. "Yeah, her mother's something else."

Simon got the impression that wasn't a compliment.

He looked at the pictures long enough to seem interested, even though he didn't want to become embroiled in the family dynamic. "They're pretty girls. You're going to have your hands full when they get older."

"Ain't that the truth," Joe said.

"You planning to do another movie soon?" This question came from Martin.

"I'm thinking of accepting another romantic thriller in March, one called *Last Train to Georgia*."

"A thriller, huh? Sort of like *Shiver?*" Joe asked.

Simon couldn't help glancing at Gail. She was definitely familiar with his work in that movie. She turned red every time someone mentioned it, which made him want to laugh. If only she knew how hard he'd worked to get that love scene right. Tomica, the actress he'd been paired with, had worn the same perfume as his mother, which made it revolting for him to kiss her. He was proud of his performance simply because no one seemed to be aware of his repugnance. He'd considered demanding they hold off and shoot another day, but it would've cost the production company a shitload of money. "More or less."

"Who else is in the new one?" Joe asked.

"An actress by the name of Viola Hilliard-Paul."

Joe washed his food down with a sip of his wine. "Never heard of her."

"She's new. But she's got talent." And she didn't remind him of his mother. He had slept with Vi a number of times—although he couldn't remember whether he'd enjoyed it. He'd been drunk more often than not and had broken it off the minute she began taking it seriously.

Joe looked at Gail. "How are you going to feel about your husband doing love scenes, baby sister?"

She got up to put some more bread on the table. "He's an actor. That comes with the territory."

"You won't be jealous?"

"Why would I? It's not real."

Martin lifted his glass. "Better not be," he muttered.

Gail promptly changed the subject. "We found a place to live today."

"Where at?" Joe signaled for more wine, and since Gail had just filled Martin's glass, she came around to pour it.

"You know that little Victorian where the Widow Nelson used to live?"

"The white one? All by itself at the end of Autumn Lane?"

"That's it."

A nostalgic smile curved Joe's lips. "How could I forget? She used to give out caramel apples at Halloween."

"Yeah, her place was always our first stop," Gail said.

Apparently in this area they didn't have to worry about someone putting razor blades in the apples. That was definitely an upside to such a small community. *Another* upside. Simon was finding quite a few of them.

Martin pushed back his chair. "I thought you wanted to rent. That house is up for sale."

"We've decided to buy," Gail informed him as she put the wine back on the counter.

"How much are they asking?"

Simon tried not to let his eyes latch on to the bottle. "Two hundred and fifty thousand."

"That's not bad," Martin told him, "considering the land."

"The house needs some work," Gail said.

Joe carried his plate to the sink. "You could have Riley fix it up before you move in."

Gail motioned in Simon's direction. "Actually, Simon is planning to do the renovations once he gets his stitches out. He's very good with his hands." She cleared her throat when she realized how that had sounded. "With wood," she clarified.

Joe turned off the faucet and set his plate on the counter. "Holler if you need any help with that," he said to Simon. "I'm not so bad with my hands, either." He grinned at Gail but seemed serious about the offer of help.

"Will do." Simon relaxed despite the relentless pull of the alcohol. There was something about Whiskey Creek *and* its people. Even with a wife who wouldn't let him touch her and the doubt Gail's father and brother had to be feeling about their marriage, Simon was beginning to feel comfortable. As a matter of fact, he hadn't felt this good, this *whole,* in months.

Maybe he was through the worst of it, he thought.

But then he got another text from Bella.

Gail could tell this night wasn't going to go as well as the last one. Simon had been fine for most of the day. Better than she'd ever seen him. There'd been times when they'd talked and laughed as if he was just an average person and not a celebrity desperate to recover his son.

But now he was restless, fidgety. He couldn't seem to shut down and sleep. After tossing and turning for a while, he seemed to doze off. But when she woke sometime during the night, she found him standing at the window, gazing pensively out into the yard.

"Is anything wrong?" she mumbled.

He glanced over his shoulder. He was still wearing the pajama bottoms he'd had on earlier but not his T-shirt. Gail had no idea where that had gone.

"No. You can go back to sleep," he said.

Unwilling to leave him up alone, she slid over to his side of the bed. Getting closer to him meant she could keep her voice down. "We could talk, if you like."

He shrugged. "There's nothing to talk about."

The moon outlined his profile in silver. Gail stared at his bare back, his broad shoulders, hunched just enough to show he was brooding even if he pretended otherwise. His hair stood up as though he'd run his fingers through it several times. Obviously he wasn't okay.

Could she get him to tell her what was troubling him? Or…somehow…help him stop worrying? She didn't want him to backslide. He'd made so much progress in the two weeks since they'd reached their agreement.

"Come here," she said.

Suddenly wary, as if he didn't trust what she might be offering, he glanced at her again. "What for?"

"I'll give you a massage. It might help you sleep."

"That's not necessary."

Under normal circumstances, he would've had a flip answer for her, or some sort of sexual innuendo; the fact that he didn't told her he was hurting too badly to accept help. Maybe he thought accepting help would be revealing he needed it, and heaven forbid he *need* anyone, especially a woman.

"Come on," she coaxed. As much as she hated to admit it, she'd been looking for an excuse to touch him ever since he'd kissed her earlier. No, before that. From the beginning. He'd just never shown any interest in her—not when he was a client, so she'd never allowed herself to seriously entertain the thought.

"There's no reason for you to be up all night," she said with a little more authority.

Sighing, he sat on the edge of the bed, and she got up to fetch the lotion from the bathroom across the hall.

But when she returned and put a hand on his shoulder to urge him to lie down, he resisted.

"What is it?" she asked.

He gave her such an intense look she knew he wanted something other than a massage. "Kiss me instead."

Gail swallowed hard. Today, every one of his smiles, every touch of their fingers or accidental brush of their arms, had sent her nerves into a jangling riot of desire that reminded her of those few minutes when he'd cupped her breasts. It didn't help that she was beginning to really care about him, that seeing him healthy and happy was becoming more important to her every day.

She was in a very precarious position, had no reason to even consider his request. But she wanted to ease his discomfort. And she *wanted* to kiss him.

"You'd just like to check out of reality for a while," she said, forcing them both to face the truth. "And I'm convenient. But…whatever you're feeling…it'll pass by morning."

"Damn it, don't say that like I'm trying to use you," he snapped. "I'm tired of being psychoanalyzed, tired of being found lacking. I know more about what's wrong with me than anyone else does. I don't need you to tell me what I want or what I'll do."

He was impatient, irritable, probably unsure how to end the pain. He wasn't even in familiar surroundings. Gail feared that might weaken his determination, cause him to turn back to alcohol.

But if she gave in and had sex with him tonight, where would she be in the morning?

She'd be no better off than the other women who'd come before her.

"Relax," she said gently. "And lie down."

"One kiss," he pressed. "Show me you trust me enough to give me one kiss."

"You kissed me at the house today."

"That doesn't count. I want you to kiss me back, here in private, where we're not putting on a show. I won't take advantage if you do. I'm not as big a bastard as you seem to think I am."

"I know you're not a bastard."

"Then prove it."

"Fine." Planning to allow him a quick peck, nothing more, she leaned forward, already braced to pull away. But he was as good as his word. He didn't attempt to draw her up against him. With his left hand lightly touching her cheek, he kissed her so tenderly she wasn't sure he was looking for a sexual escape so much as he wanted human contact, someone to hang on to.

"That wasn't so bad, was it?" he asked, surprising her by breaking off the kiss before she was even tempted to pull away.

His gentleness and honesty shattered her resistance. As she stared into his face, she nearly slid her arms around his neck to kiss him again. *More.* That was all she could think about. "Not at all."

"You liked it."

"Yes," she whispered.

He raised his hands. "See? And you're no worse for wear. You're not contaminated or anything."

"I never said you'd…*contaminate* me." She *had* accused him of carrying disease, but that was back when they'd been fighting. He'd told her he was clean and had the test results to prove it.

"You believe I'm morally beneath you, that I don't care about anything except myself."

Because she *needed* to think that. It was her only defense against the onslaught of desire she had to battle on a daily basis. She tried to conjure up an appropriate response, one that explained without giving too much away. But he didn't allow her the chance.

"Now I'm ready for my massage," he said, and flopped down on his stomach.

Twenty

When Gail woke up Simon was wrapped around her. She could feel the warmth of his bare chest at her back, feel his breath graze her ear and remembered the excitement she'd felt while touching him last night. As he'd begun to relax and fall asleep, she'd remained completely awake and vitally aware of him as a man. There'd been moments when she'd been so aroused, she'd nearly nudged him so he'd turn over.

She was pretty sure there'd been one moment when he knew that, too. She'd leaned down, kissed his jaw, then the side of his mouth. But as soon as she'd felt him stir as if he might respond, she'd pulled back.

They hadn't done anything. So why was his hand sliding up her shirt now?

At first, she thought it was purposeful, but the cadence of his breathing didn't change. He wasn't awake.

She considered removing his hand as soon as it touched her breast, but there was no intention behind his caress. He burrowed closer as he touched her, and she liked that. Liked all of it—so much that her body seemed to melt into his.

She wasn't sure how long she lay there, telling herself to stop him. But she never did, and eventually she must've slept because when she woke up again, Simon had left.

There was a note on the nightstand. "Went to the coffee shop. Join me when you wake up."

So this was Matt.

Transferring his laptop to his other hand, Simon turned to get a better look. But it was difficult to be discreet when he had to tilt his head so far back. The guy standing in line three people behind him had to be six-foot-six. He towered over Simon, over everyone, easily weighing two hundred and sixty pounds.

Simon sort of wished the guy had a crooked nose, or a gut that hung over his belt like some linemen, but Matt was all muscle. Not only that, he was blond, tan, with chiseled features—what most women would consider handsome. To top it off, he had a quick smile and was obviously well-liked. Three different people had hailed him since he walked in, which was what had drawn Simon's attention to him in the first place.

Gail had gone out with this guy. She'd almost slept with him. And Lord knew Gail didn't take off her clothes for just anyone.

"How's the knee?" someone asked.

While Simon took note from behind his Ray-Bans, Matt gestured at the brace on his right leg. "Hurts like hell, but... I'm in therapy. I'll get it back eventually."

"I can't believe you're gonna miss the rest of the season."

"Me, neither."

"Good to see you, man."

"Good to see you, too."

"You think the Packers can take the Raiders on Monday?"

A woman broke in. "Excuse me? Can I help you?"

Simon had been listening so intently to Matt's conversations it took him a moment to realize that this voice came from a different direction. The barista was asking for his order. Forced to shift his attention, he requested his usual—an espresso.

Several more people approached Matt while Simon waited for his coffee, all of them excited to see their favorite football player.

"Your coffee's ready," a girl called, dimpling as she handed Simon the cup. On one side she'd written her number. But she barely looked eighteen. That wasn't a call he would've made even at his worst.

"Thanks," he said, and headed to a table. He'd been planning to read some scripts. There hadn't been much time for that this past year. He hadn't had much interest, either. But even with the new picture Bella had texted him last night still fresh in his mind—of her completely naked and posing with her hands on her breasts—he was eager to find a gem among the files Ian had sent, a character he was dying to play, a film that would get him excited about his career again.

He hadn't had a drink in two weeks, was doing everything he possibly could to get Ty back. As long as he stayed the course, he'd look a lot better in the coming hearing. No need to worry about Bella's threats. She could pose and taunt him all she wanted. He wasn't going to let her rub salt in his wounds anymore.

For a second, he debated turning that sex video and this latest picture over to his attorney, who would then present them to the judge deciding Ty's future. The way Bella was acting meant she cared more about hurting him than protecting her parental rights. But she knew he'd never tell on her. He couldn't. Because that might make the court decide neither one of them was fit to care for Ty. Then they might put him in a foster home, and that was the last thing Simon wanted. At least Bella was a loving parent. Ty was better off with her than complete strangers.

He opened a script called "To The Bone," yet another thriller, but he couldn't concentrate. His eyes kept wandering to Matt, who had his own drink now and was sitting with an audience in the same booth where Simon had joined Gail and her friends yesterday.

"You going to the crab feed over at the school?" one of his admirers asked.

"Of course."

"You give 'em anything to auction off?"

"A signed jersey, but I do that every year. Hell, everyone in town has my jersey by now," he joked.

"You'll have to go for a jockstrap next year," someone quipped.

Suddenly Matt glanced up and met Simon's eyes. Something passed between them. Simon wasn't sure what. An acknowledgment of their interest in the same woman, perhaps. Simon expected Matt to realize he was being rude if not confrontational by staring at him with that challenging expression, but he didn't seem to care. He didn't glance away until someone addressed him again.

"You heard about Gail, right?" A man at Matt's table had noticed the exchange. Seeing Simon had obviously reminded him of Gail.

Lowering his gaze to his computer as if he was no longer paying attention, Simon strained to hear Matt's response, but it was impossible. The football player mumbled his words while turning in the other direction.

Simon almost got up to leave. There was no point in staying if he was too distracted to comprehend what he was reading, but before he could sign off his computer, Gail walked in.

The memory of waking with his hand up her shirt brought a deluge of testosterone. He hadn't touched her on purpose, but once he came awake he'd known instantly what he was doing. He'd stayed where he was for a few minutes, savoring the feel of her. It'd been an effort not to roll her onto her back so he could put his mouth where his fingers were. But then he grew so hard he was afraid she'd be able to feel his erection. So he'd gotten up and left before she could accuse him of trying to seduce her.

"Over here," he called with a wave.

She smiled brightly—until she saw Matt. Then she almost missed a step.

Wanting to be sure she came to him first, Simon stood to regain her attention. But Matt had spotted her, too. Getting up, he limped quite handily past Simon, despite his knee, and swept her into his arms. His bigger body all but engulfed hers, reminding Simon of the comment she'd tossed at him yesterday: *He's so big.*

Even with the memory of that statement ringing in his ears, Simon might not have minded. It was just a hug. Except that Matt held on a little too long—and Gail closed her eyes during the embrace, making Simon feel he was witnessing a far more intimate exchange.

When Matt finally released her, they had a short conversation. Then, without even glancing at Simon, Gail headed to the counter to place her order and Matt started back to his seat. Simon thought he'd pass right by. He'd already put on a show that underscored his importance in her life, which, Simon suspected, was exactly what he'd hoped to achieve. But he stopped, and he seemed more upset than smug when he rapped his knuckles on Simon's table. "She's a good woman," he said.

He gave Simon no clue how he was supposed to interpret that remark, but Simon could guess. And he didn't like the implication: *She's too good for you.* "Is that why you backed off last summer?" he asked.

A flicker of surprise appeared on Matt's broad face. "Damn right. It's the *only* reason. She's the type you take seriously."

"You don't call marriage serious?"

"Not when you don't have any idea what marriage means."

Leaning back, Simon crossed his arms. "You're saying you do?"

"Damn right."

"Then I guess your loss is my gain."

"We'll see about that," Matt retorted.

"Excuse me?" he said, abandoning his relaxed pose.

Matt lowered his voice. "I'll be waiting when you screw up. And if I know you, that won't be long."

Simon couldn't help clenching his jaw. "You *don't* know me. That's the point."

"Everybody knows you," he said, and moved on.

Gail joined Simon a second later. She must have seen their interaction, but didn't ask what her old flame had to say. Obviously she didn't want to talk about Matt. "How do you feel this morning?" she said instead.

Simon felt as if he'd just been slugged in the stomach, which was an odd reaction considering his fear that *she* might get too attached to *him.* "As if I'm standing in your way," he admitted.

"Why?" Lines of confusion appeared on her forehead, but then understanding dawned. "You mean…" She dropped her voice to a whisper. "You're not standing in my way. I told you, it was one date. And he never called me after."

Simon sipped his espresso. "I think he's regretting not making his intentions clearer."

"I doubt it."

He *definitely* was, but Simon didn't argue. He wasn't used to being with a woman who wanted someone else. His ex had cheated on him almost from the start, but only because she relished his jealous reaction. No matter how much he professed his love, making him prove it was the one thing that reassured her he still cared. She'd thrived on getting him so angry he was ready to kill whatever man she'd been with, and the second their relationship settled into a calm or even semiregular routine she'd pull something else. Especially after Ty was born, because threatening to split up and take him with her instantly threw Simon into the panic she was hoping for.

Gail wasn't like that. She was emotionally stable, didn't indulge in theatrics. But she'd married him even though she was in love with someone else, and he wasn't quite sure what he should do about it.

Maybe nothing. In two years she'd be free to marry Matt. Still, making her put her life on hold for so long felt pretty selfish, particularly now that Matt seemed ready to step up.

Somehow Simon had lost interest in reading scripts. "Have you heard from Kathy?" he asked.

"I have." She put her cup on the table. "She left a voice mail while I was in the shower. She has a purchase agreement for us to sign, said we can drop by her office anytime." She motioned to his computer. "What have you been working on?"

"Nothing." He closed his laptop. "Can we get the key today? Move in?"

"If we sign a rental agreement covering the period until escrow closes, I don't see why not."

If they were in their new place, he couldn't wake with his hand up her shirt again because they'd be sleeping in separate beds. Now, more than ever, they needed to give each other space. "What about furniture?"

"We could head over to Sacramento and do some shopping."

"Sounds good." After meeting Matt, he could use a break from Whiskey Creek.

He packed up his laptop and led Gail out of the coffee shop. To her credit, she didn't so much as turn toward Matt, but Simon could feel the other man's eyes following them all the way to the door.

Gail knew she was being too quiet. It was becoming obvious that encountering Matt at the coffee shop had left her reeling. If he hadn't seemed so upset that she'd gotten married, maybe she could've taken it in stride. In the past few months, she'd convinced herself that he wasn't interested in her. But when he hugged her he'd muttered, "I blew it," and sounded genuinely disappointed.

She hadn't responded to that. There wasn't time, and she wasn't about to undermine the believability of her marriage to Simon with a "Wait for me. This isn't real." For one thing, she'd look too mercenary, as if she'd done it for the money. She'd kept the secret for other reasons, too. Simon seemed to be stabilizing. The last thing he needed was for his new wife to become regretful or act as if she wanted to break up with him on account of an old crush.

She felt she'd handled the situation well, but she didn't have it in her to make small talk. She kept wondering...if she'd left Simon to solve his own problems and tried to figure out another way to rebuild her business, as Callie had suggested, would she and Matt have had a chance? Would they finally have gotten together? She'd planned on marrying him since she was thirteen!

As they drove to Sacramento, she stared out at the passing landscape, remembering how she and Callie used to take turns peering through a knothole in Callie's back fence while Matt threw a football with his father or older brother.

Maybe his knee injury and the possibility that his football career might be coming to an end were making him consider settling down. Maybe he wouldn't go back to Wisconsin, after all. He could stay in Whiskey Creek. He could even marry someone else while she was tied to Simon.

Wouldn't *that* be ironic? It was probably what she deserved for telling the world such a lic about Simon and her....

"You okay?" Since they'd left Whiskey Creek, Simon hadn't spoken much, either.

She dug through her purse for her lip gloss so she wouldn't have to look at him. She was afraid of what he might see in her face. "Fine, why?"

"Are we going to pretend?"

"Yes," she said simply.

He had the sunroof open. The warm, midmorning air ruffled his hair, but she'd put hers in a ponytail to keep it out of her face. "Why didn't you tell me you were in a romantic relationship?" he asked.

They were both wearing sunglasses, which helped hide their feelings and reactions. Today, Gail liked the buffer those glasses provided. She didn't necessarily want to know what Simon was thinking, and she sure as heck didn't want him to discern *her* thoughts. "I told you—I wasn't. I don't know what's going on. I think… I think Matt's return home is just bad timing."

"When you're ready, he's not. When he's ready, you're not."

"Something like that."

"We could make some changes in our…arrangement," Simon pointed out.

This was a business deal. She didn't mean anything to Simon on an emotional level so she didn't have to worry about hurting him. She understood that. But she couldn't dissolve the marriage too soon. He'd lose all the ground they'd just regained. And if that happened, it could be the trigger that would send him back to the bottle. He needed more time.

She could give him that, couldn't she? "I'm okay. I'll take one for the team."

His lips thinned. "Choosing me over him is taking one for the team? Wow, you really know how to flatter a guy."

"You have enough women drooling over you. You don't need me for that." Actually, she drooled over him plenty. She just didn't want him to know it. Whenever she was sure he wasn't aware of it, she found herself watching him. It was a good thing she understood the difference between reality and fantasy. Matt was someone she'd known her whole life, someone she had a right to hope for. Except for this brief period of time, and their very practical reasons for being together, Simon was as out of reach as the moon. Once their two years were up, he'd shoot back into orbit.

She just hoped she'd still have some semblance of her old life to resort to—and that she'd be satisfied with it.

His phone buzzed on the console, but he didn't even glance at it.

"You have a new text message," she said in case he'd been too preoccupied to hear.

"I know."

"Want me to read it to you?"

"No."

"Want me to drive so you can read it?"

"Don't worry about it. I'm not interested right now."

"Why not?" She looked down and saw the message. "It's from Bella."

He didn't seem surprised, which concerned her.

"Why would she be texting you?"

Lifting his bottom from the seat, he shoved his phone in his jeans pocket. "If you knew Bella you'd understand."

"What does she have to say?"

"Nothing new, I'm sure."

Another ripple of alarm went through Gail. "You haven't been contacting her, have you?"

"No. Not once—at least, not in several weeks." He sounded adamant. Whether she was right to take his word for it or not, she believed him. She hadn't caught him lying to her yet. He'd actually told her some pretty harsh truths—including the fact that he was incapable of falling in love again. She figured he deserved the benefit of the doubt.

"She's been reaching out to you?"

"I wouldn't call it reaching out."

"What would you call it?"

"Bella's own brand of torture."

"Which means…"

"Doesn't matter."

"Sure it matters. Why is she texting you?"

"She sends shit she thinks will make me mad."

"Such as…"

He grimaced. "'Meet Ty's new daddy.' 'Before long your little boy won't even remember your name.' Crap like that."

Outrage gnawed at Gail's soul. "That's not fair! She has a restraining order against you. How is it that you can't contact her, but she can contact you?"

"Welcome to Bella's world, where nothing ever makes sense. You can't fight emotion with logic. I learned that years ago."

"So you haven't gone to the police."

He looked at her as if she'd lost her mind. "What do you want me to say? 'My ex-wife keeps sending me upsetting texts?' How do you think that'll make me look?"

Gail supposed it did sound a little whiny. "Well… can you block her, at least?"

"I don't know. I've never blocked anyone. But even if I could, I wouldn't."

"Why not?"

His gaze slid over to her again. "Because she has my son, and I need to know if anything happens to him."

Gail adjusted her seat belt so she could turn toward him. "Does she ever send you anything to do with him?"

He passed a slower-moving Honda. "I'll get a picture every now and then."

"So she tries to be nice sometimes."

"Definitely not," he said with a laugh. "She's twisting the knife, but that's better than nothing."

Having full custody of his son had empowered his

ex-wife. It tied Simon's hands behind his back while *she* was free to slug away. That drove Gail crazy. But as long as Bella had Ty, Simon would remain defenseless. He wouldn't fight her if there was any chance Ty could get hurt.

"She's taking advantage of your love for your son."

"Is that news?" he asked.

She thought most people would be pretty surprised if they ever learned the rest of the story. Bella had done such a good job of smearing Simon as a heartless, irresponsible, selfish bastard. "We're going to get him back."

He slid his glasses down until he could see over the top of them. "And Matt?"

"Matt's going to Green Bay to play football."

"While you keep up appearances with me."

"Yes."

"I can depend on that?"

She slipped her hand inside his and felt far more gratified than she should have when his fingers curled through hers. "You can depend on it."

"*What* is it you want me to do?"

Simon checked to make sure Gail was still engaged with the furniture salesman across the display area. Ian sounded understandably shocked, but what good was money if Simon couldn't use it to assuage his conscience? "I want you to call Mark Nunes, the diamond guy."

"I heard that part. But then I thought you said to buy Gail a five-carat diamond."

"That *is* what I said. Have him design the setting himself. Tell him it better be good, too."

Just out of hearing range, the salesman was having

Gail try out another leather couch, one with a recliner at both ends.

"Why are you doing this?" Ian asked. "You got away with a gold band, man. Why would you buy her anything else? You know she'll just want to keep it when this is over, don't you?"

He didn't care about that. She was sacrificing more than he'd expected so she deserved a nicer ring. Or maybe it was the sudden competition. He wanted to appear more favorable than some dysfunctional movie star destined to devastate the town sweetheart. He had his shortcomings but he wanted people like Matt to know that at least he was generous with his money. Professional athletes made a fair amount, but chances were good, *very* good, that Matt couldn't give Gail a diamond of quite the same value. There weren't a lot of men who could.

"Just do it."

"Okay, but…how am I supposed to get it to you?" Ian asked. "I can't imagine the insurance company would cover it if it got lost in transit. They have stipulations on stuff like that."

They'd learned a few of those stipulations when Bella had lost her wedding ring and demanded that he replace it with one twice as expensive. Turned out, the insurance company was right to be careful. She'd been lying about losing the ring, had merely wanted to get another rise out of Simon.

"Drive it to me if you have to," he said, and hung up because Gail was coming toward him.

"Who was that?" she asked when she was close enough. "Not Bella…"

"No. Ian."

"What did *he* want?"

He could tell by her tone that she didn't hold Ian in the highest esteem. "He was giving me an update on some business at home."

"Everything okay?"

She was searching his face so he manufactured a bland smile. "Fine."

"Do you like this?" Drawing him over to the brown leather couch he'd seen her sit on, she insisted he try it out.

"Feels comfortable to me," he said as he settled into the recliner at one end.

"I like it, too," she mused. "But…it's almost ten grand."

The salesman, an older guy with a toupee, stood at a respectful distance so they could discuss their buying decision. If he recognized Simon as a celebrity, he didn't show it. He probably hadn't seen a movie since *Casablanca*.

"Would you quit that?" Simon murmured.

"Quit what?"

"Worrying about price!" Bella hadn't thought anything was too much if she wanted it. Buying her the best of everything was just another way he was required to prove his love. Gail acted as if she didn't want to be a burden.

She leaned down to whisper in his ear. "I don't see any point in wasting money. Who buys a ten-thousand-dollar couch when there are starving children in Africa?"

"I'll make a donation to compensate. We need a couch, and we need one today."

"We don't *have* to have one today," she hedged. "We could shop for something we like that's a bit cheaper."

"No. Enough shopping already." He was done traipsing through one showroom after another. "Let's have them ring it up. Otherwise, they'll close before we get anything at all."

"Fine," she grumbled.

Bedroom furniture came next. By the time they'd picked out two beds, including mattresses and box springs, and a kitchenette set, which was all that would fit in their small house, plus a couple of coffee tables and side chairs, they'd been gone all day. They arranged to have it delivered on Monday, since the store didn't offer that service on the weekend, and headed out, tired but happy.

"We still need a TV, a washer and dryer and some patio furniture." Gail ticked these items off on her fingers as they walked.

"It's after nine o'clock," he said.

"I know. At least we made a dent in it."

"Furnishing a house by yourself is a lot of work," he complained as he held the door for her.

"You probably haven't done it in a while."

"Not in a long while."

"But it feels good, doesn't it?"

He studied her tired smile. Being with her felt good. He was beginning to think it didn't matter what they were doing.

Twenty-One

"Should we stay in our house tonight?" Gail had fallen asleep against the door of the car, so this was spoken through a yawn while Simon was still driving. But she seemed excited by the idea. Simon was sort of excited by it himself. He didn't know why such a simple thing—camping out at their new home—would sound remotely enjoyable to someone who'd traveled the whole world and had the finest of everything. But the idea made him feel light and free, unshackled for the first time in years. When was the last time he hadn't had to watch over his shoulder for determined paparazzi, an overly zealous fan or his ex-wife, who felt she could show up at his house whenever she wanted, despite the restraining order? Maybe his past was still following him around. He had to remain vigilant for more than a couple of weeks before he could outdistance his previous behavior. But he was feeling more like his old self. He wasn't even craving alcohol as much as he had in the past several days, which proved he wasn't an alcoholic. With enough determination he could let it go.

"Stay there without furniture?" he said.

"We could borrow my dad's blow-up mattress and a couple of sleeping bags."

"And get out from under his roof? I don't know—" he pretended to be giving it a great deal of thought "—you'd really have to twist my arm to do that."

This bit of sarcasm elicited a playful slug from Gail. "Stop. He was better to you last night."

"Considering how things began, there was only one way he could go."

"It was my brother who was rude," she argued. "My dad didn't say anything."

"Your dad was stoic. But he kept shaking his head as if he just couldn't believe his wonderful daughter would be stupid enough to hook up with me. I wouldn't call that polite."

When she laughed, he did, too. He'd once thought she was so much more appealing when she let down her guard and relaxed. Now she was appealing all the time.

How had he worked with her for so long and been unable to detect her charm?

He'd been blinded by his own troubles. Or by the glitz and glamour of Hollywood. Maybe he was as subject to following the crowd as anyone else, despite how jaded he'd become.

"How's your hand?" she asked.

"Starting to itch."

"That's a good sign." She tightened her seat belt. "You're leaving the stitches alone, though, aren't you?"

He shot her an are-you-kidding-me look. "What am I—five?"

"Sometimes you don't know what's good for you."

"I can't argue with that."

She cleared her throat. "So…about Matt."

Surprised that she'd return to this subject, he adjusted the volume on the radio so it wouldn't be distracting. "What about him?"

"I'm fine with our arrangement. You don't have to worry that I'll regret our deal or anything. My commitment hasn't changed."

He wasn't sure how to respond. He didn't want her to stay with him because she felt obligated—and yet that would make it easiest to split up when the time came. "How did you know I was worried?"

She pursed her lips in a smug fashion. "I'm starting to figure you out."

"Which means…"

"You're not as tough as you act."

"Oh, God. Now I'm losing all my mystery? How much worse can things get?"

He'd been joking, but she answered seriously. "Things are only going to get better. There hasn't been one negative article printed about you in two weeks."

"What about the windows?" Simon asked as they were packing up.

"What about them?" Gail responded.

He pictured how easy it would be to peer in at them in their new place. "They aren't covered."

"So? There aren't any neighbors." She said this while struggling to get her suitcase zipped. Simon chuckled at the sight of her sitting on it before waving her off so he could finish.

"What about the paparazzi?" he said. "They'll find us eventually."

She'd already moved on to closing down her laptop. "How would they trace us to Autumn Lane? No paperwork's been recorded—not yet."

Once he'd succeeded in closing her suitcase, he gathered up their bags. "We aren't making it a secret where we live. Pretty soon everyone in town will know."

"But not tonight," she said. "So far only a handful of people even know we bought a house."

Something else occurred to him. "What about water?"

She glanced up. "Don't you want to go over there?"

He did. Definitely. But he didn't want to be miserable. "If the utilities are on."

"Even if there's no water we can make it for one night, can't we?" She slipped her power cord in her briefcase. "We'll use the bathroom here before we go. At least we'll have a few hours of privacy without constantly worrying about how we're coming off to my father and brother." She grinned. "I'd hate to get you all excited about skipping out on my family and then renege on the deal."

He lowered his voice. Her brother wasn't home, but her father was asleep in his bedroom. "Too bad you'll never meet my family so you can see what meeting the in-laws is *really* like."

"You plan on avoiding them for two years?"

He thought of his father and how their relationship had flip-flopped through the years. When he'd married Bella, they'd actually been close for the first time in his life. He could hardly believe that now. "I don't have to avoid my family. They know to stay away."

"You're willing to give them up for good?"

"They gave me up first," he said. *Especially my father.* He started down with the suitcases, leaving her to get her computer and makeup bag from the bathroom.

Her brother walked in as Simon was going out to load the car. "You guys moving already?"

Simon stepped aside to avoid a collision. "Got our own place now."

Joe shook his head. "For the life of me I can't believe you're staying in Whiskey Creek."

"Why not? The people here are so friendly."

It was a joke, but Joe's ears turned red. "I meant since you're famous. Matt Stinson, who plays ball for the Packers, has been our only claim to fame. He probably hates it that you're in town."

"In more ways than one," Simon muttered, crouching to fix a wheel on Gail's suitcase.

"What'd you say?"

He lifted his head. "I said I'm going to get your sister a new suitcase."

"Oh." Joe lowered his voice. "You love her, don't you?"

For a moment, Simon felt tongue-tied. How could he respond to this? It was a question that begged an honest answer.

Fortunately, when he hesitated, Joe added, "You'd never do anything to hurt her...."

Grateful for the slightly different slant, Simon stood. "No. I would never do anything to hurt her," he said, and he meant it.

Her brother seemed relieved. "Good."

Gail hurried down the stairs with the last of her belongings and gave her brother a hug. "How'd it go at the station today?"

"Fine. I think Robbie's getting the hang of it. I stayed with him tonight so I could keep an eye on things while he did his homework."

"That was nice of you." She gestured toward the stairs. "Dad was asleep when we got home. Will you tell him we'll see him tomorrow?"

"Sure. By the way..." He caught them before they could leave. "There were some people asking about you at the station earlier."

Leaving the suitcases at the door, Simon turned. "People?"

"Reporters, I think. They didn't identify themselves. They wanted to know if Simon O'Neal had been in town."

"What did you tell them?" Gail asked.

"That I hadn't seen him. They didn't seem to realize I was your brother. But... I get the impression word is out that you're in Whiskey Creek, so...keep your eyes open for an ambush."

"So much for our short reprieve," she said to Simon. "Do we dare sally forth? We could always roast marshmallows here and watch a movie on Netflix or Hulu."

"Wouldn't be the same," he said. "I'm willing to risk it."

Someone knocked on the door of their new house even sooner than Simon had expected. They'd just hauled in their bags. Gail was in the bathroom brushing her teeth. He'd been wrong about the utilities; they had both water and electricity. But because of the late hour—it was nearly eleven—and what Joe had said, there was a greater chance of their visitor being someone Simon didn't want to see than someone he did. He couldn't imagine many people staying out so late on a weeknight here in the town that time forgot.

It had to be a reporter from one of the tabloids. Or some obsessed fan who'd managed to track him down. Simon had experienced both and didn't want to deal with either, especially considering his injured hand, which limited his ability to protect Gail, if it ever came down to that.

He peered out the window. He could see the dark shape of someone standing on the porch, but he couldn't tell who it was or anything about why he or she had come. The outdoor light wouldn't go on. He figured it was burned out, since the rest of their lights worked.

"Gail? It's me!" their visitor called. "I—I know it's late, but Joe said you'd be here. And I wanted you to have this while it's still warm."

Suddenly more curious than defensive, Simon opened the door to find Sophia—the woman he'd met at the coffee shop, the one who'd alienated everyone years ago with her behavior.

"Sorry to bother you." She was carrying what looked like an apple pie and seemed flustered that he'd answered instead of Gail.

"It's fine." He held the screen door. "Would you like to come in?"

She ducked her head as she stepped past him, which brought her hair forward, concealing much of her expression. "I made you both a housewarming gift." Her gaze briefly met his. She was even prettier up close, but he felt no attraction to her. He wasn't sure if that was because she was married, or because he was.

"Thank you," he said as he took the pie. She had oven mitts on her hands, but the ceramic dish was no longer hot enough to need them. "Apple?"

"Yes."

"Smells delicious. I'll put it in the kitchen."

"Where's Gail?" she called after him.

"In the bathroom. She'll be out in a sec."

Gail came into the room as he was returning. "I thought I heard a woman's voice."

Sophia smiled in relief. She obviously didn't feel comfortable around Simon. But he didn't resent that. He was relieved to know she hadn't come because of him. "I brought you another pie. You really liked it the last time you were home."

Gail's eyebrows shot up. "Oh, right. I did. Thank you."

"I've been baking a lot lately."

"The last time we talked, you mentioned that you were thinking about getting a job. How did that go?"

She shrugged. "I decided against it."

"Why?"

"Skip doesn't think it's a good idea, not while Lexi's so young. He's worried about me not being around enough as she goes through puberty."

Simon couldn't help noting the double standard. Hadn't she told him at the coffee shop that her husband was frequently gone himself?

"But…you were talking about a few hours a week at the B and B with Chey and Eve—nothing too time-consuming."

"Turned out they didn't need the help."

Simon guessed that was a lie, but Gail quickly covered for her friends. "I think they're having a tough time staying in the black."

Sophia let it slide. "You're probably right."

"Anyway, I'm sorry you have to put off the job search."

"It's not a big deal. Really."

Gail motioned to the empty room. "And I'm sorry we can't offer you a seat…."

"That's okay. I can't stay. Skip will be wondering where I went—if he ever gets off the phone."

After shooting Simon a glance, Gail said, "He's home this week?"

"Got home late last night. He does that sometimes. Just shows up out of the blue." She laughed, although there was no real mirth in it, and when she tucked her hair behind her ear she immediately untucked it—but not before Simon saw the bruise on her cheek.

"What happened?" he asked.

She acted confused. "What do you mean?"

"To your cheek."

"Oh, that." She rolled her eyes. "I ran into the door. Can you believe it? Clumsy, huh?"

Gail stepped up to inspect her injury. "Looks painful."

"It's not. Not really. It'll heal."

"When did this happen?" Simon asked.

"Last night."

Before or after her husband came home? Simon had no reason to assume that Skip might be abusing his wife. Except that her excuse seemed flimsy. And the way she talked about her husband, as if he had the last say in everything, sounded suspect.

"I know this weekend isn't good for you with everything you've got going, but let me know if you can come to dinner sometime next week," she said, and headed for the door.

When Gail asked, "What day were you thinking?" Simon almost laughed out loud. He'd been right about how hard it was for her to withhold her friendship.

"Tuesday? Wednesday?"

"Tuesday should work. What time?"

"Six?"

Gail's smile grew more certain. "Perfect. Can we bring dessert? Or the wine?"

"There's no need. I've got everything. Thanks. Thanks a lot." Seemingly excited to have obtained a commitment, she left.

"Way to hold your ground," Simon teased after Gail had closed the door. "You showed her."

She groaned. "I know. I'm such a sucker."

"That's okay." He tweaked her nose. "I like suckers. Especially when they're as cute as you are."

"Because I'm a sucker for you, too," she said with a disgruntled look.

"Since when?" he asked with a grin. "If I'd known that, I'd have been taking advantage of it."

She was too busy berating herself for caving with Sophia to respond. "Why did I say yes?"

"Because you had to. She was trying so hard. And it'll be okay. I just hope she can cook." He took the mattress out of the box and began to assemble the pump.

"She can bake. I don't know about anything else. We've never been friends. I just agreed to have dinner with the girl who stole my date for junior prom simply because she could."

"You didn't tell me about that."

"Because it's not what matters. Not compared to Scott."

"Something like that is pretty traumatic to a teenager...."

"I couldn't blame the guy who ditched me. My dad was so strict I had to be home by eleven o'clock, which counted out the after-party. And my prom dress would've looked like a gunnysack compared to everyone else's. He wouldn't let me show an inch of skin."

Simon smiled at the image she painted of herself as an embarrassed girl with a domineering father. "Ah, now I see where you developed your penchant for the boxy business suit."

Her eyebrows came together. "Why don't you like my suits? They're stylish."

He had to speak over the whine of the air pump. "It'd be nice to see you in something sexy for a change."

"That won't fix the red hair and freckles. I'm sure you can see how I might get passed over."

She had a lot more to offer than most women. But he didn't say so. *He'd* passed over her, hadn't he? It took a second look to really see her beauty. "There's nothing wrong with your appearance. Anyway, I'm glad you gave in on dinner."

"Why?"

"Beats kicking Sophia while she's down."

"Like people have kicked you?"

"Deserving it only makes it worse," he said with a wry grin. He squeezed the mattress to see how firm it had become. Almost done. "What about her husband? Is he any more popular than she is?"

Gail sat near him and pulled her knees to her chest like a child. She was so unaware of the assets she did possess. It was refreshing. Beyond refreshing—endearing.

"He keeps everyone at arm's length," she said. "But he has a good reputation. Most of Whiskey Creek has invested with him at one time or another. Even my father. And Martin's about as conservative as a person gets."

"I can only imagine," he said wryly. "What does Skip do?"

"Puts together venture capital partnerships, so he meets with investors all over the world."

Simon turned off the air pump. "Did you see that bruise on her face?"

"I did." She frowned. "The way she kept trying to hide it makes me think it didn't come from a door."

"Have there been rumors about abuse?" Simon rolled out the sleeping bags while she got up and plugged in her laptop.

"A few. She's been seen with other injuries. But it's hard to believe Skip would strike her. He acts like the perfect husband and father—makes sure his family always has the best of everything."

"Maybe they only look perfect in public."

"Or maybe we're jumping to conclusions," she said as she queued up the movie they'd selected, which was another indie film. Unless they were particularly well done, Simon had a hard time watching big, commercial movies like the ones he worked on. After being in the industry for so long, and being exposed to its inner workings even as a child, they seemed too predictable and formulaic to him. He preferred the off-beat humor or unusual situations and settings he could find in indies or foreign films.

"Could be." Lighting the instant log they'd bought on the way over, Simon started a fire. "Has anyone ever come out and asked her if he gets violent?"

Finished prepping the movie, Gail left her computer to warm her hands above the flames. "She'd never admit it, even if they did."

The smell of smoke and accelerant filtered into the room, chasing away some of the mustiness of the old home.

"Maybe she's afraid to leave him for fear he'll *really* hurt her," Simon said. "Or that she'll wind up with nothing. Does she have any education or job skills?"

"Not that I know of. Just her looks, but that's always been enough in the past."

As far as Simon was concerned, she was too Barbie-like, which reminded him of so many of the women he'd met in Hollywood. "I guess she could always become a Playboy Bunny."

Gail arranged her laptop next to the bed he'd made and slipped into her sleeping bag. "I bet you could put her in contact with the right folks."

"I've been invited to the mansion."

"How was it?"

"I didn't go."

"Why not?"

He found that whole scene to be a little too misogynistic. Anyway, it was his father's crowd. But he didn't see any point in denying involvement, however minimal. Having avoided *one* mistake was hardly enough to improve his reputation. "I must've been busy that night."

"How unfortunate for you."

"Should I make the offer?" he asked, just to see what she'd say.

She glared at him. "Stay away from her."

Leaning over, he peered into her face. "Do I detect a note of jealousy?"

"Of course not. I'm just trying to keep you out of trouble."

"Then you won't be interested in this, but—" he caught a lock of her hair between his fingers "—I'd rather make love to you than her any day."

He probably shouldn't have said it. The admission made him that much more aware of her sexually. He wanted to touch her to see if she'd welcome it, to see if she'd respond with the same earthy realness she brought to everything else. She was so different from any of the other women he'd known, most of whom stripped before he could even suggest it. They wanted the bragging rights of having slept with someone famous, wanted to gain entrance to his world or to feel they had the right to ask him to recommend them for an acting role. His partners had used him as much as he'd ever used them. Even his ex had used physical access to her body like a weapon. Or an incentive.

But maybe he was merely justifying what he'd done....

Gail wanted something more from that aspect of a relationship, and that made him eager to see what "more" might feel like. He'd been so empty when she assumed her new role in his life, so disillusioned. But she'd made the little things important again.

He was trying to tell her that he felt differently about her, that making love with her would be different, too, but she wasn't listening.

"You just feel that way because I'm the only woman who's ever refused you," she said with a dismissive laugh, and reached for the hangers they'd brought for their marshmallows. "The second I give in, you won't be interested anymore."

When he didn't say anything, she glanced over to see his response and he forced a smile. "You've got me all figured out."

She studied him for a second. "I didn't offend you, did I?"

"Of course not." What she'd said shouldn't have bothered him. It wouldn't have, except he was beginning to care what she thought of him. Which was crazy. She'd seen him at his absolute worst. The past year he'd been her client, he'd done everything possible to let her know just how little he cared what she or anyone thought. So how could he expect her to see even a glimmer of something worthy in him now?

"Everyone knows what a shitty person I am," he added with a shrug. Then he straightened her hanger, stuck a marshmallow on the end and handed it back to her. "But I can roast a mean marshmallow."

Twenty-Two

Simon didn't talk much the rest of the evening. He was polite but the casual camaraderie they'd established since coming to Whiskey Creek was gone. Gail hadn't realized how much she'd enjoyed his companionship until that warmth was replaced with the old indifference.

Accusing him of wanting her only because he couldn't have her hadn't seemed like a big deal at the time, but it'd hurt him somehow. She was afraid it kept him from changing, becoming a better person. Every time he tried, every time he started to believe he could, she held up the mirror of his past and reminded him that there was no way to outdistance his deeds, that she'd never forget and therefore he couldn't, either.

He was probably confused and disappointed. So was she. She didn't want to send mixed signals. But no one had ever frightened her in quite the same way as Simon O'Neal. Charisma rolled off him in waves. If she let it carry her away, there was no telling where she'd end up.

"You okay?" she said at one point.

"Fine." He offered her another perfectly roasted marshmallow. But his emotional withdrawal made her feel as if the sun had suddenly disappeared behind a cloud.

Simon dozed off before the movie ended, but Gail lay next to him long after, wide-awake and feeling... she didn't know what. Remorseful. Conflicted. And attracted. Always attracted.

In the light of the log's dying embers, she admired the contours of his face while trying to decide how to keep this "marriage" on track. She was supposed to care about Matt. She'd yearned for him for years. The flutter she'd felt in her stomach when she'd seen him earlier had made her wonder what she'd done. Yet she'd scarcely thought of him since their encounter in the coffee shop. As long as Simon was around, nothing else seemed to matter.

But Simon wouldn't be around forever....

Suddenly he opened his eyes as if her intense regard had dragged him from sleep. She told herself to roll over and pretend she hadn't been watching him, but she refused to be that much of a coward. Even after his eyes met hers, she continued to stare just as intently and allowed him to do the same.

Finally he broke the silence. "What are you thinking about?"

"You," she admitted with a sigh.

"Don't waste your time on that." He turned over, but she refused to let him exclude her so easily. She put her palm on his back, and when he didn't move, she slid it up and into his hair. The thick, silky locks felt so good....

"What do you want from me?" he murmured without moving. "Sometimes the way you look at me...it's as if you want to be with me. And yet...the second I act on that, you shut me down."

"I'm sorry," she said.

After another strained pause, during which she went on touching his hair, he turned to face her again and unzipped his sleeping bag. "Come here."

Gail's heart pumped hard and fast. She'd done it now; she'd started down the path of no return. But she couldn't blame Simon. He was right about the way she looked at him. And what else could he assume when she kept touching him?

"Maybe...maybe we should lay down some ground rules first," she said.

"What kind of ground rules?"

"How about this can only happen once. And it doesn't mean anything. Those kinds of rules."

"There isn't any need."

But the next few minutes would change everything. At least for her. She wet her lips. "Are you sure?"

"Positive. You coming or not? Because it's cold, and I'm going to zip this thing up if you're not."

Supremely conscious of the fact that she'd chosen to wear a T-shirt and pajama bottoms—nightclothes that weren't the slightest bit sexy just so she wouldn't be tempted to do exactly what she was about to do—she took a deep breath and wiggled out of her own bag. Fleetingly she wondered if her underwear was attractive enough. She thought so. She'd recently bought new ones. Just marrying Simon was enough to make her worry about her underclothes.

Thinking of her panties made her question whether she should undress before climbing inside his bag. They already had *his* T-shirt and pajama bottoms to remove, which wouldn't be easy in such a confined space.

The practical side of Gail suggested she strip now. But maybe that was unromantic. He didn't tell her to....

In the end, she didn't have the nerve. She figured he could get creative; after all, he had a lot more experience than she did.

"I'm a little self-conscious," she admitted.

"Everything will be fine," he said.

"But...talk about pressure." She worried her lip. "You've been with supermodels and actresses and Olympic athletes."

He surprised her with a laugh. "Where did you get Olympic athletes?"

"Just guessing. Some of them are pretty hot, right? And you can take your pick."

Sobering, he lowered his voice. "It's not a contest, Gail. You don't have to compete with anyone."

"I wouldn't want to be your worst. I'd at least like to hit somewhere in the middle."

"God, no wonder you don't want to sleep with me."

"What do you mean?"

"Never mind. Come on."

The nerves in her stomach were making her jittery. "I'm just trying to tell you it's been a long time for me. I'm out of practice."

"How long has it been?"

"Three years."

He shoved a hand through his hair. "Wow, you really are selective. How many men have you been with?"

"At one time?"

He raised his eyebrows.

"That was a joke."

"You had me for a second. How many?"

She considered lying. Too few might make her seem like she wasn't playful or sexy enough—or someone guys sought out. But she figured he should know what he was getting into. "Two."

"That makes it easy to see why you're self-conscious. But it's just me, right? You don't have anything to worry about."

"Just you…" she repeated, and somehow managed to suppress a nervous giggle. She was going to sleep with one of the biggest movie stars on the planet. She figured she had a right to be anxious about it. But after he'd helped her inside his bag and managed to zip it up, he simply enfolded her in his arms. He didn't even kiss her.

"Simon?" she said when minute after minute ticked away and he didn't move. He seemed to be going to sleep.…

"What?" he mumbled.

Sure enough, he sounded as if he was just on this side of sleep. "Aren't you going to take off your clothes?"

"No."

Shocked, she blinked at the darkness. She couldn't look into his face. The way he was holding her kept her cheek against his chest. "Why not?" she whispered.

"Because you'll only regret it in the morning."

This was not the answer she'd been expecting. He'd tried to make sex part of her contract, for crying out loud. "How do you know?"

"You don't trust me."

She considered that before breaking the silence again. "So…what are we going to do?"

His hand swept her hair back as his lips brushed her forehead. "Isn't it obvious? We're going to sleep."

"Have you ever just…slept with someone like this before?"

"Only my wife."

So she hadn't gone *too* far. He was offering her the comfort of his body in an asexual way and she sort of liked that. It certainly eased her fear and anxiety, even her self-consciousness.

As she closed her eyes and breathed in the scent of warm male, she experienced a strange sense of satisfaction. Maybe this wasn't as exciting as a sexual encounter, but it was oddly gratifying. "You smell good," she whispered.

His hand slipped up the back of her shirt. But he didn't bring it around to her breasts. He merely flattened his palm against her bare skin. Then, slowly but surely, his breathing evened out and hers must have, too, because the next thing she knew it was morning.

Gail had slept deeply. But when she came to full awareness, she realized that the contentment she'd felt the night before was gone. She liked being in Simon's arms just as much as before—didn't want to be anywhere else. But after spending the night pressed to his body, the awkwardness of climbing into his sleeping bag had vanished. So had her reluctance to touch him and be touched by him. As a matter of fact, all she could think about was getting naked so she could feel more of him.

The love scene in *Shiver* played in her mind as Simon's chest rose and fell with each breath. She imagined him making love to her as he and his costar had depicted, imagined his mouth moving down her stomach—

"What's wrong?"

Her breath caught in her throat. He was awake. But his thoughts didn't seem to be going in the same direction as hers. He didn't sound happy to be disturbed. "Nothing, why?"

"You keep moving."

"Oh. Sorry," she said, but shifted again—to bring their hips into full contact.

She noted his surprise as she glanced up at him, felt his irritation fall away as he came almost instantly to full attention. She'd attracted his interest; she could tell by his growing erection. He opened his mouth to say something. Then the doorbell rang.

"No way," she grumbled.

He rolled onto his back and covered his face with one arm. "Already?"

She pulled her cell phone closer to check the time. It was barely eight.

"Who do you think it is?" he asked without looking over.

"Probably Kathy," Gail guessed. "She said she'd bring us copies of the fully executed real estate contract, but I don't know why she has to do it this early. I'm sure she couldn't wait to see *you* again. I'll get it."

As soon as she left the sleeping bag, Simon got up, too, and went into the bathroom. She heard the door close just as she peered out the window. But the person on her porch wasn't Kathy. It was a man.

Did she know him? There was something familiar about him, but he was turned away from her....

"Who is it?" she called through the door.

"Tex O'Neal." At the sound of her voice he'd turned back to face her. It was Simon's father.

"Oh, God," she muttered. "Simon?"

She'd had to whisper his name. Simon probably couldn't hear her over the running water. In any case, he didn't answer.

"I need to talk to Simon," Tex called.

Gail pivoted to head down the hall. She wanted to check with her husband before letting Tex in. She knew he and his father weren't on good terms. Their relationship had always been rocky, more so in recent years. But what was the point of asking Simon whether or not to let him in? They couldn't sit inside their house and refuse to open the door when she'd already given away the fact that someone was home.

Self-conscious about her appearance, since she'd come straight from bed, she smoothed her T-shirt and cautiously opened the door.

Simon's father wasn't nearly as attractive as Simon. He didn't have the same bone structure—the kind that made Simon almost as beautiful as he was handsome. Simon had inherited those features from his mother. But his father's face was interesting the way Clint Eastwood's was. Shrewd. Tough. Unflinching. Despite their visual differences, father and son had the same powerful personalities, however—the same magnetism and keen intellect. At least that was Gail's impression.

"I want to see my son," he said without preamble.

His gaze swept over her, then shifted away as if he found her wanting, which made Gail regret her courtesy in answering his knock. "He's in the bathroom. If you'd like to come in, he'll be out shortly."

She stepped back, half expecting to hear the jingle of spurs as Tex walked in. He'd taken a lot of acting parts over the years, but none fit him better than that of a hardened gunslinger; that, of course, was where he'd gotten his nickname. He'd been called Tex for so long she couldn't remember his real name. Even now he was wearing a pair of fancy snakeskin cowboy boots and a hat. No doubt he'd come straight from the ranch he owned somewhere farther north.

Was it near the town of Chico? Gail couldn't remember that, either.

Simon came out of the bathroom, froze as soon as he saw his father, then flipped his hair out of his eyes and ambled toward him. "What a surprise," he drawled.

Tex acknowledged him with a brief tilt of the head. "Must be, considering you disappeared without letting anyone know where you were going."

The belligerent attitude that had become synonymous with Simon over the past couple of years reasserted itself. His eyes glittered; his chin jutted forward. The transformation was so marked and immediate it caught Gail off guard. Obviously just seeing his father was enough to drag him into a dark place.

"So…how did you find me?" Simon asked.

"Ian finally got tired of me busting his balls and gave me the information I was after. But he said not to tell you it was him."

"So of course you out him first thing."

His father studied him for a second. "I'm not in the business of protecting Ian."

"No, that would require looking beyond your own concerns. But I'm afraid harassing my business manager was a waste of your time. It would've been smarter to call me."

"Why would I bother?" he said. "You won't pick up for me."

Simon shoved a hand through his hair. "Most people would take that as a sign and not show up on my doorstep."

"Ordinarily, I'd leave you in peace. You've made your wishes clear where I'm concerned." He tipped his hat to punctuate his words. "But this isn't personal. It's business. If you weren't my lead actor, I'd be banging on someone else's door."

A muscle flexed in Simon's cheek. "*Your* lead actor? What the hell are you talking about?"

With a condescending chuckle, Tex stepped forward. "You don't know? Man, you really have been in a world of hurt. I'm bankrolling your next film."

"No. Frank and Jimmy Kozlowski are bankrolling it."

"Together with a few other investors, and I happen to be one of them."

Nostrils flaring, Simon clenched his jaw. When he spoke, it sounded like he forced each word through his teeth. "*You* put up money for *Hellion?* Your name has never been mentioned in connection with the project."

Tex gave a careless shrug. "Ian knew when I came on board. I've never made a secret of it."

Gail felt her fingernails curve into her palms. Good old Ian, playing both ends against the middle. What had he been thinking? That Simon would never find out his father was involved?

That wasn't realistic. He must've been hoping the movie would be done by the time Simon learned. That was certainly possible. When there were a number of producers, a group of investors, not all of them had a say in the actual making of the film.

"Why?" Simon asked. "There are so many other projects, so many other actors. Why are you involved in *this?*"

"Frankly, it was the kind of opportunity I didn't want to pass up. A script like this doesn't come around every day. And you couldn't be more suited to the part."

Disgust etched lines in Simon's forehead. "I'm playing a serial killer, for God's sake!"

"But he's a good husband and father at the same time, very complex. That's what makes him interesting and I'm sure it's why you took the part. Anyway, not too many actors have more box office appeal than you do right now. We wait much longer, that might not be the case. So how can I convince you to get your ass back to work?"

Now Simon laughed. "You can't. I'm not going back until I gain custody of Ty."

"You won't get Ty. You've already made sure of that."

Simon folded his arms. "I wonder where I learned the behavior that brought me to this point."

"It's not your behavior I'm trying to understand. It's why you didn't bother to be more discreet."

"Maybe I'm not interested in becoming the Great Pretender, like you."

"If you had any brains you wouldn't be in this situation. You had Bella by the jugular, and you let her go. No one knows that better than me."

"That you could even suggest I go public with what happened, after the part you played, makes me want to kick your ass," Simon growled. "You were probably hoping I'd do just that. Give you a spot in the limelight again."

Tex waved his words away. "Oh, come on, your marriage to Bella would never have lasted, regardless of anything I did. It was already on the rocks." He gestured toward Gail. "This one won't last, either. One woman could never keep you happy, not when just about every female you come across is willing to lie down and spread her legs. You're too much like me."

Gail felt sick. "Out," she said. "Get out of our house. Now."

Simon grabbed her by the arm before she could get in Tex's face. "I'm nothing like you, and I'm going to prove it."

His father adjusted his hat. "Knock yourself out," he said. "But understand this—you have three days. I'll be staying at the B and B on Sutter Street until Tuesday. You don't make arrangements with me to start that damn film, I'll sue you for breach of contract and hire someone else. We'll see if the publicity from that helps you get Ty back. The judge and everyone else will think, 'Simon screwed up again, just like we figured he would.' Then hiding out here in the back of beyond will be a waste of time. Why not be realistic while you have the chance?"

"While it serves you, you mean?" Simon said. "While it gives you a film that'll make you millions more than if you hired another actor?"

"The people I talked into signing on are upset at the way this thing is going. I owe them something, too."

"But who do you owe more?" Gail asked. "Don't you care about your grandson? Don't you want a better relationship with him than you have with your son?"

Tex shifted his attention to her. "I think you shouldn't get involved," he said, and stalked out.

Rage consumed Simon. His father's nerve in showing up here and acting as if...as if he'd had nothing to do with the situation that had started everything made Simon want to put his fist through a wall.

"You okay?" Gail's voice came to him as if from far away. He knew she meant well, that she was trying to help him, but he couldn't be with her right now. Considering the rage bubbling up inside him, he couldn't be with anyone he hoped to have a relationship with afterward because there'd be no way to take back the things he was about to say.

"I need to get out of here," he muttered.

She stood in his path. "And go where? You don't even know the area."

"Who cares?"

"*I* do."

"Then you're a fool. And you'll live to regret it. Get out of my way."

"No. If you leave now you'll do something *you* regret."

On some level, he agreed with her. He thought of Ty and wanted to make him proud. But even his son wasn't enough to stem the deluge of anger whipping through him. Because trying to reclaim Ty felt like he was grasping at air. His father was right; he'd never get his son back.

He needed a liquor store, some way to dull the jagged emotions that felt like barbed wire being yanked through his heart. If he didn't do something he'd explode—or finally give his old man what he deserved. He wanted to do exactly that, but if he ever started down that road, he'd wind up in prison. He doubted he'd be able to quit slugging him.

He tried to get around Gail, but she stopped him. "No!" she said more firmly. "I won't let him take from you what you've achieved during these past two and a half weeks."

"I don't give a shit about what I've achieved. I don't give a shit about anything!" He thought his temper would frighten her. It'd certainly frightened her when he'd stormed into her office following that bogus rape accusation. But she didn't let go or back away, even when he tried to shake her off.

"I'm not giving up on you, damn it!" she cried. "Don't let him win!"

"You have no choice but to give up. Our marriage—

this joke of a relationship—is over." Determined to get through the door, he picked her up and set her aside. But she came after him again, catching his arm. When he whirled, ready to shout—to say whatever he had to say to get her to accept who and what he really was—she grabbed his hand and shoved it up her shirt.

"Stay," she breathed.

The shock of suddenly having her breast in his hand shot straight to his groin. He told himself it wasn't right to take her up on the offer she was making. Not when he knew why she was making it. But the anger was like a monster inside him, a monster with a mind of its own. It demanded some kind of physical action, a release....

Still, he hesitated for a second and almost let go. He respected her too much to use her. But there was more than anger at work. He also wanted her—badly. And when her hand clenched in his hair and she turned his head to kiss him as if she wouldn't take no for an answer, he knew he wouldn't be able to refuse.

Especially when she met his lips with an open mouth and arched into him, holding nothing back.

Twenty-Three

Gail had never experienced anything even close to what was happening. The emotions flying between her and Simon were so charged they seemed to be sparking. Desperate to come together as fast as possible, they tore at each other's T-shirts, managed to remove them and, naked from the waist up, feasted on each other's mouths, necks and chests—gasping for breath in between.

Gail felt as if she'd just climbed aboard a runaway train. The crash was coming. But she wasn't tempted to jump off. Not yet. Everything had changed. It didn't matter that they were only temporarily married. It didn't matter that sex was against the rules *she'd* established. It didn't matter that it was full daylight and, after spending the night in Simon's sleeping bag, she didn't look her best. She was keeping him safe. That was all she cared about.

Fortunately, he was too preoccupied with touching and tasting her to notice that her hair was messy. And she was too busy enjoying the pleasure he gave her to be self-conscious.

When Simon lifted her in his arms, she warned him not to pull out his stitches, but he didn't seem concerned. He carried her to the mattress, yanked her pajama bottoms off and buried his face in her breasts while touching her in other, more sensitive areas.

"I wish I had better use of my right hand," he muttered, but he was doing just fine with his left.

Recalling all the fantasies she'd had over the years that centered on Simon O'Neal, Gail could hardly believe this was real. Especially because Simon in the flesh was so much sexier than the Simon in her dreams. He was far more aggressive than either of her former lovers—more demanding, too—but he was also careful not to take it too far. She could sense whenever he'd draw back, when he'd check her expression and responsiveness to make sure she was enjoying how he touched her.

They were both walking on the far edge of control and there wasn't a more exhilarating feeling. Gail had never let herself go to this point. She *couldn't* pull back, didn't even want to.

"I was wrong about you," he told her, his voice husky as he spread her legs.

She could barely speak. She was trembling as she clung to his arm, already close to climax. "In what… way?"

"In every way." His mouth descended on hers, mimicking what he was doing with his fingers until she stopped him.

"I want *you* inside me," she whispered. "I can't wait. It feels like I've been waiting forever for the man I could desire this much."

His gaze locked on to hers. She wasn't sure if he was still angry, but there was a feral look in his eyes. He got up to get a condom from his wallet and put it on. But then he pinned her arms above her head and covered her with his hard, warm body.

Gail allowed her eyes to close at the solid weight of him, the delicious pressure as he pushed inside. She was lost. She hadn't protected herself against anything. She'd fallen head over heels for a man who was emotionally damaged and she'd done it in record time. Probably because, despite what she'd tried to tell herself, she'd been halfway in love with Simon from the beginning. Matt had been a schoolgirl crush by comparison, someone she'd only *thought* she wanted.

A trickle of fear ran through her as that truth crystallized. Because an even harder truth came right behind it. Simon was going to break her heart, and that wouldn't take very long, either. But as the friction increased and the tension mounted, future pain wasn't a concern. She'd never made love like this before because she'd never *felt* like this before. Despite all the reasons she shouldn't be, she was desperately in love, and her body *knew* Simon's touch, could distinguish it from anyone else's.

As she reached that first peak, with Simon's smell and body in and around her, she felt as if her bones would melt and somehow meld with his. She looked up to see him watching her. He was soaking up every nuance of her expression, reveling in every gasp, and the smile of accomplishment that curved his lips in that moment was probably the best part of all.

Simon was shaking with the effort of holding back, but he was determined to bring Gail to climax several times before allowing himself the same pleasure. He liked feeling her shudder when she reached that crest, liked hearing her moan his name. But he knew he was being unselfish partly to escape the guilt. He no longer had a heart to offer, so he had to deliver where he could.

He happened to be good at this. Today he was too worked up to have the stamina he wanted, but he was doing what he could to last.

"Again," he whispered, and closed his eyes. He needed to think of something other than the warm wetness, the clenching of her body, or it would all be over. But she didn't seem happy that he had to mentally check out in order to make that happen.

Encouraging him to roll onto his back, she got on top and that was the beginning of the end. When she took control, he could believe she was making love to him because she wanted the pleasure as badly as he did and would have no regrets—and that was all it took to render him helpless.

As soon as his hands found her breasts, wave after glorious wave ripped through him. Closing his eyes again, he succumbed to the release until he felt completely drained. Then he looked up at her, still breathing hard. He had no idea what to expect next. He was terrified she'd start to cry, feel angry that they'd broken her "rules," cling to him as if this was the beginning of forever, or—worse than anything—make him squirm by telling him she loved him.

Fortunately, she did none of those things. With a devilish smile, she bent her head for a quick peck that ended with a playful bite on his bottom lip.

"Not bad," she said. "Not bad at all."

He raised an uncertain eyebrow. "You've had better than that?" *He* certainly hadn't. Not in recent memory. Maybe it was because he hadn't been drunk, for a change, but he already knew he'd never forget this.

"A couple times." Her manner suggested she might

be teasing, but he couldn't be sure. "Anyway, I think you're talented enough to make the two years we're married go a lot faster."

He still wasn't convinced she felt as cavalier as she was acting, but he was willing to play along. "You thought I might not be?"

"I thought you needed a break from your stud services, but… I'm glad I decided not to worry about that," she said. Then she got up and headed into the bathroom as if what had happened was nothing more than a casual encounter.

Thank God. Covering his face with one arm, Simon breathed a sigh of relief.

Pressing herself against the bathroom door, Gail covered her face. She was shaking and couldn't seem to calm down. But she wouldn't let Simon know how deeply their lovemaking had affected her. He wasn't capable of dealing with anything that complicated right now, even if he cared about her. And she knew he didn't. Not in the same way she cared about him.

"What have I done?" she mouthed as she stared at herself in the mirror. But it was too late for regret or remonstrance. At the very least, she was infatuated with Simon. Now that she wasn't caught up in the moment, she was reluctant to call it *love.* Even if it was, she could still salvage her pride.

"Gail?"

He was outside the door.

She hurried to flush the toilet, even though she hadn't used it. "Yes?"

"You okay?"

"Of course. Why?"

"Just wanted to be sure."

"I'm fine. Thanks. You definitely know how to show a lady a good time." She bit her lip, forcing herself to stop talking before she gave away the fact that she was completely thrown by what had just happened.

"Good. Glad to hear it. Let's take a shower."

He wanted more. And, heaven help her, so did she.

Their first encounter hadn't been bad, not by any stretch of the imagination. But, thanks to practice and a growing familiarity, sex with Simon got even more enjoyable as the weekend wore on. Gail was surprised at how quickly she became comfortable with the intimacy and how easily she lost her self-consciousness. She'd been so worried about comparing unfavorably to his other lovers, but that was crazy. If their relationship wasn't going to last, what did it matter?

Other than a short stint here and there when they ran out to buy food and more condoms, they'd spent the weekend holed up in the house, making love, sleeping and eating. Ironically, it felt like a real honeymoon. Gail knew Josh would love to hear the dirty details of the past two days, but she planned to give Simon the same respect and privacy she was counting on from him. As if to confirm that, she ignored Josh's call when it came in.

"Who is it?" Simon asked when she set her phone back on the carpet.

Curling into him, she kissed his bare shoulder. "Josh."

"What do you think he wants?"

"To update me on how things are going."

"On Sunday?"

"He's a workaholic, like me. And he's probably dying to hear what's happening with us."

It was getting dark outside. Gail almost couldn't believe they'd spent the whole weekend indulging in hedonistic behavior. But she'd already crossed all the lines she'd intended not to cross. At this point, there was no reason not to enjoy Simon while she could.

"It's peaceful here, don't you think?" She'd been careful not to mention his father, but the knowledge that Tex was staying at A Room with a View and had been there for two days made her uneasy. She guessed Simon felt the same, probably worse, and wondered what he planned to do about his father's ultimatum.

Maybe she'd lose Simon much sooner than she'd expected to....

"It's been perfect." He kissed her, and his tongue met hers briefly. "You don't regret what we've done, do you?"

He'd spoken casually, but she sensed that her answer mattered.

"What's to regret? It was about time I got laid, right?" She chuckled as if it meant nothing more than that, and he didn't follow up.

"Who were the other two?" he asked at length.

She ran a hand over the contours of his flat stomach. "The other two?"

"You said you've slept with two other guys."

Rising up on one elbow, she gave him a challenging look, but she was teasing and she could tell he knew that. "Do you really want to talk about past lovers?"

He surprised her by remaining serious. "Only because I'm guessing they meant something to you."

The air mattress shifted as she rearranged the blankets, which were twisted around their feet. "Hardly."

"What does that mean?"

"The first was more of a date-rape situation. He

didn't like me saying no, felt I owed him more than a good-night kiss in exchange for dinner."

His eyebrows knitted as he helped her untangle the blankets. She liked him with his hair mussed and his jaw darkening with beard growth. She wasn't sure she'd ever seen him look sexier, even in the movies. "I hope you turned him in."

"I wish I had. At the time I felt that maybe I'd invited it by acting interested in him. I was so excited when he finally asked me out. Now that I'm older, I have no idea why I let him get away with what he did. But I was twenty-five and inexperienced. And I thought maybe I was weird for not *wanting* to have sex with him on the first date. He was really handsome, someone most girls would desire."

"Where is he now?"

"Who knows? I met him at a dance place some of my employees dragged me to. We didn't have any contact after that."

"And the other guy?"

"That was a much better experience. He was quite a bit older than me, very kind—a college professor complete with the tweed jackets." She smiled in memory of Skylar Henshaw's conservative wardrobe. "I liked his calm, trustworthy manner. We were together for several months."

"Why'd you break up?"

"He decided to get back with his ex-wife. She was a lovely woman, and they had children together. I never could understand why they split."

His hand slid over the curve of her waist and down around her hip in a gentle caress. "Was it because of you?"

"No, I met him at a Starbucks after his divorce. He

offered me his table because it was too crowded for me to use my laptop any other way."

"How romantic," he said dryly.

She smiled. "He was nice, like I said."

He kissed her neck, her ear. "Did he leave you brokenhearted, Gail?"

She closed her eyes. "Not really. I was ready to tell him I wanted to move on. I figured it was lucky he'd come to the same decision. Our relationship was…comfortable but not passionate. I liked that he didn't demand more from me than I was willing to give. I was building my business and didn't have a lot of time or energy for anything else. He took care of my creature comforts."

Simon raised his head. "Sounds more like a father figure."

"I guess he was. But we both understood that."

"And then there was Matt."

Gail stretched. "I didn't sleep with Matt, remember?"

"You wanted to."

She didn't correct him.

"Will you in the future?"

"Maybe." She glanced away so he couldn't tell how troubling she found that question. He'd spoken as if it wouldn't matter to him if she did.

"Why haven't you slept with anyone from Whiskey Creek?" he asked.

"I almost slept with Ted in high school."

"Your friend? The author?"

"That would be him."

"What happened?"

"His mother caught us getting naked and told her sister, who's the biggest gossip in town. The rumors going around afterward were enough to keep me on the straight and narrow. I couldn't bear the thought of news like that getting back to my father. My mother had already disappointed him. I didn't want to be next."

He ran his finger along her jawline. "What did your mother do?"

Oh, God, this, too? Gail almost said she didn't want to talk about Linda, but she supposed she might as well get it out of the way. "She left us for an old boyfriend from high school."

"Us?"

"There was no question that Joe and I might go with her. She packed up and disappeared while we were at school. We heard from her periodically that first year, but…she's the type who shies away from conflict whenever she can, and I think she hated having to speak to my father, to be reminded of what she'd done. So, once she remarried, the calls became more and more infrequent. Soon, it was just too awkward to talk at all, even at Christmas. *Especially* at Christmas."

"It must've been tough to lose your mother that way."

Probably not as tough as it'd been for him to lose his mother. At least she'd had her father. Besides, the last thing she wanted from Simon O'Neal was sympathy. "I've always had the love I need. The hard part was feeling I had to make up for what she did, to prove to my father that not all women are the same."

He rolled onto his back. "That's a lot of pressure. Must've been a relief to go to college." He paused. "You went to college, right?"

"I did. Stanford."

He whistled. "I'm impressed."

She adjusted the pillow so she could look into his face, but thanks to the setting sun and the fact that they hadn't yet turned on any lights, it was harder and harder to see. "What about you?"

"I was too busy rebelling to go to college."

That didn't surprise her. "Did you attend acting school?"

"Who needs acting school when you have a father as famous as mine?"

She heard the bitter edge to his voice. "The connection must have provided a few key contacts, but... the way I've heard it, the two of you have never gotten along." That was certainly how it had appeared when Tex showed up at the house. "I can't imagine he bent over backward to lend you a hand."

"We've always had a love-hate relationship. There were times when I was a kid that I desperately wanted to win his love. But too many other things stood in the way. He hated my mother with a passion, even though what happened was as much his fault."

"Why would he blame her? That hardly seems fair."

"He wanted her to terminate the pregnancy. When she refused, it made his marriage even more difficult than it already was. Then her family found out, and the rest of the world. He hates looking bad, wants everyone to admire him. But because of me he couldn't escape the consequences of his actions. I mean, don't get me wrong, there've been times when he's decided to be the father he never was, but...he can't sustain it."

"I remember seeing both of you from a distance at the premiere of *Now or Never*."

"That was shortly after I married Bella." It was also several years before he'd hired Gail. "He wanted to be part of Ty's life, so he was busy trying to be a good grandfather."

"What changed that?"

A muscle twitched in Simon's jaw. "He couldn't

maintain that, either. If there's anything consistent about Tex O'Neal, it's inconsistency."

That didn't really answer her question. It certainly gave her no details, no specifics. But she didn't push it. He was still talking but he'd gone back to the subject of his career and his father's response to his getting into acting.

"I believe that at one point he tried to limit my options, but it was too late to do the kind of damage he could've inflicted earlier on. He hates growing old, being counted out. Feels like I've stolen everything he used to have. So he's done what he can to take what's mine."

"What does that mean?"

He grew pensive. "Never mind. He's just…not your typical father. Or grandfather."

"You've climbed higher than he ever did. That probably bothers him. And Ty's an extension of you."

"Maybe, but…his name carried enough weight to open certain doors. I owe it to his career that mine ever got a start."

"Those doors would've been slammed in your face if you didn't have the looks and talent to become who you are," she pointed out. "You should be proud of yourself."

"Proud of myself," he repeated with a self-deprecating chuckle. He didn't say so, but she got the impression he didn't hear that line very often.

"Yes, you've accomplished a great deal."

"I got lucky. It worked out."

In Gail's opinion, he was a little too quick to dismiss his success. He certainly wasn't as conceited as some people accused him of being. Even she'd accused him of that. But then… Simon had been accused of almost everything at one time or another. She'd come to believe there was a lot of misconception about him.

"I think most people in America would find that an understatement." She bent her head to rub her lips against the soft skin of his chest. "If only it could work out so well for all the starving actors in L.A."

He didn't comment. He toyed with her hair, which fell down around him. "You must've had plenty of chances to experiment with boys in college."

"We're back to my sex life? Jeez, you have a one-track mind." She touched his face, kissed him. She loved being so familiar with him.

"I'm just trying to understand what your life's been like," he said, easily rolling her beneath him.

She stared up into his eyes. "By your standards, it's been boring, okay? You would've jiggled your knee all through it."

"Jiggled my knee?"

"That's what you do when you're bored, or anxious. Anyway, I didn't sleep around in college because I'd been trained to be cautious, and I was too busy with my schoolwork to socialize. I had to get straight A's so I could feel good about sending my report cards home to Daddy." She would've shrugged, except his weight pressing her into the mattress made that impossible. Her tone implied it instead. "Or maybe it was just that I didn't meet the right guy. I was kind of shy, and I've always been self-conscious about my red hair."

She was surprised she didn't mind mentioning that to him, although it was something she generally kept to herself. She supposed it was because she didn't have any hopes or expectations where Simon was concerned. Since she'd had to count him out from the beginning, there was no point in pretending *not* to have the insecurities that were as much a part of her as her desire for discipline and order. Considering who Simon was and the type of women he usually surrounded himself with, her shortcomings would be very obvious, anyway.

Supporting the bulk of his own weight with one hip and shoulder, he twisted a strand of her hair around his finger. "I like the color of your hair."

"Sure you do." She managed to push him the rest of the way off. "But for your information, I wasn't trying to solicit a compliment. Besides, you don't have any choice at the moment except to make do. I'm better than nothing, remember?"

He didn't seem pleased to have his words thrown back at him. "I was dying for a drink that day. And I was still angry over the rape accusation. I didn't mean what I said."

She kicked off the blankets that covered her feet. "Of course you did. But that's okay. I am what I am." With a smile to let him know she really didn't care if he found her lacking, she rolled off the mattress and onto the carpet. "Why don't we get dressed and head down to Just Like Mom's. I think it's time for a proper meal."

"Gail…"

He sounded too serious. She didn't want to hear what he had to say. She could only handle what was happening between them if she kept things light and didn't expect too much. "Come on." Resisting the urge to cover her nudity, she got to her feet. "Enough being lazy."

"I really *didn't* mean it," he said, but she was already on her way to the bathroom and pretended not to hear.

Twenty-Four

Just Like Mom's had purple walls, white ruffled curtains and half a dozen high chairs lined up at the entrance. The booths around the perimeter of the main dining area were done in lavender vinyl; the country-style oak tables in the middle of the floor had chairs sporting cushions with big bows that could only have been hand-sewn. Simon had never seen a restaurant that reminded him more of his grandmother's house. Not that he'd been able to spend much time there. Grandma Moffitt had been too upset about the circumstances of his birth to ever fully forgive his mother, and him by extension. She preferred her other grandkids, who were girls. But he'd always secretly liked the homey comfort of her rambler in Palm Springs.

"Smells good, doesn't it?" Gail murmured over the bell that jingled when they walked in.

The place wasn't crowded, but it was doing a brisk business for eight o'clock on a Sunday night. "Pot roast," he said.

"Mildred Davies makes the best meat loaf and beef stew imaginable. I'm sure the pot roast isn't bad, either."

Through the two-foot opening where the food came

out, he saw a short, round woman with a cap of snow-
white hair directing traffic in the kitchen. "That's the
cook? Mildred Davies?"

"Cook and owner," Gail said. "As you can tell, she's
getting on in years but she manages to keep up. After
dinner you'll have to try her carrot cake. Delicious."

"Maybe I'll *start* with it." Somehow, he felt younger,
more innocent and certainly more content than the man
he'd been in L.A. Either the paparazzi couldn't find him
or they'd been unwilling to make such a long drive on
the off chance of picking up a detail or two about his
private life. He hadn't heard from Bella for twenty-four
hours. He had less craving for alcohol than at any previous point since giving it up. And, best of all, for the
first time since the event that had caused him to un-
ravel, he was gaining confidence that he'd be able to
do what was necessary to get Ty back.

It wasn't until he thought of his father's visit yesterday morning, and the possibility of running into Tex in
Whiskey Creek, that some of the old anger and uneasi-
ness returned. His father seemed to appear every time
Simon began to get on his feet.

But he wasn't going to let Tex provoke him. Tex
could sue if he wanted. Simon would gladly pay resti-
tution for any financial loss he caused the producers of
Hellion, but he wouldn't allow his father to ruin his life
yet again. He wasn't ready to jump back into the world
that had nearly driven him crazy. Ty was the prize.
Ty—not another movie or another fifty million dollars.

Once he was granted custody, even if it was only partial, maybe he'd bring Ty to Whiskey Creek. They could
spend their summers here enjoying Gail's friendship,
whenever she came home, and maybe the friendships
of some of the people he'd met at the coffee shop. He

and Ty could forget the opulence and excesses associated with his career, they could play baseball, eat at this tacky but homey restaurant, check out the old-fashioned soda fountain down the street, hike in the mountains....

Simon wanted to take Gail's hand, to communicate his gratitude for all she'd done. Despite his initial skepticism, her involvement in his life had made a huge difference. But ever since they'd left the house, she'd been careful not to so much as brush against him, which felt odd, considering. At first, he thought he was only imagining the change. But the more minutes that went by without physical contact, the more convinced he became that she was doing it on purpose. She was determined not to expect him to act like a boyfriend.

He appreciated that she wasn't suddenly clingy. Their current arrangement was what he'd asked for from the start. Now he had what he wanted, and yet her withdrawal bothered him. In his opinion, she was being *too* vigilant about making sure there was no emotional spillover. Why couldn't they just relax and do and say as they pleased for the time being?

He was about to broach the subject. He wasn't ready for Gail to raise her defenses again. It'd been too long since he'd felt close to anyone, and he wasn't willing to lose it so soon.

But the hostess, a middle-aged woman who wore a purple uniform with a tag that said Tilly, approached before he could bring it up. Her mouth formed an *O* the minute she recognized him, but she cleared her throat and addressed Gail. "Two for dinner?" she said in a gravelly smoker's voice.

Gail seemed amused by the hostess's reaction to his presence. He was amused by it himself. True to Whiskey Creek form, she didn't gush over him or ask for his autograph, but she was obviously flustered.

"Hi, Tilly," Gail said.

"Great to see you back," the waitress responded.

"It's great to be home. We'd like a booth, please."

Pressing a hand to her chest as if her heart was beating too fast, Tilly glanced at Simon, but looked away as soon as he met her eyes. "Right this way."

She took two menus from the holder but dropped one. When Simon caught it before it could hit the floor and gave it back, she muttered, "Oh, my God. I can't believe this."

Gail sent Simon a conspirator's smile as Tilly marched ahead of them, but someone else hailed her before they could reach their seats.

"Gail!"

Simon turned at the same time Gail did to see Callie, the friend who'd made it clear she wasn't happy to have Simon in Gail's life, sitting at a table—with Matt.

Gail wasn't sure how to react. Simon wouldn't want to be waylaid by Matt or Callie, but Callie was one of her best friends, and nothing had happened between her and Matt that prevented them from being friends, too. They'd never even been a couple.

Still, it felt awkward to stand and talk at their table, and even more awkward when Callie put her on the spot by insisting she and Simon join them.

"Are you sure?" Gail asked. "I mean…haven't you already ordered?"

"Not yet. We got here just before you." The way Callie said it led Gail to suspect this might be a test to see how she'd react now that she was married to Simon.

Gail didn't want Callie to think having Simon as

her husband would make her any less receptive to her friends. "In that case…" She nearly sent Simon an apologetic glance, but knew Callie and Matt would see it, too, and recognize it for what it was. So she didn't look at him. She returned Callie's smile as she accepted, and even though Callie slid over, making a place for her, she sat on Matt's side. With Simon's right hand still bandaged, he needed to eat with his left. And Matt was so big she couldn't imagine cramming another guy into the booth next to him.

"Have you eaten here since you've been back?" Gail could feel Simon's gaze on her as she addressed Matt.

The glower that had descended on Matt's face when Simon approached the table eased, as if he'd won a small victory when she sat beside him. "Once. I plan to come as often as possible before I have to leave."

Gail took the menu Tilly handed her. "When will that be?"

"Whenever I'm capable of running without pain."

"It's terrible what happened to your knee. How's the therapy going?"

"Okay. At least I get to be home while I do it."

Tilly gave Simon his menu as Gail asked, "Who are you working with? Curtis?"

"Yeah."

Curtis Viglione was one of the best therapists in the country. He saw a lot of professional athletes. After building a reputation and a considerable clientele in the San Francisco Bay Area, he'd moved to Whiskey Creek three or four years ago—Gail couldn't remember exactly when. Now he had athletes come to his state-of-the-art center built in the hills about a mile outside town. "From what I hear, he's a miracle worker. Sounds like you're in great hands."

Matt nodded, but his eyes kept moving to Simon, who was glaring at him. Why Simon would bother with this little rivalry, Gail couldn't say. There was no point in acting possessive or jealous when he didn't really care about her. But she figured it might be part of what he felt was expected of a husband, another aspect of playing his role.

Regardless, it made her uncomfortable. She wanted her friends to like him, although she couldn't put her finger on exactly why. Maybe it was just so they wouldn't think she was foolish for marrying him.

She cleared her throat to gain Simon's attention. "What looks good?" she asked, but he didn't get a chance to answer. Tilly was still standing at the table, waiting to tell them about the daily specials. She rattled off a spiel about homemade chili and corn bread for $8.99 and beef Stroganoff with sour cream for $12.99. Then she announced that Luanne would be their server and, when she couldn't seem to think of anything else to say, finally left.

In her peripheral vision, Gail could see Tilly whispering to two waitresses at the coffee machine. They kept turning to look at Simon, no doubt excited to have a movie star in their midst. But Gail was too wrapped up in manufacturing small talk to pay much more attention than that.

"How's business at the studio, Callie?" she asked.

"Busy. I've been doing lots of family portraits. And a few weddings."

"You're a photographer?" Simon asked.

"I am." She offered him a fake smile. "I would've been happy to photograph you and Gail at your wedding—but of course you didn't really have one."

Gail jumped in before Simon could respond. "We wanted to keep it simple."

"You certainly accomplished that," Callie said. "It doesn't get any simpler than a few vows and 'I do.'"

Luanne showed up with water for Gail and Simon; Callie and Matt already had theirs. She said she'd be back to take their order in a few minutes, but Gail caught her before she could leave, insisting they were ready now. They hadn't even looked at the menu, but she wanted to get this dinner over with as soon as possible.

They all fell silent while they quickly perused the meal selections. Then Gail ordered the meat loaf, Simon the pot roast, and Callie and Matt went for the chili. After Luanne left, Matt spoke up. "So...how's married life?"

Simon gave him a smile that, to Gail's eye, looked a little too deliberately satisfied. "Second time's the charm."

"Too bad it didn't work out that way for your father. How many times has he been married, anyway?"

Gail winced at Matt's choice of subject, and the derision in his voice. She doubted he'd heard, but the fact that Tex was in town somehow made it worse.

"I haven't kept track," Simon said.

"Are you two planning to have children?" Callie asked.

Were her friends purposely trying to embarrass Simon? Gail answered, just in case. "Probably not." She'd wanted to limit the conversation on that subject by sounding resolved. But she'd seemed too reconciled to not having kids. She could instantly tell that Callie was not pleased with her response.

"Why not?" her friend demanded.

"Simon already has a son," she replied, but that didn't help.

"So?" Callie set her water down so fast it sloshed over the sides. "What about *you?* You've always wanted children."

Gail lowered her voice. "You don't have to be so defensive of me, Callie. I'm happy the way I am. Besides…maybe we *will* have children someday. We're merely saying we don't have any immediate plans, okay?"

Callie scowled at Simon. "Just because you've had it all and done it all doesn't mean you don't have to consider *her.*"

Instead of getting angry, as Gail expected, Simon validated Callie's concern. "I understand that," he said.

His calm answer seemed to take the fire out of Callie's anger. "She's one of my best friends, you know? I care about her. I want her to be happy."

"So do I," Simon said, and he sounded so sincere Gail almost applauded.

"Great." Gail used her napkin to mop up the water Callie had spilled. "You both care about me. I couldn't be in better hands. Now…maybe you can try to get along? Because *that's* what would make me happiest."

A sulky expression turned down the corners of Callie's lips.

"We're already married, Callie." Gail leaned across the table to squeeze her hand. "I know you're mad that I didn't take your advice, but…it's over. Can we leave it for the time being?"

Her friend sighed audibly. "I'm just afraid your happiness won't last."

If she only knew… "So you're going to ruin it?"

"No."

"Hollywood marriages hardly ever succeed." Matt volunteered this, but it was unclear whether he was inviting responses or simply stating a fact.

Regardless of what he meant, Gail warned Simon with a look not to put Matt in his place. Simon could've said quite a bit about the world of a professional athlete. But what was the point? Matt was right; Hollywood marriages rarely did last, and this one would turn out to be the perfect example. "Okay, everyone's aired their complaints and expressed their worry, and it's all been duly noted by me. Can we please enjoy our dinner without making me regret that I've asked my husband to sit through this?"

Callie and Matt nodded grudgingly, but it wasn't long before they were enjoying themselves. When Simon started regaling them with stories about some of the unusual and out-of-the-way locations he'd gone to shoot movies, and the stunts he'd had to perform without a double, Matt dropped all animosity. Soon, he was so mesmerized he was talking and laughing as if he'd never viewed Simon as a competitor.

When Simon got up to go to the bathroom, Gail expected Callie to tell her again why she'd been crazy to marry him. But she didn't. "He can be charming," she admitted instead. Her tone implied she had to allow him that much.

Simon had done his best to win them over, and he'd managed it quite easily. He'd had them all laughing, gasping in astonishment, asking questions and generally hanging on every word he said. When Matt seemed more interested in becoming Simon's friend than in pouting over losing her, Gail knew his reaction to her marriage hadn't been one of true regret. If she had her guess, he'd been miffed to find that the girl he'd thought would always be waiting for him had actually moved on—and that she hadn't settled for someone less famous, less attractive or less charismatic than he was. He'd been reacting to the blow her defection had dealt his ego more than anything else, which meant that even after she and Simon divorced there'd be no Matt and Gail.

After all the years she'd believed herself in love with him, that was a little depressing. But she'd learned about her own commitment to Matt, too. She doubted she would've wanted Simon so badly today if she'd really been so enamored of Matt. He'd just made a good dream, given her someone to think about while she was working too hard to date.

"He's a lot of fun," Gail said, and stood up to go to the restroom, too. She didn't want her friends to quiz her on how she felt about Simon or ask pointed questions in his absence. She had too many conflicting emotions at the moment, didn't want to acknowledge that what she felt for Simon seemed far more powerful than what she'd felt for Matt. That made her fear she wouldn't get over him quite so readily when the time came…

Simon was just walking out of the men's room as she reached the entrance to the ladies'.

"Great job," she murmured. "They love you."

"More important, are they convinced I care about you?"

"Completely! They bought every compliment you paid me."

His smile disappeared. "But you didn't."

"I would've if I hadn't known better. You're a hell of an actor."

He took her arm. "Being an actor doesn't mean I'm always acting, Gail."

Averting her gaze, she put her hand on the door. "But it certainly comes in handy when you need to," she said.

Twenty-Five

It came as a surprise in the middle of the night. One minute Simon was lying next to Gail. The next they were awakened by the sound of movement, a bright light and then a series of flashes from just outside the window.

Cameras! Simon understood what was happening as soon as he opened his eyes. He'd known staying in an empty house with no window coverings would leave them vulnerable. But they'd had it so good since coming to Whiskey Creek, he'd grown complacent.

"What's going on?" Gail asked, sounding confused.

He rolled over to shield her. "Paparazzi."

Fortunately, they were both dressed. They'd come home from the restaurant, watched some television on Hulu and eventually fallen asleep. Simon had wanted to strip off Gail's clothes, to feel her skin against his while they dozed off. But things weren't the same after the restaurant. What she'd said while they were talking outside the restrooms had set him back, made him realize that she'd taken his remark—that he wasn't capable of falling in love—to mean that he'd never feel any fondness or concern for her, either.

"They've found us," he said, and shuttled her into the hall.

She hugged herself. It was chilly without blankets. "How?"

"Don't know. Someone here in Whiskey Creek must've leaked the information."

"Or Ian. He's the one who told your father where we are."

"My father's different. He may not be doing much acting anymore. There aren't too many good parts for men his age. But he's still a force to be reckoned with in Hollywood."

"I figured that out."

He pulled her up against him, to keep her warm. "I'm sure Ian didn't feel he could refuse. But…" Suddenly the obvious occurred to him. "That's it! I'll bet you anything my father did this!"

"Why would he tell the paparazzi where you're staying?"

"He doesn't want this town to be an escape. He'd rather roust me out, get me to head back home so I'll make that damn movie."

"You have quite the father."

The images he dreaded came to mind, the ones that revealed Tex as the selfish bastard he was, but Simon shoved them away. It helped that Gail softened against him, as if she wasn't opposed to letting him hold her. Somehow that made him feel better because it convinced him he hadn't lost everything he'd gained earlier. "If you had any idea…"

"What's that supposed to mean?"

"Nothing." He hadn't told a soul about what had happened. He wasn't going to break his silence.

"So what do we do?" she asked. "We could pull our

mattress into a bedroom, but the bedrooms have windows, too. And we don't have a hammer and nails to put up a blanket or a sheet."

"You stay here. I'll take care of it."

She grabbed his hand. "You can't go out there! You're angry and defensive. What if you get in a fight?"

"Whoever it is deserves to have my fist planted in his face."

"No!" She tugged him back. "You'd only reinjure your hand. And we can't risk a scene. There can be no more pictures or stories of you losing your temper."

He felt he should have the right to defend himself—and his wife—which made it difficult to listen to reason. But he'd ignored Gail too often when she worked for him. "Your suggestion is…"

"We call the police and let them handle it."

Footsteps echoed on the wooden porch. The photographer was coming around the house, probably looking for another way to see in.

"My phone's charging in the kitchen," she added.

"Mine's in the living room. I'll get it."

"Wait."

"Why?"

"Maybe we can create an opportunity here."

She was always thinking. "Gail, whoever's outside is trespassing and invading our privacy. I want his ass kicked off the property. Our wedding pictures haven't come out in *People* yet, which means he'll have the first shots of us after our wedding. He'll be able to sell them for a fortune, and I'm not about to let some guy get rich out of sneaking pictures of me in bed with my wife."

"Maybe we can make a deal with whoever it is to release his snapshots after that."

She couldn't convince him on this. He'd dealt with the paparazzi for too many years. "Absolutely not. We can invite someone else to take pictures when *we're* ready. There's no need to let this asshole get away with what he's doing."

"Okay. You're right. It's just…if we give the press what they want, they'll be more likely to leave us alone."

"You're wrong," he argued. "They're insatiable."

"They're insatiable when they have some scandal to report. Our marriage is news because it's shocking and they think it's another bad move on your part. Once we prove otherwise and establish that you're happy and living a good life, they'll lose interest. Then, as long as nothing changes, they'll leave us alone."

He'd been hounded to the point that he had a hard time believing this. "No…"

"Yes," she insisted. "Their profits depend on showing the dirt in people's lives. If you give them nothing negative, they'll have to look to other actors, musicians, whatever, who might be screwing up."

He could see her logic. It wasn't until his marriage had started to crumble that the paparazzi had become so unbearable. They wanted a front-row seat at the destruction of Simon O'Neal. Now that he was pulling his life back together there wouldn't be so much to see or report. "Fine. We'll invite someone else out here, like I said. But this guy's not the one."

"Agreed."

He dashed into the living room for his phone. But it turned out to be an exercise in futility. By the time the cops arrived, the intrusive photographer was gone.

Knowing the culprit could very easily come back, they packed up and returned to Gail's father's.

* * *

"I thought I heard you two come in last night. What happened? Air mattress pop?"

Martin DeMarco was in the kitchen brewing coffee. That meant it was Joe who'd left earlier. It must have been his turn to open the station. Simon had heard someone tramp down the stairs and head out. The noise had awakened him from a deep sleep, but he felt rested despite the early hour and the hours they'd been up in the middle of the night. No doubt it helped that he was no longer dealing with a perpetual hangover.

"We got a little surprise," he said.

Martin's caterpillar-like eyebrows drew together. "A skunk?"

Simon laughed. "In a manner of speaking." He explained about the photographer as Martin handed him a cup of coffee.

"Who do you think told the paparazzi where you were?"

Chances were they'd never know for sure. Simon had his guess, but he didn't want to say it was most likely his own father. He could hear the protective note in Martin's voice, knew he was a different kind of man. Martin would do anything to shield his children. Just being married to Gail put Simon under that same protection.

The stark contrast between Martin and Tex embarrassed Simon. But Simon had been ashamed of his father for a long time. Maybe he'd always been ashamed of him. The story of his own conception wasn't exactly something he could be proud of. The humiliation caused by his personal history had been excruciating. It was so salacious that it was brought up again and again and again in the media.

"We don't know," he said instead of admitting his suspicions.

Martin took out a frying pan and turned on the gas stove. "I can't imagine anyone around here would give you away. The only person who could provide your exact address would be the Realtor. And Kathy's good as gold. Or—" he seemed to realize she wasn't the *only* one who knew where they were "—maybe it was one of Gail's friends."

"I don't think so." Simon tried to recall the conversation they'd had with Callie and Matt at dinner last night. They'd mentioned the house, certainly. But when they parted, Matt had clapped him on the back and told him how great it was to have dinner with him. Simon didn't think Matt would turn around and call the press. And Callie would never do anything to make Gail unhappy. She was as protective as Gail's own family. Maybe more so.

"You're right. Those kids and Gail go way back," Martin said. "You can trust every last one of 'em."

"Even Sophia?"

"Maybe not Sophia. Gail's never been too fond of her."

Smiling at Martin's blatant honesty, Simon added a splash of cream to his coffee. "She's been quite friendly. She brought us an apple pie the other night."

"Really?" He sounded more interested than Simon would've expected. "Did you bring the leftovers?"

Martin was probably joking, but with him it wasn't easy to tell. "No, but we will," Simon promised.

Gail's father dropped bread in the toaster and cracked some eggs in the pan. Then he motioned to a chair halfway around the table. "The *Gold Country Gazette*'s right there if you want to read the paper."

Now that he wasn't likely to see some terrible picture of himself doing Lord knew what, Simon thought he might. "This is local?" he asked as he retrieved it.

"It is. A weekly. They'd probably love to interview you. Maybe you'll be interested now the news is out that you're here. They always do a big spread on Matt Stinson."

"Well, I have to outdo Matt."

Gail's father actually grinned at this. "What do you have planned for today?"

Simon replied over the sizzle of eggs. "I thought I'd head over to the hardware store, see if they have the tools I'm going to need to do some remodeling. Then I've got to be at the house. Our furniture is due to arrive sometime after ten but before noon."

"What's Gail going to do?"

The comforting smells of a home-cooked breakfast rose to Simon's nostrils as he leafed through the paper. Sure enough, there was a big picture of Matt, along with an update on his knee. "When I got out of bed, she mumbled something about needing time on the computer to take care of a few details at Big Hit. It'll be easier for her to do that here, so she'll drive me and then come back."

"I can take you if you like."

Simon lowered the paper. "You don't mind stopping by the hardware store?"

"Not at all. I've got a few things I should pick up myself."

"Okay. Then I'll call her when the furniture arrives. She'll want some input on how we arrange it."

"Input?" Martin said dryly.

Simon was starting to like Gail's father. "Euphemistically speaking."

"If that means she'll need to tell you exactly where to put every single piece, then you've got the right idea."

Simon chuckled. "As far as I'm concerned, that's her prerogative. I'm not feeling any burning need to place the sofa." He trusted Gail enough to let her make much more important decisions, and he liked that.

Martin flipped the eggs. "I'm glad you two are staying here in town for a while, but I'm surprised she's willing to take so much time off work."

Simon set the small paper aside. "We were just married. Some people would call that a honeymoon."

"A three-month honeymoon? Maybe in your world, but not in Gail's. She loves the PR business. And she's done a damn fine job with that company of hers."

Setting his coffee on its saucer, Simon leaned back. Martin was so proud of his daughter. And he had every reason to be. "That's true."

When the toast popped up, Simon got to his feet. He was planning to put some in for himself, but Martin waved for him to sit down again. "I've got it."

A couple of minutes later, Gail's father sat a plate of three eggs, over easy, and two pieces of toast in front of him.

"Probably not as good as you're used to eating," he said, "but at least you won't go hungry."

Actually, the food tasted better than any Simon had eaten in a long time. But he knew the difference wasn't in the cooking. This meal told him that Martin was willing to give him a chance. All Simon had to do was prove he deserved it.

Gail paused on the landing near Simon's father's room. She knew Simon wouldn't approve of her coming to the B and B. In fact, he'd be angry if he learned.

But she wasn't about to let anyone get in the way of what they were hoping to accomplish. Even his father.

Especially his father.

Taking a deep breath, she stepped up to number six, the room number Sally at the front desk had given her, and knocked.

There was no response. Had Tex left town? She doubted they'd be that lucky. More likely he'd gotten up early and gone to the coffee shop or Just Like Mom's.

She knocked again—and this time she heard movement.

"Later, for God's sake!" he yelled, and something— a pillow?—hit the door, making it rattle. "What kind of place is this?"

Tex thought she was one of the maids. Briefly, she was tempted to leave it that way and scoot. Clearly, he was in no mood to be bothered. She didn't want to tangle with him, and she didn't want him to disturb the other guests, but she had something to say and she doubted she'd get another opportunity to say it—not without Simon around.

Calling on all her nerve, she rapped at the door again. "Mr. O'Neal? Could I talk to you, please?"

Silence met her request. Then he said, "Who is it?"

His voice had lost its gruff edge. The question held curiosity instead.

"Gail DeMarco, er, O'Neal." She wasn't sure whether or not to use Simon's name. It would bring her quite a bit of clout, especially where her business was concerned. But knowing it was only borrowed for a couple of years made her feel like a cheat. And there didn't seem to be much point here in Whiskey Creek. "Your daughter-in-law."

"You don't say." A creak suggested he was getting up. She heard the bolt slide back, then the door opened and Tex peered out at her with red-rimmed eyes. "You're here alone? Where's Simon?"

"He had some things to do this morning. I came without him."

He smelled of booze. Those eyes and the sallow look of his face also told her he'd spent the previous night drinking.

"The question is why," he said.

"If you invite me in I'll explain."

The rasp of whiskers sounded as he rubbed a hand over his jaw. "I'm not exactly dressed for company, but if you want—"

"I'll wait." She had no desire to see Simon's father in his boxers.

He chuckled softly. "I heard you were a real prude."

"Ian tell you that?"

"Among other things."

He kept laughing, but the door closed and didn't open again until he was dressed. "Madame..." he said, his voice filled with sarcasm as he waved her inside.

He hadn't combed his hair. It stood up in front, gray but still thick despite his age. She could see why some women would find him appealing. He had a devil-may-care attitude that probably attracted the type of women who liked that sort of challenge. And he still had a good physique. "What can I do for you?"

"I'm here to see if you care about your son at all," she said.

Her statement took him off guard. Obviously he hadn't expected her to be so direct. He straightened for a second—and then his eyes narrowed. "What the hell has that got to do with anything?"

"It's the only thing that matters."

"Not when it comes to business."

His room now smelled like cologne. Too much of it. "When it comes to *everything.*"

He finished buttoning his shirt. He wore that and a pair of jeans but not his belt or boots. "What are you hoping to achieve, Ms. DeMarco?"

She noted that he didn't do her the courtesy of using her married name. It was probably his way of letting her know he didn't think she'd be with Simon very long. He was right. But she didn't care what he was trying to intimate.

"Simon is doing better than he has in at least two years. I want that to continue. So I'm asking you to leave Whiskey Creek without further contact and find someone else to take his part in the movie."

A thunderous expression appeared on his face. "Who the hell do you think you are?"

"I'm his wife." *For now...*

"I don't give a shit. Do you realize how much—"

"That will cost?" she broke in. "I know it'll be a lot. I also know that Simon will compensate you."

"It's not just me. It's the people I convinced to invest in this. I have a responsibility to them."

"If they're like you, they have plenty of money. Fortunately, so does he. He'll repay you, and you can return what you'd like to your investors. But I'm asking you to let him out of the contract gracefully and not retaliate by dragging him into court."

"My friends won't be happy. Hardly any other actor has the same pull."

She couldn't help it; she raised her voice. She'd told herself this was a business meeting. She was here to protect the campaign she'd developed, to ensure its ultimate success. But it had become personal, too, because she cared about Simon. "Your friends don't matter as much as your *son!* Could you do what's best for him for a change? Just once?"

He threw up his hands. "Why should I? Simon's never given a shit about me!"

That was an excuse. He had to know it, at least in some part of his brain. "I'm afraid you have that reversed, Mr. O'Neal. It's *you* who should give a shit about *him.*"

Shaking his head, he laughed without mirth. "He's sure got you snowed, doesn't he? Don't you realize it's just a question of time before he acts out again regardless of what I do? Regardless of what *you* do? What's it been—two or three months since he stumbled into a bar, got drunk and started a fight? I may as well look after my friends and my money because Simon will go to hell in a handbasket no matter how hard you try to save him. He's the most stubborn son of a bitch I've ever met. And here you are, sticking up for him. He wouldn't thank you for it. You know that, right? Trust me on this—he's going to leave you with a broken heart, just like he did Bella."

"The divorce wasn't entirely his fault, and *you,* of all people, know it." In spite of Simon's past sins, Gail was clinging to the loyalty she felt to him. She was also relying on what Ian had intimated to her earlier, that Bella had done more to cause the divorce than anyone knew. She hoped to hell Ian was right, because she was determined to make some headway with Simon's father.

She expected Tex to continue arguing with her. But he didn't. He stepped back as if she'd slapped him, and a strange look came over his face. "He told you?"

Gail's heart began to pound. Simon hadn't told her anything particularly revealing. But she wasn't willing to admit it, wasn't about to let the power swing back to Tex. There was something at play here, something that affected everyone involved. What? "Of course he did," she bluffed. "He tells me everything."

"Then you should also know that *she* came on to *me*." Tex brought a hand to his chest for emphasis. "*She* was the one who wanted *me* in her bed."

Gail gaped at him. Had she heard correctly? She was sure of it, and yet she couldn't believe what had just come out of his mouth. *"You had sex with Bella?"*

He winced at the disgust in her voice but rallied. "It was a one-time thing. It didn't mean squat to either of us. She'd gotten in the habit of coming to me whenever she was upset. I helped her, gave her a shoulder to cry on. Simon's not easy to live with. If you don't know that yet, you'll—"

"When?" She was so shocked her voice had dropped to a whisper. "When did you do this?"

He cursed under his breath. "Two and a half years ago."

That was about the time Simon had started behaving badly. It was the reason he'd been unable to cope. His wife had had an affair with his own father, a sad echo of what had happened with his mother, and just as reprehensible. What was wrong with Tex? Did he have to be admired by *every* woman he met?

She swallowed hard. "How did Simon find out?"

Tex stared at her so long she thought he wasn't going to answer. Then his shoulders slumped and he sighed. "He came home unexpectedly."

"The *one* time you were together he caught you in bed? What are the chances of that?"

"Okay, we were together a few times. But it hadn't been going on for more than a few weeks." He jammed a hand through his hair. "I just blew it, didn't I? He didn't tell you a thing."

"No. If I had my bet he hasn't told a soul." He could've used it to excuse his own bad behavior. To get his son back. To make his ex-wife look a lot worse than he did. But he hadn't. He'd kept it inside. "You want to know why?"

Tex didn't answer.

"Because he cares too much about *his* son. He would never want Ty to grow up knowing such a terrible thing about Bella, the way *he* had to grow up knowing what his mother did with you."

"Our affair wasn't all that broke up their marriage," Tex said. "They were having trouble before. That's why she came to me in the first place."

"And you helped her out by seducing her."

"*She* wanted it."

"And that made you feel like a big man, didn't it? That Simon's wife could want *you?*"

He stepped back, nearly stumbled and knocked the lamp off the nightstand while he was trying to catch his balance. His hangover had put him at a disadvantage. "I don't have to tolerate your judgmental bullshit."

"And I don't care if you think I'm judgmental. What you did makes me sick. The fact that you're trying to justify it makes me even sicker."

"It's not like Simon and I have ever been close!"

"You were close when you did that, probably closer than you've ever been."

He winced. "Something would've ruined it."

"Is that what lets you sleep at night? He's your *son,* for God's sake! You know what I think?"

"Get out of here!" he snapped, but she wasn't finished yet.

"I think you're jealous of Simon," she said. "He's younger, stronger, better-looking, a superior actor and by far a better man. And you hate all that. You hate that he's replaced you in Hollywood, outdone you so easily. So you've been doing everything you can to destroy him—at the same time you've been trying to capitalize on his success."

Squeezing his eyes closed, he pressed a palm to his forehead as if he had too much of a headache to be having this conversation. "You shouldn't have tricked me."

She started to leave but turned back. "It was your guilty conscience that set you up, *Dad*. I only helped a little. Now get out of town before I tell Simon what you told me. It's a miracle that he's put up with you so far."

He wasn't willing to let her have the parting shot. "He won't stay with you. You're not even that pretty."

"Maybe not. But I wouldn't cheat on him in a million years. Especially with a morally bankrupt old fart like you. That's got to be worth something," she said, and slammed the door behind her.

Twenty-Six

Classic rock blasted from the old-fashioned boom box Simon had purchased at the hardware store as he tore out the sink, counters and cupboards in the kitchen. The furniture they'd purchased in Sacramento hadn't arrived—almost two and still no delivery—but that didn't affect him much. He'd been happily engaged in demolition since he got here more than three hours ago. It was a relief to be able to use his hand again. He knew he should get the stitches taken out because there was no more pain when he moved it.

Gail had brought him lunch a couple of hours ago, but she hadn't stayed long. She'd said she had more work to do. For starters, she was closing the deal on the sale of their pictures for $2.8 million.

Simon didn't mind working alone, but he frequently found himself thinking of Gail—the way she kissed or cuddled up to him in the night, or watched him when she didn't realize he was aware of it. The house seemed strangely empty without her, and yet he felt as if he could get lost in his current task for days. The physicality of the work eased some of the deep-seated tension that kept him so wound up.

Just as he was thinking about calling her to see when she might be back, a vehicle pulled up outside. Assuming it was the furniture he'd been expecting, or maybe his wife, he set down his hammer and headed into the living room.

He'd left the front door ajar, partly to enjoy the nice weather and partly to make sure he didn't miss the furniture delivery, but it was his father who stepped inside.

"You're making a damn racket," he said when he spotted Simon.

Simon dusted Sheetrock chalk from his hands and clothes. "So? This is my house. What are you doing here, anyway? Did you come to serve me papers?"

"Not this time." He slanted his head to look beyond Simon. "Where's Gail?"

"Gone, but she'll be back soon."

He tore the wrapper off a toothpick and shoved it in his mouth. "She's different from anyone you've been with before. You know that?"

Leery, Simon folded his arms. "Different in what way?"

"Better. Stronger. I can see that, now I've got some painkiller in me and I've had a chance to think."

Simon agreed with his assessment of Gail, but he wondered how his father had noticed so quickly. "What makes you say so?"

"Not hard to tell." He handed over an envelope. "Here."

"What's this?"

"A release."

"From the film?" Simon didn't bother hiding his surprise.

"Take a look." His father gestured for him to open it. Simon pulled a single handwritten sheet of paper from the envelope. It said that his contract with Excite Entertainment Production Company had been terminated and all monies paid him were due back in thirty days. It was a fair arrangement, one Simon could live with. "What changed your mind?" he asked.

A faint smile curved Tex's lips. "I guess I don't want to be a morally bankrupt old fart *all* the time."

Simon had never heard his father talk this way before. "Excuse me?"

"Never mind. I owe you that much. And…" He moved the toothpick to one side and turned to spit over the railing. "I'm sorry I, uh, got involved with Bella. Sometimes even I don't know why I do what I do."

Simon wasn't sure how to react. Tex could be agreeable and easygoing at times, but he always reverted to his more difficult, narcissistic self. Still, the pleasant moments were rare and that made this an Occasion. "So you're no longer putting all the blame on her?"

"It's takes two." Tex lifted a hand in farewell. "Tell Gail to keep fighting. Looks aren't everything."

Offended, Simon followed him down the walkway. "There's nothing wrong with Gail's looks!"

"See what I mean?" Tex said, chuckling. "She might prove me wrong, after all."

Simon stopped at the gate while Tex continued on to his truck. "Prove you wrong about what? When have you ever talked to Gail?"

"Don't worry about it," his father said. "Just know that she's the best thing to happen to you in a long time. Don't take her for granted."

"Hey, I didn't expect to see you."

Gail glanced up as her father walked into the minimart section of his gas station. She'd known he'd come. A buzzer sounded in back whenever someone stepped over the threshold.

"I just wanted to stop in and say hi." She handed him his favorite flavor of milk shake, which she'd purchased at the soda fountain down the street. "Where's Joe?"

"Got a call for a tow. Old Mrs. Reed is stranded with a dead battery over at the bingo parlor."

"That's quite an emergency." She put the shake she'd bought for Joe in the minifreezer located in the tiny break room, which was more like a closet. It also contained the mop, bucket and other supplies they used for cleaning, as well as toilet paper and towels for the restrooms.

"Like what we've done to the place?" her father called after her.

He was talking about the new section of the store, where one could buy soft drinks, fruit smoothies and snow cones. She'd been admiring the new machines when she first came in. "I do. Bet it'll be a hit come summer."

"Hope so. Cost me enough."

Gail breathed deep, taking in the scents of motor oil, grease and gasoline that brought back her youth. Oddly enough, the station felt as much like home as the house in which she'd been raised. She'd spent a lot of time here as a little girl, playing with the tools or watching a small TV behind the counter while her father ran his business. When she was a teenager, she'd stocked the shelves, co-ordinated tows and written up work orders in addition to running the register. Her father had believed in keeping his kids busy. That hadn't prevented Joe from getting into trouble now and then. She'd never gotten into trouble, but she remembered closing on many Friday nights when her friends were partying after the football game and feeling left out. As an adult she didn't begrudge her father those hours. She realized he'd probably needed her help—or maybe just her company. For some of that time Joe was away at college.

"Did your furniture ever come?" her father asked.

Gail checked her phone. "I don't think so. Simon texted me an hour ago to say it hadn't arrived, and I haven't heard from him since. He said he'd call when it did."

Her father glanced at the clock hanging on the wall. "It's almost three. I'm surprised you're not over there waiting for it."

"I wanted to see you."

Stirring his shake, he tilted his head to look into her face. "Something wrong, Gabby?"

She shrugged. "Nothing serious. I guess I just wondered what you think of Simon."

"I don't know what to think yet. He seems nice enough so far. But I don't form an opinion on nice alone. It takes more to be a good man than a smile."

She nodded.

"Don't tell me you two are having trouble already...."

"No. Not at all. He treats me really well. It's just..." She nibbled on her bottom lip while searching for the right words. "I think I'm falling in love with him."

"That's good, isn't it?" he said with a laugh. "You are married to him."

"But I'd prefer not to be head over heels."

"Why not?"

She stopped trying to hide the misery she was feeling. "Because I'm scared. What if he never feels the same way toward me?"

"If he doesn't love you, what's he doing with you?"

"Isn't it obvious? I told you I married him to help

him. He needs me right now. But that won't be the case forever."

Her father took a big spoonful of his milk shake and spoke after he'd swallowed. "No marriage is easy, Gabby."

"I know that. But…am I crazy to want more than I should expect?"

Her father set his cup aside and took her hands. "Look at me."

She forced herself to meet his gaze. He had every right to say, "I told you not to get involved with Simon," but that wasn't what she wanted to hear.

"Love is always a risk," he said instead.

"I was fully aware of that coming into this. I thought I could take…whatever. But I never knew I could fall so hard."

Her father kissed her forehead. "If Simon's as smart as I think, he'll realize what he's got."

His reassurance made her feel better. She gave him a hug despite his dirty clothes and left. But as she started her car to go over to the house, a little voice inside her head repeated what Simon's father had said: *He won't stay with you. You're not even that pretty.*

When Gail arrived at the house, Simon came to the front door to meet her with his T-shirt tied around his head like a headband. His bare torso was covered in dust, dirt and sweat.

"You've been busy," she said as she got the ribs she'd bought them for dinner from the backseat of her car.

He flopped down on the top step of the porch. "I'm exhausted. I'll probably be so sore tomorrow I won't be able to move."

Captivated by his dazzling smile, she put down the

sack and sat next to him. He was tired, but he was happy. She'd never seen him this relaxed, this carefree. Whiskey Creek had been the right place to bring him. She felt certain of that and proud of the self-restraint he'd exercised so far. "I got your text. Furniture's coming tomorrow, huh? What happened?"

"Truck got a flat. But I think it's for the best." His guilty expression made him look younger, almost boyish. "I've created a bigger mess than I expected."

She leaned over to peek through the open door and into the house. Whatever he'd been doing hadn't extended to the living room. She could see their mattress and bedding in front of the fireplace, apparently untouched since last night, but…the lighting was different. "Did you cover the windows?"

"I did. I wanted us to be able to stay here tonight."

She raised her eyebrows. "Any particular reason?"

His grin said it all.

Gail was done fighting what she felt. She had him for two years. Although she couldn't help hoping for more, she knew the chances of her marriage lasting longer than that were slim. She figured she might as well enjoy being with him while she could and if—when— she lost him, she'd let him go gracefully. That way, he'd maintain some respect for her afterward, maybe even remember her fondly. There was no way they could continue to work together—not after being married—but they'd have memories. She preferred that those memories be positive. "I thought you were beat."

"Not *that* beat." He slipped a hand under her blouse but only to caress the skin at her waist. "Getting you naked's been on my mind all day."

She untied the T-shirt on his head and smoothed his

unruly hair. "Funny, I could say the same thing about you."

"Then what took you so long to get here? I almost called you a dozen times."

Oh, boy…she was falling deeper. There was no help for her. "Weren't you busy?"

"I will be as soon as I get you in the house. But first, a shower." He started to climb to his feet, but she pushed him back and straddled him right there on the porch.

"Actually, I like you just the way you are."

"Dirty?" he teased.

"A little dirt never hurt anybody." She leaned over to whisper in his ear. "I've always wanted to get nailed by a contractor."

He laughed. "I hope Riley doesn't know that, or I might have some competition."

She ground her hips against him. "I'm not interested in his hammer."

His teeth flashed in another smile. "I'm more than happy to show you what I can do with mine."

In one fluid movement, he sat up, then carried her inside.

"What about the food?" she asked as he kicked the door shut.

He was already nuzzling her neck, telling her she smelled good and tasted good and just the thought of her had been driving him crazy. "Later," he murmured against her skin. "Right now all I want is you."

It was well after they'd showered and eaten and rearranged their bedding so they could sleep that Simon's phone awakened him. He had a new text message. At this hour, it had to be from Bella. She was the only one who ever bothered him so late. He would've ignored it.

He didn't want to leave the warmth and comfort of being tangled up with Gail. Despite her lack of experience, his new wife really knew how to make love. And this time she'd put everything she had into it. God, it was good.

But he was worried about Ty. It'd been so long since he'd talked to his son. Could something terrible have happened to him? Or maybe something not so terrible? Did he have a cold? A stubbed toe? A loose tooth?

Simon ached for the comfort of all the things he'd once taken for granted—Ty crawling into his bed early in the morning and patting his cheeks, whispering, "Daddy, wake up. I want some cereal." Ty running to him after he'd hurt himself. Ty throwing both arms around his neck and saying, "I love you, Daddy." Simon had never hurt so much over anything or anyone. The hunger to hold his son made him angry with the woman who was standing in his way, but he knew allowing that anger to overpower him would defeat everything he was doing to get Ty back. He couldn't act on it.

But thinking about Ty and Bella made it difficult to sleep.

Careful not to wake Gail, he slipped off the air mattress, pulled on his jeans and scooped up his phone, which was lying among the remains of their dinner, before going outside.

The sky was clear, the temperature cool. The stars seemed bigger than he ever remembered seeing them in L.A. He was tempted to blame it on the smog, but knew it was probably him. He hadn't been paying attention to such details. There was a lot he'd ignored in recent years. Only now was he beginning to realize that he'd filled his life with so many possessions and so much angst and clamor, so much *shallowness,* that he'd missed the quiet, still things that brought him peace.

When had he lost sight of who he really was? Of what he wanted his life to be? He was a critically acclaimed actor, but who was he on a personal level? Had he ever really known?

As he sat on the step and gazed down at his ex-wife's latest message, he frowned. Why won't you answer me? she'd written.

She had a restraining order against him, and she had to ask?

He scrolled up to read all the other messages he'd seen and hadn't responded to, but he stopped short of viewing the video she'd sent the night he cut his hand. He knew if he saw that right now he wouldn't be able to stop himself from driving to L.A. and busting into her house to get Ty.

Really? You're going to ignore me?

Maybe I should tell Ty his daddy doesn't give a shit about him anymore.

Your father's looking for you. Where the hell are you?

You said you'd never marry again. What, were you too drunk to realize you were saying "I do"? Or were you thinking with your cock again?

Who is the bitch? Your *publicist*? Were you screwing her all along?

It was hateful, spiteful garbage. He wanted to text back, to vent his anger and frustration as she felt free to do, but what would he say? That he was bitterly disappointed? That they'd created a great kid, the best, and he couldn't understand why they hadn't been able to get along?

Simon felt like such a failure—and everything he'd done to escape the self-loathing just made it worse.

Leaning back, he closed his eyes and let the autumn air calm him. He could think more clearly now than he had in months, could see that he was at a turning point. It was time to cut the past away. Sure, he and Bella had messed up their marriage. Sure, he had his regrets. But it was too late to change any of that now. So how long was he going to hang on to the wreckage?

Not anymore, he decided. He was letting go, and he wanted Bella to do the same. From here on out, they needed to handle all communication, at least any communication that didn't directly concern Ty, through their lawyers, as they'd been advised to do.

But he doubted she would. He knew why she kept jabbing him. She loved him almost as much as she hated him. As twisted as that was, he understood. He'd been struggling with the same love-hate compulsion, which was another reason he'd gotten himself into so much trouble.

Fortunately, Gail had changed everything.

His thoughts turned to his publicist and what they'd shared tonight. Something had changed, grown serious. He'd noticed it in himself as much as her. They'd approached their lovemaking with an emotional intensity that hadn't been there before, as if possessing each other mattered far more than achieving a physical release. And he'd welcomed that new emotional element, because Gail satisfied him more deeply than Bella ever could.

Somehow Gail, someone he would've considered a highly unlikely prospect, given their many differences, had managed to plug the gaping hole in his chest, to stop the bleeding caused by his divorce, his father, his mother—all of it. He wasn't sure how long being with her would feel this right. He didn't trust what he was experiencing to last. But he owed Gail enough loyalty to put an end, in *every* way, to what had come before, with Bella.

Please let me know if Ty needs anything, he typed. I will do everything I can for him. But other than that, don't contact me. He reread his words, then smiled as he added, I'm happily married.

Twenty-Seven

"Do you see it yet?" Josh's voice was even more animated than usual.

Gail moved the phone to her other ear as she opened the link he'd just sent her. There, front and center, was a picture of her and Simon on the porch last night with the heading Hot Honeymoon. As she straddled him, his hands circled her waist and he stared up at her. They weren't photographed from the front, but there was no doubting their identities. "I'm there."

"Is that really you?"

Clearly, that was her. She looked completely caught up in the moment—and she had been. She and Simon had made love again this morning, a gentle, sweet coupling that was a stark contrast to the explosion of desire last night. She couldn't decide which she'd enjoyed more. She'd liked both. Sex was so much better when you were madly in love....

"How many sites have put this up?" she asked Josh. Their furniture had arrived. She didn't yet have a desk, but she was sitting on the new couch. Until Josh had called to report the sudden influx of Google hits, she'd been comfortable. There was only one drawback to working out of their new house—it wasn't easy to hear with Simon banging away in the kitchen.

She had to admit she was glad he wasn't in the room with her, however. She'd all but attacked him last night, and in plain view of anyone who might've been hoping for just such a pic.

"It's all over the Net and spreading as we speak," Josh said. "Isn't that great? You did a fabulous job. You both look as if you're completely *into* each other. This could be an ad for Armani or Calvin Klein. It's gorgeous! Who took the picture? I even like the old Victorian in the background. Was it Ian?"

Face burning, Gail briefly covered her eyes. "No."

"Then who? Your father?"

"My *father*?" She wrinkled her nose at the thought of Martin being anywhere in the vicinity when she'd wantonly climbed on top of Simon. "That's sick."

"Why? You have your clothes on!"

It still looked very sexual—because it had been.

"You are so conservative," he said. "Well, normally." He was obviously referring to the photograph with this clarification. He chuckled at his own joke, but Gail didn't find it funny.

"Anyway, *someone* took that picture," he said. "Was it a friend?"

"No. I'm guessing it's some member of the paparazzi. Someone was trying to get a shot through the window while we were sleeping the night before last. We assumed he, or she, left after that. No one was here when the cops arrived, and we haven't noticed anyone following us since. But apparently, whoever it was hasn't given up."

"I haven't run across any shots of you sleeping."

Big Hit would know if such photos had appeared on

the internet. Google would've alerted them of that, too. "They must not have turned out—or showed our identities clearly enough. It wasn't a high-percentage shot."

Josh lowered his voice. "So…you were straddling Simon, getting him excited, and you didn't know someone was taking your picture? This *wasn't* calculated?"

She stared at the photo of her and Simon on her computer screen. Maybe Josh was happy about it, but she wasn't sure this would do Simon any favors. He needed a different slant for his new image, one that showed him as a man who'd settled down. This was far too sexy. It made him look like he was embroiled in yet another torrid affair.

"No, it wasn't calculated," she said. "As a publicist, I would've structured it very differently—maybe had him carry in the groceries or something."

"So this was spontaneous? Holy shit!" Josh cried. "Now I'm really jealous. You must be having the time of your life."

She was having the best sex of her life. No doubt about that. But she was scared to death wondering where things would go from here. And now she had to worry about how her behavior last night was going to affect the campaign and her efforts to help Simon gain custody of Ty. After they made love, he'd talked about his son for probably an hour. He missed Ty so much, he'd had to get his pictures out of his wallet and show them to her, even though she'd met Ty several times in the past and already knew what a darling little boy he was.

Could she soften the impact of this rather explicit picture? Give an interview focusing on the fact that this was, after all, their honeymoon? Passion played an important role in a marriage, but that wasn't what she'd been hoping to highlight. She doubted this picture would impress the judge who'd be ruling on Ty's fate....

"Gail?" Joshua prompted. "Did you hear me?"

She searched her memory for his question and managed to recall his last words: he'd wanted to know if she was having fun. "For now."

"So he's good in bed. As good as he seems in *Shiver?*"

Joshua wanted her to dish, but her private life with Simon was something she planned to keep to herself. "That's none of your business."

"But you *have* slept with him, even though you said you wouldn't."

"Quit digging, Josh."

"That's a yes. Oh, my God!"

She couldn't help laughing. "Stop it! We need to figure out how to spin this."

"Why? It's perfect!"

He thought so because he was one of the most sexual creatures she'd ever encountered. "We're aiming to convince a far more conservative crowd." She considered her options, then made a decision. "Call your friend at *Hollywood Secrets Revealed.* Tell her I'm willing to talk. It's time Mrs. O'Neal gave her first interview."

"Mrs. O'Neal. You're taking ownership. I like that. But what will you say?"

"I'll tell her how misunderstood Simon has been, how there's been much more going on than was reported in the media, how one side of a story is never completely accurate."

"I know the routine. But...do you really believe that?"

After what she'd learned from Tex? Wholeheartedly. Men had committed murder over less than what Simon had discovered—firsthand—about his wife and his father. It sort of made sense to her now that he'd go out looking for a good brawl, smash someone who provoked him on-set or off, pick a fight with Bella's brother. She could even understand why he might turn to alcohol to keep from thinking about what he knew, and why he couldn't tell the world that Bella had done her share of cheating. Imagine the media frenzy that would occur over something like that—Bella having sex with Simon's famous father—and how the taint of it would follow her, and Ty, for years. Gail couldn't reveal all of that information to the public, but she could certainly tell people that Bella hadn't been easy to live with and that all the blame shouldn't be assigned to one person.

"I think he deserves more credit than he's received," she said. "He's done what he can to be gallant."

"He's gone from being an ass in your opinion to being gallant? Oh, Lord."

"What?"

"You're falling for him, aren't you."

She didn't deny it. "Hard," she admitted.

Simon walked into the room as she hung up. "We've got a mess," he announced.

Of course they had a mess, but she could tell he wasn't referring to the pictures she'd just seen. He didn't know about them yet.

"What's wrong?" She closed her laptop. She'd have to tell him about the media hits, but she wanted a moment to think it through first, to be sure she was doing the right thing in offering interviews.

"The plumbing."

"The plumbing?" she repeated, somewhat relieved. After her call with Josh, she'd thought it was going to be something far more serious.

He dusted off his hands. "It's all so old. It needs to be replaced."

With Simon standing there in a T-shirt that stretched nicely across his pecs and a pair of faded jeans that fit him so well he could've stopped traffic, famous or no, it was tough to care too much about anything else. But she did her best to show the appropriate concern. "Sounds expensive."

"It probably will be. But I'm not worried about that. I just wanted to let you know the remodel might not come together as fast as I'd hoped."

"That's fine." She was about to apologize for getting him involved in a money pit. After all, he'd bought the house to please her. But then he gazed around with a speculative eye, propped his hands on his hips and said, "Maybe we should redo the electrical while we're at it."

"Is something wrong with that, too?"

"No. It's just smart to update while everything's torn apart," he replied, and that was when she realized that he didn't mind the extra work. The opposite was true; he enjoyed what he was doing enough to add items to the list.

"I see," she said as solemnly as she could. "But you wouldn't do the electrical and plumbing yourself."

"Oh, hell, no. I'll just oversee everything and do the finish work." He hitched a thumb over his shoulder. "This place is going to look great when we're done."

"I never doubted you for a minute," she said. Then she drew a deep breath and told him about the pictures.

"An interview should handle it." A shrug indicated he wasn't too concerned as he headed back to work.

When Simon returned from getting his stitches out, Ian was there, sitting in a Porsche parked in front of the house.

His business manager opened the car door as Simon approached. "Finally!" he said with mock exasperation.

"Why didn't you go in?" Simon asked. "I told you when you called that Gail should be home." He'd left her in the midst of her interview with *Hollywood Secrets Revealed* or she would've gone to the doctor's with him.

"I have the ring you asked me to get." He held up a small brown sack.

"Great. Thanks. But I was expecting that. You still could've gone in."

"I didn't want my presence to tip her off. I assume the ring's a surprise."

"It is, but seeing you in Whiskey Creek wouldn't tip her off. You also brought some things for me to sign, didn't you?"

"I did." He scratched his head. "It wasn't just the ring, Simon. I was hoping to catch you alone."

"Because "

"I'd like to talk to you." He motioned to the passenger seat of his Porsche. "Will you take a drive with me?"

Reluctantly, Simon agreed. He knew Ian wasn't happy with his decision to put his work commitments on hold. He'd probably get a list of all the deals that were going to hell because he wasn't there to make appearances and so forth, and he didn't want to hear it. He was fully aware of the risks he was taking and the losses he was sustaining. For once it was intentional. But he figured he owed his manager a few minutes. They'd worked together for a long time.

"Fine," he said with a sigh.

Ian pulled away from the curb almost before Simon could buckle his seat belt.

"What's up?" he asked as they gathered speed.

"This." Ian handed him a file that had been wedged between his seat and the console.

Simon glanced through it. It was a collection of articles and pictures on him and Gail. "Why'd you bring me this? You think Gail wouldn't show me the same thing, if I asked?"

"Have you read some of those articles?"

"Not word for word."

"Why not?"

Because it made him angry to read what was being said about Gail. He hated seeing how the Plain Jane garbage hurt her. So why raise his blood pressure? It wasn't as if he could do anything about what was being printed. He couldn't exactly tell the assholes who wrote this bullshit that they had no idea what she was really like. That would only make her more of a target. "Gail is keeping her eye on the press coverage. I've been busy with other things."

"Like getting in her pants? Is she that good a lay?"

Obviously he'd seen the pictures that had gone viral this morning. "Maybe. Why, would that bother you?"

Ian hung a left and drove out of town. "Of course not. I'm guessing she leaked the pictures of you and her on the porch to make your relationship seem more legitimate, but people aren't buying it."

Simon felt his eyebrows shoot up. "What are you talking about?"

"Come on, Simon. No one believes you could fall for a girl like her. There's speculation all over the place, even a few claims that it's a publicity stunt."

This was the first Simon had heard about that. Gail must not know, either, or she would've mentioned it. "What gave us away?"

"How should I know? Maybe we didn't take into consideration what a cynical world we live in. Your marriage was sudden. Your new wife is a PR pro. Maybe people are reading between the lines." He sifted through the stack and took out a snarky blog post that named the women Simon had been seen with in the weeks prior to his second marriage. The blog critiqued his usual choice of women and asserted that Gail was nothing like them. It even went so far as to say "industry insiders" believed he'd paid her to marry him to save him from the rape charge.

"Shit."

"Then there's this." Ian used his knee to steer while he found another blog post. This one had a photo of Gail and pictures of the women Simon had been with over the years. Almost all of them were famous themselves or were blonde bombshells. The heading read One of These Is Not Like the Others....

The campaign was falling apart already. Feeling a sense of loss, he shut the file and looked at Ian. "What are you getting at?"

"I think we should call it quits, don't you? If there's no benefit in pretending to care about her, why keep it up? I don't want you to ruin your career by breaking all your contracts just because of some misguided decision *I* had a hand in."

"So you've come out to rescue me."

He adjusted the heater. "To tell you you're making a mistake. I should never have gotten you involved in this."

"No."

"No, what?"

"You're wrong." Regardless of how it was being played in the media, being with Gail didn't feel like a mistake. "There will always be detractors, no matter what I do. I'm not changing course." He was finally feeling human again, sleeping most nights, gaining strength and a sense of purpose. He missed Ty but every day he felt more confident that he'd get him back. Maybe that was because he could finally trust himself to be the kind of father he needed to be.

So what if no one believed in his marriage?

He was starting to believe in it.

"Take me back. I want to give that ring to Gail."

Ian's mouth dropped open. "You're kidding."

Simon smiled. "Not at all."

"You're really going to Sophia's tonight?"

When Callie asked this, Gail was standing at the window, holding back the sheet so she could see outside. Her friend had arrived at her door carrying a copy of *People* magazine shortly after Simon and Ian drove off. One of the pictures Josh had taken at the wedding was on the cover, but Gail couldn't concentrate on that when she was so concerned about what Ian might be saying to Simon. She knew it wouldn't be anything that supported his staying in Whiskey Creek. The fact that Ian hadn't come to the door or even spoken to her would've told her that much, if she hadn't already been aware of it. Although Simon didn't want to accept it, she halfway believed that Ian had told Tex where they were because he was hoping Tex would drag Simon back. Then it would be business as usual for both of them.

"Did you hear me?" Callie prompted.

Distracted, worried, Gail murmured, "What?"

"I asked if you're really going to Sophia's."

She didn't see why that mattered right now. "I guess so."

"*What?* Now I know you're out of it. Sophia's the

girl who stole your prom date in junior year, remember? She's always treated us like second-class citizens."

Gail turned. "Did you see Simon in a red Porsche on your way over here?"

Callie was thumbing through the magazine. "No, why? He cheating on you already?"

"Stop it," Gail said with a scowl.

"Sorry." Callie gave her a sheepish grin. "I have to admit I sort of like him. Not only is he…shall we say… pleasant to look at, he's very engaging."

Gail curved her lips into a superior grin. "I knew you'd like him."

"I didn't say that. The jury's still out on whether or not he's going to be good for you. It's only been a few weeks. We can't take too much for granted."

Gail dropped the smile, mostly because it was hard to act as if *she* was right when she knew it was Callie who'd end up saying, "I told you so." But she did have one argument. "Well, I, for one, am going to assume complete fidelity. Not doing so would drive us both crazy. But thanks for the advice."

Callie propped her legs up on the coffee table. "So why are you gnawing on your fingernails while you stare out the front window as if he's left for good? Why haven't you even looked at these pictures, which most women would be dying to see?"

"Because his friend and business manager cannot be trusted. Simon's trying to change, improve his life."

"And you're helping him."

"Of course."

"But what could his business manager be doing? Plying him with alcohol?"

Gail had no doubt Ian would provide drugs, too, if that was what Simon wanted. But she was more con-

cerned that he might talk Simon into going back to
L.A. and starting that movie she'd gotten him out of.
Or commit him to some other project. Simon planned
to return to acting, but he needed more time. And Ian
certainly wouldn't take that into consideration. He'd
press forward with his own agenda.

If she thought he had Simon's best interests at heart,
she wouldn't mind so much, but she didn't believe he
did. "Possibly."

"If you ask me, you should be more worried about
Sophia than Ian," Callie said, still flipping pages. "She
might be more of a test than he can handle."

"Thanks a lot!" Giving up her vigil at the window,
Gail went back to the couch and grabbed the magazine.
"Let me see this."

"You know what she was like," Callie said. "No boy
was off-limits."

Gail leafed through the pages. Simon looked gorgeous, as always, and she looked…determined, like
she was executing a business deal. For good reason…

"That was a long time ago." She tossed the magazine on the table so she wouldn't obsess about her own
imperfections, which seemed obvious when she was
standing next to her movie-star husband.

Husband… She couldn't get used to thinking like
that, to feeling she had such a strong claim on him. "Sophia's been through a lot in the past few years. Maybe
she's changed."

"And maybe she wants to get lucky with your guy.
Skip's always gone. She's probably trolling for any form
of entertainment."

Gail opened her mouth to respond but didn't bother
when she heard a car pull up. "They're back," she said,
jumping to her feet.

Sure enough, Ian's red Porsche was parked by the picket fence. He wasn't getting out of the car, but Simon was.

"Looks like he's in one piece," Callie said, speaking over Gail's shoulder.

Gail breathed a sigh of relief. But she knew that the stronger Simon became, the more Ian's pleas would tempt him to return to his regular life. They'd planned on staying married for two years. But she doubted it would last that long.

Twenty-Eight

Simon wanted to give Gail the ring, but he didn't want to do it while Callie was there. The edge of the hard little box dug into his thigh as he sat down to visit, but the whole time they talked he was thinking about making love to Gail later, maybe in the shower again, and then having the ring waiting on her pillow.

He hoped she'd like it. He couldn't imagine that she wouldn't, but there was a chance. He already knew she wasn't the type of woman who'd want it just because it was expensive. Giving it to her had to mean something. And it did now. He couldn't say exactly what. Everything was too new for labels. But…he wanted her to have it. That told him there had to be a reason.

When Callie asked about the renovation, he and Gail walked her through the house and talked about some of the changes they'd planned. He was getting excited about the possibilities, enjoyed challenging himself in a whole new way. He even liked how exhausted he was at the end of the day. It made curling up with his no-nonsense, tough-as-nails wife, who'd turned out to be as sweet as a woman could be, that much more enjoyable. One thing he knew—those don't-mess-with-me suits of hers hid a very tender heart.

After about thirty minutes, Gail said they had to get ready to go to Sophia's and Callie left. They were alone at that point. He could've given her the ring then and almost did. He felt like a kid with a really great Christmas gift he couldn't wait to present. But she was in too much of a hurry for him to be able to do it right. He certainly didn't want her to think he was trying to pay her for giving in on the sex issue. He'd asked Ian to buy the diamond before they'd ever made love, but she wouldn't know that and if he had to explain it, the whole thing would be ruined.

"You all set?" When she came out of the bedroom, she was wearing a pair of tight-fitting, skinny jeans and a sleeveless black sweater with a leather jacket. With her hair pulled back and pearls at her neck and ears, she looked classy, prettier than ever. But he liked the way she looked just as much when she wasn't wearing any makeup—or clothes, for that matter. He especially loved her smooth skin and how it felt beneath his hands. He loved her eyes, too, and the emotion they conveyed. She cared about him. Maybe too much. But he didn't want to think about that.

"You look great," he murmured, and pulled her into his arms long enough to breathe in her perfume and kiss her neck.

She didn't resist, but she glanced up at him as if she was a bit hesitant to respond. "What did Ian have to say?"

"Nothing new. He wants me back in L.A. You probably guessed that."

"What for? Can't he see how great you're doing here?"

"*Great* is a relative term. In his mind I'm not working, so I can't be doing too great. I think he's mostly reacting to the fact that things have changed. He feels he's lost control of his biggest client."

"You mean he feels threatened by me."

"He doesn't like the influence you have."

She caught his face between her hands. "We'll be able to remain friends when this is all over, won't we? I mean, I know we won't be able to keep working together, but we'll still *like* each other, right?"

Why worry about later? Why not just be grateful for now? After all, he was so much better off than before. "I hope we will. The hardest part about bumping into you will probably be stopping myself from carrying you off to the bedroom."

"Why? At that point, you'll have a huge selection again."

"No one else makes love like you." There'd never been anyone with whom he could completely let down his guard, no one he could trust in quite the same way. "In case you haven't noticed, I can't get enough."

He was afraid she'd reject that compliment like she had so many others. He expected her to say he wouldn't care who he was with as long as he got what he wanted—which was what he'd heard her say before—but she didn't. Her hand cupped his cheek as she kissed him, openmouthed.

"You keep this up, we won't make it to dinner," he said.

With a laugh, she stepped away. "I can't help it. I am so..." She seemed to catch herself.

"What?" he asked.

She hesitated, then blinked. "Glad I married you. It's been the best mix of business and pleasure I've ever had."

* * *

God, she'd almost told him. Right there, while her brain frequencies were all jammed up by the sexy look on his face and her body was growing warm in anticipation of his touch, she'd almost blurted, "I am *so* in love with you!" Every time she looked at him, she grew a little more intoxicated.

Fortunately, she'd caught herself, and a few minutes of standing outside his immediate orbit had made it easier to think. He'd basically told her she was a good lay. He would not want "I love you" in response when he'd warned her not to take their relationship too seriously in the first place.

The whole time they were at Sophia's, Gail was lecturing herself on how she'd handle being alone with him once they returned home. She wouldn't say *anything,* not one word about any kind of feeling. There was no need to send him into a panic. She'd let her body do the talking, since he didn't seem able to tell the difference between sex with a woman who lived for his every smile and sex with a woman who was merely in it for another celebrity conquest. Men were obtuse that way, she decided, and Simon didn't seem to be an exception.

"Would you like more mashed potatoes?"

Gail glanced up. Sophia had put on an impressive spread—medallions of beef tenderloin, garlic mashed potatoes, asparagus, carrots and a salad—and was now standing next to the table holding a bowl. Gail had expected Alexa, Sophia's daughter, to be with them, but she was spending the night with a friend because they had a school project they'd be presenting the next day. And Skip was gone again. Gail wasn't even sure Sophia had said where. They sat in her big elegant dining room in her big elegant house and it was just the three of them. She wondered how Sophia handled being alone so much of the time.

"No, thanks." Gail smiled and tried to think of something else to say but a moment later went back to her meal. Simon was doing fine carrying the conversation. She was too busy worrying. What was she going to do after their marriage ended? She'd be looking at some long, dreary days ahead. Would she ever get over him? Be able to fall in love again? If so, she doubted it would happen soon. She'd waited thirty-one years to fall in love the first time. Now that she had, she knew what she'd harbored for Matt had been nothing by comparison.

"You're quiet. You okay?" Simon murmured when Sophia went into the kitchen to get another bottle of wine.

She swallowed the piece of asparagus in her mouth. "Fine."

His eyebrows drew together. "Maybe we should leave early. Get you into bed."

"We can't be rude. She's gone to so much work." She checked to make sure Sophia was still out of earshot but lowered her voice anyway. "And I think she's really lonely."

"I have no doubt of it."

"Callie believes she's after you."

"I can promise you she's not. She's being very polite, but she keeps looking at you as if you're the one she's hoping to impress. Take it from a fellow reprobate, she wants to win your friendship. If you weren't so preoccupied, you'd notice."

Gail *had* noticed, which was why she hadn't concerned herself with Callie's warnings. "I'm just stewing over that interview I gave *Hollywood Secrets Revealed* this morning."

"You said it went well."

"The reporter was receptive, but let's hope it was the right move. We don't want to create a backlash to our claims of peace and happiness with the media rehashing everything that happened in the past year."

"It'll be fine even if they do. We'll keep pointing to my track record since we got together. I've been perfect. That's all the judge needs to know."

For him, it really was about getting his son back. She smiled at the pride in his voice. He was feeling a lot better about himself, and that pleased her. Regardless of what she'd face in the future, at least she would know she'd made a difference to him.

"Dessert's almost ready," Sophia called.

Simon leaned halfway across the table. "I want to mention that bruise on her cheek again and see how she responds. Do you think I should?"

Gail considered whether or not it would do any good. In her opinion, it would just make Sophia uncomfortable. "No. She's too self-conscious about it. Keeps moving her hair to make sure it's covered."

"I bet her husband did it."

Gail wondered about that, too, except she couldn't picture Skip ever striking anyone. "I don't know. Maybe not. I'd hate to accuse him and be wrong, especially here. It's such a close-knit community. Gossip like that can do so much harm."

"It's a tricky situation," he agreed.

"If she's being hurt, she needs to speak up. She can't hope someone will guess."

"But not all women can—"

His cell phone interrupted them with the buzz that signaled a text message. He took it out of his pocket and glanced at it, although he didn't seem particularly interested in what might be coming in. He obviously wanted to get back to their conversation. But then he stiffened.

"What is it?" Gail asked, but that was just as Sophia walked in.

He glanced from her to their hostess. "It's Ty," he said. "If you'll excuse me."

He got up and walked out, leaving Gail to entertain her old nemesis while he placed a call in the other room. Judging by how low his voice was, how urgently he was speaking, Gail knew he could only be talking to Bella.

Simon didn't want to look at Gail. He knew she didn't agree with what he was doing, and he hated to disappoint her. She'd just started to trust him. But he had to go back to L.A. Bella had been sobbing on the phone. He'd never heard her sound quite so desperate and brokenhearted. She'd told him how much she still loved him. That she'd always love him. That she was terribly sorry about what had happened between her and his father. That her own insecurities had gotten the best of her yet again. That there'd never been anyone in her life who could even compare to him. That she and Ty needed him.

Simon was so used to running to her rescue that it seemed natural to go now, even after everything she'd done. But he wouldn't have let that sense of obligation influence him if not for Ty. He believed Bella when she said his son needed him; he'd thought so all along, and wanted to be there for him. Although Simon wasn't interested in picking up where he'd left off with Bella, as she seemed to want, he was hoping for *some* type of relationship that would enable him to see his son on a regular basis.

Gail sat against the headboard of their new bed, hugging her knees to her chest as he randomly threw clothes into his suitcase.

"The media will find it strange that you'd abandon me to rush to her side," she said, her voice a monotone. "This could ruin everything we've established so far. You realize that."

He did. They'd talked about it on the way home. He'd take Gail with him if he could. But jealous as Bella was, he knew that would only cause more problems. It was his text about being happily married and the picture of Gail and him on the porch that'd finally caused Bella to break down. She'd told him on the phone that the minute she saw that picture, she'd feared she'd lost him for good and couldn't bear the thought of it.

"She's suddenly willing to work something out." He didn't have to specify who "she" was. "I have to take advantage of that. You have no idea how hard she's been to deal with. No one does. But she promised me that if I come right away, I can see Ty."

Gail frowned. "She's using him as a carrot. She wants you back."

"Doesn't matter. I'm no longer interested in her," he said, but he could tell that Gail didn't quite believe him. She thought it was the end of their marriage, and he couldn't promise her it wasn't. What they had was a contract to work together to help him get custody of Ty. Their relationship had turned out much better than he'd ever dreamed. But if he gained custody of his son tonight, he'd have what he wanted, and there'd be no reason to stay together.

"I'm sure she thinks you *are* interested," Gail said. "She's always been able to get you back before."

Only because she was the mother of his child and

he'd so desperately wanted to maintain a regular family. "I'm not the same person I was."

"And yet you're willing to get on the same old roller coaster."

"No. She'll eventually have to face the fact that I'm over her."

In the meantime, Bella could think whatever she wanted as long as she gave him access to his son. Maybe they could build a bridge during the next few days, figure out how to put the negativity and fighting behind them. As far as he was concerned, their split didn't have to be so acrimonious. Especially now. Thanks to Gail, he was feeling healthier, more capable of dealing with the disappointment, the sense of failure and confusion caused by the divorce.

He'd gladly offer Bella more money if she'd agree to share custody. He wasn't sure what he'd be able to arrange. Bella hadn't been all that coherent on the phone; she'd just kept crying that she wanted him—but now that she'd reached out, he had to at least try.

"I don't trust her," Gail said.

"Neither do I," he responded. "But I have to do this. I'm sorry." Once he'd finished packing, he wished the limo he'd ordered while they were at Sophia's house would arrive. He had a long drive to the airport and didn't want to miss his flight out of Sacramento. It was the last one of the night. He could've arranged for his own jet to pick him up—he rarely flew commercial these days—but that wasn't easy to do on such short notice. He'd need to call his pilot, have him get the plane out of the hangar, make sure it had fuel, file a flight plan. Then Simon would have to wait for him to arrive from L.A. "Will you be coming home soon?"

"No. Not for a while."

She probably didn't want to face the media onslaught, and he didn't blame her. She'd find it embarrassing. Everyone would say that their marriage was just another fling and that he'd been in love with Bella all along. They'd say Gail should've known better than to think she could keep him. Maybe those people Ian had mentioned, who'd figured out that they'd done it for the PR, would get louder and more insistent. He dealt with the media enough—and so did she—to realize what the conjecture would be like and that it wouldn't be flattering to Gail. He already planned to offset that as much as possible by telling everyone how great she was and how much he cared about her. But he had to handle one thing at a time. "Then I'll come back here."

"No, there won't be any reason for you to do that," she said. "If you gain custody, you won't need me anymore. And if you don't, if she calls the cops because you violated the restraining order, staying married to me won't matter. After this, no one will believe you really care about me."

This was more than he could handle at the moment. He'd have to think about what to do with her later. "I just want my son. That's why I started this."

"I know. He's a great kid, so I don't blame you. What I'm trying to tell you is that I think you'll have a better chance if you stay. You should set up something consistent and reliable through the legal system, something that won't depend on her whim."

But he couldn't wait. "That could take months and months, maybe years," he said. "And even then there'll be no guarantees I'll win."

She didn't try to convince him otherwise. "True."

"That's why I have to go."

He'd dropped a shirt on the floor. She got up to fold

it. Then she handed it to him to put in his bag and went about gathering up everything else he'd left—clothes, books, toiletries. "You didn't have to call a car service, you know. I would've driven you to the airport."

"I know. I didn't want you out so late. What if you got a flat tire?" He motioned at the stuff she was still picking up. "Forget that."

"You don't want it?"

"I'll get it later."

"Okay." She put the jeans she'd taken off the floor on the bed. "But before you go, there's one more thing I want to say."

He squirmed at her somber tone. This felt like a funeral. He wanted to get out of the house as soon as possible, but she deserved the chance to tell him how rotten he was for letting her down. She'd gone to a lot of work and effort to help him, and he'd done nothing except disrupt her life. True, her business was coming back from the brink of collapse. But in the aftermath of his leaving, her family would be angry with her for marrying him and her friends would have every right to say "I told you so."

He'd even messed up her love life. He knew very well that she'd once had feelings for Matt. Maybe, if not for his involvement, the two of them would've gotten together and become the perfect hometown couple.

"I'm listening." He was prepared to hear the worst. Instead, she came to stand in front of him, kissed him tenderly and said, "I've never loved a man so much. I hope you're always happy."

Completely taken off guard, he blinked in surprise. He almost pulled her into his arms so he could feel her body against his one more time, just in case she was right and everything changed after this moment. But she didn't give him the chance. With a parting smile, she crossed to the other bedroom and closed the door.

And then the limo arrived.

Twenty-Nine

The house felt odd without Simon, probably because he'd been such a part of it. With the amount of work he'd been putting in and his excitement over the improvements, not to mention the time they'd spent here making love or simply sleeping together, it had begun to seem like a home. *Their* home. Their marriage had begun to feel real, too. But it had all ended even quicker than Gail had anticipated. He'd abstained from alcohol and behaved perfectly since they'd made their agreement, only to be drawn back to Los Angeles by Bella, the one variable Gail hadn't expected to play the part it did. She'd thought they'd have to battle tooth and nail to get Bella to let Simon see Ty. The restraining order had convinced her of it. Now she felt as if she'd been leaning hard on a door that had suddenly opened.

She should've known better than to rely on anything she'd been feeling since marrying Simon, especially the happiness and false sense of security that enveloped her while living in her hometown. She hadn't trusted it. Not really. And yet she'd embraced it—eagerly. Once she learned about Bella and Tex she should've realized that Bella had been manipulating Simon all along and would continue to do so—and that he would never be able to resist a friendly offer from her. After all, Bella had the one thing Simon cared about most. Ty trumped every other consideration.

Hugging her pillow close, Gail rolled over and squeezed her eyes shut. She'd known she'd face this day sooner or later. There was no point in feeling sorry for herself. But all the self-talk in the world couldn't ease the ache in her chest.

Maybe if she got out of 811 Autumn Lane, she'd recover faster, revert to her old in-charge, able-to-handle-anything self. If she returned to her father's place, she'd have to tell him and her brother that Simon had left her, but she'd have to do that fairly soon, anyway. Might as well get it over with.

She kicked off the covers and got up, then pulled on an old sweatshirt of Simon's. But before she could reach the hall the doorbell rang.

For a moment, she hoped it was Simon. He'd only been gone an hour. He could've come back. But she knew in her heart he wouldn't, not when he couldn't wait to see his son.

So who could be visiting at ten-thirty?

She wiped her face on her sleeve and padded out to the living room barefoot. He'd turned off the lights and locked up, but he'd replaced the burned-out porch light and left that on. Nice of him to be so considerate, she thought sarcastically, and pushed the sheet covering the front window to one side.

It was Sophia, pretty much the last person in the world she wanted to see. Wasn't dinner enough?

Gail almost didn't open the door. She wasn't sure she could put a smile on her face and pretend, as she'd done through dessert and an hour or so of small talk at

Sophia's house earlier, that everything in her life was A-OK. But she also couldn't leave Sophia standing on the porch when the Lexus was parked out front, giving away the fact that someone was home. She couldn't have done that to anybody she knew, especially in Whiskey Creek.

Hoping the woman she'd once disliked immensely, and for good reason, wouldn't be able to tell she'd been crying, she opened the door.

"Hi." Contrary to what Gail had believed possible, she managed another of the fake smiles she'd been conjuring up all evening.

Sophia didn't immediately respond. She shoved her hands in the pockets of the lightweight jacket she was wearing and studied Gail carefully.

Growing uncomfortable, Gail cleared her throat. "What brings you out so late, Sophia?"

"Alexa forgot her toothbrush so I took it over to her."

"And that brought you here because…"

"I saw a limo pass by." She paused as if she expected Gail to say something, but Gail couldn't bring any words to her mouth. Initially, she'd been tempted to whisper, as though Simon was still in the house and she didn't want to wake him, but now she was glad she hadn't. Getting caught in such a pretense would've been even more embarrassing than acknowledging the sad reality.

"It was Simon, wasn't it?" she said. "He's leaving town."

Of all people to be the first to know. Would Sophia gloat? She would have when they were in high school. Gail wasn't even sure she could complain if Sophia did. She'd been slow to respond to Sophia's attempts at friendship, and she'd been less than wise to take the risks she had. "Yes."

"I thought so. I heard him call for a car after he spoke with… I'm guessing that was his ex-wife?"

"Yes." Although Gail wasn't thrilled to see Sophia put the pieces together so perfectly, she didn't see any point in trying to present the facts in any different way. As much as she and Simon had tried to pretend that nothing had changed, Sophia had watched him make his decision from a front-row seat.

"I'm sorry," she said.

"I appreciate that. So you came because…"

"I was worried that maybe you were having a hard time. I know you don't consider me a close friend, but I didn't want you to be alone if…if you needed someone." She shifted, obviously feeling awkward, but soldiered on. "I'm sure what you're going through can't be easy. I can tell that you love him very much."

Gail wished she could deny it. She wanted to say it was fine, that she'd known she was taking a chance when she married him and had been prepared for the worst—something that would salvage a bit of her pride. *It was fun while it lasted.* But Simon's defection was too new, her emotions too raw. She couldn't seem to raise her defenses.

So she didn't try. The redness of her face had probably given her away. "You're right," she said. "I do love him, more than I ever thought I could love someone. And it hurts like hell that he's gone." How was that for full disclosure? She figured she might as well give Sophia what she'd come for. The "mean girl" from high school could gloat if she wanted to.

But Sophia didn't seem to be taking any pleasure

from her pain. Empathy filled her eyes, then she put her arms around Gail and gave her a long hug.

"I'm really, really sorry," she murmured and Gail could tell she meant it.

"Sometimes life just sucks, doesn't it?" Sophia added.

Gail got the impression she knew what she was talking about. "You're not happy with Skip, are you?"

Sophia hesitated as if it was difficult for her to reveal the truth. She'd been selling the "perfect family" illusion for so long. But eventually, she stepped back and admitted the truth. "No."

"Sometimes life sucks, all right," Gail said with a sad laugh. "Want to come in for coffee?"

Sophia returned her smile. "I'd love to."

They spent the next two hours discussing whether or not Gail should return immediately to L.A., what her father and brother would think of Simon's defection and how she should tell them, and whether or not Sophia should keep fighting to save her own marriage. She claimed that the bruise on her cheek wasn't from Skip, but Gail suspected the reality of that was too personal to share even within the confines of their new friendship.

Gail supposed she'd find out someday. She definitely planned on maintaining the relationship. Sophia as an adult was nothing like Sophia as an adolescent. She'd held back, too, hadn't told Sophia about the original reasons for the marriage. That was too risky to tell *anyone*.

"Look at the time," Sophia said, pulling out her cell phone. "I'd better go home."

"You could stay here," Gail said. "I have an extra bed."

"No. Skip might call." She grimaced. "He does that every once in a while just to check up. He's so afraid I'll cheat on him while he's gone."

"Do you think he's been cheating on you?"

It was another hard question, but they'd built up enough trust that this time she didn't hesitate. "I'm pretty sure he has."

"Why don't you divorce him?"

"Because he'd do everything he can to take Lex and leave me with nothing. Maybe when she gets older I'll be willing to brave that, but…not now. She means too much to me."

She'd be in Simon's situation, fighting over her child. "I see."

"I've got to go, but first I need to use the bathroom."

As she walked away, Gail was thinking how much it helped to have a friend who understood and didn't judge her for her decisions, and how easy it would've been to miss that friend in Sophia.

"Gail?" Sophia had reached the bathroom but was calling her.

"Yes?"

"Have you seen this?"

"What is it?"

"Come here."

More than a little curious, Gail headed down the hall. Sophia was standing outside the bathroom and gestured for her to peer in. There, on the vanity, was a plush velvet box sitting on a scrap of paper with Simon's handwriting.

Sending Sophia a look that said she had no idea what was going on, she read the note first. "I've been trying to figure out a good way to give you this. Now that I'm leaving, I realize there is no good way, but I still want you to have it."

She handed the note to Sophia while she opened the box. Inside was one of the giant-size diamonds Mr.

Nunes had brought to show her before she and Simon were married.

"Holy cow," Sophia breathed when Gail turned to show her. "I'm tempted to believe that's a cubic zirconia but I know it's not."

So did Gail. After Mr. Nunes's visit, she also knew how much it was worth.

"Try it on!" Sophia said, and held the box while Gail slid the ring on her finger. The setting was a simple one done in yellow gold, but it offset the diamond beautifully. The combination was stunning.

"See that?" Sophia said, admiring it. "He does care about you. I bet he comes back."

Gail smiled, but shook her head. "No."

"Why not?"

"He has too much going on in his life right now," she said. But that wasn't what she was thinking. She was remembering the moment when she'd bared her soul to him. He couldn't come back to "I love you," not to continue a fake relationship. After that, it would have to be for real.

And she'd always known he wasn't ready for *real*.

Ian climbed out of his car as soon as he saw Simon pass through the doors of the baggage claim area and into the pickup zone. "How was your flight?"

It hadn't been pleasant. As eager as Simon was to see Ty, he felt bad about leaving Gail. He kept picturing her sleeping in their new bed in their new century-old house—and wished he was there with her. She kept him sane, introduced an element of calm and rightness to his life that seemed to be missing without her. Just flying into Los Angeles brought back the past couple of years, which made him tense and irritable. The way Ian kept smiling bothered Simon, too. Ian acted as if he'd somehow outmaneuvered Gail in his quest for attention and control. But he hadn't. Only Ty could beat Gail.

"Fortunately, it was short," he said. "What's going on here at home?"

Ian had brought his Mercedes and not the Porsche, so he had somewhere to stow Simon's luggage. Simon shoved it in the trunk as Ian answered.

"Bella's been calling me, freaking out. She wants you to come over right away."

Simon checked the time—11:40—and walked to the passenger door. "Have you seen Ty?"

"No, I've just heard from Bella on the phone."

His cell rang as he slid into the seat. Hoping it was Gail checking to see if he'd gotten in safely, he pulled the phone out of his pocket, then frowned. It wasn't Gail. Of course it wouldn't be. She'd told him she loved him, but then she'd sent him off as if she never planned on seeing him again. He knew in his heart that unless he contacted her, he'd never hear from her again.

Instead, it was Bella. Already. "This is her," he said to Ian, and pressed the talk button. "Hello?"

"Oh, good!" Bella gushed. "You're in?"

"Just arrived."

"So…are you coming over?"

"On my way."

"Thank God." The sexy, breathless quality of her voice wasn't quite the turn-on it used to be. Actually, it wasn't a turn-on at all. She just sounded like she was trying too hard.

"Is Ty there?" he asked.

"Where else would he be?"

Simon wanted to be sure. At this hour, his son would be asleep, but it'd been so long since Simon had seen him he didn't care. He couldn't wait to hug Ty's small body against his chest. "Okay, I'll be right there."

As he buckled his seat belt, Ian pulled into the steady flow of traffic. "It's good to see you, man."

Simon eyed him. "You're kidding, right?"

"No, I'm serious. Why?"

"You just saw me in Whiskey Creek."

"That was different." He tapped the steering wheel to the beat of the rap music playing on his expensive stereo system. "Whiskey Creek isn't L.A. *This* is where you belong."

"Is it?"

Ian's hands stilled and he glanced over. "What's that supposed to mean?"

Simon didn't even know. He used to love L.A., never dreamed he'd consider moving. Now, he wasn't so sure it was the best place for him. Whiskey Creek had been such a welcome change. He liked the innocence of it, the people. He had room to breathe there. "Nothing," he said. "It doesn't mean anything."

Ian put on his blinker and changed lanes in preparation for exiting the airport. "Can you believe you got out of your bogus marriage so easily?"

Simon arched an eyebrow at him. "Excuse me?"

"Now that Bella's willing to forget about that stupid restraining order, there's no need to bother with Gail."

Simon said nothing. After the initial agreement, Ian hadn't wanted his arrangement with Gail to work. That much was clear.

"Right?" Ian prodded.

"Whatever you say," Simon muttered.

Seemingly happy, Ian turned up the radio. "It's all going to work out, buddy. The way things stand now, you'll be able to start your next project in no time."

He did a quick drum roll to the stereo. "We're back in business."

Considering the recent improvements in his situation, Simon supposed there was no reason *not* to return to work. He knew how fickle fame could be. If he pissed away the opportunities he had right now, they could disappear, and he could end up like his father. Someone who missed the spotlight. Someone who was yesterday's news. Besides, there were a lot of people who'd been disappointed when he backed out of his commitments. Maybe he could reschedule some of them. For the most part, he was interested in those projects, or he wouldn't have signed on for them.

But did he really want to fall back into his old life-style? What about the woman who'd made him happy to live in an eight-hundred-square-foot house and work as a carpenter?

Bella's house was every bit as opulent as Simon remembered. Located in Beverly Hills, not far from his, it was a fifteen-thousand-square-foot Mediterranean with plenty of palm trees and three different pools. She'd never earned much money of her own. She'd been a news anchor when he met her at an after-party, working for sixty thousand a year, but she'd quit that job as soon as they became an item.

He waited at the gate until the security guard buzzed him through, then pulled up behind her Escalade. He'd had Ian take him home to get his car, so it was after midnight, but he never knew what to expect with Bella and wanted to be able to leave at a moment's notice, if necessary.

She was waiting for him on the front stoop. Her eyes searched his face. Then she slipped into his arms. "I'm so glad you're here," she murmured, pressing her cheek to his chest.

Her perfume brought back myriad memories, both good and bad, but Simon didn't feel the poignant emotions he'd associated with that scent before. Sadness weighed on him, for what they used to have that was now lost, but he felt nothing else. Apparently a lot had changed in the past few weeks. Or maybe the changes had been taking place much longer and he just hadn't noticed because of all the drinking.

"Where's Ty?" he asked.

"In bed. Come on, we can talk in the family room." She tried to lead him into a large but cozy kitchen/family room with hardwood floors, a huge rock fireplace, granite counters and stainless-steel appliances. It was tastefully decorated, but everything about Bella was tasteful and always had been. He couldn't fault her sense of style. With her large brown eyes, olive skin and sleek black hair, she was beautiful, too.

"Would you like something to drink?" She held up a bottle of wine—a pinot noir that was one of his favorites.

The alcohol tempted him. It felt like he hadn't had a drink in forever. But he shook his head. "No. I'm fine, thanks."

"Really?"

"I don't drink anymore." He was almost as surprised as she was to hear those words come out of his mouth, but he remained committed to them. He felt more in control of himself than he'd been in a long time; he wanted to stay that way.

"I see." Although she should be acting happy about this, which could only be an improvement in his life, he saw that her smile wilted. Obviously she'd envisioned a different kind of night than this was turning out to be. Still, she adjusted and shored up her attitude. "You look tired. What about some coffee?"

"That'd be great."

"Good. Have a seat."

He stopped her as she started to walk away. "Before we do anything else, I really want to see Ty."

She hesitated. No doubt she could tell he was much more excited about seeing their son than he was her. Simon knew that wouldn't go over too well. But he wasn't willing to deal with her until she'd given him what she'd promised.

"Of course. I'll take you up. Our boy is getting so big. Every day he looks more like his handsome daddy."

Simon followed her up a set of stairs to the second story, then down a long hall to the right wing. Had they kept going they would've come to a set of double doors—he guessed that was the master but he'd never been inside it. He and Bella had certainly made love since their separation, but not since she'd bought this house.

Ty's room wasn't far from hers. "He wanted his room decorated with race cars this time," she whispered as she opened the door.

There was a night-light burning on the far wall, providing just enough of a glow for Simon to see his son's face as he moved closer.

Smiling, he sat on the bed and pulled his little boy out from under the covers and into his arms.

"Don't wake him up," Bella whispered as if she'd thought he was only going to look.

Simon ignored her. He'd anticipated this moment for too long to hold back. "Ty, it's Daddy," he whispered. "God, I missed you."

Ty opened his eyes, smiled sleepily and tightened his arms around Simon's neck. "Daddy, where did you go? Can I go with you next time?"

Simon wished, more than anything, that he could say yes. But he wasn't sure Bella would allow him to take Ty anywhere. Not once she figured out that he didn't intend to try again with her. "I hope you can come with me someday soon."

"Maybe Daddy will stay here with us." Bella looked at him as she ruffled Ty's hair. The invitation in her eyes was clear. For whatever reason, she was ready to welcome him back into her bed, into their lives, into the family.

But Simon was no longer in love with her.

Thirty

It'd taken two hours to get Ty back to sleep, but Simon hadn't minded at all. He'd played army men with his son and talked to him about his missing tooth and the money the tooth fairy had brought him. He'd asked about kindergarten and listened as Ty talked about his teacher and proudly recited the alphabet. Once Ty's eyelids began to droop, Simon had even crawled into bed, tucked his son up against his side and memorized the smell of his hair and the feel of his baby-soft skin as if he might never see him again. It wasn't until Ty nodded off that Simon got up to find Bella, who'd grown frustrated with the lack of attention and left more than an hour earlier.

Simon wasn't looking forward to their talk. He knew she wouldn't like what he had to say. But he couldn't avoid engaging her, not if he hoped to see Ty again.

He found her sitting in the living room, watching a reality show she'd recorded on her DVR. She put the program on pause when he came in and, bottom lip jutting in an exaggerated pout, turned to him. "Happy now?" she asked.

The bitterness in that question nearly set him off. How dared she think she had the right to keep his son from him? The lies she'd told to get the restraining order were bad enough. She seemed to feel she could stand behind those lies and that infuriated him. But he'd let his anger get the best of him before. He couldn't allow himself to make that mistake again. The goal was to establish a friendly relationship, not revert to the animosity of the past. "It was great to see him. Thank you."

She nodded, combing her fingers through her long hair as if she'd done him a huge favor instead of merely giving him what he deserved as Ty's father. "Your dad called."

Simon almost asked if they were still sleeping together but bit his tongue again. His father had plenty of women who were willing to do whatever he wanted. He didn't need Bella. As a rule, Bella wasn't attracted to men who were twice her age. Simon knew what they'd done had been all about him. Now that he and Bella weren't together, she and Tex didn't even like each other. "What did he want?"

"He heard you were back in town."

"How?"

"Who knows? That prick of a business manager probably told him."

Something was up there. Ian had told Tex where to find Simon in Whiskey Creek, too. There was a reason for that, just as there was a reason he was so excited to see Simon return to work—to make *Hellion.*

Simon suspected Ian had been offered a kickback of some kind. Everything in Hollywood seemed to come down to money. But he'd deal with that later.

"What did he want?" he asked.

"He told me to leave you alone."

Instead of crossing the floor to sit down with her, Simon pulled out a bar stool from the kitchen island and turned it to face the living room. "Did he say why?"

"You can't guess?"

"You know my father and I don't talk."

"He said you were finally happy. That you don't need trash like me messing up your life again."

When he didn't respond to the "trash" part, didn't defend her as she was no doubt hoping he would, her expression darkened. "As if what happened was *my* fault," she added.

"*I'm* not the one who slept with him," Simon pointed out.

"You slept with plenty!" she snapped, but whether she believed him or not, he hadn't touched another woman until he'd caught the two of them. Even then it was several months later, when he'd known he couldn't put his marriage back together, that he wound up in bed with a costar. After that, there didn't seem to be any reason to hold back. There were a few times Bella had realized she was losing him and attempted to straighten up, but those periods never lasted. She couldn't overcome the insecurities that caused her to provoke him.

But there was no use arguing. What had happened had happened. They'd both made mistakes. He just wanted to figure out how to go on. "I did," he admitted.

Evidently satisfied that he'd taken responsibility for his behavior, she clicked her nails as she stared at him. "So…where do we go from here?"

"I'm hoping we can make some arrangements where Ty is concerned."

"What kind of arrangements?"

"I'd like full custody." That was the only way he could put a definitive stop to her using Ty as a weapon against him. "But if you cooperate with me I'll settle for shared."

"You'll never get full custody. I don't have to cooperate with you."

Simon felt his muscles tense. "Why are you still being like this?"

"Because we come as a package! You can't reject me but accept him! That's not fair!"

This made no sense. She was talking out of the hurt and anger that'd gotten them into so much trouble to begin with.

Simon tried to counteract that by remaining as calm as possible. "Bella, please. I love Ty. I'd never let anything happen to him, and you know it. That should be what matters."

"What about *me?*"

Bella acted like a child herself. "What about you?" he asked.

"What will I become? Your castoff? You think you can toss me aside and take my son to start a new family with your publicist in some boondock town hours and hours away from here? Go live happily ever after when I'm miserable?"

Simon lifted his hands. "Even if I take him to Whiskey Creek, it wouldn't be for long. I plan on coming back to L.A. and making more movies. I'm not walking away from my career. We can work together, make sure we both have what we need."

She bit her lip. "Do you love her?"

As he'd suspected from the beginning, this wasn't about Ty. Bella was feeling left out, couldn't stand the thought that he'd managed to move on. She'd liked it far better when she knew he was suffering because of her, when she still had the power to hurt him.

"Do you really want to know?" he asked.

She didn't respond, but raised her chin as if she expected an answer.

He drew a deep breath. "I married her because I thought it would be good for my image."

She sagged in relief. "Of course. You would never be attracted to someone as…as plain as she is!"

"I'm not finished," he said. "That was how it started, but then…everything changed. She's the most wonderful person I've ever met. She makes me feel good in a deep-down, satisfied way. I love how she laughs and how she makes me laugh. I love that I know I can depend on her. I love the way her face lights up every time I walk into the room. I love that she pretends to be tough but she's really all heart. Most of all, I love the way she loves me." He smiled just thinking of her. "Does that mean I love her back?" He nodded. "Yeah, I guess it does. I was telling you the truth—I'm happily married."

Tears welled up in Bella's eyes, but he felt no empathy. She didn't need him to feel sorry for her; she was feeling sorry enough for herself. "You will never see Ty again," she said. "Now get out before I call the police."

Simon headed to the door. He wouldn't undo everything he'd accomplished by causing another scandal. But he paused before opening it. "I won't give up, Bella. I'll fight for Ty as long and as hard as it takes."

She grabbed his arm. "I think it's a mistake to forget about us, Simon," she said. "We could try again. We were happy once." She lifted his hand to her breast but he wasn't remotely tempted.

"Sorry, I'm not interested," he said, and pulled away.

Simon felt great when he woke up the next morning. He'd seen Ty. The time they'd spent hadn't been long enough to make up for the months he'd missed, but at least he'd had a couple of hours with him. And he was no longer conflicted about Bella or anything else in his life. She'd finally lost all power to hurt him. His visit to her place last night had been cathartic in so many ways, had crystallized what he really wanted out of life. He wasn't ready to go back to making movies. Not yet. He preferred to return to Whiskey Creek, where he'd been so content, and finish the house on Autumn Lane. When he did come back to L.A., Gail would be with him, but that wouldn't happen until they were both ready for what they'd face here.

He'd tried calling her last night, as soon as he got home. He'd wanted to tell her he'd made these decisions and couldn't wait to see her. His future was completely wrapped up with hers. Over the past few weeks he'd become healthier and happier. Why would he ever let that go or trade it for the emptiness of before?

He didn't plan to, but she didn't know that yet. It had been very late when he tried to reach her, and she hadn't answered.

Thinking of her the second he opened his eyes, he rolled over to search for his phone, but it began to ring before he could even touch it. Maybe she'd seen that she'd missed his call and was getting back to him.

He hoped so. He was eager to talk to her. But caller ID told him it wasn't Gail. It was his father.

Scowling, he studied his digital display. What could Tex possibly want with him? Simon couldn't even guess, but because his father had signed the release for *Hellion,* and because he felt as if he finally knew his own mind and had a clear sense of direction, he went ahead and answered.

"'Lo?"

"What the hell are you doing?" Tex demanded.

The harshness of his tone surprised Simon. He'd

thought they were on better terms than usual, but it didn't sound like that right now. "I'm sleeping. What the hell are you doing?"

"I'm not talking about this minute. I'm talking about last night."

"I went to see my son. Why? And why are you so mad?"

"Because I thought you'd finally straightened up and figured out your life. I thought you understood what you had and wouldn't piss it away. And then you go and do *this*."

A sick feeling curled through Simon's stomach, chasing away the last of his fatigue. Sitting up, he rubbed a hand over his face. "Slow down and tell me what you're talking about. *What* did I do last night?"

"You're going to pretend like you don't know? It's all over the internet—on YouTube, all the celebrity blogs, AOL...."

"I really don't know what you're talking about."

"Then turn on your computer and find out. You're busted, and the media's having a field day with this one. After the 'I'm a reformed man' act you put on with Gail, they're going for your jugular. Actually, some of 'em are more interested in going after a different part of your anatomy. Castration has been mentioned as a fitting punishment."

For what? He hadn't done anything!

Tossing his phone aside, Simon climbed out of bed and hurried over to his computer. After powering it up, he did a Google search on his name. Then he sank into the desk chair, staring at the screen in silent horror. The very first hit that came up was a link to a sex tape between him and Bella. The headline read Simon's Delicious Romp with Ex Last Night Proves He's No Changed Man.

* * *

Just about everyone she'd ever known had called to tell Gail about the online footage that'd gone viral. The onslaught had started with Serge at her own PR company, because he'd been helping Josh track all the media hits relating to her and Simon, and he was first in the office. He'd awakened her. But now that word of the tape had been picked up by the major news outlets, she was beginning to hear from her friends in Whiskey Creek, too.

Although Gail had her laptop in bed and knew what the tape depicted, she couldn't bring herself to watch it. Not the whole thing. The beginning footage, with Simon approaching Bella's house and going inside, as evidenced by security cameras, was clear enough to identify him. It also revealed the date and time, which was last night, shortly after he would have arrived in L.A. That was all she needed to see. He'd left her and returned to Bella's bed within hours.

"What are we going to do?" Josh asked. He'd reached the office after Serge, so this was the first chance she'd had to talk to him. His call was the only one she'd been willing to answer. The humiliation and embarrassment was too fresh, too poignant, to cope with the sympathy of those who cared about her. She hadn't even answered the phone for her father, who must've been tipped off by some patron at the gas station. She couldn't imagine how else he would've heard.

"I don't know," she said. Her heart was aching so badly she couldn't think clearly. She dared not leave her own bedroom, dared not venture out for fear she'd be cornered. It was only a matter of time before her father showed up on her doorstep. Or maybe Joe would come. She'd pleaded with them to give Simon a chance and they had. Now she felt like she'd set them up for a strong sucker punch.

She rubbed her stomach, feeling as if Simon had hit her there. Why had she believed in him? Why had she let herself fall for his looks, his charm, his playfulness and his incredible lovemaking? Of course he was good at making love. He'd had plenty of practice both on and off the screen....

It was his happiness that had convinced her he was sincere, she decided. He'd seemed so content while he was here.

She shook her head as she remembered his boyish smile when he was demolishing the kitchen. He'd left it in rubble, just like her heart.

God, all the warnings she'd ignored... On top of everything else, what Simon had done made her feel like an idiot.

"So you've seen it?" Josh said.

"Not all of it," she replied, "But what I have seen is plenty graphic."

"It gets worse. There's no way we'll be able to spin it into anything other than what it is."

"No. And we can't claim it's not him. He left me, he went there, he slept with her. Our hands are tied. We have to let this one go, see how it affects Big Hit."

It was easier to talk about the damage this might cause her business than her life. Although she'd admitted the truth to Josh, he hadn't been around to see just how hard and fast she'd fallen for Simon, so at least she didn't have to talk about her personal feelings quite yet.

"I doubt it'll cost us clients," he said. "Simon can't blame you for this."

"Doesn't matter. It makes me look foolish and inept for getting involved with him. And you and I both know how fickle Hollywood can be. If I'm perceived to be 'out,' we'll probably lose some of our clients, if not the majority."

"We're good at what we do. We'll survive," he insisted.

At least since the sale of the wedding pictures to *People* magazine, Gail would have deep enough pockets to carry the company for a number of months, if necessary. That was the one bright spot in her agreement with Simon. The contract stipulated that if he screwed up, she got the money, anyway.

Fortunately, she'd had the foresight to demand that stipulation.

She glanced at the diamond ring he'd left her. She'd gone to bed hoping it meant something, but now she knew better. She could sell it, too.

"So you haven't talked to him?" Josh said.

"No." He'd tried to call her once, at 3:00 a.m. After she'd talked to Serge, she'd noticed that missed call. But she'd been asleep when he made the attempt, and she definitely wasn't calling him back.

She couldn't believe he'd try to speak to her right after making love with Bella. Maybe he wanted to tell her before everyone else did. Maybe he had enough of a conscience to want to give her some warning.

Josh sighed into the phone. "This is sad. Except for a few naysayers who didn't really matter, your marriage was well received. The campaign was working."

"Are you talking about the naysayers who were shouting that I wasn't attractive enough for Simon? Wasn't dynamic enough? Wasn't famous?" She'd known she was a regular, average person going in. But somehow, she'd let herself get caught up in the fairy tale.

"I mean those who are too stupid to know that you're amazing, that he was actually lucky to have you."

The phone beeped, telling her she had another call. Assuming it would be her father again, or Callie—Gail wasn't looking forward to the moment Callie learned what had happened—she checked.

It was Simon.

Thirty-One

Gail told herself not to answer. After what Simon had done, she couldn't imagine why he could possibly want to talk to her. But her desire to hear *some* explanation won out.

Telling Josh she had to go, she called herself a fool for her weakness but switched over. "Hello?"

He didn't bother with a greeting. "I didn't do it, Gail."

Her hand tightened on the phone. She'd thought he might try to present an excuse, or ask for her help in bailing him out of this latest mess. She hadn't expected complete denial. "That's your face in the footage, isn't it?" she asked.

"It is. On the security video, anyway. I went there last night to see Ty. I spent a couple hours with him—"

"At midnight?"

"Yes. I woke him up. But I didn't have sex with Bella. I didn't even kiss her. She offered but I wasn't interested." He lowered his voice, which made him so much more convincing. "All I could think about was you."

The ache in Gail's chest grew worse because now the betrayal she felt was complicated by the fear that her love for him was making her vulnerable to accepting what he said over what she saw with her own eyes. "If that's not you, who is it?" she asked, trying to hold out.

"I have no idea, but I didn't sleep with her." When she said nothing, he went on. "I haven't touched anyone since I've been with you. I called last night because I wanted to tell you that I think we should stay together. I don't want to lose you."

Gail pressed her palm to her forehead. She wanted to believe him so badly. But she'd just been calling herself a fool for ever trusting him. "I don't know what to say."

"Say you believe me. I've never lied to you."

He'd done some crazy things, some ill-advised things, but he was right—she'd never known him to lie. Still, caution advised her to proceed slowly. "So where did that video come from?" she asked. "How did it get made?"

"I've been trying to work that out. All I can imagine is that she set me up. She knew if she let me see Ty I'd come over. Maybe she thought it wouldn't be that hard to get me into bed. Then she'd have the proof she needed to destroy my marriage to you and wreck my chances of ever getting custody of Ty. But I didn't go for it. I wasn't even tempted."

"So…she had to do something else."

"Yes. I've watched that damn thing so many times, trying to figure it out. I bet it's the same man in the video she sent me before."

"What video?"

"It's not pretty, but I'll forward it. I think she dubbed my face over his. Notice that once the sex starts, you don't see much to identify me."

She noticed that he'd switched her to speakerphone, which meant he was probably forwarding the video he'd mentioned.

"There's just a glimpse of my face here and there," he finished.

If what Simon said was true, whoever had manipulated that footage had done a damn fine job. "Would Bella really be capable of something like that?"

"I'm sure she would," he said. "She was very upset last night. But this time she's gone too far, crossed the line."

"But it would take someone with real technical know-how. Someone who was used to editing video."

"Right. But thanks to me, she has plenty of contacts in the movie industry."

Her phone buzzed, signaling the receipt of a text message. "Hang on." She put him on speaker, too, while she watched the clip he'd sent. It was Bella with someone else, all right. A message came with that erotic footage: Ty's new daddy.

Gail was shocked by Bella's desire to inflict pain. "When did you get this?"

"The night I cut my hand."

That made sense. Maybe she was making an earlier mistake worse by wading in even deeper, but Gail had to go with her heart on this one, too. "How do we prove it?"

He blew out a sigh. "You believe me?"

She allowed herself a wry smile. "Did you think you might have trouble convincing me?"

"I was worried. I meant what I said. I don't want to lose you, Gail."

"Be careful," she teased. "You swore you'd never marry again."

"I'll settle for avoiding another divorce."

She laughed as relief flooded through her. They were

in a mess, but they had each other. "So what do we do now?"

"We take the video to a specialist, see if they can prove it was doctored. We won't let her get away with this."

"Sounds good to me."

"Does that mean you'll come to L.A. and stay with me until I can get this cleared up?" he asked.

He wanted to know if she trusted him enough to stand by him publicly. Was she willing to go through what the next few weeks would require?

"I'll be on the next flight."

Gail thought she was coming to his rescue. Simon knew that was the quickest way to get her to return to L.A. But she'd done enough for him already. He was sober, he was innocent and he was angry. He'd get himself out of this latest scrape.

Ian squinted against the sunlight that poured into his house when he answered Simon's knock. Then he scowled. "Simon. What are you doing here? Why didn't you just call me?"

Simon didn't reply to the question, but asked one of his own. "Late night, huh, Ian?"

It was easy to tell from Ian's demeanor that he knew something had changed. "Not too late, no. I collected you at the airport and then I came home. Why?"

"Did you *stay* home?"

There was a slight pause. "Actually, I did."

Pushing past him, Simon headed into the living room. Fortunately, Ian lived alone so Simon didn't have to worry about barging in on anyone else. "Where's your computer?"

Ian followed him. "Why do you want to know?"

"Because you have about five minutes to prove that

you didn't doctor that video, or hire someone else to do it."

"What video?" he said, but Simon could tell he knew. He knew and yet he'd been sleeping. So when did he learn if not this morning, like the rest of the world?

"The one where I'm supposedly having sex with my ex-wife."

Ian tightened the belt to his bathrobe. "Simon—"

"I know you did it, Ian," he broke in.

"No."

"Then prove it."

Hands spread wide, Ian stepped closer. *"How?"*

"Give me access to your computer."

He covered his face, then dropped his hands. "Come on, you know I'd never do anything like that. If there's a video out there, Bella must've created it herself. Or your father helped."

"It wasn't my father."

"How do you know?"

Because his frustration and disappointment this morning had been too real. Because he'd meant what he'd said when he praised Gail, and he was right about her, which lent him more credibility than he'd had in years. And because he'd apologized for the incident with Bella. Tex didn't have the strongest character in the world, but Simon believed he'd been on the level about all of that.

Besides, he'd signed the release. If he wanted to force Simon back to L.A. he'd already had a way to try and do it. He'd accepted the loss of Simon's name on his movie. *Ian* was the one who felt he stood to lose if Simon stayed in Whiskey Creek and fell any more in love with Gail. "A lot of reasons."

"But he was furious when I tried to give back your part in *Hellion*."

"He signed a release, Ian."

"That doesn't mean he was happy about it."

"He wouldn't have done it if he wasn't ready to let me go. *You* want me to make that movie even more than he did. Why?"

"Sure, I want you to make that movie. I'm your manager, and that's an Oscar-worthy part. I hate to see you screw up your life just because you're suddenly pussy-whipped. But I wouldn't do anything to hurt you."

"I wish that was true, Ian. I've been good to you. Paid you well. Kept you on, even after what you did to Gail's business, since I felt somewhat responsible for that. But now I'm realizing a few things I should've seen before."

"No, you're jumping to the wrong conclusions," he said.

"Am I? Aren't you who told my father where to find me in Whiskey Creek?"

"Yes, but that's because he wouldn't leave me alone. I didn't want to piss him off. That wouldn't have helped you. We talked about this."

"Why didn't you tell me, from the very beginning, that he was one of the executive producers of *Hellion?*"

"I didn't know! He wasn't the person who approached us. They can sell an interest to anyone they want and often do, to raise money. We don't get to dictate that, and you know it. I found out before you did and didn't pass it along because I didn't want to upset you, but I didn't know at first."

That might be true, but there was more to what was going on than Ian wanted him to find out. "I don't think he had to push you very hard to get you to tell him where I was. You wanted him to press me to leave Whiskey Creek because there was something in it for you."

"Like what?"

"Money. What else?"

"Come on. Look at this place." He pointed to the furnishings that surrounded them. "I'm doing fine. I'd never betray you."

"Not unless it was worth it. What did Bella offer you? Or were you the one making the offer to her? When I didn't come home, when my dad signed that release, which you probably never expected, did it spook you? Did you promise her a chunk of change if she could get me back here?"

"Listen to yourself," he scoffed. "You're talking crazy."

"Am I?" Simon spotted what he'd been looking for from the beginning—Ian's cell phone. Snatching it off the counter where it was charging, he checked to see if he could get into it but it was password-protected. He held it up. "What's your password?"

Ian's eyes widened. "That's none of your business. Give me my phone!"

"Either you give me your password so I can see who you've been calling and who's been calling you, or I'm going to the police. They can get your records. You and Bella will both be busted."

The color drained from Ian's face.

"What's it going to be?" Simon demanded. "Do you tell the truth and take responsibility for what you've done? Or do I have to push it farther?"

"Shit," Ian breathed, and sank onto the couch.

Gail's stomach was a riot of butterflies as the plane landed. She knew it wouldn't be easy to look into the face of reporter after reporter and tell them all that she believed Simon was innocent. It wouldn't be easy to fend off all the paparazzi who'd be eager to get her reaction to Simon's "cheating," either. But she wasn't going to leave him in L.A. alone. Not only was she his wife, she was his publicist. She'd figure out some way to get the situation turned around.

She was staring down at her ring when everyone started to deplane. She'd have to flash it around, use it as a symbol of his commitment. Maybe that would help....

"Have a nice evening," one of her seat partners said. Fortunately, no one on the plane seemed to have any idea who she was.

With a smile and a nod, she collected her carry-on bag and made her way into the airport. Once she reached the gate, she stepped off to one side to call Simon and let him know she was in.

"Hey," she said when he answered.

"You here?"

"Yeah. You?"

"I'm at baggage claim."

"You could've picked me up curbside."

"No, I decided to park. Can't wait to see you."

"I'm nervous," she admitted. "This is going to be crazy."

"I won't let it get too bad. I promise."

Was there anything he could do? She didn't think so, but she appreciated the protective sentiment. "We'll get through it either way. See you in a sec."

Joining the flow of traffic, she headed down the escalator. There was a crowd at the bottom, most of them holding cameras of some kind. She could see the call letters of various television stations. Others were holding microphones, or lights.

Instinctively, she knew they were waiting for her. But how had they known when she was arriving?

Feeling her anxiety intensify, she hiked up her carry-on and searched the crowd for Simon. He'd said he was in baggage claim. But would he be there if all the media were, too?

Apparently so. It didn't take her long to find him. He was standing right in the middle of the crowd, wearing jeans and a leather jacket, watching her walk toward him. The way everyone was waiting, as if they'd all come to yell, "Surprise!" she almost got the impression he'd invited them here. What was going on?

When her gaze met his, she asked that question with her eyes, but he merely smiled and started toward her. The media hurried to keep up with his long strides while taking photographs and video of them both.

"What is this?" she murmured when they were close enough to speak.

"Ian and Bella doctored that footage. They've admitted it."

"They have?" She could hardly believe it.

"They didn't have much choice."

"You know what that means, don't you? You can prove that she was purposely keeping you from Ty. You can win custody."

"That's what I hope."

"So—" she glanced at all the media "—why are these people here?"

"I asked them to come and document this." Pulling her into his arms, he kissed her. Then he held her chin in his hand as he said, "I love you, Gail. I haven't cheated, and I won't. I would never do anything to hurt you."

The warmth of pure happiness poured through her as he kissed her again. The crowd grew thicker, the noise grew louder, lights flashed and cameras rolled, but she didn't care if the whole world looked on. He was letting everyone know he was completely committed to her.

They were just pulling apart when one of the reporters said, "Oh, my God! Is that your ring?"

Epilogue

"You're not having coffee?" Callie indicated Gail's orange juice as the usual suspects gathered in the large corner booth on a Friday morning in August. The weather in Whiskey Creek was every bit as beautiful as Los Angeles, maybe better, since it wasn't as hot. Simon was glad to be back.

"In all the years we've been coming here, I don't think I've ever seen you order anything else," Eve added, also eyeing the orange juice. "Of course, you've been gone a lot of that time, but still. No one loves coffee more than you do."

Simon covered Gail's hand with his. He wanted to catch her eye, to tell her he didn't mind if she spilled the big news, but Ty piped up and took care of that for both of them.

"Mama Gail can't have coffee," he said matter-of-factly. "Not for *n-i-n-e* months!"

This caused not only Callie but the rest of Gail's friends to look a little startled.

"Why not?" Callie asked him. Simon could tell she already suspected the truth, but was seeking confirmation.

Ty had just put a big spoonful of fruit and yogurt in his mouth. This made him difficult to understand when he talked, but Simon let him answer, curious to hear what his son would say. Gail must've wanted to hear Ty explain, too, because she didn't speak up.

"'Cause that's how long it takes to make a baby, silly!" he said with a laugh.

Simon chuckled at his son's comment but no one else did. They were too preoccupied with the meaning of his words. There were ten of them today: Kyle, who was starting to rebound from his divorce; Riley and his son; Ted; Sophia and her daughter; Eve; Cheyenne; Callie; and Noah Rackham, whom Simon had just met for the first time, due to conflicting schedules. When Noah was home, Simon had been filming his latest movie, and when Simon and Gail were in Whiskey Creek for the weekend or whatever, Noah had been racing bicycles in Europe.

With news of the baby hanging out there, all of Gail's friends leaned close, pinning her beneath their curious gazes.

"You're expecting?" Sophia asked.

A blush of excitement tinged Gail's cheeks. They'd thought they were going to wait a year or two before having a baby. But by March they'd gained partial custody of Ty, who'd immediately started begging for a baby sister, and by April they'd admitted to each other that they were just as eager for a baby as he was. They'd stopped using birth control at that point, but it wasn't until a few days ago, on August 4, that they'd learned Gail was pregnant.

"Yes," she said, a grin curving her lips.

"Oh, my gosh!" Eve cried. "That's wonderful!"

"Do your father and brother know?" Riley asked.

"We told them last night," Simon said. "As soon as we arrived in town." Although they'd lived mostly in L.A. since Christmas, Simon had finished remodeling 811 Autumn Lane when they'd come for a couple of weeks in March and he'd brought out the movie props he'd promised to provide for Eve's B and B. They loved staying at their own place when they visited Whiskey Creek, had been there several times already. But they'd begun a tradition of spending their first night back in town at Martin's. Martin loved having them, and it made Simon feel good to please her old man.

"How long have you known?" Eve asked.

Gail squeezed Simon's hand. "Since Tuesday. But it's only now starting to feel real."

"That's so wonderful!" Callie said. "What about Big Hit? Will you continue to work?"

"Not for the first few months. After that, I might go back part-time, but I'm really only doing Simon's PR these days. Josh and Serge are handling the rest of our clients."

"When's the baby due?" Kyle asked.

Gail opened her orange juice and took a sip. "February 21."

Ted added sugar to his coffee. "So what do you want? Another boy or a girl?"

"A baby sister!" Ty shouted, but Gail said she just wanted a healthy child and Simon felt the same.

"Are you excited?" It took Simon a few seconds to realize that the usually reserved Cheyenne was talking only to him. The others had Gail's attention, were asking her all kinds of questions, but Cheyenne sat next to him.

"I'm thrilled about it," he said. He'd once sworn he'd never trust a woman enough to have another child, but that was before he'd met Gail. "There's nothing like that first moment, when the nurse puts your baby in your arms."

"You and Gail seem so happy together," she said wistfully.

She was looking for a level of honesty none of the others had demanded of him so far, but they hadn't lived the kind of hard life Cheyenne had. She wanted to believe in happily ever after, wanted to know it was possible, and he felt no hesitation in building her confidence.

Placing his arm around her shoulders, he gave her a reassuring squeeze while grinning at his beautiful wife. "Gail's the best thing to ever happen to me," he said, and meant it.

* * * * *

Look for the next irresistible romance
in New York Times *bestselling author*
Brenda Novak's new SILVER SPRINGS *series,*
NO ONE BUT YOU
Available May 30, 2017
from MIRA Books.

"Are you up for a strictly physical relationship? Because if that's
all you're after, I'd be happy to accommodate you. I have no
doubt I could satisfy you there."

Cora studied him. "That's all you're interested in?"

"Yes. I'm sorry." Elijah wasn't about to go down the same
road he'd been down before. But he wasn't sure why he was
apologizing, since she sounded almost...relieved by this news.

She nodded slowly. "Okay. I'll think about it."

That didn't sound as though she'd make up her mind as
quickly as he was hoping. "Any chance you could think fast?"

He wanted to kiss her so badly; the way she chewed on her
bottom lip made him sort of light-headed. "We should probably
give it a few weeks. See how we feel," she replied.

"Weeks? Does it have to take that long? Because I've already
made up my mind."

She seemed uncertain. "There is something I should probably
tell you..."

"And that is..."

More lip nibbling. "I've never had a strictly physical
relationship."

He shifted his gaze from her lips to her eyes. "Not even a one-night stand?"

"No."

"What? You're from LA!"

Her expression changed to one of outrage—until she realized he was joking. "Don't even start with those stereotypes," she grumbled. "Or I'll go for the country bumpkin stuff."

She wasn't making it easy for him to ignore the attraction he felt. He liked her spunk. "Can you at least tell me what my chances are?" he asked, leaning a little closer.

"I'm the one who approached you, so…I'd say they're pretty decent."

"What made you approach me?" he asked, because that was a game changer. Otherwise, he would've continued to skirt around her indefinitely.

"There's just something about you."

He almost kissed her, was tempted to use his body to convince her if he couldn't allow himself to use his voice. But as soon as he dipped his head, she seemed to understand they were only seconds away from "too late."

"Like I said, I'll think about it." Pulling away, she started up the drive.

He stood there without reacting for several seconds, trying to overcome the letdown. Then he said, "Wait."

She didn't come back to him, but she turned, so he walked over and held out his hand. "Where's your phone?"

When she pulled it from her pocket and handed it to him, he put in his number and gave it back to her. "In case the answer is yes. Maybe it won't take as long as you think."

Don't miss
FINDING OUR FOREVER by Brenda Novak,
available April 2017 wherever
Harlequin® Special Edition books and ebooks are sold.

www.Harlequin.com

HARLEQUIN®

SPECIAL EDITION

Life, Love and Family

Save **$1.00**
on the purchase of ANY
Harlequin® Special Edition book.

Available wherever books are sold, including
most bookstores, supermarkets, drugstores
and discount stores.

Save $1.00

on the purchase of any Harlequin® Special Edition book.

Coupon valid from February 21, 2017.
Redeemable at participating outlets in the U.S. and Canada only.
Not redeemable at Barnes & Noble stores. Limit one coupon per customer.

52614646

5 65373 00076 2   (8100)0 12266

® and ™ are trademarks owned and used by the trademark owner and/or its licensee.

© 2017 Harlequin Enterprises Limited

HSECOUP0217

New York Times bestselling author

brenda novak

**welcomes you to Silver Springs, a picturesque
small town in Southern California where even the
hardest hearts can learn to love again...**

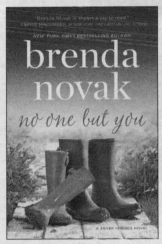

Struggling to make ends meet
after a messy divorce, Sadie Harris
is at the end of her tether.
Desperate, she accepts a position
assisting Dawson Reed—a man
who recently stood trial for the
murder of his adoptive parents.

Dawson has given small town
Silver Springs plenty of reasons
to be wary, but he's innocent
of the charges against him.
He wants to leave his painful
past behind and fix up the
family farm so he can bring his
dependent sister home.

As Sadie and Dawson's
professional relationship grows into something undeniably personal,
Sadie realizes there's more to Dawson than everyone sees—he has a
good heart, one that might even be worth fighting for.

Available May 30, wherever books are sold!

REQUEST YOUR FREE BOOKS!

2 FREE NOVELS
FROM THE ROMANCE COLLECTION,
PLUS 2 FREE GIFTS!

ROM15R